PENGUIN CLASSICS

THE THREE MUSKETEERS

Alexandre Dumas was born in 1802 at Villers-Cotterêts. His father, the illegitimate son of a marquis, was a general in the Revolutionary armies, but died when Dumas was only four. He was brought up in straitened circumstances and received very little education. He entered the household of the future king, Louis-Philippe, and began reading voraciously. Later he entered the *cénacle* of Charles Nodier and began to write. In 1829 the production of his play, *Henri III et sa cour*, heralded twenty years of successful playwriting. In 1839 he turned his attention to writing historical novels, often using collaborators such as Auguste Maquet to suggest plots or historical background. His most successful novel, *The Count of Monte Cristo*, appearing during 1844–5, and *The Three Musketeers* in 1844. Other novels dealt with the wars of religion and the Revolution. Dumas wrote many of these for the newspapers, often in daily instalments, marshalling his formidable energies to produce ever more in order to pay off his debts. In addition, he wrote travel books, children's stories and his *Mémoires* which describe most amusingly his early life, his entry into Parisian literary circles and the 1830 Revolution. He died in 1870.

ALEXANDRE DUMAS

The Three Musketeers

TRANSLATED AND
WITH AN INTRODUCTION BY
LORD SUDLEY

PENGUIN BOOKS

PENGUIN BOOKS

Published by the Penguin Group
Penguin Books Ltd, 27 Wrights Lane, London W8 5TZ, England
Penguin Putnam Inc., 375 Hudson Street, New York, New York 10014, USA
Penguin Books Australia Ltd, Ringwood, Victoria, Australia
Penguin Books Canada Ltd, 10 Alcorn Avenue, Toronto, Ontario, Canada M4V 3B2
Penguin Books (NZ) Ltd, Private Bag 102902, NSMC, Auckland, New Zealand

Penguin Books Ltd, Registered Offices: Harmondsworth, Middlesex, England

This translation first published 1952
Reprinted in Penguin Classics 1982
21

Copyright 1952 by Penguin Books
All rights reserved

Printed in England by Clays Ltd, St Ives plc
Set in Intertype Lectura

CONTENTS

PART TWO

INTRODUCTION

Alexandre Dumas

THOUGH he wrote eighty-odd novels, fifty-odd plays, and a host of other works, Alexandre Dumas the elder will always primarily be known as the author of *The Three Musketeers* and *The Count of Monte Cristo*. Both these works appeared in 1844, as serial stories in two Paris newspapers, one in the *Siècle* and the other in the *Journal des Débats*.

It was undoubtedly in 1844 that Dumas reached the zenith of his fame. That year saw him elevated to the position of uncrowned King of Paris. *Monte Cristo* and *The Musketeers* were hailed in the capital and, indeed, throughout France with the wildest enthusiasm. Long queues waited for each fresh issue of the *Journal des Débats* for the next instalment of *Monte Cristo* and in the provinces crowds assembled to meet the stage coaches which carried it. Within a few months the book was translated into ten languages, and tourists from every country thronged Marseilles, the scene of the novel, eager to visit the actual spots where the chief characters lived and acted. To what qualities does the book owe this phenomenal success? First to sheer narrative power – Dumas was a master of narrative – and secondly to the theme. It is a story for all time, a nineteenth century version of *The Arabian Nights*, a gorgeous piece of escapism from the drudgery of daily life. The glamorous figure of Dantès, who triumphs over injustice and with his limitless wealth and power can control Destiny, punish his enemies and reward his friends, is an ideal which stirs all men's repressed longings for and fantasies of personal greatness.

And *The Three Musketeers* with which we are primarily concerned? How can we explain its immediate and enduring popularity and the fact that it is as fresh and alive today as when it was first written? To quote from Mr A. Craig Bell's biography of Dumas: * *'Les Trois Mousquetaires* is first of all . . . an un-surpassed tale of adventure. It struck a new note, formulated a new technique for the historical romance. The pattern of Scott, with its labouring of details, its archaic phraseology, was thrown to the winds. Here, the background and atmosphere, instead of being carefully fabricated in the course of several tedious chapters and the characters set in motion against it, are developed side by side with the action, and achieved so subtly that some critics are still unable to see it at all and proclaim that there is no background in Dumas. The second to the seventh chapters of *Les Trois Mousquetaires* are the best retort to such criticism.' Then, as in *Monte Cristo*, one is carried along by the sweep and drive of the narrative. As Professor Saintsbury, in his *Short History of French Literature*, expressed it: '. . . the peculiar admixture of incident and dialogue by which Dumas carries on the interest of his gigantic narrations without wearying the reader is a secret of his own, and has never been thoroughly mastered by anyone else.'

But as *The Three Musketeers* is our chief concern it is of interest to examine more closely its sources and genesis. Whereas *The Count of Monte Cristo* is almost entirely a fantasy, a fairy story invented by Dumas, *The Three Musketeers* is to a large extent based on actual historical fact. In both *Monte Cristo* and *The Three Musketeers* Dumas employed a certain Auguste Maquet as his collaborator. This collaboration is, incidentally, partly responsible for the many attacks that have been made on Dumas, of which there are two outstanding examples: a libellous pamphlet published in 1845 by a certain Jacquot, who, among other accusations, openly attributed the authorship of *The Three Musketeers* to Maquet and of *Monte Cristo* to another so-called 'assistant', and a work published in 1919 called *L'Histoire d'une Collaboration — Alexandre Dumas et Auguste Maquet*, by Gustave Simon, in which the author also tries to prove that it was Maquet who wrote *The Three Musketeers* and Dumas who helped, with the implication that all their other collaborations were on the same basis. The first

* *Alexandre Dumas*, by A. Craig Bell (Cassell and Co., 1950).

attack was a purely malicious one, which ended in a lawsuit and fifteen days' imprisonment for the pamphleteer; the second was the product of genuine conviction. And though Simon's theory is utterly fantastic, he did state one indisputable truth, that Maquet, who himself had pretensions as a historical novelist, was 'a tireless searcher-out of historical documents'. And it was in this capacity that he made himself indispensable to Dumas, particularly in the writing of *The Three Musketeers*.

Sources and Genesis of 'The Three Musketeers'

Dumas, a shining light of the nineteenth-century romantic movement in France, had first tried his hand at writing plays. These were enthusiastically received by the French public, which was tired of the constantly repeated performances of its classic authors, Corneille, Racine, Molière, Beaumarchais, and Voltaire, bored with the efforts of their dreary imitators, the contemporary 'pseudo-classics', and aware that the French theatre needed livening up with a fresh vintage. Dumas' plays, however, have not survived as his novels have done. And it was not till 1842, when he was forty and had been famous in France for thirteen years, that he found his true métier as a writer of historical romances.

His first successful venture in this field was *Le Chevalier d'Harmental*, a development, or rather transformation, of Maquet's one-volume novelette, *Le Bonhomme Duvat*, which deals with the period of the Regency after Louis XIV's death. Fired with the ambition to do for France what Scott had done for England in the field of historical romance Dumas then set to work with his collaborator to study the period of Louis XIV. In the course of their researches and perusals of the memoirs and *chroniques* of the period Dumas and Maquet stumbled on the *Mémoires de d'Artagnan* by Gatien de Courtilz de Sandras, a late seventeenth-century historical novelist, in which they found the outline of the story of

d'Artagnan, the names of the musketeers and the first part of
the episode of Milady. The first volume of this work was the
main source of inspiration for *The Three Musketeers*. Being a
cunning literary plunderer Dumas slyly admits in his preface to
having used this work as a basis for the first half of the novel,
though he does not mention the author and pretends to believe
that it is a bona fide book of memoirs. In order further to throw
readers and critics off the scent he then refers to a folio manuscript found in the *Bibliothèque Royal* entitled *Mémoires of
the Comte de la Frère, relating to sundry incidents which
occurred in France towards the end of the reign of King Louis
XIII and the beginning of that of King Louis XIV*. Knowing
that no critic or philologist would ever track down this folio
manuscript, as it is in fact non-existent, Dumas declared that
the rest of his novel was merely this folio manuscript put into
print with the Government's permission and with a new title.
By this means and with the help of his current reputation in
France he hoped to get credit for an entirely original work, the
product of his own creative imagination. But this attempted
hoax had the opposite effect from what he inended, and ever
since the publication of *The Three Musketeers* has spurred on
critics and philologists to track down the true sources of this
masterpiece. And their researches have revealed many of these,
which can be summarized under the following headings:

(1) Courtilz's *Mémoires de d'Artagnan* (already referred to).
This work recounts most of the events described in the first
half of *The Three Musketeers*; d'Artagnan's journey to Paris to
seek his fortune with the letter of introduction to de Tréville
in his pocket; the quarrel with Rochefort (here called Rosnay)
on the way; the arrival in Paris, the meeting with Athos, Porthos, and Aramis; the rivalry between the Musketeers and the
Guards, the King, and the Cardinal; d'Artagnan's first love
affair with his pretty landlady; the duel of the four Frenchmen
with the four Englishmen, one of the latter being Milady's
brother; and lastly, d'Artagnan's immoral affair with Milady
herself. But Courtilz's narrative is dated sixteen years later
than Dumas's (with greater historical accuracy in regard to

d'Artagnan), and Milady is made to be one of the exiled English Queen Henrietta Maria's ladies-in-waiting.

(2) Courtilz's *Mémoires de M. L. C. D. R.* (M. le Comte de Rochefort) from which Dumas partly, but only partly, derived the idea of the branded woman, which he used for Milady.

(3) The memoirs of La Porte and those of Madame de Motteville, which relate the Duke of Buckingham's infatuation for Anne of Austria. They describe the opening incident of the intrigue when the Duke of Buckingham in the garden at Amiens attempted to seize the Queen in his arms so ardently that she was forced to summon her suite. Dumas uses this tale only indirectly, when he makes Buckingham, in a passionate secret interview with the Queen, recall to her his daring declaration in the garden at Amiens. An interesting borrowing of Dumas from Madame de Motteville is Buckingham's explanation to the Queen of his reason for seeking war with France. Madame de Motteville analyses the Duke's motives thus:

'This man (Buckingham) embroiled the two crowns in order to return to France, by the necessity of a peace treaty when, according to his purpose, he would have enhanced his reputation by the victories which he intended to obtain over the nation.'

Dumas makes Buckingham say:

'Why do you think I am planning this expedition to Ré and this league with the Protestants of La Rochelle? For the joy of seeing you! ... This war will bring a peace; there will be negotiations, and I shall be England's representative.' The memoirs of La Porte, Anne of Austria's Groom of the Chambers, also relate his own arrest, imprisonment in the Bastille, and interview with the Cardinal, in a passage which Dumas transforms into one of the most comic episodes in the novel, making the victim M. Bonacieux, whose wife, d'Artagnan's pretty landlady, he makes La Porte's ward.

(4) The memoirs of La Rochefoucauld and those of the Comte de Brienne, which relate the second incident in the intrigue between Buckingham and the Queen, the affair of the diamond tags. Both sources give the same account of the incident. Anne

of Austria as a token of her affection gives Buckingham twelve diamond tags which Louis XIII had previously given to her. An agent of the Cardinal in England, the wicked 'Milady' again, this time in a new rôle, succeeds in cutting off two of these tags, whereupon Buckingham puts an embargo on all ships anchored in English ports, has two identical stones cut and sends the present back to the Queen of France in time to foil the Cardinal's plot to dishonour her in the eyes of the King. In La Rochefoucauld the Cardinal's agent is called the Countess of Carlisle – in de Brienne, the Countess of Clarik. (Dumas calls her Lady Clarick de Winter.) In Dumas the dénouement of the whole intrigue occurs at a ball given for the King and Queen by the City Authorities, when the Queen foils the Cardinal by appearing wearing on her shoulder the bunch of ribbons with all the twelve diamonds, which d'Artagnan, with the help of his friends, has brought back from England in the nick of time. For the description of this spectacular ball given by the City Authorities Dumas is actually entirely indebted to Brienne's memoirs. Indeed, he copied whole paragraphs word for word from the memorialist. But these he fitted neatly into the pattern of his novel as a whole, and though he borrowed the background, the vivid narrative is entirely his.

(5) Volume I of *Chroniques de l'Œil de Bœuf*, by Touchard-Lafosse. This work, published in 1829, purports to be a true account of the secret activities and intrigues of the Court in the reign of Louis XIII, gleaned from a vast store of memoirs of the period. In it many so-called historical events are bred purely of the author's fancy, and the author's intention is clearly to blacken as far as possible the great personalities of the day. Nevertheless Dumas probably borrowed from it, for it records at length the affair of Buckingham and the diamond tags, with special emphasis laid on Lady de Clarick (*sic*), who is described as being enamoured of Buckingham and of appearing with him at a Court Ball at Windsor, 'armed with a stout pair of scissors' with which, at the Cardinal's behest, she proceeds to snip off two of the diamond tags. Dumas may have derived the idea of Milady's subsequent denunciation of the

Duke as her seducer from Touchard-Lafosse's hint of her un-
requited passion for him.

Fact and Fiction

Having considered the sources from which Dumas drew for
The Three Musketeers, it is now interesting to establish how
much in the novel is actual historical fact and how much fiction. In 1838, in his introduction to the *Comtesse de Salisbury*,
a work which he claimed to be the first example of the *roman-
feuilleton*, or serial novel, in French literature, Dumas first expressed his conception of the purpose and ideals of the
historical romance ... 'to interpret history rather than to
transcribe it', but not to falsify it or allow 'any imaginary personage' to 'eclipse the historical ones, who would themselves
be the prime movers of the romance and the history'. But in
the interval between expressing these views and writing *The
Three Musketeers* he had cast such principles to the winds, as
they simply did not agree with his practices. In creating 'Milady
de Winter' and allowing her to dominate the picture in the
whole of the second half of the romance he both falsified history and allowed an almost entirely 'imaginary personage' to
'eclipse the historical ones'. But apart from 'Milady' how much
of the novel can claim to be actual historical fact? Modern
research has enlightened us considerably on this point.

Very few of the millions who have read *The Three Mus-
keteers* and even of the handful who have read Courtilz's
Mémoirs de d'Artagnan, can be aware of the fact that there
really was a d'Artagnan of flesh and blood who was born in
Gascony in 1623, became a King's Musketeer and served
Mazarin and Louis XIV.* And many of these millions of readers

---

* There is irony in the fact that although Dumas, his future immor-
talizer, proclaimed in his preface to *The Three Musketeers* that Courtilz's work was a bona fide chronicle, he secretly believed that it was
entirely a work of fiction, and was therefore himself probably ignorant
of the musketeer's existence.

must have wondered why d'Artagnan's three musketeer friends had such absurd names. 'Mythical shepherds' names' is how Lord de Winter refers to them in the novel, and the Editor of the *Siècle*, who had bought the serial rights of the book in advance under the title of 'Athos, Porthos, and Aramis', feared that his subscribers would mistake them for the names of the three Fates. 'Unless you have discovered new material about these three goddesses,' he wrote to Dumas, 'your story does not promise to be gay.' Though Dumas maintained that they were assumed names, the three men actually existed under names very similar. And as for d'Artagnan, Courtilz, who was born in Paris in 1646, may have actually known him, at any rate by repute, for he was roughly thirty years old at the time of d'Artagnan's death.

Some English readers of *The Three Musketeers* may not know that Louis XIII did in fact have a bodyguard of Musketeers, a hundred or so in number. They were formed in 1622 from the old company of Carabineers, which composed the King's bodyguard and which had just been armed with the new flintlock, muzzle-loading musket. They were a sort of training-school for the élite of the officers of the French army. Père Daniel, in his *Histoire de la Milice française*, tells us that at the time of their formation they had as officers a captain, a lieutenant, and an ensign, and later two sergeants. Otherwise they were apparently all of equal rank. The Musketeer company was composed almost entirely of young aristocrats, with a sprinkling of professional soldiers, but no one was admitted who had not already had some army experience and been in some campaign. After a certain term of service every man was seconded from the company and given a commission in some ordinary regiment; he might even be granted an ensignship, lieutenancy or captaincy in the Guards, the crack infantry regiment of France. Under Louis XIII the Musketeers' peacetime duties were merely to form the King's mounted escort when he left the palace, taking precedence over all the companies of Guards. Most of the men were allowed to billet themselves anywhere in the town and made to pay for their own lodging.

On active service they were used as cavalry or infantry, serving as infantry at the relief of the fortress of St Martin on the Ile de Ré, during the siege of La Rochelle. Dumas maintains erroneously that they took no active part in that siege, and that they were present only in their capacity as King's escort. In his voluminous *Histoire* Daniel also mentions Cardinal Richelieu's company of Guards, *composés de très braves gens*, and the rivalry in regard to prowess in arms which existed between them and the Musketeers, and the jealousy of their respective patrons, the Cardinal and the King, which Dumas describes at length in the opening chapter of his romance.

M. de Tréville, though a real historical figure, was not, as Dumas makes out, the Musketeers' first commanding officer. It was not till 1634 that he was appointed their *capitaine lieutenant* under the King, Louis XIII. But he was in command of them when the real d'Artagnan, whose life story is told in Charles Samaran's scholarly work, *D'Artagnan*, published in 1912, left Gascony for Paris in 1640. Tréville was not, as Dumas makes out, the son of a comrade-in-arms of Henry IV, but of one Jean du Peyrer, a merchant of the town of Oloron in old Gascony, who had made a fortune and bought himself the manor, property and title of Troisvilles, which he passed on to his son. By the year 1636 young Troisvilles (or Tréville) had attained a position and influence at Court equal to that of the greatest seigneurs. As Dumas relates, he and Richelieu were always enemies, and Tréville was involved in the Cinq-Mars conspiracy of 1642 to assassinate the Cardinal, after which Louis XIII was forced to banish him from Court.

D'Artagnan, really Charles de Batz-Castelmore, took the name of Sieur of Artagnan, a property in the Basses-Pyrénées, from his mother's family of Montesquiou. Samaran, in *D'Artagnan*, supplies his full pedigree and life story, which he unearthed from old Gascon archives. Like Tréville he came of a prosperous bourgeois family which had bought rank and property for itself in the late sixteenth century. He left Gascony for Paris, not, as Dumas states, in 1625, but in 1640, had a distinguished career, not under Louis XIII and Richelieu, but under Louis XIV and Mazarin, became in 1667 *capitaine lieutenant* of the First Company of King's Musketeers (of which there were then two), was later made Governor of Lille and in 1673 killed by a stray bullet at the siege of Maestricht.

As for Athos, Porthos, and Aramis, Jean de Jaurgain in his study published in 1910, *Troisvilles, d'Artagnan et les Trois Mousquetaires*, has revealed their true origins, names, and life stories. All three were Gascons. Athos' real name was Armand de Sillégue, Seigneur d'Athos et d'Autevielle, Athos being a small village also in the Basses-Pyrénées. Strictly speaking he was therefore Monsieur d'Athos (the squire of Athos) who signed himself 'Athos', just as we would speak of the Duke of Derbyshire, who would sign himself 'Derbyshire'. He was first cousin once removed to de Tréville. Little is known of his career except that he was a King's Musketeer and died in Paris in 1643. His death certificate, discovered by A. Jal in the register of deaths in the church of Saint-Sulpice, in Paris, seems to indicate that he died as the result of some duel. The name 'Comte de la Fère', which Dumas declares to be his true name, under which he wrote the alleged *Mémoires* mentioned above, is an entire invention of the novelist.

Porthos' real name was Isaac de Portau, and his ancestry dates from 1590, when, as the archives of the Basses-Pyrénées have revealed, Henry IV made the Navarre treasury grant a pension to a certain Abraham de Portau, his ex 'Comptroller of the Household'. This Abraham's grandson, our Porthos, was born in Pau. When d'Artagnan arrived in Paris in 1640 he was already serving in des Essarts' company of King's Guards, and in 1642 his name is still on two King's Guards' active service lists as *Isaac de Portaut*. So he cannot have been appointed to the Musketeers until 1643. Courtilz de Sandras, in his *Mémoires de d'Artagnan*, makes his hero say that Porthos, like himself, had a mistress '*jeune, belle, et bien faite*', a lady whom Dumas travesties in the person of Madame Coquenard. There is no further mention of Isaac de Portau in any of the annals or archives of the period.

Aramis was Henry d'Aramitz, squire and *abbé laique** of Aramitz, in the valley of Baretous, of the *noblesse militaire* of Béarn. Like Athos, he was related to de Tréville, and with Athos, his fellow-Gascon, joined the Musketeers in 1640. Courtilz says in his *Mémoires* that de Tréville had summoned the two young men and Porthos to Paris because they had made a name for themselves in the province by their prowess in arms. But Jean de Jaurgain maintains that Athos' and Aramis' relationship to the Captain of the Musketeers must have had something to do with it, and the latter's sensational career would surely have been an incentive to all enterprising and impoverished young Gascons likewise to seek their fortunes in the capital. But long research work, says de Jaurgain, has brought nothing to light about Henri d'Aramitz's career in the Musketeers; we only know that he served fifteen years in the French army. The archives of the Basses-Pyrénées record that in 1650 he married Jeanne de Béarn-Bonnasse, but the date of his death is unknown.

Research having thus proved that the names of the three musketeers were in fact Armand d'Athos, Isaac de Portau, and Henri d'Aramitz, readers may wonder why Courtilz de Sandras altered them to Athos, Porthos, and Aramis, depriving them of Christian names, and why Dumas followed suit. Gailly touches on this question in his introduction to the *Mémoires de d'Artagnan*, but can only suggest that Courtilz changed the names 'for the sake of orthography and sound'. As for Dumas, we know that he maintained that they were assumed names, hiding the musketeers' proper titles.

We can therefore say that in addition to the well-known historical figures of the period whom Dumas presents to us – Richelieu, Anne of Austria, Louis XIII, Buckingham, de Tréville, Rochefort, La Porte, des Essarts, Chancellor Séguier, Felton, and others – all the chief characters of the novel – and indeed, many of the minor ones – have a basis in history. Dumas, of course, manipulates these characters at will, breathing life into

* Landlord of a property to whom tithes are paid and who is patron of the living.

them, inventing situations and dialogue for them, altering places and dates to suit them and generally fitting them into the pattern of a drama conceived in his own mind. As Parigot, writing in *Les Grands Ecrivains Français* series, observes, in paying tribute to his genius: 'Dry text-books gave him visions, which set his imagination working along historical lines . . . *La Reine Margot*, the early part of *La Dame de Monsoreau*, and two-thirds of *Les Trois Mousquetaires* are unsurpassed feats of vivid historical interpretation.' In the words of Andrew Lang: 'Dumas needed a tuning-fork to be sounded before he could begin his song; once in possession of the note his invention was inexhaustible.' And the note of the tuning-fork was supplied by the dry-as-dust memoirs and *chroniques* which his collaborator, Auguste Maquet, diligently ferreted out.

Milady

The statement that all the leading characters in *The Three Musketeers* have a historical basis needs to be qualified in one outstanding instance, that of 'Milady'. Though there is very little mention of her in any of the *chroniques*, memoirs, or pseudo-memoirs of the period which Dumas used as his sources of inspiration Lady de Winter, or Lady Clarick de Winter, as Dumas occasionally refers to her, dominates, either 'on' or 'off stage', the whole of the second half of the novel.* Courtilz de Sandras, referring to her as Milady ***, and making her one of the exiled Queen Henrietta Maria's ladies-in-waiting, certainly relates at great length the story Dumas tells of d'Artagnan's infatuation for her, of his masquerading as the Comte de Wardes, of his courtship of her maid, through whose agency he gains access to her room, and of her subsequent discovery of his low trick. But after that Courtilz never mentions her again. Then, as stated above, La Rochefoucauld and the Comte de Brienne make brief mention in their memoirs, one of a Lady

---

* Many critics, indeed, consider the enormous part she plays as detrimental to the book's merit in regard to balance and construction.

Carlisle, the other of a Lady Clarik, in connection with the theft of the diamond tags from Buckingham as Dumas relates it; and Touchard-Lafosse, no contemporary memorialist but an early nineteenth-century hasher-up of old memoirs, also refers briefly to the mysterious 'Comtesse de Clarick' in this connection. Dumas, in creating the character of Lady de Winter, combined what he read in Courtilz about Milady ***, an entirely private individual, with the references in La Rochefoucauld, de Brienne and Touchard-Lafosse to the mysterious Comtesse de Clarik, Clarick, or Carlisle, who acts as the Cardinal's agent in England. Her activities in the first half of *The Three Musketeers* are thus accounted for. But her character evidently grew on Dumas and fascinated his imagination, for from Part II, Chapter 5 onwards she takes the bit between her teeth and, as a purely fictitious character, entirely runs away with the novel.* The Cardinal sends her on a mission to England to blackmail Buckingham into deserting the Huguenots in La Rochelle and hints at the same time that if Buckingham persists in coming to their aid she might bring about what he calls 'that miracle for the salvation of France', Buckingham's murder. Then ensue the long episode of her imprisonment in her brother-in-law's castle and her gradual seduction of Felton whom she instigates to commit the murder, her subsequent return to France, her sojourn in the convent at Bethune, where she plots revenge on d'Artagnan, her poisoning of Madame Bonacieux and her final capture, trial, and rather horrifying beheading at the hands of ten men, the four musketeers, their servants, Lord de Winter, and the headsman of Lille. All this part of the tale is pure invention on the part of Dumas, and very astonishing invention too. None of his other novels or plays contain any character resembling 'Milady',† who is referred to by all the men as 'the vampire', the 'creature from

* See * note, p. 20.

† Except, perhaps, Margaret of Burgundy in the play *La Tour de Nesle*; this Queen and her two sisters solicited handsome young men, and after spending one night with them, had them murdered and their bodies thrown into the Seine.

Hell', the 'monster', the 'woman who is not a woman'; who possesses both 'leonine courage' and 'feline guile'; who coos to her lovers and yet roars with baffled rage; who is as ready to spring at men and attack them with a poniard as she is to allure them with languishing looks, siren voice, and hair studiedly dishevelled. All men who come her way are first fascinated and then repelled by her, and in the end the terror she inspires in them is, as it were, the terror of the supernatural. Even the Cardinal fears her. The fleur-de-lis on Milady's shoulder with which she was branded for having committed a felony in her extreme youth would certainly come as a shock to anyone discovering it, but does not fully account for the terror and horror which she evoked in every man who had ever known her intimately. Only her husbands (she had two) and her lovers find out her 'secret', and for that, she declares, they must die. And why was the Cardinal, who employed her as his chief secret agent, who had spies all over the country and who knew everything about everyone of importance in France, himself unaware of her criminal record? At the end of the story d'Artagnan discloses this to His Eminence, who then declares that he and his friends were perfectly justified in taking the law into their own hands and beheading her. Might not Dumas, in creating such a character, have intended to convey that Milady had that particular form of physical malformation which was regarded even in the sixteenth and seventeenth centuries as a terrifying token of divine displeasure, punishable by death – a malformation of which the fleur-de-lis was merely a symbol? This idea has led some to suppose that Dumas might have found further inspiration for the character of Milady in the life of the Chevalier d'Éon, Louis XV's secret envoy to Russia and England. This mysterious individual first masqueraded as a woman in order to become reader to the Empress Elizabeth of Russia, was condemned to wear woman's clothes for all the latter part of his life, was accused by his enemies at the time of his sojourn in England of actual physical hermaphroditism, but was discovered in a post-mortem examination to be a perfectly formed man.

Dumas's library contained the *Mémoires sur la Chevalière
d'Éon*, by F. Gaillardet, one of his earlier collaborators, dedi-
cated to 'mon cher maître' by the author, who added under
his own name, 'l'un des auteurs de *La Tour de Nesle*' (the
Dumas play already referred to), a fact which gives some backing to the d'Éon theory. But this is, of course, pure conjecture,
impossible to prove or disprove. And yet from whatever sources
Dumas drew, the character of Milady remains a puzzle, in
striking contrast to all the other characters in the novel, who
are perfectly recognizable types, portrayed by a master hand.

Problems of Translation

The fact that there are three authentic French texts of *The
Three Musketeers* with wide discrepancies between them is
likely to expose any translator to charges of inaccuracy. One
text is that which appeared in the *Siècle* in serial form, was
pirated by Belgian publishers and issued in cheap editions before the original French publisher, Baudry, had secured the
rights of the complete work. Another text is that which Dumas
himself revised before he allowed the novel to be issued in
book form by Baudry in 1844. The three earliest renderings
into English were taken from the Belgian, or *Siècle*, issue,
purely and simply because the Belgian 'pirates', paying no
royalties, published their editions at one-eighth of the price of
the Baudry edition, and translators naturally preferred the
lower-priced texts. Dumas's revised version is, on the whole,
coarser and cruder than the original *Siècle* version, especially
in the passages which describe Milady's love-affair with
d'Artagnan and her seduction of Felton, and is in many places
considerably altered, with whole paragraphs interpolated and
re-cast. Baudry's rights on the novel later reverted to Michael
Lévy or Calmann-Lévy, whose editions are now the standard
editions in France. A third text is found in the first illustrated
edition published by Fellens et Dufour (Paris, 1846). This publisher, probably with Dumas's consent, compiled his text from

both the other versions, *i.e.* he chose his wording with both before him and, where discrepancies occurred, chose the version he himself preferred, sometime even forming paragraphs by juxtaposing sentences, and sentences by combining phrases, taken from each version in turn. The Fellens edition was later issued by Marescq (1852), with many additional illustrations, and then again by Calmann-Lévy, with the same number of illustrations by Beaucé, Philippoteaux, and other artists contemporaneous with Dumas, and with the original Fellens text.

Apart from the first English and American translations already mentioned another translation by William Robson was published in London in 1853, which was definitely taken from the revised Baudry text. In all subsequent English issues up to 1903 one or other of the four previous translations were used. In 1903 Methuen published a completely fresh translation by Alfred Allinson, which, as one might expect, follows the later and current Baudry-Lévy French text. There has been no new English rendering since then. And to the average modern reader even Allinson's version sounds stilted and unnatural, especially in the dialogue. To quote one instance among many: in Chapter I, d'Artagnan's furious challenge to Rochefort: 'Tournez, tournez donc, monsieur le railleur' is rendered by Allinson as 'Right about face, Mr Impudence', which sounds arch rather than aggressive. In his historical romances Dumas made his characters talk as they would have talked in his own day, not as they talked in the period with which he was dealing. Recurrent new translations are, therefore, both justifiable and necessary, in order to keep this immortal work, *The Three Musketeers*, permanently up to date.

SUDLEY

PART
ONE

CHAPTER I

The Three Gifts of Monsieur d'Artagnan the Elder

ON the first Monday of April 1625, the market town of Meung, the birthplace of the author of the *Roman de la Rose*, was in a wild state of excitement. The commotion could not have been greater if the Huguenots had arrived to make a second La Rochelle of it. Many of the wealthier citizens, seeing the women running towards the High Street and hearing the children screaming on the doorsteps of their houses, hastily buckled on their cuirasses and, to give themselves an air of greater assurance than they really possessed, seized muskets or halberds. Thus armed they made for the Jolly Miller Inn, where they found a dense and excited throng of people swarming in from all directions.

At that time panics were frequent and few days passed without one town or another recording in its archives some event of this kind. Noblemen were at war with one another: the King was at war with the Cardinal: Spain was at war with the King. And besides these public and private wars there were other elements which kept the French countryside in a state of almost perpetual unrest, notably thieves, beggars, Huguenots, and rabble of all sorts. The citizens always took up arms against this rabble; they often fought the noblemen and the Huguenots, sometimes even the King, though never Spain or the Cardinal. So, from sheer force of habit, on this bright April morning, hearing an uproar and seeing neither the red and yellow standard of Spain nor the Duc de Richelieu's livery, the citizens rushed in a body to the Jolly Miller Inn, prepared for battle.

The moment they reached the inn, the cause of the uproar was discovered.

A young man was standing at the main gate, a young man of striking appearance. He was eighteen years of age, tall and lanky, dressed in a blue woollen doublet, faded and threadbare, brown breeches and brown top boots. He had a long, tanned face, high cheekbones – a mark of shrewdness – frank, intelligent eyes, a hooked but well-cut nose, and an enormously protruding, typically Gascon jaw. He wore the Gascon beret, decorated with a jaunty feather, though even without it there would have been no mistaking his origin. His bearing was haughty and his attitude challenging; there was an 'I'm as good as you are and tell me I'm not' look about him. An untrained eye might have taken him to be a farmer's son on a journey but for the long sword which he wore hung from a shoulder-strap and which dangled against his calves when he walked, and, when he was astride, against his horse's rough coat. Standing in front of the inn in full view of the crowd, one hand on his hip and the other holding his horse's bridle, his head erect, his legs apart, back to the wall against the world, he reminded one at once of Don Quixote, the Spanish hero of romance, the tilter at windmills, Don Quixote without his medieval accoutrements, and his horse was quite ridiculous enough to fill the part of Rosinante.

It was this horse, indeed, which had first attracted the attention of the crowd. It was a Bearnese cob, twelve to fourteen years old, with a rat tail and ulcers on its feet, which jogged along mournfully from sunrise till sunset at a steady speed of four miles an hour, drooping its head so low between its knees that it needed no curb or martingale. Unfortunately this animal's good qualities were not appreciated, so strange was its coat and so awkward its stride. At that time all men were connoisseurs in horseflesh, and the sight of this cob, which had entered Meung by the Beaugency gate some fifteen minutes earlier, caused a sensation which reflected badly on its rider.

And this sensation was very painful to our young Don Quixote (d'Artagnan was his name) because he was a good horseman and realized that he cut a poor figure on his Rosinante. And when Monsieur d'Artagnan the elder had presented it to his son as a parting gift our hero had groaned inwardly, although he knew that the animal was worth at least seven crowns and that the words of wisdom which went with the gift were beyond price.

'My son,' the old squire had said in that thick brogue which is the life-long distinctive mark of all true Gascons, 'this horse was born in your father's stables nearly thirteen years ago and has lived here ever since. Treasure it for that reason. Don't think of selling it. Let it live its normal span and die happy and respected. If you go campaigning with it treat it with the kindness you would show to an old servant. At Court, if you ever go to Court, which, of course, you're quite entitled to do, seeing who you are, be honest and above board with everyone. Always remember your rank and carry on the tradition of good behaviour which your family has been true to for the past five hundred years. This you owe to yourself and to your nearest and dearest. Stand no nonsense from anyone but the King and the Cardinal. Remember, nowadays it's only by personal courage that a man can get on in the world. If you see an opportunity don't stop to think but seize it, or you may lose it for ever. If that fails, try something else. You've got two good reasons for being brave, first that you're a Gascon and secondly that you're my son. Don't fight shy of adventures; I'd sooner you lived dangerously. I've taught you to handle a sword: you've got good strong legs and a wrist of steel. Fight at the least provocation, in season and out, because now that duelling's illegal the man who fights shows himself to be doubly brave. I wish I had more to give you, my dear boy, but here's all I have: fifteen crowns, my horse, and these few words of advice. Your mother will give you the prescription for a special ointment which she got from an old gypsy woman, and which has the miraculous property of healing all wounds except heart wounds. Make the most of these gifts and may your life be long and happy. There's just one thing I might add, by the way; I'd like to give you an example to model your life on. Not myself, for I've never been to Court and only served as a volunteer in the religious wars. Not myself, I say, but Monsieur de Tréville, who was at one time my neighbour, a Gascon like myself, and who, as a child, was the honoured playmate of our good King Louis XIII, whom God preserve. Sometimes their childish games became regular tussles and sometimes the King got the worst of it. His Majesty remembers to this day how

Monsieur de Tréville used to set about him and has as much respect for him now as he had then. Since then Monsieur de Tréville has had many another tussle; five on his first journey to Paris alone and, between the death of the late King and the coming-of-age of this one, seven more, all serious duels, not counting the various campaigns he fought in. Between this King's accession to power and the present day he's fought at least a hundred other duels, perhaps more. He's defied edicts, ordinances and decrees and see where he's got to! He's Captain of the Musketeers, in other words head of a band of dare-devil heroes who are high in the King's favour and who terrify the Cardinal, the great Cardinal, and it takes a good deal to frighten him, as we all know. Added to which Monsieur de Tréville has an income of ten thousand crowns and is therefore a very big man. He started life as you did. Go to him with this letter; do as he tells you and perhaps one day you'll get where he is.'

With these words Monsieur d'Artagnan the elder buckled his own sword round his son's waist, kissed him affectionately on both cheeks and gave him his blessing.

The young man left his father's room and went to say good-bye to his mother, who was waiting for him with the precious prescription which he was bound to need if he followed the advice of his father. The farewell scene between him and his mother was longer and more affectionate than that between him and his father; not that Monsieur d'Artagnan did not love his son, his only son, but he was a man and therefore thought it wrong to give way to his feelings. Madame d'Artagnan, being a woman and also a mother, collapsed in her son's arms and sobbed aloud. Her son tried hard to keep calm as became a future musketeer, but his warmer feelings prevailed and he too shed bitter tears, although he turned his head away as he did so.

That very day the young man set forth armed with his father's three gifts, the fifteen crowns, the horse, and the letter for Monsieur de Tréville; the good advice had been given as an afterthought.

Thus equipped and with his father's words imprinted on his mind d'Artagnan was, both morally and physically, an exact copy of Cervantes' hero with whom we at first compared him. Don Quixote mistook windmills for giants and sheep for armies, whilst our young Gascon took every smile for a sneer and every stare for a challenge. The result was that in the stretch of road between Tarbes and Meung he held his fist permanently clenched and clutched at his sword-hilt roughly ten times a day. No jaw, however, collided with his fist and his sword never left its scabbard. It was only natural that the passers-by should break into broad grins when they caught sight of the yellow nag, but they prudently stifled their mirth, or at least tried to laugh out of the corners of their mouths, like ancient masks, when they saw the good long sword which clanked above the yellow nag and then again the proud, not to say fierce, eye which flashed above the sword. D'Artagnan had, in fact, suffered no loss of dignity until he reached that wretched town of Meung.

Here, as he was dismounting at the door of the Jolly Miller without anyone, host, ostler, or stableboy, coming to hold his stirrup at the block, d'Artagnan noticed a gentleman standing at a half-open window on the ground floor of the inn, a tall, distinguished-looking man with a rather scowling expression. He was talking to two other men, who appeared to be listening to his words with deference. As usual d'Artagnan presumed that he was the object of the conversation and stood listening. This time he was only half mistaken, though it was not he but his horse which had engaged the gentleman's attention. The stranger was explaining to his listeners the animal's points one by one, and his audience appeared to agree with him. And whenever the gentleman spoke his listeners shouted with laughter. Now we know that the mere suspicion of a smile was enough to anger our young friend, so we can imagine how he reacted to these offensive explosions of mirth.

But d'Artagnan decided first to take stock of this insolent stranger's appearance. He looked at him haughtily and observed that he was a man of forty to forty-five, with shrewd dark eyes, a pale skin, a pronounced nose and a well-trimmed, black moustache, and that he wore a violet doublet and hose with aiguillettes of the same colour, with no trimmings except the usual slashes through which his shirt appeared. The doublet and hose, though new, appeared creased, like travelling clothes which had long been carried about in a valise. D'Artagnan took in all these details with the speed of an acute observer, and his instincts told him that the stranger was destined to play a big part in his life.

The gentleman chose the very moment at which d'Artagnan was taking stock of him and his violet doublet to make one of his most scholarly and profound observations about the Bearnese cob. His two listeners roared with laughter, and even he allowed the faintest flicker of a smile to pass across his face. This time there was no doubt of it; d'Artagnan had been actually insulted. Convinced of this he pulled his beret down over his eyes and, aping some of the airs and graces of a courtier which he had learnt from noblemen travelling through Gascony, stepped forward with one hand on his sword-hilt and the other on his hip. Unfortunately, as he approached his enemy, his anger increased. He completely lost his head and, instead of protesting like an insulted gentleman, shook his fist and became vulgarly abusive.

'Hi, there!' he cried. 'Yes, you Sir, skulking behind that shutter! What are you laughing at? When I see a man laughing I always like to be told the joke, so that I can laugh too.'

The gentleman slowly lifted his eyes from the horse to its rider, as though it took him quite a while to realize that he was the object of this rather strange attack; then, as there seemed to be no doubt of it, he frowned slightly and, after a longish pause, answered d'Artagnan in a tone of amused contempt:

'I was not talking to you, Sir.'

'No, but I was talking to you, Sir,' cried the young man, stung by the stranger's manner, at once easy and supercilious.

The stranger looked again at d'Artagnan with a faint smile and, leaving the window, came slowly out of the inn and took his stand a few steps away from him, facing the horse. His composed look and the sardonic expression in his eyes increased the enjoyment of his companions, who were still standing at the window. D'Artagnan, seeing him approach, drew his sword a foot's length out of its scabbard.

'This horse is definitely a buttercup, or, I should say, has been one at some time or other,' said the stranger, continuing his examination and addressing his listeners at the window, without appearing to notice d'Artagnan, who, in his rage, had backed round and was now standing between him and them. 'It's a colour common in flowers but still very rare in horses.'

'One can laugh at a horse and still be afraid to laugh at its rider!' cried Tréville's pupil in a passion.

'I don't often laugh, Sir,' said the stranger, 'as no doubt you can tell from my face. But I hold to my right of laughing whenever it suits me.'

'And I won't have anyone laughing when it doesn't suit me!' cried d'Artagnan.

'Really, Sir?' said the stranger more quietly than ever. 'Well, that's quite understandable!'

And, turning on his heel, he walked towards the main gate of the inn, under which d'Artagnan, on his arrival, had noticed a saddled and bridled horse. But d'Artagnan was not the man to allow anyone to hold him up to ridicule. He drew his sword right out of its scabbard and ran after the stranger crying:

'Turn and face me, Sir! I've had enough of your damned sneering! Turn and face me or I'll run you through the back!'

The stranger turned sharply and eyed d'Artagnan with an expression of mingled surprise and scorn. 'Run me through? Me?' he cried. 'What are you talking about? Are you mad?'

Then in an undertone, as though talking to himself, he added: 'What a pity this is! This young hothead would have made an admirable musketeer. And the King always on the look-out for fresh blood!'

Hardly were the words out of his mouth before d'Artagnan lunged at him so furiously that, had he not stepped quickly aside, he would probably not have lived to make another joke. He now realized that the affair was serious, drew his sword,

saluted his opponent and stood on guard. But at that moment
the innkeeper and the two who had been standing with the
stranger at the window fell on d'Artagnan with sticks, shovels
and tongs. This created a diversion so rapid and so complete
that, while d'Artagnan turned to defend himself against this
rain of blows, his opponent quickly sheathed his sword and
once more became a spectator instead of an actor in the drama,
a rôle which seemed to become him better. But he muttered to
himself:

'Hell take these Gascons! Why can't he get on that saffron
horse of his and be off!'

'Not till I've killed you, you coward!' cried d'Artagnan, fighting back hard against his three assailants, who were plastering
him with blows.

'Another of these swaggerers!' muttered the stranger. 'God,
these Gascons are incorrigible! Well, carry on the fight then,
since he insists on it. When he's had enough he'll let us know.'

But the stranger did not realize what an obstinate fellow he
had to deal with. D'Artagnan was not the man to give in without a struggle. So the fight went on for another few seconds
until at last d'Artagnan, in his exhaustion, dropped his sword,
which was instantly broken with a heavy blow from a stick.
Another blow, levelled at his forehead, knocked him to the
ground where he lay prostrate, bleeding, and almost unconscious.

It was at this moment that the crowd began to collect from
all sides. The innkeeper, fearing a scandal, summoned his
stableboys and had the wounded man removed from the scene
and carried into the kitchen, where his wounds were roughly
dressed. The stranger meanwhile went back to his place at the
window and stood looking with some impatience at the crowd
outside. Its presence seemed to cause him great annoyance.

'Well, how's that young lunatic?' said he, turning as the door
opened and addressing the innkeeper who had come to inquire after his health.

'I trust Your Excellency's none the worse?' asked the innkeeper.

'No, I'm all right. But I'd like to know what's happened to our young friend.'

'He's calmer now,' said the innkeeper. 'In fact he's fainted.'

'Oh, he's fainted, has he?' said the gentleman.

'Yes. But before he finally collapsed he staggered to his feet, turned in your direction and shouted a challenge.'

'That fellow's the devil himself!' cried the stranger.

'Oh no, Sir, he's not the devil,' answered the innkeeper with a sneer. 'I can vouch for that. While he was unconscious we searched him and found that he had only one shirt to his name and only twelve crowns in his purse. But for all that, before he fainted, he said that had such a thing happened in Paris you'd have been made to regret it at once whereas here you've got off, though only for the time being.'

'Oh! If he said that he must be some royal prince in disguise,' said the stranger coldly.

'I'm only telling you this to put you on your guard, your Honour,' said the innkeeper.

'Did he mention anybody's name, by any chance?'

'Oh yes! He slapped his pocket and said: "We'll see what Monsieur de Tréville thinks when he hears about this!"'

'Monsieur de Tréville!' exclaimed the stranger with a start. 'He slapped his pocket and mentioned Monsieur de Tréville! Well now, my good man, don't tell me you didn't search that pocket of his while he was lying there. What did you find in it?'

'A letter addressed to Monsieur de Tréville, Captain of the Musketeers.'

'Is that a fact?'

'Yes, Your Honour, it's as I'm telling you.'

The innkeeper, who was rather dense, did not notice the effect of his words on the stranger. The latter now left the window at which he had been standing with his elbow resting on the sill and came forward, an anxious frown on his face.

'This is the very devil!' he muttered to himself. 'Could Tréville have sent that Gascon against me? He's a bit young, I know. But a sword thrust's a sword thrust, no matter who deals it. And a boy might catch me off my guard. A small obstacle can sometimes defeat a great enterprise.'

And the stranger thought for a moment. Then, addressing the innkeeper, he said:

'Look here, my good man, can't you get this young lunatic out of the way somehow? I can't in all conscience kill him. But,' he added, frowning again, 'at present he's a nuisance here. Where is he now?'

'In my wife's room on the first floor. They're dressing his wounds.'

'I suppose he's got his clothes and his bag with him and he's still wearing his doublet!'

'No, Sir! All his things are down in the kitchen. But if this fellow's a nuisance to you . . .'

'Of course he's a nuisance. He's causing a disturbance in your inn which decent folk won't put up with. Go upstairs, make out my bill, and call my servant.'

'What, Sir? You're leaving us already?'

'You know I'm leaving! Didn't I tell you to get my horse saddled? Hasn't it been done?'

'It has been done, Sir. As your Excellency may have noticed your horse is at the main gate, all ready for the journey.'

'Well, do as I tell you then.'

The innkeeper looked at his guest with raised eyebrows as though to say:

'So you're frightened of that young whippersnapper, are you?'

But a stern look from the stranger brought him to his senses. He bowed low and left the room.

'That young scamp mustn't be allowed to see Milady,' thought the stranger. 'She'll be here at any moment. In fact she's late already. It would really be better if I rode out to meet her. If only I could find out what was in that letter addressed to Tréville.'

And the stranger, muttering these words, made his way slowly down to the kitchen.

Meanwhile, the innkeeper, who was convinced that it was

the young man's presence which had decided the stranger to leave his inn, had gone to his wife's room where he had found d'Artagnan restored to consciousness. Telling him that he was in for a load of trouble with the authorities for having provoked a nobleman (for in his opinion the stranger was certainly a nobleman), the innkeeper persuaded d'Artagnan, in spite of his exhaustion, to get up and be off. So d'Artagnan, half-dazed, with only his shirt and breeches on and with his head swathed in bandages, staggered to his feet and, urged from behind by the host, went down the stairs. But on reaching the kitchen, the first thing he saw through the window was his enemy standing at the footboard of a heavy coach harnessed to two large Normandy horses, talking to a lady seated inside.

Only this lady's head and shoulders were visible through the coach window. She was between twenty and twenty-two years old. We have already stated d'Artagnan's capacity to take in at a glance every detail of a person's appearance. He therefore noticed at once that the woman was young and beautiful. And her looks struck him more forcibly because they were of a kind entirely foreign to the southern provinces where he was born and bred. The lady was fair and pale, with long, golden ringlets which fell to her shoulders, large, blue, languishing eyes, rose-red lips and hands as white as alabaster. She was talking eagerly to the stranger.

'So, His Eminence's orders are . . .' said the lady.

'That you return to England at once, and let him know the moment the Duke leaves London.'

'And what about my other instructions?' said the beautiful traveller.

'They're here, in this box, which you're not to open till you've crossed the Channel.'

'Very well. And what about you?'

'I'm returning to Paris.'

'What! Without putting that rude young puppy in his place?' asked the lady.

The stranger was about to reply when d'Artagnan, who had heard everything, rushed into the doorway.

'You're wrong there!' he cried. 'It's the rude young puppy who's going to put you in your place! And this time I'll see you don't escape as you did before.'

'Escape?' repeated the stranger frowning.

'Yes, Sir! For I don't suppose even you'll turn tail in the presence of a woman!'

At this the stranger seized hold of his sword, but the lady quickly intervened.

'Remember the least delay may prove fatal!' she cried.

'You're right,' said the stranger. 'You go your way and I'll go mine. And let's be quick about it.'

He bowed to the lady and leapt into the saddle while the coachman whipped up his horses. And the lady and gentleman made off at top speed, disappearing down opposite ends of the street.

'Hi, there! Your bill!' shouted the innkeeper, his affection for his guest changing to scorn as he saw him make off without settling his account.

'Pay, varlet!' cried the stranger to his servant, turning sideways on his horse. The lackey threw a couple of silver coins at the innkeeper's feet and then galloped off after his master.

'Coward! Rogue! Call yourself a gentleman!' cried d'Artagnan, rushing off in turn in pursuit of master and servant.

But the young man was still too weak to indulge in such strenuous efforts. Hardly had he gone ten yards than his ears began to throb, giddiness seized him, the blood rushed to his head and he collapsed in the middle of the street still yelling:

'Coward! Coward! Coward!'

The innkeeper walked up to him as he lay prostrate. 'Yes, he's a coward all right,' he said.

He hoped by this piece of servility to get on good terms with the impoverished young man, like the heron in the fable with the snail which it had scorned the previous night.

'Yes, a proper coward,' gasped d'Artagnan. 'But she, how lovely she is!'

'She? What she?' asked the innkeeper.

'Milady,' stammered d'Artagnan.

And then he fainted for the second time.

'It doesn't really matter,' thought the innkeeper. 'I've lost two customers, but kept one, and this fellow'll be here for several days. So in any case I'm bound to be eleven crowns up.'

We know that eleven crowns was the exact sum still left in d'Artagnan's purse.

The innkeeper had reckoned on eleven days' illness at the rate of a crown a day. But he hadn't reckoned with his guest. At five o'clock next morning d'Artagnan got up, went down himself to the kitchen and asked for wine, oil, rosemary, and various other items needed for an ointment. Then, with his mother's prescription in front of him, he prepared this ointment and with it proceeded to dress and redress his many wounds, refusing all outside aid. Thanks no doubt to the healing properties of the gypsy's ointment and also perhaps to the absence of the doctor d'Artagnan was up and about that very evening, and next day almost well again.

Now it was a question of paying for the wine, oil, and rosemary. This was, in fact, our hero's only debt, for he had himself refused all nourishment, although, from what the innkeeper said, the yellow nag had devoured three times more than one would have thought possible for a beast of its size. But when the young man felt in his pocket for the money he found only his little threadbare, velvet purse containing the eleven crowns: the letter to Monsieur de Tréville had disappeared.

For a while the young man searched patiently for the letter, turning his breast and waist pockets inside out twenty times and more, rummaging about in his bag and delving into his purse. But when it dawned on him that the letter was really and truly missing he was seized with a further attack of rage which nearly called for a fresh supply of the spiced wine and oil. For when the innkeeper saw our fractious young friend getting excited and threatening to break up the whole house if his letter were not returned to him he seized hold of a pike while his wife took up a broom and his boys armed themselves with the sticks which they had so successfully wielded two days before.

'My letter! My letter of introduction!' cried d'Artagnan.

'Give it back or, by God, I'll run you all through like larks on a spit!'

Unfortunately one thing stood in the way of our young friend carrying out his threat. His sword had been split in two in the original fight, and this he had forgotten. The result was that when he grasped the hilt he found himself armed with a mere stump eight to ten inches long, which the innkeeper had carefully replaced inside the scabbard. The cook had already taken the rest of the blade to use as a larding-pin.

But our young hothead would probably have carried on in spite of this setback had not the innkeeper suddenly realized that his claim was perfectly justified.

'Now wait a moment!' said he, lowering his pike. 'I wonder where that letter is!'

'Yes, where is it?' cried d'Artagnan. 'Listen, my good man! That letter is for Monsieur de Tréville and must be found. If it's not found now you may be sure he'll get it out of you later.'

With this threat d'Artagnan succeeded in bringing the innkeeper to heel. Next to the King and the Cardinal Monsieur de Tréville was more spoken of by soldiers, and even by civilians, than any man in the kingdom. There was Father Joseph, of course, but his name was only mentioned in whispers, so great was the terror inspired by His Grey Eminence, the Cardinal's shadow.

So, throwing away his pike and ordering his wife to put back her broom and his boys their sticks, the innkeeper set to work to search for the missing letter.

'Did this letter contain anything of value?' he asked, after searching fruitlessly for some time.

'Good God! I should say it did!' cried the Gascon, who was relying on this letter to give him an entry into Court circles. 'It contained my whole fortune.'

'Spanish bonds, or what?' asked the innkeeper anxiously.

'Bonds on His Majesty's own Treasury,' replied d'Artagnan.

It was a bold statement, but his whole future was at stake.

'Oh Lord! Oh Lord!' cried the innkeeper. 'This is terrible!'

'The money's not important,' continued d'Artagnan with

true Gascon impudence. 'I don't care tuppence about the money. It's the letter that matters. I'd rather have lost a thousand pistoles than that letter.'

He could just as well have said twenty thousand, but his youthful modesty restrained him.

Suddenly the innkeeper, who was cursing himself for a fool, had an inspiration.

'That letter's not lost!' he cried.

'Not lost?' repeated d'Artagnan.

'No. It's been stolen from you.'

'Stolen? Who by?'

'By the gentleman who was here yesterday. He went down to the kitchen where your doublet was. He was alone in there. I'm ready to bet he stole the letter.'

'Oh! So you think he stole it!' replied d'Artagnan without much conviction. He knew quite well that the letter was of merely personal value and could not imagine that anyone would want to steal it. It was obvious that none of the guests or servants at present at the inn would have had any use for it.

'So you really and truly suspect that gentleman?' continued d'Artagnan.

'I repeat, I'm sure of it,' replied the innkeeper. 'When I told him your Excellency was Monsieur de Tréville's protégé and that you even had a letter with that great man's name on it he seemed very upset. He asked me where the letter was and went down at once to the kitchen where he knew he'd find your doublet.'

'Ha! So he is the thief after all!' replied d'Artagnan, 'I shall inform Monsieur de Tréville of this and he'll tell the King.'

Then, with a flourish, he drew two crowns from his pocket and tossed them to the innkeeper, who, cap in hand, went with him to the door. D'Artagnan now leapt on to his yellow horse and finally, after a long and exhausting ride, reached the Porte St Antoine in Paris. Here he sold the horse for the sum of three crowns, which was a good price considering that it had been hard pressed for the last stage of the journey. The dealer who bought the horse declared that he only paid this enormous sum because of the animal's unusual colour.

So d'Artagnan eventually entered Paris on foot, carrying all his worldly goods under his arm. He wandered about the streets until he at last found a room to let at a price which suited his slender means, a mere attic in the Rue des Fosso-yeurs, near the Luxembourg.

After paying his deposit d'Artagnan settled himself in his new quarters and spent the rest of the day sewing on to his doublet and hose certain trimmings which his mother had un-stitched from an almost new doublet belonging to his father and given to him on the sly. Then he visited the Quai de la Féraille to have a new blade fitted to his sword, later returning to the Louvre to inquire from the first musketeer whom he happened to meet the whereabouts of Monsieur de Tréville's house. When he learnt that it was in the Rue du Vieux Colom-bier, quite close to his own little attic, his spirits rose, for he considered this a good omen for the success of his journey.

Finally, thoroughly satisfied with the way he had behaved at Meung, without regret for the past, confident in the present, and hopeful for the future, he went to bed and slept the sleep of the just.

This sleep, the sleep of a rustic rather than that of a man of fashion, lasted till nine the next morning. At this late hour he got up, dressed and prepared to meet the great Monsieur de Tréville, who in his father's view was the third most import-ant man in the kingdom.

CHAPTER II

Monsieur de Tréville's Ante-Room

MONSIEUR DE TROISVILLE, as he was still spoken of in Gascony, or Monsieur de Tréville, which was the name he finally adopted in Paris, had in point of fact started life as d'Artagnan had done; that is to say, without a penny piece to his name but with a fund of quick wit, dash, and persistence which gave the poorest Gascon squires of those days a better chance of getting on in the world than all the money-bags which bulged the pockets of the stick-in-the-mud young noble-men from Périgord or Berry. His courage, assurance, and un-failing good luck had been proof against the hard knocks for which that age was so renowned, and he had soon reached the top of that difficult ladder known as Court Favour, scaling it four rungs at a time.

He was a friend of the King who, as we know, worshipped the memory of his father Henry IV. Monsieur de Tréville's father had served Henry IV well and faithfully in his wars against the Catholic League. When Paris finally surrendered the grateful monarch, who had never amassed a fortune but had always preferred to live for the day, had granted his pro-tégé in place of ready cash the right to take as his coat-of-arms gules, a golden lion passant with the motto: 'Fidelis et fortis'. This was a great tribute, to be sure, but it did not advance de Tréville's pocket very much, and when the great King Henry IV's faithful servant died all he left to his son was his sword and his motto. These two assets and the blameless name that went with them gave Monsieur de Tréville the entry into the young prince's household. Here he made such good use of his sword and was so true to his motto that Louis XIII, one of the best swordsmen in the country, used to say that if any of his friends was committed to a duel he would advise him to choose as his second himself and then Tréville, or perhaps Tréville even before himself.

Thus Louis XIII had a real affection for Tréville, a regal affection, a selfish affection no doubt, but an affection all the same. The fact was that in those unhappy days kings tried to surround themselves with men of Tréville's temper. There were many who could qualify for the epithet 'strong', which formed the second part of our friend's device, but few noblemen of that period could be called 'faithful'. 'Fidelis et fortis' was Tréville's motto, and he lived up to it. He was one of those rare people who combine a dog's obedient intelligence with reckless courage and the power of quick observation and speedy action. His eye was trained to notice only the King's enemies and his hand to strike them down: a Besme, a Maurever, a Poltrot de Méré, a Vitry, or any other nobleman you care to mention. In short Tréville had every quality and had been only awaiting his chance, which he had vowed he would seize the moment it came his way. And so Louis XIII had made him captain of his Musketeers, the bodyguard which in its fanatical devotion was for the King what his Ordinaries had been for Henry III and his Scottish Guard for Louis XI.

The Cardinal was determined not to be outdone by the King in this respect. When he saw the formidable army with which Louis XIII was surrounded he, as the joint or perhaps the sole ruler in France, was determined also to have his bodyguard. So like Louis XIII Richelieu had his musketeers, and these two rival powers were to be seen scouring the provinces of France and the neighbouring countries of Europe for men renowned for their skill in swordsmanship, to enlist them in their regiments. And King and Cardinal often wrangled in the evenings over their games of chess about the relative merits of their adherents. Each boasted of the courage and bearing of his men and, whilst they openly decreed against duelling and brawling, each secretly urged his followers to challenge the other's, grieving at any defeat and rejoicing wholeheartedly at any victory sustained by his own side. This at least is the story as told in the memoirs of a man who took part in a few of these defeats and many of these triumphs.

Tréville had always pandered to his master's weakness, and it was to this shrewdness that he owed his long period of favour with a sovereign who has left behind him a name for inconstancy. It was Tréville's habit to make his musketeers parade in front of Cardinal Armand Duplessis with an insolent air which made His Eminence's grey moustache curl with rage. Tréville had an excellent understanding of the warlike spirit of the age, in which men, when not despoiling the enemy, lived by despoiling each other. His soldiers were a regiment of daredevils, unruly in their behaviour towards everyone but himself.

The King's Musketeers, or rather Monsieur de Tréville's Musketeers were to be seen in all the taverns, walks, and fairgrounds of the city. Their faces scarred from duelling, they would lounge about with their jackets unbuttoned, shouting, twirling their moustaches and clanking their swords. They went out of their way to jostle the Cardinal's guards and would challenge them openly in the streets with a smile on their lips and mischief in their hearts. Some of the musketeers would fall in these battles; then they were sure of being mourned and avenged; more often they killed their man in the full certainty that they would not be allowed to languish in prison, for Monsieur de Tréville was there to demand their release. Thus Monsieur de Tréville's praises were sung at every street corner by these men who adored him and who, hard-bitten as they were, trembled in his presence like schoolboys in the presence of their master, ready to obey his every whim and to die to wipe out the slightest reproof from their beloved leader.

Monsieur de Tréville employed this powerful weapon firstly in the interests of the King and of the King's friends and then in the interests of himself and of his own friends. And yet in none of the memoirs of that period, which abounds in memoirs, does one see any mention even from his enemies, whether soldiers or men of letters, of this man having ever allowed his followers to be used as hirelings. With his rare talent for intrigue, in which he was a match for the most notorious intriguers of the age, he remained straight and honest in his dealings. Moreover his many duels and the hardships of his life had not coarsened him either in mind or body. On the contrary he had become a leading figure in the social life of the capital, and had a name as a philanderer and a witty talker. Monsieur de Tréville's success in love was as notorious as Bassompièrre's twenty years earlier, and that is saying a good deal. The Captain of the Musketeers was admired, feared, and loved, and what more can any man ask for in life?

All the minor stars at the Court of Louis XIV shone dim in the light of the King's own glory. But his father, a sun 'great enough to light many worlds', allowed each of his favourites to shed his own light and every courtier to show his own worth. So in the Paris of that day, besides the King's levee and that of the Cardinal, over two hundred minor levees were held, all more or less exclusive. Of these minor levees that of Monsieur de Tréville was the most frequented.

From six o'clock in the morning in summer and in winter from eight the courtyard of his house in the Rue du Vieux Colombier resembled a camp. Between fifty and sixty musketeers were always stationed there. These musketeers apparently came in relays and took alternate duty, so that the courtyard should always present an impressive display of arms and men. Up one of the great staircases which, according to our present-day ideas, occupied in itself room enough for a whole building filed an endless procession of toadies coming to ask some favour of the great man, of young gentlemen from the provinces, candidates for army commissions, and of footmen in different coloured liveries bringing messages for Monsieur de Tréville from their masters. In the ante-room, on long curved divans, waited the elect, that is to say those who had come by appointment. There was a buzz of conversation in this ante-room from morning till night, while Monsieur de Tréville, in his adjoining room, received visits, listened to petitions, gave his orders and, like the King on his balcony at the Louvre, had only to go to his window to survey his men on guard below.

On the day upon which d'Artagnan arrived the crowd was impressive, especially to a country lad straight from the provinces. It is true that our country lad was a Gascon and that at that time d'Artagnan's compatriots had a reputation for not being easily daunted. But it would have been a brave man indeed who could pass through the massive door studded with large, square-headed nails and not feel cold to the marrow of his bones when confronted with the seething mob of noisy, quarrelsome, boisterous swordsmen which composed Monsieur de Tréville's bodyguard. Only an officer, a bigwig, or a pretty woman could have forced a passage through these swirling waters.

So it was with a thumping heart that d'Artagnan advanced into the middle of this crowd, pressing his sword tight against his lanky leg, holding on to his plumed hat with one hand and wearing the forced grin of a shy country-cousin who wants to appear at his ease. Having passed one group of swordsmen he began to breathe more freely, although he realized that they were all turning to look at him. For the first time in his life our hero, who had till then thought quite highly of himself, began to feel ridiculous.

When he reached the staircase matters became even worse, for on the bottom steps four musketeers were engaged in some form of swordplay, while on the landing above stood a dozen more, waiting their turn to join in.

The game they were playing was an original one and held d'Artagnan spellbound. Of the four men fighting at the foot of the staircase one stood on a higher step than the others and tried with his sword to prevent his opponents from getting past him. All four thrust and parried with lightning agility. D'Artagnan at first mistook their blades for fencing-foils, buttoned at the tip, but, seeing the wounds inflicted, he soon realized that they were fighting with real, perfectly sharpened swords. Whenever anyone received a scratch both victim and onlookers laughed uproariously.

The musketeer who was at present on the upper step was holding his adversaries marvellously at bay. A ring had been formed round them. It was the rule of the game that the man who was touched should yield his place in the queue for audience to the man who had touched him. In five minutes the man on the step had grazed his three opponents, one on the wrist, another on the chin, and the third on the ear, whilst he himself remained unscathed. His skill had therefore put him up three places in the queue.

Though our young traveller had decided not to show any naïve astonishment this pastime made him positively gasp. There were many hotheads in his native province certainly, but even there duelling was always accompanied by certain rites, and he had never before seen anything to equal the swagger of these four bloods, even in Gascony. He felt like Gulliver, suddenly transported into a country of fabulous giants. And he had not yet reached his goal; he had still to cross the landing and the ante-room.

There was no fighting on the landing. Here the men were telling stories about women and in the ante-room tales about the Court. D'Artagnan blushed on the landing and shuddered in the ante-room. His imagination, which was lively enough and which had made him formidable to Gascon housemaids and even to their young mistresses, boggled at these tales of amorous adventures and of prowess in the arts of love, tales made more wonderful by the mention of names famous throughout France and by the daring details with which they were embellished. Our hero's morals were shocked on the landing and, worse still, his respect for the Cardinal was outraged in the ante-room. There to his amazement he heard the policy which made all Europe tremble, and the Cardinal's private life, which so many high and mighty lords had been punished for attempting to investigate, criticized aloud. This great man, revered by Monsieur d'Artagnan the elder, was a butt for the wit of Monsieur de Tréville's musketeers, who mocked his bandy legs and hunched shoulders. Some of these gentlemen made obscene rhymes about his mistress Madame d'Aiguillon and about his niece Madame de Combalet, whilst others planned all kinds of practical jokes to play against his pages and guards. All this frivolity seemed to d'Artagnan monstrous and impossible.

And yet, whenever by accident the King's name came up in the conversation, some invisible gag seemed to bind these gentlemen's mouths. They would look round timidly as though they feared that the dividing wall between them and Monsieur de Tréville's private study might betray their indiscretion. Then some new mention would be made of His Eminence, upon which the wits began once more to sparkle and all the Cardinal's actions were brought into the hard light of day and criticized.

'These people are bound to be sent to the Bastille and

hanged,' thought the terrified d'Artagnan. 'And I shall probably go with them, for the fact that I've seen them and listened
to their talk makes me their accomplice. My father taught me
to respect the Cardinal. What would he say if he saw me with
all these pagans?'

Needless to say, therefore, d'Artagnan did not dare take
part in the conversation. But he watched and listened carefully, straining his eyes and ears in order to miss nothing. And
alas his trust in his father's judgement wavered, and both
instinct and inclination prompted him to approve, rather than
blame, these monstrous goings-on.

D'Artagnan, as we know, was a complete stranger in this
crowd of courtiers and had never been seen here before, so one
of M. de Tréville's household soon came up and asked him his
business. Our hero modestly gave his name, stressed his Gascon nationality, and asked the servant to beg a moment's
audience of his master. The servant condescendingly promised
to pass on this message to his master in due course.

Our young hero had at last slightly recovered his poise and
now had leisure to look round him and take note of the appearance and dress of the Musketeers.

In the centre of the most lively group stood a tall,
supercilious-looking fellow dressed in a fashion so peculiar as
to attract attention. Though on duty, he happened at that
moment not to be wearing the regulation dress coat but was
showing himself off in a sky-blue doublet, slightly faded and
threadbare, strapped across with a magnificent shoulder-belt
trimmed with gold lace, which glittered like rippling water in
the sunlight. A long crimson velvet cloak hung gracefully from
his shoulders, revealing only the front part of the shoulder-belt,
from which hung an enormous rapier.

This musketeer had just come off guard. He complained of a
cold and coughed affectedly from time to time. It was for that
reason, he said, that he had put on the cloak. He kept talking
at the top of his voice and twirling his moustaches, exposing
his embroidered shoulder-belt to the admiring gaze of the
onlookers, d'Artagnan among them.

'It can't be helped,' the musketeer was saying. 'It's the fashion now. It's silly, I know, but there you are. It's the fashion, so one must conform. And besides, one must spend one's allowance somehow.'

'Oh, come on, Porthos,' cried one of his admirers, 'don't try and pretend that shoulder-belt was bought out of your father's allowance. I know who gave it to you; it was the veiled lady I saw you with last Sunday near the Porte St Honoré.'

'I swear it wasn't! I bought it myself, with my own money,' replied the man referred to as Porthos.

'Yes,' retorted another musketeer, 'just as I bought this new purse with the money my mistress put into my old one.'

'But it's true what I'm telling you!' cried Porthos. 'Listen! I can prove it. I paid twelve pistoles for it!'

This remark increased everyone's admiration of the belt, but it did not dispel their doubts.

'It's true, isn't it, Aramis?' cried Porthos, turning to another musketeer.

This other musketeer, Aramis, was a complete contrast to his friend, both in looks and dress. He was a young man, barely twenty-three, with a demure and innocent expression, dark, gentle eyes and downy pink cheeks like an autumn peach. His neat moustache formed a perfectly straight line on his upper lip: he seemed afraid to lower his hands for fear their veins might swell and he kept pinching the ends of his ears to preserve their delicate, shell-pink colour. He said very little and when he spoke he drawled. He was always making graceful bows, and when he laughed, he laughed noiselessly, baring pearly teeth which, like the rest of his person, he tended with care. To his friend's appeal he replied with a nod.

This confirmation seemed to settle the matter of the shoulder-belt once and for all. The company continued to admire it but referred to it no more and for no particular reason the conversation suddenly took another turn.

'What do you fellows think of the story of Chalais' equerry?' asked another musketeer, addressing the company in general.

'What story?' asked Porthos condescendingly.

'He says that in Brussels he found Rochefort, the Cardinal's private spy, disguised as a Capuchin, and that this damned Rochefort, in his disguise, had fooled that poor boob de Laigues.'

'Yes, boob's just the word for him,' said Porthos. 'But are you sure the story's true?'

'Aramis told me,' answered the musketeer.

'Oh, Aramis told you, did he?'

'Yes, Porthos! And don't pretend you don't know about it,' put in Aramis. 'I told you the story myself last night. Now let's forget it.'

'Oh! So we're to forget it, are we?' cried Porthos. 'That's what you think! The Cardinal sets spies on a gentleman, has his private correspondence stolen by a rogue, thief, or whatever you like to call him; then with the help of this spy and by searching the gentleman's private correspondence has Chalais beheaded on the fatuous pretext that he wanted to kill the King and marry Monsieur to the Queen. No one knew a word of this plot until you told us about it yesterday, and we were all pleased with you for exposing it. And now that you've got us all worked up you calmly come along today and tell us to shut up about it.'

'All right then, let's go on talking about it, if you really want to,' retorted Aramis calmly.

'If I were Chalais' equerry I'd give that Rochefort fellow something to remember me by.'

'Yes. And then the Red Duke would give you something to remember him by.'

'Ha, ha! The Red Duke! That's good!' cried Porthos, clapping loudly to acclaim the joke. 'The Red Duke! That's magnificent! I'll dine out on that, Aramis. Isn't our Aramis witty! What a pity you didn't follow your true vocation, my boy! You'd have made a perfect abbé.'

'Oh, I've only put it off for the time being,' replied Aramis. 'I'll be an abbé one day all right. You know I'm keeping up my Bible studies, don't you?'

'Yes, he'll pull it off all right one day,' said Porthos.

'Yes, and sooner than any of you think,' said Aramis.

'He's only waiting for one thing to happen before donning that cassock he hangs up behind his uniform!' put in a musketeer.

'What's he waiting for?' cried another.

'He's waiting for the Queen to produce an heir to the throne.'

'Now, gentlemen, no joking about that, if you don't mind,' said Porthos. 'Thank God the Queen's still young enough for that.'

'I'm told the Duke of Buckingham's in France,' went on Aramis with a snigger which gave a peculiar significance to this apparently harmless remark.

'Aramis, old boy, for once you're wrong,' interposed Porthos. 'And that remark wasn't witty; it was in bad taste. Monsieur de Tréville would tell you off for saying a thing like that.'

'Are you by any chance trying to teach me manners, Porthos?' cried Aramis with a sudden glint in his soft eyes.

'Come on Aramis, old boy! Be yourself! Priest or musketeer, whichever you like. But not both at the same time. Remember what Athos told you the other day; you always want two strings to your bow. Oh, don't let's lose our tempers; that would just be silly; remember the agreement we made, the three of us. We all know you visit Madame d'Aiguillon and make up to her; and we all know you visit Madame de Bois-Tracy, Madame de Chevreuse's cousin, and that she's pretty fond of you too. Oh, don't bother to deny it; we're not asking you to give away your secret and we admire your discretion. We'd merely like you to be kind about the Queen as well. Joke away about the King and the Cardinal as much as you like. But remember the Queen's sacred, and I won't have anyone saying bad things about her when I'm around.'

'Porthos, you're a pompous ass!' replied Aramis. 'How dare you lecture me! You know I'll only take that sort of thing from Athos. Anyway who are you to preach with a belt like that slung across your chest? I'll be a priest if and when I want to be. But at present I'm a musketeer and I say what I like, and just now I feel like telling you that you irritate me.'

'Aramis!'

'Porthos!'

'Gentlemen, please!' cried the musketeers in chorus.

Suddenly the door leading into Monsieur de Tréville's study opened and a lackey called out:

'Monsieur de Tréville awaits Monsieur d'Artagnan!'

At this a hush fell on everyone and in the general silence our young Gascon made his way across the ante-room and entered the Captain's study, thankful to have so narrowly escaped being involved in this curious quarrel.

CHAPTER III

The Audience

MONSIEUR DE TRÉVILLE happened at that moment to be in a very bad temper. However he greeted the young man civilly enough, and when d'Artagnan bowed low and paid his respects de Tréville smiled, for the young man's Bearnese brogue reminded him of his youth and of his native land, and whose heart is not softened at the recollection of home and childhood? De Tréville then went across to the ante-room and, signing to d'Artagnan that he would attend to him after he had dealt with more pressing business, called three times in a loud voice:

'Athos! Porthos! Aramis!'

The two musketeers to whom we have already been introduced and who answered to the names of Porthos and Aramis at once left their circle of friends and went into Monsieur de Tréville's study, and the door was closed sharply behind them. Their manner, though a trifle less assured than usual, impressed d'Artagnan by its lack of constraint, by its admirable blend of dignity and deference. He regarded these men as demigods and their leader as Jupiter in person, armed with all his thunderbolts.

When the door had closed behind the two musketeers and

the buzz of conversation in the ante-room had started again, stimulated perhaps by this sudden sharp summons, de Tré-ville began pacing up and down his study, silent and frowning, passing to and fro in front of Porthos and Aramis, who were standing stiffly at attention as though on parade. He suddenly stopped in front of them, eyed them from head to foot and said irritably:

'D'you know what the King said to me last night, gentle-men?'

'No, Sir,' replied the two musketeers after a moment's silence.

'But we'd be much obliged if you'd tell us, Sir,' added Aramis in his most ingratiating manner.

'He said that from now on he'd recruit his musketeers from the Cardinal's guards.'

'From the Cardinal's guards?' exclaimed Porthos sharply. 'Why on earth?'

'Because he realized that his wine hadn't much body to it and needed livening up with a fresh vintage.'

The two musketeers blushed scarlet. D'Artagnan was thoroughly embarrassed and longed for the earth to open and swallow him up.

'Yes, that's what the King said,' went on Monsieur de Tré-ville, raising his voice, 'and he was perfectly right. The musketeers' credit has sunk pretty low at Court, I may tell you! Last night, when they were playing chess together, the Cardinal was telling the King, with a note of mock sympathy in his voice which maddened me, how two days ago you damned musketeers, you "dare-devils", you "swashbucklers" – yes, that's what he called you, though sneeringly, mind you, and looking at me out of the corner of his eye all the time – how you swashbucklers had been loitering in an inn in the Rue Férou and that a platoon of his guards, on its rounds, had been forced to arrest you as disturbers of the peace. I really thought he was going to laugh in my face. Arresting musketeers! Who-ever heard of such a thing! You two were among that lot. You must know about this. You were recognized and the Cardinal

mentioned your names. What have you got to say for yourselves? Oh, I know it's all my fault, really. I've got a bad habit
of picking my own men. Aramis! Why the Hell did you ask for
a uniform when what you really wanted was a cassock? And
you, Porthos, with that fine lace sash of yours! What's it for,
anyway? To hang a monocle on? And Athos! Where's Athos?
Why isn't he here?'

'Athos is ill, Sir, very ill,' answered Aramis, with a mournful look on his face.

'Ill? What's the matter with him?'

'They're afraid it's small-pox, Sir,' said Porthos. 'It would be
a shame if it were, because it would quite spoil his looks.'

'Small-pox! A likely story! Small-pox at his age! Rubbish!
No, he's probably wounded or perhaps even killed. If only I
knew! Now listen, you musketeers! I won't have you visiting
low haunts, brawling in the streets and duelling in the public
squares. In fact I won't have you making idiots of yourselves in
front of the Cardinal's guards. They're good fellows, those
guards, quiet and well-behaved. They'd never land themselves
in such a mess and, if they did, they'd die rather than yield an
inch. Turn tail? Scuttle off? Oh no! That's a thing only the
King's Musketeers do!'

Porthos and Aramis were trembling with rage. They would
gladly have strangled Monsieur de Tréville on the spot, but in
their heart of hearts they knew that it was only his great affection for them which made him take that tone. They stood and
glowered at their Captain, biting their lips to control themselves and instinctively clutching at their sword-hilts. As we
have said, everyone in the ante-room had heard Monsieur de
Tréville summoning Athos, Porthos, and Aramis, and had
guessed from the tone of his voice that he was in a rage. Now
curiosity prevailed over caution and at least a dozen of the
musketeers were standing with their ears glued to the tapestry,
and their faces were white with fury for they had overheard
every word of what was being said and were repeating to the
company at large each of Monsieur de Tréville's insulting
remarks in turn as it was uttered. In an instant the news had

travelled from one end of the house to the other and all the men were fuming.

'Ha! So the King's Musketeers allow themselves to be arrested by the Cardinal's guards! God, what a story!' went on de Tréville. He was inwardly just as furious as his soldiers, but his voice was hard and clear and he clipped his words and plunged them one by one, like poisoned darts, into the hearts of his listeners. 'Six of the King's Musketeers arrested by six of the Cardinal's guards! That's the end as far as I'm concerned. I'm going straight off to the Louvre to offer my resignation as Captain of the Musketeers and to beg for a lieutenancy under the Cardinal. And if my offer's turned down I shall take to religion. Yes, by God, I'll take Holy Orders!'

At this the subdued mutterings of wrath outside changed into loud shouts, and the ante-room echoed with oaths and blasphemies. 'To Hells', 'by Christs', and 'God damns' rang through the air. D'Artagnan longed for a screen to hide behind and felt an insane desire to crawl under the table.

'Well, Sir,' said Porthos, beside himself with rage, 'it was like this. We were six against six but we were taken by surprise, and before we had time to draw our swords two of our fellows had been killed and Athos himself badly wounded. You know Athos well enough, don't you, Sir? Well, he tried twice to get up and fell back each time. Even then we didn't give in but were beaten by sheer weight of numbers. In the end we managed to escape. As for Athos they thought he was dead and didn't even bother to carry him away. There you have the whole damned business. Hang it all Sir, one can't win every battle! Great Pompey himself lost the Battle of Pharsalus, and King Francis I lost Pavia, and he was as good as the next man, I'm told.'

'And I may tell you, Sir, I ran one of the blighters through with his own sword,' said Aramis, 'for I broke mine with my first thrust. If you like you can say I stabbed him, Sir. But at any rate I beat him.'

'I didn't know that,' said de Tréville, slightly mollified. 'The Cardinal must have been exaggerating.'

Aramis, seeing that Monsieur de Tréville was calming down and wishing to put in a plea for his friend, said: 'Please, Sir, don't let it get around that Athos has been wounded. It would break his heart if the King got to hear of it. And his wound's really very serious; he was run through the shoulder and the point of the blade went into his chest. We're afraid . . .'

At that moment the curtain of the door was drawn aside and a man appeared. He was strikingly handsome but desperately pale.

'Athos!' cried the two musketeers in chorus.

'Athos!' echoed Monsieur de Tréville.

'You sent for me, Sir,' said Athos to his officer in a calm but rather weak voice. 'The fellows outside told me you wanted me. So I've come to report. At your service, Sir, now as always!'

With these words the musketeer stepped smartly into the room. He was, as usual, faultlessly turned out and showed no sign of having been in the wars. Monsieur de Tréville, moved by this soldierly display of courage, rushed towards him.

'I was just telling these gentlemen,' said he, 'that I won't have my musketeers risking their lives unnecessarily. The King rates courage very high and he knows his musketeers are the bravest fellows in the world. Athos, give me your hand!'

And before Athos had time to reply to this affectionate welcome Monsieur de Tréville took hold of his right hand and gripped it hard, not noticing the pain he was causing the young man, who, for all his self-control, winced a little and grew, if possible, even paler than before.

The door had remained half-open, for Athos' arrival had caused a sensation. Everyone knew that he had been wounded, although it was supposed to be a dead secret. A murmur of applause from outside greeted the captain's last words and in their excitement two or three musketeers actually peered through the chinks in the tapestry. At any other time Monsieur de Tréville would have dealt harshly with this breach of etiquette, but he felt Athos' hand clutch his convulsively and, looking at him, saw that he was about to faint. Athos, who had managed only with a great effort to conceal his pain, was now unable to hold out any longer and fell like a log to the ground.

'A doctor! Call a doctor!' cried Monsieur de Tréville. 'My doctor! The King's doctor! The best man that can be found! Call a doctor or, by God, our good Athos will die on the spot!'

Hearing Monsieur de Tréville's cries everyone burst into his study before he had time to stop them and crowded round the wounded man. This display of zeal and concern on the part of the musketeers would not have helped much if the doctor had not happened to be in the house at that very moment. He elbowed his way through the crowd and knelt down beside the unconscious Athos; then, as all the noise and bustle disturbed him, he insisted first and foremost on having the musketeer removed to the adjoining room. Monsieur de Tréville at once opened a door and showed the way to Porthos and Aramis, who lifted up the unconscious man and carried him out in their arms. Behind them walked the doctor and the door was then closed.

Monsieur de Tréville's study, usually so sacrosanct, had now become a mere annexe of the ante-room. Everyone was holding forth, shouting, swearing, and wishing the Cardinal and his bodyguard in Hell.

A moment later Porthos and Aramis reappeared, leaving the doctor and de Tréville alone with the wounded man.

Finally de Tréville himself reappeared. The wounded man had regained consciousness and the doctor had diagnosed his condition as not serious and his collapse as due merely to loss of blood.

Monsieur de Tréville now made a sign to everyone to leave the room. The whole company withdrew with the exception of d'Artagnan, who had not forgotten that he had been granted an audience and had stood his ground with true Gascon persistence.

When everyone had gone and the door was closed Monsieur de Tréville turned and found himself alone with the young man. The scene which had just taken place had interrupted his train

of thought. He asked our importunate hero what he could do
for him. D'Artagnan then repeated his name. In a flash Monsieur de Tréville remembered everything and was once more
master of the situation.

'Forgive me,' he said, 'forgive me, my dear fellow-Gascon.
I'd completely forgotten you! Well, you see how it is! An
officer's merely a family man burdened with heavier responsi-
bilities than an ordinary father. Soldiers are really mere children, but it's my duty to see that the King's orders are carried
out and still more the Cardinal's.'

D'Artagnan could not help smiling at this, and when de
Tréville saw him smile he realized that he had no fool to deal
with. He changed the conversation and came straight to the
point.

'Your father was a good friend of mine,' he said. 'What can I
do for you? Tell me quickly. My time's not my own, you know.'

'Sir,' said d'Artagnan, 'I left Tarbes and came here hoping
that my father's friendship with you would get me a commission in the Musketeers. But from what I've seen in the last two
hours, I realize that I'm asking a great deal of you. I'm afraid
you may think I'm not qualified for the honour.'

'Yes, it's an honour all right,' answered Monsieur de Tréville, 'but it may not be quite so far above your head as you
think. But His Majesty's made a strict ruling on this point, and
I'm sorry to say that no man can join the Musketeers until
he's first proved himself, either in some campaign, or by some
act of conspicuous gallantry, or by serving two years in some
other regiment less select than ours.'

D'Artagnan bowed and said nothing. The distinction of a
musketeer's uniform appealed to him even more now that he
knew how many obstacles stood in the way of his wearing
one.

'But,' continued Monsieur de Tréville, looking keenly at his
young compatriot as though he wanted to read his thoughts, 'I
repeat, for the sake of my old and trusted friend, your father,
I'm prepared to do you a special favour. Our young bloods in
Béarn were never very rich, and I don't suppose conditions have

changed much since I left the province. I don't suppose you've got much money to spare after paying for your board and lodging.'

D'Artagnan drew himself up proudly as though to show that he would not take charity from any man.

'All right, all right, young fellow,' went on Tréville. 'There's no need to put on these airs with me. I came to Paris myself with four crowns in my pocket and I'd have slaughtered anyone who dared say I wasn't rich enough to buy the Louvre.'

D'Artagnan remembered that the sale of his horse had made him four crowns better off than Tréville had been. So his only reply was to draw himself up higher still.

'As I was saying,' went on Tréville, 'you'd better cling on to whatever money you've got in your pocket. But you also need to learn the accomplishments of a gentleman. So I'll write today to the Director of the Royal Academy and he'll admit you free of charge tomorrow. Don't refuse this small favour. The highest and richest in the land often ask for it and don't get it. You'll learn horsemanship, fencing, and dancing. You'll meet the right people and from time to time you can look me up and tell me how you're getting on. And if there's anything I can do for you, I'll do it.'

D'Artagnan knew nothing of Court manners, but even he could tell that Monsieur de Tréville's reception of him was merely formal and would probably lead nowhere.

'I'm more than sorry, Sir,' he said, 'not to have my father's letter of introduction to give you. I see now what a help it would have been.'

'Yes,' answered de Tréville. 'I must admit I'm surprised you came all this way without something of that sort. After all, a good introduction's really the only asset we Bearnese have.'

'I had a letter when I started, Sir,' cried d'Artagnan. 'And it was all in proper form. But some scoundrel stole it from me on the way.'

And he told the whole story of the Meung adventure, giving such a lively and detailed description of the stranger's appearance that Monsieur de Tréville was completely won over.

'I agree, it's a strange thing to have happened,' he said.

He thought for a moment and then added:

'You say you mentioned my name out loud?'

'Yes, Sir. I'm afraid I was a bit indiscreet. I was counting on your name to be a kind of shield and buckler for me on the journey. I confess I did take cover behind it once or twice.'

Flattery was the vogue at that time, and Monsieur de Tréville liked praise every bit as much as the King and the Cardinal. He could not control a slight smile, but the smile quickly faded as his mind reverted to the episode at Meung.

'Tell me,' he went on, 'did this gentleman have a faint scar on his cheek?'

'Yes. The sort of mark that might have been made by a bullet grazing it.'

'He was a good-looking fellow, wasn't he?'

'Yes.'

'Tall?'

'Yes.'

'With dark hair and a sallow skin?'

'Yes, Sir. That's the man all right. How do you come to know him, Sir? Oh, if I ever catch that fellow again, and I'll get him, I swear I will, even if I go to Hell for it . . .'

'He was waiting for a woman, you say?' went on Tréville.

'Yes, Sir. The lady drove up to the inn; the fellow had a hurried conversation with her and then rode off at the gallop.'

'You didn't by any chance hear what they said, did you?'

'Yes. He gave her a box, told her she'd find her orders in it and that she wasn't to open it till she'd got to London.'

'Was she an English woman?'

'He called her Milady.'

'Yes. That's the fellow all right,' muttered de Tréville to himself. 'I thought he was still in Brussels.'

'Oh, Sir!' cried d'Artagnan. 'If you know this fellow tell me his name and nationality. I'll ask nothing more of you, I swear I won't. I won't even hold you to your promise of making me a musketeer. I'm mad to get my revenge.'

'Put that idea right out of your head, my lad!' cried de

Tréville. 'Keep well out of that fellow's way, and if ever you see him coming down the street cross over quickly to the other side. Don't go butting against that stone wall; you'll get battered to bits.'

'I don't care,' said d'Artagnan. 'If ever I see that fellow . . .'

'Take my advice and don't even look for him,' repeated Tréville.

An idea suddenly flashed across de Tréville's mind. Was this young man merely play-acting? Was his display of hatred not a sham? Why should the stranger have bothered to steal his father's letter? Was there some treachery behind this affair? Was the fellow a spy sent by the Cardinal to trap him? This would-be d'Artagnan might be in the Cardinal's pay, sent to win de Tréville's confidence and betray it again later, as had happened a thousand times before. De Tréville eyed d'Artagnan even more closely than he had done at first, and was not greatly reassured by his expression, in which he thought he read falseness and mock deference.

'I know he's a Gascon,' thought de Tréville, 'but that wouldn't prevent him being the Cardinal's agent. I'll test him.'

'Young man,' he said gently, 'I believe your story about the lost letter. And you're the son of my old friend, so I'd like to make up for my coldness towards you before I knew who you were by letting you in to a few State secrets. The King and the Cardinal are on the best of terms. All this talk of their disliking each other is just a put up job, meant to deceive fools. It's a shame to think that a Gascon, a first-class fellow like yourself with a grand career ahead of him, should be mixed up in these silly intrigues and share the fate of so many of his kind. Remember, I'm devoted to my two all-powerful masters, and the one serious aim of my life is to serve the King and His Eminence the Cardinal, who is one of the greatest geniuses France has ever produced. Take my advice, young man, and do as I do. And if you hate the Cardinal, if your family has said things against him, or if you hate him instinctively, let's say goodbye and part company. I'll do all I can for you but I won't have you in my household. Let's hope that at least you'll appreciate my frankness, for you're the first young man I've ever opened my heart to.'

As he spoke Tréville was thinking to himself:

'If the Cardinal's sent this young fox to me, knowing how I abominate him, he'll have told his young spy that the best way to get round me is by abusing him to me. So he'll ignore my praising remarks and try to convince me that he loathes the Cardinal too.'

The very opposite happened to what Tréville expected. D'Artagnan replied enthusiastically:

'Sir! You've expressed my own feelings exactly! My father taught me to respect no one but the King, the Cardinal, and yourself, whom he looks upon as the three leading men in France.'

D'Artagnan was not strictly truthful in mentioning Monsieur de Tréville in the same breath as the King and the Cardinal, but he thought no harm could come of it.

'So you see, Sir,' he went on, 'I respect the Cardinal more than any man on earth, and I think everything he does is wonderful. If you've been speaking frankly to me as you say you have, then I'm in luck, for you'll think more highly of me for sharing your views. But if you suspected me, as you may well have done, then I see I'm only damning myself by speaking the truth. But that can't be helped. At least I shall keep your respect, and that's what I value most in the world.'

Monsieur de Tréville was utterly taken aback. The boy was shrewd as well as frank, and both these qualities were admirable though not entirely reassuring. They only made him more dangerous as an enemy if he were not what he pretended to be. However de Tréville shook d'Artagnan by the hand and said:

'You're a good lad, but at present I can't do more for you than I've already promised. I shall always be glad to see you here. Later, when you're free to call on me at any time and to catch me on an off moment, you'll probably get what you want out of me.'

'In other words, Sir,' replied d'Artagnan, 'you're waiting for me to prove what I'm good for. Well, don't worry,' he added with a Gascon's cheek, 'you won't have to wait long.'

He bowed to the captain and turned abruptly to leave the room, as though the future were now his concern, and his concern alone. But Monsieur de Tréville called him back.

'Just a moment,' he said, 'I promised you a letter to the Director of the Academy. Are you too proud to take it, my lad?'

'No, Sir,' replied d'Artagnan. 'And I promise you it won't go the way the other one went. I'll see this one gets home all right, and if any man tries to steal it from me, I'll slit his throat for him.'

De Tréville smiled at this piece of swagger. He left his young compatriot at the window where they had been standing talking, sat down at a table and started to write the letter of introduction. Meanwhile d'Artagnan, who had nothing to do, tapped with his fingers on the window-pane and watched the musketeers leave the house one by one, following them with his eyes until they disappeared round the corner of the street.

Monsieur de Tréville finished the letter, sealed it and got up, meaning to hand it to the young man. But at that very moment to his great surprise the young man gave a sudden start, flushed angrily and, totally ignoring his host and the letter, rushed out of the study crying:

'Ye Gods! This time he won't escape me!'

'Who won't escape you?' cried the captain in amazement.

'The thief, of course,' cried d'Artagnan. 'Oh, I'll get him, the yellow rat!'

And he disappeared through the door.

'The fellow's a madman,' muttered de Tréville to himself. 'Unless of course that was his clever way of getting out quick, when he realized he'd messed the whole thing up.'

CHAPTER IV

Athos' Shoulder, Porthos' Shoulder-Belt, and Aramis' Handkerchief

D'ARTAGNAN in his fury crossed the ante-room in three strides and sprang on to the staircase, meaning to run down it four steps at a time. But in his mad rush he collided with a musketeer who was leaving Monsieur de Tréville's apartments by a private door, and gave him such a hard butt on the shoulder with his head that the musketeer let out a yell.

'I'm sorry!' said d'Artagnan. 'I'm in a bit of a hurry, I'm afraid.' And he tried to rush on.

But he had only gone one step down the staircase when he felt a strong grip on his shoulder which held him back. Turning round he saw the musketeer glaring at him, as white as a sheet. It was Athos, who was on his way home after having had his wounds dressed by the doctor.

'You're in a hurry, are you?' cried Athos. 'You're in a hurry, you shove me, you say "I'm sorry" and you think that's enough! Well it isn't, my lad. D'you think because you heard Monsieur de Tréville laying in to me this morning that you've got a right to lay me out now? Don't you believe it. You're not Monsieur de Tréville.'

'But I didn't do it on purpose,' answered d'Artagnan. 'It was an accident and I apologized for it. I can't do more than that. Now please let go of me. I'm in a hurry. I've got something important to do.'

Athos let go of him. 'Your manners are bad, Sir,' he said. 'You're obviously just up from the country.'

D'Artagnan had already skipped three or four steps but Athos' remark brought him up short.

'Look here, Sir,' he said. 'I may be just up from the country, as you call it, but I won't be taught manners by you!'

'Oh, won't you?'

'No, by God, I won't,' cried d'Artagnan. 'And if I wasn't in such a hurry, if I wasn't running after someone . . .'

'You may be in a hurry now, Sir, but you don't need to run to find me, you know!'

'Where shall I find you then?'

'Near the Carmelite Convent.'

'What time?'

'About midday.'

'Midday? Right! I'll be there.'

'And don't keep me waiting! I want to have those ears of yours off by twelve-fifteen.'

'Fine,' said d'Artagnan. 'I'll be with you on the stroke of twelve.'

And off he started again like a madman, hoping to overtake his enemy who, at the rate he was walking, could not have gone far.

But Porthos was standing at the street door, talking to a soldier in the King's Guards. There was just enough space between them for a man to pass and d'Artagnan, thinking he had enough room, darted between them like an arrow. But he hadn't reckoned with the wind. Just as he was passing the wind blew out Porthos' long cloak, and d'Artagnan charged straight into it. Porthos obviously had some good reason for clinging on to this important part of his dress, for, instead of letting go of it, he drew it closer to him. The result was that d'Artagnan got entangled in the velvet folds, and when he turned to loosen himself only coiled himself tighter still.

Hearing the musketeer swear, our hero tried to get out from underneath the cloak, which was blinding him, and looked everywhere for an opening. He was afraid that he might have soiled the magnificent shoulder-belt which, we remember, was Porthos' pride and joy. But when he timidly opened his eyes he found himself with his nose glued to the middle of Porthos' back, in other words right against the shoulder-belt.

Alas! Like most things in this world which are good only on the outside the shoulder-belt was embroidered with gold in front but plain buff at the back. Porthos, though a great bragger, was none too rich. He could not afford a shoulder-belt entirely of gold lace and had had to be content with a half-embroidered one, which explains why he had had a cold and had insisted on wearing a cloak.

'Look out! Look out!' cried Porthos, trying to shake off d'Artagnan who was nosing round his back. 'What the Hell d'you think you're doing, running into people like that! Are you mad?'

'I'm very sorry!' said d'Artagnan, his head reappearing under the big man's shoulder. 'I'm very sorry, but I'm in a great hurry. I'm running after someone and . . .'

'Do you always leave your eyes at home when you run?' asked Porthos.

'No,' replied d'Artagnan, stung by this remark. 'And my eyes are so good that they sometimes see things other people don't see.'

Porthos may or may not have understood the point of this remark. In any case he got angry and retorted:

'I warn you, Sir, if you go shoving musketeers about you're in for a good thrashing one of these days.'

'Thrashing! Thrashing!' said d'Artagnan. 'That's a pretty harsh word, you know.'

'It's quite common among men who face up to their enemies.'

'I daresay it is! And I know now why you're so careful not to turn your back on yours.'

And our young hero, enchanted by his little joke, ran down the street laughing uproariously.

Porthos, foaming with rage, started off in pursuit of him.

'All right! Later! Later!' cried d'Artagnan. 'When you've taken off that cloak of yours.'

'One o'clock then, behind the Luxembourg.'

'One o'clock! Fine!' shouted d'Artagnan, disappearing round the corner of the street.

But he saw no one anywhere about who in the least resembled the man he was after. His enemy may have been walking slowly but he had outdistanced him all the same; he had quite possibly gone into some house. D'Artagnan inquired from all the passers-by, went down as far as the ferry, ran back along the Rue de Seine and past the Croix-Rouge, but found no trace of him anywhere. However his mad rush did him this much good, that the more he sweated the cooler his senses grew.

He now began to reflect on the events of the day. Much had happened and all of it bad. It was not yet eleven o'clock and he had already got into Monsieur de Tréville's bad books, for Monsieur de Tréville would certainly not have been pleased by his discourteous behaviour. And he had subsequently let himself in for two good duels with two musketeers, each of whom, as he realized only too well, was capable of dealing with three d'Artagnans.

It was a depressing prospect. Certain as the young man was that Athos would kill him it was only natural that he should not be greatly concerned about Porthos. But, as we know, hope springs eternal in the human breast, so d'Artagnan soon recovered his spirits and began to feel that he might possibly survive these two duels, though not, of course, without terrible wounds. With this idea of survival in his head he gave himself a good talking-to.

'What a silly, hare-brained ass I am! Why do I have to go barging into that good fellow Athos, with that bad shoulder of his which must hurt him so? I'm surprised he didn't kill me on the spot – he had every right to, and I must have given him a frightful jar. And then Porthos! Oh well, that was rather funny, I must say!'

And at the thought of Porthos he started smiling to himself again. But he looked cautiously round to make sure that his little private joke wasn't being misinterpreted and giving offence to any of the passers-by.

'Yes, the Porthos business was certainly funny,' he muttered. 'But I'm a silly ass all the same. Do people go barging into other people like that without warning? No. Of course not! And do they go peeping under people's cloaks to find things which aren't there? No, again. And he'd have forgiven me like a shot if I hadn't mentioned that damned sash of his. It was only a joke, of course, but too good a joke by half. Oh what a silly Gascon oaf I am! I'll joke myself into the grave one day. Come on, d'Artagnan, old boy, pull yourself together. If you escape this time, which is highly unlikely, you'll have to mend your manners a bit in future. From now on you must set an example; you must be a model of what a gentleman should be. One can be kind and polite without being servile. Take Aramis, for instance; look how gentle and good-mannered he is! And has anyone ever called him a coward? Of course they haven't! In future I'll model myself on him. Well, I'm damned! Here he is!'

D'Artagnan had been walking along the street muttering to himself and was now quite close to Aiguillon House. Here he suddenly caught sight of Aramis, talking and laughing with three soldiers in the King's Guards. Aramis also noticed d'Artagnan, but he remembered that the young Gascon had been present when Monsieur de Tréville had lost his temper and hated to think that anyone had witnessed so unpleasant a scene. So he pretended not to see him.

But d'Artagnan, obsessed with his new resolve to be as polite and friendly as possible, went boldly up to the four young men, bowed low and put on his most charming smile. Aramis gave him a curt nod in return, but did not smile. And all four at once stopped talking.

D'Artagnan had enough sense to realize that his presence was unwelcome, but he was still too much of a rough diamond to know how gentlemen retire gracefully when they find themselves with people whom they hardly know and whose conversation doesn't concern them. He was thinking out some excuse to get away without looking foolish when he noticed that Aramis had dropped his handkerchief and had carelessly put his foot on it. Here was an excellent opportunity to atone for his previous lack of tact. He bent down and with a flourish pulled the handkerchief from under the musketeer's foot, although the latter tried hard to prevent him. He then handed it to Aramis and said:

'You've dropped your handkerchief, Sir. And I'm sure you'd be sorry to lose a handkerchief like that.'

The handkerchief was indeed a beautiful one, richly embroidered and with a coronet and coat-of-arms in one of the corners. Aramis blushed scarlet and snatched the handkerchief from the Gascon's hand.

'Ha, ha!' cried one of the guards. 'Aramis, you secretive old devil! Don't pretend Madame de Bois-Tracy's finished with you, when the beautiful lady's still kind enough to lend you her handkerchief!'

Aramis threw d'Artagnan one of those looks which tell a man that he has made a mortal enemy. Then in his usual mild manner he retorted:

'You're wrong, gentlemen. This handkerchief's not mine, and I don't know why our friend here chose to give it to me rather than to one of you. And to prove it's not mine I'll show you mine!'

So saying, he pulled his own handkerchief out of his pocket. It was another handkerchief made of the same fine cambric, although cambric was very dear at that time. But this one had no embroidery or coat-of-arms on it, and only a single monogram, that of its owner.

This time d'Artagnan remained silent, for he realized his blunder. But Aramis' friends refused to be convinced by his protests. One of them now put on a grave face and said:

'You know, Aramis, if that handkerchief really weren't yours by rights, I should have to ask you to give it to me. Bois-Tracy's one of my best friends and I couldn't allow anyone to make trophies of his wife's belongings.'

'I didn't like the way you said that,' said Aramis. 'You're perfectly right, of course, but I didn't like your tone. So I won't give you the handkerchief.'

'As a matter of fact,' said d'Artagnan shyly, 'I didn't actually see the handkerchief fall out of Monsieur Aramis' pocket. He had his foot on it, that's all. And I thought that as the handkerchief was under his foot it probably belonged to him.'

'And that's where you were wrong,' said Aramis coldly, unmoved by d'Artagnan's attempt to make amends. Then, turning to the soldier who had claimed to be Bois-Tracy's friend, he went on:

'Come to that, my dear chap, I'm just as friendly with Bois-Tracy as you are. Are you sure that handkerchief didn't fall out of your pocket? If it did I'd have just as much right to ask you to hand it over to me.'

'I swear it didn't,' retorted the guardsman.

'Well if you swear one thing and I swear another, one of us is bound to be lying. I've got a better idea, Monteron. Let's each take half.'

'What? Half the handkerchief?'

'Yes.'

'That's a grand idea,' cried the other two guardsmen. 'The judgement of Solomon! There's wisdom in that head of yours, Aramis, old boy.'

The young men burst out laughing and, needless to say, the subject then dropped. Very soon the conversation ended and the three guardsmen and the musketeer shook hands and parted, the guardsmen going one way and Aramis another.

'Now's my chance to make friends with this fine fellow,' thought d'Artagnan, who had been keeping quiet during the latter part of the conversation. And with this good intention in mind he followed Aramis, who was walking away without paying any more heed to him.

'Excuse me, Sir . . .' he said.

'Sir,' interrupted Aramis, 'allow me to point out that your behaviour just now was not that of a gentleman.'

'Are you suggesting, Sir . . .'

'I'm suggesting, Sir, that you're not a complete ass, and that, although you've only just arrived from Gascony, you've enough sense to know that one doesn't put one's foot on a handkerchief without good reason. The streets of Paris aren't paved with cambric, you know!'

'I shouldn't try to be funny if I were you,' said d'Artagnan, who felt his temper prevailing over his peaceful intentions. 'I'm a Gascon, as you say, and I don't need to tell you that we

Gascons are inclined to be testy. Even when we've done something silly we think one apology's more than enough.'

'Sir,' replied Aramis, 'I don't wish to have a quarrel with you. Thank God I'm no fire-eater. I'm only a musketeer, temporarily, so I don't fight unless I have to, and even then it goes against the grain. But this time it's a serious matter; you've compromised a lady.'

'We both have, you mean,' retorted d'Artagnan.

'Why were you so tactless as to return me the handkerchief?'

'Why were you so tactless as to drop it?'

'I told you once and I tell you again. That handkerchief did not come out of my pocket.'

'Now, Sir, you've lied twice! I actually saw it fall out of your pocket.'

'Oh! If you're going to take that tone, young Gascon, I see I'll have to put you in your place.'

'And I'll have to put you in yours, back at the altar, you priest! Come on, Sir, draw your sword and let's not waste any more time!'

'No, no, not here, my friend! I'm not going to fight you right in front of Aiguillon House, with all the Cardinal's men looking on. No thanks! How do I know you're not a Cardinal's man yourself sent to provoke me? If I fight here, off comes my head. And strangely enough I like my head; I don't think it looks too bad on my shoulders. I mean to kill you all right. But I want to do it somewhere nice and quiet, where we shan't be disturbed and where I shan't get into trouble afterwards.'

'That suits me!' said d'Artagnan. 'But don't be too sure of yourself. And bring that handkerchief along with you, whether it's yours or not. You may find it useful.'

'You're a Gascon all right,' said Aramis.

'Yes, I'm a Gascon. And I wouldn't let fear of a scandal stop me fighting.'

'Musketeers shouldn't ever refuse to fight, I grant you. But a churchman should and must. And I'm only a musketeer temporarily, so I shall continue to respect the law. I shall be happy to meet you at two o'clock in Monsieur de Tréville's house. From there I'll take you on to some nice quiet spot.'

The two young men bowed. Aramis then went off in the direction of the Luxembourg, while d'Artagnan, seeing how time had flown, made his way to the Carmelite Convent, muttering to himself:

'Now I'm properly for it! But if I'm killed, I shall at least be killed by a musketeer.'

CHAPTER V

The King's Musketeers and the Cardinal's Guards

D'ARTAGNAN knew no one in Paris. So he went off to fight his duel with Athos without the support of any seconds; he would have to make do with those chosen by his opponent. In any case he hoped to find some decent excuse for getting out of this duel, if he could do so without appearing weak, because he foresaw that this particular affair was bound to end disastrously for him. He was a young and active man, and his opponent was already crippled by a previous wound; if he lost, his enemy would be doubly triumphant; if he won, he might be accused of having taken a mean advantage.

It must now be obvious to the reader that our young Gascon was a man quite out of the common run of mortals. At any rate this is the impression we have tried to convey. So although he kept repeating to himself that he was going out to meet certain death, he was determined not to lie down and die without a struggle. With his courage and foresight he would save himself where another would go down. He reflected on the different characters of the men he was pledged to fight and became more sanguine. If he managed to survive the duels he would know how to deal with the men. He hoped by behaving in an honourable and generous way to make a friend of Athos. Athos was obviously a gentleman. As for Porthos, d'Artagnan was confident that he could put him in his place with the shoulder-belt incident; if he was lucky enough not to be killed outright, he could spread that story round the town and Porthos could be made to look a considerable fool. And as for that sly rogue, Aramis, he wasn't very frightened of him; if he got as far as fighting Aramis he'd soon dispose of him. What had Caesar advised his soldiers to do when fighting Pompey's? He'd strike at his face and that would spoil his beauty for him!

D'Artagnan was, in fact, determined at all costs to make an impression, and not to be dismissed as a nonentity. His father's last words still rang in his ears: 'Stand no nonsense from any-one but the King and the Cardinal.' He did not walk, he posi-tively flew to the Carmelite Convent, which had been agreed upon as the meeting-place for the first duel. The convent was a forbidding-looking building without windows, standing in a barren waste; it was in those days a fashionable meeting-place for gentlemen who had quarrels to settle in a hurry.

It was striking twelve o'clock when d'Artagnan reached the deserted little piece of ground beside the convent, and Athos had only been waiting there five minutes. So he was sharp on time. So far, so good; his conduct would have satisfied the most punctilious of duellists.

Athos was still in great pain from his wound, although it had been freshly dressed by Monsieur de Tréville's doctor. He was, however, sitting quite calmly on a milestone in his usual attitude of easy grace, aloof and unconcerned as ever. When he caught sight of d'Artagnan, he rose politely and came for-ward to meet him. D'Artagnan, not to be outdone, came up to his enemy bareheaded, and bowed low, sweeping the ground with the feather of his hat.

'Sir,' said Athos, 'I've asked two of my friends to act as my seconds, but neither of them has arrived yet. I'm surprised they should be late; they're not usually late for an affair of this kind.'

'I'm afraid I've got no seconds, Sir,' said d'Artagnan. 'I only arrived in Paris yesterday and I know no one here except Mon-sieur de Tréville. I only know him because my father gave me a letter of introduction to him.'

Athos thought for a moment.

'You know no one but Monsieur de Tréville?' he echoed.

'No, no one.'

'That's awkward,' went on Athos, talking half to himself and half to d'Artagnan. 'If I kill you I shall look a bit of an ogre, shan't I?'

'Not such a terrible ogre,' answered d'Artagnan, drawing himself up. 'Remember you're fighting me at a disadvantage. That wound of yours'll handicap you a good deal.'

'It will indeed. And I admit you hurt me a lot, barging into me like that. However, I'll fight you with my left hand as I've often done before. And don't imagine I shall be letting you off lightly. I'm ambidextrous. In fact it'll probably put you off a bit; a left-hander's always awkward to deal with, especially for beginners. I'm sorry. Perhaps I should have warned you before.'

'Of course not, Sir,' said d'Artagnan, again bowing low. 'It's very good of you even to mention it.'

'Not at all, not at all,' answered Athos, slightly embarrassed. 'And now let's talk about something else. You certainly hurt me a good deal when you ran into me. I can feel my right shoulder throbbing now.'

'May I make a suggestion . . .?' said d'Artagnan shyly.

'What's that?'

'I've got a wonderful ointment for dressing wounds. My mother gave it to me and I've already tried it on myself with great success.'

'Oh!'

'I'm certain the ointment would cure you in three days or even less. I suggest we put off our meeting till then.'

D'Artagnan spoke simply and frankly. It was obvious that he was genuinely concerned for the other's welfare and not trying to back out.

'Well said, Sir, well said,' cried Athos. 'I won't accept your offer but it proves you're a gentleman. That's the way the knights of Charlemagne spoke and behaved, and they were the beau ideal of chivalry. We should all follow their example. Unfortunately we're not living in the days of the great Emperor. The Cardinal's our master now, and if we waited three days before fighting everyone would get to know of it, however much we tried to keep it dark. They'd find out all right and stop the whole thing. What in God's name's happened to those two idle rogues, my seconds? Why aren't they here?'

'If you're in a great hurry,' said d'Artagnan, 'and would like to finish me off as quickly as possible, please don't worry but let's start without them.'

He said this with the same air of wishing to oblige with which a few seconds earlier he had suggested postponing the fight for three days.

'Well said again,' answered Athos, nodding at d'Artagnan appreciatively. 'What you say shows head as well as heart. I like fellows of your stamp, and if I don't kill you now, I hope to make your better acquaintance later. But I think we'd do well to wait for the two others; I've got plenty of time, and it's more correct that way. Ah, here is one of them, I do believe.'

At that very moment the gigantic figure of Porthos appeared, rounding the corner from the Rue du Vaugirard.

'What!' cried d'Artagnan; 'is Monsieur Porthos one of your seconds?'

'Yes. Any objection?'

'No, no. Of course not.'

'And there's my other second.'

D'Artagnan looked to where Athos was pointing and recognized Aramis.

'What!' he cried, even more astonished this time. 'Is Monsieur Aramis your other second?'

'Of course he is! Don't you know that none of us three is ever seen without the other two; that we're known by all the other musketeers and by the Cardinal's Guards, at Court and even in the town, as Athos, Porthos, and Aramis, or the three inseparables? But of course you're just up from Dax or Pau or somewhere ...'

'Tarbes,' corrected d'Artagnan.

'Tarbes, so I suppose that's why you don't know.'

'Well, Sir, I can only say you're well named,' said d'Artagnan. 'And if our little adventure gets talked about, it'll be a further proof of how much you all have in common.'

Meanwhile Porthos had come up and joined Athos and d'Artagnan. He greeted Athos with a wave of the hand; then, catching sight of d'Artagnan, he stood and stared at him in amazement. (In the interval between his two meetings with the Gascon he had taken off his new shoulder-strap and put on his old one, and also discarded his cloak.)

'Well, well!' he cried. 'And what's the meaning of all this, may I ask?'

'This is the gentleman I've had the quarrel with,' said Athos, pointing at d'Artagnan.

'But I've had a quarrel with him too!' cried Porthos. 'I'm fighting him as well!'

'Yes,' said d'Artagnan. 'But not till one o'clock.'

At that moment Aramis came up.

'And I'm also fighting this gentleman,' he cried.

'Yes, but not till two o'clock,' said d'Artagnan, still completely unruffled, and enjoying the embarrassment of the other three.

'Why are you fighting him?' said Aramis to Athos.

'I honestly don't quite know,' said Athos. 'He barged into me and hurt my shoulder. Why are you fighting him, Porthos?'

'Me? Oh, I'm just fighting him ... I'm just fighting him, that's all,' said Porthos, going rather red.

Athos, who noticed everything, saw a faint smile cross the Gascon's face as Porthos spoke.

'We had an argument about dress,' said the young man.

'And what about you, Aramis?' asked Porthos.

'I'm fighting him on theological grounds,' answered Aramis, signing to d'Artagnan to keep quiet about the real reason for their quarrel.

Athos again noticed d'Artagnan smiling to himself at this point. He turned to him and said:

'Is that really what you're fighting about?'

'Yes, we had a little dispute about a certain passage in St Augustine,' said the young Gascon.

'This fellow's no fool, no fool at all,' muttered Athos to himself.

'And now that we're all mustered, gentlemen,' said d'Artagnan, 'I'd like to make my apologies to you.'

At this surprising statement Athos frowned, Porthos smiled scornfully, and Aramis shrugged his shoulders contemptuously. And all three thought to themselves that it was a pity that this young Gascon should after all turn out to be so spiritless.

'Don't misunderstand me, gentlemen,' continued d'Artagnan, drawing himself up to his full height. At that moment the sun's rays shone on him and showed up the bold, clear-cut outlines of his face. 'I wish to apologize humbly in advance because I realize now that I may not be able to fulfil my debt of honour to you all. Monsieur Athos has the first claim on my life, a fact which greatly reduces the value of your claim, Monsieur Porthos, and makes yours virtually nil, Monsieur Aramis. So, gentlemen, let me repeat my apologies to you on that score and on that score alone. And now on guard, please! Let's waste no more time.'

With these words d'Artagnan drew his sword from its scabbard in the most elegant manner possible, like a courtier born and bred.

The young man was in a wild state of excitement. At that moment he would have challenged all the musketeers in France as boldly and coolly as he had challenged Athos, Porthos, and Aramis.

It was now a quarter past twelve. The sun was high in the heaven and its rays beat down pitilessly on the exposed plot of ground chosen as the site for the duels.

'It's very hot,' said Athos, drawing his sword in his turn. 'But hot as it is, I'm going to fight in my doublet. A moment ago I felt my wound bleeding again and I don't want to put this gentleman off by the sight of blood drawn from me by another.'

'That's most considerate of you, Sir,' said d'Artagnan. 'And I can assure you that I'd always be sorry to see the blood of a brave man like you, even if I'd drawn it from you myself. So I'll wear my doublet too.'

'Come on now, gentlemen,' said Porthos. 'Cut short the compliments. Remember Aramis and I are waiting our turn.'

'That remark was out of place, Porthos,' said Aramis. 'Speak for yourself another time. What these gentlemen have been saying does them both great credit.'

'When you're ready, Sir,' said Athos, 'on guard.'

'At your service, Sir,' said d'Artagnan, crossing swords with him.

But hardly had the two blades clinked together than a posse of His Eminence's guards appeared round the corner of the convent with Monsieur de Jussac at its head.

'The Cardinal's guards!' cried Porthos and Aramis. 'Sheath swords, gentlemen, sheath swords!'

But it was too late. The duellists had been caught in an attitude which left no doubt of their intentions.

'Hi, there!' cried Jussac walking up to them and signing to his men to follow him. 'Hi, there, you musketeers! Duelling again, I see. What about the edicts, gentlemen? What about the edicts?'

'So it's you again!' cried Athos resentfully, for Jussac had been one of the party which had set on him and his friends in the Rue Férou. 'Why don't you leave us alone? If we saw you fighting we'd take good care not to interfere with you. So leave us to fight, and you'll have a great deal of fun for nothing.'

'Gentlemen,' said Jussac, 'I'm very sorry but that's out of the question. We've our duty to do. So put up your swords, please, and come along with us.'

'Sir,' said Aramis, imitating Jussac's superior tone of voice, 'we'd be only too happy to accept your kind offer if we were our own masters. Unfortunately we have to take our orders from M. de Tréville, and he's expressly forbidden us to do anything of the kind. So run along now and leave us in peace.'

Aramis' supercilious tone stung Jussac to a fury.

'If you don't come at once we'll force you to come,' he cried.

Athos said softly, so that only his friends could hear:

'There are five of them and only three of us. We shall be beaten again and this time we shall have to die here. I could never face the captain after another licking.'

Athos, Porthos, and Aramis at once closed ranks, while Jussac drew up his men in line.

At this moment d'Artagnan made a swift decision. It was one of those occasions which determine a man's whole future for better or worse. D'Artagnan had to choose between the King and the Cardinal and, the choice once made, to abide by it. To fight was to disobey the law, and that meant risking his head, in other words, making a life-long enemy of a minister who was more powerful than the King himself. Our hero realized all this in a flash and yet, to his credit be it said, he did not hesitate for a moment. He turned to the musketeers and cried:

'Gentlemen, I think there's some mistake. Monsieur Athos said there were only three of us. I make it four.'

'But you're not a musketeer,' protested Porthos.

'I know I don't wear the uniform,' answered the young man. 'But I'm with you in sympathy, and that's all that matters.'

Jussac had evidently guessed d'Artagnan's intentions from his looks and gestures. He now shouted:

'Out of the way, young man! We won't stop you. Get out while the going's good.'

D'Artagnan made no move.

'You're a good fellow. You're a good fellow,' said Athos, delighted by his firm stand. He added on the impulse of the moment:

'Give me your hand.'

D'Artagnan held out his hand and Athos gripped it hard.

'Come on, make up your minds one way or the other,' called Jussac.

'We must do something quickly,' said Porthos and Aramis.

'It's very good of you to offer to help us,' repeated Athos to d'Artagnan.

But in his heart of hearts he thought that d'Artagnan would be more trouble than he was worth – he was so young and inexperienced. He said aside to his two friends:

'We're only three men and a boy, and one of us is wounded. And yet everyone's bound to say we were four men.'

'Yes, but we can't back out now,' said Porthos.

'We're in a bit of a fix,' said Aramis.

D'Artagnan understood why they were hesitating.

'At least give me a trial, gentlemen,' he said. 'I swear on my honour I won't leave this place alive if we're beaten.'

'What's your name, young fellow?' asked Athos.

'D'Artagnan.'

'Right! It's Athos, Porthos, Aramis, and d'Artagnan now!' cried Athos. 'We four'll have a go at them.'

'Well, gentlemen, have you at last decided to make up your minds?' cried Jussac for the third time.

'Yes,' said Athos.

'What are you going to do?'

'We're going to fight,' said Aramis.

'What! You're going to resist?' cried Jussac.

'What did you expect, you prize fool?' said Porthos.

At this the whole nine of them rushed at each other furiously. But they were all skilled swordsmen and kept their heads.

Athos, being the senior of the musketeers, chose his man – Cahusac, one of the Cardinal's favourites. Porthos had Bicarat to deal with, and Aramis found himself alone against two of the guards. As for d'Artagnan, he was face to face with the great Jussac himself.

Our young Gascon's heart was pounding in his chest; not from fright – he had no trace of that, thank God – but from his strong wish to distinguish himself. He fought like a demon, encircling his opponent ten times and more and constantly changing his stance and ground. Jussac was what was known in those days as a glutton for fighting, and was an old hand at the game. Nevertheless he had his work cut out to defend himself against an enemy of such extraordinary speed who kept bounding about and overriding the orthodox rules of the game, attacking from all sides at once and also showing quite a keen sense of self-preservation. At last he began to lose patience. The struggle was going on much too long. He was furious at being held at bay by someone whom he had dismissed as a mere child. He got ruffled and began to make mistakes. D'Artagnan in default of practice had plenty of theory, and attacked with redoubled energy. Jussac now made his longest lunge with the intention of polishing his enemy off once and for all. But d'Artagnan parried quickly and before Jussac could recover his balance glided in like a snake under his guard and drove his sword right through his body. Jussac collapsed in a heap on the ground.

The young man now turned and surveyed the battlefield, taking in the situation at a glance.

Aramis had already killed one of his opponents but was being hard pressed by the other. However he was in good fettle and could obviously hold out for a little longer.

Porthos and Bicarat had lunged together and both had hit. Porthos had been struck in the arm and Bicarat in the thigh. But both wounds were slight and had only whetted the combatants' appetite for more.

Athos had been wounded again by Cahusac and was looking paler than ever. But he had not given ground an inch; he had only changed hands, and was now fighting his man left-handed.

According to the laws of duelling which prevailed at that time d'Artagnan now had the right to help one of his friends. He was looking from one to the other, trying to decide whose part to take, when he suddenly caught Athos' eye. Athos could not actually call for help, but he could throw a look, and the look in his eye at that moment spoke volumes. D'Artagnan responded at once; he rushed at Cahusac shouting:

'Turn and face me, guardsman, or I'll run you through the back.'

Cahusac turned and faced d'Artagnan. This flank attack came only just in time. Athos now sank on one knee; his courage alone had kept him on his feet till then.

'Don't kill him, young fellow, for God's sake,' he called to d'Artagnan. 'I've got an old score to settle with him. When I'm well again I'll fight him on equal terms. Disable him – disarm him – that's right – well done, Sir, well done!'

Athos shouted this out as he saw Cahusac's sword leave his hand, fly into the air and land about twenty yards away. Both combatants immediately rushed after it, Cahusac to pick it up again, d'Artagnan to prevent him doing so. Our hero, the more agile of the two, reached it first and planted his foot on it.

Cahusac now started running towards the guardsman whom Aramis had killed, meaning to take his sword and carry on the fight with d'Artagnan. But he found his way barred by Athos, who had meanwhile recovered his breath and decided to return to the fray himself rather than allow d'Artagnan to polish off his own enemy for him. Realizing that it would be discourteous to rob his friend of the right to kill his man d'Artagnan stood aside and soon had the satisfaction of seeing Cahusac fall to the ground with a sword-thrust in the throat.

At that very moment Aramis was planting his foot firmly on the recumbent figure of his second opponent and was forcing him at the sword point to admit defeat.

Only Porthos and Bicarat were still fighting. Porthos, playing the fool, was keeping up a running fire of chatter as he fought, asking the time and even voicing his congratulations on a happy event in Bicarat's family. But he was not achieving much by these tactics; his enemy was a man of iron to whom a fight was a grim affair which could only be settled by the death of one party or the other.

But it could not go on for ever. A police patrol might come on the scene at any moment and arrest all the combatants in a body, wounded and unwounded Royalists and Cardinalists alike. Athos, Aramis, and d'Artagnan surrounded Bicarat and called on him to surrender. Bicarat was now one against four, and had a thigh wound into the bargain. He was, however, still game to carry on. But Jussac, who had in the meanwhile recovered slightly and was now leaning on one elbow, called out to him to surrender. Bicarat was a Gascon like d'Artagnan; he pretended not to hear and only laughed. Then, having parried two thrusts, he seized an opportune moment, stuck the point of his sword into the ground, and cried out in a tone of bravado, parodying a verse of the Bible:

'Here will I die gloriously, the last of my comrades to fall!'

'But you're one against four!' cried Jussac. 'Stop fighting! I order you to stop fighting!'

'That settles it then,' answered Bicarat. 'An order's an order: you're my senior so I must obey!'

With this he made a quick leap backwards, split his sword across his knee in order not to have to surrender it, threw the pieces over the convent wall and stood with his arms crossed, whistling a jaunty Cardinalist air.

Gallantry is always respected, even in an enemy. The musketeers saluted Bicarat with their swords and then returned them to their scabbards. D'Artagnan followed their example; then, assisted by Bicarat, the only guardsman who was still on his feet, he lifted up Jussac, Cahusac, and Aramis' wounded opponent, carried them over to the convent porch and left them there. The fifth guardsman, we remember, was dead. The musketeers then rang the convent bell and made off at once towards Monsieur de Tréville's house, carrying four enemy swords out of five, mad with joy at their sensational victory. They walked along arm in arm, taking up the whole width of the street, and called on every musketeer they met to join them until a regular triumphal procession was formed.

D'Artagnan was walking arm-in-arm with Athos and Porthos. He was exultant. As they reached the door of Monsieur de Tréville's house he said to his new friends: 'I may not be a musketeer yet, but at least I've been privileged to fight in your ranks.'

CHAPTER VI

His Majesty King Louis XIII

THE incident caused a great stir. Monsieur de Tréville complained bitterly in public about his musketeers and congratulated them in private. But it was important that the King should be told their version of the story without delay, so de Tréville hurried off to the Louvre. It was already too late. The King was already closeted with the Cardinal and de Tréville was informed that His Majesty was engaged in business and could not be disturbed at the moment. That evening de Tréville was present at the King's card game. The King was winning that night. He was miserly by nature, so this had put him in a good humour. As soon as he caught sight of de Tréville he called out to him:

'Come here, my dear Tréville, and let me give you a good talking to. D'you realize His Eminence came to see me today to complain about your musketeers? Their goings on have upset him so much that he's quite ill this evening and can't play cards with me. They're real desperadoes, those musketeers of yours, proper hooligans.'

'No, Sir,' answered de Tréville. 'My musketeers are thoroughly good-natured and never want to fight except in your Majesty's service. But how can they avoid fighting for the honour of their regiment when the Cardinal's Guards are always picking quarrels with them? Poor fellows, they must defend themselves!'

'Hark at him! Hark at Monsieur de Tréville,' said the King addressing the company. 'You'd think he was talking about some religious order. I've a good mind to take his captaincy away from him and hand it over to Mademoiselle de Chemerault instead of making her a Reverend Mother, as I promised. However, Tréville, don't imagine I'm taking your story as gospel truth. They call me Louis the Just, and we'll get to the bottom of it all very soon.'

De Tréville replied:

'Knowing as I do how well Your Majesty deserves the epithet I shall look forward to telling you my version of the story at your earliest convenience.'

'Right, Sir, right. But wait a little. I shan't be long.'

At that very moment, indeed, the luck of the cards changed and the King began losing as steadily as he had won before, so he was quite thankful to have a pretext for doing a Charlemagne, to use a gambler's slang expression of those days.

In a few minutes he rose, pocketed all the money that was on the table in front of him, most of which he had won in the course of the evening, and, turning to one of his suite, said:

'La Vieuville, come and take my place. I've got something important to discuss with Monsieur de Tréville. Oh, by the way, I had twenty-four louis on the table; put down the same amount yourself, it's only fair to the other players; one must always be fair.'

Then he drew de Tréville aside towards one of the windows.

'Well, Sir,' he said, 'you maintain it was His Eminence's guards who provoked your musketeers.'

'Yes, Sir, as usual.'

'Well, and how did it all happen? Tell me. A judge must always hear both sides of a question, you know.'

'It's perfectly simple, Sir. Three of my best soldiers were set upon by five of the Cardinal's Guards. I think you know them by name – Athos, Porthos, and Aramis. They've proved their devotion to Your Majesty on more than one occasion and I can swear to their loyalty. The three of them had arranged a picnic with a young fellow from Gascony, a lad I'd recommended to them that very morning. They were all going out to St Germain, I think, and had arranged to meet at the Carmelite Convent. It was here they ran into the Cardinal's men, de Jussac, Cahusac, Bicarat, and two other guards. I don't know what they were doing there in such large numbers, but I bet they were up to no good.'

'I can guess what they were up to,' said the King. 'They'd gone there to fight.'

'I'm not saying anything,' interposed de Tréville quickly. 'But one can't help wondering what five armed men might be doing in so deserted a spot, where there's no living soul for miles around.'

'How right you are, Tréville!'

'I imagine this is what happened. When they caught sight of my musketeers they sank their own quarrel in face of a common foe. Your Majesty knows, of course, that the musketeers are for the King and the King alone and therefore the natural enemies of the guards, who support the Cardinal.'

'Yes, Tréville, yes,' said the King sadly, 'and it's distressing to think there are two rival parties in France, two heads of the State, as it were. But all that will end soon. You say the guards actually provoked the musketeers?'

'I say that's what probably happened, Your Majesty. But I don't swear to anything. You know how difficult it is to get at the truth in an affair of this kind, and for people not gifted with rare insight, like Your Majesty . . . it's your insight, Sir, which has earned you the title of Louis the Just . . .'

'I know, Tréville, I know . . . But your musketeers weren't alone, you say – they had some youth with them?'

'Yes, Sir. And one of my musketeers had been badly wounded already. So that three musketeers, of whom one was wounded, plus a child, not only held their own against five of the pick of the Cardinal's Guards but actually forced four of them to surrender.'

'But that's a victory!' cried the King, flushing with delight. 'A complete triumph!'

'Yes, Sir, as perfect in its way as the victory on the Pont de Cé.'

'Four men, you say, one of them wounded and one a mere child?'

'Barely a youth. But he fought so well that I'd like to recommend him to Your Majesty's special notice.'

'What's his name?'

'D'Artagnan, Sir. He's the son of one of my oldest friends, a man who fought for Your Majesty's father in the religious wars.'

'You say this young man fought well? Tell me about it, Tréville. You know I love tales of war and valour.'

And King Louis XIII gave his moustache a proud twirl and struck an attitude, resting one hand on his hip.

'As I told you, Sir,' said Tréville, 'this d'Artagnan's virtually a child and, not being a musketeer, was wearing civilian clothes. The Cardinal's guards saw how young he was and that he wasn't in my company, so they told him to clear off before starting their attack.'

'Ah-ha, Tréville,' interrupted the King; 'so you see it really was the guards who attacked.'

'Quite right, Sir. That proves it beyond a doubt. So, as I said, they told young d'Artagnan to clear off. But he answered that he was a musketeer and a Royalist heart and soul, and that he'd stay and fight with the musketeers.'

'Good lad!' muttered the King.

'And so he did,' went on Tréville. 'And Your Majesty's got a winner in him. It was he who gave Jussac that mighty thrust which so enraged the Cardinal!'

'What? He wounded Jussac?' cried the King. 'A youth like him? No, Tréville, that's not possible.'

'It's the truth, Your Majesty. I swear it.'

'Jussac, one of the best swordsmen in the country?'

'Yes, Sir. It seems he's found his match!'

'I must meet this young man, Tréville. I'd like to do something for him.'

'When will you see him, Sir?'

'Tomorrow at twelve, Tréville.'

'Shall I bring him alone?'

'No, bring all four of them. I must thank them all. Loyalty's rare nowadays, Tréville, and one must show one appreciates it.'

'We'll all be at the Louvre at twelve tomorrow, Sir.'

'Come up by the private staircase, Tréville; the private staircase. There's no need for the Cardinal to know . . .'

'Very good, Sir.'

'But you understand, Tréville, don't you? An edict's an edict, when all's said and done. Duelling's forbidden. You must remember that.'

'Yes, Sir. But this wasn't a duel; it was a brawl, so the rule doesn't apply. Remember there were five of the Cardinal's guards against my three musketeers and d'Artagnan.'

'True, true, Tréville,' said the King. 'But come up by the private staircase all the same.'

Tréville smiled to himself. But it was quite an achievement to have persuaded this royal infant to revolt against his master for once, so he let matters rest at that, bowed to the King and asked permission to retire.

That very evening the three musketeers were told of the honour that had been done them. But they had already known the King for some time, so they were not greatly excited by the news. D'Artagnan, on the other hand, was in the seventh heaven of joy. His Gascon imagination soared to wild heights; he saw his fortune already made and spent the night building castles in the air. Punctually at eight next morning he appeared at Athos' door.

He found the musketeer already dressed and preparing to go out. Their audience with the King was not till twelve, so Athos had arranged to play a game of tennis with Porthos and Aramis on a court near the Luxembourg stables. Athos invited d'Artagnan to go with them, and he agreed. He had no knowledge of the game but did not know how else to pass the morning.

The other two musketeers had already arrived and were having a practice game on the court. Athos, who excelled at every kind of sport, chose d'Artagnan as his partner and challenged the other two. But as soon as he hit the ball his wound began throbbing again, so he had to stop playing. D'Artagnan was left alone to play against Porthos and Aramis. Porthos sent a mighty swipe across the net, and the ball whizzed past d'Artagnan's ear at a great rate.

'If that had hit me,' thought the young man, 'it would have bruised my face, and I should have to give up my audience with the King, for I couldn't appear in his presence with a black eye and a broken nose.'

And as this audience was to decide his whole future for better or worse (or so he thought), he asked Porthos and Aramis to excuse him, saying that he would prefer not to play until he was more experienced at the game. He then went and stood close to the line, in the spectators' gallery.

But as ill-luck would have it one of His Eminence's guards was also watching the game. He was still enraged at the news of his fellow-guardsmen's recent defeat and had vowed to seize the first opportunity for revenge. He now thought he saw his chance. Turning to his neighbour he said in a loud voice:

'That fellow's one of the new musketeer recruits, which, of course, explains why he's so frightened of a ball.'

D'Artagnan whipped round as though a snake had bitten

him and looked the impertinent guardsman straight in the eye.

'Stare at me to your heart's content, my lad,' said the guardsman, curling his moustache. 'I meant what I said and I'll repeat it if you like.'

'What you said was clear enough,' answered d'Artagnan. 'There's no need to repeat it, but I must ask you instead to follow me outside.'

'When?' asked the guardsman, with an ugly sneer on his face.

'At once, please.'

'I suppose you know who I am?'

'No, and I don't care.'

'You're making a big mistake. If you knew my name you might not be in such a hurry to meet me.'

'Well, what is your name?'

'Bernajoux, at your service.'

'Very well, Monsieur Bernajoux,' said d'Artagnan calmly. 'I'll be waiting for you at the gate.'

'Go right ahead. I'll follow you.'

'Don't follow too close,' said d'Artagnan, 'or we might be noticed going out together. We don't want an audience on an occasion like this.'

'True, Sir, true,' answered the guardsman, amazed to think that the young man should have been so little impressed by his name.

For Bernajoux was a notorious figure and probably d'Artagnan was the only man in Paris who had never heard of him. He was one of the most dashing of the Cardinal's guards, and hardly a brawl took place in which he was not involved. Notwithstanding the King's and the Cardinal's edicts these brawls were of almost daily occurrence, so Bernajoux was a name to conjure with.

Porthos and Aramis were so intent on their game and Athos was so busy watching them that none of the three noticed their young companion leave the tennis court. He stopped at the gate as arranged and Bernajoux joined him a moment later. D'Artagnan had very little time to spare before his audience

with the King, fixed for midday, so he looked up and down the
street, saw that it was deserted and said to his foe:

'You may be called Bernajoux, Sir, but you're lucky all the
same to have a mere recruit to deal with. However, I'll do my
best. On guard, Sir!'

'This is not a very good place to fight, you know,' objected
Bernajoux. 'We'd be much better off behind the St Germain
Abbey or in Clerk's Meadows.'

'No doubt we would, Sir,' answered d'Artagnan. 'But unfortunately I'm pressed for time; I've an appointment at twelve
o'clock. So let's get started at once, please. On guard, Sir!'

Bernajoux was not the man to need more than two invitations to fight. The next moment his sword-blade was glittering
in the sun and he was bearing down furiously on d'Artagnan,
whom he believed to be young and inexperienced. He hoped to
terrify him by this sudden onslaught. But d'Artagnan by now
felt himself quite an old hand at duelling. His previous day's
triumph was still fresh in his mind, and his heart was full of
joy at the thought of that day's audience. He was determined
not to yield an inch. So the two swords engaged right up to the
hilt and, as d'Artagnan stood his ground firmly, his opponent
was forced to take a step backwards. Bernajoux allowed his
sword to drop for a second; d'Artagnan disengaged, lunged and
touched his opponent on the shoulder. Then he, in his turn,
stepped back and put up his sword. But Bernajoux shouted that
it was nothing, lunged blindly at d'Artagnan and actually
spitted himself on his enemy's sword. Even then he didn't fall
and didn't admit defeat; he merely retreated in the direction of
the Duc de la Trémouille's house, where a close relation of his
was equerry. Bernajoux showed no sign of pain, so d'Artagnan
went on pressing him mercilessly, not realizing how serious his
second wound was. He would probably have polished him off
with a third thrust had not the noise from the street at last
reached the tennis court. Two of Bernajoux's friends, who had
seen him exchanging looks with the young musketeer and had
watched him follow him out of the tennis court, now rushed
into the street with drawn swords and fell upon the victor. But

Athos, Porthos, and Aramis, who were now also alive to the situation, followed hot on the heels of the two guardsmen, falling on them in their turn and forcing them to face about. At this moment Bernajoux collapsed. Now the guards were outnumbered two to one, so they started shouting to Monsieur de la Trémouille's household to come and help them. Hearing their cries, all who were in the house at the time came out into the street and hurled themselves at the four friends who, for their part, began shouting: 'King's Musketeers, help, help!'

This cry was usually answered. In brawls of this kind any stray guardsmen from other companies who happened to be in the neighbourhood usually sided with the musketeers against the soldiers of the Red Duke, as Aramis had nicknamed Richelieu. Three guards of Monsieur des Essarts' company happened to be passing at this moment; two of them at once came to the rescue of the four friends, while the third ran towards Monsieur de Tréville's house calling: 'King's Musketeers, help, help!'

As usual Monsieur de Tréville's house was packed with his followers. When the cry rang out they all ran at once to help their fellows in distress; the fight became a free fight for all, but the musketeers had the advantage of numbers. The Cardinal's guards and Monsieur de la Trémouille's servants finally retreated into the house, shutting the gates just in time to prevent their enemies breaking in after them. The wounded Bernajoux had been taken in some time before, and was being attended to by doctors, for he was in a very critical condition.

Now the musketeers' and their supporters' blood was up, and they were considering setting fire to Monsieur de la Trémouille's house in order to punish his servants for their impudence in daring to take up arms against the King's Musketeers. The excitement in the street was reaching fever pitch when fortunately the clock struck eleven. The four friends were at once reminded of their audience with the King at twelve, and forthwith set to work to calm things down. A couple of paving stones were hurled at the doors, but the doors stood firm. By degrees everyone got bored. And as the ringleaders had now left, the remainder of the crowd dispersed too. Meanwhile the four friends made their way to Monsieur de Tréville's house. The latter had already heard of this fresh escapade, and was waiting impatiently for them to arrive.

'Hurry, hurry,' he said. 'We must go to the Louvre at once and tell the King our story before the Cardinal gets in with his. We'll describe today's affair as a sequel to yesterday's, and slur things over like that.'

Whereupon Monsieur de Tréville and the four young men set forth to keep their appointment at the Louvre. But on arriving they were told to their astonishment that the King had gone stag-hunting in the forest at St Germain. Monsieur de Tréville refused to believe it at first, and made the servant repeat the message. When he was finally convinced his face darkened.

'Had His Majesty already arranged to go hunting yesterday?' he asked.

'No, Your Excellency,' answered the footman. 'This morning the Master of the Hunt called to tell His Majesty that they'd marked down a stag expressly for him. His Majesty at first said he couldn't go; then the temptation of a good hunt proved too strong for him and he left immediately after breakfast.'

'And has the King seen the Cardinal?' asked Monsieur de Tréville.

'Yes, Sir. I'm pretty certain he will have by now,' answered the servant. 'I saw His Eminence's horses being harnessed this morning. I asked where he was going and they said to St Germain.'

'He's stolen a march on us,' said Monsieur de Tréville.

Then, turning to the musketeers, he added: 'But I shall be seeing the King this evening in any case, gentlemen. But I think it would be wiser if you four stayed away.'

This was obviously a very sensible piece of advice. Monsieur de Tréville knew the King so well that it would have been foolish to argue. He advised the four friends to return to their various homes and wait to hear from him.

De Tréville now went home himself. He realized that he must get ahead of his opponent by telling his story first. 'Attack is the best defence.' So he sent one of his servants to Monsieur de la Trémouille with a message requesting him to turn Bernajoux, the Cardinal's guard, out of his house and to deal severely with his household for having dared take up arms against the musketeers. But Monsieur de la Trémouille had in the meantime heard the other version of the story from his equerry, who, as we know, was related to Bernajoux. So he sent back a reply to the effect that it was he rather than Monsieur de Tréville and his musketeers who had grounds for complaint; that it was the musketeers who had attacked his servants and had wanted to burn down his house. De Tréville saw that this was an argument which might go on for ever and that de la Trémouille would only become more obstinate in maintaining that he was the injured party. So he thought out a plan which would bring things to a head, and called round in person at the Duke's house early that afternoon.

The servant showed him into Monsieur de la Trémouille's room, and the two gentlemen bowed politely; there may have been no love lost between them, but they had a genuine respect for each other. They were both honest, high-principled men. Moreover Monsieur de la Trémouille was a Protestant; he never saw the King; he belonged to no particular party and was therefore on the whole unprejudiced in his social relations. This time, however, he welcomed Monsieur de Tréville rather more stiffly and formally than usual.

'Sir,' said Monsieur de Tréville, 'you and I both feel we have a grievance. I've come to ask you to co-operate with me in sorting out the rights and wrongs of this case.'

'I shall be most happy to do so,' answered Monsieur de la Trémouille. 'But I must warn you I've had first-hand information and your musketeers are definitely in the wrong.'

'You're a fair-minded man,' answered de Tréville, 'and I know you'll listen to what I have to say.'

'Of course, Sir,' answered de la Trémouille. 'Please speak out.'

'May I ask how Monsieur Bernajoux is, your equerry's cousin?'

'Very ill, Sir, very ill indeed. He has a light wound in the arm and another in the lung which the doctor regards as very serious.'

'Is he conscious?'

'Oh yes.'

'Can he talk?'

'Yes, he can just talk, but it's very painful for him.'

'Very well, Sir, I suggest that we both go and visit him, tell him his condition's critical and make him swear on his hope of salvation to tell the truth about what happened. I appoint him judge at his own trial, and agree to accept whatever he says.'

Monsieur de la Trémouille thought for a moment. Then he realized what a sensible suggestion this was, and fell in with it.

Both men immediately went down to the invalid's room. When Bernajoux saw these two great courtiers coming in to pay him a personal visit, he tried to sit up in bed. But he was too weak; the effort exhausted him and he sank back almost unconscious.

Monsieur de la Trémouille went up to him and put some smelling salts under his nose, which soon revived him. Now de Tréville invited de la Trémoulle to question the sick man himself, for fear he might be accused of influencing him.

Everything happened exactly as de Tréville had foreseen. Critically ill as he was, Bernajoux had no thought in his head but to speak the truth. He described the incident exactly as it had occurred.

Monsieur de Tréville now had all the information he wanted; he took leave of Bernajoux, wishing him a swift recovery, paid his respects to Monsieur de la Trémouille, returned to his house and sent a message to the four friends inviting them to dine with him that evening.

Monsieur de Tréville entertained all the most distinguished people in Paris, that is to say, all those with anti-Cardinalist sympathies. So it was natural that the talk at dinner should be entirely concerned with the two recent set-backs given to the Cardinal's Guards. D'Artagnan had been the hero of both these incidents, so he was the centre of interest that night, and all the toasts were drunk to him. Athos, Porthos, and Aramis were only too pleased to allow their young friend to outshine them, not only because they were generous-minded but because they had all had their full share of praise on many previous occasions.

At about six o'clock Monsieur de Tréville announced that he was expected at the Louvre. But as the King had missed the appointment which he had himself arranged for twelve o'clock, de Tréville did not insist on his right of entry by the private staircase but took his place with the four young men among the other courtiers in the ante-room. The King had not yet returned from hunting, but they had only waited a few minutes when all the doors were suddenly flung open and His Majesty was announced.

At this d'Artagnan felt a thrill of expectation. The next quarter of an hour would probably see his whole future decided for better or worse. He stood staring at the door, hardly daring to breathe.

Louis XIII now appeared, followed by a few personal attendants; he was in hunting clothes, still dusty after the day's sport; he wore heavy top boots and carried a hunting crop. D'Artagnan saw at the first glance that His Majesty was in a thoroughly bad temper. Indeed no one within a radius of twenty yards could have failed to notice His Majesty's mood. The courtiers all saw it, but this did not prevent them pressing forward as the King passed. In those days aspiring courtiers still preferred to get an angry look from their sovereign than no look at all. So the three musketeers did not hesitate, but pressed forward with the rest. D'Artagnan, however, being unfamiliar with Court ways, remained where he was, hidden behind his three friends. The King was personally acquainted with Athos, Porthos, and Aramis, but he passed them by without a look or a word of greeting, as though he hadn't noticed them. As for Monsieur de Tréville, he returned the King's angry stare with such assurance that it was the King who had to look away. After which His Majesty walked straight on into his private apartments, looking neither to right nor to left, but muttering angrily to himself.

'There's trouble in the air,' said Athos with a smile. 'We'll none of us be made knights of St Michael this time.'

'Wait here ten minutes,' said Monsieur de Tréville, 'and if I haven't come out by then, go back to my house. Not more than ten minutes, remember!'

The four young men waited ten minutes, a quarter of an hour, twenty minutes, and still Monsieur de Tréville did not come. They then went off to his house as arranged, very uneasy in their minds about the future.

De Tréville had gone boldly into the King's private room and had found His Majesty in a very bad temper, sitting on a sofa, tapping his boot impatiently with his hunting crop. De Tréville, in no way put out by this, inquired politely after the King's health.

'I'm not at all well, not at all well,' answered the King. 'I'm bored.'

Boredom was, indeed, the King's worst affliction. He had often been known to take one of his courtiers aside and say to him: 'My Lord So and So, come over here and let's be bored together.'

'Bored, Your Majesty?' echoed de Tréville. 'Didn't you enjoy your day's hunting?'

'No, Sir, I did not. Everything's going to rack and ruin, I swear it is. I don't know if it's the game that's got no scent or the hounds no noses. We started a royal, ran him for six hours, and just as he was ready to turn to bay, just as Saint-Simon was lifting his horn to sound the kill, lo and behold, the whole pack breaks away from the line and starts chasing a brocket! I can see I shall have to give up hunting just as I gave up hawking. Oh, Tréville, I'm a very unhappy man! I had only one falcon left and he died the day before yesterday.'

'Yes, Sir, I can well understand your grief, and the loss is tragic. But I thought you still had a good number of falcons, sparrow-hawks, and tercels left.'

'But not one man to train them! The falconers leave one

after the other, and now I'm the only man who takes any real interest in the science of hunting. When I'm dead there'll be no hunting or sport of any kind. All the hunting will be done with traps and snares. If only I had time to set up a training-school! But the Cardinal's always after me, pestering me about Spain, England, or Austria. He never leaves me in peace for a moment! Oh, by the way, Monsieur de Tréville, now that we're on the subject of the Cardinal, I'm seriously annoyed with you.'

De Tréville was expecting the King to wind up with this. He knew him of old; he knew perfectly well that in his previous complaints he had only been leading up to what was really on his mind and whipping up his courage to make this premeditated attack.

De Tréville pretended to be completely bewildered.

'What could I have done to displease Your Majesty?' he asked.

'Is that the way you carry out your duties?' said the King, ignoring de Tréville's question, and continuing his attack as he had planned it in advance. 'Am I to be rewarded for appointing you Captain of my Musketeers by tales of how these gentlemen have been assassinating people in the streets, setting a whole district by the ears and planning to burn down the entire city? And you yourself making no effort to stop it! However,' continued His Majesty, 'I'm probably being a bit hasty in accusing you. Probably the rioters are already in prison and you've come here just to tell me that they've been punished as they deserve.'

'On the contrary, Sir,' answered de Tréville. 'I've come to ask you to punish the people who actually do deserve punishment.'

'What people?' asked the King.

'The lying tale-bearers,' said Monsieur de Tréville.

'Well, really!' cried the King. 'You're not going to stand there and tell me that those thrice damned musketeers of yours, Athos, Porthos, and Aramis, and your young recruit from Béarn didn't provoke and attack that unfortunate Bernajoux like a lot of madmen, and cut him up so badly that he's now lying at death's door! And that they didn't then go and lay siege to Monsieur de la Trémouille's house and try to set

fire to it? In time of war, of course, that might be excusable –
it's a Huguenot stronghold. But in peace-time that sort of
thing's quite unpardonable. Come now, Monsieur de Tréville,
you're not going to deny all this, are you?'

'May I ask, Sir, who told you this pretty story?'

'Who told me, Sir?' answered the King. 'Who d'you suppose
told me? The man who watches while I sleep, who labours
while I rest, who's our guiding light in everything, at home and
abroad, in France and in Europe.'

'I suppose you mean Almighty God, Sir,' said de Tréville. 'I
can think of no one else who stands so high above Your
Majesty.'

'No, Sir, I do not mean God. I mean the guardian of the
State, my only true servant, my only friend, the Cardinal.'

'His Eminence is not His Holiness, Sir.'

'What's that you say?'

'I say that only the Pope's infallible; his Cardinals are not.'

'You mean that he's telling me lies, playing me false. Is that
what you're accusing him of? Come on, Sir, admit it. You're
accusing him of dishonesty to me!'

'No, Sir. I merely say he's been misinformed. He was too
quick to believe Your Majesty's musketeers in the wrong. He's
been unfair to them. He should have got his information from
those who really knew.'

'The complaint came from Monsieur de la Trémouille himself,' said the King. 'What have you to say to that?'

'I might say that Monsieur de la Trémouille was too personally concerned in the matter to be altogether impartial,'
said de Tréville. 'But I won't. I know the Duke to be a
thoroughly honest man. I'm willing to accept what he says.
But on one condition, Sir!'

'What condition?'

'That Your Majesty sends for him and questions him yourself, in a private interview, without witnesses, and that I should
be allowed to see you immediately after he leaves.'

'Yes, I'll do that,' said the King. 'And you'll really accept
what Monsieur de la Trémouille says?'

'Yes, Sir!'

'You'll submit to his verdict?'

'Yes, Sir!'

'And agree to pay any compensation he may ask for?'

'Most certainly!'

'La Chesnaye!' called the King. 'La Chesnaye!'

The King's confidential valet, who was always near at hand, came in in answer to this summons.

'La Chesnaye,' said the King, 'send someone at once to find Monsieur de la Trémouille, I want to see him this evening.'

'Will your Majesty give me your word not to see anyone between Monsieur de la Trémouille and myself?'

'I promise on my honour.'

'In that case, Sir, I shall wait on you again tomorrow.'

'Yes, Tréville, tomorrow.'

'What time tomorrow, Sir?'

'Whatever time suits you.'

'I don't want to come too early for fear of waking you, Sir.'

'Waking me, Sir? You don't suppose I ever sleep, do you? I never sleep at all, Tréville. I dream occasionally, that's all. So come as early as you like; let's say seven o'clock. But remember, if your musketeers are in the wrong ... Well, I'll leave it at that for the present.'

'If my musketeers are in the wrong, Sir, I'll hand them over to you at once, and you can deal with them as you think fit. Is there anything more I can do for you, Sir? I'm at your service.'

'No, Tréville, no. They call me Louis the Just, and rightly so. We'll leave it all till tomorrow. I'll see you then.'

'God keep Your Majesty till then.'

The King may have slept badly that night, but Monsieur de Tréville slept even worse. He had sent a message that same evening to the three musketeers and their companion telling them to present themselves at his house at half-past six the following morning.

Punctually at six-thirty the four young men arrived and they and Monsieur de Tréville started off at once for the Louvre. De Tréville gave evasive answers to all the young men's questions but did not conceal from them the fact that their future and his, too, hung in the balance.

When the little party reached the entrance to the private staircase, de Tréville told his companions to wait outside. If the King was in a bad temper, they could always make off without being seen; if, on the other hand, he consented to see them, they could be summoned at a moment's notice.

De Tréville walked up alone to the King's private ante-room, where he found La Chesnaye, who told him that they had missed Monsieur de la Trémouille on the previous evening, that he had returned home too late to go to the Louvre, and that he had arrived only about half an hour earlier and was at that very moment closeted with the King.

De Tréville was greatly elated at this news, for it meant that no subversive influence would be brought to bear upon the King in the interval between his hearing de la Trémouille's statement and his interview with himself.

Indeed, hardly had ten minutes passed than the door of the King's private sitting-room opened and Monsieur de la Trémouille appeared in the ante-room. He went straight up to de Tréville and said:

'Sir, the King has just summoned me and asked me to tell the whole story of what happened yesterday morning outside my house. I told His Majesty the truth; that my household was entirely to blame, and that I was quite prepared to apologize to you. Here we are face to face. So let me apologize to you now and say at the same time that I hope you'll always continue to count me among your friends.'

'Sir,' said de Tréville, 'I was so certain I could rely on your sense of justice that I wanted you to be my witness for the defence with His Majesty, you and none other. I see that my trust in you was justified, and thank you for proving to me and to the world in general that there's still one man left in France of whom one can truthfully say the things I've said of you.'

'Very nice, very nice,' said the King, who had been standing in the passage between the two doors and had overheard this exchange of compliments. 'But if he's such a friend of yours,

Tréville, tell him I'd also like to be a friend of his, but that he's neglected me; that I haven't seen him for nearly three years and that I have to summon him to get him to come here at all. Tell him all this for me, Tréville, because it's the sort of thing a King isn't allowed to say for himself.'

'Thank you, Sir, thank you,' said the Duke. 'But Your Majesty mustn't suppose that the people you see every day are necessarily the most loyal of your subjects. Naturally I except Monsieur de Tréville.'

'Oh, you heard what I said, did you, Monsieur de la Trémouille . . . Well, I'm very glad you did,' said the King, coming and standing in the doorway. 'Ah, Tréville, there you are! And where are your musketeers, may I ask? I told you two days ago to bring them here. Why haven't you done so?'

'They're down below, Sir,' said Tréville. 'And with your permission I'll ask La Chesnaye to tell them to come up.'

'Yes, yes. Let them come up at once; it's just on eight o'clock, and I've got a visitor at nine. Good day to you, Duke! And be sure and come back. Come in, Tréville.'

The Duke bowed and went out. As he opened the door the three musketeers and d'Artagnan, led by La Chesnaye, appeared at the head of the stairs.

'Come in, you scoundrels, come in,' said the King. 'I've got a bone to pick with you!'

The musketeers came up and bowed, and d'Artagnan followed behind them.

'What's all this I've been hearing?' went on the King. 'You four putting seven of the Cardinal's Guards out of action in two days? That's too many, gentlemen, too many, I say. If you go on at that rate His Eminence's whole company will be wiped out in under three weeks and I shall have to enforce the edicts much more strictly. One here and there – accidentally as it were – I wouldn't object to that. But seven in three days, no! That's far too many!'

'That's why they've come here, to apologize to you for their behaviour, Sir,' said de Tréville. 'They're all very chastened and contrite.'

'Chastened and contrite? M'm!' said the King. 'I'm not very

impressed by those mock repentant looks of theirs. And what's that young Gascon doing skulking behind the others? Step forward, Sir, if you please.'

D'Artagnan stepped forward with a mock hang-dog expression on his face.

'Why, Tréville, you told me he was a young man! He's a mere child, Sir, a mere child! And it was really he who gave Jussac that unkind thrust?'

'Yes. And two other beauties to Bernajoux.'

'Well, I'm damned!'

'Besides which he tackled Cahusac and saved my life, Sir,' broke in Athos. 'But for him I wouldn't be here now paying Your Majesty my respects.'

'A regular fire-eater, this fellow from Béarn, what?' exclaimed the King. 'Damme, Tréville, as the King, my father, would have said, at that rate we'll be seeing frayed doublets and broken swords everywhere. I suppose our Gascons are just as poor as they always were?'

'Yes, Sir. I'm afraid nobody's yet discovered any gold mines in their mountains. And yet I feel they deserve some reward for the way they supported your father's claims.'

'By that I suppose you mean that I, as the son of my father, owe my kingship to the Gascons. Very well, I'll let that pass. La Chesnaye, go and search my pockets and see if I've got forty pistoles on me. If so, bring them here. And now, young man, tell me word for word exactly what happened in your tussle with the Guards.'

D'Artagnan gave a full account of the events of the previous day: how he had been unable to sleep at the thought of the next day's audience with His Majesty and had arrived at his friends' lodgings three hours before the appointed time; how they had all gone down together to the tennis court; how he had been taunted by Bernajoux, who had nearly had to pay for his insults with his life, and how this had led to the suggestion of burning down Monsieur de la Trémouille's house, though that gentleman had himself been in no way concerned in the affair.

'Yes, that's how it was,' said the King. 'That's the story the

Duke told me. Poor Cardinal! Seven men in two days, and some of the pick of his guards too! But that's enough, gentlemen, understand? You must stop there. You've had your revenge for the Rue Férou incident, and a damned good revenge at that. You ought to be satisfied.'

'If Your Majesty's satisfied,' said Tréville, 'we are.'

'Yes, I'm satisfied,' answered the King. Then, taking a handful of gold from La Chesnaye and putting it into d'Artagnan's hand, he added: 'And here's a proof of how satisfied I am.'

In those days personal pride was not valued as highly as it is now. A gentleman could take largesse from a King and not feel humiliated. D'Artagnan pocketed the forty pistoles without any trace of embarrassment and thanked His Majesty profusely.

'Don't mention it, don't mention it,' said the King. Then he looked at his watch and said: 'And now it's half-past eight, so please leave me. As I told you, I've a visitor at nine. Thank you for your loyalty, gentlemen. I can always count on it, can't I?'

'Sir,' cried the four friends, 'we'd die a thousand deaths for Your Majesty.'

'Thank you, thank you,' said the King. 'But I'd rather have you alive; you're more useful to me alive. Tréville,' he continued in an undertone, while the others were taking their leave; 'there's no vacancy at present in your musketeers, I know. Besides, we've decided that all candidates must do a noviciate beforehand. So find a place for this young man with Monsieur des Essarts, your brother-in-law. God, Tréville, I look forward to seeing the Cardinal's face when he hears about this! He'll be furious! But I don't care. I'm quite within my rights.'

Then His Majesty dismissed Tréville with a wave of the hand. Tréville went out and joined the four friends whom he found dividing up d'Artagnan's forty pistoles into four equal portions.

The Cardinal was indeed furious, as the King had prophesied. So furious was he that for a week he refused to join the King at cards. The King, on the other hand, overwhelmed His

Eminence with his attentions whenever they met, and never failed to inquire in a caressing tone after the health of those two poor guardsmen of his, Bernajoux and Jussac.

CHAPTER VII

The Musketeers at Home

WHEN d'Artagnan and his three companions were in the street, they began at once to discuss how our hero could make best use of his pistoles. Athos advised him to order himself a good meal at the Pomme-de-Pin tavern; Porthos advised him to hire a good servant, and Aramis suggested he get himself a mistress.

The meal was arranged that very day, and the servant served it. The food had been chosen by Athos and the servant by Porthos. He was a man from Picardy called Planchet, whom Porthos had signed on that morning; he had found him on the La Tournelle bridge, making patterns in the water by spitting into it, and, maintaining that this occupation showed the man to be of an orderly and serious turn of mind, had engaged him without further recommendation.

Planchet, for his part, had been impressed by Porthos' magnificent appearance. He imagined that he was to be Porthos' own servant, and was slightly disappointed to discover that the post was already occupied by a fellow-provincial called Mousqueton, that Porthos could not afford a staff of two, and that he was to be d'Artagnan's servant instead. However, at the dinner given that very evening by his new master, he noticed him pull out a fistful of gold to pay the bill, and this sight rejoiced his heart. Planchet saw himself made for life and thanked Heaven that he had found such a Croesus for a master. He remained in this blissful state of illusion until after the supper, and made up for several days of enforced abstinence by helping himself freely to the leavings on the gentlemen's plates.

But when he went up to make his master's bed that night, his high hopes were shattered. D'Artagnan's home consisted of only two rooms and only one bed. D'Artagnan slept on the only bed in the bedroom, while Planchet had to camp on the floor of the sitting-room, with a blanket from d'Artagnan's bed drawn over him.

Athos had a servant whom he had trained in a very peculiar manner. He was called Grimaud. Athos was himself always very silent and aloof. For the past five or six years he had lived on terms of the greatest intimacy with his two friends, but neither of them had ever seen him laugh. He spoke only when he had something definite to say, and he said what he had to say in the simplest possible manner, without any frills or embroidery. His remarks were mere statements of fact.

Athos was approaching thirty, very handsome and intelligent, but was generally supposed never to have had a love-affair. He never discussed women at all. He did not actually stop people mentioning women in his presence, but it was easy to see from his unresponsiveness and from his little sneering comments whenever the subject was brought up that he took no pleasure in conversation of that kind. His general reserve and the obstinate silence he maintained on every possible occasion had made almost a recluse of him; so very set was he in his ways that he had trained his servant Grimaud to under-stand him by signs and lip-movements; in this way he avoided having to utter a word more than was necessary. He spoke to Grimaud only on very special occasions.

Grimaud was devoted to his master and had a great respect for his abilities. But he was at the same time frightened to death of him. And if he was in doubt about any order his master might give him, rather than ask to have it made clear, he would fly off and sometimes do the very opposite of what he had been told to do. Whenever this happened Athos would merely shrug his shoulders and quite cold-bloodedly proceed to give Grimaud a thrashing. On those days he would actually address a few words to him.

Porthos, as we have seen, was the complete opposite of

Athos in character. Not only did he talk a great deal, but he talked very loud. In fairness it must be said that he did not care much whether anyone listened to him or not; he talked for talking's sake and for the pleasure of hearing his own voice. He held forth on all subjects except books, pleading in excuse for this limitation that as a child he had acquired a fixed hatred for scholars. He was less distinguished-looking than Athos and knew it; his sense of inferiority in this respect had made him act somewhat spitefully towards his friend in the early days of their acquaintanceship; he used to try and outshine Athos by wearing gorgeous clothes. But Athos had only to come into a room in his simple musketeer's coat, with his indefinable air of distinction, to eclipse the resplendent Porthos at once. Porthos would try to make amends for this by trumpeting aloud his amorous successes to the other musketeers in Monsieur de Tréville's ante-room and in the courtyard of his house, a thing which Athos never did. In his love-affairs Porthos was at present transferring his attentions from the wives of professional men to the wives of the aristocracy. At the moment he was enjoying the favours of a foreign princess; this lady was apparently considering making over an enormous fortune to him.

There is an old proverb: 'Like master, like man'. So having contrasted Athos with Porthos, let us now contrast Athos' servant Grimaud with Porthos' servant Mousqueton.

Mousqueton was a native of Normandy. His real name was Boniface, but Porthos thought this sounded too namby-pamby, so he changed it to the more impressive name of Mousqueton. Mousqueton had entered Porthos' service on the condition that he was to be lodged and clothed, nothing more, but that both were to be done in great style; he was to be allowed to devote two hours a day to his appearance, upon which he relied to provide him with all the other necessities of life. Porthos had accepted Mousqueton's terms; they suited him admirably. He had the man fitted out with doublets cut out of his own old clothes and his collection of spare cloaks. Porthos' tailor was a very clever man; moreover he had a wife who was suspected of wanting to seduce Porthos away from his newly-formed aristocratic connections. The pair worked hard to please master and man, and Mousqueton was soon set up in the very latest fashion and did great credit to his employer.

As for Aramis, he has already been well enough described, and his character and that of his two friends will emerge more clearly in the course of this story. His servant was called Bazin. In anticipation of the day when his master would take Orders Bazin was always dressed in black, as became the servant of a churchman. He was a native of Berry, between thirty-five and forty, gentle, placid, and portly. He spent his leisure hours reading holy books; at a pinch he could cook a simple but excellent meal. Apart from this he was discretion personified: he saw nothing, heard nothing, and repeated nothing. And his loyalty was beyond question.

We now know, at any rate superficially, the characters of the musketeers and of their servants. So let us go on to describe their homes.

Athos lived in the Rue Férou, quite close to the Luxembourg. His quarters consisted of two small rooms, very handsomely furnished, in a lodging-house owned by a lady still young and fairly good-looking, who had persistently ogled her lodger from the day when he first came to live there, but had never had any response from him. There were a few relics of past splendours in Athos' rooms, for example a sword, richly inlaid, of the period of Francis I, of which the hilt alone, encrusted with jewels, was worth roughly two hundred pistoles. Even in times of great poverty Athos had never considered either pawning or selling this sword. Porthos had long cast covetous eyes at it, and would have given ten years of his life to possess it.

One day Porthos had had an assignation with a duchess and had actually asked Athos to lend him the sword. Athos said nothing, but collected all the jewels, gold chains, and old, dis-coloured aiguillettes he possessed and offered them to Porthos. But the sword was inviolate, he declared, clamped to its place, as it were, and should never leave the house except in the company of its owner.

Besides the sword Athos had a portrait of a nobleman of the time of Henry III, dressed in the height of fashion, and decorated with the Order of the Holy Spirit. The nobleman in the picture, resplendent with his many medals, had certain points of resemblance with Athos, a sort of family likeness which led one to suppose that he was the young man's ancestor.

The last relic of past splendours in Athos' lodgings was a very handsome wrought-gold casket engraved with the same coat of arms as the sword and the portrait. This casket stood on the mantelpiece, and was very much out of keeping with the rest of the furniture. Athos carried the key of this casket with him wherever he went. But one day he had opened it in front of Porthos, and Porthos had seen for himself that it contained nothing but letters and papers, presumably love-letters and family documents.

Porthos lived in a large apartment in the Rue du Vieux Colombier, which looked very magnificent from the outside. Whenever he happened to pass the house with a friend, he would point proudly at the windows, at one of which Mousqueton was always standing on guard, and say: 'You see that house there; that's my house!'

But if anyone called to see him, he was always out; he never invited anyone in, and not a soul knew whether the house was as grand inside as it was out.

As for Aramis, he lived in a little three-roomed apartment in the Rue du Vaugirard. All three rooms were on the ground floor and the bedroom gave on to a cool, green, shady little garden, which could not be overlooked from the windows of the neighbouring houses.

As for d'Artagnan, we know what his rooms were like, and we have already made the acquaintance of his valet, Planchet.

D'Artagnan, like all men with a gift for intrigue, was very inquisitive by nature. He made every effort to discover exactly who Athos, Porthos, and Aramis were. He realized that the names they were known by were only pseudonyms and suspected that all three were aristocrats, especially Athos, who had 'grand seigneur' written all over him. So he approached

Porthos for information about Athos and Aramis, and Aramis for information about Porthos.

Unfortunately Porthos himself knew nothing about the silent Athos' life beyond what everyone else knew. It was rumoured that he had had some unhappy love-affair and that he had been embittered for life by some terrible disillusionment. But no one had the vaguest notion what the disillusionment was or who had let him down.

Porthos' life, on the other hand, was no secret to anyone. The one thing secret about him was his name, and Monsieur de Tréville was the only man who knew that, and the names of his two friends. Porthos was vain and a braggart and as easy to read as an open book. One could only be misled about Porthos by believing what he said about himself.

As for Aramis he put on a frank, ingenuous air with everyone, but this was only a mask; he was, in point of fact, a man steeped in mystery. He never answered questions about others, and always changed the subject when anyone questioned him about himself. On one occasion d'Artagnan, who had been pestering him about Porthos and had brought up the subject of the big man's rumoured association with a princess, suddenly decided that he would like to know about Aramis' own life. So he did a verbal half-tack and asked the young musketeer point-blank:

'And what about you, my boy? You're very communicative about other people's baronesses and princesses, but very reserved about your own.'

'I beg your pardon,' answered Aramis, 'I only mentioned Porthos' private life because he advertises it so freely himself; I've heard him shouting it all out in front of everyone. But remember, d'Artagnan, if someone else had told me about Porthos' affairs, or if he'd told me about them himself in confidence, I'd have been as close as a clam about them.'

'I'm quite certain you would,' said d'Artagnan. 'However, that doesn't prevent me questioning you about your life. You needn't answer if you don't want to. I can't help feeling that you, as well as Porthos, have some fairly close connection with coats of arms. What about that embroidered handkerchief to which I owe the pleasure of your acquaintance?'

This time Aramis did not get angry. He replied apologetically:

'Don't forget I'm going into the Church and that I try to avoid all worldly entanglements. The handkerchief you saw had not been given to me; one of my friends left it in my rooms by accident. I had to pick it up and pocket it to prevent him and his mistress being compromised. I myself have no mistress and I don't want one. I'm like Athos in that respect; he's a very sensible fellow.'

'But good God! You're not a priest yet – you're a musketeer!'

'Only for the time being, as the Cardinal says. A musketeer under protest and a Churchman at heart, believe me! Athos and Porthos hustled me into the company to get me out of a fix. I was having a bit of trouble at the time with . . . but of course that wouldn't interest you. I'm only taking up your time.'

'On the contrary – I'm enormously interested,' cried d'Artagnan, 'and I've got plenty of time to spare.'

'Well, you may have, *but I haven't*,' answered Aramis. 'First of all I have to say my breviary. Then I have to compose some verses for Madame d'Aiguillon, and then I must go to the Rue St Honoré to buy rouge for Madame de Chevreuse. So you see, old boy, I'm very busy, even though you may not be.'

And Aramis gave the younger man a friendly handshake and said good-bye to him. Try as he might, d'Artagnan never managed to find out anything more about his three new friends, so he resigned himself for the time being to believing everything he heard from other people about their past lives, hoping to get more accurate and detailed information later. Meanwhile he continued to think of Athos as Achilles, Porthos as Ajax, and Aramis as Joseph.

The four young men passed their days very pleasantly, Athos spent his time gambling, but always lost. And yet he never borrowed a penny from his friends, although he was always ready to lend them whatever they wanted. And whenever he played on credit he always called early the following morning at the house of his previous night's creditor, bringing the money with him.

Porthos had his lucky days at cards; whenever he won he would put on his best clothes and go swaggering round the town. But after a bad spell at the tables he would disappear for several days, and then return looking exhausted and very chastened, but always with a fresh supply of money.

Aramis, on the other hand, never gambled at all. He was the wretchedest musketeer and the most unconvivial companion imaginable. He always had some mysterious work on hand. Sometimes, in the middle of a supper party, when everybody was beginning to liven up from the effects of wine, Aramis would suddenly look at his watch, rise from the table with a charming smile, and take leave of the others, pleading an engagement with some casuist, with whom he had an abstruse point of dialectic to clear up. At other times he would retire to his lodgings to write a thesis, and beg his friends not to disturb him.

But his friends always forgave him. Athos would smile his usual sad, aloof smile, and Porthos would pour himself out another glass of wine, declaring that Aramis would never be anything more than an obscure country vicar.

Planchet, d'Artagnan's valet, found his master's temporary affluence very much to his taste. He was paid thirty sous a day, and during the first month of his life with d'Artagnan he would return home every evening as gay as a lark, and very eager to please his master. But when the wind of adversity began to blow on the establishment in the Rue des Fossoyeurs, that is to say, when King Louis XIII's forty pistoles had been eaten up, or very nearly, Planchet started to make complaints which Athos considered revolting, Porthos indecent, and Aramis absurd. Athos advised d'Artagnan to sack the fellow at once; Porthos thought he ought to be flogged first, and Aramis maintained that valets should be seen and not heard, or at any rate that they should never speak except to pay compliments to their masters.

'It's all very well for you three to talk,' said d'Artagnan. 'You, Athos, for instance; you live with Grimaud in complete silence, and refuse to allow him to speak at all. So of course you never have any lip from him. And you, Porthos! You live in great state, and Mousqueton looks on you as a sort of god. And as for you, Aramis, you're always engrossed in your theological studies, and Bazin, being pious, looks up to you too. But I'm penniless and without credit; I'm not a musketeer, not even a guardsman. So how can I hope to impress Planchet? How can I make him love, fear, or even respect me?'

'Yes, it's a tricky situation,' agreed the three friends. 'It's a personal matter which only you can deal with. Valets are like women in domestic life; they must be put in their places at once and kept there. If you once let them get out of hand, you're done for. So think out some way of dealing with Planchet.'

D'Artagnan thought the matter well over, and decided to give Planchet a good thrashing as a provisional measure. He set about this with the thoroughness with which he tackled everything. Having subdued him physically, he proceeded to lecture him; Planchet must not leave his service without his permission; the future, he said, was bound to make up for the present and better times must surely come. Planchet was certain to prosper if he stayed with him, and he was too considerate a master to give him his notice now and let him miss the treats that were in store for him.

D'Artagnan's firm stand in regard to Planchet won him the admiration of his three friends; Planchet, too, was impressed, and never again talked of giving notice.

The four young men had now become a little community on their own. They spent their whole time together. D'Artagnan was too young to have formed any habits; moreover he was a country lad come to town, and had not yet found his feet. So he fell in with his friends' ways and did what they did.

In winter they got up every day at eight o'clock, in summer at six, and went at once to report at Monsieur de Tréville's house, to get their orders for the day, and to hear the latest news. Although d'Artagnan was not a musketeer, he paraded every day with a truly admirable devotion to duty. He never had a day off, because he went with each of his three friends in turn when it was their day on guard. He soon got known by all the other musketeers, and became very popular in the court-yard of Monsieur de Tréville's house. De Tréville himself became very fond of the boy, and was always bringing his name to the King's notice.

The three musketeers also became attached to their young companion. In fact all four young men were so devoted and so dependent on each other's company, in work as in play, that soon none of them was ever seen without the other three. Their favourite haunts were the Luxembourg district, the Saint-Sulpice Square, and the Rue du Vieux Colombier.

Meanwhile Monsieur de Tréville was being true to all his promises. One fine day the King ordered Monsieur des Essarts to enrol d'Artagnan as an ensign in his company of guards. D'Artagnan sighed inwardly as he donned this uniform; he would have given ten years of his life to exchange it for a musketeer's cloak. But Monsieur de Tréville insisted on a probation period of two years under Monsieur des Essarts, with the proviso that this period might be shortened if d'Artagnan managed in the meanwhile either to do some special service for the King or to achieve something spectacular on his own. D'Artagnan had to be content with this for the present, and entered Monsieur des Essarts' service the very next day.

Now Athos, Porthos, and Aramis took it in turns to mount guard with their young friend in return for what he had done for them. So on the day on which Monsieur des Essarts took d'Artagnan into his service he took not one man but four.

CHAPTER VIII

A Court Intrigue

IT was unfortunate but inevitable that Louis XIII's forty pistoles should, like everything else in this world, come to an end, and that our four friends should be reduced to living on practically nothing. Athos had been the first to pool his own little fortune for the common good. Then it had been Porthos' turn; he had done one of his periodic disappearing tricks and had returned with enough money to keep the four of them going for another fortnight. Then Aramis had taken on the job of financing the party; he had set himself to the task with a good grace, and had managed to find a few pistoles to carry on with. Nobody quite knew where they came from, and his own explanation that they were the proceeds of the sale of some books on theology was taken with a grain of salt.

When these additional supplies were also used up, our four friends went and appealed to Monsieur de Tréville. He made them a small advance on their pay, but this sum could not go very far to support three musketeers who were already pretty heavily in debt and one guardsman who had never had any money at all.

Realizing that they would soon be completely on the rocks they made one last effort and collected eight or ten pistoles which Porthos gambled with. But luck was against him: he lost everything he started with plus an extra twenty-five pistoles for which he had to write out an I.O.U.

Now the four young men could no longer be described as hard up — they were literally destitute. They walked up and down the streets followed by their lackeys, ravenous and with their tongues hanging out, visiting all their fellow musketeers in turn to get as many free meals as possible. In their prosperous days, prompted by Aramis, they had had the sense to sow meals right and left, and now that they were themselves in need they were able to reap a rich harvest.

Athos got four invitations, and each time he took his friends and their lackeys along with him. Porthos was asked out six times, Aramis eight, and each time the same procession of men and lackeys followed behind their leaders to get their share of the feasts.

D'Artagnan, unfortunately, knew no one in the capital, and the best he could provide was one high tea in the house of a priest, a Gascon like himself, and one dinner with a cornet in the guards. He took his motley army to visit the priest, and they ate the poor man out of house and home. They then visited the cornet, who rose nobly to the occasion. But, as Planchet remarked, however hard you try, you can't stuff down more than a certain amount at a time.

D'Artagnan felt slightly mortified at only having been able to provide a meal and a half – the tea at the priest's house could only count as half a meal – in exchange for the banquets provided by his friends. He was naïve enough to feel himself in debt to the brotherhood, forgetting that he had been providing for that brotherhood for a whole month out of his own pocket. And being worried he began to think. And it occurred to him that he and his three friends, a coalition of four, all young, active, and enterprising, should have some worthy aim in life, and not be content merely to swagger about, to indulge in occasional fencing bouts and dare-devil practical jokes, sometimes funny and sometimes not.

Here were four men, devoted to each other, sharing their luck together, ready to run any risk and dare any danger in the common cause. D'Artagnan pictured them as four arms outstretched threatening the four points of the compass or brought to bear on one particular point, and felt that they were bound to succeed in anything they undertook. They would be a live weapon in the hands of anyone who cared to use them, a kind of four-edged sword. The only thing that astonished him was that up till now none of them seemed to have realized what a formidable body they composed, and how easily they could achieve anything they set their minds to.

D'Artagnan sat in his room racking his brains to find some

use for this great driving-force. He never doubted for a moment that, if properly directed, like Archimedes' lever it could overturn the world. While he was thus ruminating there came a sudden gentle knock on his door. D'Artagnan woke up Planchet and told him to go and see who was there.

When we say that d'Artagnan woke Planchet up let not the reader suppose that it was night or even very early morning, before daybreak. No, four o'clock had just struck. Two hours previous to this Planchet had come to ask his master for food. D'Artagnan had had nothing to give him, and had advised him to go to sleep instead, to stave off the pangs of hunger, and this Planchet had done. This sleep had had to serve him for lunch.

He now went and opened the door and found a man standing outside, a rather drab-looking little man who looked like a tradesman. Planchet showed him in to his master and would have gladly stayed on and listened to the conversation as a dessert after his lunch sleep. But the man gave d'Artagnan to understand that he wished to speak to him alone; evidently his business was important and confidential. So d'Artagnan dismissed Planchet and bade his visitor be seated.

There was a moment's silence while the two men sat and sized each other up. D'Artagnan then said:

'Well, Sir, and what can I do for you?'

'Monsieur d'Artagnan,' said the stranger; 'I've heard you spoken of as a young man of great courage, and, believing as I do that the description's accurate, I've decided to let you into a secret.'

'Good, let's hear it,' said d'Artagnan, who felt instinctively that he was on to a good thing.

The stranger paused again a moment and continued:

'I've a wife, Sir, who's maid of the wardrobe to the Queen and who's both intelligent and good-looking. I was forced into marriage with her three years ago, although she only had a very small dowry, because Monsieur de Laporte, the Queen's gentleman-in-waiting, is her godfather and guardian.'

'Well?' said d'Artagnan.

'Well,' continued the little man, 'my wife was kidnapped

yesterday morning, just as she was leaving her workroom at the Louvre.'

'Who kidnapped her?'

'I don't know for certain, Sir,' answered the stranger, 'but I have my suspicions.'

'And whom do you suspect?'

'A man who has long been pestering her with his attentions.'

'That's bad, that's bad,' said d'Artagnan.

'But if you ask me my opinion,' went on the little man, 'I should say this kidnapping business has something political behind it, and isn't a mere love-affair.'

'Something political,' echoed d'Artagnan. 'I see.'

He suddenly knitted his brows and looked pensive.

'And who's the man you suspect?' he asked.

'I don't know if I should tell you, Sir.'

'Listen,' said d'Artagnan, 'I'd like to point out here and now that I'm not forcing you to tell me anything. You came of your own free will to see me. You told me you had a secret to confide in me. So do exactly as you please. You needn't stay if you don't want to.'

'No, Sir, no. You look to me an honest enough young fellow, and I'll take you into my confidence. I repeat, I don't think my wife's kidnapping concerns any love-affair of her own, but I think it concerns someone else's love affairs, someone much more important.'

'Not Madame de Bois-Tracy, by any chance?' asked d'Artagnan.

He wanted to show this little bourgeois that he was quite up-to-date in the latest Court scandals.

'More important still, Sir.'

'Madame d'Aiguillon perhaps?'

'More important still.'

'Madame de Chevreuse?'

'More important – much more important.'

'Not the . . .?' D'Artagnan stopped.

'Yes, Sir,' answered the little man in a low, quavering voice. He now seemed absolutely panic-stricken.

'Her love-affair with whom?'

'Well, Sir, I don't see who else it could be but the Duke of . . .'

'The Duke of . . .'

'Yes, Sir,' answered the little man, lowering his voice even more.

'But how can *you* know all about this?'

'How can I know, you ask? How can I know?' said the little man in a shrill, pained voice.

'Yes. Come on, speak out. I don't want any half-confidences.'

'My wife told me herself, Sir.'

'And who did she get it from?'

'From Monsieur de Laporte. I told you she was Monsieur de Laporte's ward, didn't I? Monsieur de Laporte's the Queen's confidential agent. He saw to it that my wife was given a special post near Her Majesty, so that the poor Queen could have someone at hand she could trust. She has enemies all round her; she's lost the King's confidence; the Cardinal sets spies to watch her, and she has no loyal friend at all.'

'Ah!' cried d'Artagnan. 'Now I'm beginning to see daylight.'

'My wife came to see me four days ago,' went on the little man. 'One of the conditions she imposed before taking on her new post was that she should be allowed to come and visit me twice a week. I'm lucky enough, Sir, to have a wife who's devoted to me. So, as I was saying, my wife came and confided to me that the Queen's at present in a great state of alarm.'

'Oh!'

'Yes. I gather His Eminence is pursuing and persecuting her more than ever. The Saraband incident still rankles in his mind. You know all about the Saraband incident, of course?'

'Who doesn't?' answered d'Artagnan.

In point of fact he had never heard of it, but wanted at all costs to conceal his ignorance.

'And now apparently he's no longer content merely to hate the Queen; he wants revenge.'

'Oh, he does, does he?'

'And the Queen thinks . . .'

'Go on, Sir, go on . . .'

'She thinks they've written to the Duke of Buckingham in her name.'

'What? They've used the Queen's name?'

'Yes. To get the Duke to come to Paris, and once they've got him there, to set some sort of trap for him.'

'Good Lord! But how exactly is your wife concerned in all this, may I ask?'

'They know how devoted she is to the Queen, and they're trying either to separate her from her mistress, to bully her into giving away the Queen's secrets, or to bribe her to act as a spy for them.'

'Yes, that's probably what they are doing,' answered d'Artagnan. 'But what about the man who kidnapped her? D'you know him?'

'I've told you already – I think I know him.'

'What's his name?'

'I don't know his name. All I do know is that he's the Cardinal's agent, his private spy.'

'But have you actually seen him?'

'Yes, my wife pointed him out to me one day.'

'Can you describe him? Is there anything special about him, something one could recognize him by?'

'Oh yes, he's quite unmistakable. He's a very distinguished-looking gentleman, dark-haired and sallow-skinned, with shrewd black eyes and a scar on his cheek.'

'A scar on his cheek!' cried d'Artagnan. 'Shrewd black eyes, dark-haired, sallow-skinned and distinguished-looking! That's my friend from Meung.'

'Your friend, you say?'

'Yes, yes. But that's neither here nor there. Oh yes, on second thoughts, it does simplify things a bit. If your man and mine are the same I shall be able to kill two birds with one stone, so to speak. Otherwise, it's not important. But how can we get hold of this fellow?'

'I haven't an idea.'

'You don't know where he lives, I suppose?'

'No. I was taking my wife back to the Louvre one day, and he came out just as she was going in. That's the only time I've set eyes on him.'

'That's awkward,' muttered d'Artagnan to himself. 'It's all so very vague. Who told you about your wife having been kidnapped?'

'Monsieur de Laporte.'

'Didn't he give you any details about it?'

'He didn't know any.'

'And you've had no information from other sources?'

'Yes. Actually I've had a . . .'

'A what?'

'Oh dear! I do hope I'm not being rash . . .'

'Now don't start that all over again. If you don't mind my saying so, I think you've gone a little too far to back out now.'

'In that case I won't back out, by God,' cried the little man, swearing to give himself courage. 'Besides, as sure as my name's Bonacieux . . .'

'Bonacieux, you say?' broke in d'Artagnan.

'Yes, Sir.'

'Sorry to interrupt, but the name sounds familiar.'

'Very likely, Sir. You see I'm your landlord.'

'Oh! So you're my landlord,' said d'Artagnan, half rising in his chair and bowing to his guest.

'Yes, Sir. And if I may point out, you've been under my roof for three months now, and you haven't yet paid me my rent. I imagined you were quite taken up with your grand duties and so didn't press you. But I hoped you in return would appreciate my restraint.'

'I do, Monsieur Bonacieux, I do,' said d'Artagnan. 'And as I said before, if I can be of use to you in any way . . .'

'You can indeed, Sir. And as I was about to remark, as sure as my name's Bonacieux, I feel I can trust you.'

'Good. Now get on and finish your story.'

The little man took a scroll of paper out of his pocket and gave it to d'Artagnan to read.

'A letter,' said the young man.

'A letter I got this morning.'

D'Artagnan opened it. The daylight was beginning to fade, so he went to the window to read it. The little man followed him. D'Artagnan read:

Don't try to find your wife! She will be returned to you when we've finished with her. If you make any attempt to find her it will be all up with you.

'Well, that's straight enough,' went on d'Artagnan. 'But it's only a threat after all.'

'Yes, but it terrifies me all the same. You see I'm no fighting man, and I'm frightened of the Bastille.'

'I'm not so keen on the Bastille myself, come to that,' said d'Artagnan. 'If it was merely a question of a fight I wouldn't object.'

'Oh, Sir! And I'd been thinking all the time this was just the job for you! I'd seen you constantly in the company of musketeers, Monsieur de Tréville's musketeers, who I knew were hostile to the Cardinal. I thought you and they'd be twice as ready to do our poor Queen a service when you realized you'd be annoying the Cardinal.'

'Possibly.'

'And I thought also that since you owed three months' rent . . .'

'Yes, yes, you've already suggested that reason, and I thought it excellent.'

'And I'd also made up my mind to charge you no more rent so long as you honoured me by remaining my tenant.'

'Marvellous!'

'Lastly I'd decided that if by chance you were in need of money, which of course wasn't likely, I'd make you a present of fifty pistoles.'

'Marvellous! So you're a man of means, Monsieur Bonacieux?'

'I'm comfortably off, Sir. That's the best way to describe it. I've managed to scrape together enough to bring me in about two or three thousand crowns a year. I made most of it in the drapery business, but a large portion was the result of a lucky gamble on the last voyage of Jean Mocquet, the celebrated navigator; with the result that ... you understand, Sir ...' The little man paused. 'Oh, but good gracious me!' he continued, giving a sudden start of surprise and staring goggle-eyed at some object in the street below.

'What's the matter?' said d'Artagnan.

'What do I see over there?'

'Where?'

'In the street, in that archway just opposite: a man in a heavy cloak.'

D'Artagnan looked to where the little man was pointing.

'It's the fellow himself!' cried he and the little man in one breath. They had both recognized the stranger at the same moment.

'Ye Gods!' cried d'Artagnan. 'This time he won't escape me.'

And, drawing his sword from his scabbard, he rushed head-long out of the room.

On the staircase he ran into Athos and Porthos, who were coming to pay him a visit. They both stood aside, and d'Artagnan rushed past them like a whirlwind.

'Hi, there, what's the hurry?' cried the two musketeers.

'The man from Meung,' shouted d'Artagnan and ran off.

D'Artagnan had often told his friends about his adventure at Meung, and about the beautiful lady in the coach with whom the stranger had parleyed outside the inn. Athos' explanation of the incident was that d'Artagnan had lost his letter in the scuffle. No gentleman answering to his description of the stranger would have been capable of such a mean act as stealing a letter. Porthos had summed up the whole thing as a love intrigue between a lady and gentleman who had arranged an assignation at the inn and whose plans had been upset by the arrival of d'Artagnan and his yellow horse. Aramis had maintained that things of that sort were mysteries which were better left unsolved.

So now Athos and Porthos realized at once what d'Artagnan was after and left him to pursue his enemy. They thought he was bound to return soon, whether he found the stranger and dealt with him on the spot or whether he lost sight of him in the crowd. So they went on up the stairs.

When they entered his room they found it empty. The landlord, fearing the consequences of the encounter between the stranger and the young man, had acted in accordance with the description he had given of himself to his tenant and taken to his heels.

CHAPTER IX

D'Artagnan takes Command

As Athos and Porthos had foreseen, d'Artagnan returned home after half an hour. He had lost his man a second time; the fellow had disappeared as though by magic. D'Artagnan had run down all the streets of the neighbourhood with drawn sword but had found nobody who in the least resembled the man he was after. He had ended by doing what he most probably should have started by doing; he had called at the door where he had first caught sight of the stranger. He had given the knocker about a dozen loud raps without result. No one had answered. The neighbours, attracted by the noise, had come out on to their doorsteps or had put their heads out of their windows, and had shouted at d'Artagnan that that particular house had been uninhabited for the last six months. The closed shutters were further evidence of this.

In the meantime Aramis had joined his two friends, and when d'Artagnan returned he found all of them assembled in his room.

'Well, and what happened?' they cried as d'Artagnan entered. 'Did you catch him? Have you killed him?'

'That fellow must be the Devil himself!' cried our hero. 'He vanished like a cloud, like a ghost.'

'D'you believe in ghosts?' asked Athos of Porthos.

'Me? I only believe what I see, and as I've never seen a ghost I don't believe in them.'

'The Bible tells us we must believe in them,' said Aramis sententiously. 'The ghost of Samuel appeared to Saul, and that's an article of faith I should consider it wrong to question, Porthos.'

'In any case,' said d'Artagnan, 'whatever this fellow is, man or demon, illusion or reality, he's my evil genius. He came on the scene just as I was on to a really good thing, gentlemen, something which promised to bring in a hundred pistoles, perhaps more. I caught sight of him and rushed out at the critical moment.'

'What's that? A hundred pistoles? Did we hear you say a hundred pistoles?' cried Porthos and Aramis simultaneously. Athos as usual said nothing and merely gave d'Artagnan a quick look.

D'Artagnan called to his servant Planchet, who was at that moment standing with his head pressed against the half-open door, trying to overhear as much as possible of the conversation.

'Go down and see my landlord, Monsieur Bonacieux,' he said, 'and tell him to send up half a dozen bottles of his best Beaugency – that's my favourite wine.'

'Good Lord! Does your landlord allow you credit?'

'Yes,' answered d'Artagnan, 'starting from today. And if the wine's bad we'll send it back and order some more.'

'You mustn't presume too much on the man's kindness,' said Aramis priggishly.

'I always said that d'Artagnan had more brains than the rest of us put together,' said Athos.

Having paid this tribute, which d'Artagnan acknowledged with a bow, he relapsed into his customary silence.

'Come on now, out with your story!' broke in Porthos impatiently.

'Yes, d'Artagnan,' said Aramis. 'Let us in to your secret. Unless of course some woman's honour's concerned, in which case you'd better keep it to yourself.'

'Don't worry,' answered d'Artagnan. 'No woman's honour's involved. I'll tell you everything.'

And he repeated word for word his conversation with his

landlord, explaining that the man who had kidnapped Monsieur Bonacieux's wife was the very man with whom he had had the quarrel at the Jolly Miller Inn. While he was talking Athos sipped the wine and expressed his approval of it with the authority of a connoisseur. He then said:

'That's not at all a bad proposition. We could probably get fifty or sixty pistoles out of this good man for retrieving his wife for him. It only remains to decide whether it's worth risking our heads for fifty or sixty pistoles.'

'Do remember,' pleaded d'Artagnan, 'that a woman's mixed up in this. This woman's been kidnapped; for all we know they may be torturing her at this very moment, merely because she's been loyal to her mistress.'

'Steady on, d'Artagnan,' said Aramis. 'Don't get worked up about this Bonacieux woman. Women were created for our downfall and are responsible for all men's miseries.'

At this remark Athos winced and seemed to be controlling himself with an effort.

'It's not Madame Bonacieux I'm concerned about,' cried d'Artagnan. 'It's the Queen. The poor Queen, deserted by the King, persecuted by the Cardinal, and having to stand by and watch her friends being attacked and disgraced one after the other.'

'But why does she persist in befriending the Spaniards and the English, whom we all hate?'

'Spain's her native land,' answered d'Artagnan. 'It's quite natural she should favour Spaniards; they're her fellow-countrymen, after all. And as for your second accusation, I think it would be fairer to say she befriends not the English as a whole, but one Englishman in particular.'

'And one must admit that Englishman's worthy of her friendship,' said Athos. 'I've never seen a handsomer fellow in my life.'

'Nor a better dressed one, for that matter,' said Porthos. 'I was on duty at the Louvre one day when he accidentally dropped some of his pearls. I picked up two and sold them for ten pistoles each. What do you think of him, Aramis? D'you know him?'

'I know him as well as you, gentlemen. I who arrested him that time in the garde member thinking then that the King w monstrously.'

'I don't know anything about that,' said d' can only say that if I knew where the Duke of B I'd take him by the hand and lead him straight to annoy the Cardinal, if for no other reason. Fo forget, gentlemen, that the Cardinal's our real enemy, our only enemy, and that it's war to the death with him. And if I could give him some really hard knocks I'd do it, even though it cost me my head.'

'Did the draper, your landlord, actually tell you, d'Artagnan, that the Queen suspected that Buckingham had been lured here on false pretences?' asked Athos.

'He said she was afraid of it.'

'Wait a moment!' broke in Aramis. 'Something's just occurred to me. What you said just now reminded me of something.'

'What?' asked Porthos.

'Let me think a moment. I'm trying to remember.'

'And now I'm sure,' continued d'Artagnan, 'that this woman's kidnapping is in some way connected with these Court intrigues, perhaps even with the Duke of Buckingham's presence in Paris.'

'Our young Gascon certainly has a nose for drama,' said Porthos, laughing good-humouredly, but not at all convinced.

'I like hearing him talk,' said Athos. 'His brogue amuses me.'

'Gentlemen,' broke in Aramis at this point. 'Listen to this.'

'Let's listen to Aramis,' said the other three in chorus.

'Yesterday I happened to be visiting a friend of mine, a distinguished theologian, who gives me private scripture lessons,' Aramis began.

Athos smiled.

'He lives in a rather isolated district, as he dislikes the noise of the town. I was just coming out of his house . . .'

_re Aramis stopped short.

'Well?' echoed the others. 'You were just coming out of his house . . .'

Aramis seemed to be trying to collect his wits like a man who thinks he has a clear road ahead of him but suddenly sees an unsuspected pitfall. His three companions were gazing at him expectantly, so he had to go on.

'This theologian friend of mine has a niece,' went on Aramis.

'Oh, he's got a niece, has he?' interrupted Porthos.

'A most respectable woman,' said Aramis.

At this remark the three others burst out laughing.

'Stop laughing or I shan't go on with my story,' said Aramis.

'Quiet, everyone!' cried Athos, holding up his hand in a gesture of mock severity.

Porthos and d'Artagnan controlled themselves.

'Very well then, I'll go on,' said Aramis. 'This niece sometimes comes to visit her uncle. She happened to call last night while I was there and when she left I naturally escorted her to her carriage.'

'So the theologian's niece has a carriage, has she?' interrupted Porthos, who could never restrain his tongue. 'How very convenient! What a nice friend to have!'

'Porthos,' said Aramis, 'I've told you a thousand times not to be so tactless! Women hate you for it.'

'Gentlemen, please!' protested d'Artagnan. He was beginning to see that Aramis' story, disjointed as it was, might provide some valuable clue. 'This is a serious matter, so let's try and stick to the point. Go on, Aramis.'

'As I was escorting this lady to her carriage, a tall, dark, distinguished-looking man, something after the style of your friend from Meung . . .'

'Possibly the same fellow,' interrupted d'Artagnan.

'Possibly. Well, anyway, this fellow advanced towards me, followed by five or six other men who kept about ten yards behind him. He stopped in front of me, bowed low and said: "My Lord Duke and you, Madame," turning to the lady . . .'

'The theologian's niece?' interrupted Porthos.

'Shut up, Porthos,' said Athos. 'You're becoming a bore.'

' "Please get into this carriage," said the man. "Come quietly, and don't try to resist." '

'He mistook you for Buckingham?' cried d'Artagnan.

'I imagine so,' said Aramis.

'And the lady?' cried Porthos.

'He mistook her for the Queen, I suppose,' said d'Artagnan.

'Exactly,' said Aramis.

'No flies on our young Gascon!' exclaimed Athos, looking at d'Artagnan with a glint of admiration in his eyes.

'It's true you're the same height and build as the Duke,' said Porthos. 'And yet I'd have thought your musketeer's uniform . . .'

'I was wearing a long cloak,' said Aramis.

'What? In July?' cried Porthos. 'Does the theologian make you visit him incognito?'

'I can see your clothes might have disguised you,' said Athos. 'But what about your face?'

'I was wearing a big hat,' said Aramis.

'Good Lord!' cried Porthos. 'Do you always put on fancy dress to go to your scripture lessons?'

'Gentlemen, gentlemen!' cried d'Artagnan, 'don't let's waste time on jokes! Let's get down to solving the mystery. The draper's wife seems to be the key to the problem, so I suggest we split up and go in search of her.'

'I can't believe a draper's wife can be all that important,' said Porthos superciliously.

'She's de Laporte's ward and he's the Queen's confidential agent. I've already told you that, gentlemen. Besides the Queen's probably done it on purpose. She probably thought it safer to confide in some insignificant person. Important people are always more suspect in affairs of this kind, and the Cardinal's spies are everywhere.'

'You may be right,' conceded Porthos. 'But I suggest that before we do anything we call on the draper himself and drive a hard bargain with him.'

'I don't think there's any need for that,' said d'Artagnan.

If he doesn't pay us I think we'll find plenty of others who will.'

At this moment there was a noise of hurried footsteps on the stairs. The door was suddenly flung open, and the draper himself came bursting into the room where the four young men were sitting in council.

'Gentlemen,' he cried, 'for pity's sake save me! Four policemen have come to arrest me.'

Porthos and Aramis sprang to their feet.

'Wait a moment,' cried d'Artagnan.

Porthos and Aramis had already half drawn their swords, but d'Artagnan signed to them to resheathe them.

'We've got to be cautious from now on,' he said. 'Don't let's do anything in a hurry.'

'Surely we're not going to allow . . .'

'Leave this to d'Artagnan,' broke in Athos. 'As I said, he's the clever one of us and I'm going to take my orders from him in future. Carry on with your plan, d'Artagnan, and count on me to back you.'

At this moment the four police appeared at the door of the sitting-room. When they saw the four armed musketeers they hesitated on the threshold.

'Come in, gentlemen!' said d'Artagnan. 'This is my room. Come in and make yourselves at home. We're all loyal servants of the King and the Cardinal.'

'In that case, gentlemen,' said the sergeant in charge, 'you won't object to our carrying out our orders at once.'

'Of course not, gentlemen. On the contrary, we're here to support law and order.'

'What the Hell does he think he's doing?' muttered Porthos under his breath.

'You're a nitwit,' whispered Athos. 'Shut up.'

'But you promised . . .' stammered the draper, aghast at d'Artagnan's attitude.

'We can only save you if we're free ourselves,' whispered d'Artagnan to him aside. 'If we tried to defend you they'd send more police and arrest us all.'

'But I thought . . .'

'Come on, gentlemen!' said d'Artagnan, raising his voice. 'We've got no interest in this man. I've never set eyes on him till today, and that was only because he came to ask me for the rent I owed him. Isn't that true, Monsieur Bonacieux?'

'Yes, quite true. But this gentleman hasn't told you . . .'

'For God's sake, be quiet!' whispered d'Artagnan to him aside. 'Don't say a word or you'll ruin us all and you won't help yourself either.'

Then, raising his voice again:

'Come on, gentlemen, take this man off,' he cried.

Upon which he took the wretched draper by the elbow and whisked him into the arms of the police, shouting at him:

'You're a rascal, old fellow. How dare you come and ask money from me, a musketeer! Away with him, gentlemen! To prison with him, and keep him under lock and key as long as you like, with my compliments. That'll teach him to have better manners in future.'

The myrmidons of the law were profuse in their thanks and led their victim away.

Just as the party was about to leave d'Artagnan tapped the sergeant on the shoulder.

'Why shouldn't we drink each other's healths, you and I?' he said, pouring out two glasses of Monsieur Bonacieux's Beaugency wine.

'I won't say no to that, Sir,' said the sergeant, highly gratified at the compliment.

'Good. Well, here's to you, Monsieur . . .'

'Boisrenard, at your service.'

'. . . Monsieur Boisrenard.'

'And here's to your very good health, Monsieur . . .'

'D'Artagnan, at your service.'

'. . . Monsieur d'Artagnan.'

The two glasses clinked.

'And now two extra toasts,' cried d'Artagnan, raising his glass theatrically. 'To the King and the Cardinal!'

The sergeant might have doubted the sincerity of this double toast if the wine had been bad, but it was good, so he was satisfied.

When the police squad finally took their leave and the musketeers were alone again Porthos turned to d'Artagnan.

'What a foul thing to do!' he cried. 'We four musketeers stand and watch an unfortunate man being arrested, without lifting a finger! And you, d'Artagnan, a gentleman, drinking with a policeman! Whoever heard of such a thing?'

'Listen, Porthos,' said Aramis. 'A moment ago Athos called you a nitwit, and I'm calling you one now. D'Artagnan, you're a genius! And when you succeed Monsieur de Tréville you won't forget me and my bishopric, will you?'

'Well, I'll be damned!' cried Porthos. 'You're not going to tell me you actually approve of d'Artagnan's behaviour just now?'

'Most certainly we do,' said Athos. 'Not only do we approve of it, we congratulate him.'

D'Artagnan did not even bother to explain or excuse his conduct to Porthos. Addressing Athos and Aramis he said:

'And now, gentlemen, it's one for all and all for one. That's our motto, and I think we should stick to it.'

'Here, steady on, gentlemen!' protested Porthos.

Athos and Aramis turned on him.

'Put out your hand and swear,' they shouted in chorus.

Porthos had no choice but to yield. He held out his hand but went on muttering angrily to himself. The four friends now repeated in unison the catch-phrase coined by d'Artagnan:

'All for one and one for all!'

'Excellent!' cried d'Artagnan.

Then he continued, taking command instinctively as though he had never done anything but give orders all his life:

'Now, gentlemen, we'd all better return to our quarters. And from now on beware! We've declared war on the great Cardinal himself!'

CHAPTER X

A Seventeenth-Century Mouse-Trap

THE mouse-trap is not a modern invention. From the moment when people were first organized in communities and these communities invented some form of police force, that police force invented mouse-traps. But as our readers may not be acquainted with police slang it would be best to explain what exactly a mouse-trap is.

When the police arrest someone who is suspected of a crime, they keep this arrest secret. They post four or five men in ambush in the hall of his house; these men open the door to all callers, close it at once behind them and arrest them. In this way they get all the regular frequenters of the house under lock and key within four or five days of the original arrest. This is what is known as a mouse-trap.

After arresting Monsieur Bonacieux the police proceeded to make his house in the Rue des Fossoyeurs into a mouse-trap. Everyone who came in was seized and cross-examined by the Cardinal's agents. We remember that as well as the main door the house had a side-door and passage which led to d'Artagnan's rooms on the first floor, so his callers came and went unmolested.

In any case, apart from our three musketeers, no one ever called on d'Artagnan. The three musketeers were now themselves on the hunt, each in different directions, but none of them had found anyone or discovered anything. Athos had actually questioned Monsieur de Tréville; the captain had been greatly surprised at this unusual display of curiosity on his part, for he knew Athos to be by nature aloof. But de Tréville could tell him nothing, apart from the fact that the last time he had seen the Cardinal, the King, and the Queen, the Cardinal had looked worried, the King had appeared ill at ease, and the Queen had had red eyes, which showed that she had either been weeping or not sleeping. But de Tréville had not been greatly impressed by the Queen's appearance, for since her marriage she had had many sleepless nights and had wept many bitter tears.

Monsieur de Tréville took advantage of Athos' visit to urge him to be zealous in serving the King and the Queen and to exert a stabilizing influence on his three friends.

While Athos, Porthos, and Aramis had been out on the prowl, d'Artagnan had ensconced himself in his room, which he had converted into an observation post. From his windows he could see all the callers at the front door and knew in this way who had fallen into the trap. Besides this he had dislodged one or two of the flagstones of the floor of his room and had scraped away the woodwork underneath until there was only one thin strip of board between him and the room below, where the police inquiries were taking place. By putting his ear to this hole in the floor he could hear everything that was said by the police agents and the prisoners.

The cross-examinations always began with a demand for particulars of the lives and occupations of the accused and ended with the following three questions:

'Has Madame Bonacieux ever given you anything to hand to her husband or to anybody else?'

'Has Monsieur Bonacieux ever given you anything to hand to his wife or to anybody else?'

'Has either of them ever let you into any secret?'

D'Artagnan argued that the police would not cross-examine the prisoners in that way if they knew anything. But what were they trying to find out? Probably whether the Duke of Buckingham was actually in Paris and whether he had had or was about to have a secret meeting with the Queen.

D'Artagnan stopped short at that idea. He thought it was a good enough hypothesis to go on with for the time being. Meanwhile the police agents remained in permanent session on the ground floor of the house and the young eavesdropper remained in permanent session on the floor above.

It was now the evening of the day following the unfortunate

Monsieur Bonacieux's arrest. Nine o'clock had just struck. Athos had that moment left d'Artagnan to answer the roll-call at Monsieur de Tréville's house, and Planchet was about to prepare his master's bed for the night. Suddenly there was a knock on the street door. It was quickly opened from inside and closed again. Some fresh mouse had just fallen into the trap.

D'Artagnan lay down flat on his stomach, put his ear to the hole in the floor and listened.

Soon he heard screams coming from below; then half-stifled moans. This time there was no cross-questioning.

'Ye Gods!' muttered d'Artagnan. 'I don't mind betting it's a woman they've got hold of. They're trying to search her and she's resisting. They're using violence, the brutes!'

And it was all our hero could do not to cast caution to the winds and start thumping on the floor in protest.

'But I tell you I'm the mistress of this house!' cried the unfortunate woman. 'I tell you I'm Madame Bonacieux. I work for the Queen.'

'Madame Bonacieux!' muttered d'Artagnan. 'By Jove, I'm in luck! I've found what the whole town's looking for.'

'You're the very woman we've been wanting,' said the officers of the law.

The woman's voice sounded more and more strained. Then there was a great crash which made the walls of the house shake. Madame Bonacieux was struggling as hard as any woman can struggle against four men.

'Please, gentlemen, please!' she cried. Then followed a few inarticulate sounds and then silence.

'They're gagging her! They're going to take her off with them!' cried d'Artagnan, springing up from the floor like a Jack-in-the-Box. 'My sword! Good! It's here! Planchet!'

'Sir?'

'Run and fetch Athos, Porthos, and Aramis. One of them's bound to be at home — perhaps all of them. Tell them to come along at once, armed. Oh, I remember now. Athos is with Monsieur de Tréville.'

'But where are you going, Sir?'

'I'm going to jump down from the window,' cried d'Artagnan. 'It's quicker that way. You put back the flagstones, sweep the floor, go out by the side door and do as I told you.'

'Oh, Sir! You'll kill yourself!' cried Planchet.

'Nonsense,' said d'Artagnan.

Then, hanging on by his hands to the window-sill, he proceeded to let himself down from the first floor on to the street without even grazing his fingers.

Then he went and knocked on the front door of the house, muttering:

'I'll let myself be caught in the police trap like the others. But if they try and get their claws into this mouse ... well, they'll get something they didn't bargain for.'

At the sound of the knocking the noise inside the house died down. D'Artagnan heard footsteps approach. The door was flung open and our hero rushed into Monsieur Bonacieux's room with drawn sword. The door of the room swung to sharply behind him; a spring had obviously been attached to it.

Now all the other occupants of Monsieur Bonacieux's house and the next-door neighbours heard loud cries, tramplings of feet, the clash of swords and the sound of furniture being smashed. Some of the neighbours, alarmed by the noise, had put their heads out of their windows to find out what was going on. They now saw the door re-open and four men dressed in black appear in the street, not walking in a dignified manner but rather flapping their way out like startled crows with torn and ruffled plumage, having left whole handfuls of their feathers, in other words bits of torn coats and edgings of cloaks, on the floors and tables inside the house.

D'Artagnan had not had a very hard fight, we must confess, for only one of the police-officers was armed and he had only put up a show of fighting. The three others had tried to fell the young man with chairs, stools, and china-ware, but the Gascon had given them a scratch or two with his sword which had effectively subdued them. After ten minutes' combat the whole bunch had scuttled off, and d'Artagnan had remained victorious on the battlefield.

The neighbours had opened their windows and watched the affray with the indifference common to Parisians of that date, who were accustomed to constant street brawls and riots. When they saw the four men in black leave the house they closed their windows again; their instincts told them that the trouble was over for the time being.

Moreover night was falling and in those days the inhabitants of the Luxembourg quarter kept early hours.

D'Artagnan was now alone in the room with Madame Bonacieux and turned to look at her. The wretched woman had collapsed into an armchair and was almost unconscious. D'Artagnan ran his eye over her quickly. She was a charming young woman of about twenty-five, dark-haired, blue-eyed, with a slightly tip-tilted nose, dazzling white teeth and a clear, fair complexion. In those respects she was every bit the equal of any lady of rank, but there the resemblance ended. Her hands were white but coarse, and her feet also betrayed her humbler position in life. Fortunately d'Artagnan was not yet concerned with these minor details of his protégée's appearance.

He was kneeling down beside the lady and trying to revive her when he suddenly noticed on the floor at her feet a handkerchief made of the finest cambric. His inquisitive nature prompted him to pick it up and examine it. In one of the corners he saw a monogram; it was the same monogram that he had seen on Aramis' handkerchief, and he remembered how his interference on that occasion had nearly involved him in a duel to the death.

Ever since then he had had a wholesome respect for handkerchiefs with monograms on them. So he gently slipped this handkerchief back into the pocket of Madame Bonacieux's dress.

At that moment Madame Bonacieux regained consciousness. She opened her eyes, gave a terrified glance round the room and saw to her relief that she was alone with her rescuer. She at once smiled and held out her hands to him. Madame Bonacieux had the most engaging smile in the world.

'Oh, Sir,' she said, 'is it you who saved my life? Thank you, thank you for what you've done.'

'I only did what any other man would have done in my place, so you don't owe me any thanks at all.'

'I do, indeed, Sir, and I hope to be able to prove to you that I'm not ungrateful. But what on earth were those men after? I thought at first they were housebreakers. And why isn't my husband here?'

'Those men weren't housebreakers, Madame Bonacieux,' answered d'Artagnan gravely, 'but they were equally dangerous in quite another way. They were the Cardinal's agents and I can easily explain why your husband isn't here. The police came yesterday to arrest him and took him off to the Bastille.'

'My husband in the Bastille?' cried Madame Bonacieux. 'Oh, how terrible! What could they want with him? What crime has he committed? He's as innocent as the day!'

And the faintest flicker of a smile passed across her face as she spoke. But then she began to look frightened again.

'Your husband has committed no crime, Madame Bonacieux,' answered d'Artagnan, 'apart from being your husband, which I should have said was a privilege but which apparently has its disadvantages.'

'But, Sir, do you mean to say you know . . .?'

'I know you've been kidnapped, Madame Bonacieux.'

'Oh, you know that, do you? And d'you know who kidnapped me? If so for Heaven's sake tell me.'

'A man of about forty-five, with black hair, a sallow skin, and a scar on his left cheek.'

'That's right. But who is he?'

'Ah, that I don't know.'

'And did my husband know I'd been kidnapped?'

'Yes. The man himself wrote him a letter telling him about it.'

'And has my husband any theory as to why I was kidnapped?' asked Madame Bonacieux, blushing slightly.

'I think he suspected some political motive.'

'I suspected that myself from the first, and now I know it. So it never occurred to my dear, worthy husband that there might be some other reason for my disappearance . . .'

'Far from it, Madame Bonacieux. He was too confident in your good sense and in your attachment to him to suppose that for a moment.'

Another faint flicker of a smile passed across Madame Bonacieux's face.

'But how did you manage to escape?' went on d'Artagnan.

'They left me alone for a while. I'd already discovered the reason for my kidnapping, so I made a rope by knotting my bedsheets together and let myself down from my prison window. Then I came running here, hoping to find my husband.'

'To get him to protect you?'

'Oh, no! The poor fellow's quite incapable of that. But he could have been of use to us in another way, so I wanted to let him know.'

'Let him know what?'

'Ah, that I can't tell you. It's not my secret.'

'No,' said d'Artagnan. 'Besides, though this may sound rather a cowardly thing for a soldier to say, we've got to be careful. This room's not a healthy place to sit and exchange confidences in. The four men I drove out just now are bound to return with reinforcements. If they find us here we're lost. I did send my servant to bring three of my friends along, but he may not have found them.'

'You're quite right,' said Madame Bonacieux, frightened once more. 'We mustn't stay here. We must get away at once.'

As she spoke she slipped her arm under d'Artagnan's arm and tried to drag him out of the room.

'But where can we go?' asked d'Artagnan. 'What safe place is there?'

'Let's first get well away from here and then we can think it over.'

And without even troubling to shut the front door the young couple ran quickly out of the house, down the Rue des Fossoyeurs, from there into the Rue des Fosses-Monsieur-le-Prince and on as far as the Place Saint Sulpice.

'And now what are we going to do?' asked d'Artagnan. 'Where do you want me to take you?'

'I don't honestly know where to go. What I'd meant to do was to get my husband to find out from Monsieur de Laporte what had been happening at the Louvre in my absence and whether it was safe for me to go back there.'

'Why shouldn't I go and see Monsieur de Laporte?'

'Because they know Monsieur Bonacieux at the Louvre and would have let him in. But they don't know you, and they'd only shut the gate in your face. It's unfortunate, but there it is.'

'Oh, come now! There must be some porter at one of the gates of the Louvre who's devoted to you and who'd open it to me if you gave me some password . . .'

Madame Bonacieux looked searchingly at the young man.

'And suppose I did give you the password, would you forget it again the moment you'd used it?'

'On my word of honour!' said d'Artagnan, with an unmistakable note of sincerity in his voice.

'Very well, I believe you. You look to me like a man one can trust. Besides, if you help us you'll more than likely be rewarded.'

'I'll always serve the King and help the Queen, not for any reward but because it's my duty,' said d'Artagnan. 'So use me as you would a friend.'

'And where will you hide me in the meanwhile?'

'Is there no house you can go to until Monsieur de Laporte sends for you?'

'No. There's no one I can trust.'

'We're only about a hundred yards from Athos' lodgings. You might go and wait there.'

'Who's Athos?'

'One of my friends.'

'But suppose he's at home and sees me?'

'He's not there. Come along. I'll hide you in his room and take away the key with me.'

'But suppose he comes back?'

'He won't come back. And if he does I'll tell them to tell him there's a woman in his room. That'll keep him away all right.'

'But I shall be terribly compromised. Don't you realize that?'

'Why should you mind? Nobody knows you here. Besides, in a situation like this we can't afford to be too fussy about proprieties.'

'Very well. Let's go to your friend's lodgings. Where are they?'

'In the Rue Férou, about a hundred yards away.'

'Come on then.'

And the two of them set off again. Athos was out, as d'Artagnan had said. The landlady handed over the key of his room without question, as d'Artagnan was such a regular visitor to the house. The two callers went upstairs and d'Artagnan showed Madame Bonacieux into Athos' room.

'Make yourself at home in here,' he said. 'Lock the door from the inside and don't open it unless you hear three knocks like this . . .' And he knocked three times; two loud knocks in quick succession, then a pause and a third gentle knock.

'Good. I'll remember that,' said Madame Bonacieux. 'And now it's my turn to give you instructions.'

'Carry on,' said d'Artagnan.

'Go to the Rue de l'Échelle entrance to the Louvre and ask for Germain.'

'Right. And then?'

'He'll ask you what you want and you must answer these three words: "Tours and Brussels". Then he'll do anything for you.'

'What shall I ask him to do?'

'Tell him to fetch Monsieur de Laporte, the Queen's Gentleman-in-Waiting, and when Monsieur de Laporte comes send him to me.'

'Very well. But when and how shall I see you again?'

'Do you want very much to see me again?'

'Yes.'

'Well, leave that part to me, and don't worry.'

'May I count on your promise?'

'Yes.'

D'Artagnan bowed to Madame Bonacieux, giving her such a look of love that the heart of any woman less preoccupied with her own affairs than the little draper's wife would have melted at once. When he was on his way downstairs he heard the door being shut behind him and the key being turned twice in the lock. He reached the Louvre in no time, and just as he arrived at the Échelle gate the clock struck ten. So all the exciting events that we have just described had happened within the space of an hour.

Everything went off as Madame Bonacieux had prophesied. When d'Artagnan gave the password Germain bowed and asked his instructions. Ten minutes later Monsieur de Laporte was in the porter's lodge. D'Artagnan told him the whole story in a few words and gave him the address of the house where Madame Bonacieux was hidden. Laporte asked him to repeat it twice for safety's sake, and then started off towards the house at a great rate. But he had only gone about ten yards when he turned back.

'Let me give you a word of advice, young man,' he said.

'What's that?' asked d'Artagnan.

'You may quite possibly find yourself in trouble after this. D'you happen to know anyone who has a clock which keeps bad time?'

'I might think of someone.'

'Go and see him and make him swear you were with him at half-past nine this evening. That's what's known in law as an alibi.'

D'Artagnan realized that this was a very sensible piece of advice, and ran off to Monsieur de Tréville's house as fast as his legs would carry him. Instead of joining the general company in the drawing-room he asked to be admitted into de Tréville's private study. D'Artagnan was such a regular visitor to the house that his request was granted, and the servant went off to tell Monsieur de Tréville that his young friend had asked for a special audience, as he had important news for him. Five minutes later Monsieur de Tréville came in. He asked d'Artagnan what he wanted and what could have brought him there at such a late hour.

In the interval between being shown into the study and de Tréville's entrance d'Artagnan had walked over to the clock on the mantelpiece and turned the hands back three-quarters of an hour. He now said:

'I thought as it was only nine twenty-five it wasn't too late to call on you, Sir.'

'Nine twenty-five?' cried de Tréville, looking at the clock. 'That's impossible!'

'Look at the clock, Sir! That proves it, surely,' said d'Artagnan.

'Yes, you're right. I somehow imagined it was later. But come on, tell me what I can do for you.'

D'Artagnan now invented a long story about the Queen. He said how concerned he was about Her Majesty's safety, and told de Tréville what he knew about the Cardinal's intentions in regard to Buckingham. In fact he repeated exactly what he had heard from Monsieur Bonacieux, as though it were general gossip among the musketeers, but said nothing about Bonacieux's visit, his affray with the police or his meeting with Madame Bonacieux. He spoke with such assurance that de Tréville was completely deceived about the motive for his visit and never suspected that the young man was personally involved in this intrigue. He was doubly unsuspecting because, as we remember, he himself had observed that there was trouble brewing between the King, the Queen, and the Cardinal.

When d'Artagnan heard the clock in Monsieur de Tréville's room strike ten he took his leave. De Tréville thanked him for the information he had brought, exhorted his young friend always to be loyal and zealous in the service of the King and of the Queen, and then returned to his drawing-room. D'Artagnan walked down the stairs, but when he reached the bottom step he suddenly remembered that he had forgotten his cane. So he ran quickly upstairs again, went into de Tréville's study, changed the clock back with a flick of the finger so that no one should notice next day that it had been tampered with, and then ran down and out into the street, confident that he now had an influential witness to confirm his alibi.

CHAPTER XI

The Plot Thickens

AFTER he had paid his visit to Monsieur de Tréville d'Artagnan took a very circuitous route home and appeared to be lost in thought. Our hero, usually so alert and observant, this time actually lost his way and wandered along unfamiliar streets, seeming not to care very much where he was, looking up at the stars and alternately sighing and smiling to himself. What was the cause of this sudden transformation in the young man's character, and what was he thinking of so deeply?

He was thinking of Madame Bonacieux. For a musketeer apprentice the young woman was almost an ideal object of affection. She was pretty, mysterious, and initiated into many Court secrets, which made her additionally glamorous in the eyes of a socially ambitious young man from the provinces. She appeared to be not unresponsive to admiration, and this is always encouraging to a novice in the art of love. Moreover d'Artagnan had rescued her from the clutches of those fiends who had wanted to search and use violence on her, and this had established a bond between them, a bond made doubly strong by the fact that the incident which had been the cause of it could not be confided to anyone. Thus the stage was admirably set for a romantic attachment, and it was almost inevitable that the regard which d'Artagnan and Madame Bonacieux at present felt for each other should soon ripen into some more tender sentiment.

D'Artagnan's flights of fancy knew no bounds and he was already dreaming of billets-doux and other suchlike tokens of affection which his mistress might send him. We have already mentioned the fact that in those days young cavaliers could take large sums from their sovereigns without feeling humiliated. We must now confess that they were equally brazen in regard to their mistresses, and that these ladies actually vied with each other in giving their admirers priceless tokens of their love; it was as though they wished to atone for the meagreness of their sentiments by the solidity of their gifts.

In those days young men used women quite ruthlessly as stepping-stones for their own advancement. Women who had only beauty to offer offered their beauty, and this is probably the origin of the saying that the loveliest woman in the world can only give what she's got. Those who were rich gave some of their fortune as well, and one could quote a number of instances of warriors of that stormy and romantic age who would never have won their spurs at the outset of their careers nor later their victories in the field without the well-filled purses which their mistresses tied to their horses' saddlebows.

D'Artagnan had no fortune at all. But when, through constant association with his three friends, his provincial shyness had worn off, he soon learned to behave like all other young men of the time, who acted in Paris as they acted on the battlefields of Flanders. In Flanders the enemy were the Spaniards — in Paris the women. Both had to be pursued, conquered, and despoiled.

But for the moment d'Artagnan was moved by a more noble and disinterested emotion than desire for gain. The draper had told him that he was rich, and it did not need much intelligence to guess that in a ménage with a fool like Monsieur Bonacieux as the husband the wife held the purse strings. But although d'Artagnan realized this, considerations of self-interest had little or no place in his feelings for Madame Bonacieux, and the love which now filled his heart was only very slightly tainted by the hope of gain, although, ironically enough, he had been in quest of this when he had first met the lady. We say 'only very slightly tainted' because the fact that a pretty, charming, and intelligent young woman should also be rich certainly does not detract from her appeal. Besides, as we know, d'Artagnan himself was penniless. True, he hoped to become a millionaire some day, but the date he himself had fixed for this happy change in his fortunes was rather far distant. And in the meanwhile it would have been misery for him, as indeed for any lover, to see the lady of his choice pining in vain for those little luxuries upon which all women depend for their happiness. When a woman is rich and her lover poor she can at least buy for herself what he cannot provide her with, and even though it is usually the husband who pays for these pleasures it is very rarely he who gets the thanks.

And we must remember that, though the romantic side of d'Artagnan's nature was now stirred, he still remained loyal to his friends. Obsessed as he was with the vision of the draper's wife, he did not forget Athos, Porthos, and Aramis. The lovely Madame Bonacieux would be a very suitable person to wander with through the St Denis meadows or in the St Germain fairgound, and d'Artagnan pictured himself showing off his conquest proudly to his three friends. After a long walk one is usually hungry, a fact of which d'Artagnan was at that particular moment acutely aware. In the evenings they would have little dinner parties together, in which it is so pleasant to sit with friends on one side and a charming mistress on the other. Finally d'Artagnan pictured himself as the saviour of the other three in times of need, and here the friendship of Madame Bonacieux would come in very useful.

And what about Monsieur Bonacieux, who d'Artagnan had so unceremoniously pushed into the arms of the police agents, denouncing him out loud and secretly promising to save him? We must confess that the young man never gave him a thought, except perhaps to say to himself that he was better where he was, wherever that might be. Love is the most selfish of the passions.

But though d'Artagnan may have forgotten his landlord or have pretended to forget him on the plea that he did not know where they had taken him, we have not forgotten him and we know where he is. But for the moment we'll behave like the love-sick Gascon, leave the worthy draper to his own devices and return to him later.

We left d'Artagnan star-gazing, brooding on his love-to-be and talking to the night. Absorbed in thought, he was walking up the Rue du Cherche-Midi or Chasse-Midi, as it was called in those days. This happened to be the district where Aramis lived and it occurred to him that he ought to visit his friend and explain why he had sent Planchet to him with that peremptory summons. If Aramis had been at home when Planchet called he had obviously gone off to the police-trap in the Rue des Fosso-yeurs, and having found no one there except perhaps his two companions, must have been puzzled — indeed, they must all have been puzzled — about the reason for the summons. D'Artagnan felt that he owed them an explanation for having disturbed them, and this he kept repeating to himself as he walked along the street.

But in his heart of hearts he knew that what he really wanted was an excuse to talk about the pretty Madame Bona-cieux, who at present occupied his thoughts, if not his heart, to the exclusion of all else. One must not expect discretion from a man in the throes of his first love. When a man falls in love for the first time his feelings are so tumultuous that they must be allowed to overflow or they would be too much for him.

Paris had been in darkness for the last two hours and the streets were almost deserted. The clocks of the Faubourg St Germain were striking eleven; it was a warm evening. D'Artagnan was walking along an alley which ran where the Rue d'Assas runs today, breathing in sweet scents carried by the wind from the Rue de Vaugirard and from the gardens freshened by the evening dew. From a distance came the muffled sounds of revellers drinking behind closed shutters in various taverns in the district. When d'Artagnan reached the end of the alley he turned left. Aramis' house lay between the Rue Cassette and the Rue Servandoni.

D'Artagnan had just passed the Rue Cassette and could already see his friend's house ahead of him, surrounded by sycamore trees and covered almost entirely by clematis, when he noticed a ghost-like figure coming out of the Rue Servandoni. This ghost-like figure was wrapped in a cloak, and d'Artagnan at first thought it was a man. But after a while he realized from its size and from its timid and hesitant walk that it must be a woman. Moreover the woman was apparently uncertain of her way; she kept looking up to take her bearings, stopping, turning back and walking on again. D'Artagnan's interest was aroused.

'Shall I go up and offer to help her?' thought he. 'She's young; one can tell that by her walk; she may be pretty, too. How exciting! But on second thoughts no woman's likely to be out in the street at this time of night unless she's going to meet her lover, in which case it would be more tactful to leave her alone. Damnation!'

Meanwhile the young woman was coming nearer and nearer, counting the houses and windows as she walked. D'Artagnan thought she must soon find the house she wanted; there were only three houses in that part of the street and two windows overlooking the street itself; one belonged to a detached villa opposite the house occupied by Aramis, the other was Aramis' own window.

'Ye Gods!' thought the young man, remembering Aramis and the theologian's niece. 'Might this lovely daughter of the night be calling on our friend? It looks astonishingly like it. This time, Aramis old boy, I really am going to discover something about you.'

Thus soliloquizing, he went and hid in the darkest part of the street, near a stone bench in a recess in the wall of the house opposite.

The woman came closer and closer. There was now no doubt that she was young; her light step betrayed her and at that moment she coughed, a clear, fresh cough. D'Artagnan thought this cough was probably a signal.

Either this signal had been answered, or the young night wanderer had suddenly identified the house, for she now stepped boldly up to Aramis' window and rapped three times on the shutter.

'That's Aramis' window all right!' muttered d'Artagnan to himself. 'Ha, ha, you old hypocrite! So much for your theology, my boy!'

The knocks on the shutter were immediately answered. The casement window was opened from inside and a light shone through the cracks in the shutter.

'Oh!' thought the eavesdropper. 'So the lady was expected! Now the shutter will be opened and she'll climb in through the window. Very neat.'

But to d'Artagnan's amazement the shutter remained closed. Moreover the light which had flickered for a moment inside the house disappeared and everything was now in darkness again.

D'Artagnan felt certain that something more was bound to happen, so he remained where he was, straining his eyes and ears in order to miss nothing.

He was right; a few seconds later someone inside the house gave two sharp knocks.

The young woman in the street knocked once in reply and the shutter was half opened from inside.

Needless to say d'Artagnan stood watching and listening with the greatest interest.

Unfortunately the light had been removed to another room. But d'Artagnan's eyes had meanwhile grown accustomed to the darkness. And it is well known that Gascons have eyes like cats, and can see in the night.

The young man now observed the lady pull something white out of her pocket and quickly unfold it – a handkerchief. She then held up one corner of it to the person inside the house.

D'Artagnan was at once reminded of the handkerchief which he had found at Madame Bonacieux's feet, which in its turn had reminded him of the one he had found at Aramis' feet.

What could be the meaning of this handkerchief?

In his present position d'Artagnan could not see Aramis' face. (He was, of course, convinced that it could be no one but Aramis who was having this tryst with the lady.) Curiosity now prevailed over caution and, seeing that the attention of the two conspirators was closely fixed on the handkerchief, the young man darted like lightning out of his hiding-place and squeezed up against the wall at a spot from which he could see clearly inside the room.

What he saw surprised him so much that he almost cried out. It was not Aramis inside the room after all; it was a woman. Unfortunately he could not see her face but only her clothes.

At that moment the woman inside the house pulled a second handkerchief out of her pocket and the two women exchanged handkerchiefs. Then another short conversation ensued, after which the shutter was closed again. The woman outside the window turned and walked down the street, passing within a few feet of d'Artagnan. She drew the hood of her cloak over her head, but not in time to prevent d'Artagnan catching a glimpse of her face. He saw to his amazement that it was Madame Bonacieux.

The idea that it might be Madame Bonacieux had already flashed across the young man's mind when he saw her producing the handkerchief from her pocket. But he had dismissed it as absurd. Was it likely that after summoning Monsieur de Laporte to escort her safely back to the Louvre Madame Bonacieux would then go out and tramp the streets alone at night, and run the risk of being k' napped a second time?

Now he had seen her with his own eyes. He guessed at once that only something very important could have tempted her out. And what, he argued, is the most important thing to a woman of twenty-five? Love, of course.

But was it for her own sake or for someone else's sake that she was thus endangering her life? The young man pondered this question deeply. The demon of jealousy gnawed at his heart as though he were already Madame Bonacieux's accepted lover.

He realized that it would be quite easy to find out where she was going simply by following her. And this he proceeded to do as though by instinct.

But when Madame Bonacieux saw the young man emerging from the wall like a statue stepping off its pedestal and when she heard the noise of his footsteps behind her she cried out and started running down the street like a hunted hare.

D'Artagnan set off in pursuit of her. It did not take him long to overtake her, handicapped as she was by her long cloak. She had darted down an alley, and he caught up with her after about a hundred yards. The unfortunate creature was exhausted, not by her exertions but by sheer terror, and when d'Artagnan laid his hand on her shoulder she fell on one knee and cried out in a strangled voice:

'Kill me if you must. I'll tell you nothing.'

D'Artagnan put his arm round her waist and lifted her up. Then he realized from the dead weight of her body that she was on the point of fainting, so to reassure her he told her of his love for her. But this did not reassure her at all; men who swear undying love sometimes have the worst intentions in the world. In this case, however, the voice was everything. Madame Bonacieux recognized it at once; she opened her eyes, saw d'Artagnan and gave a cry of relief.

'Oh, it's you!' she said. 'God be praised!'

'Yes,' said d'Artagnan. 'And God has sent me to protect you.'

'Was that why you were following me, in order to protect me?' cried Madame Bonacieux, smiling mischievously. Now that she knew that her pursuer was a friend her fears vanished and the flirtatious side of her nature reasserted itself.

'No,' said d'Artagnan, 'I admit that was not the reason. My meeting you tonight was a mere chance. I saw a woman knocking on my friend's window.'

'Your friend's window?' interrupted Madame Bonacieux.

'Yes. Aramis is one of my best friends.'

'Aramis? Who's Aramis?'

'Oh, come now! You're not going to tell me you don't know Aramis.'

'Know him? I've never even heard of him!'

'You mean this is the first time you've ever been to that house?'

'Certainly.'

'And you didn't know there was a young man living there?'

'No.'

'A musketeer?'

'Certainly not.'

'So it wasn't him you were looking for?'

'Of course not. You saw yourself who I was talking to; a woman.'

'I know. But the woman was a friend of Aramis.'

'I know nothing about that.'

'But they live in the same house. They must be friends.'

'Possibly. But that's no concern of mine.'

'Who was the woman?'

'I can't tell you that; I should be giving someone else away.'

'Dearest Madame Bonacieux, you're a most charming person, but if I may say so, you're extremely mysterious too.'

'Does that make me less attractive?'

'No, more. You're altogether adorable.'

'Give me your arm, then.'

'With pleasure, dear Madame Bonacieux. And now what?'

'Now you can take me where I want to go.'

'Where's that?'

'You'll see when we get there.'

'Shall I have to wait for you there?'

'No.'

'Are you going home alone, then?'

'Perhaps. Perhaps not.'

'I see. You may have someone with you. Will it be a man or a woman?'

'I don't know yet.'

'I'll find out, all right.'

'How?'

'I'll wait and watch you come out.'

'Oh, in that case good-bye!'

'What d'you mean?'

'I don't need you. I can manage quite well alone.'

'But you wanted . . .'

'I wanted to be helped by a gentleman, not dogged by a spy.'

'That's putting it a bit strongly.'

'Well, how would you describe people who follow others unasked?'

'I'd say they were a bit inquisitive, perhaps.'

'That's putting it much too mildly.'

'Very well, Madame Bonacieux. I see I shall have to obey you in everything.'

'Why did you deny yourself that privilege in the first place?'

'In order to acquire the added merit of the sinner who repenteth.'

'Have you repented?'

'I don't honestly know myself. But I do know, that if you'll allow me to escort you where you're going I'll do everything you ask.'

'You'll leave me afterwards?'

'Yes.'

'You won't stay and watch me come out?'

'No.'

'On your word of honour?'

'On my word of honour.'

'In that case take my arm and let's be off.'

D'Artagnan offered his arm to Madame Bonacieux. Half-laughing, half-trembling she put her arm through his and together they walked to the far end of the Rue de la Harpe. Here she seemed to hesitate, as she had done in the Rue du Vaugirard. She examined several doors and at last seemed to recognize one from certain marks on it. Turning to d'Artagnan she said:

'And now, Sir, I've got some private business in this house. Many, many thanks for coming with me and protecting me. Now please remember your promise and go.'

'You won't be frightened coming back by yourself?'

'Apart from thieves, there's nothing to be frightened of.'

'Well, are they nothing?'

'They can't take anything from me. I've got nothing worth taking.'

'What about that embroidered handkerchief with the monogram on it?'

'What handkerchief?'

'The one I found at your feet after you'd fainted and put back in the pocket of your dress.'

'Be quiet, be quiet, will you!' cried the young woman in terror. 'You'll ruin us all, you miserable man!'

'Ah, I thought so! You're not nearly so safe as you pretend to be. You get frightened at the mere mention of a handkerchief! And you admit that if anyone heard us talking about it, we'd be lost. Dearest Madame Bonacieux,' cried d'Artagnan, seizing her hand impulsively, and giving her an adoring look, 'be more generous. Take me into your confidence. Look at me! Can't you see how I love you, how I long to share the secrets of your heart?'

'Yes,' said Madame Bonacieux, 'and I reply that I'd gladly share my secrets with you, but other people's secrets, no.'

'Never mind,' said d'Artagnan, 'I'll find them out for myself. Since they're so important to you I must know them.'

'You'll do nothing of the kind,' said the young woman in so emphatic a tone that even d'Artagnan was quelled. 'Don't get mixed up in my affairs. Don't try and help me in any way. I ask you this for the sake of our friendship, remembering all you've done for me, for which I shall always be grateful. Try and believe what I'm telling you. Don't bother about me from now on. Try and forget I ever existed.'

D'Artagnan was nettled by this.

'Has Aramis got to try and forget you too?' he asked angrily.

'That's the third time you've said that name,' said Madame Bonacieux, 'and I keep telling you I've never heard of the man.'

'What? You knock three times on a man's window at dead of night and then you say you've never heard of him! Madame Bonacieux, I'm not a complete fool!'

'I see your little game. You've invented this man in order to trick me into telling my secret. That's it, isn't it?'

'I've invented nothing, Madame Bonacieux,' answered d'Artagnan. 'I'm telling the plain truth.'

'You say a friend of yours lives in that house?'

'I do say so. In fact I'm repeating it for the third time. A friend of mine lives in that house, and his name's Aramis.'

'Well, I expect all that'll be cleared up later. In the meantime keep quiet about everything that's happened tonight.'

'If I could open my heart to you like a book you'd read so much curiosity in it you'd take pity on me, and such devotion that you'd satisfy that curiosity at once. You needn't mistrust someone who loves you as I do.'

'You're very quick to talk of love, Sir!' said Madame Bonacieux reproachfully. 'We hardly know each other.'

'Well, I'm only nineteen, and I've never been in love before.'

The young woman gave him a quick glance.

'I think I've already got a clue to your secret,' went on d'Artagnan. 'Only three months ago I nearly fought a duel with Aramis over a handkerchief very like the one you showed the woman in that house. I don't mind betting it had the same initials on it.'

'Please don't try and probe into things,' said the young woman. 'You only upset me.'

'But do listen, Madame Bonacieux. You're very clever and you must realize that if you were arrested with that handkerchief on you you'd be badly compromised.'

'Not at all. It's got my initials on it. C. B. Constance Bonacieux.'

'Or Camille de Bois-Tracy.'

'Be quiet, will you, you terrible man!' cried the young woman, again terrified. 'But I see my safety doesn't mean much to you, or you'd be more careful. So I can only advise you to be careful for your own sake.'

'For my sake?'

'Yes. You could be sent to prison, beheaded even, merely for having known me.'

'In that case I'll never leave you from now on.'

'Sir, I implore you to go,' said the young woman, clasping her hands and looking at d'Artagnan in an agony of entreaty. 'In the name of Heaven, go! I appeal to your honour as a soldier and a gentleman! Listen, there's twelve o'clock striking. That's the hour they're expecting me.'

'Very well, Madame Bonacieux,' said the young man, bowing gravely. 'If you ask me like that I can't refuse. I'll go at once.'

'And you won't follow me? You won't spy on me? Promise?'

'I'll go straight home.'

'Oh, I knew it! You're a good, kind young man,' cried Madame Bonacieux, holding out her hand. D'Artagnan seized it and covered it with kisses.

'Oh, I wish I'd never met you!' he cried with that naïve brusquerie which women often prefer to the affectations of good manners, because it is spontaneous and revealing.

'Well,' answered Madame Bonacieux with a new note of gentleness in her voice, 'I won't go quite as far as to say that of you. What's lost today's not lost for ever. One day, when I'm released from my ties, I may satisfy your curiosity.'

'And my love too?' cried d'Artagnan in the seventh heaven of joy.

'Oh, I won't promise that, Sir. How can I know what my feelings for you will be then?'

'What are your feelings for me now?'

'At the present I feel grateful to you, nothing more.'

'Oh, Madame Bonacieux,' said d'Artagnan. 'You're very charming but very cruel.'

'No, I'm merely presuming a little on your kindness. But don't worry. We'll meet again one day.'

'You make me very happy when you say that. Don't forget this evening. Don't forget your promise.'

'I won't. When the time comes I'll remember everything. Now go, go, for Heaven's sake! They were expecting me sharp at midnight. I'm late already.'

'Only five minutes.'

'Yes, but to some people five minutes are five centuries.'

'To people in love, yes.'

'How do you know the man who's expecting me's not in love?'

'So it's a man who's expecting you!' cried d'Artagnan.

'There you go again! Argue, argue, argue,' cried Madame Bonacieux.

She was still smiling but losing patience at the same time.

'Don't worry! I'm off,' said d'Artagnan. 'I trust you. I want to get full credit for my devotion, even though it may be foolish. Good-bye Madame Bonacieux, good-bye.'

And the young man gave his adored one a final look of love and then turned and walked off down the street. He had only gone a few steps when he heard her give three gentle knocks on the door of the house. On reaching the corner of the street he turned and looked back; the door had already opened and closed again and Madame Bonacieux had disappeared.

D'Artagnan walked straight on. He had given his word that he would not spy on Madame Bonacieux, and he meant to keep to it, even though she might be in the most deadly peril. He was sad to think that she did not need his help, but this was a grief he would have to bear. Five minutes later he was in the Rue des Fossoyeurs.

'Poor Athos,' he muttered to himself. 'He'll either have gone to sleep waiting for me or he'll have returned home, in which case he'll discover there's been a woman in his rooms. A woman in the great Athos' rooms! And he so grand and aloof! What next! But, come to think of it, there was one in Aramis' room too. The whole business is very mysterious, and I wish to God I knew how it would turn out.'

'It'll turn out badly, Sir, mark my words,' said a voice which the young man recognized as Planchet's. He had been so occupied with his thoughts that he had forgotten his surroundings. Now he was surprised to find himself standing in front of his own doorstep and disconcerted to think that he had been expressing his thoughts aloud.

'What d'you mean, idiot?' he said to Planchet. 'Why should it turn out badly? What's been happening?'

'All sorts of terrible things, Sir!'

'What things?'

'In the first place Monsieur Athos has been arrested.'

'Arrested? Athos arrested? What on earth for?'

'They found him in your rooms. They mistook him for you.'

'Who arrested him?'

'The police. The four men in black whom you turned out came back with them.'

'But why didn't Athos say who he was? Why didn't he just say he knew nothing about it?'

'Monsieur Athos was too clever for that. In fact he let himself be arrested on purpose. As they were taking him off he whispered to me: "It's better your master should be free at this moment than I. He knows everything and I know nothing. They'll think they've got him safely under arrest and that'll give him time to act. I'll go on pretending to be d'Artagnan for three days; after that I'll tell them who I am and they'll have to release me." '

'Good old Athos! Well done! That's just like him. And what did the police do with him?'

'Five of them took him off, I don't know where; either to the Bastille or to the For-l'Evêque. Two stayed behind with the men in black; they made a thorough search of the room and removed all the papers. The last two stood on guard at the door while the others were ransacking the room, and finally the whole lot packed up, leaving the house empty and all the doors and windows open.'

'And what about Porthos and Aramis?'

'They never came. I didn't find them.'

'But I presume you left my message for them, so they may turn up at any moment.'

'Yes, Sir.'

'Good. And don't you stir from here. If they come, tell them the news and ask them to meet me at the Pomme-de-Pin tavern. It would be dangerous to meet here; the house is probably being watched. I'm going off now to see Monsieur de Tréville and tell him the news; I'll join them after that.'

'Very good, Sir,' said Planchet.

'You'll stay here, won't you? You won't get frightened by yourself?' asked d'Artagnan.

'Don't worry, Sir,' said Planchet. 'You don't know me yet. You don't know what I'm good for. I'm brave when I set my mind to it; it's just a question of setting my mind to it. Besides, I'm a Picard, Sir, and you, as a Gascon, know what that means.'

'That's agreed then. You'll stick on here like grim death.'

'Yes, Sir. I'll do anything to prove my loyalty to you.'

'Good lad,' said d'Artagnan.

And he thought to himself that his methods in dealing with Planchet had been remarkably successful.

He now made his way to the Rue du Vieux Colombier as fast as his legs would carry him, tired as they were after all the running he had done that day.

Monsieur de Tréville was not at home; his company of musketeers had been summoned to the Louvre to do guard duty and he had gone with them.

D'Artagnan was determined at all costs to see Monsieur de Tréville and report what had happened. So he decided to try and get into the Louvre, hoping that his guardsman's uniform would serve as a passport. He made his way along the Rue des Petits-Augustins with the intention of crossing the river by the Pont Neuf. He thought for a moment of crossing by the ferry, but then remembered that he had no money to pay the fare. When he reached the corner of the Rue Guénégaud he noticed two people, a man and a woman, coming out of the Rue Dauphiné. His attention was at once arrested for there was something familiar about them. The women had the figure and walk of Madame Bonacieux and the man was exactly the build of Aramis. Moreover the woman was wearing a black cloak very like the one which d'Artagnan could still see in his mind's eye outlined against the shutters of the house in the Rue du Vaugirard and against the door of the house in the Rue de la Harpe, and the man was wearing musketeer's uniform. The woman had pulled the hood of her cloak over her head and the man was holding his handkerchief in front of his face; it was obvious that they did not wish to be recognized.

The pair started to walk across the bridge. That was the way d'Artagnan happened to be going, so he followed them at a discreet distance. As he walked along he became more and more obsessed by the idea that the woman was Madame Bonacieux and the man Aramis. And as he watched them he felt the pangs of jealousy gnawing at his heart.

He had been doubly betrayed, by his friend and by the

woman whom he already loved like a mistress. Madame Bonacieux had sworn by all she held most dear that she did not
know Aramis, and here she was half an hour later walking arm
in arm with him!

We remember that d'Artagnan had only known the pretty
draper's wife for three hours, that she owed him nothing but a
little gratitude for having rescued her from the men in black,
and that she had promised him nothing. We remember these
things but d'Artagnan entirely forgot them. He saw himself in
the rôle of an injured, betrayed, flouted lover. Rage seized him
and he resolved to clear up the whole business there and then.

The young man and woman noticed that they were being
followed and quickened their pace. D'Artagnan started running, got ahead of them and turned back to meet them as they
reached La Samaritaine, where a street lamp shone, lighting
up all that part of the bridge. He stopped in front of them and
barred their way.

'What do you want, Sir?' asked the musketeer, retreating a
step. He spoke with a foreign accent, and d'Artagnan at once
realized that he had been mistaken in at least one half of his
suppositions.

'So you're not Aramis!' he cried.

'No, Sir, I'm not Aramis. I see you've been mistaking me for
somebody else. That explains and I suppose excuses your
extraordinary behaviour. So we'll say no more about it. And
now please let us pass.'

'My extraordinary behaviour, you say?' cried d'Artagnan.

'Yes, Sir. And now that you realize I'm not the person you're
after please stand aside.'

'Just a moment, Sir. I may not be concerned with you but I
am concerned with this lady here.'

'This lady? You don't know her!'

'On the contrary! I know her very well.'

'Oh, Sir!' cried Madame Bonacieux, highly indignant, 'you
gave me your word as a soldier and a gentleman! I thought I
could trust you!'

D'Artagnan suddenly felt ashamed.

'Well, ma'am, you did promise . . .' he stammered.

'Come, ma'am, take my arm and let's get on,' said the stranger.

D'Artagnan was by now utterly bewildered. He stood motionless in the middle of the road, still barring the way to Madame Bonacieux and the musketeer.

The musketeer now stepped forward angrily and tried to push d'Artagnan aside with his arm. This insult brought our hero to his senses. He leapt back and drew his sword, at which the stranger quickly drew his, and the two naked blades gleamed in the moonlight.

'Stop, stop, Your Grace, this is lunacy!' cried Madame Bonacieux, throwing herself between the two men and grasping the two naked blades, one in each hand.

'Your Grace?' echoed d'Artagnan in amazement. 'Did you say Your Grace?'

Madame Bonacieux, in her excitement, had let slip a vital clue. The truth suddenly dawned on d'Artagnan and he cursed himself for his folly in not having realized it earlier.

'I ask your pardon, Sir!' he said. 'Is it possible you're . . .?'

'The Duke of Buckingham,' whispered Madame Bonacieux. 'And now we shall all be ruined if . . .'

'Your Grace! Madame Bonacieux!' cried d'Artagnan, 'I ask you both to forgive me. The fact is, Sir, I'm in love, and I was jealous. You know what it is to be in love, Sir. Please forgive me, and tell me how I can best serve Your Grace.'

'You're a good fellow,' said Buckingham, holding out his hand to d'Artagnan, who took it respectfully. 'You say you'd like to do me a service, so I'll take you at your word. Follow us to the Louvre, keeping about ten yards behind us all the way. If you see anyone spying on us, kill him.'

D'Artagnan was thrilled to have the chance of serving the great and famous Duke of Buckingham, Charles I's trusted minister. He unsheathed his sword and slipped the naked blade under his arm, waited until the Duke and Madame Bonacieux had got ten yards ahead and then followed them, prepared to obey the Duke's instructions to the letter. Fortunately there was no occasion for the young hired assassin to commit any act of violence to prove his devotion. Madame Bonacieux and her handsome escort in musketeer's uniform reached the Louvre in safety and were admitted by the Échelle Gate without question.

When d'Artagnan had seen them safely inside the palace he went straight off to the Pomme-de-Pin tavern, where he found Porthos and Aramis waiting for him. He did not bother to explain the reason for his earlier summons, but merely told them that, having at first thought he would need their help, he had later decided he could manage the business better alone, and that they could return home.

And now that we are well embarked on our story let us leave the three friends to return each to his own quarters and follow the Duke of Buckingham and his guide along the dark and tortuous passages of the Louvre.

CHAPTER XII

George Villiers, Duke of Buckingham

MADAME BONACIEUX and the Duke were admitted into the Louvre without question. Madame Bonacieux was known to the lodgekeepers as one of the Queen's household and the Duke was wearing the uniform of Monsieur de Tréville's musketeers who, as we know, were on guard that night. Moreover Germain was in the Queen's pay and, if the worst came to the worst, he would swear that Madame Bonacieux had brought her lover into the Louvre; nothing more than that. Madame Bonacieux would take the crime on to her own shoulders. Her reputation would be gone, certainly, but what does the reputation of a little draper's wife count for in this world?

The Duke and Madame Bonacieux went into an inner courtyard of the palace and felt their way for about twenty yards along a wall. At last they reached a little side door which was always open in the daytime but usually locked at night. This time, however, it opened at a lift of the latch. The Duke and his guide went inside and found themselves in darkness. But Madame Bonacieux knew every nook and cranny of this part of the palace, which was reserved for the household. She shut the door behind her, took the Duke by the hand, felt her way forward, caught hold of a banister, put her foot on a step and began climbing a staircase. The Duke followed her unquestioning. His guide walked up two floors, then turned to the right, led the way along a passage and down another flight of stairs and eventually stopped in front of a little door. She now took a key out of her pocket, unlocked the little door and showed the Duke into a room which was dimly lit by a single lamp. She then turned to him and said: 'Wait here, Your Grace. Someone will come for you.'

Then she went out by the same door, locking it from the outside. The Duke found himself a prisoner.

Dangerous as the situation was the Duke of Buckingham felt no fear; for love of adventure and romance was his strongest passion. He was brave and enterprising to the verge of rashness and this was not the first time he had risked his life in an exploit of this kind. He had discovered on reaching France that the supposed message from Anne of Austria had been a trap set by the Cardinal, but instead of returning to England he had decided to take advantage of this awkward situation, and had sent a message to the Queen to say that he would not return to England until he had seen her. At first the Queen had refused point blank, but then, in terror lest he might do something rash, she had decided to grant him a moment's audience and to beg him to return to England forthwith. But on the very evening for which their meeting had been arranged Madame Bonacieux, who had been entrusted with the task of finding the Duke and bringing him to the Louvre, was kidnapped. For two whole days no one knew what had happened to her and everyone was kept in a state of suspense. But as soon as she was free again and Monsieur de Laporte had found her the scheme was taken up where it had been left off and brought to a successful conclusion only three days later than had been originally intended.

Buckingham was now alone in the room where Madame Bonacieux had left him. He went up to a mirror on the wall to take a look at himself. The musketeer's uniform suited him to perfection. He was at that time thirty-five years old and was rightly considered to be the handsomest man and the most accomplished courtier in France and England.

The favourite of two kings, possessed of immense wealth, all-powerful at a Court which he could manipulate at will, making war or peace as his whim dictated, George Villiers, Duke of Buckingham, had had one of those fantastically brilliant careers which contemporary chroniclers love to describe and which, reported from father to son through generations, become legends to posterity. He was supremely self-confident, sure of his position, and convinced that the laws which govern other men's lives could have no control over his. Whenever he saw and coveted a prize, which to others might appear unattainable, he made straight for it, and where others flinched and shrank back he pressed on. It was this quality which had emboldened him to pay court to the beautiful and aloof Anne of Austria, and enabled him to rouse her interest and to infatuate her.

George Villiers, standing alone in front of the mirror, arranged his hair, which in those days was worn long, curled his moustache and smiled at his reflection. His heart was bursting with joy and pride at the thought of this meeting: what he had yearned for so long, what he had pictured in his waking thoughts and dreamed of at night was at last to be fulfilled.

Suddenly a hidden door in the tapestry opened and a woman appeared. Buckingham saw her reflection in the glass and gave a cry. It was the Queen.

Anne of Austria was at that time about twenty-six years old, in the full splendour of her beauty. She carried herself like a true Queen. Her eyes were emerald green, gentle but full of dignity. Her mouth was small, her lips a lovely red, and although her lower lip protruded slightly (a feature common to all Hapsburg princes), her smile was wonderfully sweet, though on occasion her face could express the profoundest scorn. Her skin was soft as velvet, her hands and arms so dazzlingly white that all the poets of the age wrote sonnets to them. Her luxuriant hair, blonde in her early youth, was now chestnut and was curled and powdered; it was a marvellous frame for her face, which was faultless save for a slightly over-heightened colouring and a nose not perfectly classic.

Buckingham stood for a moment transfixed. Never at any of the balls, fêtes, or pageants at which he had met her had she appeared to him so lovely as she did now, dressed in a simple white satin gown and attended by one lady, Doña Estefania, the only Spanish lady of her suite who had not been exiled by the King or the Cardinal.

Anne of Austria came slowly forward into the room. Buckingham was overcome. He flung himself at her feet, and, before the Queen could prevent him, kissed the hem of her dress.

'My Lord Duke,' said the Queen. 'You realize that it was not I who summoned you to France!'

'Yes, Your Majesty,' cried the Duke. 'I know I was a fool, a madman to suppose for a moment that the snow of your reserve would melt, the marble of your indifference grow warm. But that's how it is. When one loves, one is only too ready to believe one's love returned. And yet how glad I am I came, for I now have you before my eyes!'

'Yes,' replied Anne. 'But please understand that I only consented to see you under great stress, because you insisted on staying in Paris, although you knew that in so doing you were risking your life and my good name. I'm only seeing you to try and convince you that our ways lie apart, that everything stands between us, not only the sea and the hostility that exists between our countries, but also the vows we've both made, which are, or should be, inviolate, and our conflicting loyalties. To try and override these is sacrilege, Your Grace. In short, my object in seeing you is to tell you we must never meet again.'

'Go on talking, Ma'am! The sweetness of your voice makes me forget the harshness of your words. You talk of sacrilege!

What's sacrilege if not the separation of two hearts whom God has destined for each other?'

At this the Queen cried out:

'You forget, Sir, that I've never said I loved you.'

'Nor have you ever said you did not. And to say you didn't love me would be the cruellest heartlessness. For where in the world could one find a love greater than mine, a love which neither time nor absence nor rebuffs can in any way diminish? A love which is content with a stray glance, a chance word, from you, a ribbon off your dress? It's three years since I first set eyes on you, and for all those years I've loved you as I do now. Shall I tell you how you looked the first time I saw you? Shall I describe in detail the clothes and jewellery you wore? I can see you clearly as you were then. You were seated on high cushions in the Spanish fashion; you were wearing a green satin dress embroidered with gold and silver, with full sleeves looped on your lovely arms, and enormous diamonds. You wore a closed ruff and on your head a small cap with a heron's feather in it, the same colour as your dress. Oh, my cup of happiness is full, for I have only to close my eyes to see you as you were then, and to open them again to see you as you are now, that is, a hundred times more lovely still!'

'How foolish, Sir, to feed a hopeless passion on such memories,' murmured Anne of Austria.

She had not the heart to chide him for having preserved so faithful a likeness of her in his mind.

'Then what would you have me live on?' replied Buckingham. 'I have only my memories. They're my happiness, my joy, my hope. Each time I see you it's as though I'd found a fresh diamond to treasure in the casket of my heart. This is the fourth you've let fall at my feet. To think that I've only seen you four times in the three years I've known you! Our first meeting I've just described; our second was in Madame de Chevreuse's house, our third in the garden at Amiens.'

'Please let's not talk of that evening, Your Grace,' said the Queen blushing.

'Oh yes, let's talk of it! Let's talk of nothing else! It was the loveliest and most enchanted evening of my life. Do you remember what a magic night it was? Do you remember the soft scented air, the clear sky, and the glittering stars? That night, Ma'am, I managed to snatch a moment with you alone. That night you were in a mood to open your heart to me, to tell me of your loneliness and grief. You had your arm through mine; I bent my head to listen to you, your soft hair lightly brushed my cheek and as I felt it I trembled. Oh, my Queen! How can I describe the ecstasy, the heavenly joy of such a moment? I'd give all my wealth, possessions, reputation, all that remains to me of life for another such hour, for another such night. For on that night, Ma'am, I vow you loved me.'

'It's possible, Sir, that the beauty of the spot, the radiance of the night and your own charm combined to cast a fleeting spell on me, that for an instant I yielded to my feelings as a woman and forgot my position as Queen of France. But remember, Sir, my weakness was but momentary; that when you spoke to me of love I summoned my suite and left you.'

'Alas, yes. And most men would have been crushed by that rebuff. But your attitude only inflamed and strengthened my passion. You thought you would escape me by returning to Paris, that I wouldn't dare leave the treasure which my royal master had set me to guard. What do you suppose I care for all the kings and treasures of this world? I was back in Paris a week later. Then you had nothing to reproach me with. I'd risked my career, my very life, to see you for one second. That time I didn't even touch your hand, and when you saw me so humble and repentant you forgave me.'

'Yes, but as you know, Sir, all the slanderous tongues in Paris seized on those follies of yours to put the worst construction on our friendship. The Cardinal played on the King's feelings and the King made a terrible scene. Madame de Vernet was dismissed, Putange was exiled, Madame de Chevreuse disgraced. And if you remember, you tried later to be appointed Ambassador to France and the King refused to accept you?'

'Yes, and France must pay the penalty of war for her King's stubbornness. If I'm not allowed to see you, Ma'am, at least you shall hear me spoken of. I'll make all France talk of me! Why do you suppose I'm planning this expedition to Ré and this alliance with the Protestants of La Rochelle? Merely to see you again. I know I've no chance of entering Paris at the head of an army. But this war will end one day and then there'll be a peace and I'll get myself appointed my country's representative to discuss terms. They'll have to accept me then. I shall return to Paris: I shall see you again and then I shall be happy for a moment. Thousands will have paid for my happiness with their lives. I know that. But what do I care provided I see you again! All this may seem to you folly – madness. But did any woman have a more devoted lover, any Queen a more fanatical adherent?'

'Your Grace, what you're saying in your own defence only adds to your guilt. What you propose to do to prove your love for me's outrageous, almost criminal!'

'You only say that, Ma'am, because you don't love me. If you loved me you'd see it in a different light. If you loved me – ah, but if you loved me my happiness would be too great, and I should go mad! Just now you mentioned Madame de Chevreuse. She was less cruel than you. Holland loved her and she returned his love.'

Anne of Austria was moved against her better judgement by Buckingham's ardour.

'Madame de Chevreuse was not the Queen of France,' she murmured.

'So you'd love me if you weren't the Queen of France? You'd love me then, Ma'am? Can I believe that it's only your high position which makes you so cruel? If you were merely Madame de Chevreuse, might the wretched Buckingham have cause to hope? Oh, thank you for those sweet words, Ma'am. Thank you, thank you and thank you!'

'Sir, you mistook my meaning. I . . .'

'Stop!' cried the Duke. 'Say no more. If a mistake has made me happy it would be cruel to undeceive me. I've been enticed over to France – you admitted that yourself. I may not escape alive. Strangely enough I've been having presentiments lately that I'm soon going to die.'

As Buckingham said this he smiled a sad, charming smile.

'Oh God!' cried Anne of Austria with a note of terror in her voice which proved that she was more attached to the Duke than she cared to admit.

'I didn't say that to alarm you, Ma'am. In fact it was just a piece of nonsense, and I don't myself attach great importance to dreams. But what you said just now, when you almost gave me cause to hope, is ample reward for anything I may suffer, even for death itself.'

'It's strange,' said the Queen, 'but I too have had presentiments and dreams. I dreamt I saw you lying on the ground covered in blood.'

'With a wound in my left side – a knife-wound?'

'Yes, a knife-wound on the left side of your body. Who could have told you that dream of mine? I've told it to no one in the world, and have only confided it to God in my prayers.'

'Ah, now my cup of happiness is full! You love me and nothing else counts.'

'I, Sir? Love you?'

'Yes, for would God send us both the same dreams, the same presentiments, if we did not love each other, if our hearts were not one? You do love me, my Queen, and you'll mourn for me when I'm gone.'

'Oh God!' cried Anne of Austria. 'This is more than I can bear! Go in Heaven's name, Sir! I don't know if I love you or not, but I do know that I won't lie to you. So take pity on me and go! To think you might be murdered in France and die on French soil! And that your love for me might be the cause of your death! I should never recover! I should go mad! So go, go! I implore you to go!'

'How beautiful you are when you're roused! And how I love you!' cried Buckingham.

'Go, I beseech you, and come back at a better time. Come back as ambassador or minister of the Crown with a bodyguard and servants to protect you. Then I shall have the joy of seeing you without any fears for your safety.'

'Can I believe it? Do you really mean what you've just said?'

'Yes.'

'Oh joy, oh bliss! And now give me some token of your favour, something which will prove to me in the days to come that I've not been dreaming. Give me something you yourself have worn and I in turn can wear – a ring, a bracelet, a necklace.'

'And if I do will you go?'

'Yes.'

'This very instant?'

'Yes.'

'You'll leave France? You'll return to England?'

'Yes, yes, I swear it.'

'Wait then while I find something for you.'

Anne of Austria now left the room, went into her apartments and returned almost immediately carrying a little rosewood box with her initials engraved in gold on it.

'Take this box, Sir, and keep it in memory of me,' she said.

Buckingham took the box and once more knelt before the Queen.

'You promised you'd leave now,' said Her Majesty.

'And so I will. This very instant. Just give me your hand and I'll go.'

Anne of Austria held out her hand, closing her eyes as she did so and resting her other hand on Doña Estefania's arm to support herself, for she was afraid she might faint, so great was her emotion.

Buckingham seized her hand and kissed it passionately. Then he got to his feet and said:

'If I escape alive I shall see you again before six months have passed, even if I have to set the world ablaze to reach you.'

Then, true to his word, he turned and left the room.

In the passage he found Madame Bonacieux waiting to escort him out of the Louvre. She performed this task with her usual brisk efficiency, and did not leave him until she had seen him safely outside the precincts of the palace.

CHAPTER XIII

Monsieur Bonacieux

THE reader may be thinking that we have meanwhile forgotten the existence of one of the humbler participants in the drama, Monsieur Bonacieux, whom we left in the hands of the police, an innocent victim of an intrigue typical of that immoral yet elegant age, in which the high and mighty used their lowlier compatriots as pawns in the furtherance of their own aims, political or amorous. True, we have lately neglected the little draper. But we promised not to lose touch with him for good, so let us now return to him.

The myrmidons of the law who arrested him took him straight off to the Bastille and led him past a squadron of soldiers who were loading their muskets, which terrified the poor man to death. He was then taken to an underground cell where he was hustled about and sworn at by the guards. They realized that he was not a gentleman and consequently treated him worse than a dog.

After about half an hour a magistrate's clerk came in and ordered the guards to lead their prisoner into the Court Room to be cross-examined. This put an end to the bullying of Monsieur Bonacieux, but did not allay his fears. Political prisoners were usually cross-questioned in their own cells, but Monsieur Bonacieux was not considered sufficiently important to be thus favoured.

Two guards took hold of the unfortunate draper and marched him first across a courtyard, then along a passage where three sentries were on duty and finally into a low, bare room containing only two chairs and one table. A magistrate was sitting at the table writing.

The two guards marched the prisoner up to the table and then, at a sign from the magistrate, retired to the back of the room.

The magistrate, who until then had been sitting with his head bent over the table, engrossed in his writing, now looked up to examine the prisoner. He was a forbidding-looking man with a pointed nose, a sallow skin, small, gimlet eyes, and the look of a fox and a ferret combined. He had a long, thin neck, and his habit of twisting his head about above his black lawyer's gown reminded one of a tortoise peering out of its shell.

He began by asking Monsieur Bonacieux his Christian and surnames, his age, occupation and place of residence. The prisoner replied that his name was Jacques Michel Bonacieux, that he was fifty-one years old, a retired draper, and that he lived at No. 11 Rue des Fossoyeurs.

Instead of continuing his examination the magistrate then proceeded to give the prisoner a long lecture, telling him how dangerous it was for a humble member of the middle-classes like himself to get mixed up in affairs of state. His discourse was interlaced with eulogies of the Cardinal, that incomparable genius, greater than any statesman of the past and an example to all statesmen of the future, whom no man could thwart with impunity.

Having finished his speech the magistrate gave the unfortunate Bonacieux a diabolical look and bade him reflect on the seriousness of his position.

Monsieur Bonacieux knew exactly how serious his position was. He cursed the day on which Monsieur de Laporte had married him off to his ward, and still more the day on which she was appointed seamstress to the Queen.

The three basic components of Monsieur Bonacieux's character were egotism, avarice, and cowardice. The love which he bore his young wife was an entirely secondary passion with him and therefore could not prevail against the three other much stronger passions.

Monsieur Bonacieux thought for a moment before answering his inquisitor.

'Sir,' he said at last, 'I hope you realize how greatly I admire and revere His Eminence the Cardinal, whom this country is privileged to have as its ruler.'

'Is that so?' replied the magistrate sarcastically. 'Then how d'you come to be in the Bastille?'

'Surely, Sir, that's a question you, rather than I, are in a position to answer. I can only say that it's not for having displeased the Cardinal or, at any rate, not wittingly.'

'And yet you must have committed some crime or you wouldn't be here on a charge of High Treason.'

'High Treason!' cried Monsieur Bonacieux aghast. 'But that's preposterous! How could I, a poor harmless draper who hates the Huguenots and abominates the Spaniards, be guilty of High Treason?'

'Monsieur Bonacieux,' replied the magistrate, looking at the prisoner with his little gimlet eyes which seemed to pierce right through the other's skull, 'you have a wife, have you not?'

This question struck terror into the draper's heart. He understood now where the trouble lay and what the authorities were after, and trembled at the thought of what this cross-examination might reveal.

'Yes, Sir,' he said, 'I have a wife, or rather I had a wife.'

'How do you mean, you had a wife? Have you lost her?'

'She's been kidnapped, Sir.'

'Has she, indeed?'

To Bonacieux that 'Has she, indeed?' was ominous. He felt that, innocent as he was, he was being dragged little by little into a quagmire.

'So she's been kidnapped?' went on the magistrate. 'And do you happen to know who kidnapped her?'

'I think I know.'

'Well, who was it?'

'Remember, Sir, I'm not making any definite statement. I have my suspicions, that's all.'

'And whom do you suspect? Answer truthfully, please.'

Monsieur Bonacieux was in a quandary. Should he tell everything or nothing? If he denied everything his examiner might well infer that he was scared of admitting how much he did know; if he confessed everything he would at any rate show a willingness to oblige. He decided to confess everything.

'I suspect a tall, dark aristocratic-looking man who's been following me and my wife about for some time. He used to dog our footsteps when we walked home from the Louvre, where I called every evening to fetch my wife.'

The magistrate seemed slightly uneasy on hearing this.

'What's his name?'

'I don't know his name. But if I ever saw him again I'd recognize him out of a thousand others. That I can promise you.'

The magistrate's face darkened.

'Oh, so you'd recognize him, would you?' he echoed.

Bonacieux saw that he had blundered.

'By that I mean, I mean . . .' he stammered.

'You said you'd recognize him,' said the magistrate. 'That's all I wanted to know. That'll do for today. Before I continue your cross-examination I must report the fact that you know the man who kidnapped your wife.'

'I never said I knew him!' cried Bonacieux in despair. 'I said . . .'

'Take the prisoner away,' cried the magistrate, addressing the two guards.

'Where shall we put him?' asked the corporal.

'In one of the cells.'

'Which cell?'

'Any, provided the door locks properly,' replied the magistrate. He shrugged his shoulders as though he had no further interest in the prisoner, and poor Monsieur Bonacieux was appalled.

'Oh dear, I am in a mess!' he moaned to himself. 'My wife's obviously committed some terrible crime, and they think I'm concerned in it. They'll punish me as well as her. She's probably confessed; she probably said she'd told me everything, in order to appease them; women are so weak. Any cell! Any cell's good enough for me for tonight. And one night's soon over, and tomorrow I suppose it's away with me to the gallows or the wheel. Oh God in Heaven, take pity on me!'

The two guards seized their prisoner each by one arm and hurried him off; he was still moaning to himself but they paid no heed. As the three of them left the room the magistrate quickly scribbled a note which he dispatched by a messenger.

Bonacieux never closed an eye all night, not because his cell was too uncomfortable, but because his terror was too great. He sat up all night on a wooden stool, trembling at the faintest noise; and when the first rays of daylight appeared he crept away into a corner of the cell so that they should not fall on him, for he felt that this dawn was heralding his doom.

Suddenly he gave a violent start. He had heard the bolts of the door being drawn back and was sure that they were coming to take him to the scaffold. However no executioner appeared but only the magistrate and his clerk, his acquaintances of the previous day. Monsieur Bonacieux was so relieved that he could have embraced them.

'Since yesterday serious complications have arisen in your case, my friend,' said the magistrate. 'The only thing for you to do now is to tell the whole truth. If you show yourself willing to make amends, the Cardinal may forgive you.'

'But of course I'll tell the truth!' cried Bonacieux. 'I'll tell you anything you want to know.'

'Very well. I want first of all to know where your wife is.'

'I've already told you she's been kidnapped!'

'Yes, but at five o'clock yesterday afternoon she escaped – with your connivance.'

'My wife's escaped?' cried Bonacieux. 'Oh blast the woman! What did she go and do that for? But I assure you, Sir, I had nothing whatever to do with it.'

'If that's so will you please explain why you called yesterday on Monsieur d'Artagnan, your lodger, and spent two hours alone with him? What were you discussing with him?'

'Oh yes, Sir! I do admit I called on Monsieur d'Artagnan. I shouldn't have done so. It was wrong of me.'

'What made you go?'

'I went to ask him to help me to find my wife. I thought I had a right to try and get her back. But I see I was wrong, and I ask your pardon.'

'Did Monsieur d'Artagnan agree to help you?'

'Yes, but I discovered later he was playing a double game with me.'

'You're lying, Sir! You bribed Monsieur d'Artagnan to find your wife for you. He agreed and subsequently assaulted four policemen who were holding your wife in custody, abducted her and hid her away from justice.'

'Monsieur d'Artagnan's abducted my wife? Oh no, Sir, I'm sure you're making a mistake there.'

'Luckily we've found and arrested Monsieur d'Artagnan, and we're going to confront you with him.'

'You may be sure I've no objection to that,' cried Bonacieux. 'I shall be delighted to see someone from the outside world again.'

'Bring d'Artagnan in,' said the magistrate to the two guards. The guards went out and came back with Athos.

'Now, Monsieur d'Artagnan,' said the magistrate, addressing Athos. 'State what took place between you and this gentleman.'

'That's not Monsieur d'Artagnan!' cried Bonacieux.

'Not Monsieur d'Artagnan?' cried the magistrate in surprise.

'Definitely not!'

'Then what is this gentleman's name?' asked the magistrate.

'I can't tell you. I don't know him.'

'You don't know him?'

'No.'

'You've never seen him before?'

'Yes, I've seen him, but I don't know his name.'

'What is your name?' asked the magistrate, addressing Athos.

'My name's Athos,' answered the musketeer.

'That's not a man's name; that's the name of a mountain!' cried the magistrate furiously. He was quite bewildered by now, and began to lose his head.

'And yet I assure you it's my name,' answered Athos calmly.

'But first you said your name was d'Artagnan,' protested the official.

'I never said so.'

'Yes, Sir. You did.'

'No, Sir, I did not. Your men came up to me and said, "You're Monsieur d'Artagnan." I replied "That's what you think." The men replied, "We don't think it, we know it." Not wishing to annoy them, I left it at that. Besides there was always a chance they might be right.'

'You're making fun of the law, Sir!'

'Not at all,' replied Athos calmly.

'You are Monsieur d'Artagnan.'

'Very well, Sir. Since you insist.'

'Listen, Sir!' cried Bonacieux, butting in. 'This matter can be cleared up at once. Even though Monsieur d'Artagnan doesn't pay his rent he lodges in my house, so it's obvious I must know him. Monsieur d'Artagnan's a young man of about twenty, and this gentleman's at least thirty. Monsieur d'Artagnan's in Monsieur des Essarts' company of guards, and this gentleman's one of Monsieur de Tréville's musketeers. Look at his uniform, Sir!'

'By God, he's right,' muttered the official.

At that moment the door was flung open and one of the Bastille lodge-keepers appeared, ushering in a messenger with a letter, which the magistrate took and read.

'Curse the woman!' he cried.

'Who? What woman?' cried the unfortunate draper. 'I do hope it's not my wife again?'

'That's exactly who it is, my friend. You're in a proper mess now, let me tell you!'

'But this is intolerable!' cried Bonacieux in a passion. 'What my wife does while I'm in prison can't affect my position either way. I will not be held responsible for that woman's follies.'

'She's only pursuing a prearranged plan, a devilish plan worked out by the two of you together.'

'Sir, I do assure you you're making a very big mistake. I haven't the faintest notion what my wife's been doing. I'm in no way involved. If she's been acting wickedly I renounce her, I curse her, I . . .!'

'Look here, Superintendent,' broke in Athos. 'If you don't

need me I'll be glad if you'll let me go. Your Monsieur Bonacieux's getting on my nerves.'

'Take Monsieur "What's-his-name" back to his cell,' said the magistrate to the two guards. 'And leave Monsieur Bonacieux here. And this time put an even closer watch on both prisoners.'

'If Monsieur d'Artagnan's your man, Sir,' said Athos with his habitual calm, 'I don't understand why you're bothering with me so much.'

'Do as I say,' shouted the magistrate to the guards. 'And remember to keep your mouths shut. We want this thing kept as dark as possible.'

Athos followed the guards out of the room, imperturbable as ever. Then the magistrate himself went out, leaving Bonacieux alone again.

The latter remained alone in his cell the whole day. He sat on his stool sobbing in the most unmanly fashion. For, as he has himself told us, he was no fighting man, but a mere draper.

At nine o'clock in the evening, just as he had decided to go to bed, he heard footsteps in the passage outside. The footsteps approached; the door of his cell was flung open and two guards came in, followed by an officer.

'Come along with me,' said the officer.

'Now? At this hour of the night? Where on earth are you taking me?'

'You'll see when you get there.'

'Come, come, that's no answer,' said the little man in a great state of alarm.

'I'm afraid it's the only answer you'll get.'

'Oh God, oh God,' moaned the draper. 'This time it really is the end. My last hour's come.'

He turned and followed the guards in a dazed fashion, making no attempt to resist. The guards led him down the same passage and across an inner courtyard to one of the gates of the prison, where a carriage was waiting with an escort of four armed guards. They made Bonacieux get into the carriage; the officer got in beside him; the door was locked and the carriage started. Bonacieux now found himself in a prison on wheels.

As they drove along, Bonacieux peered out through the barred windows but could see nothing except the pavement and the houses opposite. But he was a Parisian born and bred, so he recognized each street by the railings, the shop signs, and the lamps. When they reached St Paul, the place of execution for the Bastille prisoners, Bonacieux all but fainted and crossed himself twice, for he was convinced that they were stopping there. However the carriage drove on.

After a little while they reached the St John cemetery, and now Monsieur Bonacieux was again seized with panic, for this was where all state criminals were buried. The only thing that reassured him was that the prisoners were usually beheaded before being brought here, and his head was still on his shoulders. But when he saw then that they were making for the Place de la Grève, when he caught sight of the pointed roofs of the Town Hall, and when the carriage actually passed under the arcade he was convinced that this was really the end. He tried to persuade the police officer to hear his last confession, and when the officer refused, uttered such loud and piteous cries that his guard threatened to gag him if he did not stop immediately.

This threat pacified Bonacieux considerably. He argued that if they intended to behead him in the Place de la Grève they would not bother to gag him first. And, in fact, the carriage continued on past the ill-omened spot. Now there was nothing to fear but the Croix-du-Trahoir, but this, alas, was their very next port of call.

Now there could be no doubt. The Croix-du-Trahoir was where all minor criminals were executed. Bonacieux had exaggerated his importance in thinking that they would do him the honour of beheading him at St Paul or the Place de la Grève; his little excursion would end at the much more squalid place of public execution at the Croix-du-Trahoir, and with it his life. The ill-fated cross was not yet in sight, but he saw it in his mind's eye advancing to meet him. When they were only about twenty yards away he heard the shouts of a crowd and then the carriage drew up. This was more than the unfortunate fellow could bear, stunned as he was by the sudden disruption of his humdrum life and the rapid succession of shocks he had endured since that morning. He let out a low moan, which sounded like a dying man's last gasp, and fainted.

CHAPTER XIV

The Man of Meung

THE crowd in the street which had held up the carriage containing Bonacieux had not collected to watch a man being hanged, as our unfortunate friend had supposed, but to gaze at the body of a man already hanged. The carriage itself was held up for a few seconds only; it then continued on through the crowd, entered the Rue St Honoré, turned up on the Rue des Bons-Enfants and stopped in front of a low door, which was at once opened from inside at a signal from some invisible watcher at a window. Two guards appeared, carried the semi-conscious Bonacieux into the house, bundled him along a passage and up a staircase and finally deposited him in an ante-room. The little man had walked along mechanically like someone in a dream; there was a mist in front of his eyes and a humming in his ears. At that moment he would have gone to the scaffold like a lamb to the slaughter, without a word of protest.

Now he lay back on the divan where the guards had seated him, with his head resting against the wall and his arms hanging lifeless at his sides.

For a few moments he sat there like one dead. Then he opened his eyes and looked apathetically round the room. He saw nothing at all terrifying, nothing which in any way seemed to threaten his life. The divan was comfortably upholstered, the walls of the room were covered in fine Cordova leather, the windows were framed with heavy red damask curtains caught up by gold rings. Bonacieux began to take courage again and shook his head violently from side to side as though to rid himself of the spell of his previous terror.

At that moment one of the wall hangings was drawn aside and a uniformed officer appeared. He turned to exchange a few words with someone in the adjoining room, and then walked up to the prisoner.

'You're the prisoner Bonacieux, are you not?'

'Yes, Sir, yes,' stuttered the draper, still half paralysed with fear. 'Bonacieux at your service.'

'Go in there,' said the officer, standing aside to let the prisoner pass. Bonacieux did not need to be told twice, but scuttled like a rabbit into the next room.

He found himself in a large office, the walls of which were curiously adorned with an assortment of weapons. The room was stuffy as there was a fire burning in the grate, although it was not yet October. In the middle of the room was a square table, covered with books and papers, over which was spread a huge map of the town of La Rochelle.

In front of the fireplace stood a man of medium build but of commanding presence. He had shrewd eyes, a high forehead, and a thin, drawn face, and he wore a small beard which made his face look even longer than it was. He was not more than thirty-six or thirty-seven years old, and yet his moustache and beard were already greying. He carried no sword and yet he looked every inch a soldier, and his buff boots had dust on them, which showed that he had quite recently been in the saddle.

This man was Armand Jean Duplessis, Cardinal Richelieu. Standing with one arm resting on the mantelpiece he bore no resemblance to the stereotyped portraits of him that have been handed down to us, which depict him as an old man broken in health, racked with pain, frail of body and feeble of voice, buried in a huge tomb-like armchair, holding on to life by sheer force of will and maintaining the struggle with Europe only by a ceaseless exercise of his indomitable genius. In point of fact, at the particular period of which we write, Cardinal Richelieu was in outward appearance a prototype of the man of fashion of the age, and was still physically active though not robust. What raised him head and shoulders above his contemporaries and made him one of the most remarkable figures of all time was his spiritual strength. Just now he was in the heyday of his glory. He had recently won the Duchy of Mantua for the Duc de Nevers by force of arms; he had just captured Nîmes, Castres, and Uzés, and was now preparing to drive the English from the Ile de Ré and to lay siege to La Rochelle.

In outward appearance Richelieu was, as we have said, a typical courtier of his age and nothing in his looks or dress would have betrayed his identity to any ordinary citizen seeing him for the first time. The little draper remained standing near the wall, thoroughly cowed, while the stranger by the mantelpiece fixed his penetrating gaze on him, as though he would read his very thoughts.

'Is this the man Bonacieux?' he asked after a moment's silence.

'Yes, Monseigneur,' replied the officer.

'Good. Just hand me his papers and go.'

The officer took the papers off the table, handed them to the stranger by the mantelpiece, bowed low and left the room.

Bonacieux recognized the papers as the forms which the magistrate at the Bastille had filled in in answer to his questions. Every now and then the stranger by the fireplace would look up from these papers and fix his eyes on Bonacieux; so fierce was his gaze that the wretched man felt his knees quake beneath him.

The Cardinal took about ten minutes to read the files and ten seconds to examine his prisoner and was then apparently satisfied.

'That man's no conspirator,' he said to himself. 'He hasn't the wit for it. However, I'll question him first to make sure.'

'Monsieur Bonacieux, the charge against you's High Treason,' he said, speaking slowly and sternly.

'So they told me, Monseigneur,' cried Bonacieux, addressing his examiner by the title used by the officer. 'But I swear I knew nothing about it.'

The Cardinal smiled inwardly at this.

'You plotted with your wife, with Madame de Chevreuse, and with His Grace the Duke of Buckingham.'

'I certainly heard my wife mention those names,' answered the draper.

'In what connection?'

'She said that Cardinal Richelieu had lured the Duke of Buckingham to Paris in order to expose him and the Queen with him.'

'Oh, she said that, did she?' cried the Cardinal furiously.

'Yes, Monseigneur. But I told her she shouldn't say such things, that the Cardinal wouldn't stoop so low as that . . .'

'Hold your tongue, Sir. You're a fool,' interrupted the Cardinal.

'That's just what my wife said, Monseigneur.'

'D'you know who kidnapped your wife?'

'No, Monseigneur.'

'But I understand you suspect somebody.'

'I did, Monseigneur. And I confided my suspicions to the magistrate. But what I said only seemed to annoy him, so I don't suspect anyone now.'

'Your wife's escaped. Did you know that?'

'No, Monseigneur. I only heard about it when I was in prison, and then only because the magistrate was good enough to tell me. A most kind and considerate man, the magistrate, if I may say so, Sir.'

At this the Cardinal again smiled to himself.

'So you don't know where your wife went after she escaped?'

'I haven't a notion, Monseigneur. I can only suppose that she returned to the Louvre.'

'She hadn't returned at one o'clock this morning.'

'Oh dear, oh dear! Where can she have got to?'

'We'll find out, never fear. The Cardinal finds out everything sooner or later. He knows everything.'

'In that case, Monseigneur, d'you think the Cardinal will consent to tell me where my wife is?'

'He may. But first of all you must tell us everything you know about your wife's connection with Madame de Chevreuse.'

'I know nothing about it, Sir. I've never seen Madame de Chevreuse.'

'When you went to fetch your wife from the Louvre did you always go straight home with her?'

'No, hardly ever. She always had a call or two to make at drapers' shops with orders for the Queen.'

'How many of these drapers' shops were there?'

'Two, Sir.'

'Where were they?'

'One was in the Rue de Vaugirard; the other in the Rue de la Harpe.'

'Used you to go in to the shops with her?'

'Never, Sir. I always waited outside in the street.'

'What excuse did she give for not allowing you to go in with her?'

'She gave no excuse. She told me to wait and I just waited.'

'My dear Monsieur Bonacieux, you appear to be a most accommodating husband,' said the Cardinal.

'Now he's calling me his 'dear Monsieur Bonacieux'',' thought the little man. 'Things seems to be looking up a bit.'

'Would you recognize the doors of these shops?'

'Yes, Monseigneur.'

'D'you know the numbers?'

'Yes. 25, Rue de Vaugirard and 75, Rue de la Harpe.'

'Excellent,' said the Cardinal.

He now rang a little silver bell which stood on the table in front of him, and the officer came in.

The Cardinal spoke to him aside.

'Go and find Rochefort,' he said. 'If he's already back bring him in here at once.'

'Count de Rochefort's here,' answered the officer, 'and wants to see Your Eminence urgently.'

'Bring him in, then, and hurry,' said the Cardinal sharply.

The officer left the room with the alacrity which distinguished all the Cardinal's servants.

'His Eminence!' muttered Bonacieux under his breath, looking thoroughly scared. 'So it's the Cardinal himself!'

In a minute or two the door opened again and a new visitor was ushered in.

'That's the man!' cried Bonacieux.

'What man?' asked the Cardinal.

'The man who kidnapped my wife.'

The Cardinal rang the bell a second time, and again the officer came in.

'Put the prisoner Bonacieux in charge again,' said the Cardinal, 'and keep him here until I send for him.'

'No, Monseigneur, no! That's not the man after all,' cried Bonacieux in terror. 'I was wrong. The man who kidnapped my wife was quite different – nothing like this gentleman at all. This gentleman's a good, honest gentleman – anybody could tell that . . .'

'Take this idiot away,' cried the Cardinal.

The officer took Bonacieux by the arm, led him back into the ante-room and handed him over to the two guards.

The new arrival watched impatiently until the rat-like figure of Bonacieux had left the room. The moment the door closed he turned to the Cardinal and said sharply:

'They've been seeing each other.'

'Who?' asked the Cardinal.

'She and he.'

'The Queen and the Duke?' cried Richelieu.

'Yes.'

'Where?'

'At the Louvre.'

'You're sure of that?'

'Positive.'

'Who told you?'

'Madame de Lannoy, who's absolutely trustworthy.'

'Why didn't she report it sooner?'

'For some reason or other the Queen made Madame de Surgis sleep in Madame de Lannoy's bedroom that night and stay with her all the next day. She may have suspected her. I don't know . . .'

'Well, that's that! We've been outwitted. Now we must get our revenge.'

'I needn't tell you, Monseigneur, that you can count on my loyal support in everything.'

'How was the meeting arranged?'

'Just after midnight, when the Queen was in her bedroom with her ladies-in-waiting, a messenger came in with a handkerchief. Apparently one of the Queen's maids had given it to him to give to Her Majesty.'

'Well?'

'When the Queen saw the handkerchief she was terribly upset and went deathly pale.'

'Go on!'

'She got up and in a stifled voice said to her ladies, "Wait for me please, I'll be back in ten minutes." She then left the room.'

'Why didn't Madame de Lannoy come and report to us then and there?'

'She hadn't found out anything definite by then. Besides the Queen had told all the ladies to wait for her, and she didn't dare disobey.'

'How long did the Queen stay away?'

'Three quarters of an hour.'

'Did none of her women go with her?'

'Only Doña Estefania.'

'And did she return to her room after that?'

'Yes, but only to fetch a little rosewood box with her initials on it. She then went out again.'

'And when she returned later did she bring the rosewood box back with her?'

'No.'

'Does Madame de Lannoy know what was in the box?'

'Yes. The diamond tags which the King gave the Queen for her birthday.'

'And you say she returned without the box?'

'Yes.'

'Does Madame de Lannoy think she gave the box to Buckingham?'

'She's convinced of it.'

'What makes her so sure?'

'In her capacity as Mistress of the Robes she spent the next day searching for the box, pretended to be greatly concerned about its loss and finally mentioned the matter to the Queen.'

'And what did the Queen do?'

'She looked extremely embarrassed and invented some story about having broken one of the tags the previous day and having sent the box to her jeweller to have the tag repaired.'

'We must call on the jeweller and find out if the story's true.'

'I've done that already, Your Eminence.'

'Oh, and what did the man say?'

'He knew nothing whatever about it.'

'Excellent. The game's not lost yet, Rochefort, not by any means. In fact what's happened may turn out to be all for the best.'

'I'm confident Your Eminence's genius will . . .'

'Make good my agent's blunders, eh?'

'That's just what I was going to say, Sir, if you'd allowed me to finish my sentence.'

'And now another thing. D'you know where the Duchesse de Chevreuse and the Duke of Buckingham have been hiding all this time?'

'No, Monseigneur. My men haven't been able to get any definite information about that.'

'I know where they've been hiding.'

'You, Excellency?'

'Yes. At any rate I've a pretty shrewd idea. One of them was at No. 25, Rue de Vaugirard, the other at No. 75, Rue de la Harpe.'

'D'you wish me to arrest them both?'

'It's too late. They'll have left by now.'

'It would be as well to find out for certain.'

'Very well. Take ten men of my company and search both houses.'

'I'll go now, Sir.'

And Rochefort turned and left the room.

The Cardinal stood alone in silence for a moment. Then he rang the bell for the third time, and the same officer came in again.

'Bring back the prisoner,' said the Cardinal.

Monsieur Bonacieux was led in once more and at a sign from the Cardinal the officer left the room.

'You've been lying to me, Sir,' said the Cardinal sternly.

'I?' cried Bonacieux. 'Lie to your Eminence? Never!'

'Those addresses in the Rue de la Harpe and the Rue de Vaugirard where your wife used to call weren't drapers' shops at all.'

'What were they then, in Heaven's name?'

'They were the headquarters of enemy agents. Madame de Chevreuse was hiding in one of them and the Duke of Buckingham in the other.'

'Oh yes, Your Eminence,' cried Bonacieux, recollecting everything in a flash. 'You're perfectly right. I remember often saying to my wife that it was a queer district for drapers' shops, and wondering why there were no signboards outside. My wife used always to laugh at me, Oh, Monseigneur,' he continued, suddenly throwing himself at His Eminence's feet, 'you are indeed the Cardinal, the great Cardinal, the world-famed man of genius.'

To have won the admiration of a drab little fellow like Bonacieux could not be counted as a great triumph, and yet the Cardinal was flattered for a moment. Then almost immediately his eyes lit up as though an idea had suddenly struck him. He looked down at the prostrate figure of the draper, held out his hand to him and said affably:

'Get up, my friend. You're a good, honest fellow and I like you.'

'The Cardinal's taken my hand,' cried Bonacieux in a positive frenzy of joy. 'I've touched the great man's hand. The Cardinal's called me his friend.'

He was shouting at the top of his voice, as though haranguing an invisible crowd.

'Yes, my friend, yes,' said the Cardinal, in the 'benevolent father' tone which he liked to adopt on certain occasions and which deceived only those who did not know him well. 'And I'm afraid you've been sadly misjudged and most unfairly treated, so some compensation's owing to you. Take this purse of three hundred pistoles. And please forgive me the wrong I've done you.'

Bonacieux was quite overwhelmed. He was frightened at first to take the purse, suspecting that the Cardinal was playing a joke on him.

'I forgive you, Your Excellency?' he cried. 'But that's absurd! You had a perfect right to arrest me; you've a perfect right to torture me, to have me hanged if you wish. You're Lord and Master and it's not for a humble citizen like myself to criticize or blame. You ask me to forgive you, Sir? The very idea!'

'Monsieur Bonacieux, you're very good, and I appreciate your generosity. I take it then that you'll accept this purse and leave with not too bad an impression of me?'

'I'm more than content, Your Excellency.'

'Well good-bye for the time being. I hope we shall meet again before long.'

'Whenever and as often as Your Eminence pleases. I'm entirely at your service.'

'Don't worry. I think we shall be seeing quite a lot of each other. I find you a most interesting companion.'

'Oh, Sir!'

'Good-bye for the present, then, Monsieur Bonacieux.'

And the Cardinal nodded genially to his guest. Bonacieux bowed to the ground and walked backwards out of the room. When he was in the ante-room he shouted at the top of his voice:

'Long live His Excellency. Long live His Eminence. Long live the great Cardinal.'

The Cardinal, alone in his study, smiled when he heard this somewhat naïve display of enthusiasm on the part of the worthy draper. Then as his guest's cries died away in the distance, he said to himself:

'Good, I've got another staunch supporter in that man, fool though he is. He'd give his life for me.'

Then he turned to the map of La Rochelle which was spread

out on his desk and stood staring at it, deep in thought. Taking up a pencil he traced a line across the map at the place which eighteen months later was to be the site of the famous dyke which barred the harbour to the city's rescuers.

He was still deeply immersed in his strategical imaginings when the doors opened again and Rochefort came in. The Cardinal looked up at once from his desk.

'Well?' he said.

He stared at Rochefort so sharply that it was obvious he attached great importance to the result of his mission.

'Well, Sir,' answered Rochefort, 'I've discovered that a young woman of about twenty-eight and a man of thirty-five to forty did stay at each of the two houses mentioned by Your Excellency, the woman five days, the man four. But the woman left last night and the man this morning.'

'They were the Duke and Madame de Chevreuse!' cried the Cardinal. Then he looked at the clock and said:

'The Duchess'll have reached Tours by now and the Duke'll be in Boulogne. We shall have to catch up with them in London.'

'What do you suggest as the next move, Sir?'

'The whole thing must be kept absolutely dark. The Queen must suspect nothing. She must never know we know her secret. She must think we're trying to investigate some political plot. Bear that in mind. And now I've thought of something. I want you to fetch Séguier, the Keeper of the Seals.'

'What about the other fellow? What did Your Eminence get out of him?'

'Who?'

'The fellow who was here just now, Bonacieux.'

'I've got as much as anyone can hope to get from anyone else in this world. I've got him to act as a spy against his own wife.'

Count Rochefort gave the Cardinal a look of awe and admiration.

'Once again I bow to your genius, Sir,' he said.

Then he turned and left the room.

Alone once more the Cardinal sat down at his desk and wrote a letter which he sealed with his own private seal. Then he rang the bell for the fourth time.

'Send Vitray to me,' he said, 'and tell him to put on travelling clothes.'

A few minutes later Vitray was standing before the Cardinal, booted and spurred.

'Vitray, you're to set off post-haste for London. You must make the journey in one stretch, and not stop anywhere. The moment you reach London go to Milady with this letter. Here's a bill for two hundred pistoles; my treasurer will cash it for you. There'll be another bill for you for the same amount if you succeed in your mission and get back within six days.'

The messenger took the letter and the treasury bill and went out.

This is what was written in the letter:

Milady. When the Duke of Buckingham next attends a ball go to it. He will be wearing twelve diamond tags on his doublet. You must manage somehow to get near him and to cut off two.

Let me know the moment the studs are in your possession.

CHAPTER XV

Soldiers and Magistrates

On the day following these events Athos had not returned home, so Porthos and d'Artagnan reported his disappearance to Monsieur de Tréville. Meanwhile Aramis had asked for five days' leave, and had gone to Rouen on the plea that he had some family business to settle.

Monsieur de Tréville was like a father to his soldiers. The least of them, provided he wore the musketeers' uniform, could be as certain of his support and protection as any member of his family. So directly he learnt of Athos' arrest he called at the Office of Criminal Investigations and asked to see the officer in charge of the Croix-Rouge district. Inquiries were

made and it was eventually discovered that Athos had been
provisionally detained in the For-l'Evêque prison.

Meanwhile Athos had been put through a cross-examination
similar to that imposed on Bonacieux. We have described the
scene in which the two prisoners were brought face to face. Till
that moment Athos had refused to say anything for fear of
implicating d'Artagnan and getting him arrested before he had
had time to act. But from then on he confessed and stead-
fastly maintained that his name was Athos and not d'Artagnan.
Moreover he declared that he knew neither Monsieur nor
Madame Bonacieux; that he had never spoken a word to either
of them; that at about ten o'clock on the evening of the assault
on the police he had called on his friend d'Artagnan, previous
to which he had been in Monsieur de Tréville's house where he
had dined; that he could call at least twenty witnesses to prove
his statement, several of whom were men of note, among them
the Duc de la Trémouille.

The second magistrate was quite as taken aback as his colleague by Athos' clear and straightforward statement. He had
hoped to be able to humiliate this musketeer in some way; in
those days there was a permanent underlying antagonism between soldiers and civil servants. But the names of Monsieur
de Tréville and Monsieur de la Trémouille quoted by Athos as
witnesses for his defence cowed the magistrate not a little.

Like Bonacieux Athos had then been driven off to see the
Cardinal. But unfortunately the Cardinal was at that moment
with the King at the Louvre.

At precisely the same hour Monsieur de Tréville also called
to see the King. After leaving the Office of Criminal Investigations he had called on the Governor of the For-l'Evêque prison
but had not been able to get Athos released. So he now went
off to plead his case with the highest authority. In his capacity
as Captain of the Musketeers he had a right of audience with
the King at any hour of the day.

Everyone knows how prejudiced the King was against the
Queen, and how these prejudices were cleverly played upon by
the Cardinal, who feared women far more than men in matters

of intrigue. One of the King's main causes of complaint was the Queen's friendship with Madame de Chevreuse. The two women caused him more anxiety than the Spanish wars, the strained relations with England, and the country's financial difficulties combined. The King was convinced that Madame de Chevreuse helped the Queen not only in her political intrigues but, what was far more galling to him, in her love-affairs.

When the Cardinal told the King that Madame de Chevreuse, whom everyone supposed was living in permanent exile in Tours, had in fact spent five days in Paris and had managed to keep her whereabouts secret from his police, His Majesty flew into a violent rage. Louis XIII was a man of moods and fickle in his loves, and yet he liked to be known as Louis the Just and Louis the Virtuous. Posterity will find it hard to apply these epithets to him, for posterity judges by facts and not by pretensions.

Having thus successfully kindled the King's wrath the Cardinal kept the flame alight by recounting in detail Madame de Chevreuse's subsequent activities in the capital. He described how she had got in touch with the Queen through her secret agents, how he, the Cardinal, had been on the point of unravelling the more obscure threads of the plot and of arresting the little seamstress, the Queen's intermediary with Madame de Chevreuse, with all the proofs of her guilt on her, when an obscure musketeer had interfered with the course of the law by making an armed assault on four police officers who were carrying out their duty of examining criminal witnesses and collecting evidence of the plot for His Majesty's personal perusal. When the King heard this his anger knew no bounds. He got up and strode across the room to the door which led to the Queen's apartments, meaning to go straight to Her Majesty and accuse her to her face of intriguing against him and of being privy to a plot which defied his authority.

But at that moment Monsieur de Tréville came in. His mood contrasted strangely with the King's mood, for he was calm and perfectly controlled. Seeing the Cardinal there and observing the King's agitation he realized at once what had happened and felt as strong as Samson going out to meet the Philistines.

Louis XIII was just turning the handle of the door which led to the Queen's apartments when he heard Monsieur de Tréville enter and looked round.

'So it's you, Sir, is it?' said the King, his voice trembling with rage. 'You've come to see me! Yes. And high time too! What about these damned musketeers of yours now? I've been hearing some fine stories, I can tell you. Monstrous behaviour! Kindly explain at once!'

There was no beating about the bush this time, for when the King was really roused he always gave vent to his feelings.

Monsieur de Tréville replied coldly:

'And I, Sir, have been hearing some fine stories about your police force, for which I'd also like an explanation from the proper quarter.'

'I beg your pardon, Sir?' said the King haughtily.

'I have the honour to inform Your Majesty,' continued Monsieur de Tréville in the same tone, 'that a party of State police and detectives, admirable men, no doubt, but with a strong personal prejudice against soldiers, took it into their heads to break into a house, arrest one of my musketeers, drag him through the streets and throw him into the For-l'Evêque dungeon, on an order which they refused to show even to me, his Commanding Officer. This musketeer is, I may say, a man of the highest character, with a most distinguished record, and is known personally to Your Majesty. His name's Athos.'

'Athos,' repeated the King absent-mindedly. 'Yes, I certainly recall the name.'

'Let me remind Your Majesty that Athos was one of those involved in that unfortunate brawl the other day, and that he was unlucky enough to wound Monsieur de Cahusac rather severely. By the way, Monseigneur,' continued de Tréville turning to the Cardinal, 'I was most relieved to hear that Monsieur de Cahusac had completely recovered.'

'Thank you,' replied the Cardinal, biting his lip to control his annoyance.

'To continue my story,' went on de Tréville, 'Monsieur Athos had gone to call on one of his friends, a young recruit from Béarn in de Essarts' company of Your Majesty's Guards, and finding him out had sat down in his room to wait for him. He had only been there a few seconds when a mixed party of police and detectives laid siege to the house, forced several doors . . .'

Here the Cardinal made a sign to the King to show that this was part of the investigation to which he had previously referred.

'We know all about that,' said the King. 'Those gentlemen were acting in my interests.'

'So I'm to believe, Sir,' retorted de Tréville, 'that it was in your interests that they arrested one of my musketeers on no charge at all, put him in the hands of two guards like a common thief and paraded him up and down the streets in front of a yelling mob, a gallant soldier who's shed his blood in Your Majesty's service ten times and more and has no thought but to serve his King.'

'H'm!' said the monarch, slightly shaken by this. 'Did all that really happen?'

Here the Cardinal broke in:

'Monsieur de Tréville doesn't mention the fact that his innocent musketeer, his gallant subordinate, had an hour previous to his arrest attacked and wounded four police officers who were carrying out an important secret inquiry by my special order.'

'I defy Your Eminence to prove that,' cried de Tréville sharply. His bluff address, typical of a soldier, was in striking contrast to the Cardinal's studied suavity. 'I'd like to point out that one hour previous to his arrest Monsieur Athos, who, let me assure Your Majesty, is as fine a fellow as you could meet, was honouring me with his company in my house. He had previously dined with me and stayed on afterwards to talk to Monsieur de la Trémouille and Monsieur de Chalus, who were my other guests that night.'

The King glanced quickly at the Cardinal as though asking for support.

'An official report's proof positive in law,' said the Cardinal in answer to the King's mute appeal. 'The injured parties have drawn up their report – here it is, Sir.'

'I should have thought a soldier's word of honour counted above a mere police report,' said de Tréville haughtily.

'All right, Tréville, that'll do, that'll do,' said the King irritably.

'If His Eminence suspects one of my musketeers of some crime I suggest that a public inquiry be made. I know His Eminence won't refuse this, for I'm sure he's as anxious as anyone to see justice done.'

The Cardinal ignored de Tréville's remark and continued calmly:

'I believe I'm right in saying that two of the rooms of the house where the police raid took place are occupied by a young man from Béarn, a friend of your musketeers.'

'Your Eminence means Monsieur d'Artagnan, I suppose.'

'I mean a young man who's a protégé of yours, Monsieur de Tréville.'

'Yes, Your Eminence, that's the man.'

'Don't you think it possible that this young man might have made some wild suggestion to . . .'

'To Monsieur Athos? A man almost twice his age?' broke in de Tréville. 'No, Monseigneur, I do not. Besides Monsieur d'Artagnan spent that evening at my house.'

'Really, Monsieur de Tréville,' said the Cardinal. 'To hear you talk one would think the whole of Paris spent that night at your house.'

'Your Eminence is not questioning my word by any chance?' cried de Tréville, flushing angrily.

'God forbid,' said the Cardinal. 'But may I ask you exactly what time Monsieur d'Artagnan was in your house?'

'Yes, I can tell you that to a minute, Cardinal. Just as he came in I happened to look at the clock – it was half-past nine, and I remember being surprised as I thought it was later.'

'And what time did he leave your house?'

'At half-past ten, an hour after the assault on the police.'

The Cardinal could not doubt Monsieur de Tréville's honesty, and he now began to feel that he was losing ground.

'How d'you explain the fact that Monsieur Athos was found and arrested in that house in the Rue des Fossoyeurs?' he asked.

'Surely there's no law forbidding friends to call on each other, or musketeers to associate with men of Monsieur des Essarts' company!'

'Yes, if the house where they meet's being watched by the police.'

'That house *was* being watched, Tréville,' said the King. 'Perhaps you didn't know that?'

'As a matter of fact I didn't, Sir,' answered de Tréville. 'And I don't know which part of the house is being watched, but I'm sure it's not the part where young d'Artagnan lives. For I assure you, Sir, as he's told me himself, he's a loyal and devoted servant to Your Majesty and a staunch supporter of His Eminence.'

'Wasn't it d'Artagnan who wounded Jussac in that unfortunate affray near the Carmelite Convent the other day?' asked the King.

As he spoke he cast a sly look at the Cardinal, who flushed an angry red.

'Yes, Sir. And on the following day Bernajoux. That's the fellow. Your Majesty has a good memory.'

'Well, and what are we to conclude from all this?' asked the King.

'It's for Your Majesty to decide, not me,' said the Cardinal. 'I myself would be prepared to swear to the guilt of the accused.'

'And I deny it absolutely,' cried de Tréville. 'But you have your judges and your Courts of Law, Sir, and the matter had better be referred to them.'

'I agree, I agree,' said the King. 'We'll leave it for the law to decide.'

'And yet it's sad to think that in this year of grace no man, however virtuous, should be safe from arrest and persecution,' said de Tréville. 'And speaking as a soldier, I can assure you that the army will feel insulted to a man that one of its members should have been forcibly detained by the police on a false charge, and cross-examined about some sordid political crime of which he knew nothing.'

This was a very challenging remark and Monsieur de Tréville made it with the deliberate intention of provoking the Cardinal. He wanted an explosion, because explosions cause fire, and fires light up the surrounding landscape.

'Political crime?' echoed the King. 'What do you know about political crimes, may I ask? Confine your attentions to your musketeers and don't meddle in what doesn't concern you. To hear you talk one would think that to arrest one of your musketeers was to lay the country open to a threat of immediate invasion. All this fuss about one miserable musketeer! By God, I'll have ten of them arrested at once, a hundred of them, the whole damned company if it comes to that, and let one soul in France dare question my action!'

'Musketeers are guilty from the moment they're suspect in the King's eyes,' said de Tréville. 'So now I'm going to ask you, Sir, to kindly accept my resignation. It's better so. The Cardinal has accused my soldiers of criminal activities, and I don't doubt he'll end by accusing me too. So I prefer to forestall events and go to prison now, when I'm certain of having the company of Athos, who's there already, and probably of d'Artagnan too, for he's bound to be charged within a day or so.'

'Shut up, you pig-headed Gascon!' thundered the King.

At this de Tréville changed his tone. The expression on his face was stern and his voice hard and cold as he said:

'Sir, I must beg you to command either that my musketeer be returned to me at once or that he be fairly tried in a Court of Law.'

'He will be tried,' said the Cardinal.

'So much the better, for in that case I'll ask Your Majesty's permission to plead for him myself.'

The King was afraid that the interview might end in a

quarrel between the two men. In an attempt to smooth matters down he now said:

'If His Eminence hadn't reasons of his own for wanting . . .'

The Cardinal saw what was coming and quickly interrupted:

'Excuse me, Sir, but if I thought you considered me in any way prejudiced in this matter I'd withdraw my indictment at once.'

'Listen, Tréville,' said the King. 'Do you swear on the memory of my father that young Athos was in your house while the assault was going on and that he took no part in it?'

'I swear it by your father, Sir, and by you, who are what I love and respect most in the world.'

Here the Cardinal broke in:

'Remember, Sir, if you let the prisoner go without a cross-examination we shall never discover the truth.'

'Athos will always be at hand,' said de Tréville. 'I guarantee that. He won't desert, and he can be summoned at any time to answer questions.'

'No, I'm sure he won't desert,' said the King. 'And as Tréville says, we can get hold of him whenever we want him. Besides,' he added in an aside to the Cardinal, giving him an almost imploring look, 'let's be lenient in this case; it's good policy.'

Louis XIII's idea of good policy made Richelieu smile.

'You've only to say the word for the prisoner's release, Sir,' he replied. 'You have the right of pardon.'

'The right of pardon's only used when the party concerned's guilty,' put in de Tréville, who was determined to make his point clear. 'My musketeer's innocent, Sir, so if you release him you'll only be enforcing the law. You won't be exercising your special right.'

'And he's in the For-l'Evêque prison, you say?'

'Yes, Sir, in solitary confinement in a cell, like a common criminal.'

'Oh damnation take it!' muttered the King. 'What am I to do?'

'Sign the order for the prisoner's release, Sir,' said the

Cardinal. 'I think it'll be better that way. Like you I consider Monsieur de Tréville's guarantee a sufficient safeguard.'

De Tréville acknowledged the compliment with a bow. He was delighted at his success and a little frightened too. Why had the Cardinal suddenly decided to climb down? He would have been happier if his enemy had shown more stubbornness.

The King signed an order of release and handed it to Tréville. As the captain was leaving the room the Cardinal smiled and waved to him in a most friendly manner. Then he turned to the King and said in Tréville's hearing:

'It's pleasant to see how good a relationship exists between officers and men in your company of musketeers, Sir. It's an example to the army as a whole and does credit to everyone concerned.'

'He'll have his knife into me from now on,' thought de Tréville as he left the palace. 'It's impossible to have the last word with a man like that. But I must hurry now. The King may change his mind at any moment and at least I've achieved something. It's more difficult to get a man back into prison once he's escaped than to keep him there when you've got him.'

So Monsieur de Tréville called immediately at the For-l'Evêque prison and carried off Athos in triumph. He then went home and sent for d'Artagnan.

'You only escaped by the skin of your teeth, my lad,' he said. 'This is what you get for wounding Jussac. You're still one up on the score of Bernajoux, certainly, but you may soon expect to see that little account settled as well.'

Monsieur de Tréville was perfectly justified in his mistrust of the Cardinal and quite correct in supposing that there was further trouble brewing in that quarter. For hardly had the good captain closed the door of the King's study behind him than His Eminence turned to His Majesty and said:

'And now that we're alone, Sir, let's have done with trivialities and talk seriously. I have to inform Your Majesty that the Duke of Buckingham arrived in Paris five days ago and left again early this morning.'

CHAPTER XVI

In which Séguier, the Keeper of the Seals, looks again for the Chapel Bell which in his youth he rang so furiously

IT is almost impossible to describe the effect produced on Louis XIII by the Cardinal's words. First he flushed scarlet, then he went very pale, and the Cardinal saw at a glance that with one stroke he had regained all the territory he had lost.

'Buckingham in Paris?' cried the King. 'And what was he doing here?'

'Probably plotting with your enemies, the Huguenots and the Spaniards.'

'No. I'll swear he wasn't doing that. He was most likely plotting with Madame de Chevreuse, Madame de Longueville, and the Condés to dishonour me privately.'

'Oh no, Sir! That's a terrible suggestion and quite absurd. The Queen's much too sensible to do anything so rash. Besides, she's devoted to Your Majesty.'

'Women are weak, my dear Cardinal,' said the King. 'And as for her attachment to me, well, I've got my own views as to that.'

'Even so, Sir, I stick to my view that the Duke of Buckingham came to Paris for political reasons,' said the Cardinal.

'And I say he came for personal reasons, Cardinal. And, by God, if the Queen's guilty, she'll be made to pay for it.'

'I hate to let such an idea enter my mind for one moment,' said the Cardinal. 'And yet when you talk like that, Sir, you half persuade me there may be something in what you say. I remember now something Madame de Lannoy said to me when I cross-questioned her as you suggested. She said that last night the Queen had stayed up very late, that this morning she cried a lot, and that she spent the whole of today at her desk writing.'

'That proves it! She was obviously writing to him. Cardinal,

I must get hold of the Queen's correspondence at once.'

'I don't think we can do that, Sir. Neither Your Majesty nor I has the right to examine the Queen's private papers.'

'How was it done in the case of Marshal d'Ancre's wife?' shouted the King, now in a state of uncontrollable rage. 'I'll tell you how it was done; they ransacked her house, searched all her drawers, and in the end searched the lady herself.'

'Marshal d'Ancre's wife was a Florentine adventuress, Sir, whereas Your Majesty's Royal Consort's Anne of Austria, Queen of France, in other words one of the greatest princesses in the world.'

'That only makes her conduct worse, Cardinal. The higher her position the more she should try to be worthy of it. And in any case I've decided once and for all to put a stop to all these petty political intrigues and secret love-affairs. The Queen has a certain de Laporte in her employ . . .'

'Yes, and I must confess I think he's the chief agent in this particular plot,' said the Cardinal.

'So you agree that the Queen's being unfaithful to me?' asked the King.

'I've already told Your Majesty what I think. I think the Queen's plotting against Your Majesty politically but not privately.'

'And I say she's plotting against me in both ways. I say she doesn't love me; she loves that unscrupulous rogue, Buckingham. Why on earth didn't you arrest him while he was in Paris?'

'Arrest the Duke of Buckingham! Charles I's Prime Minister? I couldn't possibly do that! Just think of the scandal! And if your suspicions turned out to be justified, which of course I still don't believe, what a mortifying position you'd be in, Sir!'

'But he was behaving like a common thief, a criminal, so you'd have been perfectly justified in . . .'

The King paused, suddenly afraid to express aloud the thought that had entered his mind. Richelieu raised his eyebrows expectantly, waiting for the King to finish his sentence.

'Perfectly justified in . . .' he prompted.

'Nothing,' said the King, 'nothing. But at least you had him watched all the time he was in Paris?'

'Yes, Sir.'

'Where did he stay?'

'At No. 75, Rue de la Harpe.'

'Where's that?'

'In the Luxembourg district.'

'And you're sure the Queen and he didn't meet?'

'I think the Queen's too wise to stoop to such folly.'

'But we know they've been corresponding; it was to him the Queen was writing when she spent all that time at her desk. Cardinal, I must have the Queen's letters.'

'But, Sir . . .'

'I want those letters, Cardinal. I'll do anything to get hold of them.'

'Be reasonable, Sir . . .'

'Look here, Cardinal, are you plotting against me too? You must be, otherwise why try and thwart me at every turn? Are you too in league with Spain and England, with Madame de Chevreuse and the Queen?'

The Cardinal looked pained.

'I didn't think I'd ever be accused of that, Sir,' he said.

'You heard what I said just now, Cardinal,' said the King. 'I want those letters.'

'I can think of only one way of getting them.'

'What's that?'

'To get Séguier, the Keeper of the Seals, to do it. It's quite within his province.'

'Good. Send for him at once.'

'He should be at my house at this moment, Sir. I asked him to call on me just now, and when I went out I left a message telling him to wait for me.'

'Send for him at once, I say,' shouted the King, banging the table with his fist.

'Very good, Sir. Only . . .'

'Only what?'

'The Queen may refuse to allow it.'

'Refuse to obey my orders?'

'Yes, unless she knows for certain that they are your orders.'

'Well, to make sure there's no mistake I'll go and tell her myself now.'

'I know Your Majesty will agree that I've done all I can to prevent a quarrel between you and Her Majesty?'

'Yes, Cardinal. You're always very lenient to the Queen, if anything too lenient. That, by the way, is a thing we'll have to go into thoroughly some time.'

'Whenever Your Majesty pleases. But please believe that I'd always sacrifice my own interests rather than jeopardize the chances of a permanently good relationship between you and the Queen of France.'

'Well said, my dear Cardinal, well said indeed. But now be good enough to send for the Keeper of the Seals. I'm going in at once to see the Queen.'

Whereupon the King opened the door which led from his study to the Queen's apartments.

The Queen was surrounded by her ladies-in-waiting, Madame de Guitaut, Madame de Sablé, Madame de Mont-bazon, and Madame de Guéménée. The Spanish lady-in-waiting, Doña Estefania, whom the Queen had brought with her from Madrid, was seated in the corner of the room. Madame de Guéménée was reading aloud and all the other ladies were listening attentively, with the exception of the Queen, who had purposely suggested the reading so that she might be free to pursue her own thoughts without appearing noticeably pre-occupied.

The Queen's life was almost perpetually burdened with care and loneliness. Her recent romantic encounter with Bucking-ham had given her temporary joy and solace, but this joy was only a very thin overlay to the habitual, deep-set melancholy of her mind. Indeed she had every cause for melancholy. She no longer enjoyed the King's trust; she was persecuted by the Cardinal who hated her for having once rebuffed his attempt to arouse a warmer emotion in her heart, and she had always before her eyes the example of the Queen Mother, Marie de Medicis, who had had to suffer under that hatred all her life, although, if we are to believe the chroniclers of the age, Marie de Medicis had, during the early part of her reign, granted the Cardinal those favours which her daughter-in-law subsequently refused him. The Queen had seen her most devoted supporters, her most intimate friends, disgraced one by one. She was one of those unhappy souls cursed by Fate, who seem destined to spread misfortune in their path. To win her friendship was always a prelude to disaster; all who found favour with her suffered for it. Madame de Chevreuse and Madame de Vernet had been exiled, and now Laporte openly admitted that he was expecting arrest from one day to another.

The Queen was sunk in melancholy reverie when the door opened and the King appeared.

Madame de Guéménée stopped reading at once. All the ladies got up and a dead silence fell on the company.

The King rudely ignored the ladies, walked straight up to the Queen and said in a voice harsh with anger:

'The Keeper of the Seals will shortly be paying you a visit, Ma'am. I've asked him to do something for me, and I wish you to know he's acting under my orders.'

The unhappy Queen, who was constantly threatened with divorce, exile, and even impeachment, turned pale and said:

'What can the Keeper of the Seals do for you that you couldn't do for yourself, Sir?'

The King turned on his heels without answering and at that very moment Monsieur de Guitant, the Captain of the Guard, came in to announce Monsieur de Séguier's arrival. As he entered the Queen's room the King left by another door.

De séguier came in blushing and with a sheepish smile on his face. We shall probably meet him again in the course of this story, so it is as well to know something about him.

He was an altogether ludicrous figure. Des Roches le Masle, the Canon of Notre Dame, who had formerly been His Eminence's Groom of the Chambers, had mentioned him to the Cardinal as a trustworthy man. The Cardinal had made him

one of his confidential agents, and had never had cause later
to regret his choice.

There are many stories current about his early life. I am
reminded of one in particular:

After a riotous and debauched youth he retired for a while
to a monastery to expiate the sins of his adolescence. Unfortunately he was not quick enough in shutting the monastery
door behind him when he entered, and the passions from
which he was fleeing entered the holy place with him. They
tormented him remorselessly, and the Father Superior, to
whom he had confessed his shame and who wanted to help
him in his struggle against the flesh, advised him, every time he
felt the passion of lust within him, to run to the vestry and ring
the monastery bell hard. The monks would be warned that
their unfortunate brother was at that moment wrestling with
temptation and would congregate and offer up prayers for his
redemption.

The young man agreed to the Father's proposal to call the
monks to his aid to fight the Evil One. But the Evil One had
once occupied Master Séguier in force and regarded him as a
key-position which he would not surrender without a struggle.
The greater the efforts to exorcize him, the more fiercely he
returned to the attack, with the result that the monastery bell
rang out at all hours of the day and night, a witness to the
battle raging between the young penitent's loftier ideals and
his baser passions. The monks had now not a moment's rest.
They could be seen running up and down the stairs which led
to the chapel at all hours of the day; at night they would be
summoned from their beds time and again by the tolling of the
bell and forced to prostrate themselves in prayer on the floor of
their cells.

Nobody knows whether it was the devil who finally yielded
or the monks who succumbed from sheer exhaustion; we only
know that at the end of three months the penitent reappeared
in the world with the reputation of having been the most devil-
ridden man ever received into the monastery.

After leaving the monastery our friend trained as a lawyer.

eventually becoming President of the High Court in succession
to his uncle. He became a Cardinalist, which proved that he
was a shrewd enough fellow, was appointed Keeper of the Seals
and served His Eminence zealously in his campaigns against
the Queen Mother and Anne of Austria successively. He
worked behind the scenes in the Chalais affair, helped on the
reforms of Monsieur de Laffemas, the Grand Verdurer of France
and, in fact, wormed himself thoroughly into the Cardinal's
favour. At the particular period of which we write the Cardinal
relied on him so much that he could think of no better man to
entrust with the most irregular duty of searching the Queen's
private papers.

The Queen was still standing when the Keeper of the Seals
came in, but when she saw him she at once sat down again and
signed to her ladies to do likewise. Then she turned to the
intruder and said very haughtily:

'What's the explanation of this visit, Sir, and why have you
presumed to come into my private apartments?'

'I've come in the King's name, Ma'am, and with all due
respect for Your Majesty, to make a thorough search through
your papers.'

'I beg your pardon, Sir? You've come to search my papers?
How dare you, Sir! That's a downright insult!'

'Forgive me, Ma'am. I'm only acting for the King in this. And
hasn't he prepared you for my visit? Didn't I see His Majesty
leave the room as I came in?'

'Very well, Sir, proceed with your search. It appears I'm a
common criminal now, and am to be treated as such. Doña
Estefania, give this gentleman the keys of my tables and
bureaux.'

The Keeper of the Seals went through all the bureaux as a
matter of form, although he knew only too well that the important letter of which he was in search would not have been
put away in an odd drawer.

Having completed his search of the room and found nothing,
Séguier now had to bring his mission to its logical end, in other
words, to search the Queen herself. This would have been an

embarrassing task for any man, and was ten times more so for a man as susceptible as Séguier. So he approached Her Majesty with mincing steps, and in a shamefaced, hesitant manner said:

'And now, Ma'am, I still have my principal task to perform. You'll remember I was told to make a thorough search.'

'What do you mean, Sir?' asked the Queen.

Séguier did not know whether she was pretending not to understand or whether he had not made his intention clear.

'His Majesty's convinced you wrote a letter yesterday, and he knows it hasn't yet been given to the courier. That letter's not in any of your tables and yet it must be somewhere in this room.'

'Would you presume to touch your Queen, Sir?' asked Anne of Austria, drawing herself up to her full height and staring at the Keeper of the Seals, her eyes ablaze with hatred.

'I'm a loyal subject of the King, Ma'am, and everything he tells me to do, I do.'

'Very well, I admit it,' said the Queen. 'I see the Cardinal's spies have served him well. I did write a letter today and I've still got it. It's here!'

And the Queen laid her lovely hand on her breast.

'In that case please give it to me, Ma'am,' said Séguier.

'I shall give it to no one but the King,' answered Anne.

'If the King had wanted you to give it to him, Ma'am, he'd have asked you for it himself,' replied the Keeper of the Seals. 'He said you were to give it to me and if you don't . . .'

'Well?'

'His Majesty told me to take it from you by force.'

'What do you mean?'

'I mean I've got instructions to search Your Majesty herself for that letter.'

'How horrible!' cried the Queen.

'So please don't make things too difficult, Ma'am.'

'You've been ordered to lay hands on the Queen, Sir,' cried Anne. 'But that's outrageous!'

'The King's orders, Ma'am. Forgive me.'

'I won't allow it. I'd sooner die!' cried the Queen, the hot blood of Imperial Spain and Austria mounting to her temples.

Séguier bowed low, but stood his ground. It was obvious he meant to carry out his orders to the letter. And now he advanced slowly towards the Queen, one step, two steps, like an executioner bearing down on the prisoner in the condemned cell.

Tears of rage sprang into the Queen's eyes. She was, as we know, a remarkably beautiful woman, and the Keeper of the Seals had certainly been given an embarrassing task. The King was so jealous of Buckingham that he forgot to be jealous of anyone else. No doubt Séguier was at that moment reaching out in imagination for the rope of the monastery bell to give it a good tug. But it was not there, so instead he put out his hand to claw at that part of the Queen's dress into which she had stuffed the precious letter.

Anne of Austria backed away in horror. Her face was deathly pale and she was trembling so much that she had to rest her left arm against a table to support herself. With her right hand she took the letter out of her dress and handed it to the Keeper of the Seals.

'Here's your letter, Sir!' she cried, her voice harsh with rage. 'Take it and remove your odious presence from my sight.'

Séguier, who was just as overwrought as the Queen, though for a different reason, took the letter, bowed low and retired. As the door closed behind him the Queen collapsed half-fainting into the arms of her ladies.

The Keeper of the Seals went straight to the King with the letter. The King took it with a shaking hand, looked for an address on the envelope, found none, went very white, slowly opened the letter and began to read. When he saw that it was to the King of Spain he gave a deep sigh of relief and read on rapidly.

The letter was entirely concerned with the organization of a large-scale plot against the Cardinal. The Queen proposed that her brother and the Emperor, who were irritated by Richelieu's never-ceasing attempts to humiliate Austria, should threaten joint hostilities against France, and make the Cardinal's dismissal a condition of peace. There was no mention of love in the whole letter.

The King was delighted. He inquired for the Cardinal and when they told him His Eminence was waiting in his study he at once went off and joined him.

'My dear Cardinal,' he said, 'I see you were right all the time, and I was wrong. The plot was entirely political, and there's not one word of love in the whole letter. It's entirely concerned with you. Look, read it.'

The Cardinal took the letter and read it twice through from beginning to end with the closest attention.

'You see, Sir,' he said at last. 'My enemies stop at nothing. They threaten you with a war on two fronts unless you get rid of me. I can only say that if I were in your place I'd agree at once to any demand backed up by such force. And speaking for myself, I'd really be quite happy to retire from public life.'

'My dear Cardinal! What are you saying?'

'These perpetual quarrels and this never-ending work's sapping my strength. I don't think I shall be able to stand the strain of the siege of La Rochelle; you'd much better appoint Monsieur de Condé, Monsieur de Bassompierre, or some other able soldier for that job, not me. I'm a prelate; I should be left to my clerical work and not called away to do other work which I'm unfitted for. You'd be much more popular in the country, Sir, and probably more respected abroad if you got rid of me.'

'All right, Cardinal!' said the King, 'I know how you feel. I promise you all the people mentioned in this letter shall be punished as they deserve. Even the Queen.'

'Not the Queen, Sir! God forbid the Queen should suffer the smallest injury for my sake! Her Majesty's convinced I'm working against her, although as you know I always take her side, even against you. Of course if I thought she was being unfaithful to you privately it would be different, and I should be the first to say she should be punished. Fortunately there's no question of that, and Your Majesty's just had a further proof of her innocence.'

'That's very true, Cardinal,' said the King. 'You were right again this time as usual. But the Queen's transgressed in another way and should be punished for that.'

'You've punished her enough already, Sir, and now she has a right to be angry with you. If she sulks with you now I shall sympathize with her. You've really treated her most unkindly.'

'I shall always treat my enemies like that, Cardinal, and yours, too, for that matter. I don't care how powerful they are or what risk I run in doing so.'

'The Queen's hostile to me, Sir, but not to you. To you she's a devoted, obedient, and loyal wife. So let me beg Your Majesty not to be too harsh with her.'

'Let her come and make it up with me then.'

'No, Sir. Remember you were in the wrong this time, as you suspected her of something she hadn't done. In this case I think you should go and make it up with her.'

'I'd never do that!' cried the King.

'I wish you would, Sir!'

'In any case how can I make it up with her?'

'By doing something you know will please her.'

'What, for instance?'

'Give a ball. You know how the Queen loves dancing. I guarantee she'll forget her grievances very soon if you do that.'

'Cardinal, you know how I hate balls!'

'Then the Queen will be doubly grateful to you, knowing you're making a sacrifice for her sake. Besides it'll be an excuse for her to wear the magnificent diamond tags you gave her for her last birthday. It'll be the first time she's worn them.'

'Very well, Cardinal, we'll see,' said the King.

He was delighted to have discovered the Queen guilty of a crime which he considered of little importance and innocent of a fault which meant a great deal to him, and was quite prepared to patch up their quarrel.

'We'll see,' he repeated. 'But I must say I think you're asking me to be too lenient to Her Majesty.'

'Leave it to your ministers to be harsh, Sir,' said the Cardinal. 'It's a King's privilege to be lenient. You'd do well to use that privilege more freely.'

At that moment the clock struck eleven. The Cardinal got up, and after repeating his request to the King to make peace with the Queen, bowed and begged leave to retire.

After Séguier's visit Anne of Austria had been expecting some stern rebuke from the King. She was not a little surprised, therefore, to find him making overtures of peace to her on the day following the seizure of the letter. She at first refused to respond, for her woman's pride and queenly dignity had been cruelly insulted. But in the end her ladies-in-waiting persuaded her that it would be better policy for her to suppress her resentment and agree to forget the whole matter. Louis took advantage of her change of mood to tell her of his intention to give a ball in the near future.

A ball was such a rare event in the poor Queen's life that when she heard this news the last trace of vexation left her, as the Cardinal had prophesied, and she appeared radiant. She asked what day the ball would be held, and the King replied that that would have to be settled with the Cardinal. And from then on he kept pestering His Eminence to fix a date, and His Eminence kept putting him off with excuses.

Ten days passed in this way.

A week after Séguier's visit to the Queen and the Cardinal's interview with the King His Eminence received a letter with a London postmark on it, which contained these few lines:

I have got them. But I can't leave London as I have no money. Send me five hundred pistoles and I'll be in Paris in four or five days.

On the day on which this letter arrived the King put his usual question to the Cardinal:

'Have you fixed a date for the ball yet?'

Richelieu started to count on his fingers and muttered to himself:

'She says she'll be here four or five days after getting the money. It'll take the messenger four or five days to reach her;

that makes ten days. Allow another two for contrary winds and tides and the dangers of the road; that makes twelve.'

'Well, Cardinal, have you finished your calculations?' asked the King.

'Yes, Sir,' replied His Eminence. 'Today's September 20th. The City Councillors are giving a ball on October 3rd. That'll do admirably. You and Her Majesty can go to their ball and then it won't look as though you were giving way to her.'

He paused. Then he added:

'Oh, and by the way, Sir, don't forget to remind Her Majesty just before the ball that you'd like to see how she looks in the diamond tags you gave her.'

CHAPTER XVII

The Bonacieux at Home

THIS was the second time the Cardinal had mentioned the diamond studs. Louis XIII was struck by this insistence and scented some mystery behind it.

More than once the King had been mortified to discover that the Cardinal, who had an admirable secret service at his disposal, knew more of what was going on in his own household than he did himself. This time he was determined to get even with the Cardinal on this point. He decided to visit the Queen, have a long talk with her and bully her into making some confession. Armed with this he would return to the Cardinal. Richelieu might already know the secret, but even so he would rate his sovereign's intelligence more highly in future.

So he went off at once to talk to the Queen, and as usual began the conversation with threats of new measures to be taken against her intimate circle of friends. Anne of Austria sat with lowered eyes, making no protest, allowing the torrent of the King's abuse to flow on uninterrupted, hoping that he would soon grow tired and stop. This was just what the King did not want. He wished to provoke the Queen into revealing something, for he was convinced that the Cardinal had secret information and was preparing to spring some unpleasant news on him, as he had so often done before. So he went on attacking the Queen and abusing her friends and eventually succeeded in provoking her to speak.

'Sir,' she cried, exasperated by his vague threats, 'why don't you say exactly what's on your mind? What have I done? What crime have I committed? I don't think Your Majesty has a right to insult me like this. After all, that letter of mine was a private letter written to my brother. You took it from me by force — I didn't ask you to read it.'

The King was quite disconcerted by this sudden counter-attack. He could think of nothing to say, so to cover his confusion he mentioned the subject which the Cardinal had told him not to mention till the eve of the ball.

'Ma'am,' he said haughtily, 'there's to be a ball very soon at the City Hall. I wish you to appear in full Court dress in honour of our good City Councillors and also to wear the diamond tags I gave you for your birthday. That's an answer to your question as to what was really on my mind.'

The answer was indeed a shattering one. Anne of Austria imagined that the King knew everything and that the Cardinal had persuaded him to feign ignorance during the past week, in order to lull her into a false sense of security. This was one of his favourite tricks. She went very pale, leant her lovely hand, now waxen-coloured, against a little table to support herself, and stood staring at the King, speechless with terror.

'I hope you heard what I said, Ma'am,' repeated the King.

He stood watching the Queen, thoroughly enjoying her discomfiture, without, of course, guessing the reason for it.

'Yes, Sir, I heard you,' stammered the Queen.

'You'll come to the ball?'

'Yes.'

'Wearing the diamonds?'

'Yes.'

Her Majesty was now so deathly white that she appeared to be about to faint. The King noticed her perturbation and rejoiced at it. There was a streak of cruelty deep down in him, which sometimes came uppermost.

'That's settled then,' he said, 'and that's really all I wanted to say to you.'

'What day's the ball to be held?' asked the Queen.

Her voice was so weak and quavering that the King looked at her sharply. Something warned him that he would be wise not to answer that question.

'Very soon, Ma'am,' he said. 'I can't for the moment remember the date. I shall have to ask the Cardinal.'

'So it's the Cardinal who proposed the ball!' cried the Queen.

'Yes, Ma'am,' answered the King, looking slightly abashed. 'And why not?' he added defiantly.

'Was it the Cardinal who suggested I should wear my diamonds?'

'Ma'am . . .'

'It was the Cardinal! It was the Cardinal!'

'And what if it was? Why shouldn't he suggest it? It's surely no crime to ask you to wear them! Or is it?'

'No, Sir.'

'So you'll come?'

'Yes, Sir.'

'Good,' said the King. 'Remember, I'm relying on you. Don't fail me.'

With these words he turned and left the room. The Queen curtsied to him, less for reasons of etiquette than to hide the fact that her knees were giving way beneath her.

The King went back to his apartments, thoroughly satisfied with the result of the interview.

'I'm lost!' thought the Queen. 'The Cardinal knows everything and he's got the King's ear. The King knows nothing yet, but the Cardinal will tell him sooner or later. Oh God, oh God, I'm lost!'

She knelt down on a cushion on the floor and started to pray, resting her head on her hands.

Her position was indeed terrible. Buckingham had returned

to London, and Madame de Chevreuse was in Tours. She was now more closely spied on than ever, and she sensed vaguely that one of her ladies was betraying her, though she did not know which. Laporte was not allowed to leave the Louvre, and there was not a soul in the world she could trust. An appalling disaster threatened her and she was alone. She felt that her burden was too great to bear and started to weep helplessly.

'Can I do anything for Your Majesty?' said a voice suddenly.

The Queen gave a start of surprise and looked quickly round to see who had spoken. There was no mistaking the expression of the voice; it was gentle, friendly, and reassuring. In the dim light the Queen saw a woman's figure faintly outlined in one of the doors. It was Madame Bonacieux. She had been hanging up her mistress's dresses in a cupboard when the King had walked in. She had not dared cross the room while the King was present, and had in consequence stayed behind and overheard everything.

The Queen did not at first recognize her as Laporte's protégée. She thought she was a stranger and cried out.

'Please don't be frightened, Ma'am,' pleaded the young woman. Tears of sympathy at the Queen's distress stood in her eyes. 'I'm heart and soul for Your Majesty. I shouldn't be speaking to you, Ma'am, for I'm only a working woman. Indeed I wouldn't presume to if I didn't feel certain I could do something for you.'

'Do something for me?' cried the Queen. 'Oh, if I could believe that! I'm surrounded by traitors. How do I know I can trust you?'

'Oh Ma'am,' cried the young woman, falling on her knees. 'I'd die for you!'

There was no mistaking her sincerity.

'The palace is full of traitors, I know,' continued Madame Bonacieux. 'But I swear by the Holy Virgin I'm heart and soul for Your Majesty. Those tags the King was asking about — you've given them to the Duke of Buckingham, haven't you? They were in the little rosewood box he was carrying under his arm when he went out, weren't they, Ma'am?'

When she realized that yet another knew her secret the Queen started to tremble.

'We must get those tags back at all costs,' went on Madame Bonacieux.

'Yes. But how?' asked the Queen in despair.

'We must send someone to the Duke.'

'Yes, but who? Who can I trust?'

'You must trust me, Ma'am. Do me the honour of trusting me. I'll find a messenger.'

'But I shall have to send a letter!'

'Yes, you'll have to do that, Ma'am. Just a line or two in Your Majesty's handwriting, sealed with your own private seal.'

'But if the letter were found it would be the end of me. I should be exiled.'

'Yes, if our enemies got hold of it. But I guarantee to get that letter delivered safe and sound.'

'Oh God in Heaven! So I'll have to entrust my life and my good name to you!'

'Yes, Ma'am. And I'll answer for the safety of both.'

'How in Heaven's name can you do that? Explain your plan, if you have one.'

'My husband was released from gaol about three days ago, and I haven't yet had time to see him. He's a good, honest fellow, very steady and stolid. He'll do anything I ask. He'll set off with the letter directly I tell him. He'll ask no questions and he'll deliver it safe and sound. I guarantee that.'

The Queen seized Madame Bonacieux's hands impulsively and looked searchingly at her as though she wanted to read her very soul. Seeing the expression of sweet sincerity in her eyes, she kissed her tenderly.

'If you do this for me,' she cried, 'you'll save my life and my honour. I shall owe everything to you, everything.'

'Oh Ma'am, don't exaggerate. I shall only be doing you a small service. You still have your good name. You're merely the victim of traitors' plots.'

'Yes, child, that's true,' said the Queen.

'Now give me the letter, Ma'am. We must be quick.'

The Queen hurried to her writing-table and dashed off a few lines. She then sealed the envelope with her own private seal and handed it to Madame Bonacieux.

'There's one important thing we've forgotten,' said the Queen.

'What's that?'

'Money.'

Madame Bonacieux blushed.

'Yes, Ma'am, you're right,' she said. 'And I must confess that my husband . . .'

'Has no money at all. Is that it?'

'Oh yes, he has money. But he's very miserly. That's his great fault. But don't worry, Ma'am. We'll find some way of getting round that.'

'I suppose you realize I've no money either!' said the Queen.

(Anyone who has read Madame de Motteville's memoirs will realize that this astounding statement was literally true.)

'However,' Her Majesty continued, 'I think we can solve that problem.'

So saying she walked across the room, opened her jewel-case and took out a ring.

'Take this ring,' she said. 'They tell me it's very valuable. My brother, the King of Spain, gave it to me, and it's mine to do what I like with. Take it, pawn it and give the money to your husband for his journey.'

'I'll have everything ready within an hour, Ma'am.'

'Can you read the address on the letter, child?' asked the Queen.

She spoke in such low, hushed tones that Madame Bonacieux could barely hear her. 'To His Grace the Duke of Buckingham, London.'

'The letter will be delivered to him personally.'

'Dear, good child!' cried the Queen in an ecstasy of gratitude.

Madame Bonacieux kissed the Queen's hands, hid the letter in her bodice and slipped quietly out of the room.

Ten minutes later she was at home. What she had told the

Queen was true; she had not seen her husband since his release. She knew nothing of his change of heart with regard to the Cardinal, nor that the Comte de Rochefort had paid him two or three visits subsequent to his interview with His Eminence and had managed to convince him that there had been no evil purpose behind the kidnapping of his wife and that it had been purely a precautionary State measure.

Madame Bonacieux found her husband alone, trying to restore order in the house; the wretched man had come home to find all his furniture broken up and his cupboards practically bare, Justice not being one of the three things which the Scriptures record as leaving no trace of their passing. The maid-servant had fled shortly after her master's arrest; she had been so terrified that she had walked all the way from Paris to her native province of Burgundy.

The little draper's first act on his release had been to call at the Louvre and inform his wife of his return. She had sent a message congratulating him on his escape and saying that she would come and see him as soon as her duties allowed her a few hours of freedom.

That time had been long postponed. It was five days before Madame Bonacieux came. In ordinary circumstances Monsieur Bonacieux would have fumed at the delay, but his visit to the Cardinal and the visits he had received from de Rochefort had given him plenty to think about, and, as we know, meditation makes the time pass quickly.

Moreover Bonacieux's meditations were all pleasant. Rochefort had called him his friend, his good friend, and had kept assuring him that the Cardinal thought very highly of him. The little draper already saw himself on the road to fame and fortune.

Madame Bonacieux had also been meditating, but on very different lines to her husband. She was less avaricious and more romantic than he and her thoughts had centred almost entirely on the figure of the dashing young musketeer who had seemed so greatly taken with her. She had been married off to Monsieur Bonacieux at the age of eighteen and since then had seen no one but her husband's friends and associates in trade, who were not the type to stir the senses of a young woman with tastes above her station in life. So she had escaped the more sordid adventures which are usually the lot of women of her temperament tied to husbands they do not love. But in the age of which we write the title of gentleman had a peculiar appeal for women of the wealthier citizen class, and d'Artagnan was a gentleman. Moreover he wore the uniform of a guardsman, the uniform which, next to that of the musketeers, caused the most havoc in the hearts of the fair sex. And as we know he was handsome, young and high-spirited, and a very persuasive lover. So, all things considered, it was not surprising that he should strongly impress a susceptible young woman like Madame Bonacieux, who was suffering from the disillusion of a loveless marriage.

So, preoccupied as each was with his own thoughts, neither husband nor wife was greatly excited at the idea of meeting, although they had been separated for over a week and many startling events had occurred during that time. And yet Monsieur Bonacieux was genuinely pleased to see his wife and came forward to greet her with outstretched arms. She accepted his kiss but did not return it.

'And now let's talk,' she said. 'I've got something very important to say to you.'

'Well, if it comes to that,' replied Monsieur Bonacieux rather nettled, 'I've got something very important to say to you. I want to hear the whole story of your kidnapping.'

'I'm afraid that'll have to wait for the present,' said Madame Bonacieux. 'There's something far more urgent to discuss than that.'

'What, may I ask?' said Monsieur Bonacieux, rather peeved. 'Ah yes,' he continued more complacently; 'I suppose you mean my imprisonment.'

'No. I heard all about that the day it happened. But I knew you were innocent of any crime and that you knew nothing compromising to yourself or to anybody else, so I didn't take your arrest very seriously.'

Bonacieux was hurt by his wife's attitude.

'I don't know why you should take it so calmly,' he said. 'D'you realize I spent a whole day and night in a cell in the Bastille?'

'That's not very long,' replied Madame Bonacieux. 'So let's forget that and get down to the other much more important subject. After all, my chief reason for coming to see you was to discuss that.'

'I should have thought a wife's chief reason for coming to see her husband after a week's separation was to be with him again,' replied Bonacieux, now thoroughly offended.

'Yes, that first and this next.'

'Well, what is it, Madam?'

'Something terribly important, something which may affect our whole future.'

'Our hopes for the future have brightened considerably since I last saw you, Madame Bonacieux,' said the little draper, 'and I shouldn't be surprised if a few months hence we were the envy of all our neighbours.'

'Yes. That is, provided you do exactly as I tell you.'

'As *you* tell *me*?'

'Yes. I've a very difficult and responsible mission for you and the promise of a lot of money if you succeed in it.'

Madame Bonacieux was careful to mention the money because she knew her husband loved money more than life.

But no man living in those days, certainly not a draper, could have half an hour's conversation with Richelieu and not have his head turned. The Bonacieux of a week ago and the Bonacieux of today were two different people.

'A lot of money? H'm!' he replied, pursing his lips contemptuously.

'Yes. A lot of money,' repeated Madame Bonacieux.

'About how much?'

'A thousand pistoles perhaps.'

'And for that I've got to do something very difficult?'

'Yes.'

'Well, what is it?'

'To leave Paris at once with a letter which must be delivered to one particular person and not shown to anyone else.'

'And where am I to go?'

'To London.'

'To London? Are you mad? What would I be doing in London?'

'Nothing for yourself but a great deal for somebody else.'

'Who? I warn you, Madam, I'm not embarking on anything with my eyes shut. I shall want to know not only what risks I have to take, but also for whose sake I shall have to take them.'

'You'll be working for someone very high up, and the person to whom the letter's addressed is also very high up. Your reward'll far exceed your wildest hopes. That's all I can tell you.'

'Intrigues. More intrigues. Nothing but intrigues. No thank you, Madam, I'm not going to be mixed up in anything like that. The Cardinal's given me very sound advice on that point.'

'The Cardinal!' cried Madame Bonacieux. 'You've seen the Cardinal!'

'He sent for me,' replied Monsieur Bonacieux, with a proud smirk on his face.

'And you actually went to see him? Oh, you foolish man, you foolish man!'

'The fact is I had no choice in the matter. I was taken to see him by two guards. I admit that if I'd had the choice at the time I'd have declined the invitation. You see I didn't know His Eminence then.'

'What did he do to you? Manhandle you, browbeat you, or what?'

'Not at all. He shook hands with me and called me his friend, his personal friend. What d'you think of that, Madam? I'm the great Cardinal's personal friend.'

'The *great* Cardinal? H'm!' said Madame Bonacieux doubt-fully.

'You're not disputing his greatness, by any chance?'

'I'm not disputing anything. But I do say that statesmen and politicians are turncoats, and that their favours aren't worth a fig. There are people higher than politicians, people whose power and influence don't depend on the moods of crowds or the success or failure of policies. Those are the people one should cultivate.'

'I'm sorry, Madam. I can recognize no authority but that of the great man I'm privileged to work for.'

'You're working for the Cardinal?'

'Yes, Madam. And I therefore forbid you to enter into plots calculated to undermine the security of the state, and to work for a woman who is herself a foreigner and whose sympathies are with Spain. Fortunately the great Cardinal's there to protect us all. His keen eye sees everything and can read into the souls of men.'

Bonacieux was repeating word for word a phrase which he had heard from the lips of the Comte de Rochefort. But stereotyped as his words might be they had a most upsetting effect on his poor wife, who had counted on her husband's wholehearted support and had won the Queen's confidence by promising to have her letter safely delivered. She now felt completely helpless. However she knew her husband's weak point, his avarice, and still hoped, by trading on that, to use him for her own purposes.

'So you're a Cardinalist, are you, Monsieur Bonacieux?' she cried. 'You work for the man who persecutes your wife and insults your Queen?'

'The individual must always be subservient to the State,' said Monsieur Bonacieux sententiously. 'I work for those who uphold the constitution.'

This was another of Rochefort's sayings which Bonacieux had memorized. He introduced it here with what he considered most telling effect.

'Who are you to talk about the State, Sir?' cried Madame Bonacieux scornfully. 'Remember your position in life. Don't try to be something you're not and meddle in things far above your head.'

'Now, now, Madam, no preaching from you, please,' cried the little draper furiously. 'Wait till you see what I've got in here,' he added, jingling a fat, round purse which was on the table beside him and which obviously contained money.

'Where did you get that?' asked Madame Bonacieux.

'Can't you guess?'

'The Cardinal gave it to you, I suppose.'

'He and my other friend, the Comte de Rochefort.'

'The Comte de Rochefort? But that's the man who kid-napped me!'

'Quite possibly, Madam.'

'And you mean to say you accepted money from that man?'

'Why not? You told me yourself your kidnapping was en-tirely political.'

'Yes, but the idea behind it was to get me to betray my mis-tress, to torture me into revealing secrets which would damage the Queen's reputation and even endanger her life.'

'Let me remind you, Madam, that your Queen, whom you adore so much, is a sly Spaniard, and that whatever the Car-dinal does is right.'

'Sir,' replied Madame Bonacieux, 'I always knew you were a coward, a miser, and a fool, but I didn't realize you were a rogue too.'

Bonacieux had never seen his wife angry before. He flinched and shrank back in face of this sudden outburst.

'Madame Bonacieux, you don't know what you're saying!' he cried appalled.

'I'm saying you're a miserable specimen of a man,' continued Madame Bonacieux, pressing home her advantage. 'You a poli-tician, and a Cardinalist! D'you know what you're doing? You're selling your soul to the devil!'

'Not to the devil! To the Cardinal.'

'What's the difference? None that I can see. Satan and Richelieu are two names for the same thing.'

'Hush, Madam! Someone might hear you!'

'Yes. And if anyone came in I'd have no one to defend me. You're no man – you're just a rat, a sneaking, crawling rat.'

Bonacieux was by now completely cowed.

'Very well, Madam,' he exclaimed. 'Say no more. But at least tell me exactly what you want me to do.'

'I've already told you. You're to set off at once with a letter for London. And consider yourself honoured to have been chosen for such an important errand. If you succeed in it I'm prepared to forgive and forget everything – more than that – I'm prepared even to become attached to you again.'

Bonacieux was a coward and a miser but he loved his wife and was moved by her words. A man of fifty cannot long feel vindictive towards a woman of twenty-three. Madame Bonacieux saw that he was weakening.

'Well, have you decided?' she said, hoping to clinch the matter quickly.

'My dear good wife,' he replied. 'D'you realize what you're asking me to do? London's a long way from Paris, you know, and you're probably sending me on a very dangerous mission.'

'That doesn't matter if you avoid the dangers.'

'Now listen, Madame Bonacieux. I refuse point blank to have anything to do with it. I will not be mixed up in political plots; they terrify me. Remember, I've seen the Bastille. It's horrible! My flesh creeps even to think of it. They told me I was going to be tortured. Have you any idea what the Bastille tortures are like? They stick wooden wedges between your legs and force them apart till your bones crack. No thank you, Madam. Not for me! And now I come to think of it, why shouldn't you go yourself? I believe I've been wrong about you all the time. I think you're really a man in disguise, and a desperate one at that.'

'And you're a woman, a miserable, stupid, useless woman. You're frightened of the journey, are you? Well, here's my ultimatum. If you don't do as you're told and leave at once I'll have you arrested by order of the Queen and sent to the Bastille, your beloved Bastille, where I'm sure you'll be very happy.'

Bonacieux rapidly reviewed the pros and cons of the situation. He put the Queen's anger in the balance against the Cardinal's, and the Cardinal easily tipped the scale. He counter-attacked:

'Very well, Madame Bonacieux,' he said. 'Get me arrested by

the Queen's order and we'll see what His Eminence will have to say.'

Madame Bonacieux now realized that she had gone too far, and deeply regretted having told her husband so much. She stole a quick, horrified glance at him; on his face was an expression of blank, frightened obstinacy; he looked like some stupid, butting animal at bay. The situation had to be saved at all costs.

'Very well,' she said. 'Let's forget it. Perhaps you're right after all. Men are shrewder than women about politics, and you've actually met the Cardinal, which, of course, gives you an added advantage. And yet,' she went on, 'it upsets me to think that my husband, who I thought was fond of me, doesn't care for me enough to indulge my whims.'

'Your whims are a great deal too extravagant, Madame,' replied Bonacieux in triumph. 'It would be madness even to think of indulging them.'

'Very well,' replied his wife with a sigh of resignation. 'We'll say no more about it.'

At that moment Bonacieux suddenly remembered that Rochefort had recommended him to wheedle as much information as possible out of his wife.

'If you'd only tell me what I was supposed to do in London!' he said.

Some instinct now bade Madame Bonacieux beware and not let slip any more secrets.

'There's no point in my telling you now, Sir,' she said. 'The Queen wanted some trinkets which could only be got in London and which she'd have paid very handsomely for.'

But her reticence only increased her husband's suspicions. He felt certain now that his wife was keeping back some important secret. So he decided to call at once on Monsieur de Rochefort and tell him that his wife was on the look-out for a messenger to send to London.

'Will you excuse me if I leave you now, dear Madame Bonacieux,' he said. 'I didn't know you were coming to see me today, so I arranged to visit a friend of mine. I shall only be gone a few minutes and I'll return in time to escort you back to the Louvre. It's already late and you shouldn't go alone.'

'Pray don't trouble, Sir,' replied Madame Bonacieux coldly, 'I can manage quite well on my own. Besides you'd be no protection for me – you're too timid – you need protecting yourself.'

'Just as you please, Madame Bonacieux,' replied the draper. 'Shall I be seeing you again soon?'

'I expect so. Next week I shall probably get some time off, and I'll come back then to help put the house straight.'

'Good. I shall expect you. You're not angry with me?'

'Not in the slightest.'

'Good-bye, then, for the present.'

'Good-bye.'

Bonacieux kissed his wife's hand and hurried out of the room.

Madame Bonacieux waited until she heard the street door close behind her husband and she was alone. Then she burst out:

'Well, that's the last straw! I always knew my husband was a fool, but I never thought he'd sink so low as to become a Cardinalist. And here am I pledged to deliver the Queen's letter to London! Her Majesty trusted me and I've failed her! Oh misery, misery! She'll think I'm one of those horrible spies who infest the palace, that I'm a Cardinal's agent like the rest. Monsieur Bonacieux, I was never very fond of you. Now I positively hate you! I'll make you pay dearly for letting me down like this.'

Suddenly, in the middle of her soliloquy, she heard a rap-tapping on the ceiling above her head. She looked up and heard a man calling to her from the room above; his voice came muffled through the floor-boards.

'Madame Bonacieux!' he called. 'If you'll open your front door and let me in I'll come down to you.'

CHAPTER XVIII

The Lover and the Husband

MADAME BONACIEUX ran to open her front door and found d'Artagnan standing in the street. She quickly let him in and brought him into her sitting-room, closing the door behind him. The young man first made sure that no one was eavesdropping, and then turned to her and said:

'Well, Madame Bonacieux, you seem to have chosen a pretty poor specimen of a man for a husband.'

'Oh, so you overheard our conversation?' replied Madame Bonacieux, looking at d'Artagnan anxiously.

'From beginning to end.'

'How on earth?'

'Just as I overheard your other conversation with the Cardinal's agents. By a little secret method of my own.'

'And what did you make of it?'

'Quite a lot. Firstly that your husband's a fool, which is a good thing. Secondly that you're in trouble yourself, which pleased me, because now I can offer to help you, and Heaven knows I'd go through fire and water for you. Lastly that the Queen wants a brave, intelligent and reliable man to go to London on a mission. I think I can claim to have at least two of those qualities, and here I am at your service.'

Madame Bonacieux did not at first answer, but her heart leapt for joy and a fresh look of hope shone in her eyes. At last she said:

'If I did decide to trust you with this mission what guarantee could you give?'

'My love for you. Come on, tell me what I've got to do!'

'Oh dear, oh dear!' cried the young woman in terrible doubt. 'Ought I to entrust such a secret to you? You're hardly a man yet!'

'I see I shall have to get someone to vouch for me.'

'I confess that would make me feel happier.'

'D'you know Athos?'

'No.'

'Porthos?'

'No.'

'Aramis?'

'No. Who are they?'

'Three King's Musketeers, friends of mine. D'you know Monsieur de Tréville, their Commanding Officer?'

'Oh yes! I know him. Not personally but through hearing the Queen speak very highly of him.'

'You don't suspect him of being secretly in league with the Cardinal?'

'Of course not.'

'Very well. Go and tell him your secret, however deadly it is, and ask him if it's safe for you to entrust it to me!'

'But it's not my secret. I can't give it away to a stranger like that.'

'You hadn't any qualms about giving it away to Monsieur Bonacieux,' d'Artagnan reminded her. 'You were quite prepared to give him the letter.'

'In his case it was different. He's so stupid. It was like putting the letter in a hole in a tree, or tying it to a pigeon's wing, or a dog's collar.'

'And in my case it's different too, because I love you.'

'So you say.'

'Besides, I'm a man of my word.'

'Yes. I think you probably are.'

'And I'm brave!'

'Yes, that I'm sure of.'

'Well, then, put me to the test.'

Madame Bonacieux still wavered. She gave the young man a long, searching look as though to read into his soul. He looked so frank and eager and there was such a pleading note in his voice that she felt irresistibly drawn towards trusting him. Moreover she was in a situation in which half-measures were ruled out. She must dare all to win all. The Queen's interests would be jeopardized as much by over-suspiciousness as by over-credulity. But, truth to tell, what weighed with her most in her present state of doubt were her personal feelings for the young man, which were instinctive. On a sudden impulse she decided to speak.

'Listen,' she said, 'I'm going to take you at your word, and tell you everything. But I swear before God, who is our witness, that if you play me false and my enemies spare my life I shall kill myself and my blood'll be on your head.'

D'Artagnan replied:

'And I swear before God that if I'm captured on this mission I'll die rather than say anything which could compromise anyone.'

Now Madame Bonacieux told the young man her deadly secret, the first part of which he already knew through his chance encounter with the Duke of Buckingham and his guide on the Pont-Neuf. Then she handed him the Queen's letter. The fact of their sharing this secret and that she had entrusted the all-important letter to his care was their mutual declaration of love.

D'Artagnan's pride and joy knew no bounds. The precious secret and letter were now his and the woman he loved trusted and loved him. He had a sense of double possession which uplifted him and gave him the strength of ten.

'I'll leave now,' he cried. 'This very moment!'

'But what about your regiment?' asked Madame Bonacieux. 'Won't you have to report to your Commanding Officer?'

'Good Lord, I'd forgotten all about that! Yes, I shall have to get leave.'

'Oh dear, that means more delay,' said Madame Bonacieux unhappily.

'Don't worry,' replied d'Artagnan. 'I think I know how to get round that.'

'How?'

'I'll call on Monsieur de Tréville this evening and ask him to put in a word for me with Monsieur des Essarts, his brother-in-law.'

'And there's another thing,' said the young woman.

'What?' asked d'Artagnan, seeing her hesitate.

'I was wondering if you had any money.'

'What do *you* think?' replied d'Artagnan with a smile.

'Come over here then,' said Madame Bonacieux.

She walked up to a cupboard, opened it and took from a shelf the purse of silver which her husband had been caressing so fondly half an hour before.

'Take this,' she said, handing it to the young man.

D'Artagnan, as we know, had had his ear pressed to the floor of the room above during the interview between the draper and his wife, and had overheard everything. So he realized at once what this purse was.

'The Cardinal's present to your husband!' he cried.

'Yes, the Cardinal's present. Feel it, it's pretty heavy.'

D'Artagnan burst out laughing.

'So I'm to save the Queen with the Cardinal's money!' he cried. 'That's magnificent! That'll make my mission doubly enjoyable.'

'Oh, you're kind!' cried Madame Bonacieux. 'You can be sure the Queen won't forget what you're doing for her.'

'If you mean she'll reward me, I say I've already had my reward. I love you and you've allowed me to tell you so. That's more than I ever dared hope for.'

Madame Bonacieux gave a sudden start.

'Hush!' she whispered.

'What is it?'

'I heard voices in the street. Listen! That's my husband. Don't you hear?'

'Yes. I recognize his voice,' whispered the young man.

Upon which he ran to the door and bolted it.

'He mustn't come in till I've gone,' he said. 'When I've gone go down and open the door for him.'

'But I don't want him to find me here either. And what about the purse? How shall I explain its disappearance?'

'I hadn't thought of that. You're right, we must both get out and be quick about it.'

'How can we? He'll see us.'

'Well, then, you must come up to my room.'

'Oh dear,' cried Madame Bonacieux. 'I'm so frightened!'

As she spoke her eyes filled with tears. D'Artagnan noticed her tears and was moved. He knelt in front of her.

'Dearest Madame Bonacieux, I promise you you'll be quite safe with me,' he cried.

'Very well, Monsieur d'Artagnan, I trust you,' she replied. 'Let's go.'

D'Artagnan very quietly drew back the bolt of the door and the two glided out of the room like shadows, down into the hall and up the stairs which led to d'Artagnan's room. The young man barricaded the door with sofas and chairs, and the two crept to the window and peered out into the street through a chink in the shutter. Immediately below them they saw Monsieur Bonacieux talking to a man wrapped in a heavy cloak.

When d'Artagnan saw the man in the cloak he gave a start, half drew his sword, and rushed to the door. It was the man from Meung.

'What on earth are you doing?' cried Madame Bonacieux. 'Have you gone mad? D'you want to ruin us all?'

'I've sworn to kill that man! Don't you understand?'

'Your life's no longer yours to risk as you like,' cried she. 'You're pledged to someone else now and you should only think of your mission. In the Queen's name I order you not to leave this room.'

'Any orders in your own name?'

'In my own name I order you not to risk your life unnecessarily. But listen,' she added, lowering her voice. 'I think I heard them say something about me just then.'

D'Artagnan went back to the window and listened. Monsieur Bonacieux had meanwhile gone into the sitting-room, and, finding it empty, had rejoined his companion in the street.

'She's not there,' he was saying. 'She's obviously gone back to the Louvre.'

'You're sure you didn't make her suspicious by leaving her so suddenly?'

'Quite sure,' replied Monsieur Bonacieux, complacently. 'She's too stupid to notice a thing like that.'

'Is the young guardsman at home?'

'I don't think so. Look! His shutters are closed and there's no light shining through the chinks.'

'All the same we'd better make sure.'

'How?'

'By going and knocking on his door.'

'I'll ask his servant.'

'Yes. Do that, please.'

Bonacieux went back into the house, this time through the side door in the alley. He walked up the stairs which led to d'Artagnan's landing and knocked on his door.

There was no reply. Porthos happened that day to have arranged a tryst with a lady of rank and had borrowed Planchet for the evening to make an impression. And, needless to say, d'Artagnan and his companion did not respond to the gentle rap-tapping of Monsieur Bonacieux's knuckles on the door. They stood motionless like two statues, waiting in agonized suspense for what seemed hours, until at last they heard his footsteps retreating down the passage.

The little draper went out again into the street.

'There's no one there,' he said.

'Never mind,' said the man in the cloak. 'We'd better go into your sitting-room in any case. We're less likely to be overheard in there than out here in the street.'

'What a nuisance!' whispered Madame Bonacieux. 'Now we shall miss the rest of the conversation.'

'On the contrary,' replied d'Artagnan, 'we shall hear even better now.'

He proceeded to take up four or five already loosened flagstones from the floor of the room, thus converting it into a second Dennis's ear. He then spread a mat on the floor, knelt down on it and leaned over the hole, signing to Madame Bonacieux to do the same.

'You're sure there's no one in the house?' said the stranger.

'Positive,' replied Monsieur Bonacieux.

'And you think your wife . . .'

'Has gone back to the Louvre.'

'You're certain she talked to no one but you?'

'Quite.'

'That's a very important point, as I hope you realize.'

'So the information I brought was really of some value?'

'Of great value, Monsieur Bonacieux. I can promise you that.'

'So the Cardinal will be pleased with me?'

'He's bound to be.'

'Long live His Eminence!'

'You're sure your wife didn't mention anybody by name when you were talking?'

'No.'

'Not Madame de Chevreuse, the Duke of Buckingham, or Madame de Vernet?'

'No. All she said was that she wanted to send me on a mission to London on behalf of someone very high up.'

'Vile beast!' hissed Madame Bonacieux from her vantage-post in the room above.

'Hush!' said d'Artagnan. He took her hand and she allowed him to hold it.

'Never mind,' went on the stranger. 'But you were foolish to let such a chance slip. You should have agreed to go; she'd have then given you the letter and you could have given it to us. You'd have helped to defeat a dangerous plot, and you yourself would have . . .'

'What?'

'Well, you'd have benefited considerably. The Cardinal was prepared to honour your name.'

'Did he tell you that?'

'Yes. He wanted to give you a token of his esteem.'

'Don't worry,' replied Bonacieux. 'My wife thinks the world of me, and it's not too late to put things right.'

'Silly old fool!' hissed Madame Bonacieux.

'Hush!' said d'Artagnan again, squeezing her hand hard.

'How do you mean?' asked the man in the cloak.

'I'll go at once to the Louvre, ask for Madame Bonacieux, tell her that after thinking things over I've decided to go, get her to give me the letter and take it straight to the Cardinal.'

'Good. Hurry and do that. I'll go now and return in an hour or so to find out how you got on.'

With these words the stranger turned and left the room.

'Vile, vile beast!' hissed Madame Bonacieux, for the third time. She was by now in a thorough passion against her husband.

'Hush, my dear, hush!' said d'Artagnan for the third time, giving her hand an even harder squeeze.

Suddenly a series of horrible howls rent the air. D'Artagnan and Madame Bonacieux were quite startled at first. Then they realized what had happened. Monsieur Bonacieux had gone to the cupboard, missed the purse of silver and was now trying to waken the neighbourhood to stop the thief.

'Gracious Heavens!' cried Madame Bonacieux. 'He'll set all the neighbours on our trail!'

Bonacieux kept up his howling for quite a time. But the inhabitants of that particular district of Paris were so accustomed to hearing cries of distress that they paid little heed. In despair Bonacieux then went out into the street and ran off, still howling, in the direction of the Rue du Bac, and his wife and d'Artagnan heard his cries gradually growing fainter in the distance.

'Now that he's gone you must hurry and be off yourself,' said Madame Bonacieux. 'I don't need to tell you to be brave, but I'd like to remind you again that your life's no longer yours to risk as you like, now that you've pledged it to the Queen.'

'To the Queen and to you!' cried d'Artagnan. 'But don't worry, I fully realize how serious this thing is. I'll put the Queen's interests first and the memory of you will help me to success.'

Madame Bonacieux made no reply. But she flushed deeply and in so doing betrayed her true feelings for the young knight-errant.

A few minutes later d'Artagnan himself left the house, also

wrapped in a heavy cloak, under which could be seen the stiff, menacing outline of a long rapier. He carried the Queen's letter in the pocket of his doublet.

Madame Bonacieux, standing in the window, gazed long and intently at the young man's retreating figure. Deep down in her heart she knew she loved him. But when he finally disappeared round the corner of the street her thoughts turned elsewhere: she fell on her knees, joined her hands in prayer and cried:

'O God in Heaven, I beseech thee, protect the Queen from her enemies and let no harm come to me.'

CHAPTER XIX

The Plan of Campaign

AFTER leaving Madame Bonacieux, d'Artagnan went at once to call on Monsieur de Tréville. He realized that the stranger in the black cloak, who was apparently the Cardinal's agent, would go straight to His Eminence to report the proposed mission to London, that His Eminence would then take immediate action and that there was therefore not a moment to be lost.

The young man was in the seventh heaven of joy. He had struck lucky at last. A road was open to him which would lead to both fame and fortune; moreover he had been sped on his way by the woman he adored, and this he considered a good omen for the success of the venture. In the space of a few hours Fate had held out to him the promise of a more dazzling future than he had ever contemplated in his wildest dreams.

Monsieur de Tréville was in his drawing-room with several gentlemen of his suite. D'Artagnan was such a regular frequenter of the house that he was admitted into the study without question. A lackey went off to tell his master that the young man wanted to see him urgently.

Our hero had hardly been in the room five minutes when Monsieur de Tréville came in. He took a quick look at the young man, saw his eyes shining with excitement and guessed at once that he had some startling news for him.

On his way to the Rue du Vieux Colombier d'Artagnan had turned over in his mind the question whether to take the captain into his confidence or whether to ask him for carte blanche leave to go on a secret mission. Monsieur de Tréville had always been very good to him; he was staunchly loyal to the King and the Queen, and bitterly hostile to the Cardinal. The young man knew all this very well and finally decided to tell him everything.

'You wished to see me, my lad?' asked de Tréville.

'Yes, Sir,' answered d'Artagnan. 'Please forgive me for disturbing you but it's a matter of vital importance.'

'What is it?'

'It concerns the good name and perhaps the life of Her Majesty the Queen.'

'What?' asked Monsieur de Tréville sharply, darting a quick glance at his guest. He looked round to make sure that they were alone and then again eyed the young man closely.

'I've been entrusted with a deadly secret which . . .'

'Which I hope you'll guard with your life, my lad.'

'Yes, Sir, but which I must be allowed to confide in you, because you're the only person who can help me. Sir, Her Majesty has honoured me by sending me on a mission.'

'Have you the Queen's authority to confide the details of this mission to anyone?'

'No, Sir. I've been told to keep the whole thing dark.'

'Then why were you proposing to tell me about it?'

'Because, Sir, as I said before, I can do nothing without your help, and I was afraid you might refuse it if you didn't know why I wanted it.'

'Keep your secret, my lad, and tell me what you want me to do.'

'I want you to ask Monsieur des Essarts to give me a fortnight's leave.'

'Starting from when?'

'From this evening.'

'You want to leave Paris?'

'Yes. On this mission.'

'May I ask where you're going?'

'To London.'

'Do you know anyone who might want to stop you?'

'I think the Cardinal might.'

'Were you proposing to go alone?'

'Yes, Sir.'

'Then you'll get no further than Bondy. That I can promise you.'

'Why not?'

'Because you'll be murdered on the way.'

'Then I shall die doing my duty.'

'Yes, but that won't help the Queen much.'

'No, Sir, you're right.'

'Take my word for it,' went on Tréville, 'in an affair like this you must start four to arrive one.'

'Yes, Sir, I see that. And that's where I'm lucky. I've got Athos, Porthos, and Aramis, and they're game for anything.'

'Are they game for something they know nothing about? You realize you're not entitled to tell your secret to them any more than to me?'

'We've sworn an oath to trust each other in everything, Sir. Besides they won't worry when they know I've got your backing.'

'The best thing I can do then is to give them all a fortnight's leave. Athos needs a rest as his wound's still troubling him, so he can go and take the waters at Forges, and Porthos and Aramis must go with him, as they can't leave him alone in his present state of health. My leave permits will serve as passports for any town or province you want to visit.'

'That's very good of you, Sir. Thank you a thousand times.'

'Go and collect your friends at once, and leave tonight. Oh, and write out your application to Monsieur des Essarts here. It's quite likely you're already being followed, in which case the Cardinal will soon know about your visit to me. If anyone calls to inquire about it I can show your application for leave.'

D'Artagnan wrote out his application and handed it to de Tréville. The latter promised that all four permits would be sent round to the men's billets before two o'clock in the morning.

'Would you please send mine to Athos' rooms, Sir,' said d'Artagnan. 'If I went home I might find some unpleasant surprise waiting for me.'

'Very well,' said de Tréville. 'And now good-bye, and God be with you. Oh, by the way,' he added, as d'Artagnan turned to leave, 'have you any money?'

D'Artagnan took the Cardinal's purse of silver out of his pocket and jingled it.

'Is there enough in there?' asked de Tréville.

'Three hundred pistoles.'

'Excellent. You could go round the world on that. Good-bye again and good luck!'

So saying Monsieur de Tréville shook d'Artagnan warmly by the hand. D'Artagnan suddenly felt extremely grateful to this man, who had been a tower of strength to him ever since he first entered Paris; he was full of admiration for his upright and generous nature.

The young man called first on Aramis. He had not been near the house in the Rue de Vaugirard since the night of his chance meeting with Madame Bonacieux. Indeed he had only once set eyes on his friend since and had then been struck by the sad look on his face.

That evening Aramis still seemed plunged in gloom. D'Artagnan tried to pierce this reserve, but Aramis explained that he had an abstruse commentary on the eighteenth chapter of St Augustine to translate into Latin, and that the work had exhausted him. D'Artagnan was not convinced by this explanation.

The two friends had been talking for about ten minutes when one of Monsieur de Tréville's personal staff came in with a sealed envelope which he handed to Aramis.

'What's this?' said Aramis.

'The leave you applied for, Sir,' answered the servant.

'I never applied for leave!'

'Take it and say nothing,' whispered d'Artagnan.

Then, turning to the servant, he added:

'Here's a half-crown for your pains. Go back and say Monsieur Aramis thanks Monsieur de Tréville for his kindness. Good-day to you.'

The servant bowed and left the room.

'What's the meaning of this?' asked Aramis.

'Pack up a few things, enough to last you a fortnight, and come along with me.'

'But I can't leave Paris just now without knowing . . .'

Aramis hesitated.

'Without knowing what's happened to her?' prompted d'Artagnan.

'Who?'

'The woman who was here, in this house, the woman with the lace handkerchief.'

'Who told you there'd been a woman here?' asked Aramis, going very white.

'I saw her myself.'

'And you know who she is?'

'I've a pretty shrewd idea.'

'Look here,' said Aramis, 'as you seem to know so much, perhaps you can tell me what's happened to the lady.'

'I imagine she's gone back to Tours.'

'To Tours. Yes. I see you do know who it is. But what made her go back to Tours without letting me know?'

'Her fear of being arrested.'

'Why didn't she write then?'

'She didn't want to incriminate you.'

'Oh, d'Artagnan, you've made me happy again!' cried Aramis. 'And I was thinking all the time she'd lost interest in me and grown fond of someone else. And it had been so glorious seeing her again! I couldn't somehow believe she'd risked imprisonment merely to see me, and yet I couldn't think what other motive she could have for returning to Paris.'

'Her motive was the very motive which is driving us to England today.'

'And what's that?'

'You'll know one day, Aramis. At present I'm going to be as discreet as you were when you told us your story about the theologian's niece.'

Aramis smiled at the recollection of that evening.

'Very well, d'Artagnan. If you're certain the lady really has left Paris there's nothing to hold me here any longer, and I'll gladly go with you. Where did you say we were going?'

'First to call on Athos. And if you're really coming you must be quick; we've already wasted a lot of precious time. Oh, and by the way, let Bazin know.'

'Is Bazin coming with us?' asked Aramis.

'I'm not sure yet. But in any case I'd like him to come with us as far as the Rue Férou.'

Aramis called Bazin and told him to follow them to Athos' house. Then he collected his cloak, his sword, and his three pistols, rummaged about in all the drawers in all the tables in his room in the faint hope of finding a stray crown or half-crown and finally followed d'Artagnan downstairs. He kept racking his brains to think how a callow young ensign in the guards could have discovered the identity of the lady who had been his guest, and be better informed about her movements than himself.

Just as he and d'Artagnan were leaving the house he put his hand on his young friend's shoulder, looked searchingly at him and said:

'You haven't mentioned this lady's name to anyone?'

'Not to a soul.'

'Not even to Athos and Porthos!'

'No.'

'Thank God for that.'

His mind at rest on this important point Aramis walked on with d'Artagnan and the two were soon at Athos' door. They went into his room and found him holding his leave permit in one hand and Monsieur de Tréville's letter in the other. He looked bewildered.

'Can either of you explain the meaning of this?' he asked his two friends. He then read out as follows:

My dear Athos,

Since your health is still so bad I would like you to take a fort-night's leave. So go and take the waters at Forges, or somewhere else if you prefer, and get well as soon as possible.

Yours always sincerely,

Tréville.

'That letter and the permit mean you've to come with me on a jaunt, Athos,' explained d'Artagnan.

'To take the waters at Forges?'

'There or elsewhere.'

'Under orders from the King?'

'The King or the Queen. We serve both Their Majesties, don't we?'

At that moment Porthos came in.

'Listen, all of you,' he cried. 'Here's a problem! Since when have musketeers been issued with leave permits without their applying for them?'

'Since their friends began applying for them on their behalf,' answered d'Artagnan.

'Ho, ho!' said Porthos. 'I see there's something going on here. You all look thoroughly conspiratorial.'

'Yes, we're all going on a little trip – and you're coming with us,' said Aramis.

'Where?'

'Frankly I don't know,' replied Aramis. 'Ask d'Artagnan.'

'We're going to London, gentlemen,' said d'Artagnan.

'To London?' cried Porthos. 'And what might we be doing in London?'

'That's just what I can't tell you. I'm sorry. You've got to come as it were blindfolded under my aegis, and take my word for it everything's in order.'

'But you've got to have money to get to London,' said Porthos, 'and I'm broke.'

'So am I,' said Aramis.

'And I,' said Athos.

'I've got money,' said d'Artagnan.

And he pulled the purse of silver out of his pocket and laid it on the table.

'This purse contains three hundred pistoles,' he said. 'I suggest we each taken seventy-five. One can get to London and back on that. Besides it's very unlikely we shall all get to London.'

'Why?'

'Because one or two of us are pretty well bound to fall out on the march.'

'Good Lord! Are we forming the vanguard of an advancing army?'

'No. We're off on a little campaign of our own, and a dangerous one at that.'

'If we're going to have to fight I think we ought at least to be allowed to know what we're fighting about,' said Porthos.

'I don't see that that would help much,' said Athos.

'All the same I agree with Porthos. I think we ought to be told,' said Aramis.

'Have you ever known or expected the King to give reasons for his orders?' said d'Artagnan. 'Of course not. He merely says "Gentlemen, I'm starting a campaign in Spain, Flanders, or wherever, and I want you to take part in it." And what do you do? D'you ask why? No. You just go.'

'D'Artagnan's right,' said Athos. 'We've got our leave permits from Monsieur de Tréville and three hundred pistoles from God knows where. Now it's up to us to go to whatever front they send us and stop a bullet a-piece for them. After all, our lives aren't as precious as all that. D'Artagnan, you can count on me for one.'

'And me for another,' said Porthos.

'And me,' said Aramis. 'In any case I shall be quite glad to leave Paris. I'm getting bored here.'

'I can promise you you won't be bored where I'm taking you, gentlemen!' cried d'Artagnan. 'Whatever else you may be you won't be bored.'

'When do we start?' asked Athos.

'This very instant,' said d'Artagnan. 'There's no time to be lost.'

'Hi, there, Grimaud, Planchet, Mousqueton, Bazin,' cried the four young men to their lackeys. 'Grease our boots and fetch our horses from the courtyard!'

(The musketeers used to leave their horses and their servants' horses tied up all day in Monsieur de Tréville's courtyard, treating it as a sort of stables.)

Planchet, Grimaud, Mousqueton, and Bazin set off at the double.

'And now let's think out our plan of campaign,' said Porthos. 'Where are we making for first?'

'For Calais,' said d'Artagnan; 'that's the straightest route from here to London.'

'Well, gentlemen, shall I tell you my idea?' asked Porthos.

'Yes,' said the others.

'To my mind four men travelling together would arouse suspicion at once. So let d'Artagnan give us our orders now. I propose that I start off first by the Boulogne road, that Athos leave two hours later by the Amiens road, Aramis two hours after Athos by the Noyon road, and d'Artagnan after Aramis by any road he likes. I suggest that d'Artagnan, being in command, should be disguised in Planchet's clothes, and that Planchet should follow us all dressed in d'Artagnan's uniform.'

'I don't think our servants should be given any responsibility at all,' said Athos. 'State secrets entrusted to gentlemen have been known to go astray accidentally, but if you put servants in a position of trust they nearly always let you down deliberately.'

'I'm afraid Porthos' plan's unfeasible,' said d'Artagnan, 'because I've got no orders for any of you. I'm to deliver a letter, that's all. That letter's sealed, so I can't make three copies of it. We've no choice but to travel together. I've got the letter here, in this pocket,' he said, tapping the pocket of his doublet. 'If I'm killed one of you must take the letter and ride on. If he's killed the man next to him must take the letter, and so on to the end. All that matters is that one of us should reach London with the letter.'

'Good, d'Artagnan,' said Athos. 'That's much the best idea. Besides, we must be consistent. We've got to have our story ready for whoever tries to interfere with us. I'm supposed to be taking the waters at Forges. I've been told I can go elsewhere if I like, so I decided to go to the sea instead. If anyone tries to arrest us I show Monsieur de Tréville's letter and we all show our leave permits. If they try to use force we resist. If they question us we swear black and blue we were merely going to the sea to bathe for our health's sake. One man travelling alone's easily dealt with, but four together stand a better chance. I suggest we arm the servants with pistols and muskets. If we're attacked in force we fight and whoever escapes goes on with the letter as d'Artagnan said.'

'Bravo, Athos,' said Aramis. 'You don't talk much but when you do you talk sense. I agree with Athos' plan. What about you, Porthos?'

'I agree too,' said Porthos, 'if d'Artagnan approves. D'Artagnan's in charge of the letter so naturally what he says goes. Let's hear his final word and abide by that.'

'I suggest that we adopt Athos' plan and leave in half an hour,' said d'Artagnan.

'Agreed,' cried the three musketeers.

Upon which they all set to work to divide up the silver, each taking seventy-five pistoles. They then dispersed to equip themselves for the journey.

CHAPTER XX

The Journey

AT two o'clock in the morning our four adventurers left Paris by the Saint-Denis gate. They rode through the night like shadows, swift and silent. They were all brave men, but the darkness had a sobering effect on their spirits, and they imagined ambushes behind every clump of trees along the road.

When dawn broke their tongues were loosened. The sun brought good cheer. All four felt the elation of soldiers on the eve of an attack. Their hearts raced, the light of battle shone in their eyes, and their love of life was enhanced by the knowledge that they might soon be leaving it.

The little cavalcade had a distinctly warlike appearance. It had 'troop on the march' written all over it. The musketeers' black horses with their glittering harness and their habit of keeping in line, acquired from long training on the barrack square, would alone have betrayed their riders.

The lackeys followed behind their masters, armed to the teeth.

The party arrived safely in Chantilly at eight that morning. Here the four friends decided to breakfast. They dismounted at an inn with a painted sign depicting St Martin sharing his cloak with a beggar. The servants were told not to unsaddle the horses and to be ready to leave again at a moment's notice.

The four men went into the communal dining-room and sat down to have their breakfast. A gentleman who had just arrived by the Dampmartin road was breakfasting at the same table. He bowed to the four friends, made some polite remarks about the weather and then drank to their healths. They responded and the atmosphere seemed friendly enough.

But just as Mousqueton came in to say that the horses were ready and they were all preparing to leave, the stranger turned to Porthos and proposed the health of the Cardinal. Porthos agreed and then in his turn proposed the King's health. The stranger cried out that he knew no king but His Eminence. Porthos called him a drunken sot, at which he at once drew his sword.

'That was a damned silly thing to do,' said Athos. 'However, it can't be helped. You can't back out now. Polish the fellow off quickly and come on after us.'

The three others then mounted again and rode off at the gallop, while Porthos squared up to his enemy and began threatening to carve him in pieces with every thrust known to the duellist.

'There's one of us gone already,' said Athos after they had ridden on a little way.

'Why d'you suppose that fellow fixed on Porthos rather than on any of us three?' asked Aramis.

'Porthos talks so loud he probably thought he was in command of the party,' said d'Artagnan.

'I always said our Gascon was a bright lad,' said Athos.

And the three of them galloped on.

They made a halt of two hours at Beauvais to give the horses a rest and also to wait for Porthos. When the two hours were up and Porthos had not appeared they continued their journey.

A mile or so beyond Beauvais they reached a narrow stretch of road with an embankment on either side. Here they came face to face with a party of eight men who were apparently engaged on some kind of road work. The road was not paved here and the men were digging holes in it and appeared to be trying to make the way passable by clearing away the mud and slush. Aramis noticed the quagmire ahead, feared for his boots and began cursing the men roundly for their clumsy work. Athos tried to restrain him but it was too late. The workmen now hurled insults at the riders and actually succeeded in provoking the imperturbable Athos, who spurred his horse at one of them to get him to stand aside. At this the whole gang retreated into the ditch at the side of the road, reappearing a moment later with eight loaded muskets which they had concealed there and which they now proceeded to discharge point blank at the party of riders. Aramis got a bullet through the shoulder and Mousqueton one through the buttock. Aramis kept his seat on his horse but Mousqueton fell off; his wound was not serious, but being unable to see it, he thought it was worse than it was and fell off from fright rather than pain.

'It's an ambush,' said d'Artagnan. 'Don't fire! Let's get on quick.'

Wounded as he was, Aramis managed to cling on to his horse's mane and to ride on with the others. Mousqueton's horse cantered along behind them riderless.

'We've now got a spare horse to use as a remount,' remarked Athos.

'I'd rather have a spare hat,' said d'Artagnan. 'Those devils shot mine off. Thank God I wasn't carrying the precious letter in it.'

'When poor old Porthos gets there they'll murder him,' said Aramis.

'If Porthos were on his feet he'd have caught us up before now,' said Athos. 'I'm rather afraid that drunkard turned out to be sober enough when it came to fighting.'

The little cavalcade galloped on for another two hours, although by now the horses had been ridden almost to death.

The travellers had struck across country, hoping to avoid any further unpleasant encounters. But when they reached Crèvecœur Aramis declared that he could go no further. In fact only the grim courage which lay behind his rather foppish appearance and affected ways had kept him going until then. He had gone whiter and whiter in the face and the two others had had to support him on his horse. Now they helped him to dismount in front of an inn, left with him Bazin, whom they could well do without in an adventure like this, and rode on, hoping to reach Amiens before nightfall.

The party was now reduced to two masters and two servants, Grimaud and Planchet.

'I won't be had like that again in a hurry,' cried Athos. 'Nothing on God's earth'll make me utter another word or lift a finger between here and Amiens. Damn those swine!'

'Don't let's waste our breath swearing,' answered d'Artagnan. 'Let's just ride on, that is if the horses don't collapse under us.'

The four dug their spurs into their horses' flanks and urged them on. They reached Amiens at midnight and dismounted at the Golden Lily Inn.

The innkeeper looked a thoroughly honest fellow. He received his guests holding a lighted candle in one hand and his nightcap in the other, explaining that he had been roused from sleep by the knocking on the door. He wanted to put the two new arrivals in two charming rooms, one at one end of the inn and the other at the other. This offer they refused. The innkeeper then declared that he had no other rooms worthy of two such grand guests, at which the latter replied that they would sleep in the dining-room on mattresses. The innkeeper tried to dissuade them, but they insisted, so he finally had to yield.

Athos and d'Artagnan arranged their beds on the floor and then proceeded to barricade the dining-room door from the inside. Suddenly they heard the window shutters being violently rattled by someone in the courtyard. They called out to inquire who was there and two familiar voices answered them, the voices of their two servants, Planchet and Grimaud. Athos immediately unfastened the shutters and parleyed with them in the dark.

'Grimaud can perfectly well manage the horses by himself,' said Planchet. 'If you agree, Sir, I'll come and lie down across the door of your room, so that no one can get in during the night without disturbing me. That ought to make things quite safe for you two gentlemen.'

'What do you propose to sleep on?' asked d'Artagnan.

'On this,' said Planchet, holding up a bundle of straw.

'Yes, I think you'd better do that,' said d'Artagnan. 'I don't like our host at all. He's too obsequious for my taste.'

'And for mine!' said Athos.

Planchet climbed in through the window and lay down across the door, while Grimaud went off to spend the night in the stables, promising to come round with the four horses punctually at five o'clock next morning.

The night passed fairly quietly. The only disturbance occurred at two in the morning, when someone tried to open the door. But Planchet woke with a start and cried out. 'Who's there?' At which the intruder mumbled some apology and shuffled off.

At four o'clock they heard a great hullabaloo in the stables. Grimaud had tried to waken the stable boys and they had turned on him and were beating him. Athos and d'Artagnan opened the windows and saw the wretched fellow lying unconscious in the courtyard with head wounds. They had belaboured him out of his senses with the handles of their pitchforks.

Planchet went round to the courtyard and tried to saddle the horses himself. But he found them still quite unfit for work. Only Mousqueton's horse, which had been riderless for the last five or six hours of their journey, was in a fit state to travel, but by some extraordinary accident the veterinary surgeon, who had apparently been summoned to bleed the innkeeper's horse, had bled Mousqueton's horse instead.

Athos and d'Artagnan now began to be alarmed. These disasters following one upon another might have been coincidental, but they might also be the work of some hostile organization. Planchet was sent to inquire from the innkeeper whether there were any horses for sale in the neighbourhood, while his master and Athos went out. At the main door of the inn Planchet noticed two saddled and bridled horses, fresh and obviously ready for the road. They exactly fitted the bill. Planchet inquired about them and was told that they belonged to two gentlemen who had spent the night at the inn and were at that moment settling their account in the host's private room.

Athos now went himself to pay his bill, leaving d'Artagnan and Planchet standing at the main door of the inn. One of the inn servants took Athos down a long passage, at the far end of which was the host's room. Athos entered the room unsuspecting.

He found the innkeeper alone, seated behind his desk, one of the drawers of which was half-open. Athos handed him two crowns in settlement of the account. The host took them and examined them closely, turning them over in his hand and clinking them on a piece of metal on his desk. Suddenly he sprang to his feet, cried out that the money was false and that he would have Athos and his companion arrested as coiners.

'You rogue, you!' cried Athos, advancing on him menacingly. 'Just you try and arrest me! I'll slit your throat for you.'

But the host ducked down, snatched two pistols out of the half-open drawer of his desk, levelled them at Athos and called out for help.

Instantly four men armed to the teeth rushed into the room through two side doors and threw themselves on Athos.

Athos called out at the top of his voice:

'They've got me! Get away quick, d'Artagnan. Ride like the devil!'

And he raised his pistol and fired two shots into the air.

D'Artagnan and Planchet heard his cry and the two shots, and the same idea occurred to them both. They swiftly untethered the two saddled and bridled horses which were standing at the main gate, mounted them, dug their spurs into their flanks and galloped off.

'Did you see what happened to Athos?' d'Artagnan asked Planchet, as they reached the outskirts of the town.

'Well, Sir,' answered Planchet, 'I saw him run two of the blighters through and he seemed to be defending himself very well against the other three, though it was difficult to see through the glass of the door.'

'Good old Athos!' said d'Artagnan. 'It's rotten having to leave him like that. However we've probably got something equally nasty waiting for us ahead. So let's get on, Planchet. You're game enough, I must admit.'

'I told you I could rise to an occasion, Sir,' answered Planchet. 'We Picards are best ridden on a loose rein. Give us our heads and we'll do marvels. Besides. I'm back on my native soil now, and it thrills me.'

The two rode on without slackening speed and reached St Omer in a single stretch. Here they gave their horses a rest, but stayed beside them the whole time for safety's sake, eating a scrap meal standing in the crowded street; after their experience at Amiens they thought it unwise to let the animals out of their sight. They then remounted and continued their journey.

When they were within a hundred yards of the gates of Calais d'Artagnan's horse collapsed and remained lying in the road with blood oozing from its nose and even from its eyes. Noth-

ing d'Artagnan or Planchet could do would get it on its feet
again. Planchet's horse was still on its feet but it, too, refused
to move. The riders had no choice but to leave both horses
on the high road and to run the rest of the way to the harbour.
As they approached Planchet noticed a gentleman and his valet
passing through the harbour gate about fifty yards ahead of
them – apparently also travelling to England – and pointed
them out to his master. The gentleman was evidently in a great
hurry; his boots were covered in dust and he was talking excitedly to the captain of a ship which was about to set sail.
D'Artagnan approached to within a few feet of him and
stood behind him saying nothing, trying to overhear his conversation and also to make it appear that he was travelling with
him.

'I'd have liked to take you across, Sir,' the captain was saying, 'but an order came through this morning forbidding anyone to embark on any ship without a permit from the Cardinal.'

'I've got one,' said the stranger, pulling a paper out of his
pocket. 'Here it is.'

'You must have it stamped and signed by the Governor of
the Port,' said the captain. 'Then I'll take you on board.'

'Where does the Governor live?'

'About a mile outside the town. You can see the house from
here, that tiled roof underneath the hill.'

'Right,' said the stranger, 'I'll go at once.'
And he and his servant started off on foot towards the house.

D'Artagnan and Planchet turned and followed them, keeping
about a hundred yards behind them.

When they reached the outskirts of the town d'Artagnan
quickened his pace and overtook the stranger as he was entering a wood.

'Sir,' he said, 'you seem in a great hurry.'

'I am in a great hurry,' answered the stranger.

'I'm sorry about that, Sir,' went on d'Artagnan, 'because I'm
also in a hurry and I wanted to ask a favour of you.'

'What's that?'

'To allow me to pass ahead of you.'

'Impossible, Sir,' said the stranger. 'I've travelled a hundred and eighty miles in forty-four hours, and I've got to be in London by noon tomorrow.'

'I've covered the same distance in forty hours,' answered d'Artagnan, 'and I've got to be in London by ten tomorrow.'

'I'm sorry. I can't do it,' replied the stranger. 'I arrived in Calais first and I intend to leave first.'

'I regret too, Sir. I know I arrived second but I also intend to leave first.'

'Are you on a mission?'

'No, I'm travelling on my own.'

'Then I see no excuse for your offensiveness,' said the gentleman.

'I've got a very good excuse if you only knew.'

'What's that?'

'I want your travel permit. I haven't got one and I must have one.'

'Are you mad?'

'Not at all. I simply want your travel permit.'

'Let me pass at once!'

'No, Sir,' said d'Artagnan.

And he stood barring the stranger's way.

'In that case, Sir, I shall have to blow your brains out. Hi, there, Lubin, my pistols!'

'Planchet,' said d'Artagnan, 'you deal with the servant and I'll deal with the master.'

Planchet had been encouraged by his first success and now sprang at Lubin and, being young and hefty, bore him down, laid him flat on his back, straddled him and gripped him by the throat. He then called out to d'Artagnan:

'My job's done, Sir. Now do yours.'

When the stranger saw his servant overpowered he drew his sword and bore down on d'Artagnan. But the Gascon proved more than a match for him. In under ten seconds he had given him three thrusts through the body, saying after the first, 'One for Athos', after the second, 'One for Porthos', and after the third, 'One for Aramis'.

The stranger collapsed in a heap on the ground. D'Artagnan, supposing him dead, or at any rate unconscious, came up to him, meaning to take the permit from him. But just as he was putting out his hand to search through his pockets the wounded man, who still had hold of his sword, raised himself on one elbow and stabbed our hero through the chest, crying:

'And one for you!'

'And one more for myself! And a good long one to end with!' cried d'Artagnan in a rage, this time nailing his enemy to the ground with a sword thrust through the belly driven right up to the hilt.

And now the stranger's eyes closed and he lost consciousness.

D'Artagnan searched through his pockets and drew out the travel permit. It was made out in the name of the Comte de Wardes. He then looked down at the young man lying at his feet unconscious, perhaps dead, whom he fully intended to leave to his fate, and began to ponder over the strange destiny which governs men, driving them to kill each other in the service of strangers, who often do not know of their existence.

But he was soon roused from these musings by Lubin, who had recovered from the shock of Planchet's onslaught and was now yelling for help like a maniac.

'As long as I keep my hand round his throat he won't yell,' said Planchet. 'But directly I let go he'll start again. He's a Norman, I can see that from his face. The Normans are stubborn devils.'

He was right. Even with Planchet's fingers squeezing his throat Lubin managed to let out a few howls.

'This ought to fix him,' said d'Artagnan, taking out his handkerchief and gagging him.

'Now let's tie him to a tree,' said Planchet.

This they proceeded to do with great thoroughness. Then they lifted the prostrate Comte de Wardes and laid him down beside his servant. It was now growing dark and the bodies of the two victims were hidden well inside the wood, so it was unlikely that anyone would discover them before morning.

'And now on to the Governor's house!' cried d'Artagnan.

'But you're wounded, Sir.'

'That's nothing. Let's deal with the more urgent things first. My wound can wait. It's only a scratch.'

The two of them started off, half running, half walking, and before long found themselves at the door of the Governor's house. The servant led them up a wide staircase, opened the door of a large sitting-room and announced:

'The Comte de Wardes.'

'You have a signed permit from the Cardinal?' asked the Governor.

'Yes, Sir,' answered d'Artagnan. 'Here it is.'

'Yes. That's valid all right,' said the Governor.

'I know that,' said d'Artagnan. 'You see I'm on fairly close terms with His Eminence.'

'I gather His Eminence is interested in preventing one particular man from reaching England.'

'Yes, a certain d'Artagnan, a Gascon from Béarn, who left Paris with three friends a day or two ago, bound for London.'

'Do you know him personally?' asked the Governor.

'Very well indeed.'

'Then you could help me a lot by describing him to me.'

'I'll do so with pleasure,' replied d'Artagnan.

And he proceeded to give the Governor a detailed description of the Comte de Wardes.

'Has he got anyone with him?"

'Yes, a valet called Lubin.'

'I'll send a report based on your description to the local authorities and if they're lucky enough to catch the fellow I'll see to it that he's sent back to Paris under a strong escort.'

'If you do that the Cardinal will be very pleased with you, Sir.'

'Shall you be seeing His Eminence when you return, Comte?'

'I shall indeed.'

'Will you mention my name to him as one of his most loyal supporters?'

'I won't forget you, Sir. Don't worry."

The Governor was delighted with this promise, and countersigned the travel permit forthwith.

D'Artagnan wasted no time in an exchange of futile compliments. He snatched the permit from the Governor and hurried out of the room. He and Planchet then made their way back by a circuitous route, avoiding the wood and entering the town by a different gate.

The ship was still waiting to start, and the captain was standing on the quay.

'Well,' he said, as d'Artagnan approached.

'Here's my pass counter-signed,' said the young man.

'What about the other gentleman?'

'He's not leaving today after all,' said d'Artagnan. 'But I'll pay the two fares.'

'In that case we'll start right away, Sir,' said the captain.

'Excellent,' said our hero.

And he and Planchet jumped into the rowing-boat. Five minutes later they were on board.

They were only just in time. The ship was about a mile out to sea when d'Artagnan, who was looking back to shore, saw a flash of light and heard the report of a gun. It was the signal for the closing of the harbour.

Now d'Artagnan was at last free to attend to his wound; the point of his enemy's sword had struck a rib which had deflected its course, and his shirt had adhered to the open sore and acted as a dressing, so he had lost very little blood.

But he was exhausted from his efforts. They spread out a mattress for him on the deck, and he sank down on it and fell fast asleep.

When dawn broke the ship was still about twelve miles off the English coast. There had been only a light wind and they had made very slow progress.

At ten o'clock the ship dropped anchor in Dover harbour.

At ten-twenty d'Artagnan set foot on foreign soil and cried out:

'England at last!'

But he and Planchet still had to get to London, and the

language problem made the last part of the journey difficult too. But at that time in England stage travel was fairly reliable. The two men were soon in the saddle, with an outrider to escort them, and in six hours were at the gates of the capital.

D'Artagnan did not know London. Nor did he know a word of English. But he wrote the Duke of Buckingham's name on a piece of paper and showed it to various people on his route, all of whom knew exactly where the great man lived and directed him on his way. Before long he found himself at the Duke's front door.

The Duke was at Windsor that day, hawking with the King.

D'Artagnan asked to see His Grace's confidential servant. This man, Patrick, always travelled with his master abroad and therefore spoke excellent French. He explained to the man Patrick that he had come from Paris on a matter of life and death and that he must see his master at once.

D'Artagnan's brusque manner and the note of urgency in his voice convinced the servant that his business was really important. He ordered two horses to be saddled at once and declared that he would himself escort the young man to Windsor. As for Planchet, he had had to be lifted off his horse. The poor fellow's limbs were completely cramped and he was speechless with exhaustion. D'Artagnan seemed to be made of iron.

When they arrived at the castle they were told that the King and the Duke were hawking in the marshes about six miles out.

The two men rode off at the gallop and reached the marshes in under half an hour. Soon the servant heard his master's voice in the distance, calling his falcon.

'How shall I announce you to His Grace?' he asked.

'Tell him I'm the young man who insulted him one night on the Pont Neuf, opposite La Samaritaine.'

'Won't he think that rather odd?'

'No. I think it'll make him want to see me.'

The servant put spurs to his horse, approached the Duke and announced d'Artagnan in the manner suggested. Upon this the

Duke left his hawking and quickly rode over to greet the messenger from France. He recognized d'Artagnan at a glance and suspected at once that he had come with some sensational news which directly concerned himself. The servant tactfully stood aside to allow Buckingham and the young man to converse in private.

'What have you to tell me, Sir?' said the Duke. 'Has something happened to the Queen?'

This question and the note of anxiety in Buckingham's voice proved both that he loved the Queen and that this love was an obsession with him.

'No harm's come to Her Majesty yet, Sir,' answered d'Artagnan. 'But I understand some danger's threatening her from which only Your Grace can save her.'

'I save her?' cried Buckingham. 'Would to God I could be of the smallest use to her! How can I save her?'

For answer d'Artagnan put his hand into the inner pocket of his doublet and pulled out the Queen's letter.

'Read this, Sir,' he said.

'What's this letter? Who's it from?' cried the Duke.

'From Her Majesty, I believe,' answered d'Artagnan.

'From Her Majesty?' echoed Buckingham, going deathly pale.

He took the letter and mechanically broke the seal, staring at the envelope like a man in a trance.

'Who's been tampering with his letter?' he asked at length, pointing to a small neat tear on the corner of the envelope.

'Good Lord! I never noticed that, Sir,' answered d'Artagnan. 'That must have been done by the Comte de Wardes, when he ran me through the chest.'

'Are you wounded?' asked Buckingham.

'It's nothing, Sir. Just a scratch.'

Buckingham now opened the letter and read, one page, two pages. Suddenly he looked up and there was terror in his eyes.

'Good God!' he cried. 'The position's desperate! Patrick, go and make His Majesty my humblest apologies and tell him I have to leave for London at once on a matter of life and death. Come, Sir,' he added to d'Artagnan, 'let's be off.'

And the Duke and the young man put spurs to their horses and galloped off at breakneck speed in the direction of the capital.

CHAPTER XXI

My Lady de Winter

ON their way to London Buckingham plied d'Artagnan with questions. He was careful not to disclose anything he thought the young man might not know, and questioned him only on what had been happening recently, since he, Buckingham, had left Paris. When he compared what the young man said with what he himself knew and with what the Queen had said in her letter, he realized how serious the position was. He was amazed that the Cardinal, concerned as he was to prevent the young man from reaching England, should have allowed him to slip through his fingers. He expressed his surprise openly, whereupon d'Artagnan described his journey in detail, stating that various attempts had been made to hold up the party, that all his three devoted friends had succumbed, and that by offering them to the pursuers, like Atalanta's golden apples, he had been able to push on and reach his goal, having suffered nothing worse than the sword-thrust from the Comte de Wardes which had torn the Queen's letter, and for which his enemy had had to atone heavily. The Duke listened attentively and shot quick glances from time to time at the Gascon as he told his tale, for he was astonished to find such resource and courage in a man so young.

The horses went like the wind, and the Duke and his companion were soon at the gates of the capital. D'Artagnan thought that the Duke would slacken speed as he rode through the streets, but he galloped on, heedless of the thronging crowds. Once or twice, as they passed through the city, he

actually rode people down and did not even look round to see
if his victims were badly injured. On each occasion there were
angry shouts from the crowd and d'Artagnan saw people shaking their fists.

When the two riders reached the Duke's house they rode
straight into the courtyard. Buckingham dismounted, flung his
horse's reins over its neck and strode indoors, leaving the animal unattended. D'Artagnan did the same, but was not happy
about it, for he hated to see horses ill managed. At that
moment, however, three or four grooms came running from
the stables at the far end of the yard to take charge of the
mounts, so his mind was set at rest.

The Duke walked so fast that d'Artagnan could scarcely keep
pace with him. He led the way through a succession of State
rooms more magnificent than the State rooms of any of the
great contemporary French houses and came at last to a bedroom which was a marvel of luxury and good taste. There was a
door in a wall recess at the far end of this room; the Duke went
over to this door and opened it with a little golden key which
he wore on a gold chain round his neck. D'Artagnan had
thought it more respectful to remain outside the bedroom, but
the Duke happened to look round before going through the
inner door and, seeing his guest's hesitation, said:

'Come in, young man. And if you're lucky enough to have
an audience with the Queen when you get back you can tell her
what you've seen.'

D'Artagnan walked into the bedroom and followed the
Duke through the inner door, which the latter closed behind
them.

The young man found himself in what looked like a small
chapel, the walls of which were hung with beautiful gold-
embroidered Persian tapestries, and which was brilliantly lit
by rows of candles. At the far end of the room was a sort of
altar, surmounted by a blue velvet canopy; in between the altar
and the canopy hung a life-size portrait of Anne of Austria, so
excellent that d'Artagnan gave a start of surprise; it was as
though the Queen herself were present, and he expected the
portrait to come down from the wall and speak.

On the altar, immediately below the portrait, was the rose-wood box containing the diamond tags.

The Duke went up to the altar and knelt down in front of the portrait like a priest before the figure of Christ. Then he opened the box.

'Look,' he said to d'Artagnan, pulling out a large bow of blue ribbon glittering with diamonds. 'Here are the precious tags. I'd vowed to take them to the grave with me. The Queen gave them to me, and now she wants them back. Let her will, like the will of God, be done in all things.'

The Duke gazed in rapt silence at the diamonds he was to see no more. Suddenly he started back and gave a cry.

'What is it, your Grace?' asked d'Artagnan in alarm. 'Are you ill?'

'Good God, is it possible!' said Buckingham in a hoarse whisper, turning pale as death. 'Yes, two of the tags are missing. There are only ten here. Oh horror!'

'Did you lose them, Your Grace, or d'you think they've been stolen?' asked d'Artagnan.

'They've been stolen,' answered the Duke. 'It's a plot of the Cardinal's. Look, the ribbon they were fixed to has been cut with scissors!'

'Who can have done it and when?' cried d'Artagnan. 'Doesn't Your Grace suspect anyone? If you could think of someone who might have done it the diamonds might be traced. The thief might not yet have got rid of them.'

'Let me think!' cried the Duke. 'Ah, yes, I remember now. I only wore the tags once and that was last week at the King's ball at Windsor. I recollect that Lady de Winter was particularly pleasant to me that night and I was surprised because we'd had a quarrel. I realize now that her attitude was a pretence – a prelude to an act of revenge for an imagined slight. She's one of the Cardinal's agents.'

'What? Has he agents abroad as well as in France?' cried d'Artagnan.

'He has agents everywhere,' replied the Duke. 'He's a fiend. But we may defeat him yet. When's this ball to be held in Paris?'

'Next Monday.'

'In five days. That just gives us time,' said the Duke.

He went to the door, opened it and called:

'Patrick!'

The servant came in.

'Send my jeweller and my secretary to me at once,' ordered the Duke.

The servant bowed and left the room in silence. Like the rest of the Duke's staff he had been trained to obey orders promptly and without a word.

When the secretary came in a few minutes later he found Buckingham seated at a table in his bedroom, writing.

'Jackson,' said the Duke. 'Take this letter to the Lord Chancellor and tell him with my compliments to see that this order's carried out at once.'

Jackson read the letter through. Then he looked up, startled.

'But Your Grace,' he protested, 'if the Lord Chancellor asks me your reasons for putting through such an extraordinary measure what shall I tell him?'

'Tell him I want it done, and why I want it done is my business.'

'And suppose His Majesty gets to hear that no ships are to be allowed to leave any of the English harbours and wants to know why? Is the Lord Chancellor to give him that answer, that what you do is your business?'

'No, Jackson. You're right,' answered Buckingham. 'If the King gets to hear of it let the Chancellor say I've decided on war, and that this is my opening move in the campaign against France.'

The secretary bowed and went out.

'We're safe in that respect at any rate,' said Buckingham, turning to d'Artagnan. 'If the diamonds haven't already left the country they won't get out now until after you.'

'How can you know that, Sir?'

'I've just put an embargo on all ships at present in His Majesty's harbours, and none may leave without a special permit.'

D'Artagnan gave a gasp of astonishment. Here was a man ruthless and unprincipled enough to use the unlimited power vested in him by a trusting sovereign for his own private ends! Buckingham noticed the expression on the young man's face and realized what was passing through his mind. He smiled.

'Yes,' he said. 'You realize now that Anne of Austria's my true sovereign. To please her I'd betray my country, my King, my God even. She asked me not to send help to the Protestants of La Rochelle as I'd promised, and I obeyed. I broke faith with the Protestants but I didn't care, for it was her wish. And to show her gratitude the Queen gave me this portrait. Haven't I been repaid a thousand-fold for what I did for her?'

D'Artagnan was amazed to think that the destinies of nations and the lives of men sometimes hung on such slender and unsuspected threads.

He was still reflecting in this vein when the jeweller was announced. He was an Irishman, very skilled in his trade, and earned a hundred thousand livres a year in the service of the Duke of Buckingham alone.

The Duke greeted him and led him straight into the little chapel.

'O'Reilly,' he said. 'Take a look at these diamonds and tell me what each is worth.'

The jeweller took one look at the tags, noticed their beautiful settings, and replied:

'Fifteen hundred pistoles apiece, Your Grace.'

'You notice that two of the tags are missing? How long would it take you to make two others exactly the same?'

'A week, Your Grace.'

'I'll pay you three thousand pistoles apiece for them if you'll have them ready by the day after tomorrow.'

'Your Grace shall have them.'

'You're a treasure, O'Reilly. But there's another point. These tags mustn't be given to anyone outside; they must be copied in this house; the work must be done here.'

'That's impossible, Your Grace. I'm the only man qualified to do the work. No one else could make facsimile copies.'

'That's why I'm going to make you my prisoner, O'Reilly,' answered the Duke. 'You couldn't leave this house now if you wanted to. So make the best of it. Tell me what men and what tools you need for the work and I'll send for them.'

The jeweller knew the Duke of old, and saw that it was useless to protest.

'Very good, Your Grace,' he said. 'May I let my wife know?'

'Of course,' answered the Duke. 'In fact you may see her if you like. I'll make your stay here as comfortable as possible. And of course I shall compensate you for the inconvenience caused you. That's only fair. So here are another thousand pistoles besides what I already owe you for the tags.'

D'Artagnan was more and more astonished at the cool effrontery of this English aristocrat, who manipulated men and millions to suit his own ends.

The jeweller now proceeded to write a letter to his wife, enclosing the bill for a thousand pistoles and asking her to send in exchange his best assistant, a selection of diamonds of various weights and all the tools needed for the work.

Buckingham then showed the jeweller to the room which was to be his workshop, and locked him in. He posted a sentry at each door, with orders to admit no one but his own confidential servant, Patrick, and on no account to allow either the jeweller or his assistant out at all.

When all these arrangements had been made the Duke returned to d'Artagnan.

'Now, young fellow,' he said, 'England's yours. Say what you want and you shall have it.'

'I confess, Sir, that what I want most at the moment's a bed. I'm very tired.'

Buckingham showed d'Artagnan to a bedroom adjoining his own. He wanted to keep the young man near him, not because he suspected him of treachery but because he liked to have a companion to whom he could talk about the Queen.

An hour later a decree forbidding all ships, including mail ships, to leave British harbours was published in London. Everyone interpreted it as a declaration of war against France.

On the second morning after d'Artagnan's arrival in London the two diamond tags were ready. The work was so perfect that Buckingham himself could not distinguish the old from the new; moreover the greatest experts could not have said which were the copies and which the originals.

The Duke immediately summoned d'Artagnan.

'Here are the diamond tags you came for,' he said. 'Take them and bear witness that all that was humanly possible to do I've done.'

'Your Grace, I promise to give an exact report of everything I've seen. But am I to take the tags without the box?'

'The box would only be a nuisance to you. Besides it's all I've got left now of the Queen's gift and therefore doubly precious to me. Please say I insisted on keeping it.'

'Very well, Your Grace.'

'And now,' continued Buckingham, giving d'Artagnan a searching look, 'how am I to reward you for the immeasurably great service you've done me?'

D'Artagnan flushed hotly. He saw that the Duke wanted to persuade him to accept something for himself, and the idea that his and his friends' blood should be paid for in English gold was abhorrent to him.

'Let's be clear on this point, Your Grace,' he said, 'and get the facts straight to avoid misunderstanding. I'm in the service of their Majesties the King and Queen of France and attached to Monsieur des Essarts' company of guards. Monsieur des Essarts and his brother-in-law Monsieur de Tréville are both intimate friends of their Majesties. And there's another thing. I might have refused to take on this mission at all if I hadn't wanted to please a lady whom I love as dearly as you love the Queen.'

'Yes,' replied the Duke with a smile. 'And I think I actually know the lady in question.'

D'Artagnan broke in quickly.

'I never mentioned her name, Your Grace,' he said.

'No, and you may be sure I won't either,' said the Duke. 'So I have this lady to thank for your loyalty and courage?'

'Yes, Sir. For I make no bones of the fact that just at this time, when there's talk of war between our two nations, I think of Your Grace purely as an Englishman, an enemy whom I'd rather meet on the battlefield than in Windsor Park or the Louvre. I won't of course allow this personal feeling to interfere with my mission which having started I mean to finish. But I'd like to assure Your Grace that you yourself have no reason to feel under more of an obligation to me now than you did when we first met on the Pont Neuf.'

Buckingham listened to this speech with mixed feelings. He was irritated and at the same time impressed by the young man's independence.

'And we say "proud as a Scotsman",' he murmured.

'And we say "proud as a Gascon",' retorted the young man. 'The Gascons are the Scotsmen of France.'

This final sally ended the conversation. D'Artagnan rose, bowed to the Duke and prepared to leave.

'Oh, so you're going just like that, are you?' said the Duke. 'And how d'you propose to get out of England?'

'I don't know, Sir. I hadn't thought of that.'

'Ye Gods. Do you Frenchmen never think ahead at all?'

'I'd forgotten that England was an island and that you were its ruler.'

'Go to the Port of London. Ask for a brig called the *Sund* and give this letter to the captain. He'll sail you into a little French port where there's no chance of anyone looking out for you, and where usually only fishing-boats put in.'

'What port's that, Sir?'

'Saint-Valéry. But wait. There's more to come. When you go ashore at Saint-Valéry look out for a cheap-looking inn without name or signboard. You can't mistake it; there's only one. Call in there and ask to see the landlord.'

'And then?'

'Say the word "Forward" to him. That's the password. He'll have a saddled horse ready for you and tell you the road you're to take. You'll find three similar remounts at intervals along your route. If you like give your address in Paris to the innkeepers at each stage of your journey and the horses'll be sent on after you. You know two of them already; you're obviously a good judge and can appreciate their quality. They were the horses we rode from Windsor to London. You'll find the two others every bit as good. All four are fully trained for the field. I know you're proud but you'd be doing me a great honour by accepting these mounts, taking one for yourself and the three others for your three friends. Don't forget, by the way, that these horses are weapons of war, and I think you French have a saying, "the end justifies the means".'

'It's very good of Your Grace, and I shall be honoured to accept,' said d'Artagnan. 'And with God's help we'll make good use of your gift.'

'And now give me your hand, young man. Perhaps we shall soon be meeting on the battlefield. But in the meantime I hope we part friends.'

'Yes, Your Grace, but in the firm hope of soon becoming enemies.'

'Don't worry. I think I can guarantee that.'

'I count on your promise, Sir,' said d'Artagnan.

Upon which he bowed to the Duke, took his leave and went straight down to the port, where he found the brig *Sund* berthed opposite the Tower of London. He handed the Duke's letter to the captain, who took it to the Governor of the port for counter-signature and then promptly hoisted sail.

There were fifty other outward-bound ships in the port waiting for permission to weigh anchor. The *Sund* sailed close alongside one of these and d'Artagnan fancied he saw seated in the stern the lady from Meung, with whom the stranger had had a hurried conversation at the inn, the lady of the long, golden ringlets, lustrous blue eyes, and lily-white hands. But the brig was borne swiftly downstream by a strong wind and tide and the other vessel and its occupants were soon out of sight.

At about nine o'clock on the following morning the brig dropped anchor in the little port of Saint-Valéry. D'Artagnan immediately set off in search of the inn. Distant shouts guided him in his quest, and he soon found the inn, where a crowd of sailors had assembled to discuss the latest news, using the likelihood of imminent war with England as an excuse for a little extra celebration.

D'Artagnan elbowed his way through the crowd, approached the landlord and gave the password 'Forward'. The host immediately signed to him to follow him, took him out through a back door and into a stables where he found a horse ready saddled and bridled. The host then asked him if he could oblige him in any other way.

'Tell me what road I'm to take,' said d'Artagnan.

'From here you must make for Blangy and from Blangy for Neuchâtel. When you get to Neuchâtel go to the 'Golden Harrow', give the password to the landlord and he'll have another thoroughbred like this waiting for you.'

'Do I owe you anything?' asked d'Artagnan.

'Everything's already been paid for, and handsomely,' said the landlord. 'So good-bye, Sir, and God speed.'

'Amen,' said the young man.

Then he leapt into the saddle and galloped off.

Four hours later he was in Neuchâtel. He obeyed his instructions to the letter. At Neuchâtel, as at Saint-Valéry, he found a saddled horse awaiting him. He had wanted to transfer the pistols from his old saddle to his new, but found that the holsters of the new saddle also contained pistols.

'What's your address in Paris, Sir?' asked the landlord of the inn at Neuchâtel.

'Headquarters, Des Essarts' Company, King's Guards.'

'Very good,' replied the host.

'What road do I take from here?' inquired d'Artagnan.

'Take the Rouen road but branch off to the left before reaching the town. You'll come to the little village of Ecoins, where there's only one inn, the 'French Crown'. It's a cheap-looking place, but don't be put off by that. Ask there and you'll find another thoroughbred waiting to do the next stretch with you.'

'Same password?'

'Yes.'

'Good-bye, mine host!'

'Good-bye, young gentleman. Anything more I can do for you?'

'Nothing, thanks,' cried d'Artagnan, vaulting into the saddle and galloping off at breakneck speed.

At Ecoins the same performance took place; d'Artagnan found another solicitous host who provided him with another magnificent mount. He again left his address in Paris with the landlord and again galloped off towards Paris at breakneck speed. There was another change of mounts at Pontoise, the last on his journey, and by nine that evening his horse's hoofs were clip-clopping on the cobbles of Monsieur de Tréville's courtyard in the Rue du Vieux Colombier. He had travelled about a hundred and eighty miles in twelve hours.

When Monsieur de Tréville welcomed the young man he showed nothing of whatever inner excitement he might have been feeling. He may have gripped his protégé's hand a little harder and looked at him a little more searchingly than usual but that was all. He asked him no questions and told him nothing. He merely suggested that as Monsieur des Essarts' company was on special guard at the Louvre that night d'Artagnan had better report for duty at once.

CHAPTER XXII

The Merlaison Ballet

ON the day following d'Artagnan's return the whole of Paris was talking about the ball which the City Councillors were giving for the King and Queen, at which Their Majesties were to dance the famous 'Merlaison', the King's favourite ballet.

The various merchant guilds had sent representatives to the Town Hall a week in advance and elaborate arrangements had been made to deck out the building in a manner worthy of this festive occasion. The city carpenters had erected tiers of benches to accommodate the Court ladies; the city grocers had provided two hundred white wax candles to illuminate the hall – an unheard-of luxury in those days. And no less than twenty violinists had been hired to play – they were to be paid double their normal fee and were to play all night.

At ten o'clock on the morning of 3 October Monsieur de la Coste, Ensign in the King's Guards, came to the Town Hall with an escort of two sergeants and a platoon of archers of the Guard to perform the ceremony of demanding from the City Clerk the surrender of the keys of all the outer and inner doors and cupboards in the building. The keys were handed over forthwith, each with an identifying label attached, and from then on the soldiers took formal possession of the building, with the duty of guarding all the doors and approaches. At eleven o'clock Captain Duhallier, of the King's Guards, arrived from the Louvre with a company of fifty archers; these were stationed at all the entrances. At three o'clock two Guards' companies arrived, one French and one Swiss. The French company was composed half of Duhallier's and half of des Essarts' men.

At six o'clock the guests began to arrive and were all in turn ushered into the great hall and shown to their places on the raised benches.

At nine o'clock the President's wife arrived. She was the most important woman guest at the ball after the Queen, so she was received by the City Councillors and conducted to a box immediately opposite the Queen's box.

At ten o'clock a special light supper for the King was laid in the little hall near the Saint-Jean Church and placed in front of the sideboard on which stood the city plate, which was guarded by four archers.

At midnight the people near the Town Hall heard distant shouts and cheers. The King had started from the Louvre and was being acclaimed by the people lining the route to the Town Hall. All the streets were lit with coloured lanterns.

Now the City Councillors, dressed in their robes and preceded by six police officers carrying torches, went out on to the steps of the hall to greet the King. The Mayor made a short speech of welcome and the King made another in reply, in which he apologized for arriving late and blamed the Cardinal for having detained him with State business until eleven.

His Majesty was in full Court dress and was accompanied by Monsieur his brother, the Comte de Soissons, the Grand Prior, the Duc de Longueville, the Duc d'Elbœuf, the Comte d'Harcourt, the Comte de La Roche-Guyon, Monsieur de Liancourt, Monsieur de Baradas, the Comte de Cramail and the Chevalier de Souveray.

Everyone remarked that the King was looking worried and depressed.

One private room had been prepared for His Majesty and another for Monsieur. The fancy dresses which they were to wear had been laid out in the rooms. The same arrangements had been made for the Queen and for the President's wife. Changing rooms had also been provided for the ladies- and gentlemen-in-waiting on their Majesties, which they had to share two and two.

Before entering his room the King gave orders that he was to be informed the moment the Cardinal arrived.

Half an hour after the King's appearance fresh shouts and cheers were heard along the route from the palace. This time the crowd was acclaiming the Queen. The City Councillors again went out on the steps to welcome Her Majesty.

As the Queen entered the ballroom everyone remarked that she, too, looked sad and tired. At that very moment the curtains of a small gallery, which had been closed till then, were drawn back and the Cardinal's head appeared in the aperture. He was wearing a Spanish nobleman's plumed hat and looked pale and anxious. His eyes were riveted on the Queen, and suddenly a look of fiendish glee came into his face. Her Majesty was not wearing her diamond tags.

The Queen stood for some time in the ballroom receiving the compliments of the city magnates and their wives.

Suddenly the King appeared with the Cardinal at one of the entrances to the hall. His Eminence was saying something to him in a low voice and His Majesty was very pale. Before anyone had grasped what was happening the King had forced his way through the crowd in the ballroom and was at the Queen's side. He had not changed his dress and the ribbons of his doublet were half untied. Everyone standing near the Queen remained transfixed as His Majesty came up and addressed his consort.

'Why aren't you wearing your diamonds, Ma'am?' he asked in a strained voice. 'I expressly asked you to.'

The Queen noticed the Cardinal standing behind the King with a diabolical smile on his face. She replied falteringly:

'I was afraid I might be jostled by this crowd, Sir, and that the diamonds might get lost.'

'And you were wrong, Ma'am. When I gave you those tags it was my wish you should wear them. You should have done as I asked.'

By now the King was almost trembling with rage. Everyone was watching the scene with amazement, quite in the dark as to the cause of it.

'I'll have the diamonds fetched from the Louvre at once, if that will please Your Majesty,' said the Queen.

'Do so, Ma'am, and quickly. The ballet starts in an hour.'

The Queen curtsied in token of submission. Then she turned and followed the ladies who were to escort her to her dressing-room.

The King walked off in the other direction and made for his private room.

And now an awkward silence fell on the company and for a few moments no one dared stir. Everyone had noticed that the King and the Queen had had a quarrel, but Their Majesties had spoken so low that those within earshot had retreated a few steps out of respect, not wishing to intrude. So not a word of their conversation had been heard. The violins were playing sweet melodies but no one was listening.

The King was the first to come out of his private room. He and his suite were all dressed in picturesque hunting clothes. It was the style of dress which suited the King best, and turned out as he now was he certainly ranked as the first gentleman in France.

Then the Cardinal appeared, went up to the King and handed him a box. The King opened it and found two diamond tags inside.

'What's the meaning of this?' he asked.

'If the Queen has her diamonds, Sir, which I doubt,' answered the Cardinal, 'count them, and if you find she has only ten ask her if she remembers who stole these two from her.'

The King looked sharply at the Cardinal as though he wished to question him further. But at that moment there was a loud burst of applause in the hall. The Queen had just appeared in her fancy dress. If the King ranked as the first gentleman the Queen certainly ranked as the first lady in the land.

Her hunting clothes suited her to perfection. She wore a beaver hat with blue feathers, a long hunting-coat of pearl-grey velvet fastened with diamond clasps and a blue satin skirt embroidered with silver. On her left shoulder she was wearing the diamond tags attached to her dress by a blue velvet bow which matched her skirt and the feathers in her hat.

When the King saw the diamonds sparkling in the light of the two hundred candles he gave a start of joy, while the Cardinal gave a start of rage. At that distance, however, neither could count the number of tags on the Queen's shoulder. Her Majesty was certainly wearing the tags, but was she wearing all twelve or only ten?

At that moment the violins struck up the opening chords of the ballet. The King offered his arm to the President's wife, whom he was to partner in the dance, while Monsieur, his brother, offered his arm to the Queen. All the dancers then took their places on the floor of the hall, and the ballet began.

The King was dancing opposite the Queen, and every time he passed close to her he stared hard at the glittering constellation on her shoulder, in a vain attempt to count the diamonds. The Cardinal's forehead was bathed in sweat.

The ballet was composed of sixteen figures and lasted an hour. To a handful of people in the ballroom that night that hour seemed like an eternity.

When the dance finally ended the gentlemen led their part-

ners back to their seats amid the applause of the crowd. The
King, however, rudely left his partner, the President's wife,
standing alone on the floor of the hall and walked up to the
Queen.

'Thank you, Ma'am,' he said, 'for obeying me so promptly.
But I understand you've lost two of the tags and I'm returning
them to you now.'

So saying he handed the Queen the two tags which the Cardinal had given him.

The Queen pretended to be surprised.

'What, Sir?' she cried. 'You're giving me two more? But that
makes fourteen!'

The King now counted the tags on Her Majesty's shoulder
and, sure enough, there were twelve! He turned and beckoned
to the Cardinal; he was by now furious.

'Well, Cardinal,' he cried, 'what is all this about? Is it a joke
or what?'

'No, Sir,' replied the Cardinal. 'The truth is, I wanted to
make Her Majesty a present of these two tags. I didn't dare
offer them to Her Majesty myself so I thought out this plan for
getting her to accept them.'

The Queen replied with a smile which proved that she was
not deceived by this ingenious improvisation:

'Your Eminence is too good. And believe me, Sir, I value your
present to the full, for I realize that these two tags alone must
have cost you as much as the other twelve cost His Majesty.'

Upon which she curtsied to the King and the Cardinal and
retired to her private room to change out of her hunting dress.

The great ones of our story have lately occupied the entire
foreground of the picture, and the splendour of the scene in
the City Hall has diverted our attention for a time from the
young man to whose efforts Anne of Austria owed the superb
triumph she had just scored over the Cardinal. But this young
man was also in the tableau, and though he looked and felt
obscure in this great gathering, standing alone in a throng of
guests gathered at the main entrance to the hall, he was nevertheless one of the only four present who wholly understood

the drama that had just been enacted in full view of several hundred of the highest in the land.

The Queen had just retired to her room and d'Artagnan was preparing to leave when he felt a light touch on his shoulder. He turned round and saw a young woman in a black velvet mask beckoning to him. The mask was but a poor disguise and d'Artagnan at once recognized the woman as his beloved Constance Bonacieux.

On the previous night d'Artagnan had asked Madame Bonacieux to meet him at the Louvre in the lodge of Germain, the Swiss porter. But the lovers had hardly had time to say a word to each other, for Madame Bonacieux's first thought had been to let her royal mistress know that her messenger had returned and that all was well. So now the young man was only too glad to follow her; both love and curiosity drove him on. Madame Bonacieux led him along empty, winding corridors towards the back of the building. D'Artagnan tried once or twice to stop her, take hold of her and gaze into her eyes. But she always eluded him and whenever he tried to speak put her finger imperatively to her mouth, which reminded him at once that she was his mistress and he her slave. He followed her meekly and in silence until at last they came to a door. Madame Bonacieux opened it, led the young man into a little room which was completely dark, and closed the door behind them. After warning him again not to make a sound she opened a second door hidden by a tapestry, through the folds of which a light shone suddenly, slipped through it and disappeared, leaving the door ajar.

D'Artagnan stood stock still and tried to imagine what this room could be. As his eyes became accustomed to the gloom he saw a ray of light shining through the half-open door. Then he smelt a faint scent, and heard women's voices speaking in low, respectful tones and using the word "Majesty" from time to time. He realized then that he must be in a room adjoining the Queen's private dressing-room.

The young man hid himself in the darkest corner and waited.

The Queen appeared to be in a gay mood, which astonished her ladies, who were accustomed to seeing her worried and depressed. She herself gave as reason for her high spirits the beauty of the ball and the pleasure of dancing the ballet, and as it is the first duty of a Queen's entourage to reflect her moods, all the ladies now vied in praising the courtesy and generosity of the City Councillors.

Although d'Artagnan did not know the Queen he was able to distinguish her voice from the other voices by her slight foreign accent and by the natural authority in her tone, which is peculiar to all princes and princesses. He could trace her movements from her voice; now and then she seemed to be standing quite near the open door and once or twice her shadow actually fell across the floor of the room in which he was hidden.

Suddenly, as the young man stood in the darkness, watching and waiting, an outstretched arm appeared in the opening in the tapestry, an arm superbly white and lovely in outline. D'Artagnan stood for a while transfixed. Then he realized that this was his reward. He rushed forward, fell on his knees, took the fair white hand in his and pressed it to his lips. As he held the Queen's hand he felt something slip from her fingers into his; then she withdrew her hand again and the door was closed. The young man was now in complete darkness. He clenched his hand and realized that what he held was a ring. He slipped it on to his finger and stood waiting, convinced that his little adventure was not yet over. He had been rewarded for his courage and now expected to be rewarded for his love. Moreover the night was yet young, and the ball had only just started. Supper was at three and the St Jean clock had struck the three quarters some little time before.

The sound of the voices in the adjoining room grew gradually fainter, and finally ceased. Then the communicating door opened again and Madame Bonacieux came tiptoeing in to the little room where d'Artagnan was imprisoned.

'You, at last!' cried the young man.

'Hush!' said his guide, putting her finger to her lips. 'Don't make a sound and go back the way you came.'

'But when shall I see you again?' cried d'Artagnan.

'You'll find a note in your room when you get home,' said Madame Bonacieux. 'Now go quickly!'

And with these words she opened the door leading into the passage and pushed the young man out of the room.

D'Artagnan obeyed like a child, without a word of protest. And this shows how very deeply in love he was.

CHAPTER XXIII

The Tryst

D'ARTAGNAN ran all the way home from the City Hall. Although it was three o'clock in the morning and he had to cross all the most disreputable districts of Paris, he had no unpleasant encounters. As everyone knows there is a special guardian angel for drunkards and lovers.

He found the little side door into his house ajar. He ran up the stairs and gave the special knock on his door which he and his servant had arranged together. He had sent Planchet home two hours previously, and now the faithful fellow was there to greet him.

'Did anyone call with a letter for me?' asked d'Artagnan quickly.

'Nobody called with a letter, Sir,' answered Planchet, 'but one came by itself.'

'What do you mean, idiot?'

'I mean that although I had the key to this place in my pocket all the evening, when I came in I found a letter on the table in your bedroom.'

'Where is the letter?'

'I left it where I found it, Sir. It's not natural for letters to come in to people's houses on their own, like that. If the window'd been open or even on the latch I wouldn't say no. But everything was bolted and barred. I should take care, Sir, if I were you. There's something queer about that letter.'

While Planchet had been talking d'Artagnan had rushed into his bedroom and opened the letter. He read as follows:

I have my own and other people's thanks to convey to you. Come to St Cloud at ten o'clock to-night, and wait opposite the summer-house at the corner of Monsieur d'Estrées' house.   C. B.

As he read this letter d'Artagnan felt his heart leap for joy. It was the first love-letter he had ever received and the first tryst that had ever been granted him.

Planchet had seen his master's face change colour as he read.

'Well, Sir,' he said, 'didn't I guess right? Isn't there some evil attached to that letter?'

'No, Planchet, you're wrong,' answered d'Artagnan, 'and to prove how wrong you are here's a crown for you. Go out and drink my health.'

'Thank you, Sir. You're very generous. I'll do that with pleasure. But I say all the same that letters which get into houses by themselves . . .'

'Fall from Heaven, Planchet, from Heaven.'

'So you're happy, Sir?'

'I'm the happiest man alive.'

'In that case, Sir, perhaps you'll allow me to go to bed.'

'Yes, run along.'

'May everything turn out for the best, Sir. But I still say that letters . . .'

And Planchet went off shaking his head and muttering to himself, still uneasy in spite of his master's generosity and the prospect of a good tipple.

D'Artagnan was now alone. He read and re-read the letter, pressed it to his lips and kissed it passionately. He finally went to bed, fell fast asleep and dreamed golden dreams.

At seven next morning he got up and called for Planchet. The faithful servant appeared at the second summons, but it was obvious from the expression on his face that his night's rest had not dispelled his misgivings about the letter.

'I shall probably be out all day, Planchet,' said d'Artagnan.

'So you'll be free till seven this evening. But be ready punctually at seven with two horses.'

'So that's it, is it?' said Planchet. 'We're going to have a few more holes put through us!'

'Bring your musket and pistols with you.'

'What did I say?' cried Planchet. 'I knew it! That accursed letter!'

'Listen, idiot. We're going on a little jaunt, that's all.'

'Yes, I know. Like that little jaunt we took the other day, when bullets rained on us and swords were brandished in our faces.'

'You needn't come if you're frightened, Planchet,' said d'Artagnan. 'I'd rather go alone than with a fellow who's frightened.'

'That's not fair, Sir,' said Planchet. 'You've already seen me in action! You know what I'm good for.'

'I thought perhaps you'd used up all your courage then and had none left for now.'

'Oh, I can still pluck up a little at a pinch, Sir,' replied the servant. 'But don't be too wasteful of it if you want it to last out.'

'D'you think you've got any to fall back on for this evening?'

'I hope so.'

'Good. I'm counting on you.'

'I'll be ready punctually at seven, Sir. But I thought we only had one horse in the stables.'

'There may still be only one there now. But there'll be four by this evening, I promise you.'

'So that was why we went to England! To get remounts!'

'Exactly,' said d'Artagnan.

Then he went out, waving a good-humoured farewell to Planchet.

He found Monsieur Bonacieux standing at his front door. His first impulse was to ignore the little draper. But Bonacieux made him such a deep and courteous bow that he felt obliged, as his tenant, not only to return the bow but to go up and speak to him.

And after all, he thought, there's every reason to be friendly to a man whose wife has made a tryst with one at St Cloud for that very evening! He therefore greeted his landlord with his most pleasant smile.

Their conversation naturally turned to Bonacieux's imprisonment in the Bastille. The draper did not know that d'Artagnan had overheard his conversation with the stranger from Meung, and described the persecutions of Monsieur de Laffemas, whom he kept referring to as a monster of iniquity and the Cardinal's hired assassin. He then discoursed at length on the Bastille, with its bolts, barred windows, air-holes, grilles, and instruments of torture.

D'Artagnan listened with exemplary patience. When the little man at last stopped talking he said:

'And what about Madame Bonacieux? Did you ever discover who kidnapped her? You remember it was the kidnapping that first brought us together.'

'Ah,' said Monsieur Bonacieux, 'you may be sure they took good care not to tell me that, and my wife swears she has no idea who the man was. And now how about you, young Sir?' he continued, rubbing his hands good-humouredly. 'What have you been up to lately? I haven't seen you or your friends for some time, and I can't believe all that dust and mud which Planchet was wiping off your boots yesterday was picked up on the paved roads of Paris.'

'You're quite right, Monsieur Bonacieux. My friends and I've been on a little trip.'

'Did you go far?'

'Oh no. Only about a hundred miles. We escorted Monsieur Athos to Forges, where he went to take the waters. My other two friends stayed on with him there.'

'And you had to return, I suppose?' said Monsieur Bonacieux, putting on a knowing look. 'I don't suppose a handsome young fellow like you gets much time off. The ladies would have something to say if you left Paris for long. Eh, Monsieur d'Artagnan?'

The young man laughed heartily. 'Ha, ha, Monsieur Bonacieux,' he replied. 'I see one can't hide much from you. You're quite right, the ladies would have something to say; one in particular was keen to have me back.'

Monsieur Bonacieux's face darkened slightly at this, but so slightly that d'Artagnan never noticed it.

'So now you're to be rewarded for your constancy, I suppose,' continued the draper, this time with a slight quaver in his voice, which again d'Artagnan did not notice.

'Well, don't pretend you've never had a tryst!' said d'Artagnan with a laugh.

'No, I only asked because I wanted to know if you'd be coming back late tonight.'

'Why d'you want to know that, Monsieur Bonacieux? Are you proposing to wait up for me?'

'No. But the fact is, since my arrest and the entry of the police I get terrified every time I hear the door opening, especially at night. You can't really blame me, Sir. I'm not a fighting man.'

'No. But you don't need to be frightened when I come in, however late it is, one, two, or even three in the morning. You'll know it's me. Even if I don't come home all night you needn't be frightened.'

This time Bonacieux turned so chalky white that even d'Artagnan noticed it. He asked him what was the matter.

'Nothing,' said Bonacieux. 'Since my recent misfortunes I've been liable to sudden fainting attacks; I had one just then, that was all. Don't worry about me. Your only concern should be to try and enjoy yourself.'

'There's no effort needed for that. I am enjoying myself.'

'Don't be too sure. You don't know what may happen this evening.'

'Very well. I'll wait till this evening. But I'm not worried about it. Come to that, you're probably looking forward to this evening as much as I am. Madame Bonacieux is probably paying you a visit.'

'Madame Bonacieux's not free this evening,' her husband replied gravely. 'She's being kept at the Louvre.'

'That's bad luck, Monsieur Bonacieux. I'm sorry. When I'm happy I like to see the rest of the world happy. But apparently that's impossible in this case.'

And the young man went off, laughing aloud at the irony of the situation, and imagining that he was the only one who saw the joke.

'Laugh while you may,' muttered Bonacieux ominously at his retreating figure.

But d'Artagnan was already too far away to hear, and even had he heard he was in too merry a mood to pay attention to anyone so unimportant as Monsieur Bonacieux.

He walked off in the direction of Monsieur de Tréville's house; as we know, his previous day's visit to the Rue du Vieux Colombier had been short and not very explanatory.

He found de Tréville in the highest spirits. Both the King and the Queen had been most gracious to him at the ball. The Cardinal, on the other hand, had been most disagreeable, but that had not worried him very much. He had gone home at one o'clock, pleading indisposition. The King and the Queen had stayed at the ball till six in the morning.

'And now,' said de Tréville, lowering his voice and looking round to make sure that they were alone, 'now we've got you to consider, my lad. I gather that Their Majesties' and the Cardinal's sudden change of mood is somehow connected with your return from wherever you've been. You'll have to mind your step from now on.'

'Surely I'm all right if I've got Their Majesties' support.'

'You're not all right, believe me. The Cardinal never forgets an injury till he's had his revenge. And I think in this case the man he's after is a certain young Gascon I know.'

'D'you really think His Eminence knows it was I who went to London?'

'Oh, so you've been to London, have you? Was that where you got that diamond ring you're wearing? Take care, d'Artagnan. It's not healthy to accept presents from enemies. I believe there's some Latin epigram about that. Let me think now . . .'

'Yes, I'm sure there's something about it in Latin,' echoed d'Artagnan, who had never been able to master even the rudiments of that language, and had been the despair of his tutor. 'I'm sure there's something.'

'There is indeed,' said de Tréville, who had a flair for poetry. 'Monsieur de Benserade was quoting it to me only the other day. Ah, yes, I remember it now. "Timeo Danaos et dona ferentes", which means roughly, "Beware of enemies who make gifts".'

'This diamond wasn't given me by an enemy, Sir,' answered d'Artagnan. 'It was a present from the Queen.'

'From the Queen?' echoed Monsieur de Tréville. 'Yes, now I look at it I see it's magnificent – a real Crown jewel. I should say it was worth at least a thousand pistoles. Whom did the Queen send with it?'

'She didn't send anybody. She gave it to me herself.'

'Where?'

'In a room next to her dressing-room in the City Hall.'

'How did she give it to you?'

'She was holding it when she gave me her hand to kiss.'

'You've actually kissed the Queen's hand?' cried de Tréville, gazing at his young protégé in amazement.

'Yes, Her Majesty did me the honour of offering me her hand.'

'What? With everyone looking on? Oh, that was unwise of her! Most unwise!'

'No, Sir, no one saw anything,' answered d'Artagnan.

He then told Monsieur de Tréville exactly what had taken place.

'Oh these women!' cried the old soldier. 'These women with their romantic ideas, their love of mystery and intrigue! That's typical of them. So all you saw was the Queen's arm, which means that if ever you meet you'll neither of you recognize each other!'

'No, Sir. But I've got this diamond and . . .'

'May I give you a piece of advice, my lad?' broke in de Tréville.

'Of course, Sir.'

'Go in to the first jeweller's shop you pass on your way home and sell him that diamond for whatever price he offers you; however mean he is he can't give you less than eight hundred pistoles for it. Pistoles have no name and no history, d'Artagnan. But that ring has a history, a terrible history, and could bring disaster to anyone found wearing it.'

'Sell this ring!' cried d'Artagnan. 'The ring given me by my sovereign! Never!'

'Well, at least wear it back to front. Penniless Gascons don't find diamond rings in their mothers' jewel-cases. Everyone knows that.'

'So I'm really in some danger, am I, Sir?'

'A man asleep on a mine with the fuse alight is safe compared with you.'

Monsieur de Tréville spoke so seriously that d'Artagnan began to be alarmed.

'What d'you think I ought to do, Sir?' he asked.

'You must keep your eyes skinned and never be caught napping. The Cardinal has a long memory and enormous power. Take my word for it, he'll play some dirty trick on you all right.'

'What'll he do, for Heaven's sake?'

'He might do anything. He's got the devil's whole armoury at his disposal. The least bad thing that can happen to you is that you'll be arrested.'

'Would they dare arrest someone in the King's service?'

'They didn't worry much about Athos, did they? Take the word of a man who's had thirty years' experience of Court life, and don't lull yourself into a state of false security. Go to the other extreme and see potential enemies everywhere. Don't be led into an argument with anyone, not even a child. If anyone attacks you give way and don't feel ashamed about it. When you're crossing a bridge feel the planks to see there's not a loose one; when you walk under a scaffolding look up first to see that no one's holding a stone ready to throw down on your head; if you come home late get your servant to dog your footsteps, and arm him, that is, of course, if you can trust him.

Don't confide in anyone, friends or relations, not even in your mistress, in fact least of all in her.'

D'Artagnan blushed at this.

'Why least of all in her?' he asked.

'Because mistresses are the Cardinal's favourite weapons of attack; they bring the quickest and cheapest results. A woman'll sell you for ten pistoles. Witness Delilah. You know the Scriptures, of course?'

D'Artagnan thought at once of his assignation that night with Madame Bonacieux. But he was fond enough of his pretty landlady not to let Monsieur de Tréville's bad opinion of women in general shake his confidence in her.

'By the way, that reminds me,' went on de Tréville, 'what's become of your three friends?'

'I was just going to ask you, Sir, if you'd had any news of them.'

'I? No, I've heard nothing.'

'Well, Sir, I had to leave them all in turn on the journey. I left Porthos at Chantilly with a duel on his hands, Aramis at Crèvecœur with a bullet in the shoulder, and Athos at Amiens held up by a party of rogues on a trumped-up charge of coinage.'

'You see!' cried de Tréville. 'What did I tell you? And how did you get through?'

'Only by the skin of my teeth, I confess, Sir. I got a sword-thrust through the chest from the Comte de Wardes and left him half dead on a road near Calais.'

'De Wardes! There you are! Another of the Cardinal's agents; Rochefort's cousin. Listen, my lad, I've just thought of something. The Cardinal will be pretty well combing Paris for you for the next few days, so why not go quietly off to Picardy and look up your three friends? Damn it, that's the least you can do in return for what they've done for you.'

'That's a good idea, Sir. I'll go tomorrow.'

'Why not tonight?'

'Tonight I've got an appointment in Paris, which I simply must keep.'

'Oh, foolish fellow, foolish fellow! Some love-affair, I

suppose. Well, I can only repeat, take care! Women are our downfall, always have been and always will be. I wish you'd leave tonight!'

'Out of the question, Sir.'

'Have you promised to meet someone?'

'Yes, Sir,'

'Then you must keep your promise. But will you also promise me that if you're not killed tonight you'll leave tomorrow.'

'I promise, Sir.'

'D'you need any money?'

'I've still got fifty pistoles. I think that should do me.'

'What about your friends?'

'They should have enough too. We had sixty-five pistoles each when we left Paris.'

'Shall I see you again before you leave?'

'I shouldn't think so, Sir, unless I hear any fresh news in the meanwhile.'

'In that case, good-bye and good luck to you.'

'Thank you, Sir.'

And the young man took leave of Monsieur de Tréville with a feeling of intense gratitude to him for his unfailing loyalty and support.

He now called at the lodgings of all his three friends in turn. None of them had returned, nor had any of their lackeys, and no one had had word of them. D'Artagnan would not have hesitated to call on their mistresses to get news of them, but unfortunately he did not know either Porthos' or Aramis' mistresses, and as for Athos he had no mistress.

As he passed the Guards' barracks he took a look inside the stables and found to his delight that three of the four horses promised by the Duke of Buckingham had already arrived. Planchet was busy grooming them, and was staggered at their magnificent appearance.

'Ah,' he cried, catching sight of d'Artagnan. 'Thank goodness you've come, Sir.'

'Why?' said d'Artagnan. 'What's the matter?'

'I want to talk to you about our landlord, Monsieur Bonacieux. D'you feel you can trust him, Sir?'

'No, I can't say I do. Why?'

'I'm glad to hear that, Sir.'

'Why? What's on your mind?'

'While you were talking to him this morning I was watching him, not listening to your conversation, Sir, just watching. And I saw his face change colour no less than three times.'

'Oh, nonsense.'

'You didn't notice it, Sir, because your mind was full of the letter you'd just received. But if you remember, Sir, I was very worried at the time about how that letter'd got into your bedroom, and that had put me doubly on my guard. I suspected our landlord might know something about it, so I studied his face carefully.'

'And what did you make of it?'

'I thought it was a sly, crafty face.'

'Did you, now?'

'And what roused my suspicions still further, Sir, was that the moment you left him Monsieur Bonacieux rushed into the house, came out again with his hat on, locked his front door and ran off down the street in the opposite direction to the way you'd gone.'

'Yes, Planchet. All that looks mighty suspicious. Never mind. We'll refuse to pay our rent till we've had the whole thing thrashed out.'

'You're laughing at me, Sir. But just wait and see.'

'Well, anyway, Planchet, we can't do anything about it. What's to be, will be. I'm a fatalist.'

'You wouldn't consider cancelling your appointment for this evening, Sir?'

'No, Planchet. If there's really a good reason for disliking Monsieur Bonacieux I'm all the more keen to keep it.'

'So you've quite made up your mind, Sir?'

'Quite, Planchet. Be ready for me here, at the barracks, at nine o'clock tonight.'

Planchet realized that there was no hope of getting his

master to give up his plan. He sighed and set to work to groom the third horse.

D'Artagnan, who at bottom was a sensible fellow enough, decided not to return to his lodgings that night, but instead to go and beg a meal off his friend the Gascon priest, who had provided the four young men with high tea at the time of their financial crisis.

CHAPTER XXIV

The Summer-House

D'ARTAGNAN arrived at the barracks at nine o'clock and found Planchet booted and spurred. The fourth horse had arrived at last. Planchet had his musket and his pistol with him; D'Artagnan put on his sword and tucked his two pistols into his belt.

The two now mounted the horses and rode quietly off. It was already dark and no one saw them leave the barracks. Planchet kept at a respectful distance of about ten feet behind his master.

D'Artagnan led the way along the quays and out through the Porte de la Conférence, and then struck down the St Cloud road, which was much more beautiful in those days than it is today.

So long as they had houses on either side of them Planchet rode along in rear of his master. But as the road became darker and more deserted he gradually lessened the distance between them, and when they entered the Bois de Boulogne he drew level with him and they rode along side by side in silence. Planchet was frightened by the swaying of the big trees above their heads and by the shadows cast by the dark copses in the moonlight. D'Artagnan noticed his alarm.

'What's the matter, Planchet?' he asked.

'Don't you have the feeling that woods are like churches, Sir?'

'In what way, Planchet?'

'They both make one feel one must talk in whispers.'

'Why d'you feel you must talk in whispers? Are you frightened?'

'Frightened we may be heard, yes.'

'Why, Planchet? Our conversation's perfectly proper. Nobody could find anything to object to in it that I can see.'

Planchet said nothing to this. After a while he returned to the thought that was uppermost in his mind.

'Oh that Bonacieux with his crafty eyebrows and his nasty mean little mouth!' he cried.

'What on earth makes you think of him all of a sudden?'

'Horrid thoughts sometimes spring into my mind uninvited, Sir.'

'That's because you're a morbid fellow, Planchet.'

'It may be morbid to think of Bonacieux at this moment, Sir. But I know I'm right about him.'

'I dare say you are, Planchet.'

'Look over there, Sir. Isn't that a musket barrel gleaming in the moonlight? Shall we duck down?'

Fear is infectious. D'Artagnan remembered Monsieur de Tréville's warning and began to feel a little uneasy himself. He spurred his horse into a trot. Planchet did likewise, copying his master's every movement like a shadow.

'Are we going on like this all night, Sir?' he asked.

'No, Planchet. In fact you're stopping here. This is where you've got to wait.'

'What? You want me to wait here, Sir? And what are you going to do?'

'I'm going on a little further.'

'You're going to leave me alone, Sir?'

'Are you frightened, Planchet?'

'No, Sir. But I'd like to point out that it's going to be a very cold night, that cold nights spent in the open make people rheumaticky, and that a lackey with rheumatism's a poor thing, no use at all to an active man like yourself.'

'Very well, Planchet. If you're cold go and spend the night

in one of those inns over there and be ready for me outside the main door at six o'clock tomorrow morning.'

'I spent the crown you gave me last night, Sir, eating and drinking your health as you told me to. If I'm cold tonight I haven't got a sou to get warm with.'

'Here's a half a pistole. And now good-night.'

D'Artagnan dismounted, tossed his horse's reins to Planchet, wrapped his cloak round him and made off through the wood.

Planchet followed his master's retreating figure until it was out of sight and then muttered:

'Br-rr! It's cold.'

Then, without waiting a moment, he rode up to the most comfortable-looking inn he could find and booked accommodation for himself and the horses for the night.

Meanwhile d'Artagnan was walking rapidly along the little forest path which led to St Cloud. When he reached the town he avoided the main street and turned instead up a side street which led to the back of the Castle and then swung down a narrow lane which led straight to the summer-house where Madame Bonacieux had arranged to meet him. It was in a completely deserted neighbourhood. One side of the lane was bordered by a high wall, at a corner of which stood the summer-house, the other side by a hedge, behind which stood a tumble-down hut, fronted by a small garden.

The young man had kept his tryst. He had had no instructions about giving a signal so went and stood opposite the summer-house and waited.

It was a still night and not a sound was to be heard. Paris might have been a thousand miles away. D'Artagnan peered cautiously into the darkness to make sure that no one was lurking there and then leaned back against the hedge. Beyond the hedge, the garden, and the hut lay the vast expanse of sleeping Paris, now cloaked by a thick mist, a yawning gulf in which a few pinpoints of light still glittered, sinister sparks rising from that inferno.

But for d'Artagnan at this moment every prospect charmed, every thought cheered, and every cloud was silver-lined. The hour of his tryst was at hand.

Indeed at that very moment the belfry bell of St Cloud struck the magic hour of ten in its slow, booming tone. To an ordinary ear there would have been something uncanny in the clanging of that bronze clapper in the darkness. But not to d'Artagnan. His heart sang in harmony with the tolling of the bell which was to him as an angel's trump proclaiming the opening of Heaven's gates. He was standing with his eyes fixed on the little summer-house in the recess of the wall. All the windows of the house were shuttered except one on the first floor, through which a soft light shone, shedding a silvery gleam on a little cluster of lime-trees whose branches reached out beyond the high park wall. Behind that window, in that softly lit room, his beloved Madame Bonacieux was obviously waiting for him.

Enchanted by this thought, d'Artagnan stood contentedly leaning against the hedge for half an hour, his eyes riveted on that latticed window. As much as he could see of the ceiling of the room was gilded, and this testified to the beauty of the room as a whole.

And now the St Cloud clock struck ten thirty.

This time d'Artagnan felt a sudden shiver go through him which he could not account for. Was it merely the cold night air striking through his clothes and had he mistaken a physical sensation for a pang of fear?

He now began to think that he must have misread the letter, and that the appointment was for eleven. He went and stood under the window in a ray of light and took the letter out of his pocket. No, there was no mistake; the appointment was for ten o'clock.

He put the letter back in his pocket and returned to his place by the hedge. And now even he began to be a trifle cowed by the silence and by the loneliness of the spot.

Eleven o'clock struck.

D'Artagnan was now convinced that Madame Bonacieux had had an accident. He clapped his hands three times loudly, which is the acknowledged signal of lovers. But no sound came in reply, not even an echo.

His next thought was a sobering one; perhaps Madame

Bonacieux had grown tired of waiting for him and had fallen asleep. He went up to the wall and tried to grip hold of it to climb up it. But it had been freshly plastered and he only succeeded in tearing his hands.

At that moment he noticed the branches of the trees shining silver in the lamplight, and saw that one of them jutted out over the road. He decided to climb the tree and sit on the branch, from where he hoped to get a good view into the summer-house.

The tree proved easy to climb; moreover d'Artagnan was barely twenty years old and still remembered his schoolboy devices. In a few seconds he was comfortably perched on the branch, gazing through the glass panes of the window into the interior of the room.

What he saw made him start and tremble. The soft light which looked so peaceful from outside shone not on an orderly and cosy room but on a scene of incredible confusion. One of the panes of the window had been smashed; the door at the back of the room had been broken down and was hanging lopsided on its hinges; a table which had obviously been laid for supper was lying on its side and broken decanters and crushed fruit were strewn all over the floor. Everything pointed to the fact that the room had been the scene of a desperate struggle. D'Artagnan thought he saw shreds of torn clothing scattered about the floor and bloodstains on the tablecloth and curtains.

The young man now clambered down the tree and proceeded to examine the ground under the summer-house for further traces of violence. His heart was pounding in his chest and beads of sweat stood on his forehead.

A little gleam of light still shone out into the tranquil darkness. D'Artagnan now noticed something which had at first escaped his attention because his eyes had been riveted on the summer-house. The ground under the window was trampled down in places and had large potholes in it. Moreover there were footprints and horses' hoof-prints on it, and two deep carriage-wheel ruts which d'Artagnan traced for a certain distance along the road from Paris; these stopped and made an about turn in front of the summer-house.

Pursuing his researches d'Artagnan eventually discovered a woman's torn glove lying close under the wall. It was mud-stained in patches, but d'Artagnan could tell that it was new and there was a faint scent on it which seemed familiar. It was the sort of glove that lovers steal from their mistresses as keepsakes.

The more d'Artagnan explored the more his fears increased. He broke out in a cold sweat, and his breath came in gasps. He tried to console himself by reflecting that there might be no connection between Madame Bonacieux and the summer-house itself, that she had perhaps only used it as a landmark in making the appointment and that she had really intended to meet him outside; that her duties at the Louvre had probably kept her in Paris; it was even possible, he thought, that her husband had suddenly turned jealous and locked her in the house.

But these arguments could not prevail in his mind against a profound emotional conviction that some disaster had occurred: an inner voice, which speaks only to our instincts, kept telling him that some great unhappiness hung over his head.

This conviction drove the young man to a frenzy. At all costs he must make inquiries in the neighbourhood. He started to run wildly down the road towards the path which he had followed after leaving Planchet, turned right, tore down this path and did not stop until he had reached the ferry. Here at least was a fellow-creature, the ferryman, who could tell him something.

In answer to his inquiries the man told him that at about seven that evening he had ferried over a woman wrapped in a black cloak, who had seemed particularly anxious not to be recognized. For that very reason he had observed her more attentively than he did his other passengers, and had noticed that she was young and handsome.

In those days numbers of young and pretty women flocked to

St Cloud for one particular purpose, and they were all equally anxious to avoid recognition. Nevertheless d'Artagnan was at once convinced that the woman described by the ferryman was Madame Bonacieux.

Standing under the lamp in the ferryman's shelter, d'Artagnan once more took Madame Bonacieux's letter out of his pocket and read it through again to make sure that the assignation had really been at St Cloud and not in some other suburb, in front of Monsieur d'Estrées' summer-house and not in an entirely different street. No, there was no mistake, and there seemed to be no doubt now that d'Artagnan's presentiments were right and that there had been some calamity.

He now started to run back to the summer-house, hoping that something fresh might have occurred in his absence which would give some clue to the mystery.

The little lane was as deserted as before and the lamp in the window still shed its gentle light over the scene. Its rays lit up the hut at the bottom of the garden opposite the summer-house. That hut looked dead and desolate enough, but it must have been a silent witness of the drama. And perhaps not such a silent witness after all, thought d'Artagnan. Perhaps it could be made to speak.

With this thought in mind the young man leapt over the hedge and walked up to the hut. As he approached, a dog which was fastened to a chain at the door started barking furiously.

D'Artagnan knocked loudly twice, but there was no reply. The same deathly silence reigned in the hut as in the summer-house. But this hut was d'Artagnan's last hope, so he knocked again and then again. After a few seconds he fancied he heard a faint creaking noise inside the hut, a noise so timid that it seemed to regret having allowed itself to be heard at all. Now d'Artagnan stopped knocking and instead called out in a voice apologetic and anxious enough to reassure the most timorous. In a moment or two he saw the old worm-eaten shutter to the right of the door swing slowly back on its hinges. It opened only a few inches and was then pushed quickly to again; not, however, before d'Artagnan had caught a glimpse of an old man's head reflected in the dim light of an oil lamp which was burning inside the room. The old man had obviously seen d'Artagnan's shoulder-belt, sword-hilt, and pistol butts and had been frightened.

'In Heaven's name listen,' called out d'Artagnan. 'I'd arranged to meet a friend here, but my friend hasn't arrived. I'm very worried about it. Has there been some trouble in the neighbourhood? Have you seen or heard anything? Speak! Answer me.'

The shutter swung back again slowly on its hinges and the old man's head and shoulders appeared in the opening; he was very pale and seemed panic-stricken. He stood in silence in the window while d'Artagnan explained to him what he had come for, what he had discovered and what he suspected. The old man listened attentively, nodding his head from time to time to corroborate certain details in d'Artagnan's narrative. When the young man had finished his tale the old man remained standing in the window, saying nothing but shaking his head lugubriously.

'Why are you shaking your head like that?' cried d'Artagnan. 'For Heaven's sake speak! Tell me what's been happening here!'

'Don't question me, Sir, please,' answered the old man. 'If I told you what I'd seen no good would come of it.'

'So you have seen something!' cried d'Artagnan. 'Then for God's sake say what it was. I swear on my honour to repeat nothing.'

To reinforce his request d'Artagnan threw a pistole to the old man.

It was obvious from the young man's face and voice that he was genuinely distressed and the old peasant was reassured and decided to trust him. He signed to him to come closer and began talking in a low monologue.

'At about nine o'clock this evening,' he said, 'I heard a noise on the road outside. I went up to my door to find out what was happening and saw three men in my garden. I'm poor and therefore not afraid of thieves, so I opened the door and asked the men what they wanted. A carriage-and-four and three saddled horses were drawn up under the trees. The three saddled horses obviously belonged to the three men who were booted and spurred.'

' "Well, my good Sirs," I said to them, "what can I do for you?"

' "Have you a ladder you can lend us, old man?" said the spokesman of the party.

' "Yes, Sir," I answered; "the one I use for picking fruit."

' "Give it to us, and go back indoors," said the man. "And here's a crown for your pains. I may warn you you're going to see something quite out of the usual very soon. I know it's no good telling you not to look or listen, but remember if you repeat a word of what you see and hear you're a dead man."

'So saying the gentleman threw me a crown and all three went off with the ladder.

'I shut the garden gate behind them and pretended to go back into the cottage. But I went out again at once by the back door and, keeping in the shelter of the trees, managed to creep forward as far as yonder clump of elders; standing in the shadow there I could see everything without being seen.

'The three men had managed to draw the carriage up right opposite the summer-house without making a sound. Now a short, stout, shabby-looking man with grey hair stepped out and began climbing slowly up the ladder. When he got to the level of the first-floor window he took a quick look inside the room, crept stealthily down the ladder again and said to the others in a low voice:

' "It's she!" '

'At this the man who'd spoken to me walked up to the door of the summer-house, opened it with a key which he took out of his pocket and went in, closing the door behind him. His two followers, acting like soldiers rehearsed in a drill, then began climbing up the ladder. The little grey-haired man remained standing at the carriage door, while the coachman held the carriage horses and a groom the saddled mounts.

'Suddenly I heard screams coming from the summer-house

and a woman rushed to the window, flung it open and seemed to be preparing to throw herself out. But when she saw the two men on the ladder she fell back into the room and the two men climbed in through the window after her.

'I saw nothing more after that, but I heard the noise of furniture being thrown about the room. The woman kept screaming and shouting for help. But then her cries were stifled and the three men reappeared at the window carrying her in their arms. Two of them then came down the ladder with her and lifted her into the carriage and the little grey-haired man stepped in after her. The man who'd remained inside the house now closed the window and came out a moment later by the door. He looked into the carriage to make sure the woman was inside; then he joined his two companions who were waiting with their horses and all three swung together into the saddle. The groom jumped on to the box beside the coachman, the carriage drove off at breakneck speed escorted by the three riders, and that was the end. Since then I've seen no one and heard nothing.'

D'Artagnan was stunned by this terrible news and remained speechless, while the demons of fury and jealousy raged in his heart. The look of dumb despair on his face impressed the old man much more than any tears or wild outbursts could have done.

'Don't despair, Sir,' he said. 'They didn't kill the young lady, and that's the most important thing after all.'

'Can you tell me anything about the ringleader of this damnable plot?' asked the young man.

'No, Sir, I don't know him.'

'But you say he spoke to you. You must have seen what he looked like.'

'Oh yes, Sir. He was tall, a lean man, dark-skinned, with a black moustache, dark eyes, and with the dress and manners of a gentleman.'

'That's the fellow all right!' cried d'Artagnan. 'Him again. It's always him! He's my evil genius, I swear. And what about the other man?'

'Which man?'

'The little man with grey hair?'

'Oh him? He's no gentleman, I can promise you. For one thing he wasn't carrying a sword, and the others ordered him about like a nobody.'

'Some servant, I suppose,' said d'Artagnan. 'Oh, poor woman, poor woman! What have they done with her?'

'You promised you'd repeat nothing, Sir,' the old man reminded him.

'Don't worry,' answered d'Artagnan. 'I won't. On my honour as a gentleman.'

D'Artagnan walked off in the direction of the ferry, utterly sick at heart. His mind was numbed with horror and he could still hardly believe that the woman was really Madame Bonacieux. He tried to persuade himself that it was all a dream and that tomorrow he would call at the house and find her there as usual. Then he felt convinced that she was the victim; that she had been having a love-affair with another man and that this other man had abducted her in a fit of jealousy. He was distracted with grief and despair.

'If only I had my friends with me I might have some hope of finding her,' he muttered to himself. 'But they're all prisoners themselves.'

It was now almost midnight. The most urgent thing was to find Planchet. D'Artagnan knocked at the doors of all the inns in the neighbourhood in which a light was showing, but Planchet was in none of them.

After he had inquired at about six inns he realized that his quest was likely to prove fruitless; he had given Planchet leave until six the next morning and until then he was perfectly entitled to go where he pleased. And the young man did not wish to go far afield in his quest, for he thought that by remaining somewhere near the scene of the crime he might hear something which would throw light on the mystery. So he stopped at the sixth inn, ordered a bottle of the best wine the host could provide and sat down at a table in a dark corner of the room. He meant to spend the whole night awake, listening to the talk of the workmen, lackeys, and grooms, who were the inn's only customers. But he was disappointed in his hopes of hearing something, for though the talk was coarse enough not a word was said about the crime. D'Artagnan realized that there was nothing more he could do that night, so he drank down his bottle of wine, made himself as comfortable as possible in his corner and prepared for sleep. He was only twenty years old, and young men of twenty, even though heartbroken, are apt to fall asleep during periods of leisure or, as in this case, of enforced inactivity.

At about six the next morning he awoke, not much rested after his fitful slumbers. He dressed quickly, made sure that he had not been robbed of his diamond, his purse, or his pistols during the night, paid his bill, left the inn and went off in search of Planchet. He was more successful in his quest that morning than he had been the previous night, for the first living soul he glimpsed in the dawn mist proved to be his faithful lackey, who was standing with the two horses at the door of a disreputable-looking inn which his master had passed the previous night and not even noticed.

CHAPTER XXV

Porthos' Mistress

D'ARTAGNAN stopped at Monsieur de Tréville's house on his way home. He had decided this time to tell him everything as he badly needed his advice. Moreover he knew that Monsieur de Tréville saw the Queen practically every day, and he hoped he might persuade Her Majesty to make inquiries about the unfortunate woman who was obviously paying the price of her loyalty to her mistress.

Monsieur de Tréville listened closely to the young man's story, which proved that he saw more in the kidnapping of Madame Bonacieux than a mere love intrigue. When d'Artagnan had finished his account de Tréville said:

'That sounds to me very much like the Cardinal's work.'

'But what can we do?' asked d'Artagnan.

'Absolutely nothing at present. The best thing you can do is to leave Paris, and that quickly. I'll see the Queen and tell her all the details of the kidnapping which she probably knows nothing about. That'll give her something to go by when she starts making inquiries. I may possibly have some good news for you when you get back. At any rate I'll do all I can.'

D'Artagnan knew that Monsieur de Tréville, although a Gascon, was not one to make rash promises, and that one could always reckon on his achieving more than he said. And as he now took leave of his officer his heart was full of gratitude for his past acts of kindness and for his pledge of support for the future. De Tréville was also greatly attached to his brave and enterprising subordinate; he bade him an affectionate farewell, and wished him the best of luck.

D'Artagnan decided to follow Monsieur de Tréville's advice and leave the capital without delay. He walked straight back to his lodgings to give Planchet his marching orders. As he approached the house he saw Monsieur Bonacieux dressed in morning clothes standing at his front door. He suddenly recalled everything that the wily Planchet had said the previous day about their landlord and observed the little draper much more attentively than usual. And he did in fact notice that Monsieur Bonacieux's face was unhealthily yellow in colour, though that, of course, might have been due to an excess of bile in his blood and have had an entirely physical cause. But he also observed something in the pattern of the wrinkles on his face which he thought denoted shiftiness. Rogues laugh differently from honest men and crocodile tears do not flow like real tears. All falseness is a mask and a shrewd observer can detect a man's true character beneath the most cleverly constructed mask.

D'Artagnan was convinced that Monsieur Bonacieux wore a mask and thought that even with his mask he was a most repellent-looking object. He felt so strongly hostile towards him that he pretended not to see him and tried to push past him without a word. But Monsieur Bonacieux hailed him as heartily as he had done the day before.

'Well, young man,' he said. 'We're having one or two nights out, I see. D'you realize its seven o'clock? You seem to be turning normal behaviour upside down, and coming in at an hour when most people go out.'

'Of course you don't need to transgress in that way, do you, Monsieur Bonacieux?' retorted the young man. 'You've got your happiness at home, haven't you?'

Bonacieux turned as white as a sheet and tried to force a smile.

'You're a great one for jokes, young man, a great one indeed,' he replied. 'But where on earth can you have been last night?' he continued, staring at d'Artagnan's boots. 'It must have been pretty heavy going in the lanes.'

D'Artagnan looked down at his boots and saw that they were covered in mud. But at the same time he happened to glance at the little draper's shoes and stockings and noticed that they were just as soiled as his boots; moreover the pattern of the stains was exactly similar. They might both have been dipped in the same mud-pit.

Suddenly an idea flashed across d'Artagnan's mind. The short, squat man with greying hair, described by the cottager as wearing shabby clothes and being treated with contempt by the ringleaders of the plot! Could it be – yes of course it was – Bonacieux himself! He had played a leading part in the abduction of his own wife.

The young man felt a sudden wild impulse to spring at the draper's throat and strangle him. But caution forbade this and with a great effort he restrained himself. Nevertheless his change of expression and the sudden light of anger in his eyes had been so noticeable that Bonacieux was frightened and shrank back. But he was standing close to his own front door, which was shut, so he could not retreat very far.

'Monsieur Bonacieux,' said d'Artagnan, 'before you start chaffing me you'd better take a look at your own shoes and stockings; they seem to be in much the same state as my boots.

Don't tell me you've been having nights out too! At your age and with a young and pretty wife like you've got! Shame on you, Monsieur Bonacieux!'

'No such thing, no such thing, Sir,' answered Bonacieux. 'If you want to know where I've been, I've been to St Mandé to make inquiries about a servant whom I urgently need. The roads were very bad and that's where I picked up all this mud. I haven't had time to get it cleaned off yet.'

That Bonacieux should mention St Mandé as his destination was further evidence in support of d'Artagnan's suspicions. He had obviously chosen it because its position on the map was diametrically opposed to that of St Cloud.

The probability of Bonacieux having collaborated in the plot gave d'Artagnan his first ray of hope. If the draper knew where his wife was it would be possible, in an emergency, to force his secret out of him by physical violence. But first he must try and turn the probability of his guilt into a certainty.

'May I presume on your kindness, Monsieur Bonacieux?' he asked. 'Lack of sleep makes one hoarse and I'm feeling very thirsty at the moment, so with your leave I'll go into your room and help myself to a glass of water. I think we can regard that as a tenant's privilege.'

And before Monsieur Bonacieux could reply d'Artagnan pushed past him into the house, walked into his bedroom and took a quick look at his bed. It had not been slept in. So Bonacieux had been out all night and could only have returned an hour or two before. He had obviously gone with his wife to where they had taken her, or at any rate part of the way.

'Thank you, Monsieur Bonacieux,' said d'Artagnan, emptying his glass. 'That's all I wanted from you. Now I'm going up to my own room to get Planchet to clean my boots for me. When he's finished I'll send him down to do your shoes for you.'

So saying he walked round to the side door and entered the house. The little draper stared after him, quite taken aback by this extraordinary farewell and feeling that he had got the worst of this duel of wits.

D'Artagnan found Planchet standing at the top of the stairs. The fellow was all of a fluster.

'Oh, Sir,' he cried, 'there's no end to our troubles. I thought you were never coming back.'

'What's happened now?'

'You've had a visitor, Sir. You'll never guess who it was, not if you try till Kingdom come.'

'Well, who was it and when did he come?'

'About half an hour ago, when you were with Monsieur de Tréville.'

'And who was it? Come on, Planchet, tell me!'

'Monsieur de Cavois.'

'Monsieur de Cavois? The captain of the Cardinal's Guards?'

'Yes, Sir. In person.'

'Did he come to arrest me?'

'I suspected so. I didn't like those fawning ways of his. Not one bit I didn't.'

'Oh, he fawned, did he?'

'Well, Sir, he was most affable. Let's put it that way. He said he'd called on His Eminence's instructions to escort you to the Palais Royal; that His Eminence was most anxious to meet you as he'd heard such excellent accounts of you.'

'And what did you say?'

'I said I was afraid you wouldn't be able to go, as you were not at home.'

'What did he say to that?'

'He told me to tell you not to fail to call on him some time today. Then he added in a whisper: "Tell your master His Eminence has a very high opinion of him and that his whole future may depend on this interview".'

'That little dodge was a bit transparent,' said d'Artagnan with a smile. 'Don't you agree, Planchet? Not up to the Cardinal's usual standard of wiliness.'

'I saw through the dodge all right, Sir. I answered the gentleman that I knew you'd be disappointed to have missed his visit when you heard about it on your return. He then asked where you'd gone and when, and I said you'd gone off last night to Troyes in Champagne.'

'Planchet, you're a marvel,' said d'Artagnan. 'You couldn't have done better.'

'I knew that if it turned out you did want to see Monsieur de Cavois I could always take back what I'd said about your having gone away. I'd have been the liar, not you. And I'm not a gentleman, so no one thinks the worse of me for telling lies.'

'Don't worry, Planchet. As it happens you won't have lied. We're leaving Paris in half an hour.'

'That's the best news I've heard yet, Sir,' said Planchet. 'And may I ask where we're going?'

'In the opposite direction to where you said I'd gone, of course. Incidentally, aren't you keen to find out what's happened to your pals Grimaud, Mousqueton, and Bazin? I know I'm very keen to get news of Athos, Porthos, and Aramis.'

'Yes indeed, Sir,' said Planchet. 'And I'm ready to leave the moment you say. The air of the provinces would be better for us at present than the air of Paris. I'm sure of that.'

'Good,' said d'Artagnan. 'Pack our bags then, and let's be off. I'll leave the house ahead of you; I'll take nothing in my hand so that no one will suspect. You follow on with the luggage and join me at Guards' Headquarters. And by the way, Planchet, I think you're quite right about our landlord. He's a thoroughly nasty piece of work.'

'I'm always right about that sort of thing, Sir,' answered Planchet. 'I'm a physiognomist.'

D'Artagnan left the house first, as arranged. On his way to Headquarters he called once more at his three friends' lodgings to make sure they had not returned. No news had been received of any of them. A letter had arrived for Aramis in a scented envelope addressed in an elegant hand, and that was all. D'Artagnan took charge of this letter. Ten minutes later he and Planchet met in the Guards' stables, and each proceeded to saddle his own horse to save time.

'Now, Planchet,' said d'Artagnan. 'Saddle the other two horses and let's be off.'

'The idea being, I suppose, that we shall travel faster with two horses apiece, Sir,' said Planchet with a mock innocent expression on his face.

'No, idiot,' answered d'Artagnan, 'but with four horses we'll be able to bring back my three friends, that is, if they're still alive.'

'Which to my mind's most improbable,' answered Planchet. 'However, we must trust in God!'

'Amen to that,' said d'Artagnan, setting spurs to his horse.

And master and man galloped out of the barracks. When they got into the street they turned in opposite directions. D'Artagnan was to leave the capital by the la Villette gate and Planchet by the Montmartre gate, and they were to join forces again beyond St Denis. This manoeuvre, timed to the minute, was entirely successful and they entered Pierrefitte together.

Planchet, it must be confessed, was bolder by day than by night. And yet his native canniness did not desert him for a moment. He remembered every detail of their journey to England and was wary of everyone they met on the road. In fact he held his hat in his hand almost the whole time and apologized so much that d'Artagnan pulled him up more than once, for he feared that such servility might lead people to suppose that he was the servant of a nobody.

Either the other occupants of the road were genuinely touched by Planchet's courtesy or this time no hired assassins had been posted on the route to intercept the young man, for the two travellers reached Chantilly without mishap and dismounted in front of the Grand-Saint-Martin inn as they had done on their first journey.

The landlord of the inn, seeing a young man at his door with a lackey and two spare horses, came out hat in hand. The pair had already travelled about thirty miles, so d'Artagnan decided to put up at this inn without bothering to inquire first whether Porthos was still there or not. He thought that in any case it would be better policy to try and impress the host first by putting on a few airs, and start making inquiries later. So with a flourish he handed over all four horses to Planchet, and asked to be shown into a private room, saying that he wished to be alone. He then ordered the most expensive dinner and the best bottle of wine which the inn could provide. In this way he confirmed the good impression his host had formed of him at first sight.

It was well known that the Guards regiments were recruited from the best families in France, and d'Artagnan with his lackey and four magnificent mounts naturally created a stir in the inn. The host asked to be allowed to serve the young man's meal himself, and our hero took advantage of this to invite the fellow to share his bottle of wine with him and to engage him in conversation.

'Listen, my good host,' he said, filling the two glasses. 'I ordered a bottle of your best wine and if you've cheated me you'll be paid out in your own coin. You see I hate to drink alone, and I'm going to ask you to split the bottle with me. Take your glass now and let's drink. What d'you suggest as a toast? Something we're not likely to quarrel about. I suggest we drink to the prosperity of your inn.'

'You're doing me a great honour, Sir,' said the host, 'and I thank you for your goodwill.'

'Not at all,' said d'Artagnan. 'You see I'm just as interested in the success of your inn as you are yourself. I travel along this road a good deal and I'd like to see it lined with prosperous inns at convenient intervals.'

'Now I come to look at you, Sir,' said the innkeeper, 'and now you tell me you use this road a lot, I've a feeling we've met before.'

'More than likely,' answered d'Artagnan. 'I must have passed through Chantilly at least ten times and must have stopped at least four times at your inn. Oh yes, I remember now, I was here quite recently, only about a fortnight ago, in fact, with three friends of mine, three musketeers. I remember the occasion very well because one of my friends had a quarrel with a stranger, who'd annoyed him in some way.'

'Yes, indeed, Sir,' said the host. 'I remember that day very well. I think you must be referring to a Monsieur Porthos.'

'Yes, that's the fellow,' said the young man. 'And now I'll be obliged if you'd tell me exactly what happened to him.'

'He never got further than Chantilly, Sir.'

'No, I gathered that. You see we were expecting him to follow us but never saw him again.'

'He did us the honour of staying on here.'

'Here?'

'Yes Sir, in this very hotel. At present we're all rather worried, Sir.'

'What about?'

'About the little account he's running up with us.'

'He'll pay you. You don't need to worry about that.'

'Oh Sir,' said the innkeeper. 'You can't think how relieved I am to hear you say that. We've allowed Monsieur Porthos a great deal on account already, and only this morning the surgeon who attends him came to me and said that if Monsieur Porthos didn't pay him soon he'd get his fees out of me because it was I who originally sent for him.'

'What? Is Porthos wounded?'

'I can't answer that question, Sir.'

'Why not? You obviously know more about it than anyone else.'

'Yes, Sir, but people in my station in life can't always tell what they know, especially when they've been threatened with having their ears cut off if they allow their tongues to wag.'

'In that case may I go and see Porthos myself?'

'Most certainly, Sir. Go up to the first floor, if you please, Sir. Monsieur Porthos' room is Number 1. But tell him first who you are.'

'Why?'

'Because otherwise there might be an accident. Monsieur Porthos might think you were one of my staff and run you through or blow your brains out.'

'Why, what have you done to annoy him?'

'We asked him to settle some of his account.'

'Ah yes. I bet that annoyed him! Porthos doesn't like being asked to pay up when he's out of pocket. And yet he shouldn't be out of pocket just now.'

'That's what we thought, Sir. And as this is an orderly house and we make our accounts up weekly we sent him in a bill at

the end of the first week. But we must have caught the gentleman at a bad moment. He returned the bill without a word,
and when I ventured to bring the matter up he told me and my
staff to go to Hell. Of course he'd been gambling the night
before, which might account for it.'

'Gambling? Who with?'

'With a nobleman who was spending the night here. I understand they played lansquenet.'

'How typical of Porthos! Of course he lost everything.'

'Yes, Sir, everything; even his horse.'

'How very typical!'

'When I realized that Monsieur Porthos had nothing left,'
continued the host, 'and that I wasn't likely ever to be paid
my bill, I sent a message asking him to be good enough to
transfer his custom to my colleague at the "Golden Eagle". But
Monsieur Porthos replied that my hotel was the better of the
two and that he intended to stay here. I was so flattered by
this that I didn't insist on his going but merely asked him if
he'd be good enough to leave the room he was now in, which
was the best in the hotel, and move into a nice little room on
the third floor. To this Monsieur Porthos replied that he was
expecting his mistress at any moment from Paris, that she was
a lady of rank and that he'd have me know that his present
room might be the best in the hotel, but that it was a very poor
room to receive so grand a lady in. I thought Monsieur Porthos
was probably right, and yet I felt I must insist. But he refused
even to discuss the matter. He put his pistols on the table by
his bed and said that if I or my staff tried to move him from
where he was he'd blow our brains out. Since then no one's
dared go into his room except his servant Mousqueton.'

'Oh, Mousqueton's here, is he?'

'Yes, Sir. He came back five days after you left, also rather
the worse for wear. Unfortunately he's less crippled than his
master and turns the house upside down in his efforts to provide his master with everything he wants.'

'I've always thought Mousqueton unusually intelligent and
loyal,' said d'Artagnan.

'No doubt he is, Sir,' replied the innkeeper. 'But I can only say that if I were to meet many others as loyal as Mousqueton I'd be a ruined man in no time.'

'Porthos'll pay you. Don't worry.'

'H'm,' answered the innkeeper doubtfully.

'That lady of rank he mentioned is devoted to him and wouldn't stint him of the small sum he owes you,' said d'Artagnan.

'If only I dared tell you what I feel about that, Sir!' replied the host. 'Not only what I feel, what I know.'

'What do you know?'

'What I know for a certainty.'

'Well, what is it? Out with it!'

'I happen to have met that lady of rank.'

'Met her? Where on earth?'

'If only I could be sure it would go no further than you, Sir!'

'Speak out. I promise on my honour to repeat nothing.'

'Well, Sir, you can perhaps understand that when a man's worried he does things he wouldn't do ordinarily.'

'What have you been doing?'

'Nothing a creditor hasn't a perfect right to do.'

'Well, what is it?'

'Monsieur Porthos gave me a letter addressed to that duchess friend of his. That was before his servant arrived. As the gentleman couldn't leave his room he naturally asked us folk at the inn to do all his errands for him.'

'Well?'

'I didn't put Monsieur Porthos' letter in the post, knowing how unreliable it is, but instead gave it to one of my staff who happened to be going to Paris, with orders to deliver it to the duchess in person. I was only doing what Monsieur Porthos had asked me to do, wasn't I? He'd told me to take special care of the letter.'

'You were doing more or less what he asked you to do.'

'Well, Sir, d'you know who this great lady really is?'

'No. I've only heard Porthos talking about her.'

'She's not a duchess at all! She's the wife of an attorney at

Le Châtelet, called Madame Coquenard. She's at least fifty but still makes jealous scenes. I thought it odd that a duchess should live in the Rue aux Ours.'

'How d'you know so much about her?'

'Because I was told that when she read the letter she flew into a violent rage and said that Monsieur Porthos was being unfaithful to her and that he'd been wounded in a fight over another woman.'

'What? Is Porthos wounded?'

'Oh dear, oh dear!' said the innkeeper. 'What have I gone and said now?'

'You've gone and said that Porthos was wounded.'

'Yes, and he told me not to mention it.'

'Why?'

'Well, Sir, I suppose because he's only human, and after boasting that he was going to trounce the fellow you left him to deal with, he was mortified to find himself being trounced instead. Monsieur Porthos is a very vain man and didn't want anyone to know he'd been beaten in a duel, except, of course, his friend the duchess, who he hoped would sympathize.'

'So his wound's bad enough to keep him in bed, is it?'

'Yes, Sir. It's pretty bad. What a mighty lunge it was too! Your friend must be made of iron to have survived at all with a wound like that.'

'So you saw the fight?'

'Yes, Sir. I followed the two gentlemen out of sheer curiosity, and saw them fight without their seeing me.'

'What happened exactly?'

'The whole thing was over in a few minutes, Sir. They stood on guard; the stranger feinted and lunged so quickly that Monsieur Porthos had three ounces of steel in his body before he even had time to parry. He collapsed and the stranger at once put his sword to his throat and forced Monsieur Porthos to admit defeat. He then asked him his name, and when he discovered that he was Monsieur Porthos and not Monsieur d'Artagnan he helped him up and brought him back to the inn. Shortly after he paid his bill and left.'

'Oh, so this fellow was really after Monsieur d'Artagnan, was he?'

'Apparently.'

'Did you hear anything more of him?'

'No, Sir. I'd never set eyes on him before and I've never seen him since.'

'Never mind. You've told me all I want to know. And now I'll go upstairs. Porthos' room is on the first floor, you say?'

'Yes, Sir, the handsomest bedroom in the inn; I could have let it ten times over since Monsieur Porthos has been here.'

'Never mind, never mind,' said d'Artagnan with a laugh. 'Porthos'll pay you all right, with the Duchess of Coquenard's money.'

'Oh, Sir, I wouldn't care what she was if I thought she'd pay up. Titled lady or attorney's wife, I wouldn't care! But she didn't even reply to Monsieur Porthos' letter! She merely sent a message by Pathaud to say that she was tired of financing his love-affairs and that she wouldn't send him a penny.'

'Did you repeat her message to Porthos?'

'We took good care not to, Sir. If we had he'd have found out how I'd sent his letter.'

'So he still thinks the money's coming.'

'Yes, Sir. He wrote again yesterday to the lady, but this time his servant took the letter to the post.'

'You say this attorney's wife's old and ugly?'

'Yes, she's fifty if she's a day, and not at all good-looking, so Pathaud says.'

'Then you certainly needn't worry. She'll soon relent. In any case I don't suppose Porthos owes you very much.'

'Not very much indeed! He owes me twenty pistoles already, not counting the doctor. You see he doesn't stint himself; I bet he's always done himself well.'

'Well, if his mistress does leave him in the lurch you can be quite sure his friends won't. So don't worry about payment; just go on giving him everything he wants.'

'You'll remember your promise not to mention the attorney's wife or the wound, won't you, Sir?'

'I will indeed. I gave you my word and I won't go back on it.'

'He'd kill me if he knew I'd told you, Sir.'

'Don't worry. He's not such a fire-eater as he looks.'

So saying d'Artagnan walked up the stairs, leaving the inn-keeper slightly reassured on the two points which were clearly of paramount importance to him, his money and his life.

Facing d'Artagnan at the top of the staircase was a big door with 'NUMBER ONE' written on it in large ink lettering. D'Artagnan knocked on this door; a voice bade him enter and he entered.

Porthos was in bed playing a game of lansquenet with Mous-queton to keep his hand in. There were partridges roasting on a spit in the fireplace and two pans were boiling on two oil-stoves in front of the fire, giving out a delicious mixed smell of grilled fish and fricassée of game. The various tables and chests in the room were stacked high with empty bottles.

When Porthos recognized d'Artagnan he gave a shout of delight. Mousqueton got up respectfully, offered the young man his chair and went over to the fireplace to see how the meal was progressing.

'Well, well my boy,' said Porthos, 'I certainly am glad to see you again. I'm only sorry I can't get up to welcome you properly.'

As he said this he cast a quick suspicious look at d'Artagnan.

'I suppose you know what happened to me?' he asked.

'No,' said d'Artagnan.

'Didn't the landlord say anything?'

'I merely asked him where your room was and came straight up.'

Porthos seemed greatly relieved.

'Well, and what did happen to you?' asked d'Artagnan.

'I'd already given that fellow three prize wounds and was just lunging at him for the fourth time to give him the *coup de grâce* when I tripped up on a stone and sprained my knee,' replied Porthos.

'Did you really?'

'Yes, on my honour. It was very lucky for the rascal I did; if I hadn't he'd be dead meat now, I can promise you.'

'And what happened to him?'

'I've no idea. He'd had about enough when I'd finished with him and just scuttled away. And now tell me about yourself, d'Artagnan.'

'So it's merely your sprained knee that's keeping you in bed, Porthos?'

'God, yes, that's all. In any case I'll be up and about again in a few days.'

'If that's all that's wrong with you why on earth didn't you hire a carriage to take you back to Paris? You must be terribly bored here.'

'I'd planned to do that. But I've got an unfortunate confession to make to you, old boy.'

'What?'

'I was, as you say, terribly bored here with my sixty-five pistoles and nothing to do, so last night I thought I'd try and relieve the monotony by inviting a fellow who happened to be staying at the inn to throw the dice with me. He accepted, and before I knew what had happened the blighter'd won all my sixty-five pistoles and my horse into the bargain. But now let's hear about you, d'Artagnan.'

Ignoring his friend's attempt to change the subject d'Artagnan replied: 'Well, Porthos, one can't have everything in this world. You know the proverb, "Lucky in love, unlucky at cards", and you can't complain of being unlucky in love. And in any case how can the loss of a few pistoles affect you? What about that duchess of yours? She won't fail you, I'm sure.'

Porthos tried hard to conceal his embarrassment.

'Well, d'Artagnan,' he replied, 'if you want to know I wrote to her the other day telling her what a run of bad luck I'd had and what a fix I was in and asking her to send me fifty louis without fail . . .'

'Well?'

'She never answered! I can only suppose she's in the country.'

'How odd!'

'Yes. I wrote her another letter yesterday, even more strongly worded. But let's stop talking about me and talk about you for a change. I confess I was beginning to be a bit anxious about you.'

D'Artagnan again refused to be sidetracked. Pointing to the steaming pans and the empty bottles, he said:

'Your landlord seems fond enough of you at any rate.'

'Not particularly,' answered Porthos. 'Only three days ago the rogue had the cheek to bring me a bill; of course I sent him packing pretty quick, him and his bill, with the result that I'm now entrenched in here more or less like an army of occupation. As you see, I'm armed to the teeth to resist any attempt to dislodge me.'

D'Artagnan laughed.

'But you evidently make sorties from time to time,' he said, pointing to the bottles and the saucepans on the fire.

'No, I don't; I wish I did,' answered Porthos. 'My blasted knee keeps me in bed. But Mousqueton here goes on marauding expeditions through the country and brings back supplies. Mousqueton, you see we've got reinforcements now, so we shall need extra rations.'

'Mousqueton,' said d'Artagnan, 'I want you to do something for me.'

'What's that, Sir?'

'I want you to give Planchet your recipe. One day I might also find myself in a state of siege, and I'd like him to do as well for me then as you're doing for Monsieur Porthos now.'

'Nothing easier, Sir,' said Mousqueton, with an air of mock modesty. 'You've only got to keep your eyes skinned. I was brought up in the country, and my father in his spare time was a bit of a poacher.'

'What did he do the rest of the time?'

'He practised a trade which I used to think most ingenious.'

'What was that?'

'It was at the time of the religious wars, when Catholics were busy killing Huguenots and Huguenots Catholics, all in the name of religion. My father thought the best idea would be to have a sort of mixed creed which would allow him to be a Catholic sometimes and a Huguenot other times. He would wander along behind the hedges which line the main roads, armed with a blunderbuss, and whenever he saw a Catholic coming along the road alone his Huguenot feelings would get the upper hand. He'd level his blunderbuss at the approaching figure and when he was about ten yards away would start a discussion which almost always ended by the man having to hand over his purse to save his skin. Likewise whenever he saw a Huguenot coming he would feel ardently Catholic and amazed to think that only half an hour before he'd had doubts about the supremacy of our Blessed Faith. You see I'm a Catholic myself, Sir; my father, in accordance with his principles, made my elder brother a Huguenot.'

'And what was the end of your worthy parent?'

'He had a most unfortunate end, Sir. One day he found himself caught in a narrow lane between a Catholic and a Huguenot, with both of whom he'd previously had discussions and both of whom recognized him. They decided to form a temporary alliance in face of their common foe, my father, whom they proceeded to string up to the nearest tree. They then walked together to the village inn where my brother and I happened to be and began boasting in our hearing of what they'd just done, which they described as a neat little job.'

'And what did you and your brother do?' asked d'Artagnan.

'We just let them talk,' answered Mousqueton. 'Then we noticed them leave the inn and go off in different directions. My brother ran ahead and lay in wait for the Catholic, while I did the same with the Protestant. Very soon we'd both done our own neat little jobs and joined in praising our father's wisdom in educating us each in a different faith.'

'Yes, Mousqueton, your father must have been a most intelligent fellow. And you say that in his spare moments he was a poacher?'

'Yes, Sir, and it was he who taught me to lay a snare and sink a line, so that when I saw what our rascal of a host intended to feed us on, hotch-potches of coarse butcher's meat fit only for yokels and quite unsuitable for impaired digestions like Monsieur Porthos' and mine, I felt the urge to return to what I might describe as my old profession. When I took my daily walks through the woods belonging to the local Squire I'd casually set a snare or two in the runs, and when I lay down and rested beside the lakes and ponds on His Lordship's estate I'd slip a sly line into the water. In that way I managed, as you see, Sir, to lay in a rich stock of partridges, rabbits, eels and carp, all of which form an excellent light diet, suitable for invalids.'

'But what about the wine?' asked d'Artagnan. 'Does the host provide that?'

'Well, he does and he doesn't.'

'What d'you mean, Mousqueton?'

'What I mean, Sir, is that he does provide it but he doesn't know he does.'

'Please explain, Mousqueton. Your conversation's both amusing and instructive.'

'I'll try and explain, Sir. In my youth I happened to fall in with a Spaniard who'd travelled a great deal and had actually visited the New World.'

'What on earth's the New World got to do with the rows of empty bottles on those chests and tables over there?'

'Wait and you'll see, Sir.'

'Very well, Mousqueton. Carry on.'

'This Spaniard had a servant whom he'd taken with him on a trip to Mexico. This fellow was a compatriot of mine and he and I soon became great friends because we'd many tastes in common. We were both very fond of sport and he used to tell me how in the pampus plains of Mexico the natives caught tigers and buffalo with nooses. At first I refused to believe it was possible to throw the end of a rope twenty or thirty feet and make it land exactly in a certain spot, so to prove it he gave a demonstration. He stood about twenty feet away from a bottle, threw a slip-knotted rope at it and caught the neck of the bottle in the noose. I began practising rope-throwing myself and having a naturally good eye soon learnt to throw as neat a lasso as any man. Now d'you see what I'm driving at, Sir? Our landlord has a very well stocked cellar but carries the key about with him.

But this cellar has a hole in the roof to let in air and light. I throw my lasso down through this hole. By degrees I got to know exactly where the best bottles were and I now fish there every day. So now, Sir, you see the connection between the New World and those bottles on the tables and chests over there. And I'd be most happy, Sir, if you'd consent to sample our wine and tell us quite frankly your opinion of it.'

'Thanks, Mousqueton. I'd have liked to but I've just lunched.'

'All right, Mousqueton,' said Porthos. 'Lay the table in any case and while we're lunching Monsieur d'Artagnan can tell us what he's been doing since we parted company with him ten days ago.'

'Right,' said d'Artagnan. 'Now I'll tell you my story.'

Porthos and Mousqueton set to on the fish and partridges with ravenous appetites and with the friendliness of men brought close by a misfortune shared. While they ate d'Artagnan talked. He told them how Aramis had been wounded and had stayed behind at Crèvecœur, how he had left Athos at Amiens engaged in a life-and-death struggle with the four rogues who had accused him of passing bad money, and how he himself had only managed to reach England over the Comte de Wardes' dead body.

At that point, however, he stopped his narrative, and disclosed none of his subsequent adventures. He merely told Porthos that he had brought four magnificent horses back with him from England, one for himself and the three others for his three friends, and that Porthos' horse was actually in the hotel stables.

At that moment Planchet came in to tell his master that the horses were now sufficiently rested and that if they started at once it would be possible to reach Clermont that night.

D'Artagnan was now fairly happy about Porthos and keen to get news of his other two friends. So he took leave of the sick man on the plea that he wished to continue his search. But, he said, he intended to take the same road back and if Porthos were still at the inn in a week or so he would pick him up on his return. Porthos replied that he did not think his knee would be cured before a week and that in any case he had to stay on at Chantilly as he was expecting an answer from his duchess. D'Artagnan said he hoped the answer would come soon and that it would be a kind one. Then, having congratulated Mousqueton on his skill and devotion in attending his master and having settled his account with the landlord, he took the road again with Planchet, leaving one of the spare horses behind for Porthos.

CHAPTER XXVI

Aramis' Thesis

D'ARTAGNAN had said nothing to Porthos either about his wound or his mistress. The Gascon was young but possessed tact beyond his years. He had pretended to believe every detail of the story that Porthos, in his vanity, had told him, for he was convinced that if Porthos knew that his secret, his so jealously guarded secret, had been discovered, his pride would be sorely hurt and he would turn hostile to his former friends. Besides, d'Artagnan argued, to know about a man's private life always gives one a moral advantage over him. And, being ambitious and determined to use his three friends as instruments for his and their advancement, he was glad to have at the outset of their careers the control of those invisible threads by which he hoped later to make them dance to his tune.

Everything seemed to be progressing satisfactorily and yet d'Artagnan was sad and sick at heart as he rode along with Planchet at his side. He was thinking of the young and pretty Madame Bonacieux, who on that fateful night was to have given him his due reward. And to his credit we can say that his despondency was due less to regret at the joys which had been denied him than to concern about what had happened to her. He was inwardly convinced that she had been a victim of the Cardinal's plan of revenge, and everyone knew how terrible the Cardinal's revenges were. How, he wondered, had he himself

managed to win the Cardinal's favour? No doubt Monsieur de
Cavois, the Captain of the Guards, could have explained this
mystery to him had he found him at home when he called.

Absorbing thoughts speed up the passage of time and
shorten journeys miraculously. D'Artagnan, obsessed with
thoughts of Madame Bonacieux, covered the twenty-odd miles
between Chantilly and Crèvecœur almost in a state of trance,
paying no heed to the country or the passers-by. Only when he
reached the village did he come to his senses. He looked along
the street and soon caught sight of the inn where he had left
Aramis. He jerked his horse into a trot and pulled up at the
main door.

This time he was received by a landlady instead of the usual
landlord. D'Artagnan was a good judge of character. He saw at
a glance that 'mine hostess' was a simple, friendly soul and
that he had no need to put on airs with her.

'Ma'am,' he said, 'can you give me news of a friend of mine
whom I left at your inn a fortnight ago?'

'A handsome, well-spoken young gentleman of about twenty-
five, dark and of slight build?'

'Yes, and with a wound in his right shoulder.'

'I know the gentleman you mean. He's still here, Sir.'

D'Artagnan at once dismounted and threw his horse's reins
to Planchet.

'Ah, that's good news, good news indeed,' he said. 'Tell me
where I can find the rascal. He's a very dear friend of mine,
Ma'am, and I'm longing to see him again.'

'If you'll pardon me, Sir, I don't think Monsieur Aramis will
be able to see you just at present.'

'Why ever not? Has he got a woman with him?'

'A woman? Good gracious me, no, Sir! A woman indeed! I
should say not!'

'Well, who is with him then?'

'The Curé of Montdidier and the Superior of the Jesuits of
Amiens.'

'Good Lord!' cried d'Artagnan; 'is he very ill? Is he dying?
Tell me the worst, Ma'am.'

'No, Sir, he's better. But after his recovery he had a moral crisis and decided to enter the Church.'

'Of course,' said d'Artagnan. 'I'd forgotten he was only a musketeer for the time being.'

'D'you still wish to see him, Sir?'

'More than ever now.'

'Very well. Go up the staircase on the right of the courtyard. His room's number 5, on the second floor.'

D'Artagnan went out into the courtyard. Here he saw one of those outdoor stairways which are still to be found in the courtyards of old inns. He ran up two flights of stairs and then re-entered the house. But it was no easy task to gain access to the future abbé's room. The passes to it were as well guarded as the gardens of Armida. Bazin had been posted in the passage and was barring the way with the determination of a man who, after many years of strain and stress, at last sees his goal within reach and will not be driven back from it.

Poor Bazin's dream had always been to serve a Churchman and he had been waiting anxiously for the moment when Aramis would finally exchange his musketeer's cap for a cassock. It was only his master's almost daily reassurance on that point that had kept him in his service for so long, for in his heart he thought that a soldier's life was vicious.

So Bazin was now in the seventh heaven of joy. It was unlikely that his master would go back on his word this time. The combination of mental and physical suffering had had the desired effect on him, for in his double affliction he had turned his thoughts to religion, and had taken the sudden disappearance of his mistress, and his wound, as warnings from above.

Nothing could have annoyed Bazin more, in his present hopeful state of mind, than the appearance of d'Artagnan. The young man would, he felt, persuade his master to return to the whirlpool of life which had held him for so long. So he resolved to defend the door bravely against him. He could not pretend, after what the landlady had said, that Aramis was out, so he tried instead to convince d'Artagnan that it would be in the worst of taste to disturb his master in the middle of the religious discussion in which he had been engaged since early morning and which was likely to occupy him till nightfall.

But d'Artagnan was not in the least impressed by Master Bazin's eloquence and, not wishing to embark on a long controversy with his friend's servant, merely pushed him aside, turned the handle of the door of room number 5 and walked in.

He found Aramis seated at an oblong table covered with scrolls of parchment and several enormous volumes. He was wearing a black robe and on his head a round flat cap like a priest's skull-cap. The Superior of the Jesuits was sitting on his right and the Curé of Montdidier on his left. The curtains were half drawn and only a faint, mysterious light filtered into the room. All those worldly objects which one usually sees in young soldiers' quarters, swords, pistols, plumed hats, embroidered doublets, silk sashes, and lace cravats, had disappeared as though by magic, for Bazin, fearing that the fascination of their presence might lead his master's thoughts astray from higher things, had swept the room clean of them. In their place d'Artagnan fancied he saw, nailed to the wall, in a far corner of the room, a cord of self-discipline like those used in monasteries.

Aramis looked round as the door opened and recognized his friend. But to d'Artagnan's amazement he showed very little emotion on seeing him; apparently his thoughts were no longer on things of this world.

'Good-day to you, my dear d'Artagnan,' he said. 'I'm delighted to see you.'

'And I'm glad to see you too,' answered the Gascon. 'I must confess, however, that I'm not yet quite convinced that it's Aramis I'm talking to.'

'Aramis at your service. Aramis and none other. What made you doubt it?'

'I thought at first I'd come to the wrong room and that you were a clergyman. And when I saw these two gentlemen I guessed wrong again; I thought then you must be seriously ill.'

The two men in black scented an enemy in d'Artagnan and looked daggers at him. But the young man ignored them.

'I'm afraid I'm disturbing you, my dear Aramis,' he

continued. 'From what I see I can only suppose, as a third possibility, that you're confessing to these gentlemen.'

Aramis coloured slightly.

'Disturbing me?' he said. 'On the contrary, my dear chap. As I said before, I'm delighted to see you. And to prove it let me say how relieved I am to think that you're still safe and well after what you've been through.'

'Ah, he's becoming his old self at last,' thought d'Artagnan. 'And high time too.'

'This gentleman's a friend of mine,' went on Aramis, addressing the two men in black. 'He's just had a narrow escape from death.'

'Give thanks to the Lord,' said the two men in black, bowing to d'Artagnan.

'I have not failed to do so, Reverend Sirs,' replied the young man, returning their bow.

'You've arrived at an excellent moment,' said Aramis. 'You'll be able to join us in debate and match your wits with ours. The Reverend Father, the Curé, and I are debating certain abstruse theological points which have interested us for some time. I'll be glad of your opinion and I'm sure these gentlemen will too.'

D'Artagnan did not like the turn the conversation was taking.

'A soldier's opinion's not worth much, I fear,' he answered. 'You'd better argue the matter out between yourselves.'

'On the contrary,' replied Aramis. 'Your opinion will be of the greatest value to us. We were arguing whether my thesis should be dogmatic and didactic. The Reverend Father thinks it should.'

'Your thesis?'

'Yes,' answered the Jesuit. 'All candidates for ordination must write a thesis.'

'Ordination!' cried d'Artagnan.

Bazin and the landlady had already warned him of Aramis' plan, but he still could not believe it. He stood and stared in amazement at the three figures seated at the table.

Aramis was reclining at ease in an armchair, for all the world as though he was in a lady's boudoir; he was holding up one hand to let the blood drain from it, and gazing at it with affection; it was as white and dimpled as a woman's hand. He now went on in his habitual drawl.

'As I was saying, d'Artagnan, the Principal would like my thesis to be dogmatic, whereas I think it should be idealistic. In his regard for dogma he has proposed the following subject as full of splendid possibilities:

' "Utraque manus in benedicendo clericis inferioribus necessaria est".'

D'Artagnan, as we know, was not very erudite. He was just as bewildered by this quotation as he had been by Monsieur de Tréville's classical reference to illustrate the folly of accepting gifts from enemies.

'Which means,' interpreted Aramis, ' "The lower orders of clergy should always use both hands in giving benediction".'

'An admirable subject,' cried the Jesuit.

'Admirable and dogmatic,' echoed the Curé.

His knowledge of Latin was about on a level with d'Artagnan's, so he was always careful to take his cue from the Jesuit before speaking.

The clerics' enthusiasm left d'Artagnan cold.

'Yes, admirable,' went on Aramis. 'Prorsas admirabile, but one which calls for a deep study of the Fathers and of the Scriptures. Now I've confessed to these learned gentlemen, in all humility, that as a result of many hours spent in the King's service I've somewhat neglected my religious studies. For that reason I'd feel more at home, "facilius natans", in a subject of my own choosing which would stand in the same relation to these tough theological problems as morality stands to metaphysics in philosophy.'

D'Artagnan was by now thoroughly bored. So was the Curé.

'A remarkable exordium,' cried the Jesuit.

'Exordium-exordia,' echoed the Curé mechanically.

'Quem ad modum inter coelorum immensitatem,' exclaimed the Jesuit.

Aramis took a quick look at d'Artagnan out of the corner of his eye and noticed that he was yawning.

'Let's talk French, Father,' he said, 'so that Monsieur d'Artagnan won't miss any of the finer points of our talk.'

'I must confess I'm tired after my journey,' said d'Artagnan, 'and I'm not enjoying the flavour of your Latin as I should.'

'Very well,' said the Jesuit.

He seemed rather disappointed; the Curé, on the other hand, looked immensely relieved and shot a quick look of gratitude at at d'Artagnan.

'Let's now consider what can be developed from this theme,' continued the Father. 'Moses, the servant of the lord ... he's only the servant, mark you. Moses blesses with both hands; he makes his followers hold up both his arms to enable the Hebrews to defeat their enemies, in other words, he blesses with both hands. Besides, what does the Baptist say: "Imponite manus", not "manum" – he talks of the laying on of hands, not of the hand.'

'The laying on of hands,' echoed the Curé. 'You see the hands,' he repeated, stretching out his own hands.

'And yet,' went on the Jesuit, 'when referring to St Peter, who is the Father of the Popes, the Scriptures say "Porrige digitos". Offer the fingers. D'you follow me?'

'Yes, Father, I do,' answered Aramis, warming to the discussion. 'But it's a subtle point.'

'The fingers,' answered the Jesuit. 'St Peter blesses with his fingers, so the Pope also blesses with his fingers. And how many fingers does he use? Three, one for the Father, one for the Son, and one for the Holy Ghost.'

Everyone crossed themselves and d'Artagnan felt impelled to do the same.

'The Pope is St Peter's successor and represents the three Divine Powers; the rest, the "ordines inferiores" in the priestly hierarchy, bless in the name of the Holy Angels and Archangels. The humblest servants of the Church, deacons and sacristans, bless with sprinklers, which symbolize an indefinite number of blessing fingers. There you have the subject of your thesis in rough outline, "argumentum omni denudatum ornamento". I shall write two large volumes on it one day, each the size of this.'

And in his excitement the Jesuit thumped a Saint Chrysostom folio which lay on the table in front of him, weighing it down with its enormous bulk.

D'Artagnan shuddered.

'I'm the first to acknowledge the beauties of that theme, Father,' said Aramis, 'but at the same time I must confess I feel unworthy of it. I myself had chosen this as a theme; listen, d'Artagnan, and tell me if it's not to your taste:

' "Non inutile est desiderium in oblatione", which means roughly:

' "It is not unfitting to season offerings to the Lord with a little regret".'

'Stop!' cried the Jesuit. 'That theme borders on heresy. There's an almost similar theme in the heretic Jansen's *Augustinus*, a book which is bound sooner or later to be burnt by the public hangman. Take care, my young friend, you're tending towards false doctrines; you're falling away!'

'You're falling away,' echoed the Curé, shaking his head dolefully.

'You're touching on the controversial subject of Free Will, which is a deadly snare. Your theme's suggestive of the innuendoes of the Pelagians and the Semipelagians.'

Aramis was a trifle abashed by the broadside of reproof which he had unwittingly called down on himself.

'But, Father . . .!' he protested.

The Jesuit continued in a stern tone:

'How do you propose to prove that one must regret the world when one gives oneself to God? How do you propose to solve this problem: God is God and the world is the devil? To regret the world is to regret the devil. That's my conclusion. Irrefutable!'

'My conclusion too,' said the Curé.

'But for Heaven's sake!' broke in Aramis, 'how . . .?'

'Desideras diabolum! Oh poor misguided soul!' cried the Jesuit.

'He regrets the devil!' echoed the Curé in mournful tones. 'Oh my young friend! Pray do not regret the devil!'

D'Artagnan felt his brain reeling. He began to think he was

in a madhouse and feared that he would himself shortly become mad like the others. But he could not protest, for he did not know how to address the three men in a language they would understand.

'Please listen, Father,' continued Aramis. His manner was still courteous but now slightly impatient. 'I won't say I regret – I won't use that word if it's unorthodox . . .'

The Jesuit raised his hands to Heaven – the Curé likewise.

'No, Father. But you must admit that it's not very gracious to offer the Lord something one doesn't value oneself. Don't you agree, d'Artagnan?'

'I most emphatically do,' cried the young man.

The Jesuit and the Curé sat bolt upright in their chairs.

'That's my premise. It's a syllogism. The world has its attractions. I'm leaving the world. Therefore I'm making a sacrifice. And it's written in the Scriptures "Make a sacrifice to the Lord".'

'That's true,' admitted the holy men.

'Besides,' Aramis continued, 'I composed a little rondeau on that subject only last year, and sent it to Monsieur Voiture. The great man complimented me on it.'

'A rondeau!' scoffed the Jesuit. The Curé echoed:

'A rondeau!'

'Recite it to us,' cried d'Artagnan. 'It'll be a welcome change.'

'No, it won't,' said Aramis. 'It's religious. Theology in verse.'

'Well, I'll be damned!' muttered d'Artagnan.

'If you insist, I'll recite it for you,' said Aramis, with an air of modesty, which, if a pose, was a most becoming one.

> 'Waste not the hours in vain regret,
> For loves departed and affections slain.
> Offer thy tears to God and pain
> Shall cease and thou shalt find comfort yet.
>   Waste not the hours.'

> ('Vous qui pleurez une vie pleine de charmes
> Et qui trainez des jours infortunés
> Tous vos malheurs se verront terminés
> Lorsqu'à Dieu seul vous offrez vos larmes.
>   Vous qui pleurez.')

D'Artagnan and the Curé seemed delighted with the verse, but the Jesuit still looked shocked.

'The style's too florid for the subject,' he said. 'Remember St Augustine's injunction, "Severus sit clericorum sermo".'

'Yes, the sermon should be clear,' said the Curé, meaning as usual to echo and support his more learned colleague.

The Jesuit, seeing that he had blundered over the Latin, broke in quickly:

'Your thesis will please the ladies, that's all; it will have the sort of success that Maître Petru's pleadings have.'

Aramis' eyes lit up.

'Would to God it might!' he cried. The idea seemed to enchant him.

'You see!' cried the Jesuit. 'The world still has its hold on you. I fear you may yet fail to find grace.'

'Don't worry, Father. I've no fears on that score.'

'Presumptuous youth!'

'I know my own mind, Father. My decision's final.'

'So you insist on adopting that thesis?'

'I feel inspired to write on that theme; no other theme appeals to me. So with your leave I'll start work on it. I hope to show it to you tomorrow, Father, set out in the form you've suggested.'

'Don't hurry over the work,' said the Curé. 'We shall leave you in a proper frame of mind for the subject.'

'Yes, the soil's well sown,' said the Jesuit. 'We need not fear that some of the seed has fallen on stony ground, some by the wayside, and that the birds of the air have devoured the rest, — "Aves coeli comederunt illam".'

D'Artagnan was by now at the end of his tether.

'To Hell with you and your blasted Latin,' he muttered.

'Good-bye, my son, until tomorrow,' said the Curé.

'Good-bye, headstrong young man,' said the Jesuit. 'You give promise of being one of the shining lights of the Church. Let's pray that that light won't become a devouring fire.'

For the last half-hour d'Artagnan had been gnawing at his nails to control himself, and had bitten them almost down to the quick.

The two clerics got up, bowed to Aramis and d'Artagnan and walked towards the door. Bazin, who had been listening to the whole debate in a trance of spiritual fervour, rushed towards them, took the Curé's breviary and the priest's missal and walked ahead of them in solemn procession to clear their path.

Aramis accompanied them to the bottom of the stairs and then returned to his visitor. He found him seated in a chair in a semi-dazed condition.

Now that they were alone together an embarrassed silence fell on the two friends. One of them had to break it sooner or later, and as d'Artagnan showed no sign of doing so, Aramis did.

'You see I've returned to my true vocation,' he said, 'like the lost sheep who returned to the fold.'

'Yes, true grace has been bestowed on you, as the gentlemen said just now.'

'I always meant to take Orders, you know. You've heard me mention it often enough, haven't you?'

'I have indeed. But I must confess I always thought you were joking.'

'Joking on a serious subject like that? Oh, d'Artagnan!'

'Hang it all, people joke even about death.'

'They oughtn't to, d'Artagnan. Death's the gate which leads either to damnation or to salvation.'

'Possibly. But please don't let's talk theology now, Aramis. You must have had enough of it for one day, and I've forgotten every word of the little Latin I ever knew. Besides which I'd like to remind you that I've eaten nothing since ten this morning and I'm hellishly hungry.'

'We'll dine in a moment, my dear fellow. But let me remind you in turn that today's Friday, and that on Fridays I mayn't look at or taste meat of any kind. However perhaps you won't object to sharing my meal of fruit and boiled tetragones.'

'What exactly are tetragones?' asked d'Artagnan anxiously.

'Spinach,' answered Aramis. 'But for your sake I'll infringe the rule for once and add a few eggs as well. But it's a serious offence; eggs are technically meat, because they hatch chickens.'

'It doesn't sound a very appetizing meal. But I'll put up with it for the pleasure of your company.'

'Thank you,' said Aramis. 'And remember, though the meal may not please your palate it'll do your soul good.'

'So you've really made up your mind to enter the Church, Aramis,' said d'Artagnan. 'I wonder what your friends and Monsieur de Tréville are going to say to that. You'll be called a deserter, you know.'

'I'm not entering the Church. I'm re-entering it. It was the Church I deserted when I went into the world. You knew, of course, that it was a great grief to me to have to put on uniform.'

'No. I didn't know.'

'You don't know why I left the Jesuit college?'

'I've no idea.'

'Then I'll tell you the whole story. Don't the Scriptures exhort us to hear each other's confessions? I'm going to confess to you now, d'Artagnan.'

'And I'm going to give you absolution in advance. You see what a good-natured fellow I am.'

'Don't joke about serious subjects, d'Artagnan.'

'Fire away, then. I'm listening.'

'I was nine when I first went to the college. At the time I'm talking of I was just twenty; I was going to be a priest; everything was fixed. I'd gone one evening to a certain house which I used to visit from time to time. I was young, you know, and no less human than my fellows. There was a certain officer who also used to visit the house, and who was jealous of me. That night he came in unexpectedly and caught me reading to the mistress of the house. I'd finished translating a passage from *Judith*, and when the fellow came in I and the lady were reading my verses together, sitting on the sofa, she with her head resting on my shoulder. Our attitude was certainly compromising, and the officer was furious. He said nothing at the time, but when I left the house he rushed out after me and said:

' "Well, young priest, does the idea of a good thrashing appeal to you?"

' "I can't answer that," I said, "as no one's ever dared try to give me one."

' "Well, listen, little priest," he replied, "if ever I catch you in that house again I'll give you one, and a proper one too."

'I think I was frightened. I went very white and I felt my knees trembling. I tried to think of some retort but could think of nothing, so I just stood there looking foolish. The officer waited for me to say something; then seeing I had nothing to say he laughed in my face, turned on his heels and went back into the house. I returned to the college.

'I'm a gentleman born, as you know, d'Artagnan, and I felt this insult terribly, though no third party had witnessed it. I could do nothing about it at the time, but it rankled. I told the Superiors at the college that I didn't yet feel properly prepared for ordination, so they postponed the ceremony for a year.

'I then called on the best fencing-master in Paris and arranged for him to give me a lesson regularly every day for the next year. I never missed a time with him. On the anniversary of the day on which I'd had the scene with the officer, I hung my cassock to a nail on the wall of my cell, dressed up in the height of fashion, and went to a ball given by a lady of my acquaintance where I knew I should meet the officer who'd insulted me. Directly I caught sight of him I went up to him — he was singing a love-song to a lady and I interrupted him in the middle.

' "Sir," I said, "are you still determined that I shan't go back to a certain house in the Rue Payenne, and would you still dare give me a thrashing if I took it into my head to defy you?"

'The officer stared at me in amazement; then he said:

' "What are you talking about? I don't think I know you, Sir."

'I replied:

' "I'm the little priest who reads the lives of the Saints and translates the Book of *Judith* into verse."

' "Oh yes, I remember!" said the officer with a sneer. "And what can I do for you now, Sir?"

' "You can spare me a few minutes of your time and come for a little walk with me."

' "Tomorrow morning, yes. I'll be delighted to oblige you then, but not now."

' "Yes, now, please."

' "If you absolutely insist . . ."

' "I absolutely insist."

' "Very well, I'll come," said the officer. Then he added: "Excuse me a moment, ladies, while I polish this fellow off. Then I'll come back and sing you the last couplet."

'We went out together. I took him to the Rue Payenne, to the very spot where a year previously he'd insulted me. It was a bright moonlight night. We crossed swords and I killed him stone dead with my first thrust.'

'Did you, by Jove?' said d'Artagnan.

'The ladies at the ball waited for the officer to return. After an hour or so they began to get frightened and reported his disappearance. A search was made and his body was eventually found in the street, with a sword-thrust through it. Everyone, of course, suspected me and there was a scandal. After that I had to give up all idea of entering the Church for some years. I'd got to know Athos just at that time, and I'd also made a friend of Porthos, who'd taught me a few sword tricks of his own besides what I'd learned from my fencing-master. These two persuaded me to join the Musketeers. My father, who was killed at the siege of Arras, had been a personal friend of the King, and I was enrolled at once. So you see the time's now come for me to return to the Church.'

'Why now more than any other time? What's happened to you today to put these shocking ideas into your head?'

'I regard this wound of mine as a warning from Heaven.'

'That wound? Rubbish. It's almost healed. No. I'm sure there's something that's making you suffer much more than that.'

'Oh? And what d'you think that is?' asked Aramis, flushing.

'A heart-wound, Aramis, a wound given you by a woman.'

A sudden look of pain crossed Aramis' face. But he forced a laugh and replied:

'Don't talk nonsense, d'Artagnan. Do you think I'd allow a woman to upset me for very long? Me love-sick! Absurd, my dear chap. Vanitas vanitatum. So you think I've allowed a woman to turn my brain! And who do you think it is? Some prostitute? Some barmaid I made up to in some provincial town?'

'No, Aramis. I think your ambitions lie higher than that.'

'High ambitions? Me, a penniless soldier of fortune? You know how I hate ties of any kind and how out of place I feel in the great world.'

D'Artagnan repressed a smile at this.

'Dust to dust, ashes to ashes,' went on Aramis. 'Man is born to sorrow; happiness lasts but a day. Take my advice, d'Artagnan; when you're in trouble hide it. Silence is the only refuge of the unhappy. Don't let others into the secrets of your heart; prying folk feed on your tears as vampires feed on human blood.'

It was now d'Artagnan's turn to sigh.

'You might be describing my own state, telling my own story,' he said.

'What do you mean?' asked his friend.

'A woman I loved has just been kidnapped. I don't know where she is; they may have taken her anywhere. She's certainly in prison – may be dead for all I know.'

'At least you've the comfort of knowing she didn't leave you of her own accord, and that why she doesn't write to you is because she can't. Whereas . . .'

'Whereas what?'

'Oh, nothing, nothing,' answered Aramis quickly.

'So you've definitely decided to leave the world? You'll never change your mind about that?'

'Never! Today you're a friend of mine; tomorrow you'll be only a memory – not even that – you'll cease to exist for me. As for the world, it's an empty tomb.'

'That's the most depressing remark I've ever heard!'

'I can't help it. My calling's clear to me, and I put it before everything.'

D'Artagnan smiled and said nothing. Aramis went on:

'And yet, before leaving the world for good, I'd have liked to hear what happened to you and the other two.'

'And I'd have liked to talk about you and your affairs,' replied d'Artagnan. 'But I see you're quite detached from everything; love you despise; friends are just memories to you, and the world's an empty tomb.'

'Yes, and one day you'll see how right I am,' sighed Aramis.

'Very well, we'll say no more about it. And knowing how you feel I see no object in keeping this letter addressed to you. It's probably only one of your prostitute or barmaid friends writing to confess some fresh infidelity. I'll tear it up.'

'What letter?' cried Aramis, starting up in his chair, his eyes glittering with excitement.

'A letter which came for you while you were away and which they gave me to give you.'

'Who's it from?'

'Some heartbroken barmaid or love-sick prostitute, I expect. It's postmarked "Tours", so it might be from Madame de Chevreuse's maid; I imagine she returned there with her mistress. I don't know why the paper should be scented and the envelope have a duchess's coronet on the back; I suppose the poor girl stole those from her mistress to make herself look important.'

'What on earth are you talking about, d'Artagnan?'

'Oh Lord! Now I've gone and lost it,' said the young man, pretending to search through his pockets and then throwing up his hands. 'But never mind. We know the world's an empty tomb for you, men and women merely shadows, and love an emotion you despise. So we needn't worry about the letter.'

'Oh d'Artagnan, you're torturing me! For God's sake find it,' cried Aramis.

'Ah, here it is,' said d'Artagnan, pulling the letter out of his pocket. 'I wonder why I couldn't find it before?'

Aramis sprang out of his chair, seized the letter and opened it. He did not read it, he positively devoured it with his eyes. Then his face lit up.

D'Artagnan with difficulty controlled his mirth.

'Your barmaid friend seems to have a pretty style in writing,' he said.

'Oh d'Artagnan, you can't think how grateful I am to you for bringing this letter,' cried Aramis, beside himself with joy. 'She had to return to Tours; she hasn't left me for someone else; she still loves me. Come here, you old devil, and let me hug you; I'm so happy I don't know what to do.'

And the two friends started dancing a wild jig round the works of the venerable St Chrysostom, trampling recklessly on the scribbled-on sheets of paper which composed Aramis' thesis and which lay strewn about on the ground.

At that moment Bazin came in carrying two dishes of omelette and spinach.

'Clear out, you gloomy old wretch!' cried Aramis, throwing his skull-cap in his face. 'Take that filthy omelette and that revolting green mess back to the kitchen, and order a roast hare, a nice fat capon, a leg of mutton, and four bottles of old Burgundy.'

Bazin was utterly baffled by his master's sudden change of mood. He stood there speechless, like a man in a trance, and, forgetting that he held two steaming dishes, allowed his hands to drop slowly to his sides, so that the omelette and the spinach rolled on to the floor.

'Now's the moment to offer your life to the King of Kings,' said d'Artagnan, 'if you want to do Him a real favour. Don't forget "Non inutile est desiderium in oblatione".'

'To Hell with you and your Latin!' cried Aramis. 'Come on, d'Artagnan, let's drink, and you can tell me all the latest news from the great world.'

CHAPTER XXVII

Athos' Wife

THE excellent dinner of meat and mellow wine served by the chastened Bazin soon made Aramis forget his thesis and d'Artagnan his fatigue. When d'Artagnan had finished acquainting his friend with the latest news from Paris, he said:

'Our next task is to find Athos in Amiens.'

'I can't see Athos allowing anyone to get the better of him,' said Aramis. 'He's a first-class swordsman and not one to lose his head, I should have thought.'

'I agree,' answered d'Artagnan, 'and I'm sure he gave a good enough account of himself. But I don't mind betting he'd have felt happier if he'd had steel and not wood against his steel — I know I should. Those rogues were all armed with sticks, and lackeys usually hit hard and keep on hitting hard. I'm not too happy about him, I'm afraid, and I'd like to make as early a start for Amiens as possible.'

'I'll try and come with you,' said Aramis. 'I can't say I feel very happy at the idea of getting into the saddle again. I tried a little self-flagellation yesterday with that cord hanging on the wall over there, but it was too painful and I had to give it up.'

'Well, really!' said d'Artagnan. 'Trying to cure a blunderbuss wound with a cat-o'-nine-tails! That's the craziest notion I ever heard! However, you were ill, and illness always makes one a bit light-headed, so I forgive you.'

'When are we leaving?'

'At dawn. Try and get as much rest as possible tonight and see how you feel tomorrow.'

'Right,' said Aramis, 'I'll say good night to you now, d'Artagnan. I expect even you need a bit of rest, man of iron that you are.'

When d'Artagnan went into Aramis' room next morning he found his friend standing at the window.

'What are you looking at?' he asked.

'I was admiring those three magnificent horses in the charge of those grooms; what a joy it would be to have mounts like that!'

'Well, Aramis, that joy's to be yours. You see, one of those mounts is yours.'

'Ha ha! Very funny! Which?'

'Whichever you like. I personally don't care which I have.'

'And that smart harness is mine, too, I suppose?'

'Most certainly.'

'You're not serious!'

'I became serious the moment you started talking French again.'

'What, those gilt holsters, that velvet saddle-cloth, and that silver-mounted saddle? All for me?'

'All for you. And the horse pawing the ground's for me and the other one's for Athos.'

'But they're the finest mounts I've ever seen!'

'Glad you like them.'

'Who gave them to you? The King?'

'Well, you may be sure it wasn't the Cardinal. Don't worry about where they came from; just concentrate on the fact that one of them's yours.'

'I'll take the one in the charge of the red-haired groom.'

'Fine!'

'Glory be!' cried Aramis. 'That's cured all my aches and pains. I'd get astride a horse like that with twenty bullets in my carcase. Just look at those stirrups! What a dream! Hi, Bazin, come here!'

Bazin came in looking listless and dejected.

'Polish up my sword, Bazin, put my hat into shape, brush my cloak, and load my pistols.'

'Don't bother about the pistols, Bazin,' said d'Artagnan. 'There are already two in your holsters.'

Bazin gave a moan of despair.

'Cheer up, Bazin, cheer up,' said d'Artagnan. 'There's room in Heaven for soldiers as well as priests, you know.'

'Monsieur Aramis was showing such promise as a theologian,' said Bazin with tears in his eyes. 'He'd have been a bishop for certain; he might even have been a Cardinal. Oh, it is a shame!'

'Listen, Bazin. By becoming a priest you don't avoid having to go to war. Look at Cardinal Richelieu! He's going off on the first campaign with a helmet and halberd like the rest of them. And what about Monsieur de Nogaret de la Valette? He's a cardinal, and just ask his servant how many times he's dressed his wounds for him.'

'Alas, Sir, yes,' replied Bazin. 'Everything's topsy turvy nowadays.'

The two young men and the wretched Bazin now went down to the courtyard where the horses were.

'Hold my stirrup for me, Bazin,' said Aramis.

He leapt into the saddle with his usual grace. But his high-spirited mount started bucking and soon the young man felt his wound throbbing again. He went very white and reeled in the saddle. D'Artagnan had foreseen that this might happen and now ran forward, caught him in his arms and helped him back to his room.

'Never mind, Aramis. You'd better stay here and look after yourself,' he said. 'I'll go on to Amiens alone.'

'What are you made of?' said Aramis. 'Does nothing ever tire you?'

'Oh I'm lucky, that's all. But how are you going to pass the time while I'm away? No more scripture commentaries or prayers, I hope.'

Aramis smiled.

'No. I'll write poetry,' he said.

'Yes, verses redolent of Madame de Chevreuse's maid's letter. Teach Bazin to versify; that'll console him a bit. And I should try out the horse a little every day to get used to his tricks.'

'Don't worry,' said Aramis. 'I'll be in fine fettle by the time you get back.'

The two friends shook hands. Then d'Artagnan took leave of

Bazin and the landlady, and ten minutes later was jogging along the road to Amiens.

How was he going to find Athos? Indeed would he find him at all?

He had left him in a very ticklish situation, and the chances were that he had not come out of it alive. At this thought d'Artagnan's face darkened and he began to devise various plans for revenge. Athos was the oldest of his three friends and one would have supposed from that that he would be the one with whom he had least in common. In fact the reverse was the case. D'Artagnan had a greater affection for Athos than for either of the other two. The older man's distinguished appearance, the wit and wisdom he displayed on those rare occasions when he dropped his habitual reserve, that unfailing good humour which made him the best possible companion, his coolness in face of danger which might have been thought foolish had it not been the fruit of self-discipline, all these talents and virtues had won d'Artagnan's respect, friendship, and admiration.

On his good days Athos could stand comparison with that most accomplished courtier, Monsieur de Tréville. He was of medium height, but so well-knit and well-proportioned that he had often floored Porthos in friendly wrestling matches, though Porthos was renowned among the musketeers for his physical strength. His well-shaped head, his shrewd dark eyes, his clear-cut, aquiline nose, his firm chin, all contributed to his air of distinction. Reserved as he was, his most outstanding gift was an innate social tact, a knowledge of how to deal with men in every walk of life. He was superior to all his friends in this, and here they followed his lead instinctively.

Like all aristocrats of that period he rode well and was a skilled swordsman. He was also very well grounded in the Classics, and in this he was exceptional; so learned was he that he used to smile at the odd scraps of Latin which Aramis had managed to glean after months of study and had more than once been able to correct his friend on some elementary point of grammar or syntax.

Last but not least of Athos' qualities was his integrity. This quality was specially praiseworthy in that lax age, in which soldiers readily compromised with their consciences, lovers fell far short of the standards of honour which prevail nowadays and poor men often failed to observe the seventh commandment. Athos at his best was, in fact, a paragon of knowledge and virtue.

And yet, for some extraordinary reason, this man, so richly endowed by nature with gifts of head and heart, was drifting slowly but surely into a life of sloth and self-indulgence, as old men drift into physical and mental decrepitude. All his friends knew it and none of them could account for it. In Athos' hours of gloom, and they were many, a heavy cloud seemed to fall on him, dulling his lively intelligence and numbing his moral sense, so that he utterly forgot the high principles upon which, in his tranquil moods, he based his life. The demi-god would then change into something less than a man. His eyes would grow lacklustre, his speech become thick and laboured, and he would sit for hours in a hunched attitude, gazing either at the bottle of wine on the table beside him or at his servant Grimaud. The latter, trained to obey by signs, was never baffled by his master's expressionless look but knew exactly what he wanted as soon as he wanted it. If the four friends had arranged to meet on a day on which Athos was attacked by melancholy none of the other three could get his companion to contribute anything to the talk beyond a word here and there, produced with a violent effort. But if at these meetings he talked less than half a man he drank enough for four, and the only effect this excess produced on him was that he frowned more deeply and became more sottishly taciturn as the evening wore on.

D'Artagnan, as we know, was extremely inquisitive and had tried hard to discover the cause of his friend's bouts of gloom. But in vain. Athos never received any letters, had no secret trysts and never disappeared suddenly as Porthos was in the habit of doing. And his sadness could not be attributed to drink, for it was the sadness that drove him to drink, although, as we have seen, the remedy was worse than the disease. It could not be explained by his gambling habits for, unlike Porthos, who boasted when he won and grumbled when he lost, Athos remained unmoved alike by success and by failure at the tables. In his tussles at cards with his fellow musketeers he had been known to win a thousand pistoles in one evening, lose them all again and his gold-embroidered sword belt, and finally win the whole lot back, plus an extra hundred louis, without raising an eyebrow.

Nor could his low spirits be attributed to changes in weather. Unlike our neighbours, the English, who become sad with the approach of autumn and the decline of the year, Athos was at his most melancholy during the loveliest seasons; June and July were the months in which his sufferings reached their climax. There was no immediate cause to account for his gloom, and the future obviously did not concern him at all. His secret must lie in the past, and this had already been hinted to d'Artagnan by his other two friends. And this aura of mystery which surrounded him made him an even more interesting study, for he had never in his most drunken moods betrayed his inner feelings either by looks or speech, even when subjected to clever cross-questioning.

'Poor Athos is probably dead now,' thought d'Artagnan as he jogged along the road to Amiens. 'And I'm responsible because I dragged him into this affair without giving him the why or the wherefore of it; he knew he didn't stand to gain anything and followed me from pure friendship.'

He expressed his fears and his remorse to Planchet as they rode along.

'And don't forget, Sir,' replied the lackey, 'that we probably owe our lives to him. You remember how he yelled out: "Get away quick, d'Artagnan! They've got me!" And how he fired off his two pistols and then began laying about him with his sword. He was like a man possessed, that he was.'

Planchet's words brought the scene back vividly to d'Artagnan's mind and made him more eager than ever to reach his friend. He put spurs to his horse, which was high-spirited enough as it was, and drove it into a gallop.

At about eleven in the morning they sighted Amiens and at eleven-thirty pulled up at the gate of the ill-fated inn.

D'Artagnan had often meditated taking revenge on the treacherous landlord. He had got some satisfaction merely from imagining the scene, and had rehearsed it so often in his mind that now, on entering the inn, he acted as though by instinct; he pulled his hat well down over his eyes, gripped his sword-hilt in his left hand, and with his right cracked his riding-whip imperiously.

The landlord came forward to greet him.

'Do you recognize me?' asked d'Artagnan.

The landlord was dazzled by his guest's brilliant turn-out.

'I haven't that honour, Sir,' he replied, bowing low.

'You mean to say you don't know me?' repeated d'Artagnan. 'In that case I must refresh your memory. What have you done with the gentleman you had the cheek to detain here a fortnight ago on a charge of passing bad money?'

As he spoke he looked the landlord sternly in the eye. The landlord turned pale.

'Oh, don't mention that unfortunate episode, Your Honour,' he said in whining, cringing tones. 'God knows I've had to pay dearly for that blunder. What a time I've had!'

'I repeat, what have you done with the gentleman?'

'Pray be seated, Sir, and be good enough to listen to my story.'

D'Artagnan was white with fury. He sat down, as stern and silent as a judge, while Planchet stood behind his chair, eyeing the landlord with the utmost scorn.

'I'll tell you exactly what happened, Sir,' went on the host nervously. 'I recognize you now. It was you who rode off while I was having that unfortunate scene with the other gentleman, your friend.'

'Yes, it was. So you see unless you tell the truth you can expect no mercy from me.'

'No, Sir. And if you'll kindly listen I'll tell you the whole sad tale.'

'I'm listening.'

'I'd been warned by the local authorities that a party of notorious coiners were going to put up at my inn, and that they'd all be wearing Guards' or Musketeers' uniforms. I'd been given a full description of all you gentlemen, your horses and your servants.'

D'Artagnan realized at once from what source this description had come.

The landlord continued:

'I'd been given six extra men by the authorities to help me arrest this party of coiners.'

'Go on,' said d'Artagnan. The term 'coiners' as applied to himself and his friends irritated him greatly.

'Forgive me, Sir, for daring to say such things, but they're my defence. The authorities had frightened me and you realize that a poor landlord must always keep in with the powers that be.'

'For the third time, mine host, I ask you; what's become of the gentleman? Where is he? Is he alive? Is he dead?'

'Patience, Your Honour,' went on the host. 'We're just coming to that. Well, you know yourself what happened next. And if I may say so, Sir,' he added, with a sudden crafty look on his face which was not lost on d'Artagnan, 'your own hurried departure made me think that what I'd been told about you might be true. At any rate the other gentleman, your friend, fought like a demon. His servant had unfortunately annoyed the men sent to me from headquarters, who were disguised as grooms . . .'

'You miserable blackguard!' cried d'Artagnan. 'You were all in the plot together! I've a good mind to slaughter the whole lot of you here and now.'

'No, Sir. We were not all in the plot together, as you'll soon see. The gentleman, your friend (forgive me for not giving him his proper title, which, alas, I don't know), put two of my men out of action with the two shots from his pistols and kept the rest of us at bay with his sword, retreating all the time, and, what's more, maiming another of my men with the point and knocking me senseless with the flat end of it.'

'Curse you, landlord! Will you never come to the point?' cried d'Artagnan. 'Athos! What happened to Athos?'

'He retreated in the direction of the cellar, Your Honour. The door happened to be open and he darted in like a flash, banging the door to behind him. Then he started to barricade himself in. Knowing that he couldn't escape from there, my men left him alone.'

'I see,' said d'Artagnan. 'You didn't intend to kill him outright; merely to keep him a prisoner.'

'Keep him a prisoner, Your Honour? Great Heavens! He kept himself a prisoner. I swear that was his doing, not ours. In any case he'd laid about him in earnest before he reached the cellar at all; he'd killed one man outright and seriously wounded two others. The dead man and the two wounded men were taken away by their fellows and I've never heard a word of them from that day to this. When I got my senses back I went to see the Governor, told him the whole story and asked him what he wished me to do with the prisoner. The Governor just gaped at me; he swore that my story meant nothing to him at all, that he'd never given me any instructions, and that if I dared mention his name to anyone in connection with the scuffle he'd have me hanged. It turned out that I'd blundered, Sir, that I'd arrested the wrong man and that the real culprit had escaped.'

'But Athos?' cried d'Artagnan in despair. The knowledge that the authorities had let the whole thing drop only increased his concern for his friend's welfare.

The landlord continued:

'My one thought now was to make my peace with the prisoner, so I went back to the cellar to let him out. Oh, Sir, he wasn't a man any more; he'd become a wild beast! When I suggested setting him free he said it was a trap and that he'd consent to come out only on certain terms. I realized that I'd put myself in the wrong by attacking one of His Majesty's Musketeers and therefore agreed to accept any terms.'

' "I insist first and foremost on having my servant returned to me armed", said he.

'We were only too glad to do this — you see, Sir, we now

wanted to please your friend in every way. So Monsieur Grimaud was taken down to the cellar, wounded as he was, and when his master'd got him safely inside he barricaded the door again and told us to go away.'

'But where is he now?' cried d'Artagnan. 'For God's sake tell me where Athos is now.'

'He's in the cellar, Sir.'

'What, you rogue? You've kept him in the cellar all this time?'

'We keep him! Good Heavens no! What an idea! Don't you realize what he's doing in there, Sir? If you could make him come out I'd be grateful to you all my life.'

'So he's in there now, is he? I shall find him there, shall I?'

'Yes, Sir. He insisted on staying there. Every day we've had to hand down bread to him through the skylight on a pitchfork, and meat whenever he asked for it. If it were only bread and meat he wanted it wouldn't be so bad. But there are other things still more to his taste. One day I tried to break in to the cellar with two of my boys, but he flew into a terrible rage and I heard him loading his pistols and his servant priming his musket. We tried to parley with him through the door, but he said he and his servant had forty rounds of ammunition between them and that they'd fire off the whole lot before they'd let any of us in. I then went off again to complain to the Governor, but the Governor said I'd only got what I deserved and that this would teach me in future not to insult honest folk who came to me for food and lodging.'

The landlord's look of woe was so comical that d'Artagnan could hardly contain his laughter.

'From that day to this,' the man continued, 'this inn's been the most miserable place in the world. You see, Sir, all my stores are in the cellar: my bottled and my casked wine; my beer, oil, and groceries, my bacon and sausages. We can't get down there at all now; I can't feed my guests and I'm steadily losing custom. If your friend stays in the cellar another week I shall be ruined.'

'And you deserve to be, you rogue! You ought to have known

from our looks that we were gentlemen and not coiners. Any-one with any intelligence could have seen that.'

'Yes, Sir, I realize that now,' said the host. 'Listen! Did you hear that? Monsieur Athos is in a rage again about something.'

'I expect they've been disturbing him.'

'They'll have to disturb him!' cried the host. 'Two English gentlemen have just called.'

'Well? What about it?'

'The English love good wine, Sir, as you know, and these two gentlemen have just ordered some of our best wine. I expect my wife's been asking Monsieur Athos to allow her in to the cellar to get them their wine and Monsieur Athos has told her to go away, as usual. Oh good Heavens! Did you ever hear such a noise? What is going on?'

D'Artagnan did, in fact, hear loud oaths coming from the other side of the house. He got up and walked in the direction of the noise, preceded by the host, who was wringing his hands, and followed by Planchet, who was holding his musket at full cock.

The two Englishmen were at the end of their patience; they had done a long stretch on the road and were ravenous and parched with thirst.

'What on earth next?' they shouted. 'Why should a madman be allowed to keep these good people out of their own cellar and we die of thirst? Come on! Let's break down the door! If the monster's too fierce we'll shoot it.'

'Steady on, gentlemen!' said d'Artagnan, drawing his pistols from his belt. 'I've a feeling you won't be shooting anyone.'

'All right!' called a calm voice from the cellar, which d'Artagnan recognized as the voice of Athos. 'Let those English blighters try to get in and they'll find something waiting for them they won't like.'

The two Englishmen looked at each other. They had been bold enough at first, but the hollow voice from the cellar seemed to intimidate them. In their mind's eyes they pictured some half-starved ogre crouching inside that vault, one of those giant creatures of folklore who jealously guard their lairs.

There was a moment's silence. Then the Englishmen plucked up courage and the bolder of the two walked down the six steps which led to the cellar and gave the door a kick hefty enough to break down a wall.

D'Artagnan began loading his pistols.

'Planchet,' he said, 'I'll deal with the one up here and you deal with the other. Since you want a fight, gentlemen, you shall have one.'

'Ye Gods!' boomed the hollow voice from the cellar. 'I do believe I heard young d'Artagnan!'

'You did, you did!' shouted back the young man. 'Athos, it's me, d'Artagnan!'

'Good!' shouted Athos. 'Now we'll tickle these English blighters up!'

The two Englishmen had meanwhile drawn their swords, but now they found themselves between two fires. They hesitated again, but personal pride prevailed once more and the Englishman standing below gave the door another mighty kick which made its timbers fairly shiver.

'Stand back, d'Artagnan!' shouted Athos. 'Stand back – I'm going to fire.'

At this point d'Artagnan's presence of mind came to the rescue.

'Gentlemen,' he said, addressing the two Englishmen. 'Aren't you being a little foolish? The odds are heavily against you and you'll be dead men before you even start to fight. My servant and I've got three rounds between us and there'll be three more coming to you from the cellar; after that we've got our swords, and we're pretty handy with them too. Leave me to settle the matter with Athos and our host here. I'll see you get your wine – don't worry!'

'If there's any left,' came Athos' growling voice from the other side of the door.

At this the landlord felt himself break into a cold sweat.

'What do you mean, if there's any left?' he quavered.

'Oh don't worry, there'll be plenty left,' said d'Artagnan. 'They can't have drunk the whole cellarful between them. Gentlemen, sheathe your swords, I beg you.'

'Very well, if you'll put away your pistols.'

'Of course,' said d'Artagnan, sticking his pistols into his belt and signing to Planchet to unload his musket.

The Englishmen now followed suit and reluctantly resheathed their swords. D'Artagnan then told them the story of Athos' imprisonment. They were gentlemen, so they put the blame on the landlord.

'Now, Sirs, kindly go back to your rooms and I guarantee that within ten minutes you'll be served with everything you can possibly want in the way of food and drink.'

The Englishmen bowed and went out.

'They've gone now, Athos!' shouted d'Artagnan through the cellar door. 'So please let me in. I'm alone.'

'Right away,' answered Athos.

D'Artagnan heard a noise of crashing beams and creaking joists; the besieged warrior was demolishing the bastions and counterscarps of his own privately constructed fortress.

A moment later the door split in two and Athos' head appeared in the opening. His face was ashen white as he stood there, trying in a dazed fashion to take stock of his surroundings.

D'Artagnan rushed towards him and hugged him affectionately. His first impulse was to drag his friend out of his dank cave into the daylight, but as he took his arm he noticed that he was staggering.

'Are you wounded?' he asked.

'No, I'm not wounded. I'm dead drunk, and so I deserve to be after my noble efforts of the past few days. Well, landlord, I must have accounted for at least a hundred and fifty of your bottles on my own.'

'Heaven help me!' cried the landlord. 'If the servant's drunk only half as much as the master, I'm ruined!'

'Grimaud's a servant of the old type,' said Athos. 'He wouldn't presume to drink the same quality wine as I. No, he drank from the barrel; incidentally I rather think he forgot to replace the stopper. Listen! I hear wine flowing now!'

D'Artagnan gave a shout of laughter while the landlord groaned and wrung his hands.

At that moment the figure of Grimaud emerged from the darkness. He had his musket slung over one shoulder and his head was lolling from side to side. He looked like a drunken satyr in a study of a Bacchanalian orgy. He was smeared from head to foot with a greasy fluid, which the host recognized as his best olive oil.

The four in procession, d'Artagnan and Planchet, Athos and Grimaud, now crossed the main hall and were shown into the best room in the inn, where they proceeded to make themselves comfortable. Meanwhile the landlord and landlady took lamps and rushed into the cellar, their own cellar from which they had been so long evicted. A hideous sight met their gaze.

The entrance was piled high with beams, joists, and empty casks which had composed Athos' fortification works. Beyond were stagnant pools of oil and wine in which floated bones and pieces of fat, the remains of the devoured hams. The left-hand corner of the cellar was stacked high with empty and broken wine-bottles and in the centre was a barrel from whose unstoppered pipe trickled a steady stream of wine, the last remains of a precious vintage. As the poet says of the battlefield, the spirit of death and devastation reigned over the scene.

Of the original fifty sausages which had hung from the rafters barely ten remained.

Now the voices of the landlord and lady were raised in lamentation, and the sound of their moans reached d'Artagnan and his companion. Even our hero was moved to pity, but Athos did not so much as look round.

Then the victims' grief turned to rage. The landlord armed himself with a skewer and with the courage of despair rushed into the room where the two friends were seated.

When Athos saw him he called out:

'Wine!'

'Wine!' cried the host in horrified amazement. 'You've already drunk a hundred pistoles' worth of my best! I'm ruined, lost, destroyed entirely.'

'Nonsense,' said Athos. 'We didn't even drink our fill.'

'And you didn't only drink; you broke all the bottles as well!'

'That was your fault. You shoved me against a case of bottles which collapsed.'

'And all my oil gone!'

'Oil's a sovereign remedy for sword-wounds. It was only natural the wretched Grimaud should dress the wounds you'd given him, and quite fair that he should use your oil to do it with.'

'And all my stock of sausages gone!'

'That cellar's full of rats, you know!'

'You'll have to pay back every penny of damage you've done,' cried the host in a passion.

'You scoundrel, you rogue, you . . .!' shouted Athos.

He tried to get to his feet but fell back at once; he had reached the limit of his capacity. D'Artagnan went to his rescue with his riding-whip raised.

The host shrank back and began to sob.

'This'll teach you to be more civil in future towards the guests whom the good Lord sends to you.'

'The good Lord! The Devil, you mean!'

'Listen, landlord,' said d'Artagnan. 'If you don't stop pestering us with your ridiculous complaints we'll all four go down into your cellar and make quite sure the damage really is as great as you say it is.'

'Very well, Sir,' whimpered the host. 'I confess I was wrong to behave to you as I did. But confession should bring absolution. You're both great lords and I'm only a poor innkeeper; you should have pity on me.'

'Oh, if you take that tone,' said Athos, 'I shall burst into tears; the tears'll flow from my eyes as the wine flowed from your barrels. Don't look so mournful! Our bark's worse than our bite. Come here and let's talk.'

The host approached nervously.

'Don't be frightened,' said Athos. 'When I was in your room, preparing to pay your bill, I put my purse down on your desk. D'you remember that?'

'Yes, Sir.'

'There were sixty pistoles in that purse. Where is it?'

'I handed it in to the Magistrate's Office, Sir. I was told it contained false money.'

'Well, go and fetch it back and keep the sixty pistoles.'

'The Magistrate's Office won't release anything. Surely you know that, Sir? If the purse had really contained false money they might have given it up. But the money was good.'

'Oh, you must work that out for yourself, my dear fellow,' said Athos. 'That's your funeral. In any case I haven't a sou left.'

'I've got an idea,' said d'Artagnan. 'What about Monsieur Athos' old horse. Where is it?'

'In the stables, Sir.'

'What's it worth?'

'Fifty pistoles at the most.'

'Nonsense! It's worth at least eighty. Take it and let's forget the whole business.'

'What's this?' said Athos. 'You're selling my horse for me? My Bajazet? But that'll leave me with nothing to ride in the campaign! Or are you suggesting I ride Grimaud?'

'I've brought another horse for you,' said d'Artagnan.

'Another horse?'

'Yes. A magnificent horse,' cried the host.

'Well, if I'm being presented with a brand new horse, by all means take the old one. And now get us something to drink.'

The host was now all smiles.

'What do you fancy, Sir?' he said.

'Some of the stuff at the back of the cellar, near the slats. There are still twenty-five bottles of that stuff left – all the others were broken in my fall. Bring up six of those.'

'This fellow's a perfect well,' muttered the host to himself. 'If he'd only stay another fortnight here and pay for all he drank I'd retrieve my fortunes.'

'And don't forget to send up two bottles to the English lords,' went on d'Artagnan.

The host bustled off to carry out his orders.

'And now, my dear d'Artagnan,' said Athos; 'while we're

waiting for our wine tell me about the other two. What happened to them?'

D'Artagnan described how he had surprised Porthos in bed with a sprained knee and Aramis at a table with two theologians. In a few moments the host returned with the bottles and a ham which he had fortunately omitted to store in the cellar.

'Well, so much for Porthos and Aramis,' said Athos, filling his and his friend's glasses. 'And what about you? What's been happening to you? There's a sinister look in your eye which I don't like much.'

'If you want to know,' said d'Artagnan, 'I'm the most unhappy of the lot of us.'

'You unhappy?' asked Athos. 'What have you got to be unhappy about?'

'I'll tell you another time,' said d'Artagnan.

'Why not now? I know, because you think I'm drunk. Actually I'm never so clear-headed as when I've had a bottle or two. So come on, tell me. I'd like to know.'

D'Artagnan described his experience with Madame Bonacieux in detail. Athos listened with the closest attention. When the young man had finished his tale Athos said:

'A wretched business – an altogether wretched business.'

It was his one and only comment on all love-affairs.

'You always say that, Athos,' said d'Artagnan. 'How can you make a remark like that when you know nothing about it? You've never been in love!'

Athos' lack-lustre eyes lit up for a second. But only for a second. They then became dull and lifeless again.

'You're right,' he said quietly. 'I've never been in love.'

'Stony-hearted fellows like you've no right to be hard on poor soft-hearted fools like us,' said d'Artagnan.

'Soft hearts – broken hearts,' muttered Athos.

'What's that you're saying?'

'I'm saying that love's a lottery in which the prize is death. You're very lucky to have lost, d'Artagnan, believe me. And if you're wise you'll take care always to lose.'

'And I thought she loved me!'

'You thought!'

'I know she loved me!'

'So gullible! Every man thinks his mistress loves him and every man's mistress is unfaithful to him.'

'Except yours, Athos, because you've never had one.'

'No,' said Athos after a moment's pause. 'I've never had one. Come on, let's drink.'

'Well, you old Socrates,' said d'Artagnan. 'Teach me your philosophy. Let me drink at the fount of your wisdom. I need to know and be comforted.'

'Comforted in what?'

'In my sorrows.'

'Your sorrows are nothing,' answered Athos. 'I wonder what you'd say if I told you a love story, in return for the one you've told me.'

'Your own love story?'

'Mine or a friend's. It doesn't really matter.'

'Come on, let's hear it, Athos. I'm dying to hear it.'

'Let's drink instead. It's more fun.'

'Let's do both. You can drink and tell me your story at the same time.'

'Yes, I could do that,' answered Athos. 'Drinking and talking go well together.'

'Good. I'm listening,' said d'Artagnan.

Athos sat lost in thought for a moment and d'Artagnan noticed that his thoughts were agitating him; he had reached the stage of drunkenness at which the common run of drinkers collapse and lose consciousness. Athos was like a man in a trance; he was dreaming and yet awake. When he spoke he seemed to be talking as much to himself as to his companion. There was something uncanny about this state of somnambulism.

'You really want to hear the story?' he asked.

'I long to hear it,' said d'Artagnan.

'Very well then, you shall. A friend of mine – a friend of mine, you understand, not I – one of the counts of my native province

of Berry, as grand as any d'Andelot or Montmorency, fell in
love at the age of twenty-five with a young girl of sixteen, as
beautiful as the dawn. Child as she was, she was marvellously
gifted; she had not a woman's but a poet's mind; she was more
than charming – she was enchanting. She lived in a little village
with her brother, the local priest. Neither brother nor sister
were native to the province; they'd settled there a short while
back. No one knew where they came from, but the sister was
beautiful and the brother good, so no one bothered to inquire.
They were said to be of good birth. My friend was the Seigneur
of the district and could have seduced the girl or even ravished
her, had he wished; he had sovereign rights and no one would
have bothered to protect two strangers from another province.
Unfortunately he was an idealist and like a fool went and
married the girl!'

'Why a fool if he loved her?' asked d'Artagnan.

'Wait and you'll see,' answered Athos. 'He took her to his
home and made her the first lady in the province. And in fairness it must be said she did full justice to her position.'

'Well?' asked d'Artagnan.

Athos lowered his voice and began talking very fast.

'One day she was out hunting with her husband and had a
fall,' he said. 'Her horse threw her heavily and she lost consciousness. The man rushed to help her and seeing that her
tight riding-habit was stifling her slit it open with a knife as
she lay on the ground and exposed her shoulder.'

Athos paused; then he suddenly gave a shout of laughter.

'Guess what she had on her shoulder, d'Artagnan!' he said.

'I can't guess. Tell me,' replied the young man.

'A fleur-de-lis,' said Athos. 'She was branded!'

And he tilted up his glass and drained the contents at one
draught.

'How horrible!' cried d'Artagnan. 'What a horrible story!'

'The truth, my dear fellow. The angel was a fiend, the innocent child a thief; she'd stolen the Communion plate from a
church.'

'What did your friend do?'

'He was sovereign ruler in his province, with rights of criminal and civil justice. He stripped his wife of the rest of her clothes, tied her hands behind her back and hanged her to a tree.'

'Good God, Athos! You mean he murdered her?' cried d'Artagnan.

'Yes,' replied Athos.

He was as pale as death.

'But look,' he went on, 'my glass is empty. That won't do at all.'

And he seized the last remaining bottle, lifted it to his mouth and drained the contents as though it were a glass.

Then he leaned over the table and buried his head in his arms. D'Artagnan sat facing him, speechless with horror.

After a moment's silence Athos looked up and continued:

'That cured me for ever of women, of enchanting creatures lovely as the dawn and with the souls of poets. God grant you the same experience!'

At last he had admitted his identity as the hero of the tale.

'So the woman died?' stammered d'Artagnan.

'Of course. But come on, reach me your glass. What, no more wine? Well then, bring the ham, landlord! And hurry!'

D'Artagnan was still horror-struck and hardly dared speak. At last he asked timidly:

'But what happened to her brother?'

'Her brother?' echoed Athos.

'Yes, the priest.'

'Oh I sent for him to have him hanged too. But he'd stolen a march on me; he'd left his parish the previous night.'

'Did you ever discover who he really was?'

'Yes, he was the creature's first lover and her accomplice. A worthy fellow who'd posed as a priest in order to marry his mistress off and ensure her and himself a livelihood. I trust he's also been hanged by now.'

D'Artagnan could only mutter to himself:

'How horrible!'

'Have some of this ham, it's delicious,' said Athos calmly, carving a slice and laying it on his friend's plate. 'If only there'd been four more hams like this in the cellar I'd have polished off fifty more bottles of wine!'

D'Artagnan felt he could bear no more. The conversation was driving him mad. It was his turn to bury his head in his arms and pretend to go to sleep. Athos observed him pityingly and muttered to himself:

'The youth of today certainly can't drink. That fellow's one of the best. And just look at him!'

CHAPTER XXVIII

The Return

D'ARTAGNAN had been stunned by Athos' terrible story. There were a great many details about which he was not yet clear. Although Athos had been drunk when he told his tale and d'Artagnan half drunk, the latter on waking next morning remembered all that his friend had said as clearly as though the words had been planted one by one in his mind as they were uttered. He was very anxious to know more and knocked early on his friend's door with the object of continuing their previous night's conversation. But he found Athos back in his normal state of mind, that is to say urbane and inscrutable.

Moreover, after wishing d'Artagnan good morning, the older man took the bull by the horns and himself brought up the topic of their night's debauch.

'I'm afraid I was very drunk last night, d'Artagnan,' he said. 'I realized that this morning from the state of my tongue and the fact that I'd a bad headache. I bet I said a great many very silly things.'

As he spoke he stared at d'Artagnan so hard that the young man was embarrassed.

'I don't remember your saying anything at all odd,' replied the latter.

'That's funny,' said Athos. 'I thought I remembered telling you a most deplorable story.'

And he gave his friend a searching look.

'I can only think I must have been even drunker than you then,' replied d'Artagnan. 'I remember nothing about it.'

Athos was not deceived by this. He continued:

'I expect you've noticed, d'Artagnan, that drink affects people differently. It makes some cheerful, others sad. I'm the kind that gets sad, and the moment I'm drunk I start repeating all the lurid stories my fool of a nurse stuffed into my head when I was a boy. That's my failing; a very bad failing, I grant you. But apart from that I'm a good drinker.'

Athos spoke so simply and naturally that d'Artagnan began to have doubts. Wishing to find out the truth, he said:

'So that's the explanation! I do remember now your telling me some story about someone being hanged. I wasn't sure if you really had told it me or if I'd dreamt it.'

Athos went very white. But he tried to hide his feelings and replied with a laugh:

'I was sure I'd said something! People being hanged is one of my nightmares.'

'Yes, that's right,' said d'Artagnan. 'It's all coming back to me now. It was a story about some woman being hanged.'

Athos went ashen-coloured. He stammered:

'Yes, yes! That's my great story! The hanging of the fair woman. When I start telling that story it's a sign I'm dead drunk.'

'As far as I remember,' said d'Artagnan, 'she was a tall, fair, lovely girl with blue eyes and a poet's soul.'

'Yes, hanged.'

'Hanged by her husband, a fellow you used to know,' continued d'Artagnan, staring closely at his friend.

Athos shrugged his shoulders and replied:

'You see how indiscreet one can be when one's drunk. I shall never get drunk again, d'Artagnan. I always regret it afterwards.'

D'Artagnan said nothing. Then, to change the conversation, Athos remarked:

'By the way, thanks very much for the horse you brought me.'

'D'you like it?'

'Yes, but it's no cart horse. I mean it isn't very strong.'

'Oh yes, it is. I did thirty miles on it in an hour and a half and it was as fresh at the end as though I'd only trotted it round the square.'

'Oh Lord, you're making me feel guilty.'

'Guilty? Why?'

'I've got rid of it.'

'Got rid of it? How?'

'I'll tell you. I woke up at six this morning. You were sleeping like a log and I didn't know how to pass the time. I was still feeling the effects of last night's debauch. I went down to the hall where I found one of the Englishmen buying a horse from a coper. His had had a stroke in the night. I went up to him and heard him offering a hundred pistoles for a red bay. I said to him: "If you want a horse I've got one for sale".'

' "And a very fine one too!" replied the Englishman. "I saw your friend's servant exercising it yesterday."

' "D'you think it's worth a hundred pistoles?" I said.

' "Every sou of it," he replied. "Will you let me have it for that?"

' "No," I said. "But I'll play you for it."

' "What at?"

' "Dice."

'We set to at once and I lost the horse.'

D'Artagnan looked rather vexed.

'Never mind, I won back the harness,' said Athos to console him.

D'Artagnan still seemed upset.

'Are you annoyed?' inquired Athos.

'I must confess I am rather,' replied d'Artagnan. 'That horse was supposed to make us conspicuous on the battlefield. It was a token of friendship – a souvenir. You shouldn't have done that, Athos.'

'Put yourself in my place, my dear fellow. I was bored to death. Besides, I don't like English horses. And if it's only a question of being recognized on the battlefield the saddle'll do that for me all right. God knows it's striking enough. And we'll find some excuse for the disappearance of the horse. Damn it all, horses are mortal. We'll say mine got glanders or farcy.'

D'Artagnan still looked upset.

'I'm sorry you should set such store by those mounts,' continued Athos. 'You see I've got something even worse to confess to you.'

'Good Lord! What?'

'When I lost my horse nine to ten (you see how close it was!) I suddenly had the bright idea of staking yours.'

'That doesn't strike me as a very bright idea.'

'Well, bright or not I did it. I staked your horse too.'

'Well, really, Athos!' exclaimed d'Artagnan in great annoyance.

'I staked your horse and lost it.'

'Lost it?'

'Yes. Seven to eight. By one point . . . you know the proverb.'

'Athos, you're mad. I swear you are.'

'You ought to have told me that when I was spinning you those silly yarns last night. Not this morning. As I was saying I lost your horse, harness, saddle and all.'

'But don't you realize that's very serious?'

'Wait! You haven't heard the end yet. I'd be an excellent gambler if I weren't so obstinate. But I find myself getting obstinate gambling just as I do drinking. I can never stop.'

'But you'd nothing more to gamble with. You'd lost everything.'

'There was still one thing, the diamond ring I noticed you wearing yesterday.'

D'Artagnan put his hand quickly over the ring.

'Not this ring!' he cried.

'Yes. And I'm a bit of a connoisseur in rings, having owned quite a few in my time. I'd valued yours at a thousand pistoles.'

D'Artagnan was now thoroughly alarmed. He said, looking sternly at Athos:

'I trust you didn't mention this ring to the Englishman.'

'Of course I did,' replied Athos. 'Don't you see that ring was the only other asset I had? I could get back our horses and our harness with it – might even make something to pay for our journey back.'

'I don't think that's funny at all, Athos. You're upsetting me very much.'

'As I said, I mentioned the diamond to my Englishman. He'd noticed it himself. You can't wear a jewel like that and expect people not to notice it, d'Artagnan.'

'For God's sake finish your story,' said d'Artagnan. 'You're killing me – springing all these frightful surprises on me.'

'Well, we divided the diamond into ten parts, each valued at a hundred pistoles.'

D'Artagnan now began to grow really angry.

'You're inventing all this, aren't you? You're trying to see how much I'll take from you.'

'Not at all,' replied Athos coolly. 'I only wish you'd been there. I'd been quite alone for a fortnight and was getting sottish draining down all that drink by myself.'

D'Artagnan was biting his lip to control himself.

'That's no reason to go gambling with my diamond,' he said.

'Let me finish. It was to be ten throws of a hundred pistoles each, no revenge. I lost the whole diamond in thirteen throws. Thirteen, if you please! That always has been an unlucky number for me. It was on July 13th . . .'

'Ye Gods!' cried d'Artagnan, jumping up from the breakfast table. What he had heard that morning had driven the previous night's debauch completely out of his head.

'Wait a minute, there's more to come,' said Athos. 'I wasn't beaten even then. I'd thought of a plan. That Englishman was a queer devil. I'd seen them talking to Grimaud that very morning and Grimaud told me he'd been asking him to leave me and go to him. So I now staked Grimaud, the silent Grimaud, divided into ten parts, like the diamond.'

At this d'Artagnan momentarily forgot his annoyance and burst out laughing.

'Well, I'll be . . .' he cried.

'Yes, I actually staked Grimaud,' went on Athos. 'The whole of him's not worth a ducat, but I played him in ten parts and won back the diamond with him. What d'you think of that?'

D'Artagnan was quite cheered up by this news.

'Magnificent!' he exclaimed, still convulsed with laughter.

'I now felt my luck had returned, so of course I re-staked the diamond.'

D'Artagnan's face fell again.

'I won back your harness first and then your horse; then my harness and my horse. And then I lost them all again. To cut a long story short I ended up with your harness and mine. It was a superb stroke of luck. I thought I'd let it rest at that.'

D'Artagnan heaved a sigh of relief. Then he inquired weakly.

'I hardly dare ask, but have I still got my ring?'

'Intact, old boy. And your harness and mine into the bargain.'

'But what's the use of harness without horses?'

'I've got another bright idea about that.'

'What's it this time?'

'Listen, d'Artagnan. You haven't gambled for ages, have you?'

'No, and I've no wish to.'

'Don't interrupt. I was saying that you hadn't gambled for ages, so your luck should be in.'

'Well, what about it?'

'The two Englishmen are still here. I saw they were sorry to lose the harness, and I see you're sorry to lose your horse. Why not stake your harness against your horse?'

'What would they want with one harness?'

'Stake both harnesses. Mine as well. I'll gladly hand over mine in a good cause.'

D'Artagnan hesitated.

'Would you really do that?' he said.

He was beginning to catch his friend's gambling fever.

'On my honour. On one throw.'

'But we've lost the horses, and I don't want to lose the harness too.'

'Well, stake your diamond then.'

'No, that I will not do!' said d'Artagnan firmly.

'Oh damn!' cried Athos. 'I'd suggest your staking Planchet,

but I've already staked Grimaud so the Englishman probably wouldn't fall for that.'

'I think I'd really rather not risk anything, Athos.'

'What a pity! That English fellow's stuffy with pistols. Come on, be a sport! Just one throw!'

'And if I lose?'

'You won't.'

'But if I do?'

'You'll lose the harness, that's all.'

'Very well, one throw.'

Athos set off in quest of the Englishman. He found him in the stables, gazing covetously at the harness. It was an opportune moment. Athos proposed the stakes: the two harnesses against one horse or a hundred pistoles. The Englishman made a swift calculation. The two harnesses together were worth every sou of three hundred pistoles. He accepted.

D'Artagnan's hand was shaking as he threw the dice. The number three came up and he went as white as a sheet. Athos said calmly:

'That's a pretty poor throw, my lad. It looks as though you're going to get horses, harness and all, Sir.'

The Englishman looked triumphant. It was now his turn to throw. He did not even rattle the box, but threw the dice out carelessly without bothering to look at them, so sure was he of victory. D'Artagnan had turned his head away to hide his chagrin. Suddenly he heard Athos remark coolly:

'Well, that's an extraordinary throw! I've only seen it four times in my life, two aces.'

The Englishman looked at the dice aghast. D'Artagnan also looked and flushed with pleasure.

'Yes, four times only,' went on Athos. 'Once at Monsieur de Créquy's house; once in my house in the country, when I had one; once at Monsieur de Tréville's house, where everyone remarked on it, and once in an inn, where I threw it myself and lost a hundred louis and a supper on the strength of it.'

'I suppose you'll take your horse back, Sir,' said the Englishman.

'Definitely,' replied d'Artagnan.

'You won't give me my revenge?'

'We agreed no revenge.'

'Very well, Sir, I'll have your horse returned to your servant.'

'Just a moment, gentlemen,' broke in Athos. 'If you'll excuse me,' he added, turning to the Englishman, 'I'd like a word with my friend in private.'

'Right.'

Athos took d'Artagnan aside.

'I suppose you're going to try and tempt me again, Athos?' said d'Artagnan. 'You want me to stake another throw, I suppose.'

'No. But listen. You're taking your horse back, aren't you?'

'Definitely.'

'I think you're wrong. You ought to take the hundred pistoles. You were staking the harnesses against the horse or a hundred pistoles, remember?'

'Yes.'

'I'd take the hundred pistoles.'

'Oh, you would, would you? Well, I'm taking the horse.'

'I think you're being very foolish. What's the good of one horse between the two of us? I can't ride pillion to you; we'd look like two sons of Aymon who'd lost their brothers. And I'd feel very small with you capering about on that charger of yours. I wouldn't hesitate; I'd take the hundred pistoles every time. We need money to get back to Paris.'

'I'm very fond of that horse, Athos.'

'You're making a mistake. Horses shy and stumble, get glanders and farcy and God knows what. Then they're dead meat and there's a hundred pistoles gone down the drain. And owners have to feed their horses, remember, whereas pistoles feed their owners.'

'But how shall we get back at all without a horse?'

'On our servants' horses, of course. People will know from our looks we're gentlemen.'

'We'll look pretty silly on a couple of mules, with Porthos and Aramis capering about on their chargers.'

'Porthos and Aramis!' echoed Athos.

And he suddenly started chuckling to himself.

'What's the joke?' asked d'Artagnan rather irritably.

'Nothing, nothing. What were we saying?'

'You were saying I ought to take the hundred pistoles.'

'Yes. With the hundred pistoles we can celebrate till the end of the month. We've had a pretty strenuous time lately; we deserve a little relaxation.'

'Me celebrate? Not on your life!' said d'Artagnan. 'Directly I get back to Paris I'm going to start searching for Constance.'

'Well, a hundred pistoles will be much more use to you than a horse. I'd take the pistoles every time.'

D'Artagnan only needed a good excuse to give in. That seemed an excellent one. And if he held out any longer his friend might think him selfish. So he agreed and took the hundred pistoles from the Englishman in place of the horse.

Now the two friends' one wish was to be off. The landlord agreed to settle for six pistoles plus Athos' old horse. D'Artagnan and Athos took Planchet's and Grimaud's horses, and the two latter set off on foot, carrying their masters' saddles on their heads.

Badly mounted though they were the masters soon outdistanced their servants and arrived at Crèvecœur. They spied Aramis from a long way off; he was seated at his bedroom window, with his elbow on the sill, like Sister Anne, watching the landscape shimmering in the sunlight.

'Hullo, there, Aramis!' cried the two friends. 'And what d'you think you're doing?'

Aramis shouted back:

'Oh, it's you, d'Artagnan and Athos! I was merely pondering. I've just seen my English horse leave me and disappear in a cloud of dust; to me it symbolized the transitory nature of this world's goods. Life itself can be summed up in three words: Erit, est, fuit.'

D'Artagnan began to suspect what had happened.

'Cut out the poetry, Aramis, and tell us what you're driving at,' he begged.

'Just this,' replied Aramis. 'I've been badly done. Sixty louis for a horse which I could tell from its canter could do a steady fifteen miles an hour comfortably.'

D'Artagnan and Athos burst out laughing.

'Don't be too angry with me, d'Artagnan,' said Aramis. 'Needs must where the devil drives. Anyway I'm the chief sufferer – that damned coper's done me out of fifty louis at least. But I see you're cleverer, you two. Good idea of yours riding your servants' horses and sparing your own. I suppose you're having yours brought along by slow stages, on leading reins.'

At that moment a market-cart came rumbling down the high road and drew up opposite the inn. Out of it stepped Grimaud and Planchet, carrying their saddles on their heads. The cart was returning empty to Paris and the driver had agreed to give the two lackeys a lift on the condition that they stood him plenty to drink on the road.

'Hullo, what's this?' asked Aramis. 'Planchet and Grimaud and two saddles? Where are the horses?'

'Where yours is, of course,' said Athos.

'My dear fellow, great minds think alike,' said Aramis. 'Some instinct made me keep my harness too. Hi, there, Bazin, fetch my new harness and put it in the cart with these two gentlemen's!'

'And what have you done with your Reverend Fathers?' asked d'Artagnan.

'I asked them to dinner the evening you left,' replied Aramis. 'Incidentally there's some delicious wine here. I made them as drunk as Lords. The Curé actually forbade me to leave the army, and the Jesuit begged me to get him a commission in the Musketeers.'

D'Artagnan burst out:

'He mustn't bring his thesis! We can't allow that!'

'Since then I've been leading quite a pleasant life,' went on Aramis. 'I'm composing a poem in words of one syllable. It's rather difficult, but the merit of a composition is in overcoming difficulties. I'll let you see the first canto: it's got four hundred verses and takes a minute to read.'

D'Artagnan hated poetry almost as much as he hated Latin. He observed:

'You say the first canto's difficult. Let's hope the second'll be impossible.'

'I'm sorry you feel like that about it,' replied Aramis good-humouredly. 'But now we're returning to Paris, my lads, aren't we? Fine! I'm ready when you are. And we're going to pick up that old devil Porthos on the way. Fine again! I've really missed the old boy quite a lot. I like him, conceit and all; he makes me feel more pleased with myself. I'll bet he hasn't sold his horse; not he! I'm really looking forward to seeing him on it and the new saddle and all. He'll put the Grand Mogul's nose right out of joint.'

They stopped for an hour at Crèvecœur to give the horses a rest. Aramis settled his account at the inn and saw Bazin into the cart with Grimaud and Planchet. Then the whole party set off to pick up Porthos.

They found him almost restored to health and with much more colour in his face than at d'Artagnan's first visit. He was sitting alone at a table laid for four, on which were spread various meat dishes, bottles of expensive wine, and bowls of delicious fruit.

'Welcome, gentlemen!' he said, getting up from his chair. 'You've timed your arrival well. I was just starting on the soup and now you can all join me.'

'Just look at those bottles!' said d'Artagnan. 'I bet they weren't lassoed by Mousqueton. And don't I see larded veal and fillet of beef?'

'I'm building myself up again,' said Porthos. 'Nothing pulls one down more than these damnable sprained knees. Have you ever sprained a knee, Athos?'

'Never,' replied Athos. 'But in one of our scraps with the guards I remember getting a sword wound and about a fort-night later feeling exactly as you feel now.'

'Surely you didn't order that banquet just for yourself, Porthos!' said Aramis.

'No,' said Porthos. 'I'd invited three fellows who live near here to dine with me, but they all put me off at the last moment. Now you three can share it with me instead. Hi, there, Mousqueton! Bring three more chairs and another dozen bottles.'

The four friends set to work on the meal with a will. They ate in silence for a few minutes. Then Athos said suddenly:

'D'you know what we're eating, gentlemen?'

'I know what I'm eating,' said d'Artagnan. 'I'm eating larded veal.'

'I'm eating fillet of lamb,' said Porthos.

'And I white of chicken,' said Aramis.

'You're wrong, all of you,' said Athos gravely. 'You're all eating horse.'

'Athos, don't be absurd!' said d'Artagnan.

'Horse?' cried Aramis with a look of disgust.

Porthos alone of the four said nothing.

'Yes, horse,' repeated Athos. 'We're eating horse, aren't we, Porthos? We're probably eating harness too.'

'No, gentlemen, I kept the harness,' replied Porthos.

'My God, we're all as bad as each other!' cried Aramis. 'You'd think there was telepathy between us.'

'I couldn't help it, gentlemen,' said Porthos. 'That horse made everyone round here jealous, and I didn't want to upset them.'

'And I suppose your duchess is still in the country,' suggested d'Artagnan. 'Which, of course, doesn't help.'

'Yes, she's still away,' replied Porthos. 'And the Governor of this province, who was to have been my guest this evening, seemed to want the horse so much that I hadn't the heart to refuse him.'

'What, you gave it to him?' cried d'Artagnan.

'As good as,' said Porthos. 'It was worth at least a hundred and fifty louis and the brute wouldn't give me more than eighty for it.'

'Saddle and all?' asked d'Artagnan.

'No, without the saddle.'

'You see, gentlemen,' said Athos; 'Porthos has done the best deal of all of us.'

Whereupon Athos, Aramis, and d'Artagnan burst into shouts of laughter which completely bewildered Porthos. But they soon told him the reason for their mirth, and he laughed louder than anyone.

'So now we're all rich,' said d'Artagnan.

'I'm not,' said Athos. 'I found Aramis' Spanish wine very much to my taste and ordered sixty bottles to be loaded into the van, which put me down again a good deal.'

'I'm afraid I've been a bit extravagant too,' chimed in Aramis. 'D'you realize I'd offered every sou I possessed to the Montdidier Church and the Jesuits of Amiens? And I committed myself in other ways which also cost money. I ordered masses for myself and all of you. They'll be read and I'm sure we shall be the better for them.'

'And you don't suppose my sprained knee cost me nothing, do you, gentlemen?' said Porthos. 'And Mousqueton's wound? I had to have the surgeon twice a day to treat him.'

Athos exchanged secret smiles with d'Artagnan and Aramis.

'That was very generous of you,' he said. 'I see Mousqueton's got a good master.'

'So what with all that and my debt to this inn I've only got thirty crowns left.'

'And I've got about ten pistoles,' said Aramis.

'Why, we're millionaires, all of us!' exclaimed Athos. 'How many of your hundred pistoles have you got left, d'Artagnan?'

'Well, I had to give you fifty to start with.'

'Me?'

'Yes. Don't you remember?'

'Oh yes, I'd forgotten.'

'Then I paid another six to the landlord.'

'That rogue! Why on earth?'

'You told me to.'

'Did I? I'm too generous, I swear. Well, after all that what have you got?'

'Twenty-five pistoles.'

Athos pulled some small change out of his pocket.

'And that's what I've got,' he said.

'Is that all?'

'Yes. And it's so little it's not worth counting.'

'Well, let's add up what we've all got together,' said Athos. 'Porthos?'

'Twenty crowns.'

'Aramis?'

'Ten pistoles.'

'D'Artagnan?'

'Twenty-five pistoles.'

'Which makes a total of . . .?'

'Four hundred and sixty-five livres,' said d'Artagnan, who was a quick reckoner.

'We'll have about four hundred when we get to Paris,' said Porthos. 'Plus the harness, of course.'

'But what about our battle chargers?' asked Aramis.

'We can buy ourselves two good horses with our servants' four, which we'll draw lots for,' said Athos. 'Of our four hundred livres we'll give half to one of the horseless ones, and the scrapings from our pockets to d'Artagnan, who's lucky at dice and can go and stake them at the first gambling-house we meet. So that settles that.'

'Good,' said Porthos. 'And now let's get on with our dinner. The second course is getting cold.'

And the four friends, now easier in their minds about the future, did full justice to the meal, leaving the remains to be devoured by their four servants.

When they arrived back in Paris d'Artagnan found a letter from Monsieur de Tréville telling him that the King had decided to open the campaign on 1 May, and that he must start buying his equipment at once. Though he had only parted from his friends half an hour before he ran off at once to find them again. He discovered them all in Athos' rooms; they all looked worried, and d'Artagnan suspected at once that they had had some fairly serious news.

It turned out that they had all received letters from Monsieur de Tréville telling them about the campaign and ordering them to buy their equipment. All three looked despondent; they knew that Monsieur de Tréville was very strict in matters of discipline and the problem of how to buy equipment for the campaign with their little stock of money seemed insoluble.

'How much d'you think this equipment will cost?' asked d'Artagnan.

'At least fifteen hundred livres each,' said Aramis. 'And we can't raise more than a hundred each at the most.'

'Four times fifteen's sixty, in other words six thousand livres for the four of us,' said Athos.

'I think we ought to try and manage on a thousand apiece,' said d'Artagnan.

'And how d'you think we're going to get that much?' asked Porthos. Then his face suddenly brightened.

'I've got an idea,' he said.

'You're lucky,' said Athos. 'I haven't the faintest shadow of one. As for d'Artagnan I think he's mad. A thousand livres indeed! I tell you all here and now I'm not spending a sou less on my outfit than two thousand livres.'

'Four times two thousand's eight thousand,' remarked Aramis. 'So to get properly turned out we need eight thousand livres. Quite a tidy sum! Of course we've got our saddles. We can count those as credit, which is something.'

CHAPTER XXIX

In Search of Equipment

D'ARTAGNAN was undoubtedly the most harassed of the four friends, although as an ordinary guardsman his campaign equipment presented far less of a problem than that of the musketeers, who formed the King's personal bodyguard. The young Béarn recruit was, we know, thrifty almost to the point of avarice, but strangely enough, he was vain too. The question of how to cut a good figure in the campaign worried him a lot, and he was also concerned about Madame Bonacieux. The efforts he had made on her behalf had so far led to nothing. Monsieur de Tréville had mentioned the matter to the Queen, who had promised to make inquiries. But d'Artagnan had regarded this promise as a mere formality, which would probably lead nowhere.

Athos would not leave his room; he was determined to make no effort at all to find equipment.

'We've got another fortnight,' he said to his friends. 'If I haven't found anything by then, or rather if nothing has found me by then, I can see only one way out. My religion forbids suicide, so I shall pick a quarrel either with five of the best of His Eminence's Guards or with eight Englishmen and go on fighting till one of them kills me, which is pretty well bound to happen with those odds against me. Then the world will say I died in the King's service, and I shall have done my fighting without needing to get equipment.'

Porthos kept pacing up and down the room, with his hands behind his back, nodding his head solemnly and muttering to himself:

'I must think out my plan; I must get on with my plan.'

Aramis sat looking worried and saying nothing.

From this short summary we can see that an atmosphere of gloom reigned over the little community.

Like the coursers of Hippolytus the servants reflected their masters' mood, and mourned in sympathy with them. Mousqueton made it his daily task to collect crusts of bread. Bazin, who had a taste for religious observance, spent all his time in church. Planchet lay and watched the flies on the ceiling, and Grimaud, who could not be induced even now to break the strict rule of silence imposed on him by Athos, heaved a succession of sighs sad enough to melt a heart of stone.

Athos, as we have said, refused to make any effort to find equipment, but the three others were on the hunt from early morning till late evening. They wandered about the streets, examining the pavements in the hope of finding a stray purse accidentally dropped by a passer-by. They were like bloodhounds on the trail, so eagerly did they sniff the ground for booty. Whenever they met they would eye each other in silence and each knew that the question in the other's mind was:

'Have you found anything?'

Porthos had been the first to hit on a plan, so he was the first to act. He was not a man who readily admitted defeat. One day d'Artagnan noticed him wending his way towards the Saint-Leu church, and curiosity prompted him to follow him. He noticed him curl his moustache and stroke out his beard before entering the church and presumed from this that he was on an errand of conquest. D'Artagnan followed him into the church, but took care to keep out of his sight, so that Porthos should not know that he was being watched.

The big man walked up the aisle and stood beside a pillar near the chancel. D'Artagnan followed him and leant against the other side of the pillar, still hidden from his friend's sight.

A sermon was being preached that day, so the church was full. Porthos, who had a roving eye, was soon busy ogling all the female members of the congregation. With the help of Mousqueton he had managed to make himself look quite presentable and his appearance adequately belied the state of his purse. His hat was perhaps a trifle shabby, the plume faded; his gold facings were somewhat tarnished, and his lace trimmings somewhat frayed. But the half-light was kind to these little shortcomings of dress, and Porthos, reclining at ease against the tall column, was an impressive figure.

D'Artagnan soon noticed a woman seated in a pew nearby, a woman in the early autumn of life, slightly parched and wrinkled of skin, but a dignified enough figure in her black hat and dress. Porthos cast a quick look or two at this woman out of the corner of his eye and then started ogling the other ladies of the congregation in earnest.

The lady in black, for her part, let her gaze rest for a second on the handsome Porthos, upon which he, as though in answer to a signal, started fluttering his eyelashes wildly down the aisle. This manoeuvre obviously irritated the lady in the black hat, for she now began biting her lip and fidgeting uneasily in her seat.

Seeing this Porthos once more curled his moustache, and began casting sheep's eyes at a beautiful lady seated near the choir. Besides being beautiful this lady was obviously someone of rank, for in the pew behind her sat a little Negro boy who carried the cushion upon which she knelt to pray and a maid who carried the embroidered bag which contained her prayer-book.

The lady in black followed every dart and roll of Porthos' eyes and noticed his gaze rest at last on the lady with the velvet cushion, the maid, and the Negro page. Porthos played his cards cunningly; he now ogled the beauty so shamelessly that the lady in black became frantic. Finally, unable to contain herself, she did a sort of private *mea culpa*; she beat her breast and groaned like an animal in pain. So loud was her groan that the whole congregation, including the lady with the velvet cushion, turned round to look at her. Porthos alone did not turn round; he knew exactly who had groaned and why, but pretended to have heard nothing.

The beautiful lady with the velvet cushion was the cynosure of all eyes. But she impressed three people in particular; the lady in black, who saw in her a formidable rival; Porthos, who thought her ten times more attractive than the lady in black, and lastly d'Artagnan, who recognized her as the woman of Meung whom his evil genius, the man with the scar, had addressed as Milady.

The young man was determined not to let the lady out of his sight. Meanwhile he continued to watch Porthos' little comedy with considerable amusement. He deduced that the lady in black must be the attorney's wife from the Rue aux Ours, both from her appearance and from the fact that that street was quite close to the Saint-Leu church. He guessed that Porthos was now getting his revenge for his setback at Chantilly, when the attorney's wife had turned a deaf ear to his request for money.

When the sermon was over the attorney's wife stepped up to the stoup of holy water. Porthos also walked up to it, reached it just before she did and dipped not one finger but his whole hand into the water. The attorney's wife imagined that he was paying her this attention and gave him a sweet smile. But the next moment she was cruelly undeceived. When she was only three feet from him he turned away and gazed fixedly at the other lady who was at that very moment approaching with her maid and her black page. Porthos waited until she was quite close and then lifted his dripping hand from the stoup. The lady laid her slender fingers on Porthos' broad hand, smiled her thanks, crossed herself, and left the church.

This was more than the attorney's wife could bear. She was by now convinced that Porthos and her rival had a secret understanding. Had she been a lady of rank she would have fainted. But she was only an attorney's wife, so was content to hiss furiously at the musketeer:

'Well, Monsieur Porthos! Aren't you going to offer me some holy water too?'

At the sound of her voice Porthos pretended to start with surprise.

'Well, well, Ma'am!' he said. 'Fancy seeing you! And how's Monsieur Coquenard, your husband? As mean as ever? Where can my eyes have been that I never noticed you during the whole of that two-hour sermon?'

'I was only a few feet away from you, Sir,' said the attorney's wife. 'You didn't notice me for the simple reason that you had eyes only for that beautiful lady you gave the holy water to.'

Porthos pretended to be embarrassed.

'Oh, so you noticed, did you . . .?'

'I'd have had to be blind not to notice.'

'Yes,' said Porthos coolly. 'The lady's a friend of mine, a duchess. She has a very jealous husband who tries to stop her seeing me. It's been very difficult to arrange meetings with her, and today she came all the way to this church in this God-forsaken district on purpose to meet me.'

'Monsieur Porthos,' answered the attorney's wife, 'will you be good enough to take a stroll with me? I want to talk to you.'

'With pleasure, Ma'am,' said Porthos. And he smiled to himself like a gambler gloating at the thought of a trick he is about to play on an unsuspecting opponent.

At that moment d'Artagnan came out from behind the pillar and walked down the aisle in pursuit of Milady. As he passed Porthos and the attorney's wife he stole a quick look at his friend, noticed the gleam of triumph in his eye and thought cynically:

'That's one of us set up for the campaign, at any rate!'

Porthos yielded to the pressure of the lady's arm like a ship responding to a turn of the wheel and walked with her to the Saint-Magloire cloister, a deserted alley with a turnstile at either end. Madame Coquenard made sure that there was no one within earshot and then said:

'Oh, Sir, it seems you're a great lady-killer.'

'I, Ma'am?' answered Porthos, preening himself. 'What exactly do you mean?'

'All those coy looks just now and the holy water. She must be a princess at least, with her maid and her black page-boy and all.'

'No, Ma'am,' answered Porthos. 'She's no princess, merely a duchess.'

'What about the footman at the door and that carriage with a coachman in livery on the box?'

Porthos had not noticed the footman or the carriage, but nothing had escaped Madame Coquenard's jealous eye. The musketeer regretted not having made the lady with the red cushion a princess from the start.

'Oh, I can see you're the darling of the ladies,' sighed Madame Coquenard.

'Well, Ma'am,' answered Porthos. 'It's only natural a man of my physique should have a certain success.'

'Lord, how quick men are to forget!' cried Madame Coquenard, raising her eyes to Heaven.

'Less quick than women, I should have said,' retorted Porthos. 'Haven't I evidence enough for that in your case? I was wounded, dying, despaired of by the doctors. I, a man of rank, who'd given you my friendship, and who relied on yours, was nearly allowed to die miserably of wounds and starvation in a little inn at Chantilly, merely because you wouldn't condescend to acknowledge my letters and appeals to you for help.'

Madame Coquenard blushed, for she realized that she had fallen short of the acknowledged code of behaviour of the great ladies of that age.

'And you remember, don't you, that for your sake I broke with the Baronne de . . .'

'I do remember.'

'And the Comtesse de . . .'

'Monsieur Porthos, don't be harsh with me.'

'And the Duchesse de . . .'

'Please stop, Monsieur Porthos. You're being most unkind!'

'Very well, Ma'am. Let's forget all about it. You're quite right. It's foolish to indulge in recriminations.'

'It's my husband's fault. He won't hear of my lending money to anyone.'

'Madame Coquenard,' answered Porthos, 'have you forgotten the first letter you ever wrote me? If you have, I haven't. It's engraved on my memory.'

The lady moaned aloud.

'I must confess, Sir,' she said, 'that even I thought the sum you mentioned was a trifle large.'

'I appealed to you first, Madame Coquenard. I could just as easily have written to the Duchesse de . . . I won't say her name because I've never compromised a woman in my life and I don't intend to start now . . . But I will say this, that I had only to write to her and she'd have sent me fifteen hundred.'

The attorney's wife started to weep.

'Monsieur Porthos,' she said. 'You've made me feel thoroughly ashamed of myself! You really have. If you ever find yourself in such a position again you mustn't hesitate to appeal to me.'

'Please, Ma'am!' said Porthos in an outraged tone. 'Don't let's mention money now. It's most embarrassing!'

'So you don't love me any more!' moaned Madame Coquenard.

Porthos maintained an injured silence.

'So that's your answer? Oh dear,' sighed the lady, now thoroughly downcast.

'You hurt me, Ma'am, you wounded me deeply,' said Porthos. 'You wounded me here,' he added, laying his hand on his heart in a theatrical gesture.

'Dear, dear Monsieur Porthos! I'll make it up to you again. I swear I will!'

'And after all I wasn't asking so very much of you,' went on Porthos. 'A loan, that was all. I'm not unreasonable. I know you're not rich, Ma'am. I know your husband has only a few poor clients whom he has to bleed in order to eke out a miserable living for himself. If you were a lady of rank it'd be different and there'd be no excuse for you.'

Madame Coquenard was nettled by this.

'Monsieur Porthos,' she said. 'I may be a mere attorney's wife, but I'd have you know that my safe's probably just as well stocked as the safes of any of those stuck-up duchesses of yours.'

'That only makes your behaviour worse, Ma'am,' said Porthos.

As he spoke he removed the lady's hand gently but firmly from his arm.

'If you're rich,' he went on, 'you'd no reason at all to let me down.'

Madame Coquenard saw that she had gone too far.

'When I say rich, Sir, you mustn't take me too literally. I'm not exactly rich; I'm what you might describe as comfortably off.'

'It's a sordid affair altogether,' said Porthos. 'We'd better say no more about it. You slighted me and our friendship must now cease.'

'You ungrateful man!'

'Don't you start complaining, Ma'am!' said Porthos.

'Very well then. Go off with your fine duchess or princess or whatever she is. I won't keep you from her.'

'Yes, I think I'll do that. She's not at all bad-looking, you know!'

'Monsieur Porthos, for the last time, do you still love me?'

Porthos sighed deeply and looked mournful.

'Alas, Ma'am,' he said. 'You know I'm just off on a campaign and may never come back . . .'

'Don't say such terrible things, Sir,' cried Madame Coquenard, bursting into tears.

'Something tells me I shall never return,' said Porthos in increasing mournful tones.

'Oh don't say that. Say you've fallen in love with someone else. I'd rather hear that.'

'No, Ma'am. I haven't fallen in love with someone else; on the contrary, some voice deep down in me sometimes speaks your name. But as you may or may not know, this great campaign starts a fortnight from now and this next fortnight I shall be very busy finding my equipment. And I shall also have to pay a visit to my family in the heart of Brittany to get money.'

Porthos watched a final battle between passion and avarice raging in Madame Coquenard's breast.

'Incidentally,' he went on, 'the duchess who was in church just now has estates bordering on my family's, so we've arranged to travel to Brittany together; journeys are much less tedious when there are two of you.'

'Haven't you any friends in Paris, Sir, who'd save you the journey?'

'I thought I had,' said Porthos, looking excessively mournful, 'but I fear I was wrong.'

'No, Sir, you were not wrong. You have got friends,' cried Madame Coquenard, carried away by a sudden gust of feeling which surprised even herself. 'Come back tomorrow to the house. You're the son of my aunt, in other words my cousin; you come from Noyon, in Picardy; you've got several lawsuits in Paris and no solicitor. Will you remember all that?'

'I will indeed, Ma'am.'

'Come at lunch-time.'

'Very well.'

'And keep your head with my husband. He's seventy-five but as cunning as a fox.'

'Only seventy-five? That's the prime of life,' said Porthos.

'The evening of life, you mean, Monsieur Porthos,' said the

lady. 'Indeed the poor fellow may die on me at any moment and leave me a widow,' she added, with a quick, meaning glance at Porthos. 'Luckily it was agreed in our settlement that everything was to go to the surviving partner of the marriage.'

'Everything?' asked Porthos.

'Everything.'

'I see you're a woman of foresight, dear Madame Coquenard,' said Porthos, giving the lady's hand an affectionate squeeze.

'So now we're friends again, dear Monsieur Porthos,' she replied with a simper.

'For life,' answered Porthos, with a sly look.

'Well, good-bye till tomorrow, my unfaithful one!'

'Good night, my neglectful one!'

'Sleep well, my angel.'

'Pleasant dreams, love of my life.'

CHAPTER XXX

Milady

D'ARTAGNAN had followed Milady unknown to herself; he watched her get into her carriage and heard her tell the coachman to drive to Saint-Germain.

It would have been useless to try to follow the carriage on foot, for it set off at a quick trot and the horses were of powerful Normandy stock. D'Artagnan therefore made his way back to the Rue Férou.

In the Rue de Seine he ran into Planchet; the silly fellow was standing in front of a pie-shop, gazing enraptured at a most appetizing-looking meat-pie. He ordered him to go at once to Monsieur de Tréville's stables and saddle two horses, one for himself and one for his master, and to bring them to Athos' lodgings. Monsieur de Tréville, in showing favour to the young man, had now gone so far as to put his stables permanently at his disposal.

Planchet set off for the Rue du Colombier and d'Artagnan for the Rue Férou. Athos was sitting at home as usual, drinking a bottle of the precious Spanish wine which he had brought back with him from Picardy, and which seemed to increase his melancholy. He signed to Grimaud to bring a glass for d'Artagnan. Grimaud obeyed in silence.

Now d'Artagnan told his friend about Porthos' meeting with the attorney's wife in the church and how the big man was probably already well on the way to being set up for the campaign.

'Well, if that's his way, he's welcome to it,' said Athos. 'But I'm not going to have any woman paying for my equipment.'

'And yet I bet that you, with your looks and intelligence, could have any number of women running after you.'

'How absurdly young you are, d'Artagnan!' said Athos. 'However, we won't disturb these illusions.'

And he signed to Grimaud to fetch another bottle of Spanish wine.

At that moment Planchet stuck his head timidly through the half-open door and announced that the two horses were ready.

'What horses?' asked Athos.

'Two horses I've borrowed from Monsieur de Tréville to go to Saint-Germain.'

'What are you going to Saint-Germain for?' asked Athos.

D'Artagnan then described what had happened in the church, how he had seen the woman from Meung, and how he was almost as much obsessed by her as by the man with the scar on his cheek.

'In other words, you're now as much in love with this woman as you were a day or two ago with Madame Bonacieux,' said Athos. And he shrugged his shoulders and gave a contemptuous snort as though to say: 'So much for human constancy.'

'Most certainly not,' replied d'Artagnan angrily. 'I only want to solve the mystery of who she is. I've got a haunting idea, an obsession you might say, that though I don't know her and she doesn't know me she's somehow affecting my life.'

'I think you're probably right,' replied Athos, ignoring his friend's last remark. 'I know I've never met a woman who was worth looking for for very long. Madame Bonacieux's lost, so why waste time and energy searching for her? It's up to her to turn up again.'

'No, Athos, you're wrong,' said d'Artagnan. 'I love poor Constance more than ever and I'd go to the ends of the earth to rescue her if I knew where she was. But unfortunately I don't. I've done all I can to find her, but I've failed. And it's no good sitting and brooding. One must go out and try and forget about it.'

'Forget about it with this other woman then,' said Athos. 'If that's going to make you feel better don't let me stop you. Good luck to you.'

'Listen, Athos,' said d'Artagnan. 'Why not get hold of a horse too, and ride out to Saint-Germain with us instead of moping here by yourself.'

'My dear chap,' replied Athos, 'I ride when I've got a horse of my own. When I haven't I walk.'

Had the speaker been anyone but Athos d'Artagnan would have taken offence at this remark. As it was he merely smiled and said:

'I'm not so proud as you, Athos. I'll ride any horse I'm offered. So now good-bye to you.'

'Good-bye,' replied the musketeer.

At that moment Grimaud came in with the fresh bottle of wine and Athos signed to him to open it.

D'Artagnan and Planchet mounted their horses and trotted off to Saint-Germain. As the young man rode along he thought of what Athos had said about himself and Madame Bonacieux. D'Artagnan was not over-sentimental and yet he was sincere in his attachment to the draper's wife, and when he had said he would go to the ends of the earth to find her he meant it. But the earth is round and has many ends and the problem which end to aim for seemed insoluble. Meanwhile, he thought, why not try and solve another problem, the mystery of Milady? Milady had talked to the man with the scar on his cheek; the man with the scar on his cheek and the man in the black cloak

who had later parleyed with M. Bonacieux in the street were
one and the same. D'Artagnan was convinced that the man
in the black cloak was as much involved in the second kidnapping of Madame Bonacieux as he had been in the first, and
thought that if he followed Milady he might discover something about the man in the cloak. So he was only half deceiving
himself when he argued that by going in quest of Milady he
was indirectly going in quest of Constance.

Such thoughts occupied his mind during the whole stretch
between Paris and Saint-Germain. Not until he and Planchet
were passing the house where ten years later Louis XIV was
born did he wake from his reverie. They were riding along an
empty street, keeping a sharp look-out for any trace of the
beautiful Englishwoman, when he suddenly noticed a man
standing in the porch of a house by the roadside. The house
stood at a bend in the road and, like so many houses of that
period, had no windows giving on to the street. The man's face
seemed to d'Artagnan vaguely familiar, but Planchet recognized
him first.

'D'you see that fellow standing there star-gazing, Sir?' he
asked.

'Yes, who is he?'

'You ought to remember him, Sir,' replied Planchet. 'That's
Lubin, the servant of the Comte de Wardes, the gentleman you
had the duel with a month ago in the wood near Calais.'

'By Jove, so it is!' cried d'Artagnan. 'I recognize him now.
D'you think he's recognized you?'

'Well, Sir, I spent such a lively quarter of an hour with him
that I don't suppose he's kept a very clear picture of me in his
head.'

'Go and talk to him, then,' said d'Artagnan, 'and find out
whether his master's dead.'

Planchet dismounted and walked boldly up to Lubin. As he
had foreseen the man did not recognize him and the two started
chatting together quite amicably. Meanwhile d'Artagnan led
the two horses up a side-road and round the back of a neighbouring house, and approached the first house under cover of

a hazel hedge, drawing close enough to overhear the conversation of the two servants.

A few minutes later d'Artagnan heard the noise of carriage wheels, and the next moment a coach, Milady's coach, drew up in front of the house only a few yards away from him.

Yes, there was no mistake, Milady herself was seated inside!

D'Artagnan crouched down against his horse's neck and from that position could see without being seen.

Milady leaned her charming head out of the coach window and called out an order to her maid. The maid, a pretty, lively young girl of twenty, jumped down from her seat on the footboard of the coach and walked over to the terrace where Planchet and Lubin had been standing. D'Artagnan watched her from his vantage-point behind the hedge.

It so happened that Lubin had meanwhile been summoned indoors on an errand, and Planchet was now standing on the terrace alone, anxiously looking to right and left for traces of his master. The maid came up to him and, mistaking him for Lubin, handed him a letter.

'For your master,' she said.

'For my master?' replied the astonished Planchet.

'Yes,' replied the maid. 'As you see, the letter's marked "urgent", so please deliver it at once.'

So saying she turned and walked quickly over to her mistress. The coach had meanwhile been backed round and was now facing the direction from which it had come. The young girl stepped lightly on to the footboard and the coach immediately drove off.

Planchet turned the letter over in his hand, puzzled how to act. Then, trained as he was in unquestioning obedience he ran down the terrace steps, turned up the side-road, and after about twenty yards came face to face with d'Artagnan, who had seen everything and was on his way to join him.

'For you, Sir,' said Planchet, handing him the letter.

'For me?' asked d'Artagnan. 'Are you sure?'

'Positive, Sir. The maid said "For your master." You're my

only master, so the letter must be for you, mustn't it? Fine young lass, that maid!'

D'Artagnan opened the letter and read as follows:

Someone who is deeply interested in you wishes to know when you will be well enough to take a walk in the forest.

A footman in black and red livery will await your reply to-morrow at the Field of the Cloth of Gold inn.

'This is really too much!' muttered d'Artagnan. 'Milady and I seem to have a common interest in the Comte de Wardes' health. Well, Planchet, and how is the good Count? I gather he's not dead after all.'

'No, Sir. He's progressing as well as a man can hope to pro-gress after receiving four sword thrusts in the body – that was what you gave the poor gentleman, Sir. But he's still very weak, having lost nearly all his blood. As I thought, Sir, Lubin hadn't recognized me and actually gave me a graphic account of our meeting with him and his master.'

'Excellent, Planchet. You're the king and prince of lackeys. Now hop on your horse again and let's see if we can overtake that coach.'

It did not take them long; after a five minutes' ride they turned a corner and saw the coach drawn up in front of them on the wrong side of the road. A well-dressed man on horse-back was parleying with Milady through the coach door. Their conversation was so lively that d'Artagnan was able to ap-proach to within a few feet of the other side of the coach, un-observed by all save the pretty maid.

Milady and the man on horseback were talking in English, so d'Artagnan could not understand what they were saying. But from the tone of her voice he gathered that the beautiful Eng-lishwoman was in a rage. She brought the conversation to a close with a gesture which betrayed her state of mind; she rapped the stranger's knuckles very violently with her fan, shattering it. At this the stranger merely roared with laughter, which seemed to incense Milady still more.

D'Artagnan thought this an excellent moment to intervene.

He rode up to the off-side door of the coach, took off his hat, bowed and said:

'Can I be of service to you, Madame? This gentleman's apparently been annoying you and with your permission I'll teach him a lesson in manners.'

Milady had turned at the sound of d'Artagnan's voice and now stared at him in surprise. In answer to his little speech she said in excellent French:

'At any other time I'd have been glad of your support, Sir, but this gentleman happens to be my brother.'

'Then please accept my apologies, Ma'am,' replied d'Artagnan. 'If I'd known that I wouldn't have interfered.'

'What does this young idiot think he's doing?' cried the stranger on the horse, lowering his head to the level of the carriage door. 'Why doesn't he go away and mind his own business?'

'Idiot yourself!' said d'Artagnan, bending down and addressing him through the body of the coach. 'And I'm not going away to please you, Sir!'

The man on horseback now said a few words to his sister in English.

'I addressed you in French, Sir,' said d'Artagnan. 'So be good enough to answer me in that language. You're this lady's brother, I know, but you're not mine, for which I thank God.'

If Milady had been timid, like most women, she would have interfered at this point and tried to prevent the quarrel becoming serious. But she did the very opposite. She leaned back against the cushions of her seat and called out calmly to the coachman:

'Drive back to the house!'

The pretty maid threw a quick, anxious glance at d'Artagnan, whose good looks had apparently attracted her. Then the coach drove off, hiding him from her sight and leaving the two men face to face on the empty road.

The stranger was preparing to canter off after the coach when d'Artagnan rode up to him, seized his horse by the bridle and held him back. He had recognized him as the Englishman from

Amiens to whom Athos had gambled away his horse and nearly his ring too. The recollection of that incident, combined with the fellow's recent behaviour, which he chose to regard as a fresh piece of insolence, had thoroughly roused his ire.

'I think, Sir,' he said, 'that of the two of us you're the greater idiot. I fancy you've forgotten that you and I have already got a little score to settle.'

'Oh, so it's you again, is it, young fellow,' replied the Englishman. 'You seem to be always on the look-out for trouble.'

'Yes, and that reminds me, Sir; I want to have my revenge on you. I'll be interested to see if you're as handy with the rapier as you are with the dice.'

'I haven't got a sword, Sir, as you can see for yourself. You're surely not going to start blustering against an unarmed man.'

'I expect you've got a sword at home, Sir. If you haven't I've got two and I'll gladly play you for one.'

'No need for that, Sir,' answered the Englishman. 'I've got all the swords I'm ever likely to want.'

'Good,' said d'Artagnan. 'Then pick your longest and come and show it to me this evening.'

'Where?'

'Behind the Luxembourg. An ideal spot for two people who've got something urgent to discuss.'

'Right. I'll be there.'

'State your time, Sir.'

'Six o'clock.'

'Oh, and by the way, I daresay you've a friend or two in Paris.'

'I know three who'd be delighted to take my side in this dispute.'

'Marvellous! I've got three dying to take my side.'

'And now, Sir, your name, please,' said the Englishman.

'D'Artagnan, Squire of Gascony, attached to des Essarts' company, King's Guards. And yours, Sir?'

'Lord de Winter.'

'Your servant, my Lord!' said d'Artagnan. 'Six o'clock then, behind the Luxembourg!'

And putting spurs to his horse he galloped off in the direction of the capital.

As was his habit on an occasion like this he called at once on Athos. He found him lying stretched out on a large sofa, waiting, as he said, for his campaign equipment to come and find him. The young man related word for word all that had happened, but did not mention Milady's letter to the Comte de Wardes.

Athos was enchanted with the news, for, as we know, his one wish had been to fight an Englishman. The two lackeys were immediately sent off to fetch Porthos and Aramis, who arrived posthaste and were at once told the story.

Porthos was overjoyed at the prospect of the duel. He drew his sword and started making imaginary passes at the wall, lunging and feinting and capering about like a dancer. Aramis calmly retired into Athos' little writing-room to finish his poem in words of one syllable, begging his friends not to disturb him until the very moment when swords were to be drawn.

Athos signed to Grimaud to bring in another bottle of Spanish wine.

As for d'Artagnan, he sat down to work out a little private scheme of his own. From the smiles which from time to time crossed his face as he sat brooding it was clear that he was picturing some amusing intrigue which might result from his machinations.

CHAPTER XXXI

English and French

At the time appointed the four friends and their four servants arrived at the site agreed upon for the duel, an enclosed piece of meadow-land which was used as a pasturage for goats. Athos gave the goatherd some money to remove his goats elsewhere for the time being. The four lackeys were then posted as sentries at each of the four gates into the enclosure. In a few moments another silent party of four entered the enclosure and joined the musketeers. As was customary in England before duelling they gave their names and waited for their opponents to do the same. All four Englishmen were members of distinguished families, and were therefore both astonished and dismayed to hear their opponents announce themselves as Athos, Porthos, and Aramis.

'And after that,' said Lord de Winter, 'we're none the wiser as to who you really are. I'm sorry, but we can't fight men with names like those. They're mythical shepherds' names.'

'Of course you realize they're assumed names, Sir?' said Athos.

'Yes. And that's why we must insist all the more that you tell us your real names,' replied the Englishman.

'You didn't object to gambling with us under those names, Sir,' said Athos, 'and winning our two horses from us into the bargain.'

'True. But then we were only risking our pistoles whereas now we're risking our lives. A man can gamble with anyone, but gentlemen only fight with their equals.'

'True, Sir,' said Athos.

Upon which he took aside the Englishman whom he was to fight and whispered his name to him.

Porthos and Aramis did the same with their two opponents.

'Are you satisfied?' said Athos to his foe. 'D'you consider me your equal and qualified to cross swords with you?'

'Yes, Sir,' said the Englishman, bowing.

'Good,' said Athos. 'And now may I say something to you in return?'

'Pray do,' answered the Englishman.

'You'd have been wiser not to force me to tell you my real name.'

'Why?'

'Because I'm supposed to be dead and have good reasons for not wanting anyone to know I'm alive. So I shall be forced to kill you to make sure my secret never leaves your lips.'

The Englishman stared at Athos in amazement. Could he be talking seriously? Athos was, in fact, perfectly serious.

'Well, gentlemen,' he said, addressing the whole company, 'are we ready?'

'Yes,' replied the two opposing parties in one voice.

'On guard then,' said Athos.

Immediately eight sword blades gleamed in the rays of the setting sun and a fierce battle began. These eight men were fighting in a double cause, for their own personal honour and for the honour of their country.

Athos fought as coolly and warily as though he were in a fencing school. Porthos, chastened, no doubt, by his experience at Chantilly, played a cautious game, while Aramis, mindful always of his poem, fought aggressively to get the business over quickly.

Athos was the first to kill his man. He struck him only once, but the thrust was mortal and he collapsed with a wound through the heart. Porthos, the next to score, sent his man sprawling on the grass with a thigh wound. The Englishman surrendered and handed over his sword, upon which Porthos picked him up in his arms and carried him to his coach. Aramis, pressing hard, forced his man to give ground about fifty feet and finally to surrender. D'Artagnan, fighting Lord de Winter, played an entirely defensive game; he waited for the Englishman to tire and then disarmed him with a clever feint.

Lord de Winter, defenceless, retreated a few steps out of d'Artagnan's reach. But his foot caught in a stone and he tripped and fell on his back. D'Artagnan was on him in a trice; he put his sword point to his throat and cried:

'You're in my power now, Sir. I could kill you if I liked, but I'll spare you for the sake of your sister, whom I love.'

D'Artagnan was triumphant. Everything had turned out as he had planned. The scene which had caused him to smile as he had pictured it was exactly realized.

Lord de Winter was delighted to find his enemy so tractable. He embraced him with many expressions of gratitude and paid compliments to each of his three friends. So much for him.

Porthos' opponent was already ensconced in his carriage and Aramis' foe had taken to his heels. So there was now only the dead man to consider. Porthos and Aramis undressed him to make sure that his wound was fatal. In doing so they discovered a heavy purse attached to his belt.

D'Artagnan untied it and handed it to Lord de Winter.

'What d'you expect me to do with that?' asked the latter.

'Return it to his family, Sir,' said d'Artagnan.

'His family won't worry about a trifle like that,' said Lord de Winter. 'They'll be coming into an income of fifteen thousand pounds. Keep that purse for your servants.'

Then, turning to d'Artagnan, he continued:

'And now, my young friend, if you'll allow me to call you that, I shall be delighted to present you tonight to my sister, Clarice de Winter. I'd like her to know you too, for her own sake, and as she has some influence at Court she might be able to put in a good word for you.'

D'Artagnan flushed with pleasure, bowed and accepted the invitation with thanks.

Meanwhile Athos had approached the young man. He waited till Lord de Winter had stopped talking; then, taking the purse from his friend's hand, he whispered to him:

'Let's give this purse not to our servants but to the English servants.'

And he threw the purse to the coachman, crying:

'For you and your fellows.'

This act of generosity, coming from a man so poor as Athos, impressed even Porthos. The musketeer's action was later quoted everywhere by Lord de Winter as an example of French liberality and delighted everyone except Masters Grimaud, Mousqueton, Planchet, and Bazin.

Before leaving the scene of the duel Lord de Winter gave d'Artagnan his sister's address in the Place Royale, which in those days was the most fashionable district of Paris. He also promised to call for the young man at Athos' lodgings, drive him to the house and present him to his sister personally.

The knowledge that he was to meet Milady greatly excited

the young man, for he remembered how a strange Fate had already caused their ways to cross. He was convinced that she was an agent of the Cardinal and yet some peculiar instinct, of which he himself was only half aware, seemed to drive him towards her, though his better judgement told him he was acting rashly.

His only fear was that she might remember their two previous meetings, at Meung and at the Port of London. For she would then know that he was a friend and protégé of Monsieur de Tréville and therefore Royalist to the core. He would then lose all his advantage in the battle of wits with her, for from the start she would know as much about him as he about her and they would be fighting on equal terms.

The young Gascon had no qualms on the score of Milady's attachment to the Comte de Wardes, although the latter was young, handsome, rich and very high in the Cardinal's favour. We may be more ready to excuse his conceit if we remember that he was a native of Tarbes and only just twenty.

After leaving the Luxembourg he went straight home and changed into his smartest clothes. He then called on Athos and, as was his habit of late, confided everything to him. Athos listened closely to his story, shook his head disapprovingly and recommended caution.

'I can't understand you,' he said. 'You've only just parted from one woman whom you describe as good, charming, and altogether perfect, and here you are running after another.'

D'Artagnan felt the justice of this rebuke.

'I love Madame Bonacieux with my heart, and Milady with my head,' he explained. 'My only object in meeting her is to find out exactly what position she holds at Court.'

'From what you say I should have thought it was obvious what she was,' said Athos. 'She's an agent of the Cardinal, a dangerous woman who'll entrap you and get your head chopped off.'

'You're a gloomy devil, Athos.'

'My dear fellow, I'm suspicious of women. I can't help it. I've had bitter experiences with them. I'm particularly suspicious of fair women. I think you said Milady was fair.'

'She's got the fairest hair I ever saw!'

'Oh, my poor d'Artagnan!' said Athos.

'I promise you I only want to find out about her. When I've done that I'll stop seeing her.'

'Very well. Good luck to you in your quest,' replied Athos calmly.

Lord de Winter arrived at the hour arranged. Athos, forewarned, retired discreetly into the back room and the Englishman found d'Artagnan alone. It was already eight o'clock so the two men left the house at once, got into the Englishman's carriage and drove off to the Place Royale.

Lady de Winter received d'Artagnan graciously. Her house was furnished in the greatest luxury. The threat of war had already driven most English people out of France, but Milady was still busy altering her house to her taste, which proved that she was exempt from the general measure expelling British subjects from the country.

Lord de Winter, introducing d'Artagnan to his sister, said:

'Here's a young man who had my life in his hands and spared me. We were enemies on two counts; we'd had a personal quarrel and also had our countries' honour to defend. And yet he spared me. So if you've a spark of affection for me, Clarice, I'm sure you won't refuse to thank him.'

Milady frowned and her face darkened ever so slightly. Then she smiled a queer smile. That smile made d'Artagnan feel very uncomfortable. Her brother, however, noticed nothing; he had turned his back and was playing with Her Ladyship's pet monkey, which had clawed at his doublet.

'I'm indeed glad to see you, Sir,' said Milady in a voice of singular sweetness, which contrasted strangely with the expression of annoyance which d'Artagnan had noticed on her face. 'I shall always be grateful to you for what you did today.'

The Englishman now turned to her again and described the meeting in the enclosure in detail. Milady listened with the greatest attention and pretended to be delighted by the story. But it was obvious from the way she kept flushing and tapping the floor with her foot beneath her dress that she was inwardly furious.

Lord de Winter, however, noticed nothing. When he had finished his tale he walked across the room, filled two glasses from a decanter of Spanish wine on a table and invited d'Artagnan to drink with him. D'Artagnan knew that the English regarded a refusal to drink as a mortal insult. So he went over and joined his host. But at the same time he kept his attention fixed on Milady, watching her reflection in the mirror. When she thought herself unobserved an amazing change came over her. Her face was distorted by an expression of almost murderous rage and she bit savagely at her handkerchief.

At that moment the pretty maid whom d'Artagnan had noticed on the footboard of the coach came in and said something in English to Lord de Winter. The latter at once asked d'Artagnan to excuse him on the grounds of an appointment and suggested that his sister entertain his young guest in his absence.

D'Artagnan shook hands with Lord de Winter and then returned to his hostess. Milady's face, which was extraordinarily mobile in expression and seemed to reflect her every changing mood, was now gracious and smiling; there were, however, a few drops of blood on her handkerchief from her torn lips.

The conversation now took a light, easy turn. Milady seemed to have entirely recovered her spirits. She told d'Artagnan that Lord de Winter was her brother-in-law and not her brother; that she had married the younger son of the de Winter family who had died, leaving her a widow with one child. If Lord de Winter did not marry, this child would inherit the name and the family fortune.

D'Artagnan learned a little of what he wanted to know from Milady's talk. But he had an uneasy feeling that it was a screen, a camouflage, put up to hide something else. At present he could not see beyond the screen.

After half an hour's talk he was convinced of one thing, that Milady was a Frenchwoman; she spoke the purest and most polished French imaginable.

D'Artagnan laid himself out to please her with gallant speeches and professions of regard. Milady accepted all his compliments graciously.

At last the time came for him to take his leave. He bade Milady farewell and left the room the happiest of men.

At the head of the stairs he came face to face with the pretty maid. She brushed his arm lightly as he passed, blushed modestly, and asked his pardon so prettily that it was at once granted.

D'Artagnan called again next day and Milady gave him an even kindlier welcome. Lord de Winter did not appear this time and Milady entertained her young guest alone. She seemed to take a great interest in him, asked him what province he came from, who his friends were, and whether he had ever considered entering the Cardinal's service.

D'Artagnan was, as we know, quite shrewd for a man of his years, and at this point he remembered his earlier suspicions of Milady. He immediately embarked on a long eulogy of the Cardinal and declared that he would certainly have joined His Eminence's Guards and not the King's Guards if he had known Monsieur de Cavois and not Monsieur de Tréville.

Milady now skilfully changed the conversation and with studied nonchalance asked d'Artagnan if he had ever been in England. D'Artagnan replied that Monsieur de Tréville had once sent him there to buy some remount horses and that he had ridden four of them back himself to show as samples.

Once or twice in the course of the conversation Milady bit her lip with annoyance; she had hoped to be able to lead the young man on, but began to realize that he was no fool.

D'Artagnan took his leave at the same hour as before. On the stairs he again came face to face with Kitty, the pretty maid. This time she shot him a shy, admiring glance which spoke volumes. But the young man was so preoccupied with the mistress that he never gave the maid a thought.

He returned next day and the day after. Each time Milady gave him a warmer welcome, and each time, whether by accident or design, he came face to face with the pretty maid, either in the ante-room, in the passage, or on the stairs. But he continued to ignore her.

CHAPTER XXXII

Lunch at the Lawyer's

AND now to return to Porthos. The duel in which he had so distinguished himself had not made him forget his invitation to lunch with the attorney's wife.

On the morning following the duel he told Mousqueton to give his clothes an extra special brush and then wended his way towards the Rue aux Ours. His heart was beating fast, but not, like d'Artagnan's, with the excitement of a young man in love. No, a more material motive guided his footsteps to the lawyer's house; he knew that at long last he was to cross that mysterious threshold, to climb that unknown staircase which Maître Coquenard's silver crowns, the proceeds of his legal extortions, had climbed one by one before him. He was to come at last face to face with a certain cabinet-safe which he had pictured often in his mind; a long, deep chest, padlocked, bolted, nailed to the floor, a chest he had often heard mentioned. Now it was to be actually opened and its precious contents disclosed to his admiring gaze.

The lawyer's house offered another attraction besides the chest. Porthos, the penniless soldier adventurer, without family or background, accustomed to eating in taverns and inns, and depending for his livelihood mostly on chance encounters with friends, had been invited into a family circle, to partake of meals cooked by a provident housewife, and to enjoy the comfort and peace of a well-run home. He pictured himself as the cousin whom everyone is glad to welcome, seated day after day at a table laden with good food, charming the old work-weary attorney with his lively chatter, teaching the young articled clerks the finer points of basset, passe-dix, and lansquenet and winning from them in one evening all their month's earnings, in lieu of fee for his instruction. Porthos' mind was entirely taken up with these fancies as he walked towards the

Rue aux Ours, and he smiled to himself in anticipation of pleasures to come.

It is true that bad tales were told of the attorneys of those
days, tales which have survived them – tales of stinginess, of
niggling and haggling. But Porthos had always found his own
attorney's wife generous enough, apart from occasional bouts
of frugality which he had always considered unnecessary, so
he was not very worried and had every reason to hope that he
would find himself comfortably housed and fed for the next
fortnight.

When he reached the house, however, doubts assailed him.
The approach was not exactly welcoming – a narrow, dark,
fusty alley, a staircase with barred windows through which
filtered a faint daylight reflected from an inner courtyard, and
at the top of the staircase a low door studded with enormous
bolt-headed nails like the main gate of the Grand Chatelet.

Porthos knocked on the door. It was opened by a clerk, a
tall fellow with a pale face framed in a forest of unkempt hair.
He bowed low in token of respect for Porthos' stature, which
symbolized strength, for his uniform, which symbolized high
status, and for his ruddy complexion, which denoted good
living.

Behind the tall clerk stood a short clerk; behind the short
clerk stood another tall clerk, and behind him a twelve-year-old
errand boy. In all, three clerks and a half, which at that period
indicated a more than usually thriving practice.

Porthos was not due to arrive till one o'clock, but the attorney's wife had been on the alert since midday, for she calculated that her admirer's feelings for herself, combined with
the promptings of his stomach, would bring him to the house
a little before the appointed time. So she entered the hall
through the sitting-room door just after the appearance of her
guest. Her arrival was to Porthos as an answer to prayer, for
the clerks, who were an inquisitive lot, had been embarrassing
him with silent stares.

'Ah, so you've arrived, my dear cousin,' cried the lady. 'Come
in, Monsieur Porthos, come in.'

At the name 'Porthos' all the clerks started giggling. But the big man turned and gave them such a fierce look that their smiles froze on their faces.

To reach the attorney's private sitting-room Madame Coquenard and her guest crossed first the ante-room where the clerks were, and then the office where they should have been; then, leaving the kitchen on their right, they crossed the reception room. The sight of all these inter-communicating rooms depressed Porthos, for he realized that with the doors left permanently open as they were no conversation could be held in any one room and not be overheard in all the other rooms. Moreover, he had thrown a quick, appraising glance at the kitchen on his way past and had had to admit, to his own mortification and to the shame of his hostess, that he had seen none of the zeal and bustle which, in prosperous houses, usually prevail in that sanctuary of gluttony at the hour of the midday meal.

The attorney had obviously been warned in advance of Porthos' visit, for he showed no surprise at seeing him. The musketeer went up and greeted him politely but with studied casualness.

'I gather we're cousins, Monsieur Porthos,' said the old attorney, propping himself up by his arms in his cane chair. He was dressed in a black, loose-fitting doublet, which hung like a sack over his frail torso; he was dried up and wizened and had grey, gimlet eyes which shone like garnet-stones; his eyes and his grimacing mouth seemed to be the only part of him in which there was still life. His legs had recently begun to fail him, and since then he had been almost entirely at the mercy of his wife. He had accepted his cousin's visit with resignation and nothing more; had he had the use of his limbs he would have denied all relationship with Monsieur Porthos.

'Yes, we're cousins,' said the musketeer in answer to his host's greeting. He was not at all taken aback by the attorney's cool manner, for he had never expected to be received by him with anything more than tolerance.

'Cousins through the female side, I believe,' said the attorney, with a sly look at his guest.

Porthos did not notice the underlying malice of this remark; he took his host's observation as a piece of naïveté and laughed inwardly. But Madame Coquenard knew that naïveté is a quality rare in attorneys; she blushed at her husband's comment and gave a pained smile.

Ever since Porthos' arrival Maître Coquenard had been casting anxious glances at a large chest which stood immediately in front of his oak writing-table. The musketeer realized that though it did not correspond in shape or size to the picture he had formed of it in his mind this chest must be the thrice-blessed cabinet-safe of which he had so often dreamed. He was delighted to see that the reality was six feet higher than the dream.

Monsieur Coquenard did not press his genealogical inquiries very far. Instead he looked first at the chest and then at Porthos and said, eyeing his wife:

'I hope our cousin will honour us by dining with us once before he returns to the country. Eh, Madame Coquenard?'

This time Porthos understood the full sting of his host's remark and was hurt, not in his feelings but in his stomach. Madame Coquenard apparently understood it too, for she said:

'Monsieur Porthos won't come back at all if we don't fulfil his expectations as hosts. But if we do we must insist on his giving us every moment he can spare of his short and hurried stay in Paris.'

'Oh my poor legs!' groaned Monsieur Coquenard.

Madame Coquenard had come to the rescue just as Porthos' gastronomic hopes had received a death blow. He felt grateful to her.

At that moment the lunch-bell rang. They all adjourned to the dining-room, a large, dark room adjoining the kitchen. The three clerks had apparently smelled unaccustomed smells in the house that day, for they were as punctual as soldiers on parade, standing at the table with their stools in their hands, awaiting permission to sit down. Porthos noticed them licking their chops with horrible eager looks on their faces, and thought to himself:

'In your place, cousin, I would not have such greedy fellows in my house. They look like shipwrecked sailors who haven't had a meal for six months.'

Monsieur Coquenard in his arm-chair was wheeled into the dining-room by his wife, assisted by Porthos. Hardly was he in the room than he began sniffing and licking his chops just as his clerks had done.

'Ha!' he said. 'That looks a good, appetizing soup!'

'What on earth do they see so specially marvellous in that soup?' thought Porthos, looking at the tureenful of thin, watery brew, on which floated here and there a few crusts, like the islands of an archipelago.

Madame Coquenard sat down and signed to the rest of the company to do likewise. She served her husband first, Porthos next, and herself last. Then she distributed the crusts, without any soup, among the three ravenous clerks.

At that moment the dining-room door swung slowly open on its hinges and Porthos, looking out, saw the little errand-boy standing in the passage; having been forbidden to join the feast, he was eating his dry crust steeped in the combined smells from the kitchen and the dining-room.

After the soup the maid brought in a boiled fowl, a delicacy which caused the clerks' eyes to bulge out of their sockets.

'It's easy to see you love your relations, Ma'am,' said the attorney with an agonized smile. 'You're doing your cousin more than proud with a dish like that.'

The chicken was scraggy, with an outer covering of those bristly hairs through which bones can never penetrate with the best will in the world. The local poultry man must have spent a long time ferreting out the bird from the perch to which she had retired to die of old age.

'Ye Gods!' thought Porthos. 'That's a sorry-looking object. I respect old age, but I don't like to be long in its company, boiled or roast.'

He looked round the table to see if his fellow-guests shared his opinion of the fowl. But he saw that, far from despising it, their eyes were fixed in rapt contemplation of the glorious object.

Madame Coquenard pulled the dish towards her, neatly severed the bird's two feet which she placed on her husband's plate, cut off the neck and head which she set aside for herself, and sliced off a wing for Porthos. She then handed the bird back almost intact to the servant, and the servant whisked it away into the kitchen before Porthos had even had time to observe the disappointment of the three clerks, the victims of this act of economy.

In place of the bird an enormous dish of beans was now brought in, a regular sea of beans from which protruded the ends of a few mutton bones which might or might not have meat on them. The clerks, however, did not allow their hopes to be raised a second time; they waited patiently to receive whatever should be offered them. Madame Coquenard dealt out minimal portions of this dish to the young people.

Now came the drink. Monsieur Coquenard took up a thin, stone bottle and poured out a third of a glass for each of the young people and a third of a glass for himself, and then handed the bottle to Porthos and Madame Coquenard. The young clerks filled the remaining two-thirds of their glasses with water, and as they drank so they put in more water, and as the meal went on so the liquid in their glasses became paler.

Porthos ate his chicken wing daintily, shuddering as he felt his hostess' knee pressing his affectionately under the table. He then drank half a glass of the carefully apportioned wine which he recognized as the horrible vintage of Montreuil. A despairing look came on Maître Coquenard's face as he watched his guest pour the undiluted contents down his throat.

'Won't you try a few of these beans, cousin Porthos?' said the lady, with a sidelong glance at her guest as though to say: 'I'd really advise you not to.'

'Not me!' muttered Porthos to himself. Out loud he said:

'Thank you, dear cousin, I've had all I can manage.'

Silence now fell on the company. Porthos was embarrassed

and did not know where to look. The attorney repeated over
and over again:

'Madame Coquenard, I do congratulate you. Your lunch was
a real feast. I haven't eaten so much for years.'

Porthos now began to suspect that he was the victim of a
plot to make him look a fool. He frowned and began curling
his moustache. But he suddenly again felt Madame Coquenard's knee pressed against his, reassuring him and begging
him to be patient.

Now, at a sign from Monsieur Coquenard and a nod from his
wife, the clerks got up, folded their napkins, bowed each in
turn and left the room.

'Go, young men, and digest at your desks,' said the lawyer
gravely.

When the clerks had left the room Madame Coquenard got
up, went over to the sideboard and returned with a piece of
cheese, some quince jam, and a cake which she had baked herself with almonds and honey. Maître Coquenard frowned at the
sight of so many dishes.

'A feast indeed,' he cried, figdeting uneasily in his chair. 'A
regular banquet. Epulae epularum. Lucullus lunching with
Lucullus.'

Porthos looked at the bottle of wine beside him. Perhaps
after all he might make a meal of the wine, the bread, and the
cheese. But the bottle was empty and neither Monsieur nor
Madame Coquenard showed any sign of wishing to produce
another one.

'Good,' muttered Porthos to himself. 'Now at least I'm forewarned.'

And he licked a spoonful of the quince jam and stuck his
teeth into the gluey compound which Madame Coquenard
called a cake.

'And now my penance is done,' he thought. 'And I hope not
in vain.'

Maître Coquenard, after the joys of such a banquet, which
he considered an excess, expressed his desire for a siesta.
Porthos hoped that he would take it where he was. But the

attorney insisted on being wheeled back into his private sitting-
room and appeared uneasy until he was back in front of his oak
chest, upon the lower edge of which he proceeded to plant his
feet for greater safety.

Madame Coquenard took Porthos into the adjoining room
and began her task of making amends to her visitor for his
unfortunate reception.

'You can come and lunch here three days a week,' she said.

'Thanks,' said Porthos, 'but I prefer not to trespass on your
hospitality. Besides I've got to hunt round for my equipment.'

'Oh, that wretched equipment!' moaned Madame Coquenard. 'What a bore it is!'

'Yes, Madame, but it's a necessary evil.'

'What does this equipment consist of, Monsieur Porthos?'

'Oh, every sort of thing,' said Porthos. 'The Musketeers are,
as you know, a crack regiment and need a lot of stuff which the
Guards and Swiss Corps don't need.'

'Give me some idea what the stuff is, and what it would cost.'

Porthos thought it would be wise to mention the total first
and the separate items after.

'The whole outfit might easily cost . . .'

Madame Coquenard waited, tense with fear.

'Cost what?' she said. 'I do hope not more than . . .'

She paused; she could not bring herself to name a definite
sum.

'Oh, no,' said Porthos. 'It couldn't come to more than two
thousand five hundred livres. I think if I was careful I could
even manage with two thousand.'

'Two thousand livres!' cried the lady. 'But that's a fortune!
I could never get my husband to let me have as much as that!'

Porthos said nothing, but made a very expressive gesture
which Madame Coquenard understood at once. She said
quickly:

'I asked you to give me a list of the things you wanted only
because I've got connections and contacts in trade, and I'm
fairly sure I could get everything ten per cent cheaper than you
could.'

'Oh,' said Porthos. 'If that was your only reason . . .'

'Yes, dear Monsieur Porthos, that was my only reason,' replied the lady. 'Now I suppose what you need first and foremost is a horse.'

'Yes. A horse.'

'Well, I've got the very thing for you.'

'Good,' said Porthos beaming. 'So much for the horse. Then I need a complete harness which consists of various small items which I shall have to buy myself. In any case the whole lot won't come to more than three hundred livres.'

'Three hundred livres! Oh well,' said Madame Coquenard with a sigh. 'Let's put down three hundred livres for the harness.'

As we know, Porthos already had the saddle which Buckingham had given him, so he calculated that he could slip these three hundred livres slyly into his pocket.

'Then there's my servant's horse and my valise,' he went on. 'Arms you needn't worry about. I've got all the swords and pistols I want.'

'A horse for your servant!' exclaimed the attorney's wife. 'You've got very grand ideas, I must say.'

'You're not suggesting we Musketeers are a rabble regiment, are you?' said Porthos with an injured air.

'No. But it occurred to me that a pretty mule sometimes looks just as fine as a horse, and I thought if I provided your Mousqueton with a pretty mule . . .'

'Very well, a pretty mule it is!' said Porthos. 'I remember seeing Spanish grandees whose entire suites were mounted on mules. But you understand, don't you, Madame Coquenard, that I must have a mule with plumes and bells.'

'You shall, you shall,' said the lady.

'And now the valise,' continued Porthos.

'That's a simple matter!' cried Madame Coquenard. 'My husband's got several. You can have the best. There's one he's particularly fond of; he always took it with him on his travels and it's big enough to hold a house.'

'You mean it's got nothing in it?' asked Porthos slyly.

'Of course,' replied the lady innocently.

'I see. But I want a valise with something in it, my dear!'

Madame Coquenard again sighed deeply. Molière had not yet written his scene in *The Miser*, so Madame Coquenard had a considerable lead over Harpagon.

One by one the various items of the equipment were named and haggled over. It was eventually decided that Madame Coquenard should go to her husband with a request for a loan of eight hundred livres and should provide the horse and the mule which were to carry Porthos and Mousqueton to fame and fortune.

When these terms had been agreed on and the rate of interest fixed, together with the date for repayment of the loan, Porthos took leave of Madame Coquenard. The lady tried to detain him with fond looks, but Porthos pleaded the call of duty and Madame Coquenard had to yield in favour of His Majesty the King.

The big man went home hungry and in a very bad temper.

CHAPTER XXXIII

Mistress and Maid

MEANWHILE d'Artagnan had been growing daily more enamoured of Milady. His conscience, Athos' words of wisdom, happy recollections of Madame Bonacieux, none of these things had succeeded in deterring him from his pursuit of the beautiful Englishwoman and he continued to visit her and pay her compliments. He was confident enough to believe that sooner or later she would yield to his courtship.

One day he arrived at her house holding his head high and treading on air as usual. In the porch he ran into the pretty maid Kitty. This time she did not merely give him her customary fond look; she actually took him by the hand.

'Good,' thought d'Artagnan. 'She's got some special message for me from her mistress, some note proposing a tryst which the lady daren't suggest to my face.'

And he gave the pretty maid one of his most engaging smiles.

'May I say something to you, Sir?' stammered the unfortu‑nate Kitty.

'Of course, child! What is it?'

'I can't say it here, Sir. It would take too long. Besides it's a private matter.'

'Where can we go then?'

'I could take you somewhere if you'd be good enough to follow me, Sir,' said Kitty timidly.

'With pleasure, my dear.'

'Come then, Sir.'

She still had hold of his hand and now turned and led him up a narrow spiral staircase. They climbed about twenty steps and came to a little door which Kitty opened.

'Come in here, Sir,' she said. 'We can talk in here and we won't be disturbed.'

'What room's this?' asked d'Artagnan.

'It's my room, Sir. And that door there leads into my mis‑tress's room. But she never goes to bed before midnight so there's no danger of her overhearing us.'

D'Artagnan looked round him. It was a charming little room, clean and pleasantly furnished. But, as may be supposed, what interested him most in the room was the door which led into the room beyond.

Kitty guessed what was in his mind and sighed.

'You're very fond of my mistress, Sir, aren't you?' she asked.

'Fonder than I can say, Kitty. I'm madly in love with her.'

Kitty sighed again.

'I'm very sorry about that, Sir,' she said.

'Why on earth?'

'Well, Sir, my mistress doesn't love you at all.'

'Doesn't she, by Jove?' said d'Artagnan. 'And did she tell you to tell me so?'

'Oh, no, Sir! I made up my mind to tell you myself, for your own advantage.'

'Thank you, Kitty,' replied d'Artagnan. 'Thank you for your intentions, which I'm sure are good; not for your message, which is not so good!'

'So you don't believe me?'

'It's always difficult to believe things like that. One's pride revolts, if nothing else.'

'Won't you really believe me?'

'Not unless you give me some proof.'

'Well, what do you think of this?' asked Kitty.

And she pulled a letter out of her bodice, folded but un-addressed.

'For me?' cried d'Artagnan.

He snatched the letter from her hand and, before Kitty could stop him, opened it and started to read.

'Oh, Sir, what are you doing?' she cried.

'Well, don't you want me to read a note that's addressed to me?' asked the young man.

He read as follows:

You never answered my first note. Are you ill or have you for-gotten how you smiled at me at Madame de Guise's ball? Now's your chance, Comte. Don't miss it.

D'Artagnan went white. He was hurt, not, as he supposed, in his affections, but in his pride.

'This note's not for me at all!' he cried.

'No, it's for someone else. I tried to tell you but you wouldn't listen.'

'Who is it for?'

'The Comte de Wardes.'

D'Artagnan at once recalled the scene on the terrace at Saint-Germain, which confirmed what Kitty had just said.

'Poor Monsieur d'Artagnan,' said Kitty, taking the young man's hand in hers and pressing it fondly.

'So you're sorry for me, are you, my dear?' said d'Artagnan.

'Very sorry indeed. You see I know what it is to be in love.'

'You know?' asked d'Artagnan. He looked at Kitty for the first time with some interest.

'Yes, unfortunately.'

'Well, then, instead of being sorry for me you'd better help me get my revenge on your mistress.'

'What revenge do you want?'

'I want to make her fall in love with me; I want to do down my rival.'

'I'll never help you to do that, Sir,'-said Kitty firmly.

'Why not?' asked d'Artagnan.

'For two reasons. Firstly because my mistress'll never love you.'

'What makes you think that?'

'You've done her a mortal injury.'

'I? Do her an injury? But that's nonsense! Why, ever since I first met her I've been at her feet like a slave. What on earth do you mean?'

'I can't explain except to the man who can read my heart.'

D'Artagnan again eyed Kitty with interest. He saw that she had a freshness and charm for which many princesses would have exchanged their wealth and rank.

'I'll read your heart, Kitty,' said the young man. 'So don't let that prevent you talking. There!'

And he kissed her, at which the poor girl blushed a cherry red.

'Oh no,' she cried. 'You don't love me; it's my mistress you love; you told me so only a moment ago.'

'Does that prevent your telling me your second reason for refusing to help me?'

'My second reason, Sir,' said Kitty, gaining courage as she looked into the young man's eyes, 'is that in love it's everyone for himself.'

Only then did d'Artagnan remember Kitty's languishing glances, those apparently accidental encounters in the ante-room, on the stairs or in the passage, how she had brushed his sleeve with her hand and the stifled sighs she had uttered. He had noticed nothing of all this at the time, so obsessed was he with thoughts of her mistress. Who in quest of an eagle takes note of a thrush?

But now our Gascon saw in a flash all the advantages to be gained from Kitty's attachment to himself, which she had so naïvely confessed. It would now be possible, he thought, to intercept letters addressed to the Comte de Wardes, to get political news at first hand, to enter the house at any hour of the day or night by the side staircase leading to Kitty's room, which adjoined that of her mistress. The unscrupulous and ambitious young man was already planning to sacrifice the humble servant to the great lady.

'Well,' he said, in answer to her protest that it was not her he loved but her mistress. 'Shall I give you a proof of the love you seem to doubt?'

'What love?' asked the young girl.

'The love I'm prepared to feel for you.'

'How can you prove that?'

'Suppose this evening I were to spend with you the time I usually spend with your mistress?'

'Oh, that would be wonderful!' cried Kitty, clapping her hands.

'Very well, my dear,' said d'Artagnan, settling himself down in an arm-chair. 'Come here and let me tell you you're quite the prettiest girl I ever saw.'

And he continued in this vein so long and so adroitly that the unfortunate Kitty, who was already half-way to being persuaded, ended by believing him. And yet, to d'Artagnan's surprise, she put up quite a stubborn resistance before yielding to him.

Time spent in attacks and defences of this nature passes swiftly. Midnight struck and almost at once the bell rang from Milady's bedroom.

'Good Heavens!' cried Kitty. 'That's my mistress ringing for me! You must leave the house at once. Hurry!'

D'Artagnan got up and seized his hat as though preparing to leave. Then, instead of going to the door, he went over to a big cupboard in the corner of the room, opened it, stepped in, locked the door from the inside, and hid himself among Milady's dresses and night-dresses.

'What on earth are you doing?' cried Kitty.

There was no reply from inside the cupboard.

'Well,' cried Milady angrily from the next room, 'are you asleep, Kitty? Why don't you answer when I ring?'

D'Artagnan heard the communicating door being thrown open.

'I'm just coming, Milady!' cried Kitty, running forward to meet her mistress.

The two women went back into the bedroom, leaving the communicating door open, so that d'Artagnan could hear every word that was said in Milady's bedroom. Milady continued to scold Kitty for a while. Then she calmed down, and while Kitty was undressing her turned the conversation on to himself, d'Artagnan.

'Well,' she said. 'I didn't see my Gascon friend this evening.'

'Didn't he call tonight?' asked Kitty. 'Has he lost interest before getting his way with you?'

'Oh no,' said Milady. 'He hasn't lost interest. He must have been kept back by Monsieur de Tréville or Monsieur des Essarts. I'm experienced in these things, Kitty, and I know I've got that young man.'

'What will you do with him, Milady?'

'Just you wait and see, Kitty! I've a score to settle with him which he knows nothing about. He nearly made me lose my position with His Eminence. I'll make him pay dearly for that.'

'I thought you loved him, Milady!'

'Love him? I hate him! Why, the fool had Lord de Winter's life in his hands and spared him, thereby losing me an income of three hundred thousand livres.'

'Yes, of course,' said Kitty. 'Your son was His Lordship's sole heir and you'd have had control of his fortune until he came of age.'

D'Artagnan, listening from inside the cupboard, felt his blood freeze in his veins. What horror was this he heard? This creature whom he had idolized, whom he had thought as good as she was fair, was actually cursing him, in a voice unrecognizably harsh and strident, for his failure to kill a man for whom she had previously professed deep affection.

'I'd have revenged myself on him before now,' continued

Milady. 'But for some reason the Cardinal asked me to deal gently with him.'

'Yes, Milady. You've been gentle with him, but you weren't so gentle with that woman he was so fond of.'

'You mean the draper's wife from the Rue des Fossoyeurs! Oh, he's forgotten her ages ago! That's not much of a revenge.'

D'Artagnan broke out into a cold sweat. Was this woman a complete monster? He strained his ears to hear more, but Milady had now finished her toilet for the night.

'That'll do, Kitty,' she said. 'You can go to bed now. And first thing tomorrow take the letter I gave you and try to get an answer from the person concerned.'

'You mean Monsieur de Wardes?'

'Of course.'

'You may be unkind to poor Monsieur d'Artagnan, Milady, but you're certainly not unkind to Monsieur de Wardes.'

'Don't be impertinent, Kitty. Leave the room, please.'

D'Artagnan heard the door being closed again. Then he heard a noise of bolts being drawn, and a key being turned very gently in the lock. Milady was shutting herself in on one side of the door and Kitty was making assurance doubly sure on the other.

Now d'Artagnan opened the cupboard and stepped out.

'Good Heavens, what's the matter?' whispered Kitty. 'You're as white as a sheet!'

'What a vile creature!' muttered d'Artagnan.

'Hush!' said Kitty. 'Go away at once. The partition wall's very thin and Milady can hear everything that goes on in this room.'

'That's just why I'm not going.'

'What d'you mean?' asked Kitty, blushing.

'At least . . . not just yet.'

And he pulled Kitty towards him. It was hopeless to resist now, for resisting meant making a noise, so Kitty yielded.

The love-making of d'Artagnan and Kitty was to a great extent inspired by their common wish to be revenged on Milady. And d'Artagnan had good reason to agree with the old adage that revenge is a joy not scorned by the Gods. And had he had more heart and less pride and ambition he would have been content with this one triumph. But he was no saint. It can be said to his credit, however, that the first use he made of his influence over Kitty was to try and discover the whereabouts of Madame Bonacieux.

The poor girl swore on the Bible that she knew nothing, and that her mistress only let her in to half her secrets. All she could be sure of was that the draper's wife was not dead. And Milady's remark about d'Artagnan having undermined her influence with the Cardinal had completely baffled her.

But on that point d'Artagnan was better informed than she. He had caught sight of Milady on a ship anchored in the Port of London at the moment when he himself was leaving England, so he guessed that she had been referring to the affair of the diamond tags. But from what he had overheard he concluded that the main reason for her hatred of him was that he had not killed her brother-in-law.

D'Artagnan called on Her Ladyship again next day and found her in a very bad temper. He guessed that the reason for this was that she had had no answer from the Comte de Wardes. When Kitty came in Milady spoke to her very sharply, at which Kitty cast reproachful glances at d'Artagnan, as though to say:

'Look what I have to suffer on your behalf!'

However, as the evening wore on Her Ladyship calmed down and listened graciously to d'Artagnan's compliments. She even allowed him to kiss her hand.

The young man took leave of her, not knowing what to make of her behaviour. But, as we know, he was not easily flummoxed, and while paying court to Milady he was also hatching a little plot of his own. He found Kitty waiting for him at the door, and again went up to her room to hear what news she had for him. She told him she had been severely scolded and accused of carelessness in handling the letter. Milady had been upset by the Comte de Wardes' silence and had ordered Kitty to come to her next morning at nine o'clock for fresh orders. D'Artagnan suggested that she call at his lodgings afterwards to pass on her orders to him, and the poor child, in her foolish infatuation for the young musketeer, agreed to do so.

At eleven o'clock next day Kitty called on d'Artagnan, bringing another note in Milady's handwriting. This time she did not even try to prevent him reading it; she just let him have his way. She was his slave now, ready to obey him in everything.

D'Artagnan opened this second letter which was also unaddressed and unsigned and read as follows:

This is my third letter to you telling you I love you. Take care I don't write a fourth telling you I hate you.

If you repent of your behaviour the girl who brings this will tell you how you can make amends.

D'Artagnan changed colour several times as he read. Kitty kept her eyes fixed on him while he was reading.

'So you still love her!' she said.

'No, Kitty,' he replied. 'I don't love her, but I mean to have my revenge on her.'

Kitty sighed. D'Artagnan took up a pen and wrote:

Lady de Winter,

Until now I was in doubt whether your first two notes were really intended for me, so unworthy did I feel of such an honour.

But today I am compelled to believe in your goodness, for I both read in your letter and hear from your maid's lips that I have the incredible good fortune to have won your love.

I shall come at eleven this evening to make amends. To let one more day pass would be unpardonable.

Your humble servant, the man blessed above all others.

de Wardes.

This letter was a forgery. D'Artagnan, in writing it, was certainly acting unscrupulously, and nowadays his action would be condemned as criminal. But in those days a less high standard of morality prevailed. And we must not forget that when he wrote the letter the young man already knew from her own words that Milady was guilty of perfidy greater than mere signature-forging! Moreover, although madly infatuated, he had very little respect for her. He wished to be revenged on her for having falsely fostered his hopes and for her cruelty to Madame Bonacieux.

His plan was quite simple. He would enter Milady's bedroom through her maid's room and take her by surprise. He would compromise her, terrify her with threats of a scandal and force her to confess to the kidnapping of Madame Bonacieux and to disclose her whereabouts. He foresaw that if he played his cards well he might even obtain her release.

'Here, Kitty,' he said, putting the sealed note into her hand, 'give this letter to Milady; it's Monsieur de Wardes' reply.'

Kitty went as pale as death, for she suspected what the note contained.

'Listen, my dear,' said d'Artagnan. 'You must realize that you're now in this plot as much as I and that it's too late to back out. Milady may discover that you gave her first note to my servant instead of to de Wardes' servant and that I, and not de Wardes, opened the two others. If she finds that out she'll sack you, and you know her well enough to realize that she won't be content with a small revenge like that.'

'Oh dear!' sighed Kitty. 'And who am I doing all this for, d'you suppose?'

'For me, Kitty. I know that,' replied the young man. 'And I'm very grateful to you.'

'You might at least tell me what you've written in the note.'

'Milady will tell you.'

'I see you don't love me and I'm very unhappy.'

To such accusations from a woman there is only one reply. D'Artagnan replied in such a way that Kitty's illusions were completely restored. She cried a good deal before consenting to deliver his note to Milady. But at last she agreed, and that was all d'Artagnan wanted. To please her he promised that he would leave her mistress early that night and come to her.

That promise succeeded in banishing Kitty's last doubts.

CHAPTER XXXIV

How Aramis and Porthos Found their Equipment

SINCE the time when the four friends had started their hunt for equipment they had only met at intervals. They dined alone wherever each of them happened to be and only met when it was convenient to do so. Their hours of duty also took up a great deal of this valuable time, which passed all too quickly.

Their one fixed arrangement was to meet once a week at one o'clock at Athos' lodgings. They had to meet there because Athos had vowed that he would not cross his threshold. The day on which Kitty had called on d'Artagnan was one of the days fixed for their meeting.

No sooner had Kitty gone than d'Artagnan set off for the Rue Férou.

He found Athos and Aramis philosophizing together. Aramis had been toying vaguely with the idea of returning to the Church. Athos, as usual, was making no attempt to influence him one way or the other. It was his policy to let people decide for themselves; he never gave advice unless asked for it, and even then he had to be asked twice.

'In general,' he would say, 'people only ask for advice in order not to follow it or, if they do follow it, in order to be able to blame someone if things go wrong.'

Porthos arrived a few minutes after d'Artagnan, completing the party.

The four men all had different expressions on their faces. Porthos looked smug, d'Artagnan hopeful, Aramis worried, and Athos unconcerned.

They had been talking and comparing notes for a few minutes when Mousqueton suddenly appeared and begged Porthos to return to his lodgings, where apparently a surprise was awaiting him.

'Has my equipment arrived?' inquired Porthos.

'It has and it hasn't, Sir,' replied Mousqueton, looking the picture of woe.

'What d'you mean, it has and it hasn't?'

'If you come, you'll see, Sir.'

Porthos got up, took leave of his friends, and left the house with Mousqueton.

A minute or two later Bazin came in.

'What d'you want, my friend?' inquired Aramis in the soft-spoken manner he always affected when his thoughts turned towards the Church.

'There's a man waiting for you at the house, Sir.'

'Oh? What kind of a man?'

'A beggar, Sir.'

'Give him some money, Bazin, and tell him to pray for a poor sinner.'

'This particular beggar insists on seeing you, Sir. He says he's sure you'll be glad to see him.'

'Didn't he give a name?'

'No, Sir. But he said that if you seemed not to want to see him I was to tell you he came from Tours.'

'From Tours!' cried Aramis. 'Oh, then I'll come at once. Will you excuse me, gentlemen? I think this man has some very important news for me.'

And he got up and almost ran out of the room.

Athos and d'Artagnan were left alone.

'I think those two are fixed as far as equipment goes,' said Athos. 'What d'you think?'

'I know Porthos is well on the way to being fixed,' replied d'Artagnan, 'and as for Aramis I was never very worried about him. But what about you, Athos? You were very generous with that Englishman's pistoles which were yours by right. How are you going to manage now?'

'I don't regret having killed the fellow,' replied Athos, 'especially as he had the cheek to ask me my real name. But if I'd pocketed his pistoles they'd have hung like a millstone round my neck.'

'Really, Athos, your scruples astonish me!'

'Well, don't let them worry you. By the way, Monsieur de Tréville honoured me with a visit yesterday. What's this about your consorting with suspect English people, friends of the Cardinal?'

'I suppose he meant that one Englishwoman I told you about?'

'Ah yes, the beautiful blonde. I remember giving you some advice on that subject which I suppose you ignored completely.'

'I told you why I wanted to see her. I was sure she'd had something to do with Madame Bonacieux's kidnapping.'

'I see. You make up to one woman in order to find another. It's a somewhat circuitous method but no doubt amusing.'

D'Artagnan was on the point of telling Athos the whole story but suddenly thought better of it. Athos had a very strict code of honour, and there were certain elements in the plot which d'Artagnan had hatched against Milady which he knew would shock his puritanical friend. So he decided to keep the whole thing dark, and as Athos was the least curious of mortals no more was said on the subject of Milady.

The two friends had for the moment nothing more of importance to discuss. So let us leave them and follow Aramis.

The latter was so keen to meet his visitor from Tours that he ran all the way to the Rue de Vaugirard. On entering his room he found the man waiting for him, as Bazin had said. He was a sharp-looking little fellow dressed rather surprisingly in rags.

'What can I do for you?' asked the musketeer.

'I wish to see Monsieur Aramis, Sir. Are you he?'

'Yes. Have you something to give me?'

'Yes, if you'll first show a certain embroidered handkerchief.'

'I have it here.'

He took a key out of his pocket, opened a little ebony box which stood on the table and held up the handkerchief.

'That's it,' said the beggar. 'And now,' he added, pointing to Bazin, who was standing behind his master, 'send away your servant, please.'

Bazin had been so curious to know what the beggar wanted of his master that he had run almost as fast as he and had arrived at the house at almost the same moment. But his curiosity was not to be gratified, for his master now signed to him to leave the room and poor Bazin had no choice but to obey.

The beggar took a quick look round the room to make sure that he was not being spied on. Then he undid the loose leather belt which fastened his ragged coat, unpicked the stitches in the upper part of his doublet and produced a letter. When Aramis saw the seal he gave a cry of delight. He snatched the letter from the man's hand, kissed the writing on the envelope, opened it reverently and read as follows:

My friend,

Fate has decreed that we must be parted for a while longer. But the lovely days of youth are not lost for ever. Win honour and glory in the field and I'll do what I have to do elsewhere.

Please accept what the bearer of this note brings you. Good luck and don't forget me!

Adieu or rather au revoir.

While Aramis was reading the letter the beggar went on unstitching his doublet and picking one by one out of his dirty clothes a hundred and fifty Spanish doubloons,* which he arranged in a pile on the table. Then he walked to the door, opened it, bowed, and went out before the astonished young man had had time to say a word to him.

Aramis then re-read the letter and found that it had a postscript:

You can entertain my messenger as an equal. He's a Spanish Count and grandee.

'Oh joy, oh bliss!' cried Aramis. 'Oh, is life good! Yes, we're still young. Joys are ahead of us. Oh mistress mine! My love, my youth, my life are yours; everything I have is yours, everything!'

And he kissed the letter passionately, without even glancing at the gold which lay in a glittering pile on the table.

Bazin gave a gentle rap-tap on the door. Aramis had no reason to keep him at bay any longer and called to him to come in. He

* 1 doubloon=2 pistoles. – Translator's note.

stood in stupefied silence, gaping at the pile of gold and forgetting what he had knocked for. Aramis called him sharply by name, which brought him to his senses and reminded him that Monsieur d'Artagnan was waiting outside and wanted to know who the mysterious beggar from Tours was.

D'Artagnan did not stand on ceremony with Aramis and after a moment or two came in without being announced.

'Good Heavens, my dear fellow!' he exclaimed, looking at the gold. 'If Tours supplies you with plums like those I don't wonder you send down there for them.'

'You're quite wrong, d'Artagnan,' said Aramis. 'That's the fee my publisher paid me for my poem in monosyllables which I began at Crèvecœur.'

'Is that so?' replied d'Artagnan. 'Well, I can only say your publisher's very generous.'

'What, Sir?' cried Bazin. 'Can one get all that money for a poem? How marvellous! Oh, Sir, you're so clever, you could do anything! You could become a second Monsieur de Voiture or Monsieur de Benserade. I like that idea very much, Sir. A poet's almost as good as a priest. Oh, Monsieur Aramis, do become a poet!'

'Bazin, I'll thank you to keep your comments to yourself.'

Bazin, snubbed, had no choice but to bow and leave the room.

'So your literary efforts actually bring in money!' said d'Artagnan with a smile. 'You're lucky. But take care! There's a letter sticking right out your pocket. I suppose that's also from your publisher, so you mustn't lose that!'

Aramis blushed scarlet, quickly stuffed the letter back into his pocket and buttoned up his doublet.

'Well, d'Artagnan,' he said, 'I suggest we now go and find our friends. I'm rich again, so I propose we all dine together and drink to the day when you'll be rich again too.'

'That's a grand idea,' said d'Artagnan. 'It's many a day since we had a respectable meal. And I've got rather a difficult evening ahead of me so I wouldn't say no to a few bottles of old Burgundy to liven me up.'

'Old Burgundy it is!' said Aramis. 'I don't dislike the stuff either.'

At the sight of the gold his ideas of monastic seclusion had vanished like a cloud. He now put three or four doubloons in his pocket to meet the needs of the moment and locked the rest away in the ebony box from which he had produced the precious embroidered handkerchief which had served as a password.

The two friends called first on Athos. The latter still obstinately refused to leave his room, but he guaranteed to have all the ingredients of the dinner brought to his lodgings. He was something of an epicure, so d'Artagnan and Aramis agreed to leave the arranging of the meal entirely to him and set off themselves to find Porthos.

On their way to his lodgings the two young men ran into Mousqueton. The wretched fellow was driving a mule and a horse in front of him down the street and had a more than usually woeful expression on his face.

At the sight of the horse d'Artagnan gave a start of surprise.

'My yellow horse!' he exclaimed. 'Aramis, just take a look at that horse!'

'What a horrible looking object!' said Aramis.

'Well, if you want to know it was on that horse that I first entered Paris.'

'What, Sir? You recognize this horse!' exclaimed Mousqueton.

'It's a most unusual colour,' said Aramis. 'I've never seen a horse with a coat like that before.'

'I'm quite sure you haven't,' said d'Artagnan. 'That was why I managed to get three crowns for it. It must be its coat that attracts people, for I swear its carcase isn't worth three crowns. Where on earth did you pick it up, Mousqueton?'

'Don't ask, Sir, don't ask!' wailed Mousqueton. 'It's a nasty practical joke our duchess's husband played on us.'

'What d'you mean, Mousqueton?'

'You see, Sir, we're very much in favour with a lady of rank, the Duchess of . . . but I mustn't say her name; my master told me never to mention names. The lady asked us to accept a little memento from her, a magnificent Spanish jennet and an Andalusian mule. Her husband got to hear of it, seized and confiscated the horse and the mule before they reached our lodgings and sent these two eyesores in their place.'

'And now you're returning them to him?' asked d'Artagnan.

'Yes, Sir. You realize we can't put up with these monstrosities in place of what we were supposed to have.'

'No, you certainly can not,' said d'Artagnan. 'Although I must confess I'd have enjoyed seeing Porthos on my buttercup. I'd have got some idea of what I must have looked like when I arrived in Paris. But we mustn't stop you, Mousqueton. Carry on the good work. Is your master at home, by the way?'

'Yes, Sir,' answered Mousqueton. 'But he's in a very bad temper.'

So saying he whipped up the two animals and started off down the street, while the two friends walked on in the direction of Porthos' lodgings. When they reached his house they rang the bell and waited. But Porthos had seen them crossing the courtyard and purposely ignored their ring. D'Artagnan and Aramis waited for a little while and then returned to the Rue Férou.

Meanwhile Mousqueton continued on his way. He crossed the Pont Neuf, still driving the two old crocks in front of him, and finally reached the Rue aux Ours.

He now proceeded to carry out his master's orders, which were quite simple. He tied the horse and the mule to the knocker of the attorney's door and left them there. Then he calmly turned and walked back to the Rue du Vieux Colombier.

The horse and the mule, who had not eaten since early morning, began raising and lowering the knocker of the door in an effort to break loose, and caused such a disturbance in the street that the attorney sent his errand-boy to search the neighbourhood for the beasts' owner and to beg him to remove them from his property.

The noise drove Madame Coquenard to her window. She recognized her present to Porthos and could not at first understand the reason for the animals' return. But this was soon explained to her by a visit from the musketeer himself. When the lady saw the light of anger in his eye as he entered the house she was terrified.

The big man, as we know, was already irritated enough by Madame Coquenard's low trick. But when Mousqueton returned and described his meeting with d'Artagnan and Aramis, and how d'Artagnan had recognized the yellow horse as an animal which he had once sold for three crowns, Porthos had been filled with uncontrollable rage and had set off then and there for the Rue aux Ours.

After arranging for Madame Coquenard to meet him at a certain hour in the Saint-Magloire cloister Porthos once more left the house. He contemptuously declined the attorney's invitation to stay to dinner, which was, of course, only tendered after the musketeer had declared his intention of leaving.

Madame Coquenard set out for the cloister with a trembling heart, for her instincts told her she was in for a good dressing-down. And she was not mistaken. All that a man wounded in his pride can utter in the way of abuse and reproof was hurled at the unfortunate lady, who received her chastisement with bent head.

'I only did what I thought best,' she moaned. 'One of my husband's clients is a horse dealer. He owed us some money and was obstinate about paying, so I took the horse and the mule as payment in kind. He'd promised me two first-class mounts.'

'Well, Ma'am,' said Porthos, 'I can only say that if your coper owed you more than three crowns he's a swindler.'

Madame Coquenard protested:

'It's not a crime to try and get things cheap if one can, Monsieur Porthos.'

'No, Ma'am. But people who get things cheap shouldn't try and palm them off on their friends.'

So saying Porthos turned on his heels and began walking away.

'Monsieur Porthos!' cried the lady. 'I was wrong. I admit it. I oughtn't to have bargained. I should have insisted on the best of everything for someone so grand as you.'

Porthos did not answer but continued to walk away.

The lady had a sudden sharp vision of him in an aura of majesty, surrounded by duchesses and princesses throwing purses of gold at his feet. She was terrified.

'Don't go! For pity's sake don't go!' she wailed. 'Stay and let's talk things over.'

'Talking things over with you doesn't seem to get me anywhere,' answered Porthos.

'At least tell me what you want!' pleaded the lady.

'I don't want anything. It wouldn't make any difference if I did.'

Madame Coquenard clutched Porthos by the arm and cried out in anguish:

'Monsieur Porthos, I'm so ignorant about these things. What can I know about horses and harness?'

'All the more reason for letting me choose them myself,' replied the musketeer. 'I do know about these things. But you wanted to economize, in other words, to lend on interest.'

'Yes, Monsieur Porthos, I was wrong. I'm sorry. But I'll put everything right again.'

'How?' asked the musketeer.

'Listen. Monsieur Coquenard's been called out on business this evening. He'll be away at least two hours. Come round to the house then. We'll be alone and can settle everything.'

'Delighted,' said Porthos. 'Now you're talking sense, my dear.'

'You'll forgive me?'

'I may, I may,' said Porthos condescendingly.

Upon which they parted.

'Good-bye till this evening,' said Madame Coquenard.

'Till this evening,' echoed Porthos.

As he walked away he muttered to himself:

'By Jove, I really believe I'm getting somewhere near Maître Coquenard's safe at last.'

CHAPTER XXXV

All Cats are Grey at Night

THAT evening, so eagerly awaited by d'Artagnan and Porthos, arrived at last.

As usual d'Artagnan called at nine o'clock at Milady's house. He found her in excellent spirits, and more gracious than he had ever known her. He rightly attributed Her Ladyship's good humour to the fact that she had at last received an answer from the Comte de Wardes.

When Kitty came in with the sherbet her mistress smiled kindly at her, but the poor girl was so distressed to see d'Artagnan sitting there that Milady's smiles were wasted on her.

D'Artagnan looked at both women and was forced to admit that nature had made a mistake when she created them. She had given the mistress a cunning, scheming mind and the maid an affectionate and loyal heart.

At ten o'clock Milady began to show signs of restlessness. D'Artagnan guessed the reason for this. She kept looking at the clock, fidgeting uneasily in her chair and smiling at d'Artagnan in a manner which seemed to say:

'I'm sure you're very nice, but you'd be even nicer if you went away.'

So d'Artagnan got up and took his leave, and Milady gave him her hand to kiss. She pressed his hand gently, this time, as d'Artagnan guessed, not from coquetry, but from gratitude to him for leaving her.

'She loves him desperately,' he thought.

Then he went out. This time Kitty was not waiting for him either in the ante-room, in the passage, or at the front door. So the young man had to find his way alone up the staircase and into Kitty's little room.

He found the poor girl sitting with her face buried in her hands, crying. She did not look up when he came in, so he went over to her and took her hand. At this she burst into loud sobs.

As d'Artagnan had foreseen Milady had been overjoyed to receive the note which she took to be from the Comte de Wardes; in her excitement she had confided everything to Kitty and had then given her a well-filled purse as a reward for her success in obtaining an answer. Kitty had thrown the purse into a corner of her room, where it now lay unfastened, disgorging a few coins on to the carpet.

D'Artagnan, suddenly conscience-struck, begged the wretched girl to stop crying. At the sound of his voice she at last looked up, clasped her hands in front of her and sat gazing at him, not daring to say a word. Unimpressionable though he was, the young man was moved by the look of dumb misery on her face. But he was too set on carrying out his plan to allow sentiment to intervene at the last moment.

Kitty saw that it was hopeless to try and restrain him. His mind was made up. All he would do was to reassure her in regard to his motives which, he declared, were merely to take revenge on Milady for having given him false hopes and to find out the whereabouts of Madame Bonacieux; he hoped to achieve his second aim by using his one and only weapon against Milady, her fear of scandal. Fate seemed bent on furthering his designs, for that night Milady, anxious no doubt to hide her blushes from her lover, had taken it into her head to have all the lights put out in her room and in her maid's room. Monsieur de Wardes was to leave before daybreak, and he and she were to spend all the hours of their tryst in total darkness. This would enable d'Artagnan to slip into her room without her recognizing him.

In a few moments d'Artagnan and Kitty heard Milady coming upstairs. The young man immediately hid himself in the cupboard as he had done the night before. Hardly had he closed the cupboard door when Milady's bell rang. Kitty went into her mistress's room, shutting the door behind her. But the dividing wall was so thin that d'Artagnan could hear almost all that was said in the room beyond. Milady seemed to be in the seventh heaven of joy. She made Kitty describe to her every detail of her interview with the alleged Comte de Wardes; she asked if he had been glad to get her letter, if he had answered it at once, how he had looked when writing his reply and whether he had seemed very much in love. Kitty answered all these questions in a strained, stilted manner, trying to make her voice sound natural. But Milady noticed nothing unusual either in her face or voice, so absorbed was she in her own fantasies.

As the hour of her appointment with the Comte de Wardes approached Milady reminded Kitty to put all the lights out; she then told her to return to her room and to show Monsieur de Wardes in as soon as he arrived.

Kitty did not have to wait long. When d'Artagnan, peeping through the keyhole in the cupboard door, saw that everything was in darkness he stepped out of his hiding-place just as Kitty was closing the door into her mistress' bedroom.

'What's that noise?' called out Milady.

'It's I, de Wardes!' answered d'Artagnan in a low voice.

'Oh dear!' thought Kitty. 'He can't even wait till eleven, the time he fixed himself.'

'Well?' said Milady, her voice trembling with excitement. 'Why doesn't he come in?'

Then she called:

'Comte, Comte, you know I'm expecting you!'

At this summons d'Artagnan pushed Kitty gently aside and strode into Milady's bedroom.

No pain is so great as that endured by a man who listens to endearments from his mistress which he knows are intended for another. D'Artagnan now found himself in a distressing situation which he had not foreseen; he was smitten with jealousy and suffered almost as much as poor Kitty, who was weeping in the next room.

Milady was cooing in her softest voice, holding d'Artagnan's hand in hers.

'Oh Comte,' she said, 'the look of love in your eyes and the charming things you said each time we met made me so happy! I, too, love you. Send me some token to prove your devotion and I'll give you this ring so that you won't forget me.'

She took a sapphire and diamond ring off her finger and slipped it on d'Artagnan's. The young man's first impulse was to return it to her, but Milady stopped him.

'No, keep it out of love for me,' she said.

Then she added in a voice suddenly strained:

'And by keeping it you'll be helping me in another way which I can't explain now.'

'This woman's a real mystery,' thought d'Artagnan.

At that moment a sudden impulse seized him to confide everything to her, to tell her who he was and confess his true motives in visiting her. But she interrupted him as he was about to speak.

'My poor angel,' she said. 'How near you were to being killed by that frightful Gascon.'

That frightful Gascon! Himself! D'Artagnan winced.

'Are your wounds still hurting you?' asked Milady.

The young man found this question difficult to answer. He replied lamely:

'Yes, a little.'

'I'll avenge you, I'll avenge you. Never fear!' hissed Milady in a voice which made the young man shiver. He thought to himself:

'No. This would not be a good moment to confess.'

It took him quite a time to recover from this little dialogue. All his ideas of revenge had vanished. This woman had an astonishing power over him. He was drawn to and repelled by her at the same time, and was perturbed to find himself swayed by two such conflicting emotions. The passion she roused in him was uncanny and somehow evil.

Now the clock struck one and the lovers had to part. When d'Artagnan bade Milady farewell he felt nothing but strong regret at having to leave her. And as they kissed for the last time they arranged another meeting for the following week. Poor Kitty had hoped to be able to say a few words to d'Artagnan as he passed through her room. But Milady insisted on leading him through the dark room herself and out on to the landing.

Early next morning d'Artagnan paid a call on Athos. He had become involved in such a fantastic intrigue that he felt he must ask his friend's advice. He told him everything.

Athos frowned several times as he listened to the story.

'This Milady seems to be an inhuman monster,' he said. 'But even so you were wrong to play that trick on her. You've only succeeded in making an enemy for life.'

As Athos talked he kept staring at the sapphire and diamond ring on d'Artagnan's finger. The young man had put it on instead of the Queen's ring, which he had carefully locked away in a box.

'Are you looking at my ring?' he asked, proud to be able to show off such a handsome present to his friend.

'Yes,' replied Athos. 'It reminds me of a sapphire which used to belong to my family.'

'It's beautiful, isn't it?' said d'Artagnan.

'Magnificent,' said Athos. 'I didn't know there was another stone like that anywhere in the world. Have you bartered your diamond for it, or what?'

'No,' said d'Artagnan. 'It's a present from my beautiful Englishwoman. Incidentally I think she's French; I've never asked her, but I'm somehow convinced she was born in France.'

'Milady gave you that ring?' cried Athos.

His voice was suddenly strained and he was obviously struggling to hide some emotion.

'Yes, last night.'

'Let me have a look at it.'

D'Artagnan slipped the ring off his finger and handed it to his friend.

Athos examined it closely and turned pale. Then he tried it on the fourth finger of his right hand. It fitted perfectly. D'Artagnan was surprised to see a look of rage suddenly cross his face. Then he seemed to regain his self-control.

'It couldn't possibly be the same,' he said, speaking half to himself and half to d'Artagnan. 'How on earth could Lady de Winter have got hold of that ring? And yet it's difficult to believe there are two sapphires so exactly alike.'

'Have you seen that ring before?' asked d'Artagnan.

'I thought I had. But I suppose I must be wrong.'

He returned the ring to d'Artagnan but still kept his eyes fixed on it. After a moment's silence he said again:

'D'Artagnan, be a good fellow and turn that ring round so that the stone's underneath. It brings back such bitter memories that I couldn't go on talking to you seeing it glittering on your finger. And I think you said you wanted my advice. No, on second thoughts, show it to me again. The sapphire I'm thinking of had one of its facets slightly scratched from an accident.'

D'Artagnan again slipped the ring off his finger and handed it to the older man, who examined it closely and then gave a start.

'Look, d'Artagnan!' he exclaimed. 'Curious coincidence, isn't it?'

And he pointed to a scratch on the sapphire exactly as he had described it.

'But who gave you the ring?' asked d'Artagnan.

'My mother left it to me, and my father gave it to her. As I told you, it's an heirloom which should never have been allowed to go out of the family.'

'And you . . . sold it?' suggested d'Artagnan.

'No,' said Athos with a strange look on his face. 'I gave it away during . . . an hour of perfect happiness, just as it was given to you.'

Athos' words set d'Artagnan thinking in his turn. His thoughts centred round Milady, who seemed to him more than ever a creature of mystery, with dark and as yet unfathomed secrets in her soul. He took the ring back from his friend, but instead of slipping it on his finger put it in his pocket.

'Listen, d'Artagnan,' said Athos, taking his friend's hand. 'You know I'm fond of you. I'm as fond of you as though you were my son. Well, here's my advice to you; give this woman up. I don't know her, but some instinct warns me she's dangerous and that there's something evil about her.'

'I think you're right,' answered d'Artagnan. 'Very well, I'll give her up. I won't deny she even frightens me.'

'Will you have the strength of mind to do that?'

'Yes, I'll do it at once,' replied d'Artagnan.

'I really think you're wise, my dear boy,' said the older man, grasping the younger's hand affectionately. 'Thank God this woman's only just come into your life, and God grant she may not have left some curse on it already.'

Whereupon he nodded to his friend to show that he would now like to be left alone with his thoughts.

When d'Artagnan arrived he found Kitty waiting for him. A month's illness could not have ravaged the poor girl's looks more than her one hour of jealous suffering. She had come to the Rue Férou with a message from her mistress for the Comte de Wardes. Milady was mad with joy, crazed with love, and had sent to inquire when the Comte would pay her a second visit. And now poor, ill-used Kitty stood and waited for d'Artagnan's reply.

Athos had a great influence over his young friend. His advice, the promptings of d'Artagnan's own instincts, the recollection of Madame Bonacieux, which never left him for long, and the knowledge that he had saved his pride and had his revenge, combined to decide the Gascon to part finally with Milady. In reply to her message through Kitty he therefore wrote as follows:

Lady de Winter,

Do not force me at present to give you a definite date for our next meeting. Since my recovery I have had so many engagements of a similar nature that I have had to make a sort of time-table.

I will have the honour to inform you when your turn comes.

Respectfully,

de Wardes.

No mention of the sapphire.

Did the young man mean to keep it provisionally, as a sort of weapon against Milady? No, he was more likely holding on to it ~s a means of raising money for his field equipment, should all `·il. And it would be unfair to judge the actions of a man age from the standpoint of another. What we ·v as an act unworthy of a gentleman was then an every-day affair, and it was quite common for younger sons of good families to be kept by their mistresses.

D'Artagnan had handed his letter to Kitty without sealing it. The girl read it through but at first could make neither head nor tail of it. When she finally grasped its meaning she went half mad with joy. She could scarcely believe the good news and would not be satisfied until d'Artagnan had repeated word for word what he had written.

Knowing her mistress' violent temper Kitty realized the risk she ran in handing her this letter. But this did not prevent her from returning to the Place Royale as fast as her legs would carry her. Even the best-natured women are indifferent to the sufferings of their rivals in love.

Milady opened the letter with a joy as intense as Kitty felt in handing it to her. But when she read the first words she went livid. She crumpled the letter in her hand and then faced Kitty, her eyes flashing fire.

'What's the meaning of this letter?' she asked.

'It's in answer to yours, Milady,' replied Kitty, trembling from head to foot.

'Impossible,' said Milady. 'No gentleman would write a woman a letter like that.'

Then she suddenly cried out:

'Good God! Could he have seen . . .?'

She stopped. Her teeth were chattering, her face ashen pale. She now turned and tried to walk over to the window to get air, but could only raise her arms; her legs gave way under her and she collapsed into an armchair.

Kitty thought she had had an attack of some sort and rushed up to her to unlace her bodice. But Milady shrank back at her touch and glared at her.

'What d'you want?' she cried. 'Why did you take hold of me like that?'

Kitty was appalled by the expression of mingled rage and fear on her mistress' face.

'I thought you'd fainted, Milady,' she said, 'and I wanted to do something to help you.'

'You thought I'd fainted?' cried Milady. 'What d'you take me for? A silly, weak woman? No. When I'm insulted I don't faint. I strike back. D'you hear? I say I strike back. Now go!'

And with an imperious gesture she waved Kitty out of the room.

CHAPTER XXXVI

Plans for Revenge

THAT evening Milady gave orders that d'Artagnan was to be shown in to her the very moment he called. But that night for the first time he did not appear.

The next day Kitty called a second time on the young man and told him exactly what had happened the previous night. D'Artagnan smiled grimly at the description of Milady's furious outburst; that was his revenge.

That evening Milady was more impatient even than before. She repeated her orders to her household to show d'Artagnan in when he arrived. But once more she waited for him in vain.

The following day Kitty called again on d'Artagnan, but this time, instead of being gay and lively as on the two previous occasions, she was in despair. When d'Artagnan inquired the reason for her gloom she took a letter from her pocket and handed it to him without a word. It was addressed in Milady's handwriting, and this time not to the Comte de Wardes but to Monsieur d'Artagnan.

The young man opened the letter and read as follows:

Dear Monsieur d'Artagnan,

You are unkind to neglect your friends like this, especially now that you are soon going away.

My brother-in-law and I were expecting you yesterday and the day before, but you never came.

I hope it will not be the same again this evening?

Your ever grateful friend,

Clarice de Winter.

'That's just what I expected,' said d'Artagnan. 'As the Comte de Wardes' stock falls mine rises.'

'Are you going?' asked Kitty.

The young man had every intention of going but had to justify himself to himself for breaking the promise he had made to Athos. In answer to Kitty's question and to still the voice of his conscience he said:

'It would be most unwise to ignore such a pointed invitation. If I didn't go this evening Milady would wonder why I'd suddenly broken my habit of visiting her. She'd suspect something, and a woman like her might do anything to revenge herself for a slight.'

'Oh dear,' sighed Kitty. 'You always manage to put things so that everything you want to do seems right. But you're bound to start making up to her again, and if this time you succeed with her under your own name it'll be ten times worse than before.'

The poor girl had instinctively guessed what was likely to happen. D'Artagnan comforted her as best he could and assured her that he would remain impervious to Milady's charms. He then sent her back to her mistress with a message that he would be delighted to call on her that evening. (He did not dare write lest Milady's experienced eye should recognize his handwriting.)

As the clock struck nine d'Artagnan arrived at the house in the Place Royale. The servants on duty in the ante-room had apparently been warned that he was coming, for when he appeared one of them ran at once to announce his arrival before he even had time to inquire whether her Ladyship was at home.

'Show him in,' said Milady quickly and so loudly that d'Artagnan heard her in the ante-room.

'I'm not in to anyone else,' she added. 'You understand? To no one else.'

The servant went out and ushered in the young man. As d'Artagnan entered the drawing-room he took a quick look at Milady and noticed that she was pale and that her eyes were tired, either from weeping or from lack of sleep. The light had purposely been dimmed, but even so traces of her sufferings of the past two days were visible on her face.

D'Artagnan began paying court to her as usual. She braced herself to respond to his compliments, but the effort was obviously painful, and never had such haggard looks belied so sweet a smile.

D'Artagnan inquired after her health.

'My health's bad,' she said, 'very bad.'

'In that case I'm only tiring you,' replied the young man. 'I'll go now and leave you to rest.'

'No, don't go,' said Milady. 'Stay and give me the pleasure of your company.'

'I've never known her so gracious,' thought d'Artagnan. 'I'd better be on my guard.'

Milady laid herself out to delight the young man with her charm and to dazzle him with her wit. And the fire of anger which burned within her added sparkle to her eyes and colour to her cheeks. D'Artagnan felt himself falling under her spell again. Then Milady smiled and the young man knew that he would risk damnation for that smile. He even began to feel remorse for having tricked her.

From generalities the conversation gradually changed to matters more intimate and personal. Milady asked d'Artagnan if he was in love. D'Artagnan sighed deeply, laid his hand on his heart and replied:

'That was a cruel question, Lady de Winter. You know that since I first met you I've lived for you and because of you alone.'

Milady smiled a strange smile.

'So you love me?' she said.

'Do I need to tell you? You must have noticed.'

'Yes,' she replied. 'But as you know, proud hearts are hardest won.'

'I enjoy a hard fight. I only shy off if a thing's impossible.'

'Nothing's impossible to true love,' said Milady.

'Nothing, Lady de Winter?'

'Nothing.'

'Ye gods,' thought d'Artagnan. 'The tables are turning. Is the fickle creature preparing to fall in love with me? Is she going to give me another sapphire like the one she gave me as de Wardes?'

'You say you love me, Monsieur d'Artagnan,' went on Milady. 'What would you do to prove it?'

'Anything!' cried d'Artagnan, fully aware that in committing himself thus he was not risking much.

'Then come closer and let's talk,' said Milady, inviting d'Artagnan to bring his chair up to her armchair.

'Well, Lady de Winter?' asked the young man.

Milady paused for a moment, as though in doubt. Suddenly she seemed to make up her mind and said:

'I have an enemy, Monsieur d'Artagnan.'

D'Artagnan pretended to be surprised.

'You, Lady de Winter?' he cried. 'How could anyone hate you, good and charming as you are?'

'A mortal enemy.'

'Incredible!'

'A man who's insulted me so cruelly that it's open war between us. Can I count on you as an ally in this?'

D'Artagnan realized in a flash what she was leading up to.

'You can, Lady de Winter,' he said. 'My life's yours.'

'Very well,' said Milady. 'Since you're so ready to prove your love . . .'

She paused.

'Well?' prompted d'Artagnan.

'Well, never again talk of impossibilities.'

'Oh, you make me so happy!' cried d'Artagnan, falling on his knees before her and covering her hands with kisses.

Milady muttered under her breath:

'Punish that vile de Wardes for me, and then I'll get rid of you, you swaggering oaf, you sword-blade of a man!'

And d'Artagnan muttered under his breath:

'Wicked woman! How can you tell me you love me after playing me up like that? D'you think I'd fight for you after the way you've treated me?'

Then he looked up at her.

'I'm ready,' he said.

'So you know what I want you to do, dear Monsieur d'Artagnan?' said Milady.

'I could read your thoughts merely by gazing at you.'

'And you'll risk your life to avenge my honour?'

'Just say the word.'

'And what shall I do for you in return? I know men; I know they always expect some reward.'

'I only ask you to let me love you,' replied d'Artagnan.

And he drew her gently to him.

She scarcely resisted. With an enchanting smile she said:

'I don't think you really love me at all.'

At this d'Artagnan felt a sudden surge of genuine passion for this woman, the passion her presence never failed to rouse in him.

'Oh Clarice,' he cried, 'just now you said you loved me! Let me kiss you once in token of that love.'

'Do you think you deserve that pledge so soon?'

'I've offered to risk my life for you, remember.'

'And you really mean it?' asked Milady, looking searchingly at him.

'Just name the scoundrel who's dared insult your beauty!'

'Remember if I tell you his name I'm giving you my secret.'

'And yet if I'm to kill him I must know his name.'

'And so you shall. You see how I trust you.'

'How good you are! Who is he?'

'Someone you know.'

'Someone I know?'

'Yes.'

'It's not one of my three friends by any chance?'

'If it were would you think twice about it?' asked Milady.

And for an instant her eyes glinted dangerously.

'No,' cried d'Artagnan, 'not if it were my brother.'

It was a bold statement but the young man knew he was on perfectly safe ground.

'I love you for saying that,' said Milady.

'Is that the only thing you love me for?' sighed d'Artagnan.

'I love you for yourself too,' she replied, taking his hands in hers.

D'Artagnan trembled at her touch; it was as though the fever which possessed her entered into him.

'You love me!' he cried. 'Oh, if I could believe that, I should go mad!'

And he leaned forward and took her in his arms. She made no attempt to avoid the pressure of his lips on hers but did not respond to his ardour. Her lips were cold. Am I making love to a corpse? he wondered. And yet he was himself so crazed with love that he almost imagined his love returned and almost believed in the reality of de Wardes' crime. Had de Wardes been within reach of him then he would have killed him.

Milady struck while the iron was hot.

'My enemy's name is . . .' she began.

'De Wardes, I know it,' said d'Artagnan.

Milady started and drew back.

'How did you know that?' she asked, seizing his hands and staring at him as though she would read his thoughts.

D'Artagnan realized that in the excitement of the moment he had blundered.

'Tell me how you knew!' insisted Milady.

'How I knew?'

'Yes.'

'Because yesterday, in front of a crowd of people, myself included, de Wardes produced a ring which he said was a present from you.'

'The fiend!'

As may be imagined Milady's words cut d'Artagnan to the quick.

'Well?' she continued.

'Well, I'll slay this fiend for you!' cried the young man melodramatically.

'Thank you, brave friend! And when will you do it?'

'Tomorrow, today, whenever you say.'

Milady was about to cry 'Today!' But she realized that to

show such haste would be unflattering to d'Artagnan. More-over there were pitfalls to be avoided; d'Artagnan had to be warned not to say anything indiscreet to de Wardes before witnesses.

The young man now said gravely:

'Let's make it tomorrow. Tomorrow either you'll be avenged or I shall be dead.'

'I shall be avenged but you won't be dead,' said Milady. 'He's a coward.'

'With women perhaps, but not with men. I've had proof of that.'

'You got the best of it in your last fight with him.'

'Yes, but Fortune's fickle. She favours a man one day and spurns him the next.'

'D'you mean you're fighting shy of it?' cried Milady.

'God forbid! But is it fair to ask me to risk my life without giving me something more than mere hope?'

For answer Milady gave him a quick look which said, as clearly as any words could have said:

'Is that all you want? Well, come and take it.'

Then, as an accompaniment to her look, she said softly:

'You're right, it isn't fair.'

'You're an angel!' cried the young man.

'So everything's settled?'

'Everything, except what I ask of you, dear heart.'

'I've already told you you can be sure of my love!'

'Yes, but for me tomorrow may never come.'

At that moment they heard footsteps on the stairs.

'Quiet!' whispered Milady. 'I hear my brother. You'd better not meet him tonight.'

She rang the bell and Kitty appeared.

'Go out this way,' said Milady to d'Artagnan, opening a hidden door in the tapestry. 'And come back at eleven. Kitty will let you in.'

When the poor girl heard this she thought she would faint.

'Now then, Kitty,' said Milady sharply. 'Don't stand there gaping! Hurry up and show Monsieur d'Artagnan out, and show him in again at eleven. Do you hear?'

D'Artagnan thought to himself:

'She seems to make all her trysts for eleven. It must be a sort of routine.'

Milady held out her hand and d'Artagnan kissed it.

He then went out and down the stairs, almost completely ignoring poor Kitty's reproaches. He was entirely concerned with his own thoughts and kept repeating to himself:

'Don't be a fool. That woman's definitely evil. Take care!'

CHAPTER XXXVII

Milady's Secret

AFTER leaving Milady d'Artagnan went straight out of the house, ignoring Kitty's entreaties that he should wait in her room until the hour of his appointment with her mistress. He did this firstly in order to avoid the maid's reproaches, and secondly, because he wanted time to think things over and if possible fathom what was in Milady's mind.

The fact which stood out most clearly in the affair was that he, d'Artagnan, loved her madly, while she did not love him at all. A moment's calm thought told him that his wisest course would be to return home and write a long letter to Milady, explaining that he and de Wardes were the same; that he could only kill de Wardes by committing suicide and that the real de Wardes was innocent of any crime against her.

Unfortunately the young man was himself spurred on by a fierce longing for revenge. He wanted to possess this woman under his own name, and as the nature of his revenge promised to be very sweet he was reluctant to give up his plan.

He walked about a dozen times round the Place Royale, looking up every now and then at the light in Milady's drawing-room windows, which shone dim through the blinds. She was obviously not so keen to keep her tryst that night as on the first occasion.

At last the light disappeared and with it d'Artagnan's last doubts. He remembered every detail of the first night he had

spent with Milady and ran back to the house and up the stairs
to Kitty's bedroom, his heart pounding with excitement, his
senses on fire.

The little maid was standing at the door as pale as death,
trembling in every limb. She tried to bar the young man's way.
But Milady had been listening closely and had heard him arrive; she now opened the communicating door and called:

'Come in!'

The whole affair was so incredibly, monstrously brazen that
d'Artagnan could hardly believe in the reality of it. He felt he
had embarked on one of those fantastic adventures into which
we are dragged against our will in dreams. And yet, shameless
as the adventure appeared, he flung himself into it with zest.
Pushing Kitty aside he rushed towards Milady, yielding to an
irresistible urge, as steel yields to a magnet.

The door closed behind them.

Kitty, left alone on the far side, flung herself against the
door in a frenzy. She felt all the pangs of jealousy, rage, and
hurt pride, and at that moment had an overwhelming impulse
to expose the whole intrigue. But then she realized that if she
confessed her complicity in the plot she would not only be
ruined herself but would lose d'Artagnan for ever. She decided
that rather than lose him she would submit to this final
indignity.

D'Artagnan had meanwhile realized his heart's desire. His
mistress no longer loved him under the name of a hated rival; it
seemed she now loved him as himself. Some still, small voice
did indeed whisper to him that he was only an instrument of
vengeance for her, that in caressing him she was merely coax-
ing him for her own purposes. But pride and his insane passion
silenced that voice, stifled that whisper.

And, being by no means over-diffident, he now began to com-
pare himself with de Wardes and could not see that he was in
any way inferior to him. So why should the lady not love him
for himself? Satisfied that he had just as good a claim to her
affections as his rival, he yielded entirely to the sensations of
the moment. His sudden vision of Milady as an evil, designing

woman faded from his mind and she was to him now a gentle and responsive mistress, surrendering to an apparently genuine passion.

About two hours passed. Then the lovers' transports abated a little. Milady was not so deeply moved as d'Artagnan and was therefore the first to return to realities. She asked the young man if he had worked out a plan for forcing de Wardes into a duel next day. D'Artagnan had been thinking only of the love duel he was at present engaged in, and was foolish enough to reply that this was surely no time to think of duelling with swords.

This casual dismissal of the one subject which concerned her alarmed Milady. She began pressing the young man more and more. D'Artagnan, knowing that this duel was impossible and having never taken it seriously, tried to change the subject. But Milady held him to the point and persisted in her inquiries. The young man thought that this would be a suitable moment to suggest to her that she renounce her plans for revenge and forgive de Wardes. No sooner had he spoken than Milady stiffened and drew away from him.

'You're not afraid, are you, my d'Artagnan?' she asked in a shrill, mocking tone which made the young man feel most uncomfortable.

'You know I'm not, dear heart. But suppose poor de Wardes turned out to be less guilty than you thought?'

'He's insulted me,' said Milady gravely. 'That's enough in itself to warrant his death.'

'Very well, he shall die, since you've passed sentence on him.' D'Artagnan spoke so emphatically that Milady was again convinced that he loved her heart and soul. And once more she drew close to him.

We cannot say how long that night seemed to Milady. To d'Artagnan barely two hours seemed to have passed when dawn began to filter through the cracks in the blinds and gradually spread through the room. Seeing that the young man was preparing to go, Milady again reminded him of his promise to avenge her.

'Yes, I'll do it,' said d'Artagnan. 'But I'd like first to be certain of one thing.'

'What?'

'That you love me.'

'I should have thought I'd given you proof enough of that,' she replied. 'And now it's for you to prove your love for me.'

'Yes. And I'll do so,' replied d'Artagnan. 'But if you love me as you say you do, aren't you at all concerned for my safety?'

'Why? What danger is there?'

'I might be seriously wounded, killed even.'

'Not with your courage and good swordsmanship.'

'Wouldn't you prefer some other revenge which would save my having to fight a duel?'

Milady looked at the young man in silence. In the first faint rays of dawn her eyes shone with a sinister light.

'I really believe you're fighting shy of it,' she said at length.

'No,' he replied. 'But I confess I'm sorry for poor de Wardes now you no longer love him. I feel that to have lost your love is punishment enough in itself.'

'Who said I ever loved him?' asked Milady.

'Well, at least I can fairly say now that you love someone else. And I repeat, I'm sorry for de Wardes.'

'Why?'

'Because I happen to know . . .'

'What?'

'That as far as you're concerned he's not nearly so guilty as you think.'

'Not guilty?' cried Milady uneasily. 'What d'you mean? Please explain yourself.'

And she looked at d'Artagnan, who was still holding her in his arms, with eyes in which now shone a truly hostile light. D'Artagnan decided to end this ridiculous farce at once.

'I'm a man of honour,' he said, 'and now that I know you love me . . . for you do love me, dear heart, don't you?'

'Yes, yes, go on.'

'Well, to know that makes me so happy that I want to confess something to you.'

'Confess something?'

'Yes. You know how much I love you, and if I've wronged you through excess of love will you forgive me?'

'Perhaps. But what have you to confess?'

Milady's voice was hard and she was now deathly pale.

'You had an assignation with de Wardes last Thursday in this very room, didn't you?'

'Certainly not!'

Milady spoke so emphatically and showed so little concern that had d'Artagnan not known the truth he would have doubted. Instead he smiled a sickly smile and said:

'Don't lie, dear heart, it's no use.'

'What d'you mean? Explain yourself. You frighten me!'

'Don't be frightened. You've done me no wrong and I've already forgiven you.'

'Well, go on!' cried Milady.

'De Wardes hasn't been boasting at all.'

'What d'you mean? You told me yourself he was flaunting my ring about.'

'I've got that ring, dear heart. You see it was I who was here on Thursday night . . . not de Wardes!'

The rash young fellow expected nothing more from his mistress than surprise and mortification, a petulant storm which would resolve itself in tears. But he was very much mistaken and was soon to discover his mistake.

Milady started up wild and pale. She forced d'Artagnan away with all her strength and sprang out of bed.

It was now almost daylight.

D'Artagnan caught hold of her flimsy crêpe-de-Chine night-dress and held her back, meaning to coax her into forgiving him. As she tried to jerk herself free the cambric of the dress tore, leaving her beautiful white shoulders bare. And on her left shoulder d'Artagnan saw to his horror the fleur-de-lis, the mark of the criminal. Milady was branded!

The young man let go of her nightdress and lay there motion-less, paralysed with fear.

'God in Heaven!' he whispered.

Milady saw the look of horror on his face and guessed the cause of it. He had obviously seen everything; he now knew her secret, which no other living soul knew.

She turned on him. She was no longer an angry woman; she was a wounded animal at bay.

'Fiend!' she shrieked. 'You've played a vile trick on me and you know my secret! You shall die!'

She ran over to her dressing-table, half naked as she was, and with trembling hands opened a marquetry jewel-case, took out a little gold-hilted dagger with a thin, pointed blade and with one bound was back at d'Artagnan's side.

Brave as he was the young man flinched and shrank back at the sight of her. Her face was transformed. The pupils of her eyes were horribly dilated, her cheeks deathly pale, her teeth bared in a snarl. He backed away from her as far as the alcove, eyeing her warily like a wild beast, and when his hand, damp with sweat, accidentally touched his sword he clutched hold of it and drew it from its scabbard.

But Milady showed no alarm at the sight of the sword. She came nearer and nearer to the young man to strike him with the dagger and stopped only when she felt the point of his sword against her breast.

She now tried to catch hold of the naked blade with her hands. But d'Artagnan managed to keep it from her grasp and to hold her at bay by pointing it first at her eyes and then at her throat. As he did so he slid gradually down to the bottom of the bed; his plan was to get as close as possible to Kitty's door, through which he hoped to escape.

Meanwhile Milady made frenzied attempts to get near him and strike him, uttering low growls of baffled rage. So fierce was her onslaught that d'Artagnan began to feel he was duelling with a man and took courage again.

'All right, my beauty,' he kept saying. 'That'll do, that'll do. Calm down or by God I'll carve another fleur-de-lis on your other shoulder!'

'Fiend of Hell! Fiend of Hell!' shrieked Milady.

D'Artagnan's one thought was to get to the door and out of

the room, so he kept on the defensive. And now Kitty, startled
by the noise as Milady turned the room upside down in her
efforts to reach d'Artagnan, burst open the door and looked in.
D'Artagnan had by careful manoeuvring at last succeeded in
approaching to within three feet of this door. Now with one
bound he was in Kitty's room; quick as lightning he slammed
the door behind him and held it closed, while Kitty drew the
bolts across.

With a man's strength Milady now tried to break down the
door. Finding this impossible, she stabbed the door panel over
and over again with her dagger. Some of her blows drove the
point right through the woodwork and each time she struck she
cursed aloud.

When the bolts were drawn safely across d'Artagnan whispered to Kitty:

'Get me out of the house, quick. I must leave before she
calms down, or she'll set her household at me.'

'But you can't go out like that,' said Kitty. 'You're stark
naked!'

Only then did d'Artagnan notice his condition.

'Well, bring me some clothes, quick! Anything! Only hurry!
If I don't get out I shall be killed.'

Kitty understood this as well as he. In a twinkling she had
rigged him out in a flowered dress, a large bonnet and a tippet,
and put slippers on his bare feet. The two of them then rushed
headlong out of the room and down the stairs to the street
door.

They were only just in time. Milady had by now rung her bell
and wakened all the household. As the night porter was un-
bolting the door on Kitty's order Milady leaned from her bedroom window, also half-naked, and screamed:

'Don't let him out!'

And as the young man fled down the street she stood watching him, shaking her fist in impotent rage and hurling curses
at his retreating figure. No sooner had he vanished from her
sight than she fell down on the floor of her room in a dead
faint.

PART
TWO

CHAPTER I

How Athos Found His Equipment Without Bestirring Himself

D'ARTAGNAN was so horrified by his experience that he fled from the house without giving a thought to poor Kitty. He ran almost from one end of Paris to the other and did not stop until he had reached the Rue Férou. On his way he came up against several police patrols which set off in pursuit of him, but their shouts to him to stop only made him run faster.

He crossed the courtyard of Athos' house, climbed the two floors, and knocked loudly on his friend's door. Grimaud came to open it, his eyes heavy with sleep. D'Artagnan rushed past him into the room at such a rate that he almost toppled him over. Grimaud was so startled that he forgot his training in silence and cried out:

'Hi, there, missy, what's the hurry?'

D'Artagnan tilted his bonnet on to the back of his head and let his tippet fall open. Grimaud saw his moustache and his sword, realized that he was a man and concluded that he was a house-breaker.

'Help, thief, help, help!' he cried.

'Shut up, idiot!' said the young man. 'Don't you recognize me, d'Artagnan? Where's your master?'

'Monsieur d'Artagnan!' cried Grimaud, gaping at him.

At that moment Athos came out of his room in his dressing-gown.

'Did I hear you speak, Grimaud?' he said.

'Excuse me, Sir, but ...'

'Silence!'

Grimaud was silent. He merely stretched out his arm and pointed at d'Artagnan. Athos recognized his friend and, phlegmatic as he was, could not help exploding with laughter at his ludicrous appearance: bonnet back to front, skirts trailing on the ground, sleeves rucked up and moustaches bristling with alarm.

'Don't laugh, Athos, for God's sake,' said d'Artagnan. 'I can assure you there's nothing to laugh at.'

He said this so seriously and with such a look of genuine terror on his face that Athos was startled. He seized his friend's hands and said:

'You're not wounded, are you? You look very pale.'

'No, I'm not wounded. But I've just had a horrible experience. Are you alone, Athos?'

'Who d'you expect to find here at this hour of the night?'

'That's all right then.'

And the young man rushed into Athos' bedroom. Athos closed the door behind him and bolted it to make sure that no one would disturb them. Then he said:

'What is it, for Heaven's sake? Is the King dead? Have you killed the Cardinal? You look scared stiff. What's happened? Tell me! You've frightened me now.'

D'Artagnan quickly threw off his clothes and stood only in his shirt.

'Prepare to hear a really horrifying story,' he said.

'Right. But first put on this dressing-gown,' said the musketeer.

D'Artagnan shuffled into the dressing-gown and stood with it half on and half off. He was too upset to pay attention to details of dress.

'Well?' asked Athos.

D'Artagnan lowered his voice.

'Well,' he said. 'Milady's branded with a fleur-de-lis on her shoulder.'

Athos drew in his breath sharply and started back as though he had been shot.

'Listen,' went on his friend. 'Are you quite sure the other one's dead?'

'The other one?' murmured Athos in a voice so faint that d'Artagnan could hardly hear him.

'Yes. The one you told me about that day at Amiens.'

Athos groaned and buried his head in his hands.

'This woman's about twenty-eight.'

'Fair?'

'Yes.'

'With very light blue eyes, black eyebrows and eyelashes?'

'Yes.'

'Tall and beautifully made?'

'Yes.'

'The fleur-de-lis is small, reddish-brown and rather indistinct as though some sort of ointment was put on it to hide it?'

'Yes.'

'And yet you say this woman's English?'

'They call her Milady, but she might be French all the same. Lord de Winter's only her brother-in-law.'

'I must see her, d'Artagnan.'

'I should keep well out of her way, Athos. You tried to kill her once and she'll want to punish you for that. She's revengeful.'

'She wouldn't dare report me; she'd only be giving herself away.'

'She's capable of anything. Have you seen her in a rage?'

'No,' said Athos.

'She's the devil incarnate. Oh, Athos, I'm afraid I've made a terrible enemy in that woman – an enemy for both of us.'

D'Artagnan then described the scene in Milady's bedroom and her attempts to murder him.

'You're right,' said Athos. 'Our lives aren't worth a moment's purchase now. Luckily we're leaving Paris the day after tomorrow; we'll probably be going to La Rochelle and once we're on the march . . .'

'If she sees and remembers you she'll never rest till she's got even with you, Athos. So steer clear of her and let her vent her rage on me.'

'I wouldn't much care if she did kill me,' said Athos. 'I don't think this world's such a very wonderful place.'

'There's some mystery behind it all, Athos. I'm sure that woman's the Cardinal's spy.'

'In that case take care on your own account. Either the Cardinal admires you very much for the London episode, or he hates you like Hell for it. There's nothing he can openly get you for and yet he must vent his rage somehow. So take care. If you go out late at night don't go alone; don't eat or drink anything you're not sure of. Be on your guard all the time in fact.'

'Thank God we've only got two more days to get through. After that we'll be with the army and then we'll only have men to fear.'

'From now on I renounce my vows of seclusion,' said Athos. 'I propose to go about with you everywhere. The first thing you must do now is get back to the Rue des Fossoyeurs and I'm coming with you.'

'It's not far, I know,' said d'Artagnan. 'But I can't go in your dressing-gown all the same.'

'No, you can't,' said Athos.

He rang a little bell on the table and Grimaud came in. Athos signed to him to go to d'Artagnan's lodgings and bring back his clothes; Grimaud clicked his heels, bowed, and went off without a word.

'D'you realize we're worse off now than we were before as far as equipment goes?' said Athos. 'You've left your uniform in Milady's house and I don't suppose she'll be in any hurry to return it. Luckily you've still got your sapphire.'

'The sapphire's yours, Athos. Didn't you tell me it was a family heirloom?'

'Yes. My father bought it for two thousand crowns; it was one of his wedding presents to my mother. It's magnificent. My mother gave it to me, and I, like a fool, instead of treasuring it, gave it to that fiend.'

'Well, here it is. Take it. I expect you're longing to have it back.'

'I take that ring! After that fiend's had it? Never! That ring's defiled now.'

'Sell it or pawn it, then. They're bound to advance you a thousand crowns on it. That'll fix you for the time being; directly you get hold of some ready cash redeem it. It'll be undefiled again then because it'll have passed through the hands of the money-lenders.'

Athos laughed.

'You're a good fellow, d'Artagnan,' he said. 'Your wit's a tonic. Very well, we'll pawn the ring. But on one condition.'

'What's that?'

'That we share the proceeds – take five hundred crowns each.'

'I wouldn't dream of it, Athos. I don't need a quarter of that. I'm only a guardsman, remember. I can get all I want by selling that saddle of mine. All I really need is a horse for Planchet. Besides I've got a ring of my own.'

'Yes, but I think you value yours even more than I value mine.'

'True. You see that ring could be used to save our skins as well as our pockets. It's a gold mine and a talisman too.'

'I don't know what you mean, but I'll take your word for it. But as regards my ring, either you consent to take half the proceeds or I throw it into the Seine. And once there it's likely to stay there. I can't see any Polycratian fish popping up with it in its mouth.'

'Very well then. I agree,' said d'Artagnan.

At that moment Grimaud came in followed by Planchet; the latter, concerned for his master's safety, had insisted on bringing the clothes himself.

D'Artagnan and Athos now dressed. When they were ready to go out Athos struck an attitude of a man pointing a gun, upon which Grimaud ran and unhooked his musket from the wall and handed it to him. The two masters and the two servants then set off for the Rue des Fossoyeurs.

Monsieur Bonacieux was standing at his front door; he winked slily at d'Artagnan and said:

'Hurry up, Sir, hurry up. A beautiful young lady's called to see you, and women don't like to be kept waiting, you know.'

'It must be Kitty!' cried d'Artagnan.

And he rushed down the alley, in at the door, and up the stairs.

On the landing outside his room he did, indeed, find Kitty. She was standing hunched up against his door; her face was pale and she was trembling. When she caught sight of him she cried out:

'You promised to protect me; you promised to protect me from her! Don't forget it's you who got me into trouble.'

'I hadn't forgotten you,' said d'Artagnan. 'Don't worry. What happened after I left?'

'I don't know,' answered Kitty. 'She went on shouting and yelling and all the men came running up. She was mad with rage. She hurled every insult under the sun at you. Then I realized that she might remember how you always went into her room through my room and might suspect me of being in league with you. So I took what little money I had and a few things and fled.'

'Poor child! But what d'you think I can do for you? I'm leaving Paris the day after tomorrow, you know.'

'Surely you can think of something, Sir. Get me out of Paris, out of France if possible.'

'You don't expect me to take you to the siege of La Rochelle, do you?' asked d'Artagnan.

'No. But you could find me a place in the provinces somewhere, with some relation or friend of yours; in your own province, for instance.'

'Alas, the ladies of my province don't have maids. But I think I can do something for you all the same. Planchet, run and fetch Aramis; tell him to come at once; say we need his help urgently.'

'I see your idea,' said Athos. 'But why not Porthos? I should have thought his marquise friend . . .'

'Porthos' marquise friend gets her husband's clerks to do all her dressing and undressing for her,' said d'Artagnan with a laugh. 'Besides Kitty wouldn't want to live in the Rue aux Ours. Would you, Kitty?'

'I'd live anywhere provided I was well hidden and no one knew where I was,' said Kitty.

'Now that we're going to part, Kitty,' said d'Artagnan, 'and that you won't be jealous of me any more . . .'

'Oh, Sir, near or far, I shall love you always,' said Kitty.

'Is there such a thing as constancy in this world?' muttered Athos under his breath.

'And I'll always love you, Kitty,' replied d'Artagnan. 'But now I'm going to ask you a question which concerns me vitally. D'you remember ever hearing your mistress mention a young woman being kidnapped one night?'

'Let me think a moment! Oh Sir! You don't still love that woman?'

'No. One of my friends is in love with her. This fellow here, Athos.'

'Me!' cried Athos in horror.

'Yes, you,' repeated d'Artagnan, nudging his friend in the ribs. 'You know how interested we all are in that unfortunate Madame Bonacieux. Besides, Kitty won't repeat anything, will you, Kitty? D'you realize she's the wife of that revolting ape you met on the doorstep of this house?'

'Good Heavens!' cried Kitty. 'That reminds me. I knew there was something on my mind. I do hope that man didn't recognize me.'

'Recognize you? Why? Have you met him before?'

'He came twice to see Milady.'

'Oh, he did, did he? When exactly?'

'About a fortnight or three weeks ago.'

'I see.'

'And then again last night.'

'Last night?'

'Yes, only a moment or two before you arrived.'

'My dear Athos, we're caught up in a web of spies! D'you think he did recognize you, Kitty?'

'I pulled my bonnet well down over my eyes, but it may have been too late.'

'Go down and see if he's still on his doorstep, Athos. He's less suspicious of you than he is of me.'

Athos went down and came up again at once.

'He's gone,' he said, 'and the house is closed.'

'He's obviously gone to report that all the doves are safely in the dovecote,' said d'Artagnan.

'Well, the doves must spread their wings and fly,' said Athos. 'All of them. We'll leave only Planchet here to watch what happens.'

'What about Aramis?' asked d'Artagnan. 'Remember we sent Planchet to fetch him.'

'So we did!' said Athos. 'Well, we'll have to wait for him.'

At that moment Aramis came in. They told him the whole story and asked him to help them find a place for Kitty with one of his grand friends.

Aramis thought for a moment. Then he said, blushing:

'Would I really be doing you a good turn if I did that, d'Artagnan?'

'I'd be grateful to you all my life.'

'Very well then. I'll do what I can. Oddly enough Madame de Bois-Tracy asked me to look out for a lady's maid for a friend of hers who lives in the country. If you can vouch for this girl's character, d'Artagnan . . .'

'Oh, Sir,' interrupted Kitty, 'I'd do anything for anyone who'd give me a chance to leave Paris.'

'Right, that's settled then,' said Aramis.

He sat down at a table and wrote a short note, sealed it with his signet ring and handed it to Kitty.

'And now, my dear,' said d'Artagnan, 'you know it's no healthier for us here than it is for you. So let's say good-bye quickly and hope to meet again in better times.'

'Wherever and whenever that may be,' said Kitty, 'you'll find me just as much in love with you as I am today.'

'H'm,' muttered Athos to himself again.

D'Artagnan escorted Kitty to the top of the stairs. A few minutes later the three young men separated, arranging to meet again at four o'clock at Athos' lodgings, and leaving Planchet to watch the house. Aramis returned home and Athos and d'Artagnan went off to pawn the sapphire. As the Gascon had foreseen they had no difficulty in getting three hundred pistoles for it. Moreover the Jew declared that it would make a magnificent pendant for a set of earrings in his possession and that he would buy it at any time for five hundred pistoles.

So active were Athos and d'Artagnan and so knowledgeable in military matters that it took them a bare three hours to buy their two complete outfits for the campaign. Athos was, of course, very amenable and whenever he found anything to his taste would pay the price asked without attempting to bargain with the shopkeeper. D'Artagnan tried to protest from time to time, but Athos always frowned at him reprovingly, until d'Artagnan was made to feel that bargaining was all very well for a petty Gascon squire like himself but unbecoming in a true aristocrat.

The musketeer found a magnificent five-year-old Andalusian horse, a jet black thoroughbred. He fell in love with it at once and bought it for a hundred pistoles. He might have got it for less, but while d'Artagnan was disputing the price with the dealer Athos was already counting out the hundred pistoles on the table. A sturdy Picardy horse was found for Grimaud for the sum of thirty pistoles. And when this horse had been provided with a saddle and Grimaud with arms, not one sou was left of Athos' hundred and fifty pistoles. D'Artagnan tried to persuade his friend to borrow a slice of his share of the proceeds of the ring, but Athos refused point blank.

'How much did the Jew offer to buy the sapphire for?' he asked.

'Five hundred pistoles.'

'That's another two hundred, a hundred more for you and a hundred more for me. A small fortune, in fact. Go back to the Jew at once.'

'What? You mean you'll sell it?'

'That ring would bring back unhappy memories to me. Besides, we shall never have enough ready cash between us to redeem it. So if we don't sell it we shall lose two hundred pistoles. D'Artagnan, go and tell him he can have the ring, and come back with the two hundred pistoles.'

'Don't decide now, Athos. Sleep on it first.'

'No. Ready cash is our problem at the moment. We must make sacrifices. Go at once and take Grimaud and his musket with you as an escort.'

D'Artagnan went off and returned safely half an hour later with the money. Thus was Athos' purse filled for him and his equipment acquired without any effort on his part.

CHAPTER II

A Vision

AT the appointed hour the four friends met in Athos' rooms. Their concern about equipment had completely vanished and they were now all in the highest spirits. They were talking and laughing together when suddenly Planchet came in, bringing two letters addressed to d'Artagnan. One was a small letter neatly folded length-ways and sealed with a green seal bearing the mark of a dove carrying an olive branch. The other was a large, square envelope adorned with the impressive crest and coat-of-arms of His Eminence, the Cardinal Duc de Richelieu.

When d'Artagnan saw the little note his face lit up, for he recognized the handwriting. He had only seen that handwriting once before, but he had kept the memory of it in his heart. He seized the note, broke the seal and read as follows:

Could you manage to be somewhere on the Chaillot road next Wednesday evening between six and eight? I shall be driving along that road at that time, so look carefully into every passing coach. If you see me don't appear to recognize me. If you do you'll be endangering your own and your friends' lives. I myself am running a great risk in doing this but can't resist the temptation of getting a moment's glimpse of you.

No signature.

'It's a trap,' said Athos. 'Don't go, d'Artagnan.'

'I think I recognize the handwriting,' said d'Artagnan.

'It might be a forgery,' said Athos. 'Just now the Chaillot road's quite deserted at that hour. You might as well go for a walk in the Bondy forest.'

'I suggest we all go,' said d'Artagnan. 'Good God! They can't eat all of us, four lackeys, four horses, arms and all! They'd get a belly ache.'

'Besides it would be a chance to show off our equipment,' said Porthos.

'But if it's a woman writing,' said Aramis, 'and she says she doesn't want to be seen, we shall be compromising her. You can't do that to a woman.'

'We can stay in the background,' said Porthos, 'and let d'Artagnan go and wait by the road alone.'

'Yes,' added Aramis, 'but shots can be fired from a carriage even when going at full speed.'

'Don't worry about that,' said d'Artagnan. 'They'll miss me. And if they do try any dirty tricks we'll ride after the coach and slaughter everyone inside. That'll mean so many enemies the less.'

'Yes,' agreed Porthos. 'Let's risk it. We've got to try out our arms in any case.'

'It ought to be quite good fun,' added Aramis in his slow drawl.

'Very well,' said Athos, 'I'll come with you.'

'Gentlemen,' said d'Artagnan, 'it's already half-past four and if we start now we'll only just get to the Chaillot road by six.'

'And if we start too late no one'll see us,' added Porthos, 'and that would be a pity. Let's go and get ready, gentlemen.'

'How about that second letter, d'Artagnan?' said Athos. 'The one in the large envelope. You've forgotten all about that in your excitement over the first. And to judge from the seal I should say it was well worth opening.'

'Right,' said d'Artagnan, 'let's see what His Eminence wants with me.'

He unsealed the letter and read as follows:

Monsieur d'Artagnan, des Essarts' Company, King's Guards, is commanded to be present at the Palais Cardinal this evening at eight o'clock.

La Houdinière,
Captain of the Guards.

'Ye Gods,' said Athos. 'That's another exciting invitation, but in a different way.'

'I shall accept both,' said d'Artagnan. 'One's for seven and the other for eight. I can fit both in easily.'

'I wouldn't go if I were you,' Aramis advised him. 'A man can't honourably refuse a tryst with a lady, but he's quite justified in refusing one with His Eminence, especially if he knows he hasn't been asked for his charm.'

'I agree with Aramis,' said Porthos.

'Remember, gentlemen,' said d'Artagnan, 'I had one invitation from His Eminence before, through Monsieur de Cavois. That was the day after Constance was kidnapped. I ignored that and I've never seen Constance since. This time I'm going, whatever happens.'

'If you've made up your mind to go, go,' said Athos.

'But the Bastille!' objected Aramis.

'Oh, you'll get me out of that all right,' said d'Artagnan.

'Yes, we'd do that all right,' said Aramis and Porthos airily, as though rescuing a man from a strongly guarded fortress were the easiest thing in the world. 'The only snag is that we're due to leave Paris the day after tomorrow and might not be able to manage it before then.'

'We can do better than that,' said Athos. 'We can stop him getting in at all. We can stay with him all the evening. I suggest one of us waits with three musketeers at each of the three entrances to the palace, four men at each entrance. If we see any suspicious-looking carriage with closed doors drive out we'll attack it. It's a long time since we had a set-to with the Cardinal's Guards, and Monsieur de Tréville must think we're dead.'

'Athos, you're a born strategist,' cried Aramis. 'What d'you think of the plan, gentlemen?'

'Admirable!' shouted the other two.

'Well, I'll go off now to headquarters and tell the other fellows to be ready at eight o'clock,' said Porthos. 'We'll all meet in front of the Palais Cardinal; you three had better go and get the horses saddled.'

'I haven't got a horse,' said d'Artagnan, 'but I'll borrow one from Monsieur de Tréville.'

'No need for that,' said Aramis. 'You can take one of mine.'

'*One* of yours! You talk as though you'd half a dozen.'

'I've got three,' replied Aramis with a smile.

'My dear chap, you must be the best-mounted poet in all France and Navarre,' said Athos.

'You surely don't need three horses, Aramis,' said d'Artagnan. 'What on earth made you buy three?'

'Actually I only bought two.'

'The third came down the chimney, I suppose.'

'No. The third appeared at my door this morning in the charge of an unliveried groom, who said he'd come by his master's order but refused to give the master's name.'

'Or the mistress's,' broke in d'Artagnan.

Aramis blushed.

'That's neither here nor there,' he retorted. 'Anyway this third horse is a present from some anonymous friend.'

'Things like that only happen to poets,' said Athos gravely.

'Now I've got a better idea,' said d'Artagnan. 'One of your three horses is presumably for Bazin. Of the other two which are you going to ride? The one you bought or the one that was given you?'

'The one that was given me of course. I can't insult my . . .'

Aramis paused.

'Unknown patron,' suggested d'Artagnan.

'Or patroness,' put in Athos.

'So you won't need the one you bought at all?'

'No.'

'Did you choose it yourself?'

'Yes. And I took great trouble about it. You know how much depends on one's horse in a campaign.'

'Right. I'll buy it from you for what you gave for it.'

'I was going to suggest that myself, d'Artagnan. And don't hurry about paying; it's very little in any case.'

'How much?'

'Eight hundred livres.'

D'Artagnan delved into his pockets and took out a handful of gold.

'Here are forty doubloons, in other words eighty pistoles,' he said. 'I know you like to be paid in pistoles; that's how you get paid for your poems.'

'So you're in funds, are you?'

D'Artagnan jingled what remained of the pistoles in his pocket.

'I'm rich, rich as Croesus,' he said.

'Send your saddle to headquarters and they'll bring your horse back with ours,' said Aramis.

'Right. But it's just on five o'clock now. We must hurry.'

Twenty minutes later Porthos appeared at one end of the Rue Férou, riding a magnificent jennet. Mousqueton was riding behind him on a small but sturdy Auvergne pony. Porthos looked thoroughly pleased with himself. At the same moment Aramis appeared at the other end of the street, mounted on a magnificent English charger. Bazin rode behind him on a roan horse, leading a lively Mecklenburg two-year-old on a leading rein. The Mecklenburg was for d'Artagnan. The two musketeers met at the door, while Athos and d'Artagnan watched from the window.

'God, that's a fine beast you've got there!' said Aramis.

'Yes,' replied Porthos. 'It's the horse I should have had to start with. The other one, the yellow one, was the duchess's husband's dirty trick. But he's been well punished for it.'

Now Planchet and Grimaud appeared, leading their masters' mounts on leading reins. D'Artagnan and Athos at once came down and joined their companions in the saddle. The little quartette made a fine show trotting through the streets towards the quay, Athos astride a horse for which he was indebted to his wife, Aramis a horse presented to him by his mistress, Porthos one provided by the attorney's wife, and d'Artagnan one supplied by Dame Fortune, the best mistress of all.

The four servants rode along in procession behind their masters.

Had Madame Coquenard happened to live on the triumphal

route and seen her handsome lover astride his Spanish jennet she would not have regretted the severe bleeding she had given her husband's strong box.

Near the Louvre the four friends ran into Monsieur de Tréville, who was returning from St Germain. He stopped them to compliment them on their fine turn-out, and this picturesque encounter brought a crowd of about a hundred idlers running to the spot.

D'Artagnan took advantage of this chance meeting to tell Monsieur de Tréville about the letter with the large red seal and the ducal crest and coat-of-arms. Needless to say, he did not mention the other letter. Monsieur de Tréville approved the young man's decision and assured him that if he did not put in an appearance the following morning he would find him and rescue him, wherever he was.

At that moment the Samaritaine clock struck six. The four friends excused themselves on the grounds of an appointment, took leave of Monsieur de Tréville and galloped off towards the Chaillot road. When they reached it twilight was setting in and carriages were passing to and fro. D'Artagnan took up his position at the roadside, while his friends waited under the trees a few yards behind him. The young man scrutinized all the carriages closely but at first saw no familiar face.

After about a quarter of an hour, just as the daylight was fading entirely, d'Artagnan noticed a carriage approaching at a great rate along the Sèvres road. He had a presentiment that this carriage contained the person who had arranged the tryst with him and felt a thrill of excitement. The next moment the carriage swept past and he saw a woman look out of the window and hold two fingers to her lips, either to enjoin silence or to send a kiss. At the sight of her the young man gave a shout of joy, for he had recognized Madame Bonacieux. Then the carriage swept on and he was left with only the memory of what he had seen, a fleeting vision, a phantom.

Forgetting the words of warning contained in the note d'Artagnan now unthinkingly spurred his horse into a gallop and in a few strides drew level with the carriage. But the door-blind had been drawn down and the vision had disappeared. Only then did he remember the warning:

'If you see me don't appear to recognize me.'

He stopped short, suddenly terrified, not on his own account but for his beloved Constance, who had evidently run a great risk in arranging this meeting. The carriage drove on at full speed and disappeared in the maze of the city streets.

D'Artagnan let his horse's reins go slack and sat lost in thought. How was he to interpret this strange experience? If the woman were really Madame Bonacieux and if she were returning to Paris, why that fleeting tryst, that tantalizing glimpse, that farewell kiss? If on the other hand his eyes had deceived him in the faint light and it had not been Constance, this might have been the first move in a plot against himself, in which the woman he was known to love was used as a bait.

D'Artagnan's three friends now rode up and joined him. All three declared that they had also seen a woman's head at the carriage window, but of the three only Athos knew Madame Bonacieux. Athos agreed that it was she, but, being less preoccupied than d'Artagnan with her pretty face, had noticed a man's head behind hers in the carriage.

'If there was a man there,' said d'Artagnan, 'he was obviously taking her from one prison to another. Oh God, what are they doing with my poor Constance, and shall I ever see her again?'

'Remember the only people you'll never see again in this world are the dead,' said Athos. 'So if your beloved Constance is not dead and was in that carriage, you'll see her again some day, never fear.' He added gloomily: 'Perhaps even sooner than you want to.'

At that moment the clock struck seven-thirty. The carriage had been twenty minutes late arriving. D'Artagnan's friends reminded him of his second engagement for that evening, but also pointed out that he could still get out of it if he wanted to.

But d'Artagnan was by nature both obstinate and inquisitive. He had made up his mind to go to the Palais Cardinal and find out why His Eminence wanted to see him. And nothing his friends said could alter his decision.

So all four set off and soon reached the Rue St Honoré and the Place du Palais Cardinal. Here they found awaiting them the twelve musketeers whom Porthos had recruited for the evening. They were now told the reason for the summons and what they were expected to do. All the musketeers knew d'Artagnan and knew that he was destined to join their ranks one day, so they agreed unanimously to stand by him that night. It was an escapade which particularly appealed to them, for it might lead to a scrap with the Cardinal's Guards, which they always enjoyed. Athos split them into three parties, put himself in command of one, Aramis of another, and Porthos of another, and posted each party under cover opposite each of the entrances to the palace.

Thus supported, d'Artagnan walked boldly up to the main door of the palace and entered the hall. He was outwardly calm but inwardly not a little alarmed at the thought of meeting the Cardinal. He knew that he had behaved unscrupulously to Milady and suspected that she and the Cardinal were in close political contact. He also knew that de Wardes, whom he had thrashed so badly, was one of His Eminence's intimates, and that His Eminence was as loyal to his friends as he was unrelenting to his foes. He thought to himself:

'If de Wardes has described our adventure to the Cardinal and if the Cardinal recognized me from the description, which is most probable, I'm pretty well doomed. But why has His Eminence waited till today to punish me? I suppose because Milady has now got in with her story, made a scene about it and brought things to a head. Thank God I've got all my friends below. They won't stand by and see me taken off without putting up a fight. And yet one company of Musketeers can't do much against the Cardinal, who's got the whole French army to back him, the Queen in his power, and the King eating out of his hand. D'Artagnan, my lad, you're quite brave and quite bright, but women'll be your downfall!'

The young man walked up the great staircase and into the

ante-chamber in some trepidation. He handed his invitation card to the page on duty, who showed him into a smaller ante-room and then disappeared into the private apartments. About half a dozen of the Cardinal's Guards were waiting in this ante-room. They at once recognized d'Artagnan as the man who had wounded Jussac and exchanged meaning glances, which d'Artagnan regarded as ominous. But he was not easily intimidated, as we know. He summoned up his native pride, faced up to them squarely and stared them straight in the eye, showing no sign of fear.

At last the page returned and signed d'Artagnan to follow him. He led him along a passage, across a large drawing-room and into a library in which a man was seated at a table writing. The page announced him and then retired without a word. D'Artagnan stood and observed the man seated at the table. He thought at first that he was a lawyer going through some briefs. But then he noticed that he was writing, or rather correcting, lines of unequal length and scanning them by tapping his fingers on the table. He then realized that the man was a poet.

After a few moments the poet closed his manuscript, which bore the title *Mirame, a Tragedy in Five Acts*. Then he looked up. D'Artagnan recognized the Cardinal.

CHAPTER III

The Cardinal

RICHELIEU rested his elbow on his manuscript and his head in his hand and stared at d'Artagnan for a moment in silence. No one had a keener gaze than the Cardinal and under his scrutiny the young man felt his heart sink. But outwardly he seemed perfectly at ease as he stood there, holding his plumed hat in his hand, respectfully awaiting His Eminence's pleasure.

'Are you one of the d'Artagnans of Béarn, Sir?' said the Cardinal at last.

'Yes, Your Eminence.'

'There are several branches of the d'Artagnan family in Tarbes and the surrounding district. Which branch do you belong to?'

'I'm the son of the d'Artagnan who fought in the religious wars with His late Majesty, King Henry IV.'

'Quite so. You're the young man who left home seven or eight months ago to seek your fortune in Paris?'

'Yes, Monseigneur.'

'You travelled through Meung, where you had trouble of some kind. I can't remember now what it was exactly, but I know something happened.'

'I'll tell you exactly what happened if you like, Sir.'

'Don't trouble,' said the Cardinal with a smile which seemed to say that he knew the story as well as the young man himself.

'You had a letter of introduction to Monsieur de Tréville, did you not?'

'Yes, Monseigneur, but during that unfortunate episode at Meung . . .'

'Your letter of introduction was lost,' said the Cardinal. 'I know that. But Monsieur de Tréville's a good judge of character and enlisted you in the company of Monsieur des Essarts, his brother-in-law, so that you could join his own company of musketeers later.'

'Your Eminence knows my story inside out.'

'Since then a great deal has happened to you. You went for a stroll one day behind the Carmelite Convent when it would have been better if you'd stayed at home. Then you made an expedition with your friends to Forges to take the waters. Your friends stopped half-way but you went on. I know all about that – you had special business in England.'

D'Artagnan was completely taken aback. He stammered out:

'I was going . . .'

'You were going to hunt at Windsor, or somewhere,' broke in the Cardinal. 'But that's your affair. I know about it merely because it's my business to know everything. On your return you had an interview with a certain lady of high position. And by the way, I'm delighted to see you've kept the present she gave you!'

D'Artagnan put his hand quickly over the Queen's ring and turned it round on his finger. But it was too late.

'Two days later, if you remember, you had a visit from Monsieur de Cavois,' went on the Cardinal. 'He brought you an invitation from me, which you ignored. That was foolish of you.'

'Your Eminence, I thought you were displeased with me.'

'Why should you have thought that?' went on the Cardinal. 'You'd shown unusual courage and resource in carrying out your Sovereign's orders. Was that a reason for being displeased with you? I wasn't at all displeased. I admired you. I punish people when they disobey orders, not when they obey them ... too well, as you did. In proof of this let me remind you of what happened the night before I sent you that invitation which you ignored.'

D'Artagnan remembered that that had been the night of Madame Bonacieux's kidnapping. He felt a sudden chill of fear, for this in turn recalled to his mind the incident on the Chaillot road of only half an hour ago. The Cardinal's words seemed to hint that his beloved Constance was still in the hands of her enemies.

The Cardinal went on:

'I hadn't heard from you for some time, so I wanted to find out what you were up to. Besides you've some cause to be grateful to me; you've been treated very leniently so far; you must have noticed that.'

D'Artagnan bowed.

'Your Eminence is too good,' he murmured.

The Cardinal continued:

'I've been lenient with you partly because I felt you deserved it and partly because I've thought of a possible career for you.'

D'Artagnan gave a start of surprise.

'That was what I wanted to discuss with you the day I sent you that invitation which you ignored. Fortunately nothing's been lost by the delay, and we can discuss it today instead. Sit down there opposite me, Monsieur d'Artagnan. We don't need to be too formal.'

The young man was so amazed that he stood staring at the Cardinal without moving, and the latter had to repeat his invitation to him to sit down.

'You're a brave man, Monsieur d'Artagnan,' he went on. 'And you're also a man of sense – which is even better. I like men of your stamp. But you're young and inexperienced. And for someone so young and inexperienced you've managed to make some pretty formidable enemies. You'd better take care; they'll crush you if they can.'

The young man replied:

'They oughtn't to find that very difficult, Sir. They're strong and well supported, and I'm on my own.'

'Yes. But you've already done quite a lot on your own. And you'll do a lot more still, I've no doubt. But I think you need help. I think I'm right in saying you came to Paris with the idea of making your fortune.'

'I'm still at the foolishly optimistic age, I'm afraid, Sir,' said d'Artagnan.

'Only fools are foolishly optimistic,' replied His Eminence. 'And you're not a fool. Listen! What would you say to the offer of an ensignship in my Guards and a captaincy after the campaign?'

'Monsiegneur . . .!'

'Well?'

D'Artagnan looked embarrassed.

'Monseigneur!' he repeated.

'Why are you hesitating?' cried the Cardinal.

D'Artagnan replied:

'I'm in His Majesty's Guards, Monseigneur, and I'm very happy there.'

'Are you suggesting that my Guards aren't His Majesty's Guards? Remember, whatever French regiment you belong to you're in His Majesty's service.'

'That wasn't what I meant, Sir.'

'Oh, I see. You want an excuse for accepting. Is that it? Well, you've a very good excuse. Desire for promotion, the coming campaign, the chances I'm offering you — that's your excuse to the world. And your excuse to yourself is that you need protection. For let me tell you frankly, Monsieur d'Artagnan, I've had some very serious complaints about you from certain quarters. You don't devote all your days and nights exclusively to your duties as you should.'

D'Artagnan flushed. The Cardinal laid his hand on a file of papers on the table.

'I actually have a whole dossier about you here,' he said. 'But I wanted to have a word with you before reading it. You've got plenty of energy and if you'd direct it into the right channels you might make your fortune. At present you're only doing yourself harm.'

D'Artagnan replied:

'It's very good of you to take this interest in me, Sir. I don't deserve it, I know, and I'm all the more grateful to you for your kindness. But I think you said I might speak frankly . . .'

He paused.

'Go on,' said the Cardinal. 'Say what's on your mind.'

'Only this, Sir. For some strange reason all my friends seem to be either musketeers or King's Guards and all my enemies your men, Sir. If I accepted your offer I wouldn't be welcome in your ranks and all my friends would say I'd behaved badly.'

The Cardinal smiled scornfully.

'Are you so proud as to think my offer's not good enough?' he asked.

'No, Sir, I never thought that. You're being far too generous to me and I don't think I've done nearly enough to deserve your attention. The campaign's just starting, Sir. I shall be serving under your command, and if I have the good luck to distinguish myself in some way I shall feel more worthy of your interest in me. Perhaps one day I'll be in a position to offer you my services. At present I might be accused of selling myself.'

The Cardinal was irritated. At the same time he admired the young man for his integrity. He replied:

'So you refuse to join me, Sir. Very well. I can't decide for you. You're free to choose whom you want as your friends and whom you want as enemies.'

'Monseigneur . . .!'

'That's all right, that's all right,' broke in the Cardinal. 'I'm not angry. But please understand I've enough to do protecting my friends. I can't be responsible for what happens to my enemies. However, I'll give you one word of warning. Don't do anything rash, Monsieur d'Artagnan. The instant I withdraw my support from you your life won't be worth a moment's purchase.'

'I'll remember your warning, Sir,' replied the young man.

His manner was deferent but he seemed in no way cowed.

Richelieu stared at him for a moment in silence. Then he said gravely:

'If anything bad should happen to you, always remember it was I who took the trouble to get to know you and that I did my best to prevent that thing happening.'

D'Artagnan replied with equal earnestness:

'Whatever happens, Sir, I'll always be grateful to you for our interview today.'

'Right, Monsieur d'Artagnan,' said the Cardinal. 'Well then, as you say, we shall be seeing each other after the campaign. Meanwhile I'll keep my eye on you.'

He pointed to a magnificent suit of armour hanging on the wall and said:

'I shall be at La Rochelle myself, you know.'

He paused. Then he added:

'And on our return I hope we'll be able to come to some better agreement.'

'Monseigneur, I beg you not to look on me as an enemy!' cried d'Artagnan. 'I've been honest with you, Sir. I can't expect to enjoy your favour, I know. But at least bear me no malice!'

'Young man,' replied Richelieu. 'If we meet again after the war's over and I can ever repeat the offer I made you today you may be sure I shall do so.'

This last speech alarmed d'Artagnan more than any open menace would have done. It was a warning. The Cardinal was obviously hinting to him that some imminent danger threatened him. He was about to reply, but the Cardinal dismissed him with an imperious gesture.

D'Artagnan bowed and turned to leave the room. But as he reached the door he was seized with sudden panic and was on the point of yielding. Then he saw in his mind's eye Athos' stern, accusing face. If he made a pact with the Cardinal his friend would disown him and turn his back on him. This thought strengthened him in his resolve to stand firm.

He walked down the same staircase and out by the same door. At the entrance he found Athos and his four musketeers; they had had a long wait and had begun to grow anxious. D'Artagnan reassured them with a word and sent Planchet off to tell the other two parties of musketeers that they could now disperse. as his master had come out of the Palais Cardinal unscathed.

When the four friends were back in Athos' rooms Aramis and Porthos inquired the reason for the interview. D'Artagnan merely told them that Richelieu had summoned him to offer him an ensign's commission in his Guards and that he had refused.

'You were quite right!' cried Porthos and Aramis in one breath.

Athos frowned and said nothing. But when he was alone with d'Artagnan he said:

'You did the only thing you could do. But perhaps you were unwise.'

D'Artagnan was silent. He was too depressed to speak. For Athos' words strengthened his own conviction that some calamity was in store for him.

The next day was spent in preparations for departure. D'Artagnan called on Monsieur de Tréville to take leave of him. At that time it was generally supposed that the separation of the Guards and the Musketeers was to be only temporary. The King had summoned Parliament for that very day and was due to leave the day after. So Monsieur de Tréville merely asked d'Artagnan if he needed money, to which d'Artagnan replied that he needed nothing.

That night a select few of the Guards and the Musketeers had a joint farewell supper. They would be meeting again when it pleased God and if it pleased God. As can be imagined the evening was wildly hilarious, for one can only drive out care of that kind with extreme frivolity.

On the following morning as reveillé sounded on the bugles the friends took leave of each other. The Musketeers ran to report at Monsieur de Tréville's house and the Guards at Monsieur des Essarts' headquarters. The two captains then rode with their companies to the Louvre where the King was to review them.

His Majesty was obviously out of temper and looked unwell. He had, in fact, had an attack of fever the previous day while he was holding his *Lit de Justice*. He was resolved, however, to ignore his doctor's advice and to leave that very evening. Moreover he insisted on reviewing the troops in the morning, hoping to shake off his illness by remaining active.

After the review the Guards marched off alone, for the Musketeers were due to leave only when the King left. Porthos took advantage of these few hours of grace to ride in solitary state down the Rue aux Ours to show off his equipment. The attorney's wife saw him passing. So devoted was she to her gay cavalier that she signalled to him to dismount and enter the house. Porthos looked resplendent; his spurs jingled, his cuirass shone and his sword clanked impressively against his leg. This time the clerks neither dared nor wanted to laugh, for Porthos looked a proper fire-eater. Madame Coquenard took him in to see her husband, and the attorney's little grey eyes flashed fire as he saw his would-be cousin so spick and span. One thought however, consoled him – everyone said that the campaign would be hard, and there was therefore a good chance that Porthos would perish on the battlefield. With this cheering thought in mind he shook the young man warmly by the hand and wished him good luck. As for Madame Coquenard she shed bitter tears, but no one put a bad construction on her grief. Everyone knew how attached she was to her relations and how she had always had to defend them against her husband. She watched Porthos' retreating figure from her window, leaning so far out in her excitement that she almost overbalanced and fell into the street. Porthos received these demonstrations of affection coolly, as no more than his due, and only at the last moment did he trouble to turn and wave to his unfortunate mistress.

Aramis meanwhile was writing a long letter. To whom? No one knew. The document was to be given to Kitty, who was due to leave for Tours that evening, and who was waiting for it in the next room.

Athos spent the few intervening hours at home, sipping the remains of his store of Spanish wine.

Meanwhile d'Artagnan was riding out of Paris with his company of Guards. When his troop reached the Faubourg St Antoine the young man turned round and sent a challenging salute to the Bastille, from whose clutches he had so far escaped. He was so busy looking at the fortress that he failed to observe at a cross-roads a woman mounted on a bay horse, who was watching him closely. The woman was Milady, and she was pointing the young man out to two sinister-looking men. The latter immediately approached the troop of riders to take a close look at him, and then glanced back at Milady, who nodded to confirm that he was the man. Having made sure that her orders were fully understood Milady spurred her horse to a canter and rode off. The two men now turned and followed the company of guards on foot. At the end of the Faubourg St Antoine they mounted two horses which were waiting for them in the charge of an unliveried groom, and rode along in rear of the soldiers, following them through the gates of the capital and out into the country.

CHAPTER IV

The Siege of La Rochelle

THE siege of La Rochelle was one of the most important episodes in the reign of Louis XIII and one of the Cardinal's
greatest military enterprises. To understand this story properly
we must know some of the historical facts about this siege. Let
us first review shortly the events which led up to it.

The Cardinal had many far-reaching political designs in
undertaking the siege. Of the important towns given by Henry
IV to the Huguenots as places of refuge only La Rochelle remained, and this last stronghold of Calvinism had to be
destroyed, for it was a dangerous breeding-ground of wars and
revolutions. Dissentient spirits in Spain, England, and Italy,
adventurers and soldiers of fortune of all nations and sects
rushed at the first summons to join the ranks of the Protestants
and banded themselves into an organization with ramifications
over the whole of Europe. La Rochelle had taken on a new
importance after the destruction of the other Calvinist towns
and was therefore a happy hunting ground for the unruly and
the ambitious. Moreover its harbour was the last door open to
England in all France, and by closing it to France's traditional
enemy the Cardinal was continuing the work of Joan of Arc and
of the Duc de Guise. Bassompierre, one of the army leaders at
the great siege, who was officially a Catholic but by conviction
a Protestant, German by birth but French in sympathy, said
once, when planning an assault on the town with certain members of his staff who shared his Protestant leanings:

'Mark my words, gentlemen, we shall be foolish enough to
take La Rochelle.'

And Bassompierre was right. To him the cannonading of the
Ile de Ré presaged the persecution of the Huguenots in the
Cévennes. The taking of La Rochelle was the prelude to the
revocation of the Edict of Nantes.

These were the motives of statesmanship which drove Richelieu to undertake the siege. They are part and parcel of history. But the chronicler must also take account of the more ignoble motives which underlay his decision, motives of personal revenge. As everyone knows, Richelieu had been in love with the Queen. Whether his love was a mere political manoeuvre or one of those genuine passions which so many of Anne of Austria's contemporaries felt for her we shall never know. But we do know from reading this tale that Buckingham had tricked His Eminence at least once and that, thanks to the courage and devotion to duty of the three musketeers and d'Artagnan, he had quite recently outwitted him in the affair of the diamond tags. Richelieu, in undertaking the siege, was concerned not only with ridding France of an enemy but also with taking personal revenge on a rival. And he was determined that this revenge should be glorious and dazzling, worthy of a man who had the resources of a vast kingdom to back him. He knew that by fighting England he was fighting Buckingham; that if he triumphed over England he would triumph over Buckingham; in short, that in humiliating England he would be humiliating Buckingham in the eyes of the Queen.

Buckingham for his part, concerned though he was to uphold his country's interests, was also fired by personal motives in his struggle against France. He, too, sought revenge. He had failed to be appointed England's ambassador to France, so he now wished to enter the country as a conqueror. And it can fairly be said that the real stake in this war, in which two nations were involved at the arbitrary dictation of two men, was a smile from the lovely Anne of Austria.

The first honours had gone to Buckingham. He had arrived unexpectedly off the Ile de Ré with ninety ships of the line and roughly twenty thousand men; he had surprised the Comte de Toiras who was in command of the King's troops, and had landed on the island after a sharp engagement. In passing we may note that among those who lost their lives in that engagement was the Baron de Chantal, who left an orphan daughter, eighteen months old, the future Madame de Sévigné. The Comte de Toiras retreated with his garrison to the fortress of St Martin and posted a hundred of his men in a little outlying fort called the Fort of La Prée.

This setback had spurred the Cardinal on to a swift decision. La Rochelle was to be besieged. Monsieur was sent to supervise the first operations until the time when King and Cardinal were ready to take command, and all available troops were at once ordered to the scene of action. D'Artagnan's company formed part of the detachment sent to La Rochelle as an advance guard.

As we have said, the King had declared his intention of starting for the campaign immediately after his *Lit de Justice*. But when he rose on the morning of 28 June he felt feverish. He had insisted on leaving in spite of this but had become weaker as the day wore on and had to stop at Villeroy. Where the King stopped the Musketeers stopped. D'Artagnan, who was a mere guardsman and not essential to the King's welfare, had therefore found himself separated from his musketeer friends for longer than he had foreseen. He regarded this separation as a nuisance and missed them. But he did not yet realize how much he was to regret their absence during the next few days. And for the moment all was well; the young man arrived safely with his company at their destination on the date fixed, their destination being the camp before La Rochelle and the date 10 September, 1627.

Nothing had changed lately in the positions of the opposing forces. The Duke of Buckingham's troops, who were occupying the Ile de Ré, kept up their unsuccessful siege of the St Martin and La Prée fortresses; besides this a minor operation had been started by the English near La Rochelle itself against a fort recently erected by the Duc d'Angoulême.

Monsieur des Essarts' company of Guards was billeted in the Minimes. D'Artagnan's main ambition in life was, as we know, to be transferred to Monsieur de Tréville's Musketeers. He had therefore not attempted to make friends with his fellow guardsmen and now found himself isolated and a prey to his own thoughts. These thoughts were by no means cheerful. Almost immediately on his arrival in Paris a year ago he had got involved in affairs of State and had consequently been frustrated both in his love-affairs and in his ambitions. As far as his love-affairs went, the only woman he really cared for was Madame Bonacieux, and Madame Bonacieux had disappeared and he had lost all trace of her. As for his ambitions, he had succeeded, young as he was, in making an enemy of the Cardinal, a man feared by all the greatest in the land, the King included. This man could have easily crushed him and yet for some reason had not done so. D'Artagnan was shrewd enough to augur good things from the Cardinal's behaviour to him and to see a ray of hope in this direction. He had also made another enemy, one less to be feared, perhaps, than the Cardinal, but by no means to be despised. This enemy was Milady.

To set against all this he had won the Queen's favour. But at that time the Queen's favour was usually more of a curse than a blessing, and those who enjoyed it nearly always found themselves victims of persecution. The two most recent examples of this were Chalais and Madame Bonacieux. D'Artagnan's most practical acquisition in the past year was the Queen's diamond, which was worth between five and six thousand livres. But the young man was far-sighted enough to see that if he wished to make his way in the world his best course was to keep and not sell the diamond, so that he could prove his identity to the Queen later. And until then the ring was as valueless as the pebbles under his feet. We say 'pebbles under his feet' because, while brooding thus, d'Artagnan happened to be walking along a pretty little path which led from the camp to a neighbouring village. So immersed was he in his thoughts that he strayed farther than he had intended. Night was already falling when he suddenly noticed, in the last rays of the setting sun, the glint of a musket barrel behind a hedge. D'Artagnan had a quick eye and quick wits. He realized that the musket had not got there by itself and that the man who carried it, whoever he was, had certainly not hidden behind the hedge with any friendly intention. So he decided to take to his heels. But then he noticed, on the other side of the road, the end of another musket barrel gleaming behind a rock. It was obviously an ambush. The young man glanced back at the first musket and saw to his alarm that it was now pointing in his direction. Quick as lightning he threw himself to the ground and at the same moment heard the shot being fired and the bullet whistling over his head. There was no time to lose. He sprang to his feet again and now the bullet from the other musket scattered the pebbles at the exact spot where his head had been when he had been prostrate. D'Artagnan, like all sensible men, believed that there was no virtue in courage for its own sake, in standing firm against superior odds. Besides, it was not a question of courage now; he had fallen into a trap. He muttered to himself:

'The third shot'll get me.'

And he started running like the wind in the direction of the camp. But the man who had fired the first shot had meanwhile reloaded his musket and now sent a second shot, this time so well aimed that the bullet pierced d'Artagnan's hat and sent it flying in the air. D'Artagnan had no other hat, so he retrieved it and then ran on. In a few minutes he was back at the camp, breathless and dead white in the face. He retired to his billet without saying a word to anyone, sat down and started to think hard.

There were three possible explanations for this attack. The first and most likely was that it was a piece of sniping-work by the defenders of La Rochelle. His Majesty's Guards were fair prizes; they were picked soldiers and sometimes had well-filled purses in their pockets. D'Artagnan examined the bullet-hole in his hat. It had not been made by a musket bullet but by a bullet from an arquebus. The sniping was therefore not the work of soldiers as the bullet was not of regulation army calibre. Could it have been a memento from the Cardinal? This was the second possible explanation, but d'Artagnan dismissed it as unlikely. The Cardinal rarely adopted underhand methods in dealing with those powerless to defend themselves. Thirdly, the attack might have been an act of revenge on the part of Milady. This was much more likely. D'Artagnan tried to recall the faces and dress of the two assassins, but he had been too busy running away from them to notice much. He began to feel depressed and moaned aloud: 'Athos, Porthos, Aramis! Where are you? Why aren't you here to support me?'

That night he hardly slept at all. He kept starting up in bed, imagining that he saw a man standing over him with a knife. However the next day dawned and found him without a scratch. But he suspected that more trouble was in store for him. He spent all that day in his billet; the weather was bad and he welcomed this as an excuse to remain under cover.

Two days after the attempt on the young man's life there was a battalion parade. The Duc d'Orléans was making a tour of inspection of the troops under his command. The Guards paraded, d'Artagnan with the rest. Monsieur did his tour of inspection first and then interviewed all the senior officers on the parade ground, Monsieur des Essarts among them. The Duke and the officers formed a little group apart and after a while d'Artagnan saw his commanding officer beckon to him. He was surprised and at first did not move. Then came a second summons, at which he fell out of the ranks, walked up to the group and saluted.

'Monsieur needs volunteers for a piece of reconnaissance work,' said Monsieur des Essarts. 'It's a dangerous job and he wants picked men. I thought I'd put your name forward.'

'That's very good of you, Sir,' replied d'Artagnan.

He was delighted at this chance to distinguish himself and attract the Commander-in-Chief's notice. It appeared that the Rochellese had made a sortie in the night and recaptured a bastion which the Royalist army had taken two days before. A reconnaissance party was to be sent to find out in what strength the enemy was holding this bastion. Shortly after des Essarts had summoned d'Artagnan, Monsieur turned to him and said:

'I need four volunteers for this job, with a reliable man in charge.'

'I've got the very man here, Sir,' replied des Essarts, pointing to d'Artagnan. 'He'll lead the party and get the volunteers for you.'

D'Artagnan stepped forward, saluted and raised his sword.

'I want four volunteers to risk death with me!' he called out.

Two of his fellow guardsmen immediately stepped out of the ranks and two soldiers from another regiment joined them. Four was the number asked for and d'Artagnan chose these four because they were the first to volunteer and because he did not wish to pick men only from his own company. The party had to discover whether the Rochellese had evacuated the bastion or whether they had left a garrison there. To do this it had to get within fairly close range of the bastion. D'Artagnan and his men marched off along the trench, the two guardsmen marching in line with him and the two soldiers in rear. Advancing under cover of the trench they got to within about forty yards of the bastion. There they halted. D'Artagnan looked round and saw to his surprise that the two soldiers had disappeared. He thought that they had probably panicked and he and the two guardsmen continued to advance. They reached the bend of the counterscarp and found themselves within twenty yards of the bastion. They could see no one and the bastion appeared to be unoccupied. D'Artagnan and his men were deliberating whether to advance further when suddenly a cloud of smoke belched from the stone tower and a dozen bullets whistled round the heads of the three men. They now had the information they wanted; the bastion was occupied. They had done their job and now turned and ran back to the trench. Just as they reached it and were preparing to take cover a single shot rang out and one of the guards collapsed with a bullet through the chest. The other was untouched and continued his flight down the trench. D'Artagnan, not wishing to abandon his fellow guardsman, bent down to lift him up and help him back to the camp. But at that moment two shots rang out and the wounded guardsman again fell back, this time with a bullet through the head; the other bullet whizzed past d'Artagnan's ear and flattened itself against the rock behind him. The young man whipped round, for he realized that these shots could not have come from the bastion, which was masked by the angle of the trench. He suddenly recollected the two soldiers who had deserted earlier and then thought of the two assassins who had attacked him two days before. This time he was determined to discover the truth. He had a sudden inspiration and collapsed over his friend's body, pretending to be dead. In a moment he saw two heads peering cautiously over the top of an abandoned earthwork about twenty yards away. He recognized them as the two soldiers who had deserted. His suspicions were justified; the two men had volunteered with the object of killing him, hoping that his death would be attributed to enemy bullets. Now, fearing that their victim might be merely wounded and might later report them, they were coming up to him to finish him off. Luckily they had been deceived by d'Artagnan's trick and, imagining him to be seriously wounded, had not bothered to reload their guns. D'Artagnan in falling had been careful not to leave go of his sword, and when the two men were about ten feet away he sprang up suddenly and rushed at them. The assassins realized that if they fled back to the camp without having killed him he would report them, and that their only hope now was to go over to the enemy. One of them took his musket by the barrel and, using it like a club, aimed a fearful blow at d'Artagnan, which the young man managed to dodge. The bandit then rushed past him in the direction of the bastion. The Rochellese in the bastion thought he was attacking them and opened fire on him. A bullet struck him through the shoulder and he collapsed. Meanwhile d'Artagnan was at grips with the second soldier, attacking him with his sword. It was a short struggle, for the rogue had only his empty arquebus to defend himself with. In a few moments the young man succeeded in wounding his enemy in the thigh; he fell down and d'Artagnan was on him like a flash, pressing the point of his sword against his throat.

'Don't kill me, Sir, don't kill me!' cried the bandit. 'Spare me and I'll confess everything!'

'Why should I spare you? What can you confess that could interest me?'

'If you value your life at all you'll do well to listen to me.'

'You blackguard!' cried d'Artagnan. 'Well confess then. Who employed you to murder me?'

'A woman I don't know; a woman they call Milady.'

'If you don't know her, how d'you know what they call her?'

'The other fellow knows her and used to call her that. He was the one who had the dealings with her – not me. He actually has a letter from her in his pocket, which I'm sure would interest you, Sir.'

'How do you happen to be mixed up in the plot?'

'He suggested I should join him and we should do the job together.'

'And how much did the lady offer you for this . . . job?'

'A hundred louis.'

D'Artagnan laughed.

'I see she rates me pretty high,' he said. 'A hundred louis's no mean sum for a couple of rogues like you. I can well understand you're taking on the job for that much and I'll spare you. But on one condition.'

'What, Sir?' asked the soldier anxiously. His sly mind could not take such magnanimity at its face value and he suspected some trick.

'That you go back and retrieve the letter from the other fellow's pocket.'

'But that's just another way of getting me killed, Sir,' cried the bandit. 'How can I get that letter with the enemy in the bastion firing at me almost point blank?'

'You'll jolly well have to; if you don't I swear I'll kill you myself.'

'No, Sir, no!' cried the bandit. 'Spare me for the sake of the lady you love! You probably think the lady's dead, Sir. But I can tell you she's not.'

As he spoke the bandit fell on his knees, abject and grovelling. He had to support himself on one arm for his strength was giving out with the loss of blood from his wound.

'How d'you know about this lady?' asked d'Artagnan. 'And how d'you know I thought she was dead?'

'It's all written in that letter the other fellow has in his pocket, Sir.'

'All the more reason why I must have that letter,' said d'Artagnan. 'So hurry up and get it. If you don't, much as I dislike the thought of staining my sword again with the blood of a rogue like you, . . . I swear I'll . . .'

The young man accompanied his words with such a fierce look that the bandit sprang up. Sheer fright seemed to have brought life back to his limbs.

'All right, Sir, all right!' he cried. 'I'll go!'

D'Artagnan took the man's arquebus from him, stood behind him and forced him forward, prodding him in the back with the point of his sword. As the unfortunate man walked along he left a trail of blood behind him. Pale and sweating with fear at the thought of the almost certain death which awaited him, he was a piteous spectacle as he tried to slink along under cover towards his friend who lay prostrate about twenty yards away. D'Artagnan watched him for a while with scorn. Then he took pity on him.

'All right,' he said. 'Stay where you are. I'll go. And I'll show you the difference between a brave man and a coward.'

And he proceeded to stalk up to the second soldier, treading warily, watching the enemy's every movement and taking advantage of every possible piece of cover. Having reached the man he had two courses open to him: either to search him on the spot or to carry him back, making a shield of his body, and search him in the trench. D'Artagnan chose the second course. He had just lifted the man on to his back when the enemy opened fire. D'Artagnan felt the man's body jolt against his shoulder, heard him scream and give a final shudder of agony. The man had achieved the very opposite of what he had intended: he had shielded his victim and instead of killing him had saved his life. D'Artagnan jumped back into the trench and threw the corpse down beside the wounded man, who was almost as pale as his dead comrade. And now he proceeded to search the rogue's pockets. A leather wallet, a purse containing a sum of money which was evidently part of the fee paid by Milady for the crime, a dice-box and some dice composed the man's entire stock of this world's goods. D'Artagnan threw the dice and the box over the side of the trench, flung the purse to the wounded man and quickly opened the wallet.

Buried among a lot of other papers he found the following letter, the letter he had risked his life to recover:

You let the woman escape and she's now in safety in a convent. That was a bad slip. Don't fail with the man. If you do I shall see that you pay dearly for the hundred louis you got from me.

No signature. But the letter was obviously from Milady. D'Artagnan put it carefully in his pocket for future use as evidence of her guilt. He was now sheltered from the enemy's fire by the angle of the trench, so he proceeded to question the wounded man. The latter confessed that he and his friend had been hired to kidnap a young woman who was due to leave Paris on a certain day by the La Villette gate, but that they had stopped to have a drink in an inn and had missed the carriage by ten minutes.

'What were you told to do with the woman?' asked d'Artagnan anxiously.

'To take her to a house in the Place Royale,' answered the man.

'To Milady's own home; I thought so,' muttered d'Artagnan.

He was suddenly appalled to think how vindictively this woman was pursuing him and his friends, and how well versed she must be in State affairs to have discovered everything. No doubt the Cardinal had told her a great deal. On the other hand he was overjoyed to know that the Queen had at last found out where Madame Bonacieux was imprisoned and that Her Majesty herself had taken her out of that prison. The letter he had received from Constance and his glimpse of her on the Chaillot road were now explained to him. Now, as Athos had foreseen, it would be possible to find her again; convents were easily stormed. This thought rejoiced his heart and made him feel more friendly to the world in general. He turned to the wounded man, who was anxiously watching the changing expressions on his face, and, holding out his hand to him, said:

'Come on. I'm not going to leave you like this. Lean your weight on me and let's get back to the camp.'

The man was amazed at this magnanimity.

'Very well,' he said. 'But I suppose you're taking me back just to have me hanged.'

'No,' said d'Artagnan. 'You can trust me. I've decided to spare you once and for all.'

The wounded man fell on his knees again and abjectly kissed his rescuer's feet. But d'Artagnan now wanted to get away from the enemy as quickly as possible, so he cut short his expressions of gratitude. The guardsman who had run back to the camp after the enemy's first volley had reported the death of his four companions. So when the young man reappeared safe and sound he was greeted with cheers and many expressions of goodwill.

D'Artagnan accounted for the bandit's sword wound as a wound inflicted in a sortie by the enemy. He reported the other soldier's death and the whole expedition in detail. His story impressed everyone and rumours of it spread like wildfire through the camp. Monsieur sent him his personal congratulations. And besides the honour and glory which accrued to him through this act of gallantry the young man had the inner joy of an increased sense of security. Of his two enemies one was now dead and the other his friend for life.

But he was not destined to remain long in this comfortable state of mind. And the fact that his fears were so easily lulled proved one thing – that he did not yet know Milady very well.

CHAPTER V

The Anjou Wine

HAVING at first had bad news of the King's health the army now began to hear rumours of his convalescence. It was reported that he was now keen to get to the scene of action and that he intended to continue his journey as soon as he was well enough to ride.

Monsieur, who was temporarily in charge of the siege, knew that he would soon be replaced either by the Duc d'Angoulême,

Bassompierre, or Schomberg, all of whom were rivals for the post of Commander-in-Chief. He was therefore very half-hearted in his conduct of the siege; he wasted his time in small, isolated sorties and made no concerted effort to dislodge the English from the Ile de Ré, from where they were besieging the fortress of Saint Martin and the fort of La Prée.

As we have said, d'Artagnan's fears had been a trifle eased and his dread of Milady's wrath diminished as the days and weeks passed. Only one thing now grieved him – that he had received no news of his friends. But one morning early in November he got a letter which elated him. The letter was postmarked 'Villeroy' and ran as follows:

Monsieur d'Artagnan,

Your friends, Monsieur Athos, Monsieur Porthos, and Monsieur Aramis, recently spent a very good evening at my hotel and became very lively. They created such a disturbance that the provost-marshal of the Castle, who is a strict disciplinarian, sentenced them to several days' detention. Before their arrest, however, the gentlemen ordered me to send you twelve bottles of my Anjou wine which they found very much to their taste. They wish you to drink to their health in their favourite wine. I am therefore sending you the wine and remain

Your most respectful and obedient servant,

Godeau,
Innkeeper to their Honours
His Majesty's Musketeers.

'Marvellous!' cried d'Artagnan. 'They think of me when they're enjoying themselves just as I think of them when I'm bored. I'll drink their healths with all my heart, but not alone.'

And the young man ran off to invite two of the guards with whom he was on more intimate terms than the rest to join him in sampling the excellent Anjou wine which had just arrived from Villeroy. One of the two guards was on duty that night and the other the following night. So the party was arranged for midday two days ahead.

On returning to his billet d'Artagnan had the wine sent to be stored in the Guards' messroom. At nine in the morning of the

day for which the lunch party was fixed he sent Planchet off to
make preparations. Planchet was proud to be promoted to the
position of butler and, in order to make the party a success,
hired as waiters the servant of one of his master's guests,
Fourneau by name, and Brisemont, the assassin. The latter,
whose life d'Artagnan had spared, being attached to no company, had become d'Artagnan's or rather Planchet's personal
servant.

At the appointed hour the two guests arrived. The three men
sat down and the dishes were placed on the table. Planchet
served the meal, Fourneau uncorked the bottles, and Brisemont
decanted the wine. Everyone noticed that the wine was curiously cloudy, but attributed this to the effects of the journey.
The first bottle was so very cloudy that Brisemont poured the
dregs into a special glass which d'Artagnan said he might
drink himself as he was still rather weak from his wound. The
guests had just finished their soup and were lifting their glasses
to sip the wine when salvoes were fired from the guns of Fort
Louis and Fort Neuf. The three guardsmen, taking this to be a
warning of a surprise attack by the English or by the Rochellese,
seized their swords and rushed out to report at their posts.
But they soon discovered the real reason for the gun-fire. They
heard loud cries of 'Long live the King', 'Long live the Cardinal',
and the drums beating through the whole camp. The King, in
his impatience to reach the scene of action, had done two days'
marches in one and had at that moment arrived with all his
household at the head of an army of ten thousand men. His
Musketeers formed his bodyguard. D'Artagnan, drawn up in
line with his company to honour the King's arrival, signed to
his three friends in greeting as they marched past and after the
parade was over ran to welcome them.

'You couldn't have arrived at a better time!' he cried.

He then introduced them to the two guardsmen who had
been his guests and added:

'The food won't have had time to get cold yet, will it, gentlemen?'

'Ho, ho!' said Porthos. 'So you were having a party!'

'I hope there are no women at your party,' said Aramis.

'Is there any drinkable wine in your pot-house?' asked Athos.

'Well, there's your wine, you know,' replied d'Artagnan.

'Our wine?' queried Athos, astonished.

'Yes. The wine you sent me.'

'We never sent you any wine!'

'You remember! That light Anjou stuff. Twelve bottles of it.'

'Yes, I know the stuff all right.'

'Your favourite wine.'

'Yes,' replied Athos, 'next to Champagne and Chambertin.'

'Well, you won't find Champagne or Chambertin here, so you'll have to put up with Anjou.'

'So you've ordered some Anjou, have you?' said Porthos. 'That's very extravagant of you!'

'No. I mean the stuff you sent me.'

'We sent you!' cried the three musketeers.

'Did you send any wine, Aramis?' asked Athos.

'No.'

'Did you, Porthos?'

'No.'

'Did you, Athos?'

'No.'

'Well, if you didn't, your innkeeper did,' said d'Artagnan.

'Our innkeeper?'

'Yes, your innkeeper, Godeau. The innkeeper to their Worships the Musketeers.'

'Well,' said Porthos, 'let's sample it, wherever it comes from. It mightn't be too bad.'

'No,' said Athos. 'Don't let's drink any wine without knowing its origin.'

'You're right, Athos,' said d'Artagnan. 'Did none of you order wine from the innkeeper, Godeau?'

'Definitely not. Did he tell you we had?'

'Here's his letter,' said d'Artagnan, showing the note to his friends.

'That's not his writing,' cried Athos. 'I remember his writing. I settled all our accounts with him before we left.'

'That letter's a forgery,' said Porthos. 'We were never given detention.'

Aramis said reproachfully:

'D'Artagnan, can you imagine us *creating a disturbance*!'

D'Artagnan suddenly went very white and began to tremble.

'Look here, what's all this about?' said Athos sharply. 'D'Artagnan, why are you looking like that?'

'Listen, all of you!' said d'Artagnan. 'Something frightful's just occurred to me. D'you think this could be another of that woman's tricks? We must get back to the inn at once. Come on, hurry!'

Now Athos also went white. And all six men, the four friends and the two guardsmen, turned and ran hell for leather back to the inn.

The first thing d'Artagnan saw as he entered the dining-room was Brisemont lying full length on the floor, writhing in ghastly convulsions. Planchet and Fourneau were standing over him, trying to help him. But it was obvious that nothing could be done for him. He was dying and his face was distorted with pain. When he saw d'Artagnan he cried out:

'What a vile trick! You pretend to spare my life and then poison me!'

'I!' cried d'Artagnan. 'I poison you! You fool! You don't know what you're saying!'

'It was you who gave me that wine,' said Brisemont. 'You made me drink it. You were getting your revenge. It was a vile trick!'

'You mustn't think that, Brisemont!' said d'Artagnan. 'It's not true. I swear . . .'

'But the Lord is there! The Lord will punish you. Oh God, make him suffer one day what I'm suffering now!'

D'Artagnan knelt down beside the dying man.

'By all that's holy I swear I didn't know the wine was poisoned,' he said. 'I was going to drink it myself.'

'I don't believe you,' said the soldier.

Then he had another attack of convulsions and died.

'How horrible!' muttered Athos.

Porthos now proceeded to smash all the remaining bottles of

wine and Aramis sent one of the men off to fetch a priest.

'Oh, my dear friends!' cried d'Artagnan. 'That's the second time you saved my life! And you've saved the lives of these fellows as well.'

Then he added, addressing the guardsmen:

'Gentlemen, I beg you to keep this affair a dead secret. Some well-known people may be involved in it, and if you spread the story round it might be very unpleasant for us.'

Planchet was standing by, paralysed with fear. He now stammered out: 'Oh, Sir, I had a narrow escape there. Whew!'

'What, you rascal!' cried d'Artagnan. 'You were going to drink my wine!'

'To the King's health, Sir. I was going to have just one sip when Fourneau told me I was wanted.'

Fourneau was also standing by. His teeth were chattering.

'I wanted to get him out of the way so that I could have a quick one on my own, Sir,' he stammered.

D'Artagnan now turned to the guardsmen and said:

'Gentlemen, I'm sure you'll agree that after what's happened our party had better be postponed. Please accept my apologies and let's arrange it for another day instead.'

The two guardsmen agreed and tactfully went off, leaving the four friends alone.

The latter first made sure that there were no eavesdroppers about and then shot quick looks at each other, which showed that they were all alive to the seriousness of the situation.

'We'd better get out of this room first,' said Athos. 'Dead men are poor company.'

'Planchet,' said d'Artagnan, 'look after that unfortunate devil and see he's buried in consecrated ground. It's true he was a crook but he'd repented of his crime.'

The four friends went out, leaving Planchet and Fourneau to see that Brisemont received a decent burial. The innkeeper showed them into another room and served them with boiled eggs, and water which Athos drew from the well himself. Porthos and Aramis were told the whole story of Milady and her villainy in a few words. Then d'Artagnan said to Athos:

'So you see it's war to the death.'

Athos nodded.

'Yes,' he said. 'I know that. But d'you think it's really her?'

'I'm sure of it.'

'I'm still a little doubtful myself.'

'But that fleur-de-lis on her shoulder?'

'I think she's an Englishwoman who committed some crime in France and was punished for it in France.'

'Athos, that woman's your wife, I tell you,' repeated d'Artagnan. 'D'you remember how I described her to you and you agreed it must be your wife?'

'Yes. And I was so sure she was dead! I'd done the job so thoroughly!'

D'Artagnan shrugged his shoulders.

'But in any case what can we do?' he asked.

'We certainly can't go on living with a sword of Damocles hanging over our heads,' said Athos. 'We're in a fix and must get out of it.'

'Yes, but how?'

'Listen. Try and get in touch with her and have the whole thing out. Face her with the alternative "war or peace". You give your word of honour to say and do nothing against her on condition she swears to do nothing against you. If she refuses, threaten to go to the Chancellor, to the King, to the Public Executioner; say you'll rouse the Court against her, proclaim her branded and start criminal proceedings against her, and that if she's acquitted you'll take the law into your own hands, chase her to some lonely spot and destroy her like a mad dog.'

'I rather like that idea,' said d'Artagnan. 'But how can I get in touch with her?'

'We'll find some way in time,' replied Athos. 'We'll have to wait, that's all.'

'Yes, but can we afford to wait with all these murderers and poisoners about?'

'We'll have to risk that,' said Athos. 'God's protected us till now and He'll go on protecting us.'

'Yes, I expect we'll survive,' said d'Artagnan. 'Anyway we're men and it's our job to risk our lives.'

Then he added in an undertone:

'But what about her?'

'Who?' asked Athos.

'Constance.'

'Madame Bonacieux! Of course, I'd forgotten!' said Athos. 'Poor fellow, I'd forgotten you were in love with her.'

Here Aramis broke in.

'Didn't you read in the letter you found in the dead man's pocket that she was in a convent? Convents are very pleasant places, I'd have you know. I'm going into retirement myself directly the siege of La Rochelle's over.'

'Yes, Aramis,' said Athos. 'We all know how you long to hide away from the world and its wickedness.'

'I'm only a musketeer for the time being,' said Aramis primly.

Athos whispered to d'Artagnan.

'I gather he hasn't heard from his mistress for some time. But don't refer to it; we know how these moods take him.'

'I think I see an easy way out,' said Porthos.

'What's that?'

'She's in a convent, you say? Well, as soon as the siege is over we'll rescue her.'

'We've first got to find out which convent she's in.'

'True,' said Porthos.

'Listen,' said Athos. 'I've had an idea. Didn't you say the Queen had found this convent for her?'

'Yes. I'm almost sure it was the Queen.'

'In that case Porthos'll be able to help us.'

'How?' asked Porthos.

'Get your princess, duchess, or whatever she is to find out about the convent. She must have influence at Court.'

'No,' said Porthos. 'That wouldn't do at all. I suspect her of being a Cardinalist: she mustn't be told anything.'

'In that case I'll find out,' said Aramis.

'You, Aramis?' cried the three friends. 'How?'

Aramis coloured slightly. 'Through the Queen's almoner,' he said. 'I'm on fairly close terms with him.'

The other three agreed to accept Aramis' proposal. They had

now finished their frugal meal, so they parted, arranging to meet again that evening. D'Artagnan returned to the Minimes and the three musketeers went off to the King's Headquarters to settle themselves in their new billets.

CHAPTER VI

The Red Dovecote Inn

THE King as we know was anxious to start hostilities and shared the Cardinal's hatred of Buckingham. So on his arrival at the camp he pressed for immediate action, first against the English in the Ile de Ré and then against the town of La Rochelle itself. But rivalry among the generals under his command, Bassompierre, Schomberg, and the Duc d'Angoulême, was at first a serious obstacle to any concerted effort against the enemy.

Bassompierre and Schomberg were marshals of France and claimed their right to be appointed Commanders-in-Chief of the army under the King. But the Cardinal, knowing Bassompierre to be at heart a Huguenot, was afraid that he might be lukewarm in pressing the English and the besieged Rochellese, his co-religionists. His Eminence supported the Duc d'Angoulême and had persuaded the King to appoint him Commander-in-Chief. Bassompierre and Schomberg had refused to serve under the Duke, so each had been granted an independent command.

Bassompierre commanded the district north of the town, from the Leu to Dompierre. The Duc d'Angoulême commanded the district to the east of Bassompierre, from Dompierre to Périgny, and Schomberg the south district, from Périgny to Angoutin. Monsieur's headquarters were at Dompierre, the King's at Estrée and La Jarrie alternately, and the Cardinal's on the dunes, by the La Pierre bridge, in a plain, unfortified house. In this way Monsieur could keep an eye on Bassompierre, the King on the Duc d'Angoulême, and the Cardinal on Schomberg. As soon as the troops had been disposed thus in battle formation the commanders set to work to drive the English from the island. The time chosen was propitious.

The English always need to eat well to fight well. At present they had only salted meat and bad biscuits for rations, so there was much sickness in their camp. Moreover the sea was always very rough at that season along the whole coast; one or more English ships of the line foundered every day and the stretch of beach between the Aiguillon headland and the trenches was at low tide literally strewn with hulks of pinnaces, barges, and feluccas. It was obvious, therefore, that if the French army continued the siege a little longer Buckingham, who was holding on only with great difficulty, would be forced to evacuate the Ile de Ré. But Monsieur de Toiras reported that the enemy appeared to be preparing a fresh attack. The King decided that this must be nipped in the bud and ordered out enough troops to ensure a decisive engagement. Our intention is not to give a day-to-day account of the campaign but only to mention those events which concern our story. So we will merely state that the operation succeeded, to the great delight of the King and to the honour and glory of the Cardinal.

The English were driven back step by step, defeated in all the skirmishes, wiped out in the pass of the Ile de Loie and obliged to take to the ships again. They left behind them two thousand dead and wounded, among them five colonels, three lieutenant-colonels, two hundred and fifty captains, and twenty men of rank. In arms and trophies they lost four cannon and sixty flags, which were brought back to Paris by Claude de Saint-Simon and hung in state in the cathedral of Notre Dame. Te Deums were sung in the camp and echoed over the whole of France. This victory had established the French troops in a position from which they could continue the siege without any immediate fear of attack from the English. Unfortunately it was to prove but a temporary respite.

An envoy of Buckingham, one Montagu, had been captured, and in Buckingham's headquarters, which had been hastily abandoned, evidence had been discovered of a secret league between the Empire, Spain, England, and Lorraine against

France. This discovery is vouched for by the Cardinal in his memoirs. It was established that Madame de Chevreuse was a party to this plot and through her the Queen. The Cardinal had to bear all the blame for the existence of this league, because autocrats are always held responsible for everything. Henceforth all the resources of his genius were brought to bear, night and day, to discover the faintest rumours current in any of the big countries of Europe. The Cardinal knew Buckingham's energy and his hatred of himself. If the league triumphed he would lose all his influence. Spanish and Austrian policy had its champions in the cabinet of the Louvre, but so far their influence was negligible. If the league triumphed he, Richelieu, the Minister of France, his country's representative par excellence, would be lost. For the King, though he obeyed him like a child, also hated him as a child hates his master, and would abandon him to his enemies, Monsieur and the Queen. So he would fall, and perhaps France with him. All this Richelieu knew and was prepared to combat.

Day and night a stream of secret messengers poured in and out of the little house by the La Pierre bridge where the Cardinal had taken up his quarters. One saw ruffianly-looking men in ill-fitting monks' cassocks, women in pages' clothes with trunk-hose which, though wide-cut, could not conceal the curves of their bodies, and peasants with blackened hands but very shapely legs, who had 'courtier' written all over them. There were also other visitors to the little house on the dunes, less welcome perhaps to its occupier, for one heard constant rumours of attempts being made on the Cardinal's life. His enemies declared that the Cardinal had himself instigated these attempts in order to take reprisals on people he considered really dangerous. But one must never believe what politicians say of each other. In any case these attempts on his life did not prevent His Eminence, who was notoriously brave, from making countless night excursions to the headquarters of the King or the Duc d'Angoulême, or to meet special envoys whom he did not wish to receive at his own billets.

The Musketeers, who formed the King's bodyguard, were not

much used in the conduct of the siege itself. They were not under strict discipline and could lead a fairly free life. Athos, Porthos, and Aramis were even more fortunate than their fellows in this respect, for they were personal friends of Monsieur de Tréville and could get special permits from him to remain out of camp after dark. One evening, when d'Artagnan was on duty in the trenches and had been unable to accompany his three friends, the latter had ridden out to an inn on the Jarrie road called the Red Dovecote, which Athos had discovered two days before. Shortly before midnight they left the inn and were riding back to the camp on their battle chargers, dressed in their service cloaks and with their hands on their pistol butts, when suddenly, about a mile from the village of Boisnau, they thought they heard the sound of horses' hoofs coming towards them. All three immediately reined in, closed ranks and waited in the middle of the road.

At that moment the moon came out from behind a cloud, and a few seconds later two riders appeared round a bend in the road. When they caught sight of the three friends they too reined in and seemed in doubt whether to advance or retreat.

The strangers' hesitation roused the musketeers' suspicions. Athos rode forward a few yards and called out in a loud voice:

'Who goes there?'

At which one of the men called back:

'Who are you?'

'That's no answer,' replied Athos. 'Who goes there, I said! Answer at once or we charge.'

At this the stranger called back:

'I shouldn't do that if I were you, gentlemen!'

His voice rang out sharp and clear; it was obviously the voice of a man used to command.

'It must be some senior officer going his rounds,' said Athos to his friends. 'What shall we do?'

'Who are you?' repeated the stranger who had spoken last. 'Answer at once or you'll regret it later.'

The man's voice convinced Athos that he was within his rights in thus challenging them.

'King's Musketeers,' he replied.

'What company?'

'De Tréville.'

'Advance in formation and account for your presence here at this hour of the night.'

The three friends rode forward. They were by now rather crestfallen, for they were convinced that their challenger was someone of high rank. Athos, with the tacit consent of Porthos and Aramis, acted as spokesman of the party.

The stranger who had spoken had halted a few yards ahead of his companion. Athos signed to Porthos and Aramis to remain behind and rode forward.

'My apologies, Sir,' he said. 'We didn't know who we were talking to. I hope you noticed we were keeping a sharp lookout.'

The officer was holding his cloak over the lower part of his face.

'Your name?' he asked.

Athos suddenly began to feel irritated at his insistence.

'And what about you, Sir?' he asked. 'I think you might show me your warrant or give me some proof of your right to cross-question me.'

The officer now let his cloak fall and revealed his face.

'Your name!' he repeated.

Athos stared at him, stupefied.

'The Cardinal!' he cried.

'Your name?' repeated His Eminence for the third time.

'Athos,' said the musketeer.

The Cardinal turned and beckoned to his groom.

'I want these three musketeers to come with us,' he said to him aside. 'I don't want it known that I've left camp, and if they come with us they won't be able to report having seen me.'

'Monseigneur, we're gentlemen,' said Athos. 'You can trust us to keep a secret. We won't mention having seen you if you ask us not to.'

The Cardinal was annoyed to have been overheard. He frowned and replied:

'You've got sharp ears, Monsieur Athos. But please don't take offence. I'm not asking you to follow me because I mistrust you but because I need your support. Your two friends are, I presume, Monsieur Porthos and Monsieur Aramis.'

'Yes, Your Eminence.'

Porthos and Aramis now rode forward, hats in hand.

'I know you, gentlemen,' said the Cardinal. 'I know you and I know that you're not too well-disposed towards me, which I regret. But I also know you're brave and can be trusted. Monsieur Athos, if you'll honour me by accompanying me, you and your two friends, I'll have an escort which the King himself would envy.'

The three musketeers bowed so low that their heads touched their horses' necks.

'I think you're wise to take us with you, Sir,' said Athos. 'We've met some proper ruffians tonight; in fact we had a bit of an argument with four of them at the Red Dovecote inn.'

The Cardinal frowned.

'An argument?' he said. 'Why? You know I don't like brawling.'

'That's why I mentioned it, Sir,' replied Athos. 'I was afraid Your Eminence might get a wrong report of it from other sources, and think we were to blame.'

'What happened in this brawl?' asked the Cardinal, still frowning.

'My friend Aramis here got a slight wound in the arm. But that won't prevent him going on parade tomorrow if Your Eminence decides on an attack.'

'Look here, gentlemen,' said the Cardinal, 'you're none of you the kind to take blows and not return them. I'm sure you gave as good as you got. Confess! You can confess to me, you know; I've got the right of absolution.'

Athos replied:

'Speaking for myself, Sir, I didn't draw my sword at all. I took my fellow round the waist and threw him out of the window. Apparently he broke his thigh in falling.'

'H'm!' said the Cardinal. 'And what about you, Monsieur Porthos?'

'I knew duelling was illegal, Monseigneur, so I took up a bench and dealt my fellow a blow which I believe broke his shoulder.'

'I see,' said the Cardinal. 'And you, Monsieur Aramis?'

'Me, Monseigneur? Well, I'm peaceful by nature, and I don't like fighting. Besides, you may not know, Sir, but I'm on the point of taking Orders. So I was trying to smooth things over when one of the rogues thrust me through the arm when I wasn't looking. That maddened me and I simply had to draw my sword. He lunged at me again, but this time I think he must have spitted himself on my sword. I know he fell down and I think I saw them carrying him out with his two companions.'

'Good God!' said the Cardinal. 'Three men put out of action in a tavern brawl! That's a bit drastic, isn't it? And how did it all start?'

'Those rogues were drunk,' said Athos. 'They knew a woman had arrived that evening at the inn and wanted to force open her door.'

'Force open her door?' said the Cardinal. 'What for?'

'Presumably to take advantage of her, Sir,' said Athos. 'They were drunk, as I told you.'

The Cardinal frowned again.

'And what about the woman?' he asked. 'Was she young and good-looking?'

'We didn't see her, Sir,' replied Athos.

'Oh, you didn't see her!' said the Cardinal sharply. 'Excellent. And you were quite right to defend her. As it happens I'm on my way to the Red Dovecote now, so I'll soon find out if you've been telling the truth.'

Athos replied coldly.

'We wouldn't lie to you, Sir, not to save our lives. We're gentlemen.'

'That's why I don't doubt your story, Monsieur Athos. Not for a moment,' said the Cardinal.

Then, to change the conversation, he added: 'Was the woman alone?'

'No, Sir,' said Athos. 'She had a man with her in her room. That's what I couldn't understand. He never came out. He must have heard the row going on. I suppose he was a coward.'

'The Scriptures tell us not to judge rashly,' said the Cardinal. Aramis nodded approvingly.

'Very true, Sir,' he said.

'Well, gentlemen,' continued His Eminence. 'Thank you for telling me about this affair. I now know all I want to know. So let's be off.'

The three musketeers fell in behind the Cardinal. His Eminence once more pulled his cloak up over his face, put spurs to his horse and trotted off down the road, keeping about ten yards ahead of his escort.

The little party soon arrived at the inn, which at this hour of the night was quite deserted. The innkeeper had evidently had notice of the arrival of a distinguished guest, for he had cleared the inn of its usual noisy customers.

When they were about ten yards away the Cardinal signed to his groom and to the three musketeers to halt, rode forward alone and rapped three times sharply on the door. A saddled horse was tethered to the wall. In answer to the Cardinal's knock a man in a cloak immediately came out and had a hurried conversation with him. He then mounted the horse and rode off at the gallop in the direction of Surgères, which was also the direction of Paris. The Cardinal then turned to his escort and beckoned them on.

'I see you've told me the truth about what happened this evening, gentlemen,' he said. 'Our meeting has in fact been most opportune, and I'll see it turns out to your advantage. Now follow me please.'

The Cardinal and the three musketeers dismounted; the Cardinal threw his horse's reins to his groom, while the three musketeers tethered their horses to the wall. His Eminence then entered the inn, followed by his escort.

The innkeeper received him in the hall. He had no suspicion of the Cardinal's true identity and took him for an officer who had an assignation with a lady.

'Have you a room on the ground floor with a good fire where these gentlemen can wait for me?' asked the Cardinal.

The innkeeper opened the door of a large room in which he had recently replaced a worn-out stove with a large and excellent fireplace.

'The gentlemen can have this room,' he said.

'Good,' said the Cardinal. 'Kindly wait for me in there, gentlemen. I shan't keep you more than half an hour.'

The three musketeers entered the ground floor room and made themselves comfortable by the fire. Meanwhile the Cardinal, ignoring the innkeeper's offers of help, walked quickly up the stairs and entered a room on the first floor. It was obvious that he knew his way about, and from this we can infer that he had visited the inn before.

CHAPTER VII

The Advantage of Stove Pipes

THE three friends now realized that in trouncing the drunkards at the inn earlier that evening they had done a bigger thing than they supposed. They had rescued someone who was very high in favour with the Cardinal. Who was this someone? They were all agog to know. But they realized that they could never solve this problem by thought, so Porthos called the innkeeper and asked for dice. He and Aramis then sat down at a table and started to play. Athos paced up and down the room, lost in thought. As he paced up and down he kept passing the broken stove pipe belonging to the stove which had been removed, the bottom end of which hung halfway down from the ceiling, while the top end protruded into the first-floor room. Each time he passed the pipe he heard a subdued murmur of voices from above. His curiosity was aroused and he finally stopped in front of the pipe, put his ear to the opening and tried to hear what the voices were saying.

What he heard was apparently of the greatest interest, for he suddenly signed to his two companions to keep quiet and went on listening intently.

It was the Cardinal speaking.

'This is a matter of vital importance, Milady,' he said. 'So let's get it settled at once. Sit down.'

'Milady!' muttered Athos.

A woman's voice now spoke. At the sound of it the musketeer started and turned pale.

'Tell me what I'm to do, Monseigneur,' replied Milady.

'A brig with an English crew and a captain in my pay is waiting for you at the mouth of the Charente, by Fort la Pointe. It's to set sail tomorrow morning.'

'So I'm to go on board tonight?'

'At once. That is, when I've given you your instructions. There are two men waiting outside this inn to escort you to the coast. I shall leave the inn ahead of you. You'll wait on half an hour and then leave yourself.'

'Very well, Monseigneur. And now tell me what mission you're sending me on. My one wish is to succeed in it and to continue to enjoy Your Eminence's favour. So please explain very carefully what I'm to do, so that I make no mistake.'

There was dead silence for a moment. The Cardinal was obviously rehearsing in his mind what he was about to say, while Milady was preparing to grasp and memorize her instructions.

Athos meanwhile signed to his two companions to lock the door of the room from the inside and to come and put their ears to the pipe so that they could all listen together. Porthos and Aramis liked comfort so they brought their chairs with them and an extra chair for Athos. All three then sat down with their ears to the mouth of the pipe.

'You're to go to London again,' said the Cardinal. 'When you get there you're to see Buckingham.'

'I'd like to remind Your Eminence that Buckingham mistrusts me since the affair of the diamond tags,' said Milady. 'He suspects me of having stolen them.'

'This time I'm not sending you to England as a spy but as an official agent of France,' said the Cardinal. 'In that capacity you must approach Buckingham frankly and openly.'

'Frankly and openly,' echoed Milady in a tone of infinite guile.

'Yes, frankly and openly,' said the Cardinal. 'All this has to be done in the open.'

'I understand, Your Eminence,' replied Milady. 'Please go on.'

'You'll tell Buckingham from me that I know the preparations he's making and that I'm not at all concerned about them because the moment he makes a move I shall expose the Queen.'

'Will he believe you're in a position to do that, Sir?'

'Yes. You see I've got proofs of her guilt.'

'I shall have to be able to quote him the proofs so that he can judge for himself.'

'Of course. Tell him I shall publish Bois-Robert and Beautru's account of the secret meeting he had with the Queen at Madame la Connétable's house on the night of her fancy-dress ball; to show him how much I know tell him he came dressed as the Grand Mogul in an outfit which he bought from the Chevalier de Guise for three thousand pistoles.'

'Very good, Monseigneur.'

'Tell him I know all the details of his entry into the Louvre and how he left in the early hours of the morning; how he got in disguised as an Italian fortune-teller, how he wore under his cloak a long white dress embroidered with skulls and cross-bones, so that if he were seen he could pretend to be the White Lady, the ghost which appears at the Louvre before every great event.'

'Is that all, Monseigneur?'

'Tell him I also know all the details of the Amiens adventure; that I shall publish a witty skit on the subject with a plan of the garden and portraits of all the principal actors in that drama.'

'I'll tell him all that.'

'Tell him also that I'm holding Montagu; that Montagu's in the Bastille; that although no papers were found on him I can torture him into telling all he knows and even a bit more.'

'Excellent.'

'Lastly, tell His Grace that in his hurry to leave the Ile de Ré he left in his headquarters a certain letter from Madame de Chevreuse which is very compromising to the Queen, because it proves not only that she befriends the King's enemies but that she's actually plotted with the enemies of France. Have you remembered all that, Milady?'

'Yes, Your Eminence. Madame la Connétable's ball, the night in the Louvre, the evening at Amiens, Montagu's arrest and Madame de Chevreuse's letter.'

'You have a most excellent memory,' said the Cardinal.

'But suppose the Duke decides to ignore these threats and to go on with his plans against France? What then?'

Richelieu replied bitterly:

'The Duke's madly, besottedly in love. Like the Paladins of old he embarked on this war merely to get a smile from his mistress. When he sees that the war may bring dishonour to her, may even lead to her imprisonment, he'll be reluctant to go on with it.'

But Milady was not yet satisfied. She wished to be able to judge for herself how far her mission was likely to succeed. So once more she said:

'But suppose he does decide to go on?'

'That's not likely,' said the Cardinal.

'But if he does . . .'

His Eminence paused. Then he answered:

'If he does go on I shall pray for one of those events which change the destiny of nations.'

'If Your Eminence would quote a parallel in history, you might give me an idea,' said Milady.

'I'll quote one,' said Richelieu. 'In 1610, if you remember, King Henry IV was preparing to invade Flanders and Italy in order to attack Austria simultaneously on two fronts. His motives were more or less the same as Buckingham's. Didn't an incident occur then which saved Austria?'

'Your Eminence means the murder in the Rue de la Féronnerie?'

'Yes.'

'D'you think anyone would dare emulate Ravaillac, knowing what a terrible end he had?'

'In every age and in every country, particularly in countries divided in religion, you'll find fanatics who long for martyrs' crowns. And now I come to think of it, the Puritans in England hate the Duke of Buckingham; their preachers denounce him as anti-Christ.'

'Well?' asked Milady.

The Cardinal shrugged his shoulders.

'Well,' he said casually, 'the first thing would be to discover a young, handsome, intelligent woman who wanted revenge on Buckingham. Some such person might be found. The Duke's a man of many loves; his romantic nature has won him hearts enough, and his infidelities have made many hate him.'

'It shouldn't be difficult to find the woman,' said Milady calmly.

'Well, a woman like that might in turn inspire a fanatic like Jacques Clément or Ravaillac. That woman would save France.'

'Yes, but she'd be an accomplice in the crime.'

'Were Ravaillac's or Clément's accomplices ever discovered?'

'No. But that was probably because they were so highly placed that no one dared take action against them. Not everyone could have the Palais de Justice burnt down to save their own skins, Monseigneur.'

'Oh, so you think the burning of the Palais de Justice wasn't an accident?' asked Richelieu quietly, as though he were asking an entirely trivial question.

'I have no views one way or the other,' replied Milady. 'I'm merely stating a fact. I'm merely pointing out that if I were Madame de Montpensier or Queen Marie de Medicis I'd need less protection than I need as Clarice de Winter.'

'That's perfectly fair,' said Richelieu. 'Well, what would you like me to do?'

'I'd like you to give me an order ratifying in advance everything I might feel compelled to do in the interests of France.'

'But the first step would be to find a woman such as I described just now, who wanted to take revenge on the Duke.'

'She's found,' said Milady calmly.

'Then one would have to find the abject fanatic who'd serve as the instrument of God's justice.'

'He'll be found.'

'Very well,' said the Cardinal. 'Find him first and then come to me and I'll give you the order.'

'Your Eminence is right,' said Milady, 'and I was wrong to see in this mission more than it really is, which is to let the Duke know what weapons Your Eminence holds against the Queen. I'm to tell him you know the different disguises in which he succeeded in meeting Her Majesty first at Madame la Connétable's ball, and then in the Louvre; that you've composed a short and witty fantasy about the Amiens adventure with a plan of the garden where the adventure took place and portraits of the actors in the drama; that Montagu's in the Bastille and can be tortured into revealing things he knows and even things he may have forgotten; finally, that you hold a certain letter from Madame de Chevreuse which was found in His Grace's head-quarters and which seriously compromises not only the author but also her in whose name the letter was written. If he still persists in face of all this I've done all I can; my mission's at an end, and I've only to pray God to send some miracle to save France. That's right, Your Eminence, is it not? That's all you wish me to do.'

'That's all, Milady,' the Cardinal replied coldly. Then he added:

'When you've talked to the Duke return to this country at once, go to Béthune, to the Carmelite Convent there, and await further orders. I'll tell the Abbess she's to take you in.'

Milady pretended not to notice the Cardinal's sudden change of manner and replied:

'Very well, Monseigneur. And now that I have Your Eminence's instructions for dealing with your enemies, will you allow me to say a few words about mine?'

'Have you enemies?' asked Richelieu.

'Yes, Monseigneur — enemies against whom you owe me your support, for I acquired them by acting for you.'

'Who are they?' asked the Cardinal.

'First of all there's a little schemer called Madame Bonacieux.'

'She's in the Nantes prison.'

'She was,' replied Milady. 'But the Queen got an order from the King to have her removed to a convent.'

'To a convent?' said the Cardinal.

'Yes.'

'Which?'

'I don't know. That was kept secret.'

'Don't worry. I'll find out.'

'And will you tell me?'

'Yes, if you wish it,' replied the Cardinal.

'Thank you, Sir,' said Milady. 'Then I've got another enemy more formidable than Madame Bonacieux.'

'Who's that?'

'Her lover.'

'What's his name?'

Milady burst out angrily:

'You know him well enough, Sir. He's our evil genius, yours and mine. The man who helped the King's Musketeers to defeat Your Eminence's Guards in a brawl, the man who wounded your agent de Wardes three times and who thwarted us in the affair of the diamond tags. Your Eminence, this man has sworn to kill me; he knows it was I who had his mistress kidnapped.'

'Yes,' said the Cardinal. 'I know the man you mean.'

'I mean that scoundrel d'Artagnan.'

'He's a brave fellow, you know,' said the Cardinal.

'It's just because he's so brave that he's so dangerous.'

'We'll have to have proofs of his dealings with Buckingham,' said the Cardinal.

'Proofs!' cried Milady. 'I'll get a dozen at least.'

'In that case it's the easiest thing in the world,' said the Cardinal. 'Get me those proofs and I'll send him to the Bastille.'

'Thank you, Monseigneur. And after that?'

'There's no "after that" for people in the Bastille,' said the Cardinal grimly. 'Good God!' he continued. 'If I could crush my enemy as easily as I can crush yours, and if you asked for protection only against people like that . . .'

'Monseigneur,' broke in Milady, 'man for man, life for life, give me your enemy and I'll give you mine.'

'I don't know what you mean,' said the Cardinal, 'and I don't even want to know. But I'll gladly do you a favour and I'll certainly give you a free hand to deal with someone so subordinate as d'Artagnan, the more so since from what you say the fellow's a libertine, a duellist, and a traitor to France.'

'A bad character, Monseigneur, a thoroughly bad character.'

'Give me a pen and paper,' said the Cardinal.

'Here, Monseigneur.'

There was a moment's silence while the Cardinal wrote out the order. Athos, listening below, had not missed one word of the conversation. He now took his two friends by the arm and led them over to the far corner of the room.

'Why didn't you leave us to hear the end?' asked Porthos.

'Sh!' whispered Athos. 'We've heard all we need to hear. You two go on listening if you want to; I must leave this place at once.'

'Leave the inn?' exclaimed Porthos. 'And suppose the Cardinal asks for you? What shall we say?'

'Don't wait for him to ask. Directly he comes down tell him I went on ahead to reconnoitre, because I heard the innkeeper say something which made me think there was trouble on the road. I'll fix it with the Cardinal's groom. What happens after that's my affair; leave it to me.'

'Don't do anything rash, Athos,' said Aramis.

'Don't worry,' said Athos. 'I can take care of myself.'

Porthos and Aramis went back to the stove pipe. Athos left the inn, sauntered coolly over to his horse, which was standing with his friends' horses by the door, untethered it, whispered to the groom that he was going on ahead to act as advance-guard for the return journey, made a show of adjusting the flints of his pistols, unsheathed his sword and galloped off alone in the direction of the camp.

CHAPTER VIII

A Conjugal Scene

ALMOST immediately after Athos' departure the Cardinal came down; he looked into the room in which he had left the musketeers and found Porthos and Aramis deeply engrossed in a game of dice. He glanced quickly round and noticed that one of his escort was missing.

'Where's Monsieur Athos?' he asked.

'Your Eminence, he went on ahead to reconnoitre. The inn-keeper said something which made him suspect the road was unsafe.'

'And what have you been doing, Monsieur Porthos?'

'I've been busy winning five pistoles from Aramis,' replied Porthos.

'Are you ready to come back with me now?'

'Yes, Sir.'

'Well, come quickly then, gentlemen. It's getting late.'

The groom was at the door, holding His Eminence's horse by the bridle. A little further off stood a group of two men and three horses, barely visible in the darkness. These two men were Milady's escort, who were to take her to Fort la Pointe and see her safely on board. The Cardinal questioned the groom about Athos and the man confirmed Porthos' story that he had gone on ahead to spy out the land. The Cardinal nodded his approval and started off along the road to the camp, making the musketeers and the groom follow ten yards behind him as before.

Athos meanwhile had galloped a hundred yards or so down the road. When he was out of sight of the inn he plunged into the dense undergrowth at the side of the road, made a complete about turn and rode half-way back to the inn under cover of the trees. Here he halted, still under cover, and waited for the Cardinal and his escort to pass down the highway. He soon saw through the trees his friends' braided hats and the Cardinal's gold-fringed cloak glinting in the moonlight. He waited for the little procession to turn the corner of the road. Then he galloped back to the inn, dismounted and knocked on the door. The innkeeper recognized him at once. Athos said:

'My officer sent me back with a message for the lady on the first floor, something he meant to tell her and forgot.'

'Go up, Sir,' said the host, 'the lady's still there.'

Athos went up the stairs, treading as lightly as he could. When he reached the landing he saw through the half-open door Milady tying on her hat. He walked quickly across the landing, pushed open the door and walked straight into the room, closing the door behind him. Then he stood stock still, facing Milady, with his cloak wound round him and his plumed hat pressed well down over his eyes. When Milady saw this silent figure by the door she was frightened.

'Who are you? What do you want?' she cried.

Athos muttered to himself:

'Yes, it's her.'

Then he let his cloak fall open, took off his hat and walked up to her.

'Do you recognize me?' he asked.

Milady looked at him for a moment in silence. Suddenly she flinched and shrank back as though she had seen a ghost.

'Good,' said Athos. 'I see you do recognize me.'

Milady went deathly pale and retreated before him until she was standing with her back pressed against the wall.

'Comte de la Fère!' she muttered.

'Yes,' replied Athos. 'Comte de la Fère, returned from the past on a matter of vital importance. So, as the Cardinal said just now, let's get it settled at once. Sit down!'

Milady, struck dumb with terror, sat down without a word. Athos sat down facing her.

'You're a fiend,' he said, 'an evil spirit sent into this world to torture men. Your power's great, I know, but with God's help men have conquered worse demons than you. You've already come into my life once. I thought I'd crushed you then. But either I was wrong or Hell's resurrected you.'

Athos' words brought horrifying recollections to Milady's mind. She groaned and buried her head in her hands.

'Yes, the Devil's resurrected you,' said Athos. 'The Devil's made you rich; he's sent you out in a new guise with another name and almost another face and form. But he hasn't wiped out the stains on your soul nor the mark of Cain on your body.'

At this Milady sprang to her feet and stood facing Athos, her eyes blazing with rage and hate. Athos sat calmly watching her.

'You thought I was dead, didn't you?' he continued. 'And I thought you were dead. I took the name of Athos to hide the identity of the Comte de la Fère, just as you took the name of Lady de Winter to hide the identity of Anne de Breuil. Wasn't that the name you went by when your worthy brother married us?'

He smiled grimly and continued:

'Our position's really strange. You and I have both managed to exist since then only because each believed the other dead; memories are less painful than facts, although memories can sometimes be quite bitter too.'

Milady broke in in a low voice:

'For God's sake tell me why you've come here tonight and what you want.'

'I came to tell you that though you haven't seen me since those far-off days I haven't lost sight of you.'

'You know about my life?'

'I can tell you every detail of your life from the time you first became the Cardinal's agent until today.'

Milady scoffed:

'You don't expect me to believe that, do you?' she said.

'Listen,' said Athos. 'It was you who cut the two diamond tags off the Duke of Buckingham's shoulder. It was you who had Madame Bonacieux kidnapped. You were in love with Comte de Wardes and allowed my friend d'Artagnan to make love to you in the belief that he was de Wardes; you then tried to make d'Artagnan kill de Wardes, to avenge an imagined slight. When

A CONJUGAL SCENE   511

d'Artagnan discovered your shameful secret you hired two men
to murder him; thank Heaven they failed. You then sent him
poisoned wine with a forged letter which was supposed to
come from his friends; that trick failed too, thank God! To
crown all, only a moment ago, in this very room, you arranged
with the Cardinal to have the Duke of Buckingham murdered,
and he gave you in exchange an authority to kill d'Artagnan.'

Milady was livid.

'How do you know all this?' she hissed. 'Are you Satan himself?'

'Possibly,' said Athos. 'If I am I hope it'll help to impress on
you what I'm going to say. I don't care if you do murder the
Duke of Buckingham or get someone else to murder him. I
don't know him and his life's nothing to me. In any case he's
France's enemy. But d'Artagnan's my friend. If you so much as
lay a finger on him I swear on my father's head that, whether
you succeed or fail, it'll be the very last act of your life.'

There was a hard note in Milady's voice as she replied:

'Monsieur d'Artagnan's insulted me. Monsieur d'Artagnan
must die.'

Athos replied with a sneer:

'Is it possible to insult a creature like you? He's insulted you
and must die. Is that it?'

'Yes,' replied Milady. 'They must both die, she first and then
he.'

At this Athos suddenly felt a wave of fierce anger surge up in
him. As he looked at this utterly inhuman creature, to outward
semblance a woman but with nothing of a woman's soul, a
terrible picture flashed across his mind; the memory of a day
many years ago when, alone with her in a situation less critical
than now, he had not hesitated to sacrifice her to avenge his
honour.

He now felt a wild return of his murderous impulse of that
long-forgotten day. He got up in his turn, faced Milady, slowly
put his hand to his belt, pulled out a pistol and cocked it.
Milady stood as though transfixed. She wanted to cry out but
her tongue froze to her mouth and she could only utter a croak

more like an animal's death-rattle than a human voice. Against
the background of the dark tapestry, standing as though nailed
to the wall, her eyes wide and staring, her hair dishevelled, she
looked the personification of terror. Athos stretched out his
hand until the muzzle of the pistol was almost touching her
forehead, and in a coldly determined voice said:

'Lady de Winter, hand over at once the order the Cardinal
signed for you, or by God I'll blow your brains out.'

Had it been anyone but Athos Milady might have doubted his
carrying out his threat. But she knew Athos.

And yet she made no move.

'I'll give you one second to decide,' he said.

Milady saw from the contraction of his face muscles that he
was about to pull the trigger. She quickly put her hand to her
bodice, pulled out a scroll of paper and handed it to him.

'Here, take it,' she said. 'And curse you to all eternity.'

Athos took it. He then replaced the pistol in his belt and, to
make sure that what he held was really the Cardinal's order,
took the paper to the lamp, unrolled it and read as follows:

*It is by my order and for the benefit of the State that the bearer
of this note has done what he has done.*

3 December, 1627.   Richelieu.

Athos now drew his cloak round him and put on his hat.
Then, looking at Milady with loathing, he said:

'Now I've drawn your viper's fangs. Strike if you can!'

With that he turned and left the room.

Outside in the courtyard he met the two mounted men and
the spare horse which they were holding on a leading rein.

'Gentlemen,' he said, 'my officer's orders to you are, as you
know, to escort this lady at once to Fort la Pointe and not to
leave her until you've seen her safely on board.'

This order tallied with the order the men had already received, so they nodded assent.

Now Athos sprang into the saddle and galloped off. But
instead of following the high road towards the camp he
branched off across country, urging his horse forward at a great
rate and reining in from time to time to listen. At last he heard

the sound of horses' hoofs on the road a short way in rear. Convinced that they were the horses of the Cardinal and his escort, he pushed forward again a short distance, then halted and gave his own horse a good rubbing down with heather and leaves. Then he turned sharp right, rode out of the wood and placed himself in the middle of the road, a little ahead of the oncoming party of riders and facing them. The camp was now only about a hundred yards away. Directly he caught sight of the Cardinal and his escort he called out:

'Who goes there?'

'That must be Athos,' said the Cardinal.

'Yes, Monseigneur,' shouted the musketeer. 'It's Athos!'

'I'm most grateful to you for your help, Monsieur Athos,' said the Cardinal. 'Well, here we are, gentlemen, at last. You go in by the left gate; the password's "Roi et Ré!" '

With that His Eminence nodded to the three friends and turned down the road to the right, followed by his groom. For that night he, too, was sleeping in the camp.

When the Cardinal was out of earshot Porthos and Aramis turned to Athos and said:

'She got the order out of him.'

'I know,' said Athos calmly. 'And I got it out of her. In fact I've got it on me now.'

The three friends rode back in silence to their billets, only speaking to give the password to the sentry. But they sent Mousqueton to tell Planchet to beg his master to call on them the moment he came off duty.

Meanwhile Milady found the two men waiting for her at the door of the inn and rode off with them without a word. For a moment she had thought of ordering them to escort her, not to the ship but straight back to the Cardinal, for she was in a fever to tell him everything. But then she realized that any disclosure on her part would bring a counter-disclosure from Athos. If she exposed Athos as having attempted to murder her Athos would expose her as having been branded. So she decided that for the time being silence was the best policy. She would leave France as arranged and carry out her difficult mission with her usual skill. When she had achieved this she would return and claim her revenge from the Cardinal.

With this plan in mind Milady rode with her escort through the night and reached Fort la Pointe at seven the next morning. At eight o'clock she was on board and at nine the vessel, which was ostensibly bound for Bayonne with sealed orders from the Cardinal, weighed anchor and set sail for England.

CHAPTER IX

The Bastion of St Gervais

WHEN d'Artagnan received his friends' message he came round at once to their billets. He found them all in the same room. Athos was sitting in a corner brooding. Porthos was striding up and down tugging at his moustache, and Aramis was reading prayers in a charming little Book of Hours bound in blue velvet.

'Well, gentlemen,' said d'Artagnan, 'let's hope you've got something really worthwhile to say, otherwise I shan't forgive you for disturbing me. I was enjoying a well-earned rest after a night spent capturing and dismantling a bastion. You can thank your lucky stars you weren't there, all of you. God, the heat!'

'Where we were it was none too cold either, I can tell you,' said Porthos with a smug smile.

'Quiet! Not so loud!' said Athos, waking out of his reverie.

D'Artagnan was quick to notice the frown on his friend's face.

'H'm!' he said, 'I see you really have got some news for me.'

Athos said:

'Aramis, didn't you dine the night before last at the Parpaillot inn?'

'Yes.'

'What was it like there?'

'They gave me a very nasty and expensive meal. It was their bad day and they only had meat.'

'What?' said Athos. 'A harbour town and no fish?'

Aramis looked up from his prayer-book.

'Apparently the Cardinal's dyke has driven all the fish out to sea,' he said.

'That wasn't what I meant, Aramis,' said Athos. 'I meant were you left to yourself or did people keep disturbing you?'

'I was left pretty well to myself,' said Aramis. 'Yes, Athos, I see what you're driving at. I think we'd be pretty safe at the Parpaillot.'

'Well, let's go there,' said Athos. 'Here the walls are like paper.'

D'Artagnan knew his friend so well by now that he could tell at once from the tone of his voice or the expression on his face when something serious was in the air. He took his arm and went out with him without a word. Porthos and Aramis followed them, also arm-in-arm. On their way to the inn they met Grimaud, and Athos signed him to follow them. Grimaud bowed his assent as usual; the poor fellow had by now almost forgotten how to speak.

The little party soon arrived at the Parpaillot inn. It was now seven o'clock in the morning and dawn was just breaking. The four friends ordered breakfast and went into a room where the host assured them they would not be disturbed.

Unfortunately they had chosen a bad hour for a conference. Reveillé had just sounded. Everyone was shaking off the night's sleep and had come to drink a tot of brandy at the inn to drive away the effects of the early morning damp. Dragoons, Swiss mercenaries, foot-guards, musketeers, and life-guards kept passing in and out, much to the satisfaction of the landlord and much to the annoyance of the four friends, who gave very surly replies to their fellow-customers' jovial greetings.

'We shall find ourselves involved in an argument if we don't take care,' said Athos, 'and we want to avoid that at all costs. D'Artagnan, describe your night to us, and we'll describe ours later.'

A life-guard was standing by, sipping a glass of brandy. He broke in at this point.

'Yes, you were up the line last night, you guards,' he said. 'I gather you had a bit of trouble with the Rochellese.'

D'Artagnan looked quickly at Athos to inquire whether to answer this noisy intruder or not. Athos said:

'D'Artagnan, don't you see Monsieur de Busigny's talking to you? Come on, tell us what happened last night; these gentlemen want to know about it.'

'Didn't you capture a bastion?' asked a Swiss guard, who was drinking rum out of a beer glass.

'Yes,' replied d'Artagnan, nodding to the Swiss. 'We had that pleasure. As you may have heard, we also had the pleasure of stuffing a barrel of gunpowder under one of the corners of the bastion, setting light to it and making a pretty breach in the wall. The bastion was fairly old so the rest of it was badly shaken as well.'

A dragoon was also standing by; he held impaled on his sabre a goose, which he was taking to the fire to roast, using his sabre as a spit.

'Which bastion was it?' he asked.

'The St Gervais bastion,' replied d'Artagnan. 'The Rochellese were occupying it and worrying our pioneers in the trenches.'

'Quite a lively affair, wasn't it?'

'Yes, we lost five men and the Rochellese eight or ten.'

'They'll probably send their pioneers this morning to repair the bastion,' said the life-guard.

'Probably,' said d'Artagnan.

Athos broke in: 'I'll make a bet with you, gentlemen!'

'Good, a bet!' said the Swiss guard.

The dragoon laid his sabre like a spit across the two large iron dogs which supported the fire.

'Wait!' he said. 'I want to be in on this bet. Hi, there, landlord! Bring a frying-pan quickly! I don't want to lose a drop of this goose's fat.'

'Quite right,' said the Swiss. 'Goose fat is very good with bread.'

'There – that's fine!' said the dragoon. 'And now for the bet. We're waiting, Monsieur Athos!'

'Yes, the bet,' said the life-guard. 'I want to be in on it too.'

'Well, Monsieur de Busigny,' said Athos. 'I bet you that I and my three friends here, Porthos, Aramis, and d'Artagnan, will breakfast in the St Gervais bastion and that we'll hold it for an hour, no more and no less, against all opposition from the enemy.'

Porthos and Aramis threw each other quick looks. They had both grasped at once what lay behind this apparently frivolous proposal. But d'Artagnan bent over Athos and whispered:

'What's the idea? Are you trying to get us all killed?'

Athos whispered back:

'We're much more likely to be killed if we don't go.'

Porthos leant back in his chair and twirled his moustache.

'Well, gentlemen,' he said, 'how's that for a bet?'

'I'll take that bet,' cried de Busigny. 'What are the stakes?'

'There are four of you and four of us,' said Athos. 'What d'you say to a slap-up dinner for eight to be paid for by the losers?'

'Excellent!' said de Busigny.

'Excellent,' said the dragoon.

'That goes with me too,' said the Swiss.

The fourth man, who had been a silent witness of the scene, nodded to show that he, too, agreed to the terms.

At that moment the innkeeper called out:

'Your breakfast's ready, gentlemen!'

'Bring it in then,' said Athos.

The innkeeper obeyed.

Athos now summoned Grimaud, pointed to a large basket lying in the corner of the room and made appropriate gestures to show that he was to wrap up the food in napkins and pack it in the basket. Grimaud understood at once that the four gentlemen were going on a picnic. He packed up the food, placed the bottles of wine on top and lifted the basket with its contents on to his shoulder. At this the innkeeper tried to protest.

'Where are you proposing to eat my breakfast, gentlemen?' he asked.

'That's no concern of yours provided we pay for it!' replied Athos.

And with a flourish he drew two pistoles from his pocket and threw them on the table.

'Shall I bring you change, Sir?' said the landlord.

'No. Just add two bottles of champagne to the other things and keep the change as cover charge.'

The champagne would have considerably reduced the landlord's profit on the breakfast, so he put in two bottles of Anjou wine instead.

'And now, Monsieur Busigny,' said Athos, 'kindly set your watch by mine, or allow me to set mine by yours.'

The life-guard took a beautiful diamond-studded watch out of his pocket.

'I make it seven-thirty,' he said.

'And I make it seven-thirty-five,' said Athos. 'We'll remember that my watch is five minutes ahead of yours.'

Now the four young men bade the astonished onlookers good morning and set off for the St Gervais bastion. Grimaud followed them, carrying the basket; the poor fellow was quite in the dark as to their objective, but was so accustomed to passive obedience that he trotted along behind them like a dog.

While they were inside the camp area the four friends were careful not to exchange a word. They were followed all the way by a crowd of inquisitive idlers who knew about the bet and wanted to get a good view of the proceedings. But once they had crossed the line of outposts and were in open country d'Artagnan, who was as much in the dark about this picnic as Grimaud, thought it time to demand an explanation.

'Athos,' he said, 'will you tell me exactly where we're supposed to be going?'

'You know where we're going,' replied Athos. 'We're going to the bastion.'

'What on earth for?'

'You know perfectly well. We're going to have breakfast there.'

'Why didn't we have breakfast at the Parpaillot?'

'Because we've some very important things to discuss, and

we couldn't have talked in that inn with those nosey devils pestering us all the time.'

He added, pointing to the bastion: 'There's no fear of them following us in there!'

D'Artagnan, reckless as he was at times, had a strain of common sense deep down in him.

'Couldn't we have found some secluded spot on the dunes near the sea?' he asked.

'The four of us in close conclave would have attracted attention at once. The Cardinal's spies would have told him about us in no time.'

'Yes,' said Aramis, 'I agree. Animadvertuntur in desertis.'

'A desert would have been quite a good place,' said Porthos, 'but deserts aren't so easily found.'

'Even in deserts birds fly over your head; on lonely beaches fish pop out of the sea and look at you and in woods rabbits come and peer at you from their holes. And I'm sure all the birds, fish, and rabbits in France are in the Cardinal's pay. So this is our only chance. Besides we'd look perfect fools if we went back now. We've made a bet; it was quite spontaneous and I defy anyone to discover the motive for it. To win this bet we've got to hold the bastion for an hour. We may be attacked and we may not. If we're not attacked we'll have plenty of time to talk and no one'll hear us. I bet the walls of that bastion haven't got ears. If we are attacked we can settle our private affairs and win honour and glory at the same time. So you see we've got everything to gain and nothing to lose.'

'Except our lives,' said d'Artagnan. 'There's a good chance we may stop a bullet apiece, you know.'

'As to that, my lad, the bullets most to be feared are not the enemy's. And well you know it.'

'I think we might at least have brought our muskets,' objected Porthos.

'Friend Porthos, you're a fool. Why bring unnecessary lumber?'

'I don't see how a good regulation musket with twelve rounds and a powder flask can be called lumber. Most useful for keeping the enemy at bay, I should have said.'

'Didn't you hear what d'Artagnan told us?' asked Athos.

'No. What?'

'He told us that in last night's skirmish five of our fellows were killed and about eight or ten Rochellese.'

'Well, what about it?'

'They didn't have time to strip them, remember. They were too busy doing other things.'

'Well?'

'We shall find their muskets, their ammunition, and their powder flasks on them. We'll have more than we need in the way of arms, fifteen muskets and a hundred rounds at least between the four of us instead of only four muskets and twelve rounds.'

'Athos, you're a genius!' cried Aramis.

Porthos nodded assent to this. Only d'Artagnan still appeared doubtful. Grimaud evidently shared his misgivings, for when he saw that they were continuing to advance towards the bastion he went up to his master, plucked him by the coat-sleeve and gesticulated the query:

'Where are we going?'

Athos pointed to the bastion.

At this Grimaud shook his head and waved his hands about, which being interpreted meant:

'We shall never get out of it alive!'

In answer to this Athos raised his eyes and pointed to the sky. Grimaud immediately dropped his basket and sat down on the ground shaking his head and smiling grimly. Athos now advanced on him, slowly drew his pistol from his belt, looked to see that it was primed, loaded it and put the muzzle against Grimaud's ear. This was too much for the unfortunate man; he leapt to his feet like a Jack-in-the-box and stood trembling before his master. Athos signed to him to pick up the basket and go ahead.

Grimaud obeyed. The only thing he had gained by this little pantomime was promotion from rearguard to vanguard of the party.

When they reached the bastion the four friends turned round.

Over three hundred men of all arms had gathered at the gates of the camp, and they could just discern de Busigny, the dragoon, the Swiss mercenary and their companion forming a little group by themselves.

Athos took off his hat, stuck it on the end of his sword and waved it above his head. At this all the watchers in the camp raised a mighty cheer, of which the four friends heard a faint echo.

They then turned and walked into the bastion, where they found Grimaud already ensconced.

CHAPTER X

A Council of War

As Athos had prophesied there were about a dozen dead men lying in the bastion, five French and seven Rochellese.

'Gentlemen,' he said, 'while Grimaud's laying the breakfast let's start collecting the guns and the cartridges. We can talk at the same time. We're quite safe,' he added, pointing to the dead men, 'these gentlemen aren't listening.'

'Why not throw them down into the moat all the same?' remarked Porthos. 'Of course we must search their pockets first.'

'Yes,' said Aramis. 'But that's Grimaud's job.'

'Very well,' said d'Artagnan, 'let Grimaud search them and then throw them over the wall.'

'Let him search them, yes,' said Athos, 'but he mustn't throw them over the wall; they may be of use to us.'

'What possible use could they be?' asked Porthos. 'Don't talk nonsense, Athos.'

'Just you wait and see, my lad,' continued Athos. 'How many guns are there, gentlemen?'

'Twelve,' replied Aramis.

'How many rounds?'

'A hundred.'

'That's plenty. Load the guns.'

The four musketeers set to work. Just as they had finished loading the last gun Grimaud announced that breakfast was ready. Athos now signed to him to go and stand in a kind of watch-turret at one end of the bastion and act as sentry. To break the monotony of his task Athos allowed him to take a loaf of bread, two cutlets, and a bottle of wine with him.

'And now let's start eating,' said Athos.

The four friends sat down on the ground with their legs crossed like Turks or tailors.

'Look here, Athos,' said d'Artagnan. 'There's not the faintest chance of anyone hearing us now, so I insist that you tell me your secret at once.'

'I flatter myself I've both amused you and brought you into the limelight this morning, gentlemen,' said Athos. 'I've taken you for a pleasant walk and provided a delicious breakfast at the end. And over there a huge crowd's watching us – you can see them through the loopholes – taking us either for madmen or heroes; there's not much difference really.'

'But your secret, your secret!' urged d'Artagnan.

'Here it is in five words: I saw Milady last night.'

D'Artagnan was just lifting his glass to his lips, but when he heard this his hand began to tremble so much that he had to put it down.

'What!' he cried. 'You saw your . . .?'

Athos silenced him with a gesture.

'Remember these gentlemen don't know as much about my private life as you do,' he said. 'I repeat, I've seen Milady.'

'Where on earth?' asked d'Artagnan.

'Only about a couple of miles from here, at the Red Dovecote inn.'

'Oh, in that case I'm finished!' said d'Artagnan.

'No, not quite yet,' replied Athos. 'She's not staying here. In fact she must have left the country by now.'

D'Artagnan gave a deep groan of relief.

'Who is this Milady, for God's sake?' cried Porthos.

Athos sipped his glass of sparkling wine and replied:

'A charming woman.'

Then he cried out:

'That damned swine of a landlord! He's given us Anjou instead of Champagne! Does he take us for complete fools? Oh, never mind!'

Then he continued:

'Yes, a charming woman who was very kind to our friend d'Artagnan, who, to reward her, played some low trick on her for which she tried to revenge herself a month ago by hiring two thugs to shoot him, a week ago by poisoning him, and only yesterday by asking the Cardinal for his head.'

D'Artagnan went white.

'What?' he cried. 'She asked the Cardinal for my head?'

'Yes,' said Porthos. 'I can vouch for that. I heard her with my own ears.'

'So did I,' said Aramis.

D'Artagnan hid his face in his hands.

'In that case it's hopeless to fight on,' he said despairingly. 'I might as well blow my brains out here and now and put an end to it all.'

'That's the last thing you must do,' said Athos. 'That's the only thing for which there's no cure.'

'But I'll never escape now,' replied d'Artagnan. 'Not with the enemies I've got; the stranger from Meung, de Wardes, the fellow I had the duel with, Milady, and lastly the Cardinal, who hates me for the affair of the diamond tags.'

'Well, that's only four and there are four of us,' said Athos. 'That's equal numbers! Look, there's Grimaud gesticulating! If I get him right we shall be having a good many more than four to deal with in a moment. What is it, Grimaud?' he cried. 'The position's critical, so you may speak. Quick, what have you seen?'

'A party of the enemy.'

'How many?'

'Twenty.'

'What are they?'

'Sixteen pioneers and four soldiers.'

'How far away are they?'

'About five hundred yards.'

'Good. We've got time to finish this chicken and drink a bottle of wine. Your good health, d'Artagnan.'

'Your health!' echoed Porthos and Aramis.

'Right, my health it is!' said d'Artagnan. 'Not that I think your toast will help much.'

'Cheer up!' said Athos. 'As the Mohammedans say, Allah is great and the future is in his hands.'

Upon which he drained his glass, put it down, got up slowly, picked up the first musket he saw and ambled over to a loophole. Porthos, Aramis, and d'Artagnan did likewise. Athos made Grimaud stand behind them to act as loader.

In a few seconds they saw the enemy platoon; it was advancing along a tributary trench which connected the bastion to the town.

'Ye Gods,' said Athos. 'Just look at them! Did we really need to get up for rabble like that armed with picks and shovels? I bet if Grimaud'd shaken his fists at them they'd have gone away.'

'I doubt that,' said d'Artagnan. 'They look determined enough to me. And they're not only pioneers – they've got four soldiers and a sergeant with them, armed with muskets.'

'They haven't seen us yet,' said Athos. 'Wait till they see us.'

'I must confess I don't like the idea of firing on a lot of untrained civilians,' said Aramis.

'It's a bad priest who pities heretics,' said Porthos.

'I agree with Aramis,' said Athos. 'I'm going to give them a chance to go away.'

'What on earth are you doing?' cried d'Artagnan. 'Don't show yourself like that! You'll get shot!'

'No I won't,' said Athos.

Whereupon he sprang into the breach in the wall, holding his gun in one hand and his hat in the other, and began addressing the oncoming party.

'Gentlemen,' he called, 'I and a few friends are breakfasting in this bastion. As I'm sure you'll agree, nothing's so odious as to be interrupted in the middle of a meal. So if you must occupy this bastion, please either wait till we've finished or go home and come back later. That is, unless you'd consider changing sides, leaving the rebels and joining us in a toast to His Majesty.'

The enemy platoon, astounded at this remarkable harangue, had halted about thirty yards from the bastion.

'Look out, Athos!' broke in d'Artagnan. 'They're taking aim at you. Can't you see?'

'I know,' said Athos. 'But they're civilians and therefore very bad shots. They'll never hit me!'

At that very moment four shots rang out and the bullets spattered against the wall of the bastion all round Athos. But none touched him. Almost simultaneously four answering shots rang out. And these were better aimed; three soldiers of the attacking party fell dead and one pioneer was wounded.

Athos, who was still standing in the breach, called out:

'Grimaud, another musket!'

Grimaud quickly handed him one. Meanwhile the other three defenders of the bastion had reloaded and now fired a second volley. This time the sergeant and two pioneers fell dead and the rest of the party took to flight.

'Come on, gentlemen; a sally!' cried Athos.

The four friends sprang out of the bastion, ran to where the dead men were lying and collected the four soldiers' muskets and the sergeant's pike. They decided not to pursue the retreating party and returned to the bastion bearing the trophies of their victory.

'Reload the muskets, Grimaud,' said Athos. 'Good, now we're ready for the enemy's next move. And now, gentlemen, let's continue our conversation. Where were we?'

'You were telling how Milady'd left France after asking the Cardinal for my head,' said d'Artagnan.

'Yes, I remember,' replied Athos.

'Where was she going?' asked d'Artagnan anxiously.

'To England.'

'What for?'

'To get Buckingham assassinated. She was either going to do it herself or get someone else to do it for her.'

D'Artagnan cried out:

'But that's monstrous!'

'Oh, I can't worry very much about that,' replied Athos.

Then, turning to Grimaud:

'When you've finished reloading,' he said, 'take our sergeant's pike, tie one of these napkins to it and plant it on top of the bastion, to show the rebels we're loyal soldiers of the King.'

Grimaud obeyed in silence and a moment later the white flag was floating over the bastion. Its appearance was hailed with shouts and cheers from the onlookers in the camp. By now half the besieging army was collected at the gates.

D'Artagnan protested:

'D'you really mean you don't care if Buckingham's killed? He's our friend, surely.'

'Buckingham's an Englishman; he's fighting against us. Milady can do what she likes with him – he's no more to me than an empty wine bottle.'

So saying he poured the last dregs of the bottle he was holding into his glass and hurled the bottle out of the bastion.

'Oh, no,' said d'Artagnan. 'I'm not abandoning Buckingham like that; he did give us four magnificent mounts, remember.'

'And four saddles too,' said Porthos, who was at that very moment wearing the gold braid of his saddle on his greatcoat.

'Besides,' remarked Aramis piously. 'God wants the sinner's conversion, not his death.'

'Amen to that!' said Athos. 'Very well, we'll return to Buckingham later, if you like. But as you can imagine, d'Artagnan, what concerned me most at the time was to get back from that woman what she'd got from the Cardinal. And that amounted to nothing less than a full warrant to get you put out of the way, and perhaps the rest of us as well.'

'Is this woman a vampire from the lower regions or what?' asked Porthos.

Then, almost in the same breath he said, handing his plate to Aramis, who was carving the chicken:

'Cut me off a thigh like a good chap.'

'And that warrant?' asked d'Artagnan. 'Has she still got it?'

'No. I took it away from her,' said Athos. 'I can't pretend I didn't have the devil's own job getting it.'

D'Artagnan said with tears in his eyes:

'My dear fellow, that must be the fourth time you've saved my life!'

'So that was why you left us!' said Aramis. 'To go back to her.'

'Yes.'

'Have you still got the warrant?' asked d'Artagnan.

'Yes, I've got it on me now,' replied Athos. 'Here, read it!'

And he pulled the precious document out of his pocket. D'Artagnan trembled violently as he unrolled the paper and made no attempt to hide his fear. He read the order aloud:

It is by my order and for the benefit of the State that the bearer of this note has done what he has done.

3 December, 1627.   Richelieu.

'Yes,' said Aramis. 'That's complete absolution.'

As he stared at the order d'Artagnan felt that he was looking at his death sentence.

'We must destroy this at once!' he cried.

'On the contrary,' said Athos. 'We must guard it with our lives. I wouldn't part with that document for a thousand pistoles.'

'What d'you suppose she'll do now?' asked the young man.

Athos shrugged his shoulders:

'She'll probably write to the Cardinal from England to say that a damned musketeer called Athos stole her safe-conduct pass from her. She'll probably advise him at the same time to get rid of his two friends, Porthos and Aramis. The Cardinal'll remember them as the fellows who were always getting in his way. One fine day he'll have d'Artagnan arrested and send us three to keep him company in the Bastille for fear he should get bored there all by himself.'

Porthos protested.

'I think that joke's in rather bad taste,' he said. 'Incidentally I also think this chicken's horribly tough.'

'I wasn't joking,' said Athos.

Porthos replied:

'D'you know that to wring that Milady's neck would be far less of a crime than wringing the necks of those poor devils of Huguenots. What wrong have they done, apart from singing the Psalms in French instead of in Latin?'

'What does our priest say to that?' asked Athos.

'I agree with Porthos,' replied Aramis.

'To Hell! And so do I!' cried d'Artagnan.

'Thank God she's a long way off now,' observed Porthos. 'I'd simply hate to think she was anywhere near here.'

'She's just as dangerous in England as she is in France,' said Athos.

'She's a damned nuisance anywhere,' agreed d'Artagnan.

'When you had her in that room why in God's name didn't you strangle her, put her head in a bucket or string her up?' cried Porthos. 'Then we'd all be enjoying ourselves instead of worrying our heads off about her. The dead never return.'

'That's what you think, Porthos!' said Athos, throwing a quick, meaning look at d'Artagnan.

There was silence for a moment. Suddenly d'Artagnan exclaimed:

'I've got an idea!'

'Good! What is it?' cried the other three.

At that moment Grimaud called out:

'Enemy approaching!'

The young men scrambled to their feet, picked up their guns and ran to their posts. They saw a small troop of about twenty-five men approaching. This time they were not pioneers but garrison soldiers.

'How about returning to the camp?' said Porthos. 'I think the odds are rather against us this time.'

'Impossible for three reasons,' replied Athos. 'One, we haven't finished breakfast; two, we've still got a lot to discuss; three, there's another ten minutes to go before the hour's up.'

'Well then, let's work out a plan of action,' said Aramis.

'We'd better wait till the enemy's within range and then open fire,' said Athos. 'If they continue to advance we fire again, and go on firing till we run out of ammunition. If what's left of the enemy tries to attack the bastion we wait till they're in the moat and then shove this section of wall down on their heads; as you see, it's quite loose and only holding up by a miracle of balance.'

'Bravo, Athos!' cried Porthos. 'You're a born general. As a strategist the Cardinal's got nothing on you.'

'We mustn't waste our shots,' continued Athos. 'No two to fire at the same man. Each pick your man.'

'I've picked mine,' said d'Artagnan.

'And I,' said Porthos.

'And I,' said Aramis.

'Good,' said Athos. 'Now fire!'

The four shots rang out simultaneously and four men fell dead. Immediately the drum beat and the little troop advanced at the charge. From now on the shots from the bastion rang out irregularly but always accurately aimed. But the Rochellese seemed to realize their foe's numerical weakness, for they continued to advance at the double.

Three more shots rang out and two more men fell. But those who were still on their feet continued to advance at the same speed. When they reached the foot of the bastion they were still about fifteen strong.

A final salvo greeted them, but still they pressed on. They jumped into the moat and were preparing to make the final ascent into the breach when Athos cried:

'Now gentlemen, we'll crush the whole lot with one fell swoop. Man the wall, all of you, man the wall!'

And the four friends, helped by Grimaud, placed their musket-butts against an enormous detached section of wall and began shoving it with all their strength. The wall was standing at a slant, almost severed from its base, and only needed a little pressure to loosen it entirely. In a few seconds they had succeeded in dislodging it and it fell with a great crash into the moat. A terrible cry rent the air, a cloud of dust rose skywards and all was over.

'Can we have really wiped out the whole lot?' muttered Athos.

'It looks like it,' said d'Artagnan.

'No,' said Porthos. 'I see four or five of them hobbling off!'

A wretched little group covered in blood and dust was, in fact, shambling off down the trench in the direction of the town, the bedraggled remnants of the attacking force. Athos looked at his watch.

'Gentlemen,' he said. 'We've been here an hour now, so strictly speaking we've won our bet. But let's stay on a little longer and win it handsomely. Besides, d'Artagnan hasn't told us his idea yet.'

Upon which he leaned his musket against the wall and calmly sat down in front of the remains of the breakfast.

'My idea?' said d'Artagnan.

'Yes,' said Athos. 'You were just telling us you had an idea.'

'Of course,' said d'Artagnan. 'My idea was to pay a second visit to England, find Buckingham and warn him of this plot against his life.'

'No, d'Artagnan. That you will not do,' said Athos coldly.

'Why not? I did it before!'

'Yes, but we weren't at war then. At that time Buckingham was an ally, not an enemy. What you propose doing's treason.'

D'Artagnan saw that Athos was right and did not persist.

Porthos now broke in.

'I think I've got an idea,' he said.

'Silence for Porthos' idea!' said Aramis.

'I'll ask Monsieur de Tréville for leave on some pretext or other. You'll all have to think out the pretext; I'm bad at that sort of thing. I shall then go and call on Her Ladyship. She doesn't know me so she won't suspect anything. I'll manage somehow to get left alone with her and then strangle her.'

'That's not at all a bad idea,' said Athos.

'Kill a woman!' cried Aramis. 'Not on your life! No, I've got a much better idea than that.'

'Let's hear your idea, Aramis,' said Athos, who had a great respect for the young musketeer's intelligence.

'We must let the Queen know about it.'

'Yes, of course!' cried Porthos and d'Artagnan. 'That's the obvious thing to do!'

'Let the Queen know?' repeated Athos. 'And how d'you suggest we do that? We've got no connections at Court, and we couldn't send anyone to Paris without the whole camp knowing. It's two hundred and eighty miles from here to Paris. We'd all be in detention before our letter reached Angers.'

'I'd guarantee to get a letter through to Her Majesty,' said Aramis, colouring slightly. 'I know someone in Tours who'd do that for me.'

Athos smiled at this. Aramis noticed him smile and hesitated.

'Well?' asked d'Artagnan. 'And what d'you think of that plan?'

'I don't dismiss it entirely,' said Athos. 'But I'd like to point out that if Aramis left camp he'd get the rest of us into serious trouble. And if we sent anyone else with the letter two hours after he'd left all the Cardinal's spies would know it by heart and arrest both Aramis and his friend in Tours on the spot.'

'Not to mention the fact that the Queen would protect Buckingham but wouldn't bother her head about any of us.'

'True enough, Porthos,' agreed d'Artagnan.

Athos suddenly raised his hand to command silence.

'What's all that racket going on in the town?' he cried.

'That's a call to arms!'

The four friends listened and heard the ominous rumble of the drums in the distance.

'You wait!' said Athos. 'They'll be sending a whole regiment against us now.'

'You don't propose to hold out against a regiment, do you?' asked Porthos.

'Why not?' asked the musketeer. 'I feel in fine form today and if we'd had the sense to bring another dozen bottles with us I'd take on an army corps!'

'Listen!' said d'Artagnan. 'The drums are getting louder. The enemy's advancing.'

'Let them come,' said Athos. 'It'll take them a good quarter of an hour to get here. That's ample time for us to settle on a plan. If we left now we'd never find anywhere else as good as this to talk in. And if you'll all listen a moment, I think I've hit on the solution of our problem.'

'Well, let's hear it.'

'I must just say a word to Grimaud first,' said Athos.

And he beckoned to his servant to leave his look-out post and come and take his orders. Pointing to the corpses lying in the bastion he said:

'Grimaud, lift up these gentlemen and prop them against the wall. Then put their hats on their heads and their guns in their hands.'

'Oh, bravo,' exclaimed d'Artagnan. 'I see it all now!'

'Do you?' asked Porthos. 'I wish I did!'

'Do you see it, Grimaud?' asked Aramis.

Grimaud nodded. Then he set to work to lift up the corpses.

'That's right, Grimaud,' said Athos. 'Get down to it. That's all we need do as far as the enemy goes. And now for this idea of mine.'

'I wish you'd first explain what you're doing with those dead fellows,' said Porthos.

'You'll soon see.'

'Come on, Athos, we're waiting for the big idea!' cried d'Artagnan and Aramis.

'D'Artagnan, didn't you tell me this Milady of yours, woman, vampire, or whatever she is, had a brother-in-law?'

'Yes. I know him personally. And I don't think there's much love lost between him and his sister-in-law.'

'That's all to the good,' said Athos. 'If he hated her it'd be better still.'

'He's the man for us, then.'

'I do wish you'd tell me what Grimaud's supposed to be doing,' interrupted Porthos.

'Shut up, Porthos!' said Aramis.

'What's this brother-in-law's name?'

'Lord de Winter.'

'Where's he now?'

'He returned to London at the beginning of the war.'

'Well, he's the very fellow we want,' said Athos. 'He's the man we must get in touch with. We must tell him his sister-in-law's on the point of murdering someone, and advise him to keep a close watch on her. There must be some place in London which corresponds to the Madelonnettes or the Repentant Girls' Society. De Winter can shut his sister-in-law up in one of those places and we can then feel easy again.'

'Yes, until she gets out again,' objected d'Artagnan.

'D'Artagnan, you expect too much,' said Athos. 'I've racked my brains for a solution and I warn you that's the best I can do.'

'I think we'd better warn both the Queen and Lord de Winter,' said Aramis. 'I think that'll do the trick.'

'Yes, but who can we get to take the letters, one to Tours and the other to London?'

'Bazin can take one,' suggested Aramis.

'Yes, and Planchet the other,' suggested d'Artagnan.

'A good idea!' said Porthos. 'We can't leave camp, I know, but there's nothing to prevent our servants leaving.'

'Of course not,' said Aramis. 'We'll write the letters today, at once; then we'll give them both money and send them off.'

'Money?' cried Athos; 'and where's the money coming from?'

The four friends darted quick glances at each other. A moment before they had been cheerful and excited; now they were in despair again.

At this point d'Artagnan suddenly jumped up, shouting:

'Look out, look out! The enemy! I can see little black and red dots moving down there. Did you say something about a regiment, Athos? Lord! It's a whole army corps!'

'Ah yes, there they come!' said Athos. 'Look at them, the dirty dogs, sneaking along without drums or bugles. Trying to surprise us, were they! Hi, there, Grimaud, have you finished the job?'

Grimaud nodded and pointed to a dozen corpses which he

had grouped most artistically round the walls, some holding their muskets at the porte, others pointing them at the enemy, and others with drawn swords.

'Well done, Grimaud!' said Athos. 'That's excellent and does credit to your imagination.'

'I still don't understand,' said Porthos. 'Do explain to me, someone . . .'

'Let's get away first,' said d'Artagnan. 'We'll explain later.'

'We must wait till Grimaud's packed up the breakfast things,' said Athos.

'Those little black and red dots are much larger now,' said Aramis. 'I really think d'Artagnan's right; we'd better get back to camp.'

'Very well,' said Athos. 'I think we're justified in getting out now. Our bet was for an hour and we've held the fort an hour and a half. No one can complain of that. So let's go.'

Grimaud had already started off with the basket and the remains of the food. The four friends followed him. But they had only gone about ten yards when Athos suddenly stopped.

'We've forgotten something, gentlemen,' he said.

'What?' asked Aramis.

'The flag. We can't leave our flag in enemy hands, even though it is only a napkin.'

Whereupon he ran back into the bastion, climbed into the breach and removed the flag.

But the advancing Rochellese were now within range. When they saw the foolhardy young musketeer exposing himself to their bullets they immediately opened fire on him. But Athos seemed to bear a charmed life. The bullets whistled round his head but none touched him. As a final gesture before abandoning the bastion he waved the standard defiantly at the enemy and in greeting to the men in the camp.

At this loud cries came from both sides, from one side cries of anger and from the other of applause. A second enemy volley succeeded the first and three bullets pierced the flag, converting it from a napkin into a proper standard. And now all the watchers in the camp began shouting:

'Come down, come down.'

Athos jumped down from the bastion. His friends were waiting anxiously for him twenty yards away and beckoned him on.

'Hurry, hurry!' cried d'Artagnan. 'We'd better run for it. We've got everything nicely worked out now except the money business, and it'd be silly to get killed at the last moment.'

But Athos refused to be hurried. He walked along at a steady pace and his companions, seeing that argument was useless, set their pace by him. Grimaud had gone on ahead with his basket and was now well out of gunshot. In a moment or two the four friends heard a furious burst of fire behind them.

'What was all that about?' asked Porthos. 'What are they firing at? I didn't hear any bullets and I can't see anyone.'

'They're firing at our corpses,' replied Athos.

'But our corpses won't fire back,' said Porthos.

'Exactly. Then the enemy'll think there's an ambush. They'll stop and have a palaver and then send a flag of truce. By the time they've discovered the hoax we'll be out of range of their guns. So you see there's no need to strain our hearts running.'

At this Porthos cried out:

'Oh, I see now! Athos, you're a genius.'

'Glad you think so!' replied Athos coolly.

When the watchers in the camp saw the four friends returning not at the double but taking their time over it, they burst into loud cheers. The next moment there was another volley of fire from behind and this time the bullets whistled unpleasantly round the friends' ears and sent the pebbles flying round their feet. The Rochellese had just occupied the bastion.

'What an incompetent lot of devils they are!' said Athos. 'How many of them did we pot? Twelve, wasn't it?'

'About that.'

'And how many did we crush with that wall?'

'About ten.'

'In return for which we've none of us got a scratch. But what's that on your hand, d'Artagnan? Blood, isn't it?'

'That's nothing,' said d'Artagnan.

'A bullet?'

'Not even a bullet.'

'What is it then?'

Athos, as we know, loved d'Artagnan as his son and, stern and sad as he was, sometimes felt a father's concern for him.

'It's a graze,' said d'Artagnan. 'My hand got caught between two stones, the stone of the wall and the stone on my finger. The skin got rubbed off.'

Athos snorted contemptuously:

'That's what comes of wearing diamond rings, my lad,' he said.

'Look here!' said Porthos suddenly. 'We've got a diamond ring. Why are we worrying about money when we've got a perfectly good diamond ring?'

'Good Lord, I never thought of that!' exclaimed Aramis. 'Good old Porthos! You've had a brainwave at last!'

Porthos gave his moustache a proud twirl.

'What's to stop us selling the ring?' he asked.

'But it's the Queen's ring,' objected d'Artagnan.

'All the more reason for using it,' said Athos. 'It'll help the Queen to save her lover Buckingham. What better use could it be put to? And it'll help her to save us, her friends. Quite as it should be. Let's sell the diamond. What does Father Aramis say? We won't ask Porthos; we already know what he thinks.'

Aramis coloured and replied:

'The ring's not a present from his mistress and therefore not a love token. So I think d'Artagnan's justified in selling it.'

'You talk like a theological treatise, my lad. So you think we . . .?'

'Should sell the diamond,' replied Aramis.

D'Artagnan was satisfied.

'Right,' he said, 'we'll sell it then.'

Meanwhile the enemy troops were keeping up their fire. But the friends were now out of range and the Rochellese were only firing to ease their consciences. Athos remarked:

'You came out with that bright idea just in time, Porthos. Here we are back at the camp. And now, gentlemen, not another word about the whole business. We're already being watched.

They're coming out to meet us and I think we're going to be carried back in triumph.'

Indeed the whole camp was in an uproar. More than two thousand men had gazed enthralled at the four friends' spectacular feat of 'derring-do', totally unaware of the motive for it. The air rang with shouts of 'Long live the Guards, long live the Musketeers!' Monsieur de Busigny had led the procession which came to congratulate Athos and had acknowledged the loss of the bet. Behind him came the dragoon and the Swiss guard, and they in turn were followed by the whole camp. There was an endless succession of handshakes, back-slappings, and witty sallies at the expense of the Rochellese. So great, in fact, was the uproar that the Cardinal thought there was a mutiny in the camp and sent La Houdinière, the captain of his Guards, to find out the cause of the disturbance. The incident was reported to La Houdinière with many frills and furbishes, the product of the soldiers' heated imaginations.

To the Cardinal's inquiry La Houdinière replied:

'Apparently three musketeers and a guard made a bet with Monsieur de Busigny that they'd breakfast in the St Gervais bastion, and while they were breakfasting they incidentally accounted for a considerable number of Rochellese.'

'Did you find out these fellows' names?'

'Yes, Monseigneur. They're called Athos, Porthos, and Aramis.'

'Those three rogues again!' muttered the Cardinal. 'And the guardsman?'

'A Monsieur d'Artagnan.'

'That young rascal again! Well, I see there's nothing for it; I must have them all on my side!'

That evening the Cardinal himself mentioned the exploit to Monsieur de Tréville. Indeed it would have looked strange had he not, for it was now the talk of the whole camp. Monsieur de Tréville had heard the story from the lips of the men who had been the heroes of it, so he was able to relate it in detail to the Cardinal, not forgetting the napkin incident.

'Get hold of that napkin for me, Monsieur de Tréville,' said the Cardinal, 'and I'll have three gold fleur-de-lis embroidered on it and present it to your company as its camp colours.'

'That wouldn't be fair to the Guards, Your Eminence,' objected de Tréville. 'Young d'Artagnan's not in my company; he's in Monsieur des Essarts' company.'

'Well, you take him on, Sir,' said the Cardinal. 'Those four rogues are so hand-in-glove they ought all to be together.'

Later that evening Monsieur de Tréville announced the good news to the three musketeers and d'Artagnan and invited them all to lunch with him the next day. The latter was in the seventh heaven of joy. As we know, it was the ambition of his life to be a musketeer. His three friends were also delighted.

'The bastion breakfast party was certainly a brainwave of yours,' said d'Artagnan to Athos. 'As you say, we've got ourselves talked about and at the same time had a council of war of the utmost importance.'

'Which we'll now be able to carry on without anyone suspecting us,' replied Athos. 'From now on everyone's going to take us for Cardinalists.'

At ten o'clock that night d'Artagnan went to pay his respects to Monsieur des Essarts and to tell him of his promotion. Monsieur des Essarts was very much attached to d'Artagnan. He knew that this change of corps would mean a new outfit for him, so he suggested giving him a small advance on his pay. D'Artagnan declined the offer but instead asked Monsieur des Essarts to be good enough to have the Queen's diamond valued and sold for him. Des Essarts took the ring and promised to carry out the young man's commission.

At eight o'clock next morning Monsieur des Essarts' valet called at d'Artagnan's quarters and handed him a purse containing seven thousand livres in gold. This was the price of the Queen's diamond.

CHAPTER XI

A Family Affair

ATHOS' inventive genius had found the solution. The campaign against Milady was to be carried on as a family affair. Family affairs were not open to investigation by the Cardinal and his agents; they concerned no one outside the family and could be discussed in front of anyone.

It was Aramis who had had the bright idea of sending the lackeys with the letters. Porthos had had the idea of selling the diamond. Only d'Artagnan, usually the most resourceful of the lot, had suggested nothing. But we must remember that the very mention of Milady's name paralysed him. And he had not been entirely unhelpful – he had found a buyer for the diamond.

The lunch with Monsieur de Tréville was uproariously gay. D'Artagnan was already wearing his musketeer's uniform, which he had got from Aramis. Aramis had, as we know, been handsomely paid for his poem by his publisher and had had the whole of his campaign outfit made in duplicate. He was about the same height and build as d'Artagnan, and the latter had bought an entire outfit from him with some of the proceeds of the sale of the diamond.

D'Artagnan would have been in the seventh heaven of joy had he not seen in his mind's eye the figure of Milady looming on the horizon like a black cloud.

After lunch the four friends agreed to meet that evening at Athos' billet and make the final arrangements. D'Artagnan spent the rest of that day parading up and down the camp in his new uniform. That evening, at the time arranged, the four friends met. They had only three more things to settle: what to write to Milady's brother-in-law; what to write to Aramis' friend in Tours, and which of the lackeys to send with the letters.

Each of the four friends suggested his own lackey. Athos

stressed Grimaud's discretion, reminding his friends that he never spoke except with his master's permission. Porthos boasted of Mousqueton's strength, saying that he was powerful enough to take on any four average-sized men. Aramis enlarged on Bazin's cleverness, and d'Artagnan praised Planchet's courage to the skies, reminding the company of his exemplary behaviour in the affray near Calais. The argument threatened to become heated, so Athos, to smooth matters over, said:

'Unfortunately the man we send must possess all these qualities combined, tact, strength, cleverness, and courage.'

'But where shall we find a man of that sort?'

'Nowhere,' said Athos. 'I realize that. So take Grimaud.'

'Take Mousqueton.'

'Take Bazin.'

'Take Planchet. Planchet's honest and clever and that's two of the qualities needed.'

Here Aramis broke in. 'I think the important thing to decide is not which of our servants has the most virtues but which is the fondest of money,' he said.

'That's very true, Aramis,' said Athos. 'One must gamble on men's weaknesses, not on their virtues. Father Aramis, you're a psychologist!'

'I think I'm right in this case,' replied Aramis. 'We must really be able to trust the man we send. It's not a question of merely trying to succeed — we must be certain of not failing. For if we fail it's we who'll suffer . . .'

'Sh! Not so loud, Aramis!' whispered Athos.

'I say it's we who'll suffer, not the lackeys,' went on Aramis, lowering his voice. 'Do our lackeys like us enough to risk their lives for us? No.'

D'Artagnan said:

'I'm almost sure Planchet does.'

'Well, add to his natural fondness for you the attraction of a good fee and then you'll be quite sure.'

'And even then you'll be let down,' said Athos, who was optimistic about events but had a poor opinion of human nature. He continued:

'Those fellows will promise everything for the sake of the money; then, when they've started on the job, they'll panic and give up in the middle. They'll get caught; they'll be questioned and hard pressed and under pressure they'll confess everything ... Good Lord, we're not children!'

'Remember,' he continued, lowering his voice to a whisper, 'to get to England you've to cross all France, and France is teeming with the Cardinal's spies and agents. If the man succeeds in getting across France he'll need a passport to get a passage on a ship, and if he gets to England he'll need to know English to ask his way to London. The whole thing's extraordinarily complicated, if you ask me.'

D'Artagnan was very keen to see the plan carried out.

'I don't agree,' he said. 'I think it's extraordinarily easy. Of course if we fill our letter to Lord de Winter with lurid accounts of the Cardinal's crimes ...'

'Not so loud, not so loud!' whispered Athos.

D'Artagnan lowered his voice and went on:

'If we fill the letter with descriptions of State intrigues we'll certainly let ourselves in for trouble. But don't forget what you yourself suggested, Athos, that we're writing to Lord de Winter on a family matter; that our one object in writing is to get him to put Milady somewhere out of harm's way directly she gets to London. I'll compose a letter in that style now.'

'Right, let's see what you can do,' said Aramis, with a critic's superior air.

'Dear Friend,' began d'Artagnan.

' "Dear Friend" to an Englishman?' broke in Athos. 'That's a good beginning! Bravo, d'Artagnan! Those two words alone would get you hanged, drawn, and quartered.'

'Very well. I'll start quite simply "Dear Sir".'

'You must call him "My Lord",' said Athos, who was a stickler for etiquette.

'Very well, then: "My Lord, do you remember the little field near the Luxembourg?".'

'The Luxembourg? If you put that they'll think it's a code allusion to the Queen Mother,' said Athos.

'Very well, how will this do: "My Lord, do you remember a little enclosure where we spared your life?".'

'D'Artagnan, you'll never be a writer,' said Athos. ' "Where we spared your life", indeed! That's not very tactful. One doesn't remind a man of a debt he owes one. It's an insult.'

'Athos, you're intolerable! I refuse to write with you nagging at me all the time.'

'Yes, you stick to your musket and your sword. You're brilliant with those. But leave the pen work to our friend the priest here. That's his business.'

'Yes,' said Porthos. 'Leave the writing to Aramis. He writes theses in Latin.'

'Very well,' said d'Artagnan. 'You compose the letter, Aramis. But take care! I'm going to do the criticizing now!'

Aramis replied with a poet's conceit:

'Please do. I shall be glad of your help. But first tell me the whole story. I gather His Lordship de Winter's sister-in-law's a dangerous woman. I've even got evidence of that through listening to her conversation with the Cardinal.'

'Not so loud,' begged Athos.

'But I don't know the story in full,' said Aramis.

'Nor do I,' said Porthos.

D'Artagnan and Athos stole a quick glance at each other. The latter sat for a moment lost in thought. Then he looked up and nodded at d'Artagnan. D'Artagnan took this to mean that he could speak out.

'Well, this is what you must write,' he said.

'My Lord, your sister-in-law is a wicked woman. She tried to get you killed in order to inherit your fortune. But her marriage with your brother was illegal. She had been married in France before and had been . . .'

D'Artagnan paused and waited for Athos to prompt him.

'Sent away by her husband,' said Athos.

'Because she had been branded,' continued d'Artagnan.

'Branded! Good God!' cried Porthos. 'Branded and tried to get her brother-in-law murdered?'

'Yes.'

'And a bigamist?' asked Aramis.

'Yes.'

'And her husband discovered she had a fleur-de-lis on her shoulder?'

'Yes.'

'Who's actually seen this fleur-de-lis?' asked Aramis.

'D'Artagnan and I, or rather I and d'Artagnan, to keep the chronological order,' said Athos.

'And is this fiend's husband still alive?' asked Aramis.

'Yes.'

'Are you certain of that?'

'Quite.'

There was dead silence for a moment. All four men were moved, each in a different way. Athos was the first to speak.

'This time d'Artagnan's given us an excellent start,' he said. 'We must write a properly expressed letter, using d'Artagnan's suggestion as a rough draft.'

'Yes, Athos,' agreed Aramis. 'And it's a damned difficult letter to write. Even the Chancellor would be hard put to it to write a letter like that and we know how good he is at drawing up reports. Never mind. I'll do my best.'

He took up the pen and, after a moment's thought, wrote eight or ten lines in a neat feminine hand. These he proceeded to read aloud, with slow emphasis, as though he had weighed each word carefully as he wrote.

My Lord, *he read*:

The man who is writing this once had the honour of crossing swords with you in a little enclosure in the Rue d'Enfer.

As you were kind enough to give this man frequent proofs of your goodwill he, in return, feels obliged, in token of his goodwill, to send you a word of warning.

You have a close relation who has twice tried to kill you. You believe her to be your rightful heir but she is not. Before marrying in England she was already married in France.

This woman, as I say, has twice tried to kill you. The third time, this time in fact, she might succeed.

Your relation has left La Rochelle for England. Keep a close watch on her; she is engaged in dangerous intrigues. If you wish to know what she is guilty of you can read her past on her left shoulder.

'That's marvellous!' said Athos. 'Aramis, you write like an angel. That letter will put de Winter thoroughly on his guard, that is, if it ever reaches him. And if it falls into the hands of His Eminence himself we shan't be compromised. The only fear is that the fellow who takes the letter may stop at Chatellerault and pretend he's been to London. So we'll only give him half his fee with the letter and promise him the other half when he gets back with the reply. Have you got the diamond on you?'

'I've got better than that. I've got the money for it,' said d'Artagnan.

And he threw the purse on the table.

At the clink of the gold coins Aramis looked up and Porthos gave a gasp of joy. Only Athos remained unmoved.

'How much is there in that purse?' he asked.

'Seven thousand livres in twelve-franc pieces.'

'Seven thousand livres!' cried Porthos. 'That little diamond was worth seven thousand livres?'

'Apparently,' said Athos. 'There's the money all right. I don't suppose d'Artagnan's added anything to it from his own pocket.'

D'Artagnan broke in:

'But look here, gentlemen, aren't we rather forgetting the Queen in all this? We ought to show some concern for the health of her beloved Buckingham. That's the least we can do for her.'

'I agree,' said Athos. 'But for that we've got to appeal to Aramis.'

Aramis blushed.

'Very well,' he said. 'What d'you want me to do?'

'Compose another letter to that friend of yours in Tours,' said Athos.

Aramis took up the pen again, thought for a moment, and then wrote a few lines which he proceeded also to read aloud to his friends and which ran as follows:

'My dear Cousin,'

'Oh!' interrupted Athos. 'So she's a relation of yours?'

'First cousin,' said Aramis.

'Put cousin, then.'

Aramis began again:

My dear Cousin,

His Eminence the Cardinal, whom God preserve for the glory of France and the destruction of her enemies, is about to annihilate the heretic rebels of La Rochelle. It is unlikely that the relieving English fleet will even come within sight of the town. I can almost certainly prophesy that some important event will stop the Duke of Buckingham leaving England.

His Eminence is the greatest statesman the world has ever seen or ever will see. He would snuff out the sun if it stood in his way.

Pass on this good news to your sister, dear cousin.

I dreamed that this accursed Englishman was dead. I can't remember whether he died of a wound or by poison. I'm only certain of one thing – that he was dead. And as you know, my dreams are always right.

So you can count on my returning very soon.

'Magnificent!' cried Athos. 'Aramis, you're the king of letter-writers. Everything in that letter's true and it has an oracular ring about it. The only problem now is how to address it.'

'That's easy,' said Aramis.

He folded up the letter carefully, and wrote on it:

> To Mademoiselle Marie Michon,
> Seamstress,
> Tours.

The three friends looked at each other and laughed. Their curiosity had been defeated.

'So you see,' said Aramis, 'Bazin must take that letter to Tours. My cousin only knows Bazin and trusts no one but him. It would be foolish to send anyone else. Besides, Bazin's ambitious and learned, a superior type altogether. He's studied history. He knows that Pope Sixtus the Fifth started life as a swineherd. He wants to enter the Church when I do and hopes to become Pope himself one day. A man with aims like that's not going to let himself get caught, and if he does he won't talk, however hard pressed.'

'Right,' said d'Artagnan. 'By all means send Bazin on your job. But let me send Planchet on mine. Milady had him whipped out of her house one day. The fellow has a good memory and I guarantee that if one gave him a chance to get his revenge he'd jump at it and stick to it. You manage the journey to Tours, Aramis, and let me manage the journey to London. I've been there before and I know my way about. So please let me send Planchet. He's already been to London once and can say: "London, Sir, if you please", and "My master, Lord d'Artagnan" very nicely. He can get there and back quite well on that.'

'That's settled, then,' said Athos. 'And now for the money question, I suggest Planchet should be given fourteen hundred livres for the return journey to London, seven hundred when he sets off and the other seven hundred when he gets back. Bazin should get six hundred for the journey to Tours and back, three hundred in advance and three hundred on his return. That'll leave us with five thousand livres. I suggest we each take a thousand to use as we think best, and leave a deposit of a thousand which our priest here can bank for us for an emergency.'

'Athos,' said Aramis, 'you talk like Nestor, the wisest of the Greeks.'

'Good, that's agreed then,' said Athos. 'Planchet and Bazin are to go. Personally I'm not sorry to be able to keep Grimaud. He's used to my ways and I should be rather lost without him. Yesterday's little picnic must have shaken him up a good deal. The journey to London would finish him.'

The friends now summoned Planchet and gave him his instructions. D'Artagnan had already warned him that his services might be needed; he had mentioned first the glory, then the reward, and lastly the dangers attached to the errand.

'I'll carry the letter in the lining of my coat,' said Planchet. 'And if I'm caught I'll swallow it.'

'But then you won't be able to deliver the message,' said d'Artagnan.

'Give me a copy tonight, Sir, and I'll learn it by heart before tomorrow.'

D'Artagnan looked at his friends as though to say:

'What did I tell you?'

Then, turning to Planchet, he said:

'We give you a week from tomorrow to reach Lord de Winter, and another week to get back to the camp. That's a fortnight in all. If at eight o'clock on the evening of the fourteenth day you haven't returned you won't get the second half of your reward. Even if you're five minutes late.'

'In that case, Sir,' said Planchet, 'you must buy me a watch.'

'You can have this,' said Athos, handing him his watch. 'And do your job well. Remember that if you gossip or waste time on the way you'll get your master into serious trouble; he trusts you and has vouched for you with us. And don't forget that if any harm comes to Monsieur d'Artagnan through negligence or treachery on your part, I'll find you wherever you are. And when I've found you I'll carve you in pieces.'

'Oh Sir!' cried Planchet.

He was hurt by this admission of lack of confidence and frightened by the stern look on Athos' face.

'And I'll flay you alive,' said Porthos, glaring fiercely at him.

'Oh Sir!'

Aramis said softly:

'And I'll roast you on a slow fire like the cannibals do.'

'Oh Sir!'

Planchet began to snivel. Nobody knew whether it was from terror at this succession of threats or because he was moved to see the four friends so single of purpose. D'Artagnan patted him on the shoulder.

'All right, Planchet, cheer up,' he said. 'These gentlemen are only talking like this out of affection for me. They really like you.'

'Sir,' said Planchet. 'I'll be hanged, drawn, and quartered rather than let you down.'

It was arranged that Planchet was to leave at eight o'clock the next morning. This would give him time to memorize the letter first. And he was to be back not later than eight p.m. on the fourteenth day.

The next morning, as Planchet was getting into the saddle, d'Artagnan, who had a soft spot in his heart for the Duke of Buckingham, took him aside.

'Listen,' he said. 'When you've delivered the letter to Lord de Winter give him this message as well: "Warn the Duke of Buckingham that there's a plot to assassinate him!" This is a very important message, Planchet. I haven't even dared tell my friends I'm doing this and I wouldn't put that message on paper for anything in the world.'

'Don't worry, Sir,' said Planchet. 'I won't let you down.'

And he put spurs to his horse and galloped off. He was to ride for thirty miles and travel the rest of the way by mail coach. He was somewhat chastened by the musketeer's threats of what would happen to him if he failed in his mission, but otherwise in good heart.

On the morning of the day following Planchet's departure Bazin left for Tours and was given a week to carry out his mission.

As was to be expected the four friends were on tenterhooks for the whole of the period of their servants' absence. They spent their time listening to the gossip of the camp, spying on the Cardinal, and watching the various messengers going in and out of the little house on the dunes. The strain of waiting told on them, and whenever they were summoned for some special duty they would start and tremble. And they also had their own personal safety to think of. Milady was like an evil spirit which has only to appear to a man once to destroy his peace of mind for ever after.

On the evening of the seventh day, just as the friends were sitting down to supper at the Parpaillot inn, Bazin entered, fresh and smiling as usual. He went up to Aramis as arranged, held out a letter and said:

'Your cousin's reply, Sir.'

The four friends exchanged triumphant looks. Half their task was already done, although it was the easiest and the shortest half. Aramis took the letter, which was addressed in a coarse and illiterate hand. He blushed a little and said with a laugh:

'I despair of ever teaching that poor Michon girl to write like Monsieur de Voiture.'

The Swiss guard had been talking to the four friends when the letter arrived. He now broke in with:

'Who's the poor Michon girl?'

'Oh no one very important,' said Aramis. 'Only a little seamstress I was rather fond of. I asked her to write me a letter as a keepsake.'

'Well, if her handwriting's anything to go by, you've got a mistress to be proud of,' said the Swiss, laughing uproariously.

Aramis read the letter and passed it over to Athos.

'Look what she's written!' he said.

Athos shot a quick glance at the letter. Then, to allay any possible suspicions in the minds of the bystanders he started to read it aloud. It ran as follows:

Dear Cousin,

My sister and I interpret dreams very well, and are terrified of them. But let's hope we can say that your dream was just a nightmare.

Good-bye. Take care of yourself and write to us from time to time.

Marie Michon.

While Athos had been reading the dragoon had come up and joined the party.

'What dream does she mean?' he asked.

'Yes, what dream?' echoed the Swiss.

'Merely a dream I had which I told her about,' said Aramis.

'It must be great fun telling people one's dreams,' said the Swiss. 'I never have dreams so I can't.'

'Fortunate fellow,' said Athos. 'I wish I could say the same.'

Having thus diverted the curiosity of the crowd Athos got up and left the inn. D'Artagnan followed him. Porthos and Aramis remained behind for safety's sake to exchange a few ribaldries with the two soldiers. As for Bazin he went and lay down on a bundle of straw. He had more imagination than the Swiss and dreamed that his master had become Pope and was placing a Cardinal's hat on his head.

But, as we have said, Bazin's return had relieved only half the four friends' burden. Days spent in anxious waiting seem interminable and to d'Artagnan that week seemed like a year. He forgot to take account of the uncertainty of sea-travel; in his anxiety he tended to overestimate Milady's power and to regard her as a fiend with supernatural attributes. He would start at the faintest sound, imagining that the Cardinal's men had come to arrest him; he pictured Planchet captured and brought back, and himself and his three friends seized and publicly confronted with him. His confidence in the sturdy Picard waned as the days went by.

D'Artagnan's nervousness began to affect Porthos and Aramis. Only Athos remained calm and continued to behave normally.

When the fourteenth day arrived d'Artagnan and his two friends were so nervous that they could not stay still but kept wandering like lost souls up and down the road by which Planchet was expected to return. Athos gave them a good talking-to.

'You ought to be ashamed of yourselves,' he said. 'Three grown men letting a woman put the fear of God into them! What's there to be frightened of, anyway? Imprisonment? Possibly. But they'll get us out all right – they got Madame Bonacieux out, didn't they? Beheading? Why, we go up the line every day and risk worse than that. We might get a bullet through the thigh any time and I bet the doctor would hurt us more lopping off our legs than any headsman chopping off our heads. So cheer up. In two, four, six hours at the most Planchet will be here. He promised he'd be back and I've got great faith in him. I think he's a first-rate fellow.'

'But suppose he doesn't turn up?' said d'Artagnan.

'If he doesn't turn up it'll mean he's been delayed, that's all. He may have fallen off his horse; he may have slipped on the deck of the boat and sprained his ankle; he may have caught a chill. All sorts of things may have happened. We must be calm. Come on, let's sit down and drink. A glass of Chambertin will make us all feel better.'

'Yes,' said d'Artagnan, 'but it rather spoils a drink never to be quite sure that it doesn't come out of Milady's cellars.'

'You ungrateful devil, d'Artagnan!' said Athos. 'You ought to be flattered. A lovely, exotic creature like her.'

'A woman of the best brand!' said Porthos, guffawing at his own joke.

Athos suddenly began to tremble. Then he passed his hand nervously across his forehead, got up and began pacing up and down the room; even he seemed for a moment to have lost his poise.

That day was to the four friends an eternity. But evening came at last and the troops began to crowd into the taverns. Athos had pocketed his share of the sale of the diamond and spent the whole evening in the Parpaillot. De Busigny had entertained the four friends to dinner and Athos had found in him a skilled dice player. The two men were playing together when seven o'clock struck, and the sound of the patrolling pickets echoed through the camp. At seven-thirty the tattoo sounded one full stop. D'Artagnan whispered to Athos:

'We're lost.'

Athos nudged him and, to put de Busigny off the scent, said, pulling ten louis out of his pocket:

'You're right, I *have* lost!'

Then he added:

'Well, gentlemen, they've just sounded the tattoo. Let's turn in for the night.'

And he got up and left the Parpaillot, followed by d'Artagnan.

Aramis and Porthos went out shortly afterwards, arm in arm. Aramis was reciting verses under his breath and Porthos was tugging fiercely at his moustache.

Suddenly the four friends saw a figure running towards them through the shadows. And a voice which d'Artagnan recognized at once called out:

'I've brought you your coat, Sir. It's very cold this evening.'

'Planchet!' cried d'Artagnan, wild with excitement.

'Planchet!' echoed Porthos and Aramis.

'Yes, it's Planchet,' said Athos, 'and what's surprising about that? He promised to be back at eight o'clock and there's eight striking now. Bravo, Planchet, you're a man of your word. If ever you leave your master you can always be sure of a place with me.'

'Oh no, Sir!' said Planchet. 'I'll never leave Monsieur d'Artagnan.'

At that moment d'Artagnan felt Planchet slip a little note into his hand. He had a strong impulse to fling his arms round the fellow's neck, but feared that the passers-by might be surprised at such a display of affection from a musketeer to his servant. So he restrained himself. But he whispered excitedly to his three friends:

'I've got a reply in writing.'

'Good,' said Athos. 'Let's go home and read it.'

The four started off in the direction of the camp. D'Artagnan was so impatient to read the note that he broke into a run. But Athos took hold of his arm, held him back and forced him to set his pace by him.

At last they reached the tent. They lit a lamp; Planchet stood on guard outside while d'Artagnan tremblingly broke the seal and opened the long awaited letter. It contained only these four words in English:

Thank you. Be easy.

Athos took the letter from d'Artagnan and held it over the flame of the lamp until it was burned to a cinder. Then he called Planchet and said:

'Now, my lad, you can have your second seven hundred livres. And consider yourself handsomely paid. You weren't risking much carrying a note like that.'

'Well, sir, I tried to make it as short as possible,' replied Planchet.

'Come on, Planchet, tell us the whole story,' said d'Artagnan.

'It'll take a long time, Sir,' replied Planchet.

'Leave it till later then,' said Athos. 'The tattoo's sounded and we'd be noticed if our tent was the only one with its light on.'

'Right,' said d'Artagnan. 'Let's turn in. Sleep well, Planchet.'

'It'll be the first good sleep I've had for a fortnight, Sir,' said Planchet.

'Same here,' said d'Artagnan.

'And here,' said Porthos.

'And here,' echoed Aramis.

'How about you, Athos?' inquired d'Artagnan.

'Well, if you must know, "Same here!" ' said Athos.

CHAPTER XII

Disaster

MEANWHILE Milady, wild with rage, was pacing up and down the deck of the ship that was carrying her out to sea. She had more than once considered throwing herself overboard and swimming to shore; the recollection of how Athos had browbeaten her and d'Artagnan insulted her still preyed on her mind and she was furious to think that she was leaving France without taking revenge on them. This thought had so obsessed her that she had actually begged the captain to turn back and put her ashore again. But the captain was in a hurry to escape from his dangerous position between the French and English cruisers and to reach England, and refused point blank to obey what he called a woman's whim. But he knew his passenger to be a protégée of the Cardinal, so he agreed to land her, sea and French garrison permitting, at one of the ports of Brittany, Lorient or Brest. But at present the wind was contrary and the sea rough; the ship had to keep tacking and jibbing. Not until nine days after leaving the mouth of the Charente did they see the faint, blue outline of the coast of Finisterre on the horizon. Milady reckoned that it would take three days to cross that corner of France and get back to the Cardinal, and one whole day to reach the coast – four days in all. Add to these the nine days they had already spent on the sea – thirteen days in all. Thirteen valuable days lost, during which many important events might be taking place in London! Milady knew that the Cardinal would be angry with her for returning and would therefore be more inclined to listen to accusations against her than to her accusations against others. So when the ship passed Lorient and Brest she did not hold the captain to his promise, and the captain was only too glad to let the matter drop.

So Milady continued her journey and arrived in Portsmouth harbour as His Eminence's envoy on the very day on which d'Artagnan's envoy, Planchet, was embarking there to return to France. The town was all bustle and excitement. Three large ships, recently built, had just been launched. On the jetty stood none other than His Grace the Duke of Buckingham, gorgeously dressed as usual, resplendent in gold lace and diamonds, surrounded by a staff almost as magnificently apparelled as himself. It was one of those rare summer days on which England remembers that there is a sun. It was evening and the sun was just setting on the horizon; still radiant, it shed a crimson glow on earth and sky and a last golden sheen on the towers and on the houses rising behind the town, making the windows glitter like sparks from a fire.

Milady stood on the deck enjoying the ocean air which grew balmier as the ship approached the shore. She gazed at the vast concourse of ships and men in the harbour, the product of a mighty organization, and realized with awe that to her had been entrusted the task of destroying it, to her alone, armed with a few purses of gold. Suddenly exalted by the magnitude of her task, she compared herself to Judith, the avenging Jewess, when she entered the camp of the Assyrians and beheld the array of chariots, horses, men and arms which she was to disperse with one stroke.

The ship entered the roadstead. As the crew were about to drop anchor a small cutter carrying heavy guns sailed up under her lee. She announced herself as a coastal patrol vessel and signalled that her captain wished to come aboard. Then the passengers on the brig saw a long-boat being launched with an officer, a boatswain, and a crew of eight, which ploughed its way alongside their vessel. A companionway was lowered and the officer came aboard the brig. He was received with the deference due to his uniform, exchanged a few words with the captain and showed him a warrant. The captain glanced at it and immediately ordered all the crew and passengers on deck. Then, in full hearing of everyone, the officer inquired where the brig hailed from, its course, and its ports of call. The captain answered the questions promptly. The officer then proceeded to inspect the passengers, who were lined up on deck. When he reached Milady he stopped and observed her closely without saying a word. He then turned to the captain and again muttered something to him in an undertone. The captain apparently recognized the officer's authority, for he now allowed him to take command of the ship. The officer shouted an order to the crew which was at once obeyed. The brig then got under weigh again, escorted by the cutter which sailed close under her helm with its five guns trained on her side. The longboat followed in her wake.

While the officer was observing Milady, she, as we can imagine, had also been busy scrutinizing him. But, astute as she was in reading the minds of those whose secrets she wished to discover, this time she found her victim so impassive that her scrutiny revealed nothing. The officer was about twenty-five, pale, and with light-blue, rather deep-set eyes. His mouth was sensitive and well-formed, his jaw determined, his forehead the high forehead of poets and visionaries, his hair close-cropped and, like his beard and moustache, chestnut-coloured.

When the ship anchored in the harbour it was already dark. There was a fog which made the night ever darker; round the lanterns on the jetty were circles of light like those round the moon when storms threaten. The air was damp and cold. Milady, indomitable as she was, shivered.

The officer had Milady's luggage brought from the hold and lowered into the long-boat. This done he invited her to step down and held out his hand to her. Milady stared hard at him and hesitated.

'Who are you?' she asked. 'And why am I singled out for this special attention?'

'You can see who I am from my uniform, Ma'am,' answered the young man. 'I'm a British naval officer.'

'Do all English people arriving from abroad have special escorts to take them on shore? A most remarkable piece of courtesy, if I may say so!'

'Yes, Ma'am,' replied the officer. 'It's our custom. And it's not courtesy but a war-time precautionary measure. We always take foreigners to special hostels and keep them under Government supervision until we can get official reports on them.'

The officer spoke casually and without a trace of embarrassment. But he did not succeed in reassuring Milady. In faultless English she replied:

'But I'm not a foreigner, Sir. My name's Clarice de Winter and this formality . . .'

'No one's exempt from this formality, Lady de Winter,' replied the officer. 'I'm afraid you'll have to go through with it.'

'Very well, Sir, I'll go with you.'

So saying she stepped on to the companion-way and walked down to the long-boat. The officer followed her. They had spread out a large cloak in the stern of the boat; the officer invited her to sit down and took his place beside her.

'Row ashore!' he called to the sailors.

The eight oars struck the water, the boat shot forward and in five minutes they reached the shore. The officer jumped on to the quay and offered his arm to Milady. A carriage was drawn up on the jetty.

'Is that carriage for us?' asked Milady.

'Yes, Lady de Winter,' replied the officer.

'Is the hostel a long way off?'

'Yes, at the far end of the town.'

'Very well,' said Milady. And she stepped into the carriage without protest. The officer stood for a while supervising the loading of the luggage; then he took his place beside his passenger and closed the carriage door.

The carriage now drove off at a brisk trot without any order being given to the coachman and soon disappeared into the maze of streets.

Her unusual reception had given Milady ample to think about. She looked at the young officer seated beside her and saw that he was not disposed to talk. So she leaned back in her corner of the carriage and reviewed in her mind the many possible explanations for this strange turn of events.

But after a quarter of an hour she began to be alarmed at the length of the journey and leaned out of the carriage window to see where they were taking her. There were no more houses to be seen. As they drove along, the trees in the darkness looked like a procession of tall, black ghosts. Milady began to be frightened. Turning to the officer she said:

'We're no longer in the town, sir!'

The young man said nothing.

'I warn you, Sir, unless you tell me where we're going I shan't drive another yard with you!'

Still the officer said nothing. Milady exclaimed:

'This is intolerable!'

Then, raising her voice, she called out:

'Help! Help!'

No one answered. The carriage drove on through the darkness. The young officer sat like a graven image.

Milady now gave him a terrible look calculated to make the strongest man quail. Her eyes flashed fire in the darkness. But the young man remained unmoved. She then tried to open the carriage door to jump out. The officer said coldly:

'Take care, Lady de Winter. If you do that you'll kill yourself.'

Milady sank back on her cushions, her face distorted with rage. The officer turned to look at her and was startled to see such beauty now transformed into something almost hideous. Milady realized that she was only harming herself by thus betraying her feelings. With an effort she controlled herself and in a pleading voice said:

'For pity's sake, Sir, tell me why I'm being abducted! Are you acting on your own, for your Government, or for someone who has a personal grudge against me?'

'There's no question of abducting, Lády de Winter,' said the officer. 'This is a formality which everyone who lands in England has to go through.'

'So you don't know who I am?'

'I've never set eyes on you till now, Lady de Winter.'

'You swear you've no reason to hate me?'

'None whatever, I promise you.'

The young man spoke quite naturally and with obvious sincerity. Milady was reassured.

After about an hour's journey the carriage drew up in front of an iron gate. This was opened from inside and the carriage drove through and up a long avenue, at the end of which stood a grim-looking stone castle, built on the edge of a cliff. As they drove up the avenue Milady heard in the distance the sound of the sea beating against a rocky shore. The carriage passed under two arches and finally drew up in a dark courtyard. Almost immediately the carriage door was opened from outside; the young officer jumped down and offered his hand to Milady, who took it and also stepped down. She was by now fairly calm again. She looked round her and, turning to the young officer, said with her most charming smile:

'You'll have to admit now that I'm a prisoner, Sir. But I'm sure it won't be for long. My conscience and your kindness convince me of that.'

This attempt at friendliness drew no response from the officer. He now pulled out of his belt a little silver boatswain's whistle and blew three sharp blasts. Immediately three men appeared from a side door, unharnessed the sweating horses and dragged the carriage into a shed.

In the same distantly polite manner the officer now invited his prisoner to enter the house. Milady took his arm and they walked through a low arched doorway into a vaulted passage which was lit only at the far end and led to a stone spiral staircase. They stopped in front of a massive door half-way down this passage; the officer fitted a key into the lock and the door swung heavily back on its hinges, disclosing a large room. He then stood aside to allow his prisoner to cross the threshold.

'This is to be your room, Lady de Winter,' he said.

Milady took in all its contents at a glance. The room was furnished handsomely for a prison cell but very severely for an ordinary room. But the windows were barred and the door had bolts on the outside and this left no doubt that it was intended for a cell.

For one moment Milady's indomitable strength of mind failed her. She collapsed into an arm-chair and sat in a hunched, cringing attitude, fear and guilt written all over her, staring at the door as though she expected at any moment to see some inquisitor enter and arraign her for her past crimes. But none came.

Instead three sailors appeared carrying her luggage, which they put down in the corner of the room. The officer supervised this work with the same thoroughness which he had hitherto shown in everything. He gave his orders not by word of mouth but by signs or blasts from his whistle. One would have said that he and his subordinates had never exchanged a word in their lives. At last Milady could stand it no longer. She broke the silence.

'In Heaven's name, Sir!' she cried. 'What does all this mean? Explain this mystery. I can bear any danger if I know what to expect, any ill-treatment if I know the reason for it. Where am I, and why am I here? Why those barred windows and those bolts on the door? Am I really a prisoner? If so, what crime have I committed?'

'Please don't question me, Lady de Winter,' replied the officer. 'I had orders to bring you ashore and escort you to the castle. I think I've carried them out without causing you undue discomfort. Now you're no longer in my charge. I'm to hand you over to someone else.'

'Who, who?' cried Milady. 'Can you tell me his name?'

At that moment there was a noise of spurs clanking in the passage, of voices raised and then of single footsteps approaching the door and stopping.

The officer stepped aside and stood to attention. In answer to Milady's question he said quickly:

'To the gentleman who's coming in now.'

The next moment the door opened and Milady saw a man standing on the threshold. He was hatless, carried a sword, and was clutching a handkerchief in one hand. He stood for a moment out of the light and Milady fancied she recognized this shadow in the shadows. Resting one hand on the arm of her chair she leaned forward and peered into the darkness to find out if what she suspected were true.

Now the stranger came slowly into the room. As he entered the circle of light cast by the lamp Milady started back. When there was no longer any doubt she cried out in a tone of utter amazement:

'Good God, de Winter!'

Lord de Winter bowed and smiled ironically.

'Yes, Clarice,' he said. 'Your brother-in-law.'

'And what's this building?'

'My home.'

'And this room?'

'Your room.'

'And what am I? Your guest or your prisoner?'

Lord de Winter shrugged his shoulders.

'Whichever you like to call it,' he said.

'But this is an outrage!'

'Don't fly into a rage, Clarice. Let's sit down and talk things over quietly, as brother and sister should.'

So saying Lord de Winter turned and addressed the young officer who was still standing at attention by the door.

'Thank you, Mr Felton,' he said. 'That's all for the present. You may now leave us.'

CHAPTER XIII

Conversation Between Brother and Sister

LORD DE WINTER closed the door behind the young officer, opened a grille in the panel and brought up a chair close to his sister-in-law's arm-chair. Meanwhile Milady was reviewing rapidly in her mind the various possible explanations for this extraordinary turn of events. She knew her brother-in-law to be a pleasure-loving man, a sportsman, gambler, and philanderer, a man without ambition and with no talent for intrigue. How had he discovered about her journey to England, why had he had her arrested, and why was he holding her a prisoner? From what Athos had said she gathered that he, and perhaps others too, had overheard her conversation with the Cardinal. But how could they have planned such an effective counter-stroke in so short a time? A more likely and alarming explanation for her seizure was that her previous intrigues in England had been discovered. Perhaps Buckingham had found out that it was she who had robbed him of the two diamonds and was now taking his revenge. But Buckingham, she knew, was always reluctant to take revenge on a woman, especially if he thought the woman had acted from motives of jealousy.

And yet the latter explanation seemed the most probable. Milady was convinced that this attack was a piece of revenge for some past action and not a precaution against some possible future action. She was thankful at least to have fallen into the hands of her brother-in-law, for she thought she could hope for better treatment from him than from some more cunning and unscrupulous enemy.

So she decided to adopt a friendly attitude towards him, wishing to find out all she could from him, so that she would know how to act. He would obviously try to throw dust in her eyes, but she hoped to outwit him. In answer to his proposal she therefore smiled and said:

'Yes, dear brother. Let's talk.'

'So you decided to return to England after all?' said Lord de Winter. 'And what about your resolve never to set foot in this country again?'

Milady parried this question with another question.

'You tell me first how you found out so much about me,' she said. 'How you discovered that I was on my way here; not only that, but how you knew what port I was arriving at and even the date and time of my arrival.'

Lord de Winter decided to follow his sister-in-law's tactics. They must be good, he argued, as she, who was such a mistress of intrigue, had adopted them.

'No, my dear,' he said. 'You tell me first why you've come to England at all.'

'Why? to see you, of course!' replied Milady.

She little knew that by this reply she was merely confirming her brother-in-law's suspicions, which had first been roused by d'Artagnan's letter. Her object in thus lying was merely to flatter him. De Winter smiled ironically.

'Oh, so you've come to see me!' he said.

'Of course. What's surprising about that?'

'Was that your only object in coming here?'

'Yes.'

'You crossed the Channel merely to see me?'

'Merely to see you.'

'Bless my soul! What affection, Clarice dear!'

Milady said blandly:

'Well, I am your nearest relative!'

'Yes, and my sole heir!' replied de Winter.

As he spoke he leaned forward, laid his hand on his sister-in-law's arm and stared pointedly at her.

For all her self-control Milady winced at this thrust. Lord de Winter felt her tremble and realized that he had struck home.

Milady's first thought was that Kitty had betrayed her, that she had told Lord de Winter of her dislike of him and its cause, which she had so foolishly revealed. And now she recalled how she had railed to Kitty about d'Artagnan having spared de

Winter's life. To gain time and to goad her brother-in-law to talk she now replied:

'What d'you mean, my dear de Winter? Are you insinuating something?'

Lord de Winter laughed good-humouredly.

'Good Heavens, no!' he said. 'You wanted to see me and came to England. That was very friendly of you. I heard or rather suspected you wanted to come. I know how unpleasant it is arriving at night in a foreign port and how tiring the business of landing is, so I sent one of my officers with a carriage to meet you. I told him to bring you to this castle. I'm in command here. These are my headquarters. We both wanted to see each other so I had a room got ready for you. What's more surprising in that than in your saying you came to England to see me?'

'Nothing, of course,' replied Milady. 'But what is surprising is that you knew I was coming.'

'I can explain that easily enough, my dear. I expect you noticed that when your ship entered the roadstead your captain sent out a pinnace with his log-book and a list of crew and passengers to get a permit to enter the harbour. I'm the Governor of the port, so the list was brought to me. I saw your name on it. My instinct told me what you've just confirmed in your own words, that you'd risked the dangers of the crossing merely to see me. So I sent my cutter out to meet you. The rest you know.'

Milady realized that Lord de Winter was lying and this made her more uneasy than ever.

'By the way,' she asked, 'wasn't it the Duke of Buckingham I saw on the jetty this evening as I arrived?'

'It was indeed,' replied de Winter. 'You must have been very interested to see him, coming from a country where he's a great deal in people's thoughts; I know his designs against France are worrying your friend the Cardinal quite a bit.'

Milady was alarmed to see that Lord de Winter was as well informed on this matter as on all else. She pretended to be surprised.

'My friend the Cardinal?' she echoed.

'Isn't he your friend?' de Winter asked casually. 'I'm sorry; I thought he was. Never mind. We can talk about Buckingham later. He's not so important. What is important is that you've come to England to see me, which pleases me very much. You said so yourself just now, remember!'

'Yes.'

'And I reply that I've arranged things so that you'll get your wish and see me every day.'

Milady now began to grow seriously alarmed.

'You don't mean to keep me here for ever, do you?' she asked.

'Why not? Are you afraid you won't be comfortable here? You've only got to say what you want and I'll see you get it at once.'

'But I haven't got my maids or my household with me.'

'All that will be seen to, my dear. Tell me what luxury you were used to when you lived with your first husband and, although I'm only your brother-in-law, I'll see you get the same here.'

Milady looked at Lord de Winter aghast.

'My first husband?' she echoed.

'Yes, your French husband. I don't mean my brother. Incidentally, in case you've forgotten him you may be interested to know he's still alive. If you like I'll write to him. He'll tell me all I need to know about the life you led with him.'

At this Milady went rigid with fear and clutched hold of the arms of her chair.

'You can't be serious!' she said hoarsely.

Lord de Winter got up and stood facing her, eyeing her sternly.

'And why not?' he said, his voice hard and cold.

Milady half rose in her chair, supporting herself by her arms.

'If you are serious you're insulting me!' she said.

Lord de Winter replied scornfully:

'Is it possible to insult you?'

'Either you're drunk or mad, Sir,' said Milady. 'Leave the room at once. And send a maid to look after me.'

'Maids can be very indiscreet, you know, Clarice. Why not let me look after you? Then all our secrets would stay in the family.'

'You insolent blackguard!' cried Milady.

And she sprang from her chair and rushed at Lord de Winter in a wild fury. The latter stood staring at her without moving, but instinctively put his hand to his sword-hilt.

'Steady on, steady on!' he said. 'I know murder means nothing to you, but I warn you, if you attack me, I shall defend myself.'

'I'm sure of that,' said Milady. 'I know you wouldn't hesitate to strike a woman.'

'If I did I should be perfectly justified,' replied de Winter. 'And in any case I don't think I'd be the first man who'd laid hands on you.'

As he spoke he slowly raised his arm and pointed accusingly at Milady's left shoulder, almost touching it with his finger. Milady bared her teeth in a snarl of rage and shrank back into the corner of the room, where she cowered like an animal at bay.

'Snarl away to your heart's content,' said Lord de Winter. 'But don't bite. You'll get the worst of it if you do. There are no lawyers here to arrange successions in advance, no knights-errant to rescue beautiful ladies imprisoned in castles by wicked men. No. But there are plenty of law-courts competent to deal with women who marry bigamously into rich families; you'll be sent to the public executioner who'll paint another pretty flower on your other shoulder.'

There was now a look of such fiendish rage on Milady's face that, though he was a man armed and she a woman, Lord de Winter, watching her, suddenly felt a chill run down his spine. He went on talking, however, and as he talked anger at her villainy seized him again and his momentary fear of her vanished.

'Yes,' he said, 'I realize that after inheriting my brother's money it would have been pleasant indeed to get hold of mine too. But please understand that I've insured against the possibility of your either murdering me yourself or getting me murdered. Neither you nor your son will inherit a penny of my money. Aren't you rich enough already? Why, you've got about half a million! You could easily stop your career of crime. But you go on with it purely for its own sake, because you enjoy doing wrong. I tell you straight out that if it weren't for my brother's memory I'd send you to rot in a state dungeon or to swing on Tyburn gallows and then get your son declared a bastard. But I'll hold my tongue. You, in return, must be resigned to your fate. In a fortnight or so I'm leaving with the army for La Rochelle. The day before I leave a ship will call to take you on board and I'll see you on to it. You'll be deported to one of our southern colonies. And to prevent your ever returning to England or the continent, I'm sending a man with you with orders to shoot you dead if you make any attempt to escape.'

Milady listened spellbound to this speech, staring at her brother-in-law with eyes still ablaze with rage and hate. Lord de Winter continued:

'For the present you'll remain in this castle. The walls are thick, the doors strong, and the bars solid. That wall over there's built right on the edge of the cliff, and the window looks sheer down into the sea. The troop under my command are loyal to a man; they've been detailed to stand guard round this room and to guard all the passages leading to the courtyard. Even if you reached the courtyard you'd still have three iron railings to get through. My orders to the guards are on no account to let you through and if you try to slip past them to fire on you. If they kill you I'm sure the authorities will be grateful to me for saving them the trouble. But I see you're calming down again; you look quite cheerful all of a sudden. I suppose you're thinking that a fortnight's grace will give you time to evolve some plan of escape; your fiendish brain's already working out some scheme and you think you'll find some poor simpleton to help you. Well, you're welcome to try.'

Milady, seeing her thoughts had been read, dug her nails into the palms of her hands to make sure of showing no emotion but pain.

Lord de Winter continued:

'You've seen the man who'll be in charge of you in my absence. You've probably noticed he's a very conscientious and discreet fellow. I daresay you questioned him on your way from Portsmouth and I'm sure you got nothing out of him. It must have been like talking to a stone. You've seduced men enough in your time, I know. But just try your tricks on that fellow! If you succeed with him I'll say you're Messalina herself.'

He now walked over to the door, flung it open, and called to one of his subordinates:

'Fetch Mr Felton!'

Then, turning to his sister-in-law, he said:

'I'm going to tell him the whole truth about you.'

An awkward silence now ensued between brother and sister. In a few moments they heard footsteps approaching. Then a shadow fell on the floor of the passage and the next moment the young officer who had escorted Milady from the boat appeared in the doorway. He stood to attention and saluted Lord de Winter.

'Come in, John, come in and shut the door.'

The young man stepped into the room.

'Take a good look at this woman,' said de Winter. 'As you see she's young and beautiful and very fascinating. Well, she's a fiend in human form. She's only twenty-five but she's already committed as many crimes as you could read in any of our law-courts' records for a year. She has a soft, enchanting voice; she uses her beauty to ensnare her victims. She'll certainly try to seduce you; she may even try to kill you. John Felton, I rescued you from penury; I got you your commission; I adopted you; I even saved your life once – you know when that was. But I'm not appealing to you as a creditor, but rather as a friend, as a father. This woman came to England to plot against my life. Luckily I've got her in my power now, viper that she is. Well, John, as a friend, as a father, I appeal to you once more: protect me from this woman and beware of her yourself. Swear by all you hold most dear to guard her well until she can be dealt with as she deserves. I'm counting on you, John. Don't fail me.'

The young officer eyed Milady with as much suspicion and hatred as his honest soul was capable of.

'Lord de Winter,' he said, 'I promise to carry out your orders to the letter.'

Milady responded to Felton's scrutiny by lowering her eyes and sitting with head bent and hands folded in her lap. She looked the very picture of injured innocence. Even Lord de Winter could hardly believe that she was the woman whom a few minutes before he had seen in a state of maniac rage.

'You understand, John, she must never be allowed to leave this room,' continued de Winter. 'She mustn't write letters. And she mustn't talk to anyone but you, that is provided you've no objection to speaking to someone so vile.'

'I understand, Sir. I'll see that everything's done as you say.'

'And now, Clarice,' said de Winter, 'you must try and make your peace with God. This world has already passed sentence on you.'

Milady lowered her eyes again as though crushed by his words. Lord de Winter now left the room, signing to Felton to follow him. A moment later the prisoner heard a heavy step pacing up and down the passage; it was the sentry detailed to guard her, doing duty, axe in belt and pike in hand.

For a few minutes after her gaolers had left Milady sat motionless, head bowed; she dared not move, fearing that eyes were watching her through the grille in the panel of the door. Then she slowly looked up again. There was now a wild light of battle in her eyes. She got up and ran to the door to listen; then she ran over to the window and looked out. Then she returned to her vast arm-chair, sank down in it and started to meditate.

CHAPTER XIV

Officer!

MEANWHILE the Cardinal was growing alarmed. He was daily expecting news from England but none came. La Rochelle was now satisfactorily invested on land by the besieging troops and at sea by the newly-constructed dyke, which effectively prevented all ships from entering the harbour. Ultimate success seemed certain and yet the blockade might continue for many more months. This was bad for the morale of the King's troops and irritating for their commander. His Eminence, who had so skilfully sown discord between the King and the Queen, was now faced with the more ticklish task of making peace between Bassompierre and the Duc d'Angoulême. As for Monsieur, who had started the siege, he had left its completion entirely in the hands of his successor to the command.

In spite of the amazing example of fortitude shown by the Mayor of La Rochelle the citizens had once mutinied in favour of surrender. The Mayor had had all the ringleaders hanged. This measure had subdued all the worst elements in the town, who thenceforth resigned themselves to the prospect of death by starvation, which they considered a slower and less certain death than death by strangulation.

Mutinies inside and executions of spies outside the city walls were the chief events of this period of stagnation. Every day messengers sent by the people of La Rochelle to Buckingham or by Buckingham to the citizens would be captured by the besieging army and summarily dealt with by the Cardinal, who always had them hanged. The King usually attended these executions, for they helped him to pass the time and bear the tedium of the siege. He would come quite casually and choose a place from which he could watch the operation in all its details. He nevertheless constantly complained of boredom and often talked of returning to Paris. If there was ever a shortage of hangings His Eminence was hard put to it to keep His Majesty amused.

The days passed and still the Rochellese held out. The last spy captured had had a letter on him addressed to Buckingham, telling him that the town was on its last legs. But instead of adding, 'If you do not send help within a fortnight we shall surrender', it said quite plainly, 'If you do not send help within a fortnight we shall all be dead from starvation by the time it arrives'. This letter proved that the Rochellese were now relying entirely on Buckingham. He was to be their saviour. If they ever discovered for certain that Buckingham would fail them they would immediately collapse.

So the Cardinal waited with the utmost impatience for news from England, telling him that Buckingham would not set sail. The plan of taking La Rochelle by storm had often been debated by the King in Council but always rejected on both strategic and political grounds. La Rochelle was considered by the generals to be impregnable, and the Cardinal shrank from attacking it for political reasons. He realized that any battle in which Frenchmen fought Frenchmen would be a retrograde movement of sixty years, for which he, as a progressive statesman, would most certainly be criticized. Indeed the sack of La Rochelle and the massacre of three or four thousand Huguenots which would inevitably ensue would, in that year of grace 1628, have been too reminiscent of the Massacre of St Bartholomew of 1572. His Eminence was therefore debarred from any action on those lines, and his only hope was to get news from England.

But he was not happy about the fate of his envoy. He knew Milady's extraordinary capacities, her leonine courage and feline guile. She even frightened him a little. Where was she now? Why had he heard no news from her? Had she betrayed him? Was she dead? He knew her well enough to realize that whether working as friend or foe she was not one to remain inactive. What then was the explanation of her silence? He was worried. And yet he felt he could trust her. He had guessed that there were things in her past life from which only his red robes could protect her, and that she would be true to him because he was the only man powerful enough to keep her foes at bay.

So he finally decided to carry on the campaign alone and to regard anything else that would further his plan as incidental good fortune. He gave orders for the completion of the famous dyke which was intended to starve La Rochelle into submission. Meanwhile he pictured in his mind's eye the distress of the inhabitants in the unfortunate city, which was holding out so valiantly. And he remembered the maxim so often quoted by his political predecessor, Louis XI, 'Divide et impera', and saw how it could be applied to the present situation.

Henry IV, when besieging Paris, had had food thrown over the walls to the citizens. The Cardinal devised a scheme of throwing leaflets over the walls of La Rochelle which described the behaviour of the city's leaders as selfish, unjust, and barbarous. It was true that the leaders had a store of corn which they refused to issue to the population; they acted on the principle that it did not matter how many old men, women, and children died provided that the men who were defending the walls were kept healthy. So far no one had disputed this principle. But the leaflets attacked it. They reminded the citizens that these old men, women, and children who were being allowed to die were their own fathers, wives, and sons, and suggested that it would be more just if all the population were made to suffer equally, for then any edict passed would be in the interests of the community as a whole.

These leaflets had the effect which their author hoped for. They persuaded large numbers of the population to open negotiations with the King's armies. But just as the Cardinal was beginning to enjoy the fruits of his scheme and to congratulate himself on its success a citizen of La Rochelle managed to slip through the royal lines and enter the city. This man came from Portsmouth with news of a magnificent English fleet, manned, equipped and ready to set sail within a week. Buckingham had sent a special message by this man to the Mayor to say that the Grand Alliance against France was about to declare itself and that France herself would shortly be invaded simultaneously by the armies of England, Austria, and Spain. This letter was read

aloud in all the squares and copies of it were posted up at every
street corner. Even those who had begun negotiations with the
enemy now broke them off and decided to hold out until help
came.

This untoward event restored all Richelieu's previous misgivings and forced him once more to turn his attention to
England.

The besieging army was in no way affected by its commander's cares; on the contrary, the soldiers were leading a
riotous life. There was plenty of food and money in the camp
and the regiments tried to outshine each other in feats of daring. Capturing and hanging spies, making hazardous excursions
on the dyke or on the sea, devising and executing wild raids —
such exploits helped the army to pass those never-ending days,
hateful to besiegers and besieged alike.

It was the Cardinal's habit to ride through the camp and
the surrounding districts unescorted and as simply dressed as
any private in his army. He would inspect the constructions on
the dyke which progressed very slowly in spite of the fact that
he had summoned engineers from every corner of France to
work on them. If on these excursions His Eminence ever met
any musketeers of Monsieur de Tréville's company, he would
ride up and scrutinize them closely. Having assured himself
that they were none of our four friends he would ride off and
turn his attention to solving some fresh strategical problem.

One afternoon, a prey to deadly boredom, frustrated in his
efforts to negotiate with the town, still without news from
England, the Cardinal left the camp without any object except
to escape from it. He was accompanied only by Cahusac and
La Houdinière. He rode along the seashore, finding the vastness
of the ocean in harmony with the vastness of his plans. Then
he turned inland and rode along for about an hour, finally arriving at the top of a hill from where he could see a certain
distance round him. Suddenly he caught sight of a party of
seven men sprawling on the grass behind a hedge, about thirty
yards away. Four of these men were our musketeers. One of
them had a letter in his hand, which he was apparently reading

aloud to the other three, who had their heads close to his. All four looked highly conspiratorial. Their three servants were seated a little way off, busy uncorking a demijohn of Collioure wine.

As we have said, the Cardinal was in a depressed mood. And when he was depressed nothing irritated him more than to see others enjoying themselves. He always imagined that the things which depressed him were the very things which made the rest of the world laugh. The sight of the little party laughing and talking behind the hedge annoyed him and, signing to Cahusac and la Houdinière to halt, he dismounted and walked towards them. He hoped that the sound of his footsteps would be muffled by the grass, that the hedge would hide him, and that he would be able to approach to within earshot of these men and overhear their talk. When he was about ten feet from the hedge he recognized d'Artagnan's Gascon brogue, and was convinced that the other three were Athos, Porthos, and Aramis. This conviction made him all the more anxious to find out what they were discussing. A crafty look came into his eyes and he tiptoed lightly up to the hedge and stood listening. But he had managed to catch only a few words which gave him no clue when someone behind the hedge suddenly shouted out:

'Officer!'

The Cardinal was startled and the musketeers at once looked up. The shout had come from Grimaud.

Athos raised himself up on one elbow, glared at him and said:

'Did I hear you speak, rascal?'

Grimaud said not another word but merely pointed in the direction of the hedge to announce the presence of the Cardinal and his escort.

The four musketeers at once got up and saluted him. His Eminence was furious.

'Is it usual for Musketeers to post sentries to guard them?' he said. 'Are you expecting a land attack by the English, playing at being officers, or what?'

In the general panic Athos alone of the four kept his head. He replied:

'Your Eminence, when Musketeers are off duty they drink and gamble and rank as officers in the eyes of their servants.'

The Cardinal retorted angrily:

'Did you say servants? They look more like sentries to me.'

Athos replied calmly:

'You'll agree, Sir, that if we hadn't posted the men there you'd have passed without our knowing and we'd have missed an opportunity of thanking you for your kindness in appointing us all to the same regiment. D'Artagnan here was just wondering when he'd be able to thank Your Eminence. Now's your chance, d'Artagnan.'

D'Artagnan went up to the Cardinal and tried to stammer a few words of thanks. But he faltered under the Cardinal's stern gaze. The latter was in no way appeased by Athos' attempt to smooth matters over and was still determined to discover what the four men were doing.

'That's all very well, gentlemen,' he said. 'But I don't like to see private soldiers behaving like officers just because they happen to belong to a crack regiment. Army regulations apply to you as much as to anyone else.'

Athos replied:

'Yes, Sir. But I don't think we've infringed army regulations. We were off duty and thought we could do as we liked. If you've some special duty for us, Sir, we're at your service. We've come armed, as you see, so we're ready to report at a moment's notice.'

And he pointed to their four muskets which were piled in a corner of the field. D'Artagnan now broke in:

'We'd have stood to attention at once, Sir, if we'd have known it was you coming up with such a small escort.'

At this the Cardinal frowned angrily. He replied:

'D'you realize the impression you four fellows give, always together, always armed and always guarded by your servants? You look as though you were plotting.'

Athos replied:

'And so we are, Sir. And so we were the other morning in the St Gervais bastion, as Your Eminence probably noticed. We're plotting against the Rochellese.'

The Cardinal replied, still frowning:

'Politicians, eh? Yes, I don't doubt there's a lot going on in those heads of yours. I wish I could read them as easily as you were reading that letter you stuffed away so hurriedly when you saw me.'

Athos flushed angrily and strode up to the Cardinal.

'You seem to suspect us of something, Monseigneur,' he said. 'Is this a cross-examination, Sir? If you do suspect us, please say so. Then we shall know where we stand.'

The Cardinal replied:

'And what if I am cross-questioning you? I've cross-questioned others before you and they've had to answer.'

'Yes, Sir, that's why I'm asking you to put straight questions to us, so that we can give you straight answers.'

'Very well. What was that letter you were just going to read, Monsieur Aramis?' said the Cardinal. 'And why did you hide it away when you saw me?'

'It was a letter from a woman, Monseigneur.'

'I see,' replied the Cardinal. 'One mustn't flaunt women's letters about, I grant you. But one can always show them to a father confessor. And I've taken Orders, you know.'

To this Athos retorted calmly:

'That letter's from a woman, Sir, as Aramis said. But it's not signed Marion de Lorme, Madame Combalet, or Madame d'Aiguillon.'

His coolness was all the more terrifying because he knew that this piece of insolence might well cost him his head.

The Cardinal went deathly pale and his eyes flashed fire. He whipped round as though to give a swift order to Cahusac and La Houdinière. Athos saw him turn and instinctively backed in the direction of the muskets. His three friends also edged towards them, eyeing the Cardinal and his escort warily. It was obvious that all four were preparing to resist arrest, and that if attacked they would defend themselves.

The Cardinal was convinced that the four men had in fact been plotting. But he also realized that the odds were four to three against him. So to save his face he did a quick mental somersault, suppressed his anger and said with a smile:

'All right, all right! You're first-rate young fellows, all of you. I forgive you. After all you're quite entitled to guard yourselves seeing how well you guard other people. I haven't forgotten the night you escorted me to the Red Dovecote inn and back. And if I were in danger now I'd ask you to escort me again. But I'm in no danger, so stay where you are and finish your drink and your letter. Good-bye, gentlemen.'

So saying he called to Cahusac to bring up his horse, leapt into the saddle and rode off. The four young men stood silent and motionless, watching his retreating figure until it disappeared from sight. Then they turned and looked at each other. Porthos, Aramis, and d'Artagnan were badly shaken. They knew quite well that the Cardinal's friendly farewell had been a pretence and that he was still very angry with them. Only Athos smiled cynically.

At last Porthos exclaimed:

'That Grimaud of yours was damned late warning us!'

He was thoroughly unnerved and determined to vent his spleen on somebody.

Grimaud was about to apologize but Athos signed to him to keep quiet.

'Would you have handed over the letter, Aramis?' asked d'Artagnan.

'If he'd insisted on seeing the letter I'd have held it out with one hand and run him through with the other.'

'I was expecting you to do that,' said Athos. 'That's why I got between you and him. His Eminence had no right to talk to us like that. You'd think he'd only had to deal with women and children all his life.'

D'Artagnan said:

'I admire you, Athos. But you must admit we were in the wrong.'

'What d'you mean, in the wrong?' replied Athos. 'Damn it

all, who does this air belong to and the ocean over there? And the grass we're lying on? And that letter from your mistress? To the Cardinal? Of course not! That fellow thinks the whole world belongs to him. You were all standing there gaping like idiots; you looked as though the Bastille were looming in front of you and the earth about to open and swallow you up. Can being in love be called plotting? You're in love with a woman whom the Cardinal's imprisoned. You want to get her out of his hands. That's a personal matter between you and him. That letter's one of your trump cards. Why show your hand to your opponent? Let him guess it if he can. Aren't we trying to guess his?'

'Yes, Athos,' said d'Artagnan. 'That's true enough.'

'Well then, let's forget the whole incident, and let Aramis go on with the letter from where he left off when His Eminence interrupted him.'

Aramis pulled the letter out of his pocket. The three friends gathered round and the lackeys continued uncorking the demi-john.

'You'd only read a line or two,' said d'Artagnan. 'So start again from the beginning.'

'Very well,' said Aramis. And he read:

My dear Cousin,

I think I shall soon be leaving for Béthune where my sister has sent our little servant girl to the Carmelite Convent. The poor child is resigned to this move. She knows she can't live anywhere else with safety to her soul. But if our family affairs are soon settled in the way we hope I think she'll risk damnation and return to those friends she longs more than ever to see, now that she knows they still think of her.

Meanwhile she is not too unhappy. But she would like a letter from her lover. I know it's difficult to smuggle goods of that kind through barred windows. But I think I've already proved to you, dear cousin, that I am quite clever at that sort of thing, and I'll see that it's delivered safely.

My sister thanks you for your kind messages. She was very anxious for a time but is slightly more cheerful now. She has sent her agent to the place in question to see that nothing terrible happens.

Good-bye, dear cousin. Write as often as you can, that is to say whenever you think you can do so safely.

All my love,

Marie Michon.

'I'm very, very grateful to you, Aramis,' cried d'Artagnan. 'Dear Constance. At last I've had news of her. She's alive. She's safe in a convent at Béthune. Where exactly is Béthune, Athos?'

'On the borders of Artois and Flanders. When the siege is over we might visit it.'

'It oughtn't to be long now,' said Porthos. 'They hanged another spy this morning; the fellow had a message on him that the Rochellese were now eating shoe leather. I suppose when they've finished the leather they'll get to work on the soles, and after that I don't quite know what they'll live on, unless they start eating each other.'

Athos put a bottle of claret to his lips and drained the contents.

'Silly asses!' he said. 'Why won't they see that Catholicism's the best and pleasantest religion in the world? Never mind, they're a gallant lot.'

Then he went on:

'You weren't thinking of putting that letter back in your pocket, were you, Aramis?'

'For God's sake don't,' said d'Artagnan. 'That letter must be burned. I doubt if we'll be safe even then. The Cardinal's probably invented a way of making cinders talk.'

'Well, what can we do with it?' asked Porthos.

'Grimaud, come here,' called Athos.

Grimaud got up and walked over to his master.

'As a punishment for talking without leave, Grimaud, you'll have to swallow this letter. As a reward for your smart work just now you may wash it down with this glass of wine. Here's the letter first. Chew it up well.'

Grimaud smiled wryly. Then, fixing his eye on the glass of

wine which Athos was holding out to him he chewed up the piece of paper and swallowed it.

'Bravo, Grimaud,' said Athos. 'And now take this. And don't bother to say thank you.'

Grimaud drank down the claret in silence. But the look in his eyes spoke volumes.

'And now,' said Athos, 'unless the Cardinal has the bright idea of slitting Grimaud's guts open I think we can be easy.'

Meanwhile the Cardinal continued his melancholy ride. From time to time he muttered to himself:

'I must have those four men on my side.'

CHAPTER XV

First Day of Captivity

LET us now return to Milady, whom we have neglected for a time in order to attend to more pressing events in France. We find her in the same state of despair in which we left her, meditating in her arm-chair. Her position seemed hopeless and for the first time in her life she was at a loss; for the first time in her life she was frightened.

Fate had betrayed her twice. Twice she had been unmasked and outwitted, both times by the new enemy who had lately crossed her path and whom doubtless the Lord had sent against her to destroy her. She, the incarnation of Evil, who thought herself supreme, had been defeated by d'Artagnan. He had played fast and loose with her affections, humbled her pride and thwarted her ambition. Not content with that he was now endangering her inheritance, attacking her liberty, and even threatening her life. Worst of all he had discovered and exposed her secret, which she had vowed no man should know and live, and had thereby revealed the chink in her armour.

D'Artagnan had saved Buckingham, whom she now hated as she hated every man whom she had ever loved, from the check-mate with which Richelieu had threatened him through the medium of the Queen. D'Artagnan had thwarted Milady in her pursuit of de Wardes, for whom she had had a wild animal passion. Finally, when she had obtained from the Cardinal a signed warrant authorizing her to punish him it had been seized from her and she herself was now a prisoner, destined for Botany Bay or some other horrible penal settlement.

There could be no question that d'Artagnan was the active agent in this final reverse. Who but he could have given Lord de Winter a clue to the many ugly facts which a malignant Fate had seen fit to reveal to him? He knew her brother-in-law; he had obviously written to him.

What hatred, what malevolence shone in her eyes as she sat crouched in her arm-chair in her bare room in that desolate castle high on the cliff! And what a fitting accompaniment to the surf breaking in hopeless fury against the rocks were her low growls of baffled rage! Many and terrible were the plans she laid for future revenge against Madame Bonacieux, Buckingham, and above all d'Artagnan.

Yes, but to take revenge one must be free, and she was a prisoner. To escape from prison you have to make holes in walls, tear up floorboards, and loosen bolts, tasks possible for a strong and determined man but impossible for a mere woman. Besides, for attempts of that kind you need time, long months, years even. And Milady knew from what her gaoler brother-in-law had said that she had only a fortnight's grace.

Yet had she been a man no effort of that sort would have been too great for her. She had a man's courage and brain and cursed Fate for having given her a woman's frail body.

So her early moments of captivity had been terrible. Being a woman she had at first been unable to control her feelings. But by degrees she had calmed down. Now she was sitting in her arm-chair, coiled up like a snake resting after a contest and gathering strength to strike again. She gazed at the mirror which reflected the light of anger in her eyes and muttered, as though addressing her image in the glass:

'Fool, to give way like that! Never show rage! Rage is a sign of weakness and impresses no one. You might cow women with it. But you're dealing with men now and to men you're only a woman. So use a woman's weapons and make your weakness your strength.'

Then, as though testing her powers or rehearsing a part, she started to practise facial expressions in the glass, expressions of fear, despair, outraged innocence, and humble submissiveness. She then arranged her hair in the manner which became her best. Satisfied at last she muttered to herself:

'All is not yet lost. I'm still beautiful.'

It was now about eight in the evening. Milady had noticed a bed in the corner of the room. It occurred to her that a few hours' rest would refresh her mind and her ideas and remove the pallor from her cheeks. But before she lay down another and better idea suggested itself. She had heard her gaolers mention supper; they would probably soon be bringing it, as it was already so late. Time was important and she decided to make an attempt that very evening to study the characters of the men who had been put in charge of her.

At that moment a light appeared under the door. Milady guessed that her gaolers were returning. She was standing up when she first saw the light, but she now flung herself into her arm-chair and lay there with her head thrown back, her beautiful hair loose and becomingly dishevelled, one hand on her heart and the other hanging down over the arm of the chair. Now the bolts were drawn back, the door creaked on its hinges and she heard footsteps entering the room and approaching to within a few feet of her. She then heard the young lieutenant Felton say:

'Put the table down there!'

He was obeyed.

'Bring torches and relieve the sentry!' continued Felton.

Milady, hearing both these orders, realized that she was to have soldiers to wait on her as well as to guard her.

Felton's instructions were carried out silently and swiftly, which proved that he was a good disciplinarian. Till that moment the young man had not glanced at Milady. Now he turned and looked at her.

'I see the prisoner's asleep,' he said to the men. 'Never mind. She can have her supper when she wakes up.'

He was about to leave the room when one of the soldiers, who was less of a martinet than his officer, happened to glance closely at Milady and called out:

'The prisoner's not asleep, Sir!'

'Not asleep?' said Felton.

'No, Sir. She's fainted. She looks very pale and I can't hear her breathing.'

Felton made no move in Milady's direction but observed her from where he was.

'You're right,' he said. 'She has fainted. Go and let Lord de Winter know his prisoner's ill. I daren't do anything myself. I wasn't told what to do if the prisoner became ill.'

The soldier went out. Felton sat down in an arm-chair near the door and waited in silence for the man to return. Milady had the feminine trick of noticing movements in a room by reflections in mirrors or shadows on walls. Through the mirror opposite she saw Felton sitting with his back to her. She gazed at his reflection a full three minutes and for the whole of that time the inhuman fellow did not once turn round to look at her. Milady realized that Lord de Winter would soon be there and that his presence would give the young man more confidence. Her first attempt to rouse his interest had therefore failed. She lifted her head, opened her eyes and moaned faintly. Hearing her, Felton at last looked round.

'Ah, you're awake, Lady de Winter,' he said. 'In that case I won't stay any longer. If you want anything you'll call, won't you?'

Milady replied in her melodious voice, which, like the sirens of old, she used to ensnare those whom she wished to destroy:

'Oh God, where am I? Have I been ill?'

And she sat up in her arm-chair in an even more alluring attitude than that in which she had been lying. Felton got up and said drily:

'You'll be served three meals a day, Lady de Winter; at nine in the morning, at one, and again at eight in the evening. If this arrangement doesn't suit you please say what hours you would prefer and we'll fall in with your wishes.'

Milady exclaimed:

'Surely I'm not going to be left entirely alone in this great, gloomy room!'

'Lord de Winter's hired a woman from the village to wait on you and keep you company. You can have her with you whenever you like.'

'I'm much obliged to you, Sir,' replied Milady humbly.

Felton bowed, turned and walked to the door. Just as he was leaving the room Lord de Winter appeared in the passage, followed by the soldier who had been sent to tell him of Milady's illness. He held a bottle of smelling-salts. When he saw the prisoner sitting up in her chair and Felton leaving the room he said sarcastically:

'Well, what's all this about? What's been happening in here? The resurrection of the dead already? My poor Felton, didn't you see she was only pretending? That was the first scene of a play which no doubt we shall see acted out in full as the days go by.'

'I suspected it was a trick, my Lord,' replied Felton. 'But as the prisoner was a woman I wanted to show her some chivalry. I owe it to myself if not to her.'

At these words Milady felt her blood run cold.

De Winter laughed.

'What, you stony-hearted fellow!' he cried. 'Are you still impervious to her charms? Haven't her beautiful dishevelled locks bewitched you yet? Have her lily-white skin and languishing glances made no impression on you?'

'No, my Lord,' replied the young man gravely. 'I wouldn't let a woman's wiles lead me astray.'

'In that case, my dear fellow, let's leave my sister-in-law to think out some other trick and go and have supper. Don't worry, she's got an inventive mind and I don't doubt we'll have the second act of the drama soon enough.'

So saying Lord de Winter took the young lieutenant's arm and led him away, laughing uproariously.

'I'll get even with you yet!' hissed Milady through clenched teeth. 'You miserable monk! You mockery of a soldier!'

Lord de Winter stopped at the door, turned round and said:

'By the way, don't let this setback destroy your appetite, dear Clarice. Try the chicken and the fish. I promise you I haven't had them poisoned. I'm rather proud of my cook, and as he's not my heir I'm not frightened of his concoctions. You can trust him too. Good-bye, sister dear, till your next fainting fit!'

These taunts infuriated Milady. She bit her lip and clutched the arms of her chair to control herself. When her gaolers had gone and she was alone again, she was once more filled with despair. She noticed a knife gleaming on the table, rushed towards it and seized it, but to her dismay saw that the blade was silver and quite blunt. At that moment she heard a shout of ironical laughter from the other side of the door, which was then flung open, revealing Lord de Winter and Felton.

'Look, Felton, my lad!' cried de Winter. 'What did I tell you? That knife was meant for you. She'd have killed you. It's a habit of hers with people who stand in her way. If I'd listened to you the knife would have been steel and that would have been the end of John Felton. She'd have stabbed you first and the rest of us afterwards. Look, John, how well she holds her dagger!'

Milady was, in fact, still standing with her arm raised, clutching the knife. But this final taunt was too much for her. She had a sudden sense of helplessness; the strength left her body; she let her hand drop to her side and the knife clattered to the floor.

Felton replied disgustedly:

'You were right, Sir, and I was wrong.'

Upon which both men turned and walked down the passage.

This time Milady listened closely until she heard their footsteps growing faint in the distance. Then she muttered to herself:

'I'm lost! I'm in the hands of men as cold and inhuman as

granite. They know me too well; they're not deceived by me and they've got no pity for me.'

She thought for a moment. Then she muttered to herself again:

'But this little episode can't end as they want it to. No, it's impossible. It could never happen!'

This return of optimism, this instinctive revival of hope was characteristic of Milady. Fear and despair never prevailed long in her rascally mind. She sat down at the table, ate some of the supper, drank a little Spanish wine and felt all her energy return. Before she went to bed she reviewed and analysed all the words, gestures, looks, and even the silences of her two gaolers. And from this close study, carried out with all her powers of insight, she came to the important conclusion that of the two men Felton was the least invulnerable.

Milady recalled one remark in particular. Lord de Winter had said to Felton:

'If I'd listened to you . . .'

This meant that Felton had spoken in her favour, because Lord de Winter had refused to listen to him.

'That man has a spark of pity in his soul,' thought Milady. 'It may be only an ember, but from it I'll fan a blaze which may destroy him yet. De Winter knows what to expect from me if ever I get free, so it's no use trying to gull him. But Felton's another matter. He's simple, guileless, and apparently inexperienced – in fact easier prey.'

With this thought to console her Milady went to bed and fell asleep. And in her sleep she smiled. Anyone observing her would have taken her for a young girl dreaming of the wreath of roses which she was to wear at the next carnival.

CHAPTER XVI

Second Day of Captivity

MILADY was in point of fact dreaming that she had d'Artagnan in her power at last, and that she was watching him being tortured. It was the sight of his blood flowing under the headsman's axe which had brought that beatific smile to her lips. Lulled by the hope of influencing Felton she slept soundly and awoke refreshed.

When the soldiers came into her room next morning she was still in bed. Felton had brought the village woman who was to wait on her; he sent her into the bedroom while he himself remained outside. The woman went up to Milady and offered her services. Milady was naturally pale, and people seeing her for the first time often thought that her pallor was due to illness. She said to the woman:

'I'm feverish. I didn't sleep at all last night. I feel very unwell. I hope you'll be kinder to me than the others were yesterday. I only ask to be allowed to stay in bed.'

'Would you like me to fetch a doctor?' asked the woman.

Felton standing in the doorway heard this little dialogue but said nothing. Milady realized that if she had too many people to visit her Lord de Winter would suspect that she was trying to play on their feelings and would set a stricter guard on her. Moreover the doctor would discover that her illness was a sham. She had lost the first round and was determined not to lose the second.

'Fetch a doctor?' she echoed. 'What good would that do? The gentlemen said yesterday that my illness was a sham. They obviously still think it's a sham, otherwise they'd have sent for a doctor themselves long ago.'

Felton broke in impatiently:

'Please say what you'd like us to do, Lady de Winter.'

'How can I say? I only know I feel ill. You can do what you like – I don't care.'

Felton was puzzled how to act.

'Go and fetch Lord de Winter,' he said to the woman.

'Oh no, Sir, no!' cried the prisoner. 'Please don't bring him here! I'm all right. I don't need anything. Don't call Lord de Winter.'

She put such a convincing note of terror into her voice that Felton was moved against his better judgement and came into the room.

'I touched him then,' thought Milady.

'If you're really ill, Lady de Winter,' he said, 'we'll certainly send for a doctor. But if you're playing a trick you'll be punished. But at least we'll have nothing to reproach ourselves with.'

Milady did not answer. She merely laid her head back on the pillow and started to weep helplessly. Felton watched her for a while, calm and aloof as ever. Then he saw that by remaining there he was only aggravating her paroxysm, so he turned abruptly and left the room. The woman followed him. Lord de Winter did not appear.

Milady, alone once more, stopped acting. A light of triumph shone in her eyes as she murmured:

'At last I'm beginning to see a ray of hope.'

Then she covered her face to hide from any spies behind the door this surge of inner joy.

Two hours passed.

'It's now time for my illness to end,' thought Milady. 'I'll get up now and start my counter-attack. There's not a moment to lose. I've only got a fortnight to work in and by this evening two days will have gone.'

When the soldiers had come in that morning they had brought the prisoner her breakfast. She realized that they would soon be returning to remove it and counted on seeing Felton then. She was not disappointed. In a few minutes Felton came in with the soldiers and ordered them to remove the breakfast table without looking to see whether the prisoner had eaten. The young officer stayed behind after the others had gone. He had a book in his hand. Milady was sitting in an arm-chair by the fireplace, looking like a saint awaiting martyrdom. Felton went up to her and said:

'Lord de Winter's a Catholic like yourself, Ma'am, and he thought you might be unhappy if you were deprived of the solace of your religion. So he's decided to let you read your Mass every day. Here is a missal.'

Milady was struck by the odd manner in which Felton placed the book on the table and by the sneering tone in which he said 'your Mass'. She scrutinized him closely. When she noticed his cropped hair, his grotesquely simple clothes and his stern, set expression she realized in a flash that he was one of those austere Puritans whom she had so often met at the Courts of James I and Louis XIII, where, even after the massacre of St Bartholomew, they still took refuge from time to time. She then had one of those sudden inspirations peculiar to people of genius in great crises. Those two words 'your Mass' and a single glance at Felton had made clear to her that by one bold stroke she might save herself and utterly defeat her brother-in-law. She sat bolt upright in her chair and with a note of scorn which matched the scorn in the young officer's voice cried:

'My Mass? Did you say my Mass? Lord de Winter's a wicked Catholic. He knows quite well I won't have anything to do with his religion. It's a trap he's set for me.'

Felton was frankly astonished at this and started involuntarily.

'What is your faith then, Lady de Winter?' he asked.

Milady put on a rapt air.

'I shall never declare my faith until I've suffered enough for it,' she said.

She saw from Felton's looks how much her words had moved him. However he said nothing. With the same rapt air and in the intense manner affected by Puritans of that date she continued:

'I'm in the hands of my enemies. Either it will please my God to save me or I shall die for His sake. That's my reply to Lord de Winter.'

Then, pointing to the prayer-book and eyeing it askance as though it were an evil thing, she said:

'As for that book, please take it back or use it yourself. You're obviously in complete sympathy with Lord de Winter, both in his persecution of me and in his heretical beliefs.'

Felton said nothing. He took up the book with a look of disgust and left the room.

At about five o'clock that evening Lord de Winter appeared. Milady had had the whole day in which to think out her plan of campaign and received him with the confident air of a gambler who has all the cards in her hand.

De Winter sat down in an arm-chair facing his prisoner and stretched his legs out comfortably on the hearth.

'I gather you've changed your religion,' he said.

'What d'you mean, Sir?' asked Milady.

'I mean I'm surprised to hear you've become a Protestant all of a sudden. A very quick apostasy if I may say so! You haven't by chance married a third husband recently? A Protestant?'

Milady replied haughtily:

'Please explain yourself, Sir. I don't know what you're talking about.'

Lord de Winter answered with a sneer:

'I suppose you mean you've got no religion at all. It's quite a relief to hear you say that!'

'It must indeed be a relief not to have to bother about my salvation since you're so little concerned with your own,' replied Milady coldly.

'I meant I was relieved to hear you admit you've got no religion,' said Lord de Winter.

'You don't need to proclaim your ungodliness,' replied Milady. 'Your crimes and debauches speak for themselves.'

'Did you say *my* crimes and debauches, Madame Messalina? I think I must have misheard you, Lady Macbeth!'

'You're talking like this merely to impress the people listening behind the door,' said Milady coldly. 'You're trying to influence your gaolers and hired assassins against me.'

'My gaolers, my hired assassins! Well, I'll be damned! You're becoming dramatic now. Yesterday's comedy's turning into heavy drama. But it doesn't matter. In ten days you'll be where you deserve to be and I'll have done my duty.'

Milady replied in the uplifted tones of a martyr defying her judges:

'Your duty! An outrage, you mean! A crime against humanity!'

Lord de Winter got up.

'I really believe you're going mad, Clarice,' he said. 'Stop this nonsense or by God I'll have you thrown into a dungeon. My Spanish wine must have gone to your head. But don't worry. That feeling's quite usual and soon wears off. I'll go now.'

He left the room cursing aloud, a habit which in those days was considered quite in the character of a gentleman. Milady had guessed right. Felton had been listening behind the door and not one word of that scene had escaped him.

Milady called after her brother-in-law:

'Yes, go, go! This feeling won't wear off. It'll grow! Your fate will overtake you, your sins will find you out!'

Silence fell once more in the room. Two hours went by. When they brought supper they found Milady on her knees praying out loud, prayers which she had learned from one of her former servants, a die-hard Puritan. She seemed to be in a trance of fervour, unconscious of her surroundings. Felton signed to the men not to disturb her, and when supper had been laid he left without speaking. Milady suspected that they might be spying on her through the grille, so she continued her prayers to the end. She fancied that the soldier on guard outside the door was no longer pacing up and down but had stopped and was listening. Milady thought that she had achieved enough for the moment. She got up, seated herself at the table, ate a very small supper and drank only water.

An hour later they came in to remove the table, but Milady noticed that this time Felton did not come in with the soldiers. Obviously he was afraid of seeing too much of her. She smiled, but turned her head away as she did so, for the look of triumph on her face might have betrayed her. She allowed another hour to slip by. Dead silence now reigned in the castle itself and there was no sound but the endless murmur of the sea. In harmony with the waves Milady began to chant in her clear and musical voice the first verse of the hymn so popular at that time with the Puritans:

> *'Seigneur, si tu nous abandonne,*
> *C'est pour voir si nous sommes forts,*
> *Mais ensuite c'est toi qui donne,*
> *De ta celeste main la palme à nos efforts.'*

> 'Dost Thou desert us, Lord on high,
> 'Tis but to try our constancy.
> And 'tis Thy gracious hand, O Lord,
> That later doth our pains reward.'

This verse was not good poetry, far from it. But we know that the Puritans did not set great store by poetry. As Milady sang she listened. The soldier on guard at the door had stopped dead in his tracks. From this Milady could guess that her singing had impressed him. She continued with tremendous fervour and feeling. It seemed to her that her voice was echoing through the length and breadth of the castle, enthralling the guards and acting on their senses like heady wine.

But the sentry, who was no doubt an ardent Catholic, was quick to shake off the spell. He opened the grille in the door and called:

'For Heaven's sake stop, Ma'am! Your song's as sad as "De Profundis". If as well as pacing up and down this passage all night I have to listen to hymns like that I shall mutiny.'

Then a stern voice which Milady recognized as Felton's said:

'Silence, corporal! Mind your own business! You'd no orders to stop that woman singing! You were told to guard her and to shoot her if she tried to escape. Obey your orders but don't exceed them!'

A light of devilish joy shone for a moment in Milady's eyes. Then it passed. Pretending to have heard not a word of this dialogue she started singing again, putting into her voice all the witchery she could conjure:

> *'Pour tant de pleures et de misères,*
> *Pour mon exil et pour mes fers,*
> *J'ai ma jeunesse et ma prière*
> *Et Dieu qui contera les maux que j'ai soufferb.'*

> 'To recompense my tears and grief
> This bitter exile and these chains,
> My youth have I and my belief
> And God who reckoneth my pains.'

Her voice rang out full and clear and gave this crude verse a magic and meaning which even the most fanatical Puritans rarely found in the austere chants of their religion. To Felton her song was as the song of the Angel comforting the three Hebrews in the fiery furnace. Milady continued her hymn:

> *'Mais le jour de la délivrance,*
> *Viendra pour nous, Dieu, juste et fort,*
> *Et s'il trompe notre espérance*
> *Il nous reste toujours le martyre et la mort.'*

> ' "The hour will come," the Lord hath said,
> "When they shall know you for Mine own."
> Yet should that hour be long delayed
> Death waits us and the martyr's crown.'

The fiendish creature sang so thrillingly that she finally succeeded in breaking down the young man's resistance. He flung open the door and burst into the room. He was very pale and there was a tortured look on his face.

'Why are you singing like that?' he asked.

'Forgive me, Sir,' replied Milady gently. 'I forgot that my hymns were out of place in this house. I'm afraid I've offended you in your beliefs. Forgive me. It was thoughtless of me.'

Her face was so transfigured by this feigned religious ecstasy that Felton thought he was now in the very presence of the angel whose voice had so enchanted him. He repeated:

'Don't sing like that. There are people here whom it may distress.'

He was so overwrought that he did not seem to know what he was saying. Milady was eyeing him like a lynx.

'Very well, Sir,' she said gently, 'I'll stop.'

'No, don't stop, Lady de Winter,' answered Felton. 'Just sing a little less loud, especially at night.'

The young man suddenly realized that he was no longer maintaining a dispassionate attitude towards his prisoner. Panic-stricken he turned and fled from the room.

The sentry outside remarked:

'You were quite right to stop her, Sir. Those hymns upset one's morale. But one finds oneself growing to like them; she sings so beautifully.'

CHAPTER XVII

Third Day of Captivity

MILADY was triumphant. Felton had responded to her at last. But she knew that victory was not yet hers. She had to keep her hold on him and not allow his sympathies to be deflected. She must see him constantly. But what excuse could she find for requiring his presence again? And how could she persuade him to talk to her so that she could talk to him? As she well knew, her greatest attraction lay in her voice; it had always been her most effective weapon where men were concerned. And for all her charm she might yet fail, for Felton had been warned. The least slip could be fatal. From now on she was careful in everything she said and did, and behaved in his presence like an experienced actress cautiously feeling her way through a new rôle.

The part she had to play for Lord de Winter was easier. She had made up her mind about that after her previous day's meeting with him. She would remain silent and aloof; from time to time, with a scornful word or look, she would provoke him to anger and threats of violence which would contrast unfavourably with her own dignity and self-control. That would be her rôle – enacted for Felton's benefit, of course – he might say nothing but he would notice.

The next morning Felton appeared as usual, but Milady watched him supervise all the arrangements of the breakfast without addressing a word to him. Just as he was leaving she thought he was about to speak to her. Then he seemed to change his mind. He had obviously controlled himself with an effort and choked back the words which had risen to his lips. The next moment he was gone again.

At about midday Lord de Winter came in. It was a fine day and a ray of typical lukewarm English sunshine filtered into the room. Milady took up a pose by the window and pretended to be looking out and not to have heard the door open.

'Good morning, Clarice!' said de Winter. 'And what's the act today, high comedy or heavy drama? Oh, I see! A little tragedy for a change.'

The prisoner said nothing.

'Yes, I understand,' went on her brother-in-law, 'you're wishing you were free and standing on that shore. You're picturing yourself on a ship ploughing through those green waves. You're probably hatching one of those nice little plots of yours to murder me. Patience, Clarice dear. It won't be long now. Very soon you'll be down on that shore; very soon you'll be sailing across that sea. But not in the direction you'd like. You'll be sailing away from England for ever.'

Milady clasped her hands and raised her beautiful eyes to Heaven. Then she prayed aloud in a voice of angelic sweetness:

'Lord God, forgive this man as I forgive him.'

'Pray away to your heart's content, wicked woman!' cried de Winter. 'It's very noble of you to ask God to forgive me, seeing that I've no intention of forgiving you.'

With these words he turned to leave the room. As he opened the door Milady noticed someone staring at her from the passage. It was Felton. When her eyes met his he quickly stepped out of sight. This was a signal for Milady to fall on her knees and start to pray.

'O God,' she prayed. 'Thou knowest the sacred cause for which I suffer. O Lord God, give me strength to endure.'

The door opened gently. Milady, posed theatrically on her knees in prayer, pretended not to hear and continued in a voice choked with sobs:

'God of Justice, God of Right, wilt Thou suffer this man to prosper in his wickedness?'

Then only did she show that she was aware of Felton's presence. She sprang to her feet, blushing as though ashamed of having been discovered on her knees. Felton said gravely:

'I don't like disturbing people in prayer, Lady de Winter. So I'll leave you and ask you to forgive my intrusion.'

'How did you know I was praying, Sir?' said Milady, her voice still choked with sobs.

Felton replied gently:

'D'you think I'd presume to stop a fellow-creature from going on her knees to her Maker? God forbid! I respect anyone, however guilty, who truly repents.'

'I, guilty?' said Milady with a sad, resigned smile. 'O God, Thou knowest if I am guilty! Judged and sentenced perhaps, but as you know, Sir, God loves martyrs and sometimes allows the innocent to suffer.'

'If you're a martyr all the more reason to pray,' answered Felton. 'In fact I'll pray for you myself.'

At this Milady flung herself at his feet.

'Oh, you're good, you're good!' she cried. 'But I'm weak. I can't stand it any longer! I'm afraid of losing heart at the last moment when I have to confess my faith. They're deceiving you, Sir, but never mind that! May I ask you a favour? If you grant it I'll be grateful to you always.'

Felton replied:

'You should speak to my guardian, Lady de Winter. He's responsible for you, not I.'

'No, Sir, I'd rather speak to you. Listen to me and don't let them make you an accomplice in my ruin, my shame.'

'If you've deserved this shame, Lady de Winter, you must endure it and offer it up to God.'

'What did you say? Oh I see you don't understand! By shame you thought I meant some sort of punishment, imprisonment or death. Would it were that! What do I care for death or imprisonment!'

'Now I confess I don't understand, Lady de Winter,' answered Felton.

'You're pretending not to understand, Sir,' replied the prisoner with a sad, long-suffering air.

'No, Lady de Winter, I'm speaking the truth. I swear it on my Christian faith, as God is my witness.'

'You mean you don't know about Lord de Winter's plots against me?'

'I know nothing of them.'

'You, his right-hand man? You know nothing?'

'I've already said no, Lady de Winter.'

'It's so obvious I thought you'd have guessed it.'

'I don't try and guess secrets. I wait to have them confided to me. Lord de Winter's told me nothing about you apart from what you heard him say in your presence.'

'What!' cried Milady, feigning astonishment. 'So you're not his accomplice! You don't know the unbelievable horrors he has in store for me?'

Felton flushed and replied:

'You're wrong, Lady de Winter. My guardian wouldn't do a wicked thing like that.'

Milady thought to herself:

'Good, I still haven't explained what I mean and yet he calls it a wicked thing.'

Out aloud she said:

'Satan's boon companion's capable of anything.'

'Whom d'you mean by Satan, Lady de Winter?' asked Felton.

'Can there be two men in England who deserve that name?'

Felton's eyes lit up.

'You mean George Villiers,' he said.

'The man whom heathens and heretics call the Duke of Buckingham,' replied Milady. 'I should have thought you'd have known at once whom I meant.'

'The hand of the Lord's against him. He'll be punished as he deserves.'

Felton was only expressing the common feeling in England

about the Duke of Buckingham. The Catholics themselves called him the 'Extortioner', the 'Robber', or the 'Rake', and the Puritans referred to him quite simply as Satan. Milady joined her hands and cast her eyes heavenwards.

'O Lord,' she prayed fervently, 'send that man the punishment he deserves. Thou knowest, Lord, that I ask this of Thee, not from a wish for revenge but that a whole nation may be delivered from his tyranny.'

'D'you know him then?' asked Felton.

'At last,' thought Milady, 'he's becoming interested in me.'

Out loud she said:

'Know him? Yes, to my eternal shame and remorse.' And she buried her head in her hands as though in anguish.

Felton felt himself weakening again and started to walk to the door. But Milady rushed after him and held him back.

'You're kind, you're good, Sir,' she cried. 'Won't you do me one small favour? You remember the knife Lord de Winter wouldn't let me have – the steel knife – he knew what I wanted to do with it. Get that knife for me. Let me have it for one minute. I beg, I implore you! ... Oh, just hear me out! When you've given it to me go out and shut the door behind you. I've got nothing against you; my brother-in-law was lying. You're kind and good. I feel I can trust you and you may save me yet. Let me have that knife for just one minute and I'll return it to you through the grille. Just one minute, Mr Felton, and you'll have saved my honour.'

Milady still had hold of Felton's hands. He was so shocked by her words that he made no attempt to free himself from her grasp.

'You want to kill yourself!' he cried.

Milady fell on her knees as though her strength had given out and whispered faintly:

'I've told you my secret, Sir. O God, he knows everything now! I'm lost!'

Felton stood beside her, silent and frowning.

'He's hesitating,' thought Milady. 'I still haven't convinced him.'

And now footsteps sounded in the passage. Milady recognized them as Lord de Winter's. Apparently Felton recognized them too, for he made for the door. Milady flung herself at him.

'Not a word,' she whispered tensely. 'Not a word of what I've told you or I'm lost and it'll be you who . . .'

She paused. The footsteps had stopped outside the door and she did not wish her brother-in-law to hear her talking. She laid her beautiful hand across Felton's mouth and looked at him with feigned terror in her eyes. Felton forced her gently away, and she flung herself theatrically on to a sofa. The footsteps went on again; Lord de Winter had passed the room without coming in and they heard him walk on in the other direction.

Felton stood stock still, listening. He was as pale as death. When the footsteps had died away he started like a man waking from a dream and rushed out of the room. Milady heard him walk quickly away in the opposite direction to her brother-in-law. That she considered a good sign.

Then she frowned and thought to herself:

'If he repeats anything to de Winter I'm lost. De Winter knows quite well I won't kill myself. He'll put a knife in my hands in front of Felton and then Felton will see that the scene I made just now was a sham.'

She went over to the mirror and gazed at her reflection. Never had she looked more beautiful. The frown left her face; she smiled and muttered to herself:

'I needn't worry. He won't repeat anything.'

That evening Lord de Winter came in with the soldiers when they brought the supper. Milady said to him:

'Is your presence a necessary condition of my imprisonment? Must you add insult to injury by forcing yourself on me every day?'

Lord de Winter replied:

'My dear Clarice, you amaze me! Why, only two days ago you told me your sole object in coming to England was to see me! Surely you're not bored with me already? You were so anxious to see me that you risked illness, shipwreck – imprisonment even – to get to me. Well, here I am. Make the most of me. Besides, this time I've got a special reason for visiting you.'

Milady started involuntarily; she thought for a moment that Felton had betrayed her. Adventurous as her life had been, never did she remember having felt so unnerved as at that moment. Lord de Winter drew up an arm-chair close to hers and sat down facing her. He then took a scroll of paper from his pocket and slowly unfolded it. He said:

'I thought I'd show you this passport. It's not an official passport; I drew it up myself. But it'll be your identity certificate in the new life I've planned for you.'

He glanced at her meaningly. Then he read:

Order to escort to . . .

He paused.

'The name of the place has been left blank,' he said. 'You shall be sent wherever you wish, provided it's a thousand miles or more from London.'

He paused again. Then he continued:

Order to escort to . . . the undermentioned Charlotte Backson, convicted by French law but released after serving sentence. She shall remain permanently in this neighbourhood and never travel more than eight miles in any direction. If she tries to escape she shall be sentenced to death. She shall be paid the sum of five shillings a day for board and lodging.

Milady said coldly:

'That order obviously doesn't concern me. It hasn't even got my name on it.'

'Your name? You haven't got a name.'

'I've got your brother's name.'

'No, you have not. My brother was your second husband. Your first husband's still alive. If you'll tell me his name I'll put it instead of the name Charlotte Backson. You'd rather not? You prefer to keep it a secret? Very well. You'll be deported under the name of Charlotte Backson.'

Milady said not a word. She was not acting now; genuine terror had robbed her of speech. She imagined the order was

to be carried out then and there; that Lord de Winter was
hastening her departure and that he intended to send her off
that very evening. For a few seconds she thought all was lost.
Then she suddenly noticed that the order was unsigned. Her
relief at this discovery was so great that for an instant a light
of fierce joy shone in her eyes. Lord de Winter remarked it and
said:

'I see you've noticed the order's unsigned and you're probably thinking there's still hope, that I'm trying to frighten you,
that this order's not valid and that no one will ever sign it.
You're wrong. Tomorrow it will be sent to the Duke of Buckingham and I shall get it back the day after signed and sealed
by him personally. Twenty-four hours after that we shall start
putting it in force. Good-bye, Clarice. That's all I have to say to
you.'

'And I say to you, Sir, that to take the law into your own
hands like this and exile me under a false name's an outrage!'

'Would you rather be hanged under your own name, Clarice?
You know the English law's very strict in regard to bigamy.
Say frankly which you prefer. I admit that my name, or rather
my brother's name's, involved in this, but I'm quite prepared
to risk a public scandal to be rid of you.'

Milady said nothing. But she went as pale as death.

'I see you prefer exile, Clarice. Excellent. As the proverb
says, "Travel broadens the mind". I really think you're wise.
Life's good after all. That's why I'm not going to allow you to
take mine. That leaves only the question of the five shillings
allowance. I'm afraid you'll think me ungenerous, but I'm not
going to give you more – you might use it to bribe the guards.
Never mind, you'll still have your personal charm; no doubt
you'll exploit that to the full, unless your failure with Felton's
disheartened you.'

'Felton hasn't given me away,' thought Milady. 'So there's
still hope.'

Lord de Winter said:

'And now good-bye, Clarice. I'll pay you another visit tomorrow after the messenger's gone.'

He got up, bowed ironically to his sister-in-law and left the room. Milady sank back in her chair with relief. She still had three days' grace. She calculated that by that time she would have Felton at her feet.

Then a terrible thought struck her. De Winter might send Felton himself to Buckingham with the order. If Felton left now she would lose her power over him, for to complete her seduction of him she must see him every day. Not wishing, however, to appear in any way upset by her brother-in-law's threats she sat down at the table and forced herself to eat. Then, as on the previous night, she fell on her knees and started praying out loud. And again the sentry stopped in his tracks and stood listening.

Soon Milady heard lighter footsteps than the sentry's coming from the far end of the passage, and stopping outside her door. She murmured:

'It's he.'

And she began singing the hymn which had so moved Felton before. But this time the door remained closed. Milady cast a furtive look at the panel and fancied she saw the glint of the young man's eyes staring at her through the grille. She went on singing, but still he did not come. Had he really been staring at her or had she imagined it? When she finished her hymn she heard a man's deep sigh. Then quite distinctly she heard the same light footsteps retreating slowly and as though regretfully down the passage.

CHAPTER XVIII

Fourth Day of Captivity

WHEN Felton came into Milady's bedroom next day he found her standing on an arm-chair holding a cord made out of several strips of cambric knotted together. At the sound of the door opening she sprang off the chair and pretended to be hiding the cord behind her back. Felton was paler than usual and his eyes were red from not having slept. But his manner was as composed as ever. He walked slowly up to his prisoner, who fell back into the arm-chair, still holding the cord behind her back, but purposely allowing one end of it to protrude over the edge. Felton took hold of it.

'What's this, Lady de Winter?' he asked.

Milady smiled her sad, long-suffering smile.

'That's nothing,' she said. 'As you know, boredom's the prisoner's worst enemy. I was bored, so to pass the time I plaited this cord.'

Felton looked at the place on the wall where Milady's head had been when she was standing on the chair, noticed a gilt clothes-hook and gave an involuntary start. Milady saw him start, for although she was sitting with her head bent nothing escaped her.

'What were you doing standing on that chair?' asked the young man.

'What's that to you?' replied Milady.

'I want to know,' said Felton.

'Please don't question me,' said Milady. 'You know we true Christians are forbidden to lie.'

'Well, I'll tell you what you were doing or rather what you were going to do,' replied Felton. 'It was that dreadful thing you've been planning to do for so long. Don't, Lady de Winter. God forbids lying, as you say, but He condemns suicide far more.'

Milady replied in a tone of profound conviction:

'When God sees one of his creatures unjustly persecuted, faced with the alternative of suicide or shame, He forgives suicide, for in that case suicide's martyrdom.'

'Yes, Lady de Winter,' answered Felton. 'And now that you've told me so much please tell me more and explain how that applies to you.'

'If I told you you'd only say I was lying, and if i told you what I meant to do you'd report me to my persecutor. No, Sir. And in any case how can the life or death of a wretched convict concern you? You're only responsible for my body. And if you've only a dead body to show, provided it's proved to be mine, you won't be blamed. On the contrary, you'll probably be commended for having helped to exterminate me.'

Felton was horrified.

'D'you think I'd connive at your death for my own advancement?' he cried. 'You don't know what you're saying.'

Milady gave full vent to her feelings.

'Let me have my way, Felton,' she cried melodramatically. 'Soldiers should be ambitious, shouldn't they? You're a lieutenant now. If you command my funeral escort you'll get a captaincy.'

Felton cried out:

'How can you think I'd do anything so wicked, Lady de Winter! In a few days you'll be far away from here. I shall no longer be responsible for you and you can do what you like then.'

Milady pretended to be moved to righteous wrath.

'What!' she said, 'you claim to be just and yet say that all you want is not to have to answer for my death!'

'It's my duty to guard your life, Lady de Winter, and I shall do so.'

'But do you know the truth about this so-called duty of yours? It would be a cruel enough fate if I were guilty. How far more cruel, more wicked, seeing that I'm innocent!'

'I'm a soldier, Lady de Winter, and a soldier must obey orders.'

'D'you think, Sir, that when the Day of Judgement comes God will choose between those who persecute in good faith and those who persecute for their own ends? You won't allow me to destroy my body and yet take orders from the man who wants to destroy my soul!'

Felton was shaken. He replied:

'I do assure you, Lady de Winter, you're in no danger either from me or Lord de Winter. I can vouch for us both.'

Milady cried scornfully:

'You poor fool! How can you vouch for another when the wisest and best admit they can't even vouch for themselves?

You side with the strong against the weak without even knowing the facts!'

Felton saw the force of this argument. But he replied:

'I can't do as you ask, Lady de Winter. While you're alive
you're my prisoner. I can't help you to escape by any means,
not even by death.'

'Very well, Mr Felton,' cried Milady. 'You may preserve my
life but you'll be jeopardizing something I value more dearly
than life, my honour. And I shall hold you responsible for my
shame, as God is my witness!'

Now at last Felton's defences broke down and he surrendered
to this woman's fatal spell, which he had tried so hard to resist.
The sight of her, lovely and seemingly innocent as the dawn,
alternately weeping and threatening, the symbol of beauty in
distress, worked on his fevered mind, obsessed by high ideals
and fanatical beliefs. And, like a clever general who sees the
enemy preparing to retreat and bears down on him triumph-
antly, Milady, quick to take advantage of the situation, now
rose as one inspired. Like a vestal virgin, with outstretched
arm, her throat bare, her hair dishevelled, one hand chastely
holding her dress over her breasts and with a fanatical light in
her eyes, she advanced towards Felton, chanting in her deep
and thrilling voice which had already caused such havoc in his
heart:

> 'From Hell's fire the cry shall rise
> "Cast to Baal his sacrifice! . . .
> Cast the Heathen to the sword,
> To the vengeance of the Lord!"'

> 'Livre à Baal sa victime
> Jette aux lions le martyr:
> Dieu te fera repentir! . . .
> Je crie à lui de l'abîme.'

Felton stood as though transfixed.

'Who are you?' he cried. 'An angel from Heaven or a fiend
from Hell?'

'Oh, Felton, Felton,' she said, looking at him sorrowfully.

'Don't you see? I'm neither angel nor demon. I'm of this world, a follower of the true Faith, like yourself.'

'Yes, yes,' he answered, 'I believe you. How could I have ever doubted!'

'You believe me. And yet you act for that son of Belial, Lord de Winter? You believe me and yet leave me in the hands of my enemies, of England's enemy, God's enemy? You believe me and yet hand me over to the heretic whose crimes and debauches appal the world, the fiend whom the misguided call the Duke of Buckingham and true believers call anti-Christ?'

'I, hand you over to Buckingham! What are you saying?'

'They have eyes but they see not, ears but they do not hear,' chanted Milady.

Felton pressed his clenched hands to his forehead as though to wrest the last doubt from his mind. Then he looked up.

'Yes, yes,' he said. 'I recognize the voice which speaks to me in my dreams, the angel who appears to me every night, crying to my restless soul: "Strike! Save England, save yourself, or you'll die without appeasing God's wrath!" Speak, speak. I can understand you now.'

A light of terrible, triumphant joy shone for a moment in Milady's eyes. Fleeting as was this maniac gleam Felton saw it and shuddered, as though for an instant he had looked into the dark depths of this woman's soul. He suddenly remembered Lord de Winter's warnings and Milady's own previous attempts to seduce him. He instinctively shrank away from her, but continued to eye her as though hypnotized. Milady's infallible instinct warned her that this was a very critical moment. For although apparently in the throes of violent emotion she was all the time coolly assessing the effect she created. Now before Felton could speak and maintain the conversation at the same high emotional level, which was beginning to exhaust her, she quickly dropped her hands in a gesture which implied that her woman's weakness had triumphed over her moral zeal.

'Oh no,' she said, 'I'm not destined to play Judith rescuing Bethulia from that Holofernes! The sword of the Almighty is too heavy for my arm. Don't ask too much of me! Just let me die and avoid dishonour; grant me the solace of martyrdom. I don't ask you to help me escape as a guilty woman would, nor do I claim revenge as would a heathen. I only ask to be allowed to die. I beg you, on my knees I implore you! Let me die and with my last breath I'll call down God's blessing on you as my saviour.'

She spoke so humbly and looked so chastened that Felton's faith in her was restored. The enchantress had once more cast her spell on him. She was beautiful, she was in distress, she was deeply religious. And these three attributes combined had a fatal appeal for the romantic young Puritan. Milady had acted her part to perfection.

'Alas, Lady de Winter,' said Felton, 'I can only pity you if, as you say, you've been victimized. I know Lord de Winter has some deep grudge against you. You're a Christian, of the same faith as myself. I feel drawn to you, though till now I've cared for no one but my guardian, having found the world full of rogues and heretics. But you're so beautiful and apparently so good. Why should Lord de Winter want to persecute you? Have you committed some terrible crime?'

Milady repeated sorrowfully:

'They have eyes but they see not, ears but they do not hear.'

'Then please help me to see and hear, Lady de Winter!' cried the young officer. 'Confide in me.'

Milady blushed for very shame.

'Confide in you?' she cried. 'Tell you how a man brought ruin on me? How could I, a woman, describe my downfall to you, a man?'

'You can surely confide in a fellow-Puritan,' cried Felton.

Milady stared at him and said nothing. The young man thought she was trying to find courage to speak, whereas she was merely observing him. He gazed at her imploringly; it was now his turn to play the supplicant.

'Very well, brother Puritan,' she said at last. 'I'll be brave and tell you everything.'

At that moment they heard Lord de Winter's footsteps in the passage. This time he did not merely pass by as on the previous day, but stopped, spoke to the sentry and finally opened the door and came in. While he was talking to the sentry Felton crossed the room, and when his guardian entered he was standing a few feet away from the prisoner.

De Winter eyed them both suspiciously and said:

'You've been a long time in here, John. Has this woman been telling you her crimes? If so I can well understand her keeping you so long.'

Felton started to tremble and Milady realized that she must come quickly to his rescue or all was lost. She said to her brother-in-law:

'Are you afraid your prisoner's going to escape! Don't worry. Mr Felton will tell you what I was asking him to do for me.'

De Winter's suspicions were increased by this.

'So you were asking him to do something for you!' he said. 'Well, John, what did she want?'

'She wanted me to give her a knife,' said Felton. 'I was to let her have it for only one minute and she was then to return it through the grille.'

Lord de Winter smiled cynically and said:

'Oh? Is there someone hidden in this room whose throat she wants to cut?'

'Yes,' replied Milady. 'My own.'

'I gave you the choice between America and Tyburn,' replied Lord de Winter. 'Choose Tyburn, Clarice. You might only wound yourself with a knife but the hangman's rope's certain death.'

Felton remembered that only an hour ago he had seen Milady with a rope in her hand. He started and turned pale, Milady said:

'Yes. I'd thought of that.'

Then she added in an undertone, as though to herself:

'I think that is the best way.'

Felton drew in his breath sharply. Lord de Winter noticed his emotion and said:

'Take care, John. John, my friend. I've trusted you. I've warned you. Don't fail me now. You won't have to hold out much longer. In three days we shall be rid of this fiend and where I'm sending her she won't be able to harm anyone.'

'D'you hear him, d'you hear him?' cried Milady in a loud voice, so that her brother-in-law should think that she was invoking God and Felton know that she was appealing to him.

Acutely embarrassed, the young man looked down and said nothing. De Winter now took him by the arm and led him to the door, turning his head so as not to lose sight of Milady until they were both safely out of the room. Alone once more Milady reflected:

'I haven't done as well as I thought. De Winter's stopped being flippant and is being cautious for a change. I've never seen him like that before. His need for revenge has changed him. Felton's obviously wavering; luckily he's easier to manage than that fiend d'Artagnan.'

She waited on tenterhooks for Felton to return. Her instincts told her that he would return that very day. Indeed, only an hour after Lord de Winter's visit Milady heard low murmurs at the door, which was then flung open by the young man himself. He walked quickly into the room, leaving the door open, and signed to Milady to be quiet. He looked distraught.

'What do you want?' she said.

Felton replied in a low voice:

'I've just dismissed the sentry so that I could get in here without his seeing me, and so that we could talk without being overheard. My guardian's just told me a terrible story.'

Milady smiled her injured martyr smile and said nothing. Felton continued:

'Either you're wicked or my adopted father and patron's a villain himself. I've only known you four days; him I've known and loved ten years. It's only natural I should feel doubts. Please forgive me if I say I'm still not quite convinced. I'll come again tonight after midnight and you can convince me then.'

'No, Felton,' she said. 'It's too great a sacrifice for you to make. I couldn't ask it of you. My life's finished. I'm doomed. Don't you risk ruin too! Just let me die. My corpse will be more striking proof of my innocence than anything I can say, and when you see me dead you'll realize the truth.'

'Don't talk like that, Lady de Winter!' cried Felton. 'It's wicked! I've come here now to get you to promise by all you hold sacred not to kill yourself.'

'I can't do that,' answered Milady. 'Promises must be kept and I couldn't keep that promise.'

'At least swear to do nothing till you see me again,' said Felton. 'If after that you're still determined I won't stand in your way. I'll even give you the knife.'

'Very well,' said Milady. 'I'll wait for your sake. I swear that in the name of our God. Does that satisfy you?'

'Yes,' replied Felton. 'Good-bye then, till tonight.'

He turned and walked quickly out of the room, closing the door behind him. Then he picked up the sentry's pike and stood to attention as though on guard. When the man returned a few minutes later he handed it back to him.

Milady had meanwhile crept up to the other side of the door. Through the grille she saw the young man cross himself fervently and stride off down the passage in a transport of joy. She returned to her arm-chair, and there was a look of savage scorn on her face as she muttered:

'Crazy fanatic with his ravings about God! Well, let him rave! My only concern is that he should help me to escape and get my revenge!'

CHAPTER XIX

Fifth Day of Captivity

MILADY'S scheme had so far worked well, and her success had redoubled her strength. So far her amorous successes had been limited to men of lax morals who were only too ready to be seduced, Court gallants whose licentious habits made them easy prey. Milady was beautiful and intelligent enough to be fêted in any worldly society. But now she was dealing with a man by nature reserved and misanthropic and almost inhumanly austere in his mode of life – a man so obsessed with fanatical beliefs and high ideals that he had no time for love, that pastime which thrives on leisure and feeds on depravity. On such unpromising material Milady had had to stake her all. She had pitted her hypocrisy against his virtue. With her pretence of chastity she had appealed to his genuine chivalry and with her beauty touched his heart and inflamed his senses, predisposed against her though he was. Such an achievement was even more than she had hoped for.

And yet several times that evening she had despaired. She had not called God to her aid; she put her faith in Evil, that mighty force which pervades all human life and with whose help, as the Arabian legend tells, out of a pomegranate seed arose a whole lost world. Buoyed up by this faith Milady prepared for her next encounter with Felton.

She knew that she had only two more days in which to work, that once the deportation order had been signed by Buckingham – and Buckingham would be all the more ready to sign it if it bore a name unknown to him – her brother-in-law would ship her off without delay. She realized, too, that once she had been exiled she could no longer pretend to virtue, and that her attractions would be no longer marketable. Women sentenced to a shameful punishment may remain beautiful but they stand little chance of becoming powerful again. Like all clever people Milady knew what setting best suited her nature and her gifts. Poverty revolted her, squalor deprived her of almost all her dignity. To shine among her equals satisfied her pride; to dominate inferiors merely bored her – in fact it was almost degrading. She would some day return from her exile – that she never doubted. But how long would this exile last? For a creature so ambitious as Milady any day not spent in self-advancement was complete stagnation. The thought of stagnation appalled her and retrogression was even worse. She might be two or even three years abroad. And when she returned she might find the Cardinal dead or out of favour, and d'Artagnan and his friends happy and triumphant, having been rewarded by the Queen for services rendered to her. Visions of what the future might hold obsessed and tormented her.

And what of the Cardinal? What must he be thinking of her silence? He was her only ally, the only man powerful enough to protect her. With his help she hoped to crush her enemies and ensure her future. His friendship was indispensable to her, but she had failed him. She knew his character, she knew that he would have no pity for her. She might talk of her imprisonment and dramatize her sufferings to her heart's content; the Cardinal would merely reply cynically:

'You shouldn't have fallen into the trap.'

The thought of the Cardinal inspired Milady to make a supreme effort to save herself. She muttered the name 'Felton' under her breath, Felton her only hope in the dark pit into which she had fallen. And like a snake which coils and uncoils itself to test its strength she lay and indulged in fantasies of the young man at her feet.

Meanwhile time was passing. Each hour as it sped by seemed to waken the clock-tower bell, and each stroke of the bell found a jarring echo in the prisoner's heart.

At nine o'clock Lord de Winter paid his usual visit. This time he examined the bars of the windows, sounded the floor boards and the walls, and inspected the doors and the fireplace. He did all this without addressing a word to Milady, and she made no attempt to speak to him. It was clear to both that the situation was now so serious that it was beyond mere recriminations. Having finished his inspection de Winter turned to his prisoner and said:

'There now. You won't get out tonight at any rate.'

At ten o'clock Felton came to post the sentry. Milady knew his step by now as though he were her lover. And yet she hated and despised him as a weak fanatic.

It was not yet the appointed hour. Felton did not come in.

Two hours later, on the stroke of midnight, the sentry was relieved. The time had come. From now on Milady waited in a fever of suspense. The new sentry started on his rounds. Ten minutes later Felton arrived. Milady sat listening and heard him giving the man orders.

'On no account leave this door,' he said. 'You know His

Lordship punished the sentry on duty last night for leaving his post for only a few moments, although I'd agreed to take over his duty for him!'

'Yes, Sir,' replied the soldier.

'So I warn you, look alert! I'm going in for a moment to make a second inspection of that woman's room. They suspect her of wanting to kill herself, and I've been told to keep a strict watch on her.'

Milady thought to herself:

'Good, the noble Puritan's lying already.'

The soldier smiled.

'I bet you don't object to an order like that, Sir,' he said. 'You can even have a peep at her in bed.'

Felton flushed. At any other time he would have pulled the man up for insolence. But now the voice of his conscience silenced his tongue.

'If you hear me call, come in at once,' he said. 'And if you hear anyone coming along the passage warn me.'

'Yes, Sir,' answered the soldier.

And now Felton went in to Milady. She stood up to welcome him.

'It's you!' she said.

'I told you I'd come and here I am,' replied Felton.

'You promised me something else as well.'

For all his self-control the young man felt himself trembling.

'You promised to bring me a knife and to leave me alone for a minute.'

'Please don't talk about that, Lady de Winter,' said Felton. 'No crisis, however terrible, gives anyone the right to take his life. I've been thinking it over and I know I'd never do it. It's wicked.'

Milady sat down again in the arm-chair. She smiled scornfully and said:

'So you've been thinking it over, have you? Well, I've been thinking it over too.'

'What d'you mean?'

'And I've decided I'm not answerable to anyone who breaks his word.'

'Oh God,' muttered Felton.

'You'd better go,' said Milady. 'I've decided to tell you nothing.'

At this Felton pulled a knife out of his pocket. He had brought it with him as he had promised but had hoped his prisoner would have forgotten about it.

'Here's your knife,' he said.

'Let me look at it,' said Milady.

'What for?'

'I swear on my honour to return it to you at once. You can put it down on that table and stand between me and it.'

Felton handed her the knife. Milady examined the blade closely, testing the point against her finger. She then returned it to the young man.

'Good,' she said. 'That's a fine, sharp, steel knife. You're a true friend, Felton.'

Felton laid the knife down on the table as agreed. Milady watched him and nodded her approval.

'And now if you'll listen I'll tell you my story,' she said.

The young officer needed no encouragement. He was already standing over her, waiting eagerly for her to speak. In a low, sad, serious tone Milady began her confession.

'Felton, think of me as your sister, your own father's daughter. Think of my story as her story. It was like this. When I was still young and, alas, beautiful, a man fell in love with me. I was innocent then and he took advantage of my innocence to lure me into a trap. I resisted him and managed to escape. Then he pursued me relentlessly, abducted me and tried to force me to yield to him. I resisted again. Then, because I kept appealing to my God and my religion to protect me, he started to revile them. Seeing that he couldn't shake my faith he resolved to break my will. So one night . . .'

Milady paused and smiled bitterly.

'Yes?' said Felton. 'What did he do?'

'He poisoned my will-power. He drugged my drinking-water.

I'd only just finished my meal when a strange torpor came over me. I'd drunk the water in all innocence but now I felt suspicious and in my fear tried to ward off this lassitude. I tried to get to the window to call for help but my legs gave way under me. The ceiling seemed to be falling on my head. I stretched out my arms and tried to call for help but could only make inarticulate sounds. I held on to an arm-chair to prevent myself falling but my arms, too, gave way and I sank helplessly on my knees. I tried to pray but my tongue froze to my mouth. Probably God neither saw nor heard me, for I now fell into a sort of coma. I've no recollection of anything that happened while I was in this state or how long it lasted. The first thing I remember was waking up in bed in a round room richly furnished, lit only by a faint ray which filtered through a skylight, and without doors or windows. It was like a sumptuous prison. At first I had no idea where I was and couldn't take in all these details. I struggled to shake off this oppressive languor. I had a vague recollection of having been taken some long distance, of having been in a carriage, of some exhausting nightmare. But this memory was so faint as to seem part of another life.

'Everything seemed so strange that I kept thinking I must still be dreaming. I got up and staggered over to a chair to get my clothes. I didn't remember having undressed or gone to bed. By degrees I got back my sense of reality and began to be frightened. I wasn't at home and as far as I could judge from the light of the sun it was early evening. I'd lost consciousness on the evening of the previous day, so my sleep had lasted twenty-four hours. What could have happened to me during that time? I dressed as quickly as I could, but hadn't yet got control of my limbs, which proved that the effects of the drug hadn't worn off.

'I saw then that the room I was in was a woman's room, very luxuriously furnished. I was sure other women had used it before me. But as you can imagine, Felton, the luxury of the room only increased my own terror and horror. It was a prison all right. I felt along the walls but found no door or opening of any kind and the walls themselves were very thick. I walked at least twenty times round that room, looking for an opening. At last I sank back exhausted into an arm-chair.

'Meanwhile night was falling and with the darkness my terror increased. I hardly dared stir from my chair; I felt there were dangers all round me in that room and traps I might fall into if I moved at all. I hadn't eaten since the previous day but was too frightened to feel hungry. Not a sound reached me. I had no idea of the time and no way of gauging it. I guessed it was at least seven or eight in the evening; it was pitch dark but it was autumn. Suddenly I heard the sound of a door creaking on its hinges and at the same time a lamp was lowered from the ceiling which lit up the whole room. To my horror I saw a man standing a few feet away from me and in the middle of the room a table laid for supper for two, which had sprung up through the floor as though by magic. The man was the man who'd been persecuting me for the past year and who'd vowed that one day I should be his. It was obvious as soon as he spoke that he'd carried out his threat the night before.'

'The villain!' muttered Felton.

'Oh yes, Felton, he was a villain,' exclaimed Milady, gazing earnestly at him. She saw from the expression on his face what an intense interest he was taking in her story. She continued:

'He thought that by violating me in my sleep he'd make me so ashamed that I'd be resigned to my fate. He'd come to offer me his fortune if I'd become his mistress.

'I flung at him every expression of disgust and loathing that my outraged feminine heart could invent. He was clearly used to abuse of this kind, for he stood listening to me with his arms folded, quite unmoved, with a cynical smile on his face. When he thought I'd said my say he came up to me and tried to take hold of my hand. I ran over to the table, seized a knife and held it with the point against my breast.

' "Come one step nearer," I cried, "and you'll have my death as well as my shame to answer for."

'There must have been a look on my face which convinced the brute that I meant what I said, for he stopped abruptly.

' "Your death?" he exclaimed. "Oh no! You're far too charming a mistress to be wasted like that. Believe me, I know! Good-bye my lovely one. I'll leave you now and come back when you're in a better mood."

'He then raised his hand towards the skylight, which was a signal for the lamp to be drawn up to the ceiling again. For a few minutes I was left in complete darkness. Once more I heard the sound of the door creaking on its hinges; then the lamp was lowered again and I found myself alone.

'It was a terrible moment. My worst fears were realized. I was in the power of a man whom I loathed and despised and who I knew would let nothing stand in the way of his desires.'

'But who was the man?' asked Felton.

Milady ignored his question and continued her story.

'I spent that night lying awake in my arm-chair, starting at the faintest sound,' she said. 'The lamp had been put out about midnight and I was once more in darkness. But my persecutor didn't come again that night. Dawn broke at last and I saw that the table had disappeared. But I still had the knife in my hand. That knife was my only hope. I was exhausted; my eyes were smarting from lack of sleep; I hadn't dared close them all night. But with the daylight my courage returned. I lay down on my bed, still holding on to the precious knife, which I now hid under my pillow.

'When I awoke the table was there again with a fresh meal laid on it. I was by now very hungry, for I hadn't eaten for nearly forty-eight hours. I remembered the drug that had been mixed in my drink two nights before and was careful not to touch the water. Instead I filled my glass from a marble tap which was fixed to the wall above my dressing-table. Even after doing this I felt alarmed for a while, but this time nothing happened. The symptoms didn't return.

'I'd emptied half the water out of the water-jug to make it look as though I'd drunk from the jug. It was now evening, but my eyes were growing accustomed to the darkness of the room; and this time I actually saw the table disappear through the floor and reappear a few minutes later with my supper laid on it. Almost at the same moment the lamp was again lowered from the ceiling and lit up my room.

'It wasn't long since I'd eaten so I wasn't very hungry. I decided this time to eat only food into which no drug could be dissolved. I ate two eggs and a little fruit. Then I filled my glass with water from the tap in the wall and drank it. After the first mouthful I noticed it had a different taste from the water I'd drunk that morning, and became alarmed again. I drank no more but had already swallowed nearly half a glass. I waited in terror for the symptoms to return. Someone, either my enemy himself or one of his hirelings, had obviously seen me take the water from the tap that morning and had meanwhile managed to mix the drug in the water from the tap, hoping my fears were now allayed and that I'd drink freely. It was a cunning move.

'After about half an hour I felt the same symptoms as before. This time, however, I'd drunk only half a glass so I held out longer; I didn't completely lose consciousness but fell into a sort of drowse in which I knew what was going on but felt powerless to act. I staggered over to the bed to get hold of my precious possession, my knife, but couldn't reach it and collapsed on my knees at the foot of the bed, clutching one of the bedposts . . . Now I knew I was lost.'

Felton went deathly pale and began to tremble. Breathlessly, as though she were reliving the experience, Milady continued:

'What made my position worse now was that I knew what was in store for me. My mind was alert and observant; only my body was asleep. The whole thing seemed like a dream, certainly, but that made it no less frightening. I saw the lamp disappear again and gradually leave me in darkness. Then I heard the sound of the door opening, a sound which, though I'd heard it only twice before, now haunted my dreams. I felt instinctively that someone was approaching me as I sat crouched on the floor. They say lost explorers in the wilds of Africa feel something of the sort when snakes attack them. I wanted to move, to cry out. With a tremendous effort I managed to struggle to my feet but fell back again at once, this time into my tormentor's arms.'

Felton stammered:

'Who was this scoundrel? For God's sake tell me his name!'

Milady saw that she was making her story more vivid and causing the young man pain by dwelling on the details. This pleased her. The more she stirred his sympathies the more ready would he be to avenge her. So she again ignored his question and continued:

'But this time the villain had no mere corpse to deal with. As I said, I was awake and knew what was happening, though I hadn't the full use of my limbs. I struggled for as long as I could in my weak state. I heard him mutter angrily:

' "These damned Puritans! They fight as hard in bed as they do on the scaffold!"

'Alas, I couldn't struggle very long. I felt my strength failing. At last I fainted and again the fiend had his way with me.'

Felton was listening in strained silence, clenching and un-clenching his hands. His forehead was bathed in sweat and from time to time he groaned. Milady rejoiced to see him so moved. She continued:

'The first thing I did on regaining consciousness was to feel under my pillow for the knife. I hadn't been able to seize it in time to defend myself but thought I could at least use it to atone for my shame. But directly I felt the hilt in my hand a terrible thought came to me. I promised to tell you every-thing, Felton, and I'll hide nothing, though I'm afraid you'll despise me when you hear the truth.'

'You wanted to revenge yourself on the fellow, didn't you?' said Felton.

'Yes,' said Milady. 'I know it was wicked and un-Christian of me. It must have been the Devil prompting me. And I confess, Felton, my longing for revenge was so strong it obsessed me night and day. I'm ashamed to tell you this. Perhaps I'm being punished now for my murderous impulse then.'

'Go on, go on!' cried Felton. 'I only long to hear you say you did get your revenge.'

'I'd decided to do the thing as soon as possible,' went on Milady. 'I was sure my seducer would return next night. I knew I was safe during the day. So when midday came I ate and drank freely. I'd decided to eat nothing that evening but merely to pretend to eat, so I wanted to fortify myself now to make up for that evening's fast. I poured out a glass of water at midday and hid it, for I'd suffered more from thirst than from hunger during my forty-eight hours' abstinence.

'As that day wore on I became more and more determined to carry out my plan. But I had to take care not to show what was in my mind, for I suspected I was being watched. I found myself actually suppressing a smile from time to time. Felton, I daren't tell you what I was smiling at. You'd be horrified!'

'Go on, go on,' said Felton. 'I must hear your story out.'

Milady continued:

'At last evening came. The performance was repeated. As usual my supper came up when the room was quite dark; then the lamp appeared and I sat down at the table. I ate only a little fruit. I pretended to pour out some water from the jug but drank only what I'd kept in my glass from midday, changing the two glasses very cautiously so that no spying eyes should notice. After supper I pretended again to be falling into a coma, as on the previous day. But this time I acted as though I knew what to expect; I dragged myself over to the bed, lay down and pretended to go to sleep. And now I had hold of the knife and lay there with my hand clenched tightly on the hilt.

'Two hours passed and nothing happened. This time, far from being frightened of my seducer coming I was frightened he might not come. At last I saw the lamp being drawn slowly up and disappearing into the shadows in the ceiling. My room was now dark again but I tried hard to peer into the gloom. About ten minutes passed and I heard no sound but the beating of my heart. I prayed to Heaven he'd come. At last I heard the familiar groan of the door opening and shutting and the creak of the brute's footsteps on the boards. And in the gloom I saw a figure advancing towards me.'

Felton burst out:

'Go on, go on! This is agonizing! What happened then?'

'I summoned all my courage,' continued Milady. 'I remembered that this was the hour of vengeance, and saw myself as a second Judith. I was holding the knife tightly in my hand. I allowed him to come quite close to me; suddenly I sat up in bed, raised my right hand with the knife in it and with the force of desperation struck at his heart. But the knife didn't pierce his body ... it struck against something hard and glanced sideways without even grazing him. The brute had come prepared. He'd suspected I might do something desperate and was wearing a shirt of mail for protection. He now seized my wrist, tore the knife from my hand and said jeeringly:

' "So you wanted to kill me, my lovely Puritan. What ingratitude! After all I've done for you! I thought I'd tamed you. But don't worry. I'm not one of those tyrants who keep women against their will. You don't love me. For a time I was vain enough to think you might. Now I realize you don't. So I'll let you go timorrow."

'I was so wretched then that I wanted only one thing. I wanted him to kill me.

' "Take care!" I said. "If you let me go you'll lose your good name for ever."

' "What d'you mean?" he asked.

' "I mean that directly I'm free I'll tell the whole story. I'll say you seduced me by force. I'll describe how you imprisoned me. I'll denounce you and your wicked house. You're a man of rank, I know. But beware! There's a higher authority than you, the King. And there's a higher power still, God!"

'For all his self-control he gave a start of rage. I couldn't see his face, but my hand was on his arm and I felt it tremble.

' "In that case I shan't let you out of here," he said.

' "Very well!" I cried. "Then the scene of my shame will also be my tomb. I shall die here. My spirit will haunt this place day and night and prove to you that I can be a greater scourge to you dead than I can alive."

' "No. I won't let you kill yourself," he replied. "I'll keep all weapons out of your reach."

' "There's one weapon you can't keep out of my reach," I said. "Thank God I've got the courage to use that! I'll starve to death."

' "Listen," said my enemy. "Wouldn't it be more sensible to come to terms? Promise to say nothing and I'll release you at once. I'll proclaim you a virgin. I'll have you hailed as England's Lucretia."

' "And I'll have you hailed as England's Sextus Tarquinius," I replied. "I'll denounce you to the world as I've already denounced you to God. And, like Lucretia, I'll gladly sign my indictment of you with my blood."

'At this the fiend cried tauntingly: "Oh, so you're going to be obstinate. In that case you'll have to stay here. And after all you might do worse; you'll have everything you want and if you choose to starve to death, well, that's your affair."

'With these words he turned and left the room. I heard the door open and close again. I sank back on my bed, prostrated. I still minded my dishonour less than my failure to get my revenge. I confess this to my shame. My enemy kept his word. All that day and the next passed without my seeing him again. But I, too, kept my word. I touched neither food nor drink, for I was determined to carry out my threat of starving to death.

'I spent all night in prayer, imploring God to forgive my suicide.

'The next night my enemy visited me again. I was half lying on the floor with my head and arm resting on a chair, for my strength was beginning to fail. At the sound of the door opening I looked up. The brute came up to me and addressed me in his usual harsh, sardonic tone.

' "Well?" he said. "Have you calmed down, and are you going to be reasonable and buy your freedom at the price of silence? I'm a just man. I'm prepared to be generous even to Puritans. Swear on the Cross to say nothing and I promise I'll let you go."

'I got up; the voice I'd grown so to hate had given me back my strength. I cried out:

' "On the Cross I swear that no promises, no threats, no

tortures will silence my tongue. On the Cross I swear to de-
nounce you everywhere as a cowardly murderer and seducer.
On the Cross I swear that if I ever get out of here I'll rouse all
England against you!"

'My enemy glared at me:

' "Take care," he said. "I know a way of forcing you to
silence or at any rate of preventing anyone believing what you
say. I shall only use that if you compel me."

'I threw back my head and laughed defiance in his face. He
saw that from now on it was open war between us.

' "Listen," he said. "I'll give you till tomorrow evening to
decide. If you promise to say nothing I'll guarantee you wealth,
a position in the world, perhaps even rank. But if you won't
agree to my terms I'll make you an object of scorn and loathing
for ever."

' "*You* make *me* an object of scorn?" I cried.

' "Yes, a creature reviled by the world!"

'Oh, Felton, there was such hatred in his eyes then, I thought
he was mad. I cried out:

' "Leave me! Leave the room! If you don't I'll break my head
against this wall in front of you!"

' "Very well," he said. "It's for you to choose. I give you till
tomorrow evening."

'I managed to stammer out:

' "Till tomorrow evening."

'Then I collapsed on the floor from sheer weakness.'

Felton was listening spellbound. He was leaning heavily
against a table to support himself. Milady saw to her joy that
strong emotion had exhausted him and calculated that he
would probably break down entirely before she had even
finished her narrative.

CHAPTER XX

Histrionics in the Grand Manner

MILADY watched the young man for a moment in silence. Then she continued:

'I hadn't eaten or drunk anything for nearly three days. I was in great pain; every now and then mists would form before my eyes, clouding my sight. I was becoming delirious. By that evening I was so weak I kept fainting, and every time I fainted I thanked God, for I thought it was the end.

'I was going off into one of these faints when I suddenly heard the door open. I was terrified and my fear revived me. My seducer came in followed by a man in a mask; he was masked himself, but I recognized his step, his voice, and the accursed air of distinction which the Devil must have given him to spite mankind.

' "Well," he said. "Are you going to be sensible and promise what I asked?"

' "When we Puritans say a thing we mean it," I replied. "As I've already told you I'll never rest till you're brought to justice, on earth and in Heaven."

' "You swear that?"

' "I swear it before God, who is my witness."

' "You're a prostitute!" he thundered, "and shall suffer a prostitute's fate! You shall be branded! And then try and convince the world you're innocent! Try and make them believe your story then!"

'Upon which he turned to the man in the mask and said:

' "Executioner, do your duty!" '

Felton cried out again:

'His name! Tell me his name!'

'And now I began to realize that something worse than death was in store for me,' went on Milady. 'The executioner came up to me, seized hold of me and threw me on the floor. I cried out and struggled against him but was helpless and suffocated by his great weight. Sobbing, half swooning with pain, I called to God for help, but He didn't hear me. Suddenly I screamed in agony, for I felt a red-hot iron pressed against my shoulder. It was the executioner's branding iron.'

Felton gave a groan of horror. Milady got up.

'Look, Felton,' she said, 'look at the new torture they've invented for young, innocent girls who dare defy a tyrant. Learn the evil in men's hearts and never again let them make you the instrument of their unjust revenges.'

She swiftly opened her dress, tore the cambric which covered her shoulder and, flushed with spurious shame and indignation, displayed to the young man that ineradicable stigma, the executioner's brand-mark.

'But that's a fleur-de-lis!' cried Felton.

'That was the crowning infamy,' replied Milady. 'If he'd set the brand of England on me he'd have had to prove what court had sentenced me and I'd have appealed to every court in the country. But by marking me with the brand of France he left me powerless to prove my innocence.'

Felton had heard enough. He faced Milady, transfixed with horror at her tale and with wonder at her transcendent beauty and the air of sublime innocence with which she bared her breast and shoulder to him. Then he fell on his knees before her like a disciple before a martyr at the stake. He forgot the mark on her shoulder and remembered only her beauty.

'Forgive me! Forgive me!' he cried.

Milady looked into his eyes and read love in them.

'For what?' she asked.

'For siding with your persecutors.'

Milady held out her hand to him. Felton seized it and covered it with kisses.

'So young, so beautiful,' he murmured.

Milady gave him one of those looks which make a slave into a conqueror. Felton was a Puritan; he now let go of her hand and began kissing her feet. He no longer loved her, he worshipped her.

By degrees he grew calm again and Milady seemed to recover the composure which she had in fact never lost. She drew her dress back over her shoulder, thereby increasing Felton's desire for her. He said:

'And now you must keep your promise and tell me your seducer's name.'

'What?' cried Milady. 'D'you mean to say you haven't guessed?'

'Not he? Not that villain again?' cried Felton.

'Yes, that villain again. The scourge of England, the persecutor of all true Christians, the debauchee, the man who's willing to plunge two countries into war for a whim, who befriends the Protestants one day and betrays them the next.'

'Buckingham! So it was Buckingham!' said Felton in a voice cold with hatred.

Milady covered her face with her hands as though the very mention of his name was too horrible to bear.

'Buckingham's tortured this angel!' cried Felton. 'And Thou hast not destroyed him, Lord! Thou hast left him rich, powerful, and respected, for the downfall of mankind! Why, oh why?'

'The Lord forsakes those who forsake Him,' said Milady.

'The villain's courting the retribution of the damned!' cried Felton in growing excitement. 'But he'll have to answer for his crimes to mankind as well as to God.'

'Men fear him and leave him alone.'

'I don't fear him. I'll not leave him to carry on his crimes.'

Felton's words filled Milady's soul with glee. The young man continued:

'But how is my guardian, Lord de Winter, concerned in all this?'

'Alas, Felton, the good are sometimes found among the bad, as the wheat among the tares. I had a fiancé, a man who loved me and whom I loved; a man as good as you, Felton. I went to him and told him everything; he trusted me, and never doubted my word for a moment. He was a man of high position, Buckingham's equal in rank. When I told him my story he said nothing, but put on his sword and cloak and started off for Buckingham's house at once.'

'He was quite right,' said Felton. 'But a dagger's the weapon to use on a fiend like that, not a sword.'

'Buckingham had left London the night before on a mission to Spain to ask for the hand of the Infanta for Charles I, who was then Prince of Wales. My fiancé came back.'

' "The fellow's gone away and I can't settle with him till he returns," he said. "But let's be married in the meanwhile and as sure as my name's de Winter you can count on me to avenge mine and my wife's honour." '

'De Winter!' cried Felton.

'Yes, Lord de Winter,' repeated Milady. 'So now you understand. Buckingham was away nearly a year. Lord de Winter died suddenly, a week before his return, leaving me his sole heiress. Why did he die so suddenly? God, who knows everything, knows that. I accuse nobody . . .'

'To think a man could sink so low!' cried Felton.

'Lord de Winter had died without telling his brother my story. Not a soul knew my terrible secret. Your guardian hadn't approved of his elder brother's marriage to a penniless girl and I realized I could expect no support from a man disappointed in his hopes of inheritance. I crossed over to France meaning to stay there for the rest of my life. But all my fortune was in England. When war broke out I couldn't get any money over. I found myself literally destitute and had to return. Ten days ago I landed in Portsmouth . . .'

'And then?' asked Felton.

'Buckingham had obviously heard that I was coming back; he told Lord de Winter, who was predisposed against me, that I was a prostitute, that I was branded. My husband was no longer there to defend me. Lord de Winter believed everything Buckingham said, the more readily as it was in his interest to do so. He had me arrested and brought here and put in your charge. The rest you know. The day after tomorrow I'm to be banished, deported, sent to live among outlaws. Oh, the plot's well enough worked out and I'll never recover my good name! So you see, Felton, I've no choice but to die. Give me that knife, Felton. For pity's sake, give me that knife.'

As she spoke she pretended to have come to the end of her strength, and fell limp and unresisting into the young man's arms. Felton, crazed with love, anger, and sensual joys new to him, clasped her to his breast, trembling at the scent of her hair and the pressure of her body against his.

'No, no!' he cried. 'You must live honoured and with your good name restored; you must live to vindicate yourself before the world.'

Milady pushed him gently away with her hand, and at the same time beckoned to him with her eyes. Then he, in his turn, drew her to him.

'Oh, let me die, let me die,' she implored, lowering her voice and half closing her eyes. 'Let me die rather than suffer shame. Felton, my friend, my brother, I implore you, let me die!'

'No!' cried Felton. 'You shall live and be avenged.'

'Felton, wherever I go I bring calamity. Leave me to my fate, Felton. Leave me to die.'

'Then let's die together!' he cried.

And he pressed his lips to hers.

At that moment there came a loud knocking at the door. This time Milady pushed him away not in coquetry but in earnest.

'What was that?' she whispered. 'Oh God, they've overheard us! They're coming! That's the end. We're lost.'

'No,' said Felton. 'It's only the sentry warning me the patrol's doing its rounds.'

'Then go and open the door yourself.'

Felton obeyed; this woman was already all in all to him, his whole existence.

At the door he found the sergeant of the patrol.

'Well, what is it?' he asked the sentry.

'You told me to open the door if I heard anyone calling for help, Sir,' replied the latter. 'But you forgot to leave me the key. I heard you calling but couldn't hear what you were saying. I tried to open the door but it was locked from inside. So I called the sergeant.'

'I wish to report patrol present, Sir,' said the sergeant.

Felton, half demented, stood there speechless. Milady realized that it was for her to save the situation. She ran across the room and seized the knife which Felton had left lying on the table.

'What right have you to prevent me killing myself?' she said.

'Merciful Heaven!' muttered Felton, seeing the knife blade gleaming in her hand.

At that moment there came a shout of mocking laughter from the passage. Lord de Winter had been wakened by the noise and had come along in his dressing-gown, with his sword under his arm.

'So now we have the last act of the tragedy,' he said. 'Good! Just as I thought. You see, Felton, the drama's developed exactly along the lines I said it would. But don't worry, there'll be no suicide.'

Milady realized that all was lost unless she gave Felton immediate proof of her sincerity and courage.

'You're wrong, de Winter,' she said. 'There will be suicide and may my blood be on the heads of those who have caused it to be shed.'

Felton gave a cry and rushed towards her. It was too late. Milady had already stabbed herself.

But by good luck, or rather by good management, the blade had struck the steel busk which women wore in those days inside their bodices and which protected them like a breast-plate; it glanced off it, tearing her dress, and entered her body slantwise between her ribs.

But for all that Milady's dress was in one second impressively stained with blood. She fell back and appeared to have lost consciousness.

Felton drew the knife out of her body. Then he turned to Lord de Winter and said grimly:

'Look, Sir! Here you see a woman who was in my charge and who's killed herself!'

'Don't worry, Felton,' replied Lord de Winter. 'She's not dead. Vampires don't die as easily as that. Go and wait in my room.'

'But Lord de Winter . . .'

'Go. I order you to go.'

Felton had no choice but to obey his senior officer's command. But as he went out he concealed the knife beneath his coat.

Lord de Winter now summoned Milady's attendant and told her to see to her charge, who still lay unconscious on the floor. Then he went out, leaving the women alone together. He suspected that his sister-in-law's wound was not grave, but, to to make assurance doubly sure, he sent a messenger off posthaste on horseback to summon a doctor.

CHAPTER XXI

Escape

LORD DE WINTER was right. Milady's wound was not serious. In fact, no sooner was she alone with her attendant than she opened her eyes and looked round her. But she still had to pretend to be weak and in pain, no difficult task for an accomplished actress like Milady. The woman was completely deceived by her and insisted on remaining at her bedside all night.

Her presence did not, however, prevent Milady from reflecting and plotting.

She could now count on Felton. He was convinced of her innocence and was on her side. So strongly so that had an angel from Heaven appeared to him and pronounced her guilty he would have taken him for a demon from Hell. The knowledge of this was balm to Milady's soul, for Felton was her only hope, her only means of escape.

The thing most to be feared now was that Lord de Winter might suspect the young man himself and have him watched.

At about four in the morning the doctor appeared. But Milady's wound had already started to heal so he could assess neither its position nor its depth. From the state of her Ladyship's pulse, however, he was satisfied that it was not serious.

The next morning she dismissed her attendant on the pretext that she had spent a sleepless night and wished to be left alone to rest. She counted on Felton's returning at breakfast time. But Felton did not appear.

Were her fears justified? Did de Winter suspect Felton and was he keeping him away from her? Was she to be thwarted at the last moment? She had only one more day. Lord de Winter had told her that she was to be put on board on the twenty-third and it was now the morning of the twenty-second.

Her Ladyship waited impatiently till midday. She had eaten no breakfast but her midday meal was brought in at the usual hour. To her dismay she noticed that the soldiers who brought it in were wearing a different uniform. She took her courage in both hands and asked why Felton had not come. The soldiers replied that Felton had left the castle on horseback about an hour earlier. When Milady asked where Lord de Winter was the soldiers told her he was still in the castle and had given instructions that he was to be sent for when she wanted to see him. Milady replied that she was still too weak to see anyone and that she only wanted to be left alone.

The soldiers went out, leaving the meal spread out on the table.

So Felton had left and a new party of soldiers had been put in charge of her. This was the crowning stroke of ill-luck.

Alone once more the prisoner got up. In the hope that they would think her wound serious she had till then kept to her bed. But now it seemed hot and uncomfortable.

She glanced quickly at the door. Lord de Winter had had a board nailed over the grille. He was apparently afraid that by some devilish means she might succeed in seducing the guards through that small aperture. Milady was overjoyed at this, for it meant that she could now give full rein to her feelings without fear of being observed. She started pacing wildly up and down the room liked a caged tigress or a creature possessed. Had she still had the knife she would certainly have used it, not against herself this time but against her brother-in-law.

At six o'clock de Winter came in armed to the teeth. The man whom Milady had always dismissed as a rather simple type of English gentleman had become an excellent prison warder, prepared for any contingency. He had only to take one look at Milady to know what was passing through her mind.

'I know what you're thinking,' he said gravely. 'But you won't succeed in killing me even today. You're weaponless and I'm on my guard. You'd begun to corrupt poor Felton; he was on the point of succumbing to your wiles. But I was determined you wouldn't succeed with him, so I forbade him to see you any more. You're leaving us tomorrow, so have your things packed. I'd arranged for you to leave on the twenty-fourth, but on second thoughts the sooner you're on board the better. By midday tomorrow I shall have the order for your exile signed by Buckingham. If you speak a single word to anyone before embarking my sergeant has orders to blow your brains out. When you're on the ship the captain has orders to throw you overboard if you speak to anyone without his leave. That's all I have to say to you today. I'll come and say good-bye to you tomorrow.'

De Winter then turned and left the room.

Milady had listened to her brother-in-law's tirade with a smile of scorn on her lips but with rage in her heart.

An hour or two later the soldiers came in with her supper. Milady ate, for she felt she needed strength to endure what might happen that night. A storm was brewing; heavy clouds were chasing across the sky and there was distant lightning.

About ten o'clock the storm broke. Milady was comforted to see nature sharing the turmoil of her soul. The thunder roared in the heavens, a fitting accompaniment to the tempest of her emotions; it was as though the passing squalls tore at her brain as they beat and tore the leaves from the branches of the trees. She railed against Fate in harmony with the hurricane and the moan of despair in her voice was like the moaning of the wind. From time to time she glanced at a ring which she wore on her finger. The setting of that ring contained a strong and pervasive poison. In it seemed to lie her only hope.

Suddenly she heard a rap-tap on the window and a flash of lightning revealed a man's face pressed against the bars. She ran to the window and opened it.

'Felton,' she cried. 'I'm saved!'

'Yes,' he answered. 'But keep very quiet. It'll take some time to file through these bars. Don't let them see you through the grille.'

'They've nailed a plank over it,' replied Milady. 'That proves that God is on our side.'

'Yes,' answered Felton. 'God always confounds His enemies.'

'What d'you want me to do?' asked Milady.

'Nothing. Just shut the window. Get into bed, or at any rate lie down dressed on the bed. When I'm ready I'll knock on the pane. Will you be able to come down with me?'

'Oh yes!'

'What about your wound?'

'It hurts a little but doesn't prevent me walking.'

'Then get ready to leave at my signal.'

Milady closed the window again, put out her lamp and lay down on the bed, as Felton had advised.

In between the claps of thunder she heard the steady grinding of the file against the bars, and in the reflection of each lightning flash she saw Felton's shadow behind the window.

An hour passed during which Milady hardly dared breathe. She lay in the darkness, strained and tense, starting at every sound she heard in the passage.

That period of waiting seemed like a year.

An hour passed and then Felton tapped again on the pane. Milady sprang from her bed, ran over to the window and opened it. Felton had removed two bars, leaving an opening just wide enough to allow a man's body to pass.

'Are you ready?' asked Felton.

'Yes. Shall I bring anything with me?'

'Money, if you've got any.'

'Yes; they left me all I had.'

'That's lucky. I've spent all mine chartering a boat.'

'Take this,' said Milady, holding out a purse to him.

Felton took the purse and threw it down to the foot of the wall.

'Now, are you ready to come?'

'Yes.'

So saying, Milady stepped on to a sofa and manoeuvred her head and shoulders through the opening between the bars. She saw that the young officer was hanging above the cliff on a rope ladder. At the sight of the great drop below her she felt suddenly frightened and shrank back.

'I was afraid that would happen,' muttered Felton.

'It was nothing,' said Milady. 'I'll keep my eyes closed as I go down.'

'You must have confidence in me,' said Felton.

'I have.'

'Cross your hands; that's right.'

Felton tied her wrists together first with his handkerchief and then with a piece of rope.

'What are you doing?' asked Milady.

'Put your arms round my neck and don't be frightened.'

'But my weight will throw you off your balance and we'll both fall and be killed.'

'Don't worry. I'm a sailor.'

There was not a moment to be lost. Milady put her arms round Felton's neck and worked the rest of her body through the window.

Felton started to walk slowly down the ladder step by step. In spite of the weight of their two bodies the ladder swayed to and fro in the gale.

Suddenly Felton stopped.

'What is it?' whispered Milady.

'Quiet,' he answered. 'I heard footsteps.'

'Have they seen us?'

Felton did not reply for a moment. Then he said:

'No. It was nothing.'

'What was that noise?'

'The patrol doing its round.'

'Where are they?'

'Just below us.'

'They'll see us.'

'Not unless there's a lot more lightning.'

'They'll knock against the bottom of the ladder.'

'Luckily it ends six feet short of the ground.'

'Oh God, there they come!'

'Quiet!'

The two hung motionless, hardly daring to breathe, twenty feet above the ground, while below them the patrol passed, laughing and talking. For the two fugitives it was a terrible moment. Then the patrol went on. They heard their footsteps and their voices growing faint in the distance.

'Now we're safe,' said Felton.

But Milady was unconscious.

Felton continued slowly down the ladder. When he reached the bottom and felt no more support for his feet he clung to the rope with his hands only, slid down by the force of his wrists and when he reached the end of the ladder dropped to the ground. He then picked up the purse of gold and put it between his teeth. Then he lifted Milady in his arms and started off in the opposite direction to the patrol.

Soon he left the road and plunged down among the rocks towards the sea. When he reached the shore he gave a low whistle. At once there came an answering signal and five minutes later a long-boat appeared, manned by a crew of four. It came as close inshore as possible but the water was too shallow for its bows to touch the beach. Felton walked waist-deep into the water, not wishing to hand over his precious burden to another. Fortunately the storm was beginning to abate, but the sea was still rough, and the boat bobbed up and down on the waves like a cockleshell.

When the two fugitives were safely on board Felton called out to the crew:

'To the sloop. And row like the devil.'

The four men set to work with the oars, but it was heavy going and they made little headway. But they were increasing the distance between them and the castle, and that was vital.

It was a pitch dark night. The shore was now barely visible from the boat and it was reasonable to suppose that the boat was no longer visible from the shore.

Out to sea a black dot was just discernible on the water; it was the sloop.

While the long-boat was progressing slowly towards the sloop Felton untied the rope and the handkerchief which still bound Milady's hands. He then dashed salt water into her face to revive her. Milady sighed and opened her eyes.

'Where am I?' she said.

'You're saved,' replied the young officer.

'Saved!' she cried. 'Yes, I see the sky and the sea and I'm breathing the fresh air of freedom. Oh, thank you, Felton, thank you.'

The young man pressed her to his heart.

'What are these marks on my hands?' asked Milady. 'My wrists feel as though they'd been manacled.'

She lifted up her arms and showed the bruises on her wrists.

'Oh, your poor hands!' said Felton, looking at her tenderly.

'It's nothing,' said Milady. 'I remember now.'

She then looked round her as though searching for something.

'It's here,' said Felton, tapping the purse of gold with his foot.

At last they came within hailing distance of the sloop. The sailor on watch challenged the long-boat and Felton answered the challenge.

'What's that ship over there?' asked Milady.

'The ship I chartered for you,' replied Felton.

'Where's it taking me?'

'Wherever you want to go. But you must first put me ashore at Portsmouth.'

'What are you going to do at Portsmouth?'

'Carry out Lord de Winter's orders,' said Felton, smiling grimly.

'What orders?' asked Milady.

'Don't you know what happened?'

'No. How could I?'

'Lord de Winter began to suspect me and wanted to guard you himself. To keep me out of the way he sent me to Buckingham with your deportation order.'

'But if he suspected you why did he trust you with the order?'

'He didn't know I knew what I was carrying. He'd said nothing to me himself. I only learnt the truth from you.'

'I see. And still you're going to Portsmouth?'

'Yes. And I must hurry. Tomorrow's the twenty-third, the day Buckingham's due to leave with the fleet.'

'Where's he going?'

'To La Rochelle.'

Milady forgot herself for a moment and cried out:

'He mustn't!'

'Don't worry,' replied Felton. 'He won't.'

Milady felt a sudden thrill of triumph. From the tone of the young man's voice she guessed his purpose in going to Portsmouth and in his eyes she read Buckingham's doom.

'Felton,' she said, 'you're a saviour of mankind. You're a second Judas Maccabeus. If you die I'd like to die with you. What more can I say?'

'Hush,' said Felton. 'We've arrived.'

At that moment the long-boat came alongside the sloop. Felton stepped first on to the gang-plank and held out his arm to Milady, while the sailors helped her out of the boat, for the sea was still very rough.

The next moment the young man and woman were standing on the bridge and Felton was addressing the captain of the sloop.

'Here's the lady I spoke to you about,' he said. 'You agreed to take her to France.'

'Yes. For a thousand pistoles,' replied the captain.

'Of which I've already paid you five hundred,' said Felton.

'Correct,' said the captain.

'And here are the other five hundred,' said Milady, holding up the purse of gold.

'No, Ma'am,' said the captain. 'This gentleman and I agreed I was to get the other five hundred when we reached Boulogne, and I prefer to stick to that.'

'Will you get me there all right?'

'I'll get you there, sure as my name's Jack Butler.'

'Very well,' said Milady. 'If you keep your promise I'll give you not five hundred but a thousand pistoles.'

'Long life to Your Ladyship then,' cried the captain. 'And may God send me many a passenger like you.'

'You must first sail us to the bay of Chichester just this side of Portsmouth,' said Felton. 'That was part of our bargain.'

The captain shouted an order to the crew and the ship at once got under weigh. At seven next morning it anchored in the little bay of Chichester.

During the journey Felton described to Milady the previous day's events. Instead of going to London he had chartered the sloop; he had then returned to the castle, scaled the wall by putting flints in the clefts between the stones, and, as he climbed higher, staples to give him a foothold. On reaching the window he had fastened the rope ladder to the bars.

'The rest you know,' he said.

Milady at first thought she would have to inspire Felton with further courage to carry out his plan. But she soon realized that the young hothead needed restraint rather than encouragement.

It was agreed that the sloop should wait for Felton till ten o'clock. If he had not returned by then it was to set sail for France with Milady on board. Provided he escaped with his life Felton was then to join her in France, in the Carmelite Convent in Béthune, where the Cardinal had ordered her to take refuge.

CHAPTER XXII

What Happened at Portsmouth on 25 August 1628

WHEN Felton took leave of Milady he kissed her hand, assuring her that they would not be parted for long. Outwardly he seemed as calm as ever; only his eyes shone unusually bright, like the eyes of a man with fever. His jaw was set and he rapped out his orders sharply, which showed that something was preying on his mind. While he was being rowed ashore in the long-boat he kept his gaze fixed on Milady who, for her part, followed him with her eyes from the deck of the sloop. Neither was very concerned about the danger of their being pursued. The soldiers had never wakened Milady before nine o'clock, and it would take three hours to get from the castle to Portsmouth.

Felton stepped ashore and climbed the little path which led to the top of the cliff. Then he turned, waved a final farewell to Milady and started off towards the town. He walked about a hundred yards downhill until he could only see the top of the sloop's mast. Then he started off at a brisk pace in the direction of Portsmouth, whose towers and houses he could see dimly outlined in the morning mist about a mile away. The sea beyond Portsmouth was strewn with ships, whose masts swayed gently to and fro in the breeze like a forest of stripped poplars.

As he strode along Felton remembered all the charges, true and false, that he had heard levied by the Puritans against the favourite of both James I and Charles I. Comparing the minister's public crimes, which were notorious in England and abroad, with the crimes he had committed in private, which were not common knowledge and known to him only through Milady, he came to the conclusion that Buckingham the man was even more wicked than Buckingham the minister. His sudden, all-consuming passion for Milady had magnified and distorted her false accusations in his mind, as through a microscope specks of dust loom up like gigantic and grotesque spiders.

The speed at which he strode along, his experiences of the past few days, and the thought that he was leaving in danger the woman he loved, or rather worshipped, all served to inflame his senses and uplift him abnormally.

He entered Portsmouth at eight in the morning. The whole population was up and about. The drums were beating in the streets and in the harbour, and the embarking troops were being marched down to the ships.

Felton arrived at the Admiralty damp with sweat and covered with dust from head to foot. His face, naturally pale, was flushed from his exertions. The sentry tried to prevent him from entering the building, but Felton asked to see the sergeant of the guard, produced his guardian's letter and said:

'An urgent message from Lord de Winter.'

Hearing the name Lord de Winter, who was known to be one of Buckingham's most intimate friends, and seeing Felton's naval uniform, the sergeant gave the order to let the young man through.

Felton rushed up the steps. But at that moment another man appeared and made for the entrance. He was also travel-stained and out of breath. He had left his horse loose on the terrace and the beast was so exhausted that it fell forward on its knees. The stranger and Felton approached Patrick, the Duke's personal servant, at exactly the same moment. Felton gave Lord de Winter's name. The stranger refused to give any name and declared that he could only reveal his identity to the Duke himself. Each man demanded precedence. Patrick, knowing Lord de Winter to be in close military contact and on intimate terms with the Duke, decided to admit his envoy. The other man was obliged to wait, and his annoyance at this delay was plain to see.

The servant led Felton up a staircase and across a large reception room in which the deputies from La Rochelle were assembled under the leadership of the Duc de Soubise. Signing to Felton to wait he went into a private dressing-room where

Buckingham, having had his bath, was dressing with his usual care. Patrick announced:

'Lieutenant Felton, with a message from Lord de Winter.'

'From Lord de Winter?' repeated Buckingham. 'Show him in.'

As Felton entered Buckingham was exchanging a splendid gold-embroidered dressing-gown for a blue velvet, pearl-embroidered doublet.

'Why didn't Lord de Winter come himself?' asked Buckingham. 'I was expecting him this morning.'

Felton replied:

'His Lordship told me to tell Your Grace that he regretted not being able to come owing to special guard duty at the castle.'

'I know,' said Buckingham. 'He's got a prisoner there.'

'Yes, your Grace. That's what I've come about.'

'Oh yes? And what can I do for you?'

'I'd like to speak to you in private, your Grace.'

'Leave us, Patrick,' said Buckingham. 'But keep near the bell. I'll ring in a few moments.'

Patrick went out.

'We're alone now, Sir,' said Buckingham. 'So speak out.'

Felton replied:

'Lord de Winter wrote to you the other day to ask you to sign a deportation order for a young woman called Charlotte Backson.'

'Yes. And I told him that if he sent or brought the order I'd sign it.'

'Here it is, Your Grace.'

'Let me see it.'

The Duke took the paper from Felton's hand, glanced quickly at it, identified it as the order in question, and took up his pen to sign it.

'Excuse me, your Grace,' broke in Felton, 'but do you realize that Charlotte Backson's not the young woman's real name?'

'I do,' replied the Duke, dipping his pen into the ink.

'And d'you know her real name, Sir?' asked Felton gravely.

'Yes.'

The Duke put his pen to the paper.

Felton went very pale.

'You know who she is, Sir,' he said, 'and you're still prepared to sign that order?'

'Most certainly,' replied Buckingham. 'In fact knowing who she is makes me doubly anxious to sign it.'

At this Felton said sternly:

'I can't believe your Grace really knows that the lady's ... Lady de Winter.'

'I do indeed. But I confess I'm surprised you do.'

'And you'll sign that order without any qualms of conscience, Sir?'

Buckingham gave the young man a haughty stare.

'You're asking me some rather impertinent questions, Mr Felton,' he said. 'You surely don't expect me to answer them!'

'You'd better answer, Sir,' replied Felton. 'I don't think you realize how serious this matter is.'

It occurred to Buckingham that the young man might not be speaking in his own name but have had orders from Lord de Winter to find out his opinion. So he relented and said:

'Why should I have any qualms about signing this order? Lord de Winter knows as well as I that Lady de Winter's a criminal, and that merely to banish her's almost letting her off scot free.'

And he again laid his pen on the paper. Felton stepped up to the table at which he was seated.

'You will not sign that order, Sir,' he said.

'Not sign it?' cried Buckingham. 'Why in Heaven's name not?'

'Because you'll search your conscience and see that justice is done to Lady de Winter.'

'To do her justice would be to send her to Tyburn,' replied Buckingham. 'Lady de Winter's a fiend!'

'Your Grace, she's an angel and you know it. I ask you to give her her freedom.'

'Are you mad, Sir, talking to me like this?' cried Buckingham.

'On the contrary, your Grace, I'm being very forbearing with you. But don't try me too hard!'

'Well I'm damned!' shouted Buckingham. 'I do believe the fellow's threatening me!'

'No, your Grace. I'm merely warning you as man to man. A single drop can make a full cup overflow; a small offence can bring down punishment on one who, for all his crimes, has so far escaped justice.'

'Mr Felton,' said Buckingham, 'you'll kindly leave this room at once and put yourself under close arrest.'

'No, your Grace, you shall hear me out,' replied Felton gravely. 'You've seduced this young woman, outraged and defiled her. Make good your crimes against her, set her free! Do that and I'll ask no more of you.'

Buckingham looked at the young man in amazement.

'*You'll* ask no more of *me*!' he echoed. 'Huh! That's very good of you, I'm sure!'

'Your Grace,' went on Felton, his excitement growing as he spoke, 'take care. England's sick and tired of you and your misdeeds. You're abhorrent to God and man. God will punish you later, but I'm going to see that you're punished now.'

'This is intolerable!' shouted Buckingham.

He got up and made for the door, but Felton barred his way.

'Once more I ask you, Sir,' he said. 'Sign the order for Lady de Winter's release. Remember she's the woman you ruined.'

'Leave the room, Sir,' cried Buckingham furiously, 'or I'll ring for my household and have you put in irons!'

'No, Sir, you will not ring!' replied Felton, stepping between the Duke and the bell which stood on a silver inlaid table beside him.

'Take care, your Grace,' he continued, 'you're in God's hands now.'

'In the Devil's hands, you mean,' replied Buckingham, raising his voice so that his staff should hear, without actually calling them.

Felton held out a scroll of paper to the Duke.

'Sign Lady de Winter's release, Sir,' he said.

'D'you think you can force me to sign? D'you think you can browbeat me? Patrick, Patrick!'

'Sign, your Grace!'

'Never!'

Then he shouted, 'Help!' and rushed to take hold of his sword. But Felton did not give him time to draw. Under his doublet he had the knife with which Milady had stabbed herself. He sprang at the Duke.

At that moment Patrick burst into the room, crying:

'Your Grace, a letter from France!'

'From France!' exclaimed the Duke, off his guard at the sudden realization of what the letter meant.

Seeing his chance Felton stabbed him in the side, driving the knife into his body right up to the hilt.

'Villain!' cried Buckingham. 'You've killed me!'

'Help, murder!' cried Patrick.

Felton looked wildly round him for a way of escape. He saw that the door was unguarded and rushed into the next room where the La Rochelle deputies were waiting. He ran headlong through this room and dashed to the head of the stairs.

But here he came face to face with Lord de Winter, who, seeing him so haggard, wild-eyed and with his face and hands stained with blood, guessed the truth. He seized him by the throat, crying:

'I knew it, I knew it, and I've arrived just too late! Oh fool, fool that I've been!'

Felton put up no resistance. Lord de Winter handed him over to the guards, who took him on to a small terrace overlooking the sea, where they awaited further orders. De Winter had meanwhile dashed into Buckingham's dressing-room.

When the man whom Felton had met in the hall heard the Duke's cry and Patrick's call for help he also came running up. He found Buckingham lying on a sofa, trying to stem the blood from his wound by pressing his knuckles against it.

'Laporte!' exclaimed the Duke faintly. 'Have you come from her?'

'Yes, your Grace,' replied Anne of Austria's faithful servant. 'And I pray not too late!'

'Hush, Laporte! They might hear you outside. Patrick, don't let anyone in. Oh God, I shall never know what she had to say to me! I'm dying.'

Whereupon the Duke fainted.

Meanwhile Lord de Winter, the deputies, the leaders of the expedition and the officers of Buckingham's staff had all forced their way into the room. Everywhere cries of alarm were heard. The news of the assault soon reached beyond the building and spread like wildfire through the town. A salvo of guns was fired to announce that something unusual had happened.

Lord de Winter was overcome with grief and self-reproach.

'Just a minute too late,' he moaned. 'A minute too late! Oh God, what a disaster!'

He had been told at seven that morning that a rope ladder was hanging from one of the castle windows. He had at once rushed into Milady's bedroom and had found it empty with the window open and two of the bars filed away. He had then suddenly recalled the verbal warning which d'Artagnan had sent him by his messenger, Planchet. He had at once feared for the Duke's safety, had hurried to the stables, leapt astride the first horse he saw and galloped off at full speed to Portsmouth. On reaching the Admiralty he had dismounted in the courtyard, hurried up to the Duke's dressing-room and, as we know, come face to face with Felton at the top of the stairs.

Meanwhile the Duke was still struggling for life. He came to again and opened his eyes, and everyone began to hope he would recover.

'Gentlemen,' he said, 'leave me alone with Patrick and Laporte. Ah, de Winter, is that you? That was a queer fellow you sent me this morning! Look what he's done to me!'

'Oh, your Grace, your Grace!' cried de Winter. 'I shall never forgive myself.'

'That would be wrong of you,' said Buckingham, holding out his hand to him. 'No man deserves to be mourned for a lifetime. But now be good enough to leave me. I want to talk to Monsieur Laporte.'

Lord de Winter left the room in great distress. And now the Duke, Laporte, and Patrick were alone. The Duke's household were searching the town for a doctor, but none could be found. The Queen's messenger knelt at the Duke's side and repeated over and over again:

'You won't die, your Grace. You'll recover!'

Buckingham was lying on the sofa. Blood was flowing freely from his wound. But so eager was he to talk of the woman he loved that he forgot his pain and weakness. In a faint voice he asked:

'What does she say in that letter? Read it aloud to me.'

'Your Grace!' protested Laporte.

'Come on, Laporte, do as I say. Don't you see I've got very little time left?'

Laporte broke the seal and held the scroll to the Duke's eyes. Buckingham tried to read the letter but his sight was beginning to fail.

'Read it yourself, Laporte. My sight's failing. Soon my hearing'll go too, and I shall die without knowing what she had to say to me.'

Laporte made no further protest and read as follows:

Your Grace,

Remember what I have suffered through you and on your behalf since I first met you, and, if you are concerned for my happiness, stop your vast designs against France. Stop this war. You pretend to be fighting in the cause of religion, but everyone says that your real motive is your love for me. The war is bound to bring misery to our two countries and likely to bring great unhappiness to yourself, which would make me unhappy too.

Take care! Your own life is in danger. And that will be precious to me from the day when I need no longer regard you as an enemy.

Your affectionate

Anne.

Buckingham summoned up all his fast failing strength to listen to Laporte's reading. When he had heard the letter through to the end he said in a tone of bitter disappointment:

'Have you no further verbal message for me, Laporte?'

'Yes, your Grace. The Queen told me to tell you to take care. She'd been warned there was to be an attempt on your life.'

'Is that all, is that all?' asked Buckingham impatiently.

'She also told me to tell you she still loved you.'

Buckingham sighed a deep, long-drawn-out sigh.

'God be praised,' he said. 'Then my death will really mean something to her.'

At this Laporte started to weep.

'Patrick,' said the Duke, 'bring me the rosewood box which had the diamond tags in it.'

Patrick brought the box and Laporte recognized it as having belonged to the Queen.

'And now the white satin bag with her pearl-embroidered initials.'

Patrick brought the bag.

'Laporte,' said Buckingham, 'here are the only two mementos I have of her, this box and these two letters. Please return them to Her Majesty. And as a last token from me to her take . . .'

He looked round the room to find some fitting memento. But his sight was failing with the approach of death and the only thing his eyes lit on was the knife which had fallen from Felton's hand and which lay on the floor beside him, still dripping with his own blood.

'As a last token of my love take her that knife,' he said.

He still had strength enough to place the bag inside the box and to lay the knife on top of it. Then he signed to Laporte that he could no longer speak. He was now seized with a final convulsion which shook his whole frame and threw him from the sofa on to the floor.

Patrick gave a cry of horror. Buckingham smiled a last smile and then died. But the smile remained on his lips after death, as though his soul were bidding the world a glad farewell.

At that moment the Duke's doctor arrived in a great state of alarm. He had gone aboard the flagship before the murder, and had had to be brought ashore. He went up to the Duke, took his hand, held it for a moment and then dropped it.

'There's nothing to be done,' he said. 'He's dead.'

'Dead! Dead!' cried Patrick.

Hearing his cry the people in the ante-room rushed back into the dressing-room, and soon the whole building was in a turmoil.

When Lord de Winter saw that Buckingham was dead he went at once to find Felton, whom the soldiers were still holding in custody on the terrace. He found the young man calm and collected; now that the deed was done Felton seemed to be at peace with the world.

'You miserable wretch!' cried Lord de Winter. 'What have you done?'

'I've taken my revenge,' replied the young man.

'Taken your revenge? You mean you've been duped by that fiend? I promise you you're her last victim! This crime will be her last.'

'I'm afraid I don't understand, Sir. I assure you there's no woman involved. I killed Buckingham because he refused me a captaincy in spite of your recommendation. I punished him for being unjust.'

De Winter was utterly taken aback. He stared at Felton in amazement, not knowing what to make of such callousness.

Only one thing now preyed on Felton's mind. He feared in his innocence that Milady, dreading for his safety, might come in search of him, find him, fling herself into his arms and decide to die with him.

Suddenly he gave a start of surprise. The terrace commanded a view of a wide stretch of sea. He was staring at the horizon when he noticed what another man would have taken for a gull floating on the waves, but which his experienced eye told him was the sloop in full sail making for the coast of France. In a flash he realized that he had been betrayed. He went deathly pale and a wave of agony swept through him. Turning to Lord de Winter he said:

'May I ask one last favour, Sir?'

'What's that?' inquired his guardian.

'I'd like to know what time it is.'

Lord de Winter took out his watch.

'Ten minutes to nine,' he said.

Milady had set sail an hour and a half before the time agreed. Directly she heard the salvo of guns announcing the fateful event she had given orders for the anchor to be weighed. And now the sloop was scudding along under the blue sky and was already a considerable distance from the coast.

With the resignation of a true fanatic Felton murmured:

'God has willed it so.'

And yet he could not tear his eyes from the little speck on the ocean nor his mind from the vivid memory of the woman for whom he was about to give his life.

De Winter followed his gaze, saw the suffering on his face and guessed everything. The guards now seized Felton and started to drag him away. The young man put up no resistance but still kept his eyes fixed on the horizon.

'You'll be punished alone first, miserable wretch!' called de Winter after him. 'But I swear on my beloved brother's head that your accomplice will be punished too!'

Felton said nothing in reply but allowed the guards to lead him off.

Lord de Winter now left the building and made his way quickly to the harbour.

CHAPTER XXIII

In France

THE chief concern of Charles I, King of England, on learning of Buckingham's death, was that the terrible news might cause the people of La Rochelle to lose heart. Richelieu says in his memoirs that he tried to hide it from them as long as possible by closing all the English ports, and by putting an embargo on all foreign vessels at present in those ports until the army which Buckingham had raised had itself left, offering to supervise its embarkation himself in place of his late minister. So determined was he to prevent all foreigners leaving the country that he actually detained the Danish Ambassador in England after he had sent in his papers, and also the Dutch Ambassador, who was to have taken back to Flushing some ships of the Dutch East Indies fleet, which England was returning to the United Provinces.

Unfortunately it did not occur to him to take these steps until five hours after Buckingham's murder, that is to say, until about two in the afternoon. In the interval two ships had slipped out of Portsmouth harbour. One was the sloop with Lady de Winter on board; when Milady heard the salvo from the shore batteries she suspected what had happened, and when she saw the bunting on the Admiral's flagship lowered to half-mast she knew for certain that Buckingham was dead.

As for the other vessel which left the harbour we shall see later how it escaped and who was on board.

Meanwhile there had been no new developments in the La Rochelle campaign. The King was still tremendously bored, perhaps even more so than usual. He decided to go and spend the St Louis festival at St Germain, and asked the Cardinal to grant him an escort of twenty musketeers. The Cardinal, who was sometimes as bored as the King himself, gladly agreed to His Majesty's departure, and it was arranged that he should return on about 15 September.

Monsieur de Tréville heard of the King's decision from the Cardinal, and at once prepared for the journey. He knew how keen the four friends were to return to Paris, though he did not know why, and therefore detailed them to form part of the King's escort. The young men learned the news only half an hour after Monsieur de Tréville himself, for he told them before any of the others. Now d'Artagnan realized to the full his luck in having been transferred to the Musketeers; had he still been a guardsman he would have had to remain in camp while his three friends returned to Paris.

The four friends' keenness to return to the capital was due chiefly to their concern for the safety of Madame Bonacieux. We remember that Athos, Porthos, and Aramis had overheard the Cardinal tell Milady to return at once to France after her mission and to go to the Carmelite Convent at Béthune. By a most unfortunate coincidence this, as we know, was where Madame Bonacieux had been sent on the Queen's order, after her release from the Nantes prison. The friends calculated that if Lord de Winter had not succeeded in putting his sister-in-law out of harm's way while she was in England she would have returned to France by now and would shortly be arriving at the convent in Béthune. They dreaded to think of Madame Bonacieux's fate when Milady, her mortal enemy, discovered her there. In their concern for her safety they had agreed that Aramis should write again to Marie Michon, the seamstress in Tours with the grand connections, to persuade the Queen to allow the young woman to leave the convent and go into hiding either in Lorraine or Belgium. Aramis had not had to wait long for a reply. About a week after writing he received the following answer:

My dear Cousin,

    Here is my sister's authority to remove our little servant girl from the convent at Béthune, which you think is an unhealthy district for her.

    My sister sends you this authority with her best wishes for your success; she is very fond of the girl and hopes to be able to help her later.

My love,

Marie Michon.

    To this letter was attached a written authority from the Queen herself which ran as follows:

    The Superior of the Béthune Convent will please deliver the novice who was received into the convent on my recommendation into the charge of the bearer of this note.

Anne.

The Louvre, August 10th, 1628.

    We can understand how amused Aramis' three friends were at his pretence of kinship with this seamstress who referred to the Queen as her sister. Aramis blushed scarlet once or twice at Porthos' coarse innuendoes; then he got angry and declared that if the subject were ever referred to again he would refuse to employ his 'cousin' as intermediary in the plot. So the name Marie Michon was never again mentioned by any of the four friends; they were thankful to have got what they wanted from her, an authority to remove Madame Bonacieux from the Béthune convent.

But they realized only too well that this authority was useless so long as they remained in the La Rochelle camp, that is to say, at the other end of France. D'Artagnan had therefore decided to ask Monsieur de Tréville for leave on a matter of urgency. When he called on his captain great was his joy to hear that the King was travelling to Paris with an escort of twenty musketeers, of which he and his friends were to form part. His friends were equally delighted at the news. They sent their servants on ahead with their luggage, and they themselves left with the King on the morning of 16 August.

The Cardinal accompanied His Majesty as far as Mauzes, and here the King and his minister took leave of each other with a great display of affection.

His Majesty wished to do the journey as quickly as possible in order to reach Paris by the 23rd, and yet could not resist dawdling a little on the way to fly his falcon, a pastime which he had learned from de Luynes, Madame de Chevreuse's first husband, and of which he was very fond. Sixteen of the twenty musketeers were delighted with these periodic halts, but the other four, as was natural, fumed at the enforced delay, d'Artagnan most of all. He constantly complained of a mysterious burning in his ears, which Porthos interpreted as meaning that someone was talking about him.

At last, on the night of 23 August, the royal party reached Paris. The King thanked Monsieur de Tréville for his escort and promised to grant the men under his command four days' leave, on condition that none of them appeared in any public place on pain of the Bastille.

The first four to be granted leave were, of course, our four friends. Monsieur de Tréville did Athos the additional favour of giving him two days' extra leave, and generously added two extra nights as well, by post-dating the period of leave to the 25th, although the four men actually set off on the evening of the 24th.

'I think we've been making a lot of fuss about nothing,' said d'Artagnan confidently. 'It's really the easiest thing in the world. If I ride two or three horses to death (and I can afford to do that now) I can get to Béthune in two days. Then I merely hand the Queen's letter to the Superior of the convent, bring back my darling Constance and hide her, not in Lorraine or Belgium, but in Paris itself; she'll be much better hidden there, particularly now that the Cardinal's at La Rochelle. When the campaign's over we'll get what we want out of the Queen, partly through her sister's influence and partly for what we've done for her ourselves. So you fellows stay here; don't exhaust yourselves for nothing. Planchet and I can manage this little trip on our own.'

To this Athos replied:

'We've got money too, you know. I haven't yet drunk away all my share of the diamond and Porthos and Aramis haven't yet eaten up all theirs. Between us we can afford to ride twelve horses to death. And remember, d'Artagnan,' he went on in a warning tone, 'Béthune's the town where the Cardinal's arranged to meet the arch-fiend. If you were up against four men I'd say "Go alone" every time. But you've got this woman to deal with and I say let's all go and take our servants too. And even then let's pray Heaven we'll be strong enough to defeat her.'

'Athos, you put the fear of God in me,' cried d'Artagnan. 'What on earth d'you think'll happen?'

'Anything may happen,' replied Athos.

D'Artagnan looked at Porthos and Aramis and noticed that both had the same anxious expression. So he gave in and agreed to Athos' suggestion, and all four left Paris that very night for Béthune, taking their servants with them.

On the evening of the 25th they reached Arras. D'Artagnan had just dismounted at the 'Golden Harrow' inn to drink a quick glass of wine when a man rode out of the courtyard where he had been hiring a remount, and started off at the gallop on a fresh horse in the direction of Paris. Although it was August he was wearing a heavy cloak and a wide-brimmed hat. Just as he was riding out of the main gate into the street the wind blew his cloak half open and lifted the brim of his hat. The stranger immediately caught hold of his hat and pressed it down low on his forehead, but not before d'Artagnan, who had been observing him closely, had caught a glimpse of his face. The young man went very white and dropped his glass of wine.

'What's the matter, Sir?' cried Planchet. 'Gentlemen, gentlemen, come quick; my master's fainting!'

The three others came running up. They found d'Artagnan not fainting at all but running towards his horse. They stopped him at the gate.

'Where the deuce d'you think you're going?' said Athos.

'It's the fellow himself,' cried d'Artagnan, pale and trembling with rage. 'Let me get at him!'

'What fellow?' asked Athos.

'That blackguard, my evil genius. I always meet him when there's trouble brewing. You know, the fellow who was with Milady when I met her for the first time, the fellow I was after when I had the row with Athos, the fellow I saw talking to Bonacieux in the street, the day we left for England. The fellow from Meung, in fact. I recognized him when the wind blew his hat up. It was him all right!'

Athos frowned.

'The devil it was!' he said.

'Come on, all of you!' cried d'Artagnan. 'Let's ride after him. We'll catch him!'

'Listen, d'Artagnan,' said Aramis. 'He's going the opposite way to us. He's got a fresh horse and ours are worn out. If we followed him we'd ride our horses to death and never get near him.'

At that moment a stable-boy ran out into the road, calling after the stranger.

'Hi, Sir! You've left something behind. This note dropped out of your hat. Hi, Sir! Hi! Hi!'

D'Artagnan went up to the boy.

'I'll give you half a pistole for that note, my lad,' he said.

'Most happy, Sir, I'm sure,' replied the boy. 'Here it is.'

And he ran back into the courtyard, delighted at this unexpected piece of good luck.

D'Artagnan unfolded the note while his friends waited for him to read it to them.

'Well?' they asked.

'There's only one word written on it,' said d'Artagnan.

'Yes,' said Aramis. 'But it's the name of a town.'

Porthos read out:

'Armentières.'

'Armentières?' he went on. 'Where's that? I've never heard of it.'

'And it's her handwriting!' cried Athos.

'We must guard this note with our lives,' said d'Artagnan. 'Perhaps we'll find that half-pistole of mine wasn't misspent after all. And now let's be off again.'

The four young men leaped into the saddle and galloped off in the direction of Béthune.

CHAPTER XXIV

The Carmelite Convent at Béthune

ALL great criminals are known to enjoy long periods of prosperity, during which they seem to flourish in their wickedness and even to be guided by some star, which helps them to surmount all obstacles and to defy the deadliest dangers. Then suddenly an angry Providence intervenes and strikes them down. Thus it was with Milady. The sloop which carried her from England ran the gauntlet of the battleships of two nations and arrived safely in Boulogne. When she had disembarked at Portsmouth she had posed as an Englishwoman who had been driven out of La Rochelle by French persecution. Now, disembarking at Boulogne, she posed as a Frenchwoman whom the English, in their hatred of France, had been persecuting at Portsmouth. Besides this alias Milady had two assets as effective as any passports – personal attraction, and some hundreds of pistoles to scatter among greedy officials.

She was granted an interview with the Governor of the port, who immediately fell a victim to her charm and exempted her from the usual Customs formalities. Milady in fact stayed in Boulogne only long enough to post one letter. It was addressed to:

His Eminence,
    The Cardinal Richelieu,
        At the Camp of La Rochelle,

and ran as follows:

Monseigneur,
    Rest assured that the Duke of Buckingham will not leave for France.

Lady de ...

P.S. – In accordance with Your Eminence's orders I am starting at once for the Carmelite Convent at Béthune, where I will await your further pleasure.

Having despatched her letter her Ladyship set forth that same evening. She spent that night at an inn. At five the following morning she set out again, and three hours later arrived at Béthune. Here she asked to be directed to the Carmelite Convent and drove straight to the main gate.

The Mother Superior came out to meet her. Milady showed her the Cardinal's written authority, and the Reverend Mother ordered a room and breakfast to be prepared for her.

By now Milady had driven all her past experiences from her mind as a nightmare. Her thoughts were entirely fixed on the future and she looked forward to the glorious prospects in store for her as a reward for her bold stroke. She had served the Cardinal well and had not allowed her complicity in the damnable plot to be even suspected. Her life with its ever-surging passions and ambitions was like a sky swept by storm-clouds, inky black or fiery red, which pass and leave only destruction in their wake.

After breakfast the Abbess came to pay her respects to her new guest. Convent life offers few distractions, and the Reverend Mother was anxious to make Milady's acquaintance. Milady, for her part, wanted to make a good impression on the Abbess, no difficult task for a woman of her talents. She tried to be pleasant and succeeded in being fascinating, charming her hostess by her conversation and gracious manner. The Abbess's parents were aristocrats and the good lady liked to hear stories of the Court, which only rarely reached the frontiers of the kingdom and could not hope to penetrate convent walls, against which the world's turmoil beat in vain. Milady was well versed in Court intrigues, having for the past six years been closely involved in State affairs.

She now set to work to entertain the good Abbess with tales of the worldliness of the French Court, which formed such a startling contrast to the King's outward display of godliness. She told her scandals connected with names famous throughout France, names which the Abbess recognized at once; she touched lightly on the love-affair of the Queen with Buckingham, hoping by her flow of talk to encourage the Abbess to respond. But the Abbess merely listened attentively and said nothing.

By degrees Milady turned the conversation to the subject of the Cardinal. But now she had to tread warily, for she did not know whether the Abbess was a Royalist or a Cardinalist. At first she steered a prudent middle course, while the Abbess was even more cautious, confining herself to bowing low every time her visitor mentioned His Eminence's name.

Milady, fearing that she would be bored to death during her enforced stay in the convent, resolved to be a little indiscreet in order to find out quickly how the land lay. To provoke the Abbess to speak she began to talk disparagingly of the Cardinal, at first in general terms and then in particular, mentioning his love-affairs with Madame d'Aiguillon, Marion de Lorme, and other famous courtesans. The Abbess listened closely, smiled a little and gradually grew more animated.

'Good,' thought Milady, 'she's enjoying my chatter. If she's a Cardinalist she's certainly not a fanatic.'

Then she began to talk about the Cardinal's reign of terror. To this the Abbess said nothing but merely lowered her eyes and crossed herself, which seemed to confirm Milady's view that she was more Royalist than Cardinalist. She continued to embroider her theme until at last the Abbess was provoked to speak.

'I know very little about these things,' she said. 'But out of touch as we are with Court affairs and cut off from this world's problems we do come to hear of some very sad instances of what you describe. We've actually got a novice at the convent now who's being persecuted by the Cardinal.'

'A novice here?' echoed Milady in surprise. 'Poor soul! God knows I pity her!'

'And well you may. She's been through a lot; she's been imprisoned, manhandled, ill-treated in every way. But of course we mustn't judge rashly. The Cardinal may have had very good reasons for acting as he did, and though the child looks angelic enough you can't always judge by appearances.'

'Good,' thought Milady. 'I may find out something here. Perhaps I'm in luck.'

Aloud she said, with an air of disarming candour and as though she were opening her heart to the older woman:

'I know, Reverend Mother. They say one mustn't judge by appearances. But what can one judge by, if not by the Lord's fairest handiwork? I suppose I shall always be imposed upon in this world, but I shall continue to trust people if they look good and kind.'

'So you'd be inclined like myself to believe this young woman innocent?' suggested the Abbess.

'The Cardinal doesn't only punish people for crimes,' said Milady. 'Certain virtues are more obnoxious to him than the worst vices.'

'Forgive me if I say I'm surprised to hear you talk like that,' remarked the Abbess.

'Why?' asked Milady innocently.

'It's not usual to hear the Cardinal spoken of like that. You must be a friend of His Eminence since he sent you here. And yet . . .'

The Abbess paused.

'And yet I criticize him, you mean?' prompted Milady.

'Well, you haven't said anything to his credit, have you?'

Milady sighed.

'The fact is, Reverend Mother, I'm not his friend at all,' she said. 'I'm another of his victims.'

'Then how d'you explain his letter recommending you to me?'

'It's merely an order sentencing me to a form of imprisonment. He'll be sending his secret agents for me soon.'

'Why didn't you escape?'

'Where could I have gone? The whole world's within the Cardinal's grasp if he takes the trouble to stretch out his hand. If I were a man I might have managed it. But what can a woman do? Did that novice of yours try to escape?'

'No, you're right; she didn't. But with her it's different. I fancy some love-affair's keeping her in France.'

Milady sighed again.

'If she's in love then she's not altogether unhappy,' she said.

The Abbess observed Milady with increasing interest.

'So now I've got another victim of oppression on my hands,' she said.

'Alas, yes,' replied Milady.

For a moment the Abbess stared uneasily at her visitor as though some unpleasant thought had suddenly struck her.

'You're not an enemy of our blessed Faith, are you?' she stammered.

'I, a Protestant?' exclaimed Milady. 'Oh no! I'm a devout Catholic. I swear that, as God is my witness.'

The Abbess smiled with relief.

'In that case Lady de Winter,' she said, 'your imprisonment, if you can call it that, will not be hard, and we'll do all we can to make you happy. Besides, you've got a fellow sufferer here, the young novice I was telling you about. She's clearly the victim of some Court intrigue. She's a good, kind soul. I'm sure you'll enjoy her company.'

'What's her name?'

'She was recommended to me by someone very influential as "Kitty". I've never troubled to ask her her other name.'

'Kitty!' exclaimed Milady. 'Are you sure?'

'I'm sure that's the name she goes by. Yes, Lady de Winter. Why? D'you know her?'

Milady had started involuntarily at the name of 'Kitty'. She now controlled herself and replied:

'No. I don't know her. I have a close friend of the name of Kitty, but she's a very different person. The coincidence of the two names being the same struck me. That was all.'

Milady smiled inwardly at the thought that the young novice might be her former maid. On having the girl thus recalled to her mind she felt a sudden wave of anger against her. Her desire to take revenge on her was so strong that for a moment she forgot herself and allowed a spiteful look to cross her face. But in a flash she regained her composure and gave the Abbess a sweet smile.

'And when shall I have the pleasure of meeting this young woman?' she asked. 'From your description I already feel attracted to her.'

'You can meet her this evening, this afternoon, if you like,' replied the Abbess. 'But you told me you'd been travelling for four days and that you were on the road at five this morning. You need a rest. Go to bed and try and sleep. We'll wake you at lunch-time.'

Milady decided to follow the Abbess's advice, although she could well have done without sleep, elated as she was by the prospect of this new adventure; to her intrigue was the spice of life. But in the last fortnight she had lived through so many crises that, strong as was her constitution, her mind needed rest. So she asked the Abbess to leave her and lay down on her bed, lulled by secret thoughts of revenge which the recollection of Kitty had roused in her. She remembered how the Cardinal had promised her almost complete freedom to carry out her schemes if she succeeded in her mission. She had succeeded; she would therefore be able to revenge herself on d'Artagnan.

One thing alone appalled her, the recollection of her husband, the Comte de la Fère, whom she had believed dead and who had returned to her in the shape of Athos, d'Artagnan's best friend. But then it occurred to her that if he were d'Artagnan's friend he had probably been involved in the various plots which had enabled the Queen to outwit the Cardinal; as d'Artagnan's friend he was the Cardinal's foe, and could therefore be included in any plans of revenge against d'Artagnan. All these fantasies were as balm to Milady's spirit; lulled by these thoughts she soon fell into a peaceful sleep.

She was wakened by a gentle voice calling her from the foot of the bed. She opened her eyes and saw the Abbess and a young woman with fair hair and a fresh complexion, who was gazing at her with a look of kindly inquiry on her face. The new arrival was a complete stranger to her. The two women eyed each other closely as they exchanged the usual formal compliments. Both were beautiful but in different ways. Milady rejoiced to see that she was vastly more distinguished-looking than the young novice and had more poise, though she admitted that the nun's habit which her rival wore would not show a woman at her best.

The Abbess introduced them. Then, her religious duties calling her, she begged to be excused and went out, leaving the two women together.

The novice was about to follow the Abbess out of the room for, as Milady was in bed, she concluded she did not wish to be disturbed. But Milady called her back.

'Don't go, my dear!' she exclaimed. 'I've only just got to know you. I was hoping you'd stay with me a little while. I'm relying on you to keep me company for at least some part of my stay in this place.'

'I shall be delighted, Lady de Winter,' replied the novice. 'I only thought that this was a bad time, as you were asleep when we came in and you must be tired.'

'After a sleep it's nice to have a pleasant surprise on waking. You're the pleasant surprise in this case. Let me enjoy you in comfort.'

And she took the novice by the hand and motioned her to an arm-chair which was beside her bed. The novice sat down.

'Oh dear, how unfortunate this is!' she exclaimed. 'I've been here six months and my life's been almost unbearably dull. Now you arrive. I was thrilled at the idea of having you to talk to. And now I hear I'm to leave the convent at any moment.'

'Leave the convent?' cried Milady.

'Yes, at least I hope so,' replied the novice, her eyes shining with a joy which she was at no pains to conceal.

'I gather you've got into the Cardinal's bad books,' said Milady. 'That would have been an added bond between us.'

'So what the Reverend Mother told me was true!' cried the novice. 'You're another of that wicked priest's victims!'

'Hush!' said Milady. 'Don't talk of him like that even in here. You never know who's listening. All my troubles arose from my once saying more or less what you said just now in front of a woman whom I thought was my friend and who informed on me. Was that how you got into trouble?'

'No,' replied the novice. 'I got into trouble through being loyal to a woman I loved, a woman I'd have given my life for, whom I'd give my life for even now.'

'Didn't she stand by you?'

'For some time I was wicked enough to believe she'd turned against me. Then a few days ago I discovered my mistake, for which I thank God. I'd have been miserable if she really had deserted me. But you, Lady de Winter, surely you're a free agent; you could easily get out of here if you wanted to.'

'Where could I go? I've got no friends and no money, and I don't know this part of France at all.'

'I'm sure you'd never lack for friends!' cried the novice. 'You're so beautiful and I'm sure you're good too.'

Milady smiled a sad, sweet smile.

'Even so I'm alone and the victim of oppression,' she said.

The novice replied:

'Lady de Winter, we must trust in God's mercy. Sooner or later God rewards us for the good we've done in this world. Perhaps God has brought you and me together so that I can help you. If I get out of here I've got powerful friends who'll work for me. When they've finished fighting my battles I'll get them to use their influence for you.'

Milady pricked up her ears at this. She hoped that by continuing the conversation along these lines the novice would be provoked into committing some indiscretion. To stimulate her further she now remarked:

'When I said I was alone I didn't mean that I hadn't also got powerful friends. But strong as they are, they're frightened of the Cardinal. Why, even the Queen daren't do anything which might interfere with his plans, and I know for a fact that, good as she is, she's often had to sacrifice people who've done her yeoman service because the Cardinal demanded their heads.'

'No, Lady de Winter,' replied the novice. 'The Queen may appear to sacrifice these people but she doesn't really. The more victimized they are the more she thinks about them, and often when they've given up hope they suddenly find she'd been working for them in secret all the time.'

'Yes, I can well believe that,' said Milady. 'The Queen is so good.'

The novice replied enthusiastically:

'So you know her then? You know our great and good Queen? You must know her to talk of her like that!'

Milady replied evasively:

'I haven't the honour of knowing her personally. But I know a great many of her intimate friends. I know Monsieur Putange, I knew Monsieur Dujart in England, and I know Monsieur de Tréville.'

'You know Monsieur de Tréville?' cried the novice.

'Yes. Quite well, in fact.'

'The captain of the King's Musketeers?'

'The captain of the King's Musketeers.'

'Oh, how exciting!' cried the novice. 'I'm sure we'll soon discover we've got lots of friends in common. In fact at this rate we'll soon be good friends ourselves. If you know Monsieur de Tréville you must have been to his house.'

'Often,' replied Milady.

She had embarked on her policy of lying, saw that it was succeeding and decided to pursue it. She was by now thoroughly enjoying the conversation.

'When you were in Monsieur de Tréville's house you must have met some of his musketeers,' continued the novice.

'All who visit him regularly.'

'Mention a few you know by name,' said the novice, 'and I'll see if I know any of them.'

Milady was slightly disconcerted by this. After a moment's thought she said:

'Well, I know Monsieur de Louvigny, Monsieur de Courtivron, Monsieur de Férussac . . .'

The novice waited for her to continue. Seeing her hesitate she ventured:

'You don't happen to know a gentlemen of the name of Athos?'

Milady went as white as the sheets on which she was lying, and so far lost her composure as to start up in bed, seize the novice by the hand and stare at her, wide-eyed with fear. The unfortunate girl exclaimed:

'What on earth's the matter, Lady de Winter? Have I said something to offend you?'

'No, no,' replied Milady hastily. 'You see I did happen to know Monsieur Athos at one time and it seemed so strange to meet someone who also knew him.'

'I know him very well,' said the novice, 'and I know his friends too, Monsieur Porthos and Monsieur Aramis.'

Milady became more and more alarmed.

'Do you?' she replied. 'So do I.'

'As good and true a set of men as you could find,' continued the novice. 'If you know them why don't you appeal to them to get you out of trouble?'

Milady was struggling hard to control her emotion. To gain time she remarked quickly:

'When I said I knew them I didn't mean I knew any of them personally. I know of them through a friend of theirs, Monsieur d'Artagnan.'

It was now the novice's turn to start, go pale and stare at Milady in alarm.

'You know Monsieur d'Artagnan?' she cried. Then, noticing a strange look on Milady's face, she added coldly:

'Excuse me, Lady de Winter, but may I ask what exactly Monsieur d'Artagnan is to you?'

'Why, a . . . a friend, of course,' stammered Milady in great embarrassment.

'You're lying to me, Lady de Winter,' said the girl. 'You've been his mistress.'

'No,' retorted Milady, 'on the contrary, it's you who've been his mistress.'

'I!' exclaimed the novice.

'Yes, you. I know who you are now. You're Madame Bonacieux.'

The young woman shrank back and stared at the older woman in terror and surprise.

'Don't trouble to deny it,' said Milady.

'Very well, Lady de Winter,' answered the novice. 'I admit it. I love him. Are we rivals?'

A light of maniac rage suddenly shone in Milady's eyes, which at any other time would have frightened the younger woman out of her wits. But now she was entirely concerned with her jealousy. With a firmness surprising in one so gentle she repeated:

'Lady de Winter, I insist on knowing whether you've been Monsieur d'Artagnan's mistress!'

'No, never!' cried Milady in a tone of such scorn that it was obvious she was speaking the truth.

'Very well, I believe you,' said Madame Bonacieux. 'But why did you cry out like that?'

Milady had by now recovered her poise and presence of mind. Quick as a flash she said, in answer to Madame Bonacieux's question:

'What? You mean to say you don't understand?'

'How could I?' replied the girl. 'What do I know about your relations with Monsieur d'Artagnan?'

'Well, I'll explain the whole thing. It's perfectly simple. Monsieur d'Artagnan, being my friend, took me into his confidence.'

'Oh?'

'Yes. He told me everything. How you'd been kidnapped in the summer-house at St Cloud, how miserable he and his friends had been and how they'd searched everywhere but lost all trace of you. So you can imagine my surprise when I suddenly realized who you were, after the many hours we've spent discussing you. You, the woman he loves more than anything in the world and whom he'd persuaded me to love before I ever knew you! So I've found you, dear Constance! I've met you at last!'

And Milady stretched out her arms to embrace Madame Bonacieux. The poor girl was completely convinced by Milady's explanation, and having a moment ago eyed her askance as a rival now saw in her a sincere and devoted friend. She laid her head on her shoulder and cried:

'Oh, forgive me, forgive me! You see I love him so.'

For a moment the two women clung to each other. Had Milady's sinews been as strong as her feelings Madame Bonacieux would not have come out of that embrace alive. But since she could not strangle her she smiled at her.

'You dear, sweet, pretty child!' she said. 'How wonderful it is to have found you! Let me look at you!'

And she held her at arm's length and did, in fact, gaze long and searchingly at her.

'Yes, it's you all right,' she went on. 'I recognize you exactly from his description.'

The poor girl had no suspicion of the frightful thoughts that were passing through Milady's mind, of the cruel impulses that lay behind that pure brow and those limpid blue eyes, in which she read only affection and pity.

'Knowing how unhappy he's been you'll realize how unhappy I've been,' said Madame Bonacieux. 'But to be unhappy about him is to be happy.'

Milady echoed absent-mindedly:

'Yes, to be unhappy about him is to be happy.'

'And in any case my sufferings are nearly over now,' continued Madame Bonacieux. 'Tomorrow, possibly tonight, I shall see him again and then the past will be forgotten.'

Madame Bonacieux's last words startled Milady out of her reverie.

'What's that you say?' she exclaimed. 'Tomorrow? Possibly tonight? Whatever do you mean? Are you expecting news of him?'

'I'm expecting him himself.'

'Monsieur d'Artagnan? Here?'

'Yes.'

'But that's impossible! He's with the Cardinal at La Rochelle. He can't return to Paris till the siege is over.'

'It sounds incredible, I know. But I say that a man like my d'Artagnan can do anything!'

'I wish I could believe you but I can't.'

In her excitement at the thought of seeing her lover again the young woman was now so ill-advised as to take a letter out of her bodice and hand it to Milady, saying:

'Just read this!'

Milady glanced at the letter.

'Madame de Chevreuse's writing,' she muttered to herself. 'Very interesting. I always suspected they were getting information from that quarter.'

She read rapidly through the letter, which ran as follows:

My dearest child,

Get ready. You'll be seeing 'our friend' soon. He's coming to remove you from the prison where we had to hide you for your own safety. Get ready to leave at once, and never lose faith in us again.

Our young Gascon has just given us further proof of his devotion and courage. Tell him they're very grateful to him in certain quarters for his warning.

'Yes, yes,' said Milady. 'The letter's clear enough. But what do they mean by "his warning"?'

'I don't know for certain, but I suspect he warned the Queen of some fresh villainy on the part of the Cardinal.'

'Yes, that's probably what it is,' said Milady.

She returned the letter to Madame Bonacieux and laid her head back against the pillows.

At that moment they heard the sound of a horse galloping down the road. Madame Bonacieux rushed to the window crying:

'It couldn't be him already!'

Milady lay motionless on her bed, paralysed with fear. Such a rapid succession of surprises had robbed her of her usual presence of mind.

'Could it be him!' she echoed faintly.

And she lay rigid, her eyes wide and staring.

'No, alas, it's not him!' called Madame Bonacieux from the window. 'It's a man I don't know. He looks as though he's making for the convent. Yes, he's reining in his horse; he's stopped at the door; he's ringing the bell.'

Milady sprang out of bed.

'You're certain it's not d'Artagnan?' she said.

'Quite.'

'Perhaps you didn't get a proper look at him?'

'Oh, I'd know him at once. I'd know him from the feather in his hat or the edge of his cloak.'

Milady began dressing hurriedly.

'Never mind,' she exclaimed. 'The man, whoever he was, stopped here, you say?'

'Yes. And he's come into the house now.'

'He's obviously come either for you or for me.'

'You look terribly upset, Lady de Winter. Do keep calm.'

'I wish I had your courage, my dear. But I know the Cardinal. I know he'll stop at nothing.'

'Hush,' said Madame Bonacieux. 'Somebody's coming up the stairs.'

The next moment the door opened and the Reverend Mother appeared.

'A gentleman's called asking for a lady who's come from Boulogne,' she said, addressing her new visitor. 'Have you come from Boulogne?'

'Yes, yes, I have,' replied Milady. 'It must be me he wants.'

Then, struggling to keep calm, she asked:

'Who is the man?'

'He won't give his name, but he says he's under orders from the Cardinal.'

'You're sure he wants to see me?' asked Milady.

'He wants to see the lady who's come from Boulogne.'

'Well then, show him in, Reverend Mother.'

'Oh dear, oh dear!' wailed Madame Bonacieux. 'I do pray it's nothing bad for you.'

'It doesn't look too hopeful,' said Milady.

'Well, I'd better leave you now to see this gentleman, whoever he is,' said the girl. 'But if I may I'll come back when he's gone.'

'Of course you may, my dear. In fact I hope you will.'

The Mother Superior and Madame Bonacieux left the room.

Milady remained alone. She stood motionless, staring at the door. A few seconds later she heard the sound of spurs jingling on the stone stairs and of footsteps approaching. Then the door opened and revealed a man standing on the threshold. When Milady saw him she gave a cry of joy. It was the Comte de Rochefort, the Cardinal's private spy.

CHAPTER XXV

The Female and the Male

MILADY and Rochefort cried out simultaneously:

'So it's you!'

Milady went on:

'Where have you come from?'

'La Rochelle. And you?'

'From England.'

'And Buckingham?'

'Dead or seriously wounded. I'd got nothing out of him and was just leaving England when some fanatic murdered him.'

'What an incredible piece of luck!' said Rochefort, smiling ironically. 'His Eminence *will* be pleased! Have you told him?'

'I wrote to him from Boulogne. But what's brought you here?'

'His Eminence was concerned about you and sent me to find out if you'd got here all right.'

'I arrived yesterday.'

'What have you done since?'

'Quite a lot. I haven't wasted my time.'

'I'm sure of that.'

'Guess who I've met here?'

'I can't imagine.'

'The young woman the Queen rescued from prison.'

'What? You mean young d'Artagnan's mistress?'

'Yes. Madame Bonacieux. You remember the Cardinal had lost track of her.'

'That's another stroke of luck which pairs well with the first. Fate seems to be on the Cardinal's side.'

'You can imagine my surprise meeting her like that,' said Milady.

'Does she know who you are?'

'She knows my name but nothing about me.'

'She doesn't connect you with any of her troubles?'

Milady smiled.

'On the contrary, I'm her best friend,' she said.

Rochefort replied with a laugh:

'My dear Lady de Winter, no one but you could have worked a miracle like that.'

'It was lucky I did make friends with her,' replied Milady. 'What d'you think's happening tomorrow?'

'I've no idea,' said Rochefort.

'They're coming to take her away from here. They've got the Queen's written authority.'

'Oh! And who's "they"?'

'D'Artagnan and presumably his friends.'

'Those devils again! I can see we shall have to put them in the Bastille after all.'

'Why didn't you do that long ago?'

'You may well ask. I can't think why, but the Cardinal's got a soft spot for them.'

'Has he indeed? Well, I can tell him something which will harden his heart. D'you know, Rochefort, that those four men eavesdropped on his conversation with me at the Red Dovecote inn, and that after he left me one of them came up to my room and took my safe-conduct pass from me by force! Tell His Eminence that. Tell him, too, that those men got news through to Lord de Winter that I was coming to England and again all but succeeded in checkmating me, as they did in the affair of the diamond tags. Tell the Cardinal all that. And tell him that of the four only two are really dangerous, d'Artagnan and Athos. Tell him Aramis is Madame de Chevreuse's lover, and that it would be good policy to leave him alone. We know his secret and he might be useful. Tell him the fourth man, Porthos, is a pompous ass, not worth troubling about.'

'But surely those four fellows are away on the campaign!'

'I thought so too. But I saw a letter from Madame de Chevreuse to Madame Bonacieux – the little goose actually showed it to me herself – from which I gathered that none of them are at the siege at all, but all on their way to this convent to remove her.'

'The Devil they are! What had we better do?'

'What did the Cardinal want me to do?'

'He wanted you to give me a full written or verbal report which I was to take back to him at once. When he knew what you'd done he'd decide what you were to do next.'

'Does he want me to stay here?'

'Yes, here or somewhere fairly near.'

'Can't you take me with you?'

'No. His Eminence said definitely not. You might be recognized if you went anywhere near the camp, and if it was known that you were there he'd be compromised, especially after what's happened in England. You must stay either here or in this neighbourhood. If you're not going to stay here you must tell me where you'll be, so that I shall know where to find you when I've got fresh orders for you.'

'I may not be able to stay on here, Rochefort.'

'Why not?'

'I told you. My enemies may be here at any moment.'

'Yes, of course. But if you go little Madame Bonacieux may escape, and that'll annoy the Cardinal.'

Milady smiled her crafty smile.

'Don't worry about that,' she said. 'Remember I'm her best friend.'

'Yes, I forgot. As far as she's concerned, then, I can tell the Cardinal ...'

'Not to worry.'

'Will he know what that means?'

'He'll guess.'

'Very well,' said Rochefort. 'And now what must I do?'

'Leave at once. I think the news I've given you's well worth taking back.'

'My post-chaise broke down just as I got into Lilliers.'

'Good!'

'Why good?'

'I need your chaise myself,' said Milady.

'And how am I to do the journey?'

'You can ride back.'

'D'you realize it's over five hundred miles from here to La Rochelle?'

'That won't kill you.'

'Very well, I'll ride. And what about the chaise?'

'When you pass Lilliers send it and your servant here,' said Milady. 'And tell your servant he's to take orders from me in future.'

'Right.'

'I imagine you've got an authority from the Cardinal on you?'

'I've got my full warrant.'

'Show it to the Abbess and tell her someone will be coming for me either today or tomorrow and that I'm to be put in the charge of the man who comes in your name.'

'Very well.'

'Remember to speak badly of me to the Abbess.'

'Why?'

'I'm supposed to be one of the Cardinal's victims. I've got to go on pretending that for the little Bonacieux creature's benefit.'

'Of course. And now will you write a full report of everything you've done?'

'I've told you everything I've done. You've got a good head. Repeat the things I said back to me and memorize them. It's dangerous to write things down; reports get lost.'

'True. But you must tell me where I can find you again. I don't want to waste time searching all the neighbouring villages.'

'No, of course not. Let me think a moment.'

'D'you want a map?'

'Oh no, I know this district thoroughly.'

'How? When were you here before?'

'I was brought up here.'

'Were you, by Jove!'

'You see, there are advantages in being brought up outside Paris.'

'Well, where will you be waiting?'

'Let me think. Ah, I know the very place – Armentières.'

'What's that? A village, a town, or what?'

'A small town on the river Lys. From Armentières I'd only have to cross the river to be out of the country.'

'Excellent. But you won't cross the river unless you're forced to, will you?'

'No, that's agreed,' replied Milady.

'If you do have to cross it how shall I find you?'

'Can you manage without your servant for a while?'

'Yes.'

'Is he trustworthy?'

'Absolutely.'

'Let me keep him for a time. Nobody knows him. If I do cross the river I'll leave him behind and he'll bring you on to where I am.'

'And for the present you'll stay at Argentières?'

'Armentières,' corrected Milady.

'Write that place down for me to make sure I don't forget it. There's nothing compromising in the name of a town, surely?'

'Well, let's hope not.'

And Milady sat down and wrote 'Armentières' on a half sheet of paper.

Rochefort took the sheet from her, folded it and slipped it into the lining of his hat.

'Don't worry,' he said. 'I'll do what children do, repeat the name over and over again to myself as I go along in case I lose the paper. And now is that all?'

'I think so.'

'Let's see if I've got everything right . . . Buckingham dead or seriously wounded; your talk with the Cardinal overheard by the four musketeers; Lord de Winter told about your going to England; d'Artagnan and Athos to go to the Bastille; Aramis, Madame de Chevreuse's lover; Porthos a pompous ass; Madame Bonacieux found again; my chaise and servant to be sent to you as soon as possible; I'm to speak badly of you to the Abbess to gull her; you're going to Armentières on the banks of the Lys. Is that right?'

'Rochefort, your memory's phenomenal! And there's just one thing more. I've noticed some charming woods just beyond the convent garden. Tell the Abbess to allow me to walk in those woods. You never know; I might have to make a quick escape by some side door if those fiends descended on me suddenly.'

'You think of everything.'

'And you, you've forgotten one thing.'

'What's that?'

'To ask me if I need money.'

'Of course. How much do you need?'

'Every sou you've got on you.'

'I've got about five hundred pistoles.'

'And I've got another five hundred. A thousand pistoles ought to do me all right. Give me your five hundred.'

Rochefort handed her the whole sum.

'Thank you, Rochefort,' said Milady. 'And now when are you leaving?'

'In about an hour. I'll send my servant for a post-horse and meanwhile get myself something to eat.'

'Excellent. Well, good-bye, Rochefort.'

'Good-bye, Lady de Winter.'

'My respects to the Cardinal,' said Milady.

'And mine to the Devil,' retorted Rochefort.

They smiled at each other. Then Rochefort turned and left the room.

An hour later he was galloping out of the town. Five hours later he was in Arras.

We have already heard how d'Artagnan recognized him, how alarmed the four friends were to see him and how his presence in the district brought home to them the need to reach Béthune without delay.

CHAPTER XXVI

A Drop of Water

HARDLY had Rochefort left the room when Madame Bonacieux reappeared. To her surprise she found Milady looking quite cheerful.

'Oh dear!' she exclaimed. 'So your worst fears have been realized! The Cardinal's sending for you this evening or to-morrow morning.'

'How do *you* know that, dearest?'

'I heard his messenger saying so.'

'Come and sit over here, near me,' said Milady.

'Very well.'

'Now I'll just make sure no one's listening,' said Milady.

'Why all this secrecy?'

'You'll see.'

Milady got up, walked to the door, opened it, glanced down the passage and then came back and sat down beside Madame Bonacieux.

'I see he played his part well.'

'Who?'

'The man who called here, who pretended to be the Cardinal's envoy.'

'What? Wasn't he really that?'

'No, he was only pretending to be.'

'So he's not . . .'

'He's not what he said he was,' replied Milady, lowering her voice. 'Far from it. He's actually my brother.'

'Your brother!' exclaimed Madame Bonacieux.

'You're the only one who knows this, my dear, so keep it very dark. If you repeat it to a single soul I shall be lost and you too, perhaps.'

'Good Heavens! How awful!'

'Listen. I'll tell you what happened. My brother was coming to rescue me, and take me away from here, by force if need be. On the way he ran into the Cardinal's envoy, who was also coming for me. My brother followed him. When they reached a lonely part of the road my brother drew his sword and told the messenger to hand over his papers. The man tried to defend himself and my brother killed him.'

'How terrible!' cried Madame Bonacieux with a shudder.

'There was nothing else to be done, was there? My brother then decided to get me out of here not by force but by a trick. He took the messenger's papers and rode on. When he got here he pretended to be the Cardinal's agent himself. He deceived the Abbess completely and told her His Eminence would be sending a carriage for me in an hour or two.'

'I see. And the carriage will be your brother's carriage?'

'Exactly. And I've got something else to tell you. That letter you got, you think Madame de Chevreuse wrote it, don't you?'

'Yes. Why? Didn't she?'

'It's a forgery.'

'A forgery?'

'Yes. A trap to make sure you don't try to resist when the Cardinal's men come for you.'

'But d'Artagnan's coming!'

'Don't you believe it! D'Artagnan and his friends are campaigning at La Rochelle.'

'How d'you know that?'

'On his way here my brother ran into a party of the Cardinal's men dressed as musketeers. They saw he'd seen through their disguise and that spoilt their game. They were coming here dressed like that. They'd have called you to the door. You'd have taken them for friends, gone off quite happily with them and been taken back to Paris a prisoner.'

'Good Heavens! Is that really true? You're saying the most terrible things, Lady de Winter. I didn't know such villainy existed. I feel quite dazed by all these intrigues. If I hear much more I shall go mad.'

Milady suddenly started.

'Listen!' she said.

'What is it?'

'I hear a horse trotting down the street. That must be my brother going off. I must wave good-bye to him. Come and stand beside me.'

Milady opened the window, and she and Madame Bonacieux watched Rochefort riding past.

'Good-bye, George dear!' called Milady.

Rochefort looked up, saw the two women at the window and without drawing rein waved a friendly farewell.

'Good, kind George,' said Milady to her companion as she closed the window. On her face was a look of tenderness tinged with sadness. She went and sat down in her arm-chair and appeared to be lost in thoughts of an entirely personal nature.

'Dear Lady de Winter,' said Madame Bonacieux, 'forgive me for interrupting you, but what d'you advise me to do? I seem to be in a terrible fix. You've got more experience than I. Can't you suggest something?'

'Of course I may be wrong and d'Artagnan and his friends may really be coming for you,' replied Milady.

'Oh, that would be too wonderful!' cried Madame Bonacieux. 'I wouldn't deserve such happiness.'

'In that case,' continued Milady, 'it would be merely a question of who got here first. If your friends arrived first you'd be saved; if the Cardinal's men got here first you'd be lost.'

'Yes, yes. It would be all up with me then. I couldn't expect any mercy from them. What am I to do? Oh, what am I to do?'

'I can think of one possible way out for you.'

'What's that?'

'You could hide somewhere close by and wait to see who arrived.'

'But where?'

'I know a place. When my brother's carriage comes for me I'm going off in it to hide somewhere a few miles from here and wait for my brother to join me. Why don't you come too? We'll hide together and watch what happens.'

'But they won't let me leave the convent. I'm virtually a prisoner here.'

'The Abbess thinks I'm being taken away on the Cardinal's order. She's not likely to suspect you of wanting to come with me.'

'No, I suppose not.'

'The carriage will be waiting at the door with my brother's servant as outrider. You'll step on to the footboard to give me a good-bye kiss. I'll tell the servant beforehand that when he sees you there he's to sign to the coachman to whip up the horses. You'll jump in and we'll gallop off.'

'But suppose d'Artagnan does come?'

'We'll find out all right.'

'How?'

'I'll send my brother's servant back to Béthune. He's completely trustworthy. He'll disguise himself somehow and take cover where he can see the convent. If he sees the Cardinal's men arrive he'll keep hidden; if he sees Monsieur d'Artagnan and his friends he'll go up to them and bring them to us.'

'Does he know them by sight?'

'He does indeed. He's seen Monsieur d'Artagnan often enough at my house.'

'Of course. I was forgetting. Well, that sounds a very good plan. But don't let's go too far away from here.'

'A seven or eight hours' drive would get us to the frontier. That would be a good place to wait. If anything went wrong we could be out of the country at a moment's notice.'

'And what shall we do between then and now?'

'Wait.'

'And if they come?'

'My brother's carriage will get here first.'

'Suppose I'm at the other end of the building when it comes for you? Suppose I'm at lunch or supper?'

'I think we can get round that.'

'How?'

'Tell the Abbess you want to see me as much as possible, and would like to have your meals with me.'

'D'you think she'd allow that?'

'I can't see why not.'

'Marvellous! Then we'll never be separated for a moment.'

'That settles that, then. Now go down and ask the Abbess's permission. I've a slight headache and while you're seeing the Abbess I'll take a walk round the garden.'

'Where shall I find you?'

'Come back here in an hour. I'll be back by then.'

'Very well. I'll meet you here in an hour. Oh, how good you are, Lady de Winter! I'm so grateful to you!'

'Nonsense, my dear! It's only natural I should be interested in you; you're so pretty and attractive and you're the friend of one of my oldest friends.'

'Dear d'Artagnan!' whispered Madame Bonacieux. 'He'll be so grateful to you!'

'I hope so indeed. And now let's both go down.'

'You're going into the garden?' asked the novice.

'Yes.'

'Follow that passage. You'll find a little staircase at the end which'll take you to it.'

'Thank you, my dear.'

The two women exchanged affectionate smiles and parted.

Milady's headache was no sham. She had not yet perfected her plans and her brain was in a whirl. She saw her scheme in main outline but needed quiet and solitude to work out the details.

The most important thing was to carry off Madame Bonacieux to some safe place and there, if need be, use her as a hostage. Milady was beginning to have doubts about the outcome of this terrible duel, for she realized that her enemies were as relentless in their pursuit of her as she was in her resolve to take revenge on them. And as one feels the approach of a storm she sensed that the final clash was near, and that it would be terrible indeed.

Her main concern, therefore, was to carry off Madame Bonacieux, for to hold Madame Bonacieux was to hold d'Artagnan. He loved the little draper's wife with all his heart, and Milady knew that she would be a powerful weapon with which to negotiate if things went wrong. Madame Bonacieux trusted her and would go with her. Once she had her in Armentières she could easily convince her that d'Artagnan had never come to Béthune. In a fortnight at the most Rochefort would be back, and she could spend the intervening time thinking out the best means of settling her account with the four friends. She would not be bored. Not for a moment! She would have what her mind at present most craved for, leisure to devise and perfect a scheme of revenge.

As she sat thinking Milady also made a mental note of the design of the garden. Like a good general she visualized defeat as well as victory, and laid her plans accordingly.

About an hour later she heard a gentle voice calling her from the cloister door. It was Madame Bonacieux. She told Milady that the Abbess had agreed to everything and that they were to have supper together that very night.

As they were walking down the cloisters they heard a carriage drawing up at the gate. Milady stopped to listen.

'Did you hear that?' she asked.

'Yes, carriage wheels.'

'That's my brother's carriage.'

'Oh God!'

'Courage, my dear!'

At that moment the convent bell rang.

'There! What did I tell you?' whispered Milady. 'Go up to

your room quickly and collect whatever you want to take. You must have some treasures you want to keep.'

'Yes, his letters,' replied Madame Bonacieux.

'Get them and come down to my room. We'll swallow down some supper quickly; we may have to spend most of the night on the road and we must build up our strength.'

Madame Bonacieux suddenly put her hand to her heart.

'Oh God!' she exclaimed. 'My heart's beating so fast I can hardly walk. I feel stifled.'

'Courage! In a quarter of an hour you'll be free. Just think of that! And remember that what you're doing you're doing for his sake.'

'Yes, yes, for his sake! Thank you for saying that! I feel quite brave again now. Go to your room and I'll join you in a moment.'

Milady ran upstairs to her room, where she found Rochefort's servant waiting for her. She proceeded to give him his orders. He was to wait with the carriage at the convent gate. If the musketeers happened to arrive before they themselves had left he was to drive off at a gallop, circle round the convent, make for the little village of Festubert which lay beyond the wood, and there wait for Milady. She herself would meanwhile escape through the garden and, knowing the district thoroughly, would make for the village on foot. If, however, the musketeers did not appear everything was to be carried out as arranged. Madame Bonacieux was to get into the carriage on the pretext of saying good-bye to her friend, and they would then drive off with her.

At that moment Madame Bonacieux herself came in. To remove all suspicion from her mind Milady repeated the last part of her orders to the servant in front of her. She then made a few inquiries about the carriage and was told that it was a three-horse chaise driven by a postilion, and that Rochefort's servant would act as outrider.

Milady was wrong in thinking that Madame Bonacieux suspected her; the young girl was much too honest herself to believe another capable of such perfidy. Moreover the name

'Lady de Winter', by which she had heard the Abbess address the new arrival, meant nothing to her and she had no notion that any woman was involved in the intrigues against her.

When the servant had left the room Milady said:

'You see everything's perfectly arranged. The Abbess suspects nothing and thinks I'm being taken away on the Cardinal's order. The servant will pass on my orders to the coachman. Now eat and drink something to build up your strength. Then we must be off.'

Madame Bonacieux replied mechanically:

'Yes, we must be off.'

Milady motioned her to a chair by the table, poured her out a glass of Spanish wine, carved off a slice of chicken and placed it in front of her.

'Look!' she said, pointing to the window, 'it's already getting dark. Fate's on our side. By dawn tomorrow we'll have reached our hiding-place and no one will have a notion where we are. So be brave, dear heart. Everything will be all right. Just eat something to build up your strength.'

Madame Bonacieux mechanically ate a few mouthfuls of chicken and sipped a little of the wine. Milady poured herself out a glass of the wine and said:

'Drink it down as I do. It'll do you good.'

She was raising the glass to her lips when she suddenly went rigid and stood for a moment transfixed. She had heard the sound of horses' hoofs in the distance. The sound grew louder, and now she fancied she heard horses neighing. At this all her exultation vanished, and she was like a sleeper woken from a dream by a thunderclap. She went deathly pale, put down her glass and ran to the window, while Madame Bonacieux got up trembling from her chair and stood with one arm resting on the table to support herself. Milady, watching from the window, could as yet see nothing. But the sound of the galloping horses grew louder.

'O God!' said Madame Bonacieux, 'what's that noise?'

Milady replied in a hard, cold voice:

'It's either our friends or our foes arriving. Stay where you are. Don't come to the window. I'll tell you what I see.'

Madame Bonacieux remained standing by the table, pale and speechless.

The sound of the galloping hoofs grew ever louder; now the party of riders could not be more than two hundred yards away. But still Milady could see nothing as a bend in the road hid them from her sight. But the noise was now so distinct that one could have counted the horses by the clip-clop of their hoofs on the cobble-stones.

Milady was watching and listening intently. The waning light was still strong enough to enable her to identify anyone coming along the road.

Suddenly at the bend of the road she saw braided cloaks and plumed hats glinting in the twilight. She counted first two, then five, then eight riders. One of them was about two horses' lengths ahead of the others. When Milady saw the leader of the party she gave a cry of rage. It was d'Artagnan.

'O God!' cried Madame Bonacieux. 'What's the matter?'

'The Cardinal's Guards!' cried Milady. 'Eight of them. We must escape at once. There's not a moment to lose.'

'Yes, yes, we must escape,' echoed Madame Bonacieux.

But she seemed unable to move and stood rooted to the spot with terror.

The two women heard the riders dismounting under the window.

'Come on!' cried Milady. 'We can still escape through the garden. I've got the key. But hurry! If we're not away in five minutes they'll get us.'

She seized Madame Bonacieux by the arm and tried to drag her out of the room by force. The unfortunate girl tried to walk to the door, but after a couple of steps sank helplessly to her knees. Milady now tried to lift her up to drag her through the door, but the effort was too great. At that moment they heard the sound of carriage wheels rattling down the street; seeing the musketeers arrive Rochefort's postilion had, as arranged, whipped up the horses and driven off. They then heard three or four pistol shots.

'For the last time, are you coming?' screamed Milady.

'Don't you see I'm too weak to move?' cried Madame Bona-cieux. 'I can't walk a step. Save yourself; don't worry about me.'

'Leave you here alone!' exclaimed Milady. 'Never!'

Suddenly she stood stock still and a livid light of rage flashed in her eyes. She then ran over to the table, took a ring off her finger, removed the stone from its setting with her nail and dropped a little red pellet from the ring into Madame Bona-cieux's unfinished glass of wine. The pellet dissolved at once. She then took the glass, held it to the young woman's lips and said commandingly:

'Drink this. It'll give you back your strength.'

Madame Bonacieux mechanically drank down the wine. With a smile of devilish glee Milady replaced the glass on the table.

'That wasn't how I'd pictured taking my revenge,' she mut-tered. 'But it's better than nothing.'

Then she turned and fled from the room.

Madame Bonacieux watched her go but could make no move to follow her. She was like someone in a dream who knows himself pursued, yet cannot escape.

A few minutes passed. Then Madame Bonacieux heard a loud hammering at the convent gate. She expected every moment to see Milady return but Milady did not appear. She herself was still kneeling in a hunched attitude on the floor, trembling in every limb.

At last she heard the grinding of bolts on the floor below and realized that the nuns were opening the convent gate to the callers. Then came the noise of boots and spurs on the stone staircase; then a confused murmur of voices, which grew gradually louder. Suddenly she fancied she heard someone call-ing her by name and the next moment she gave a cry of joy, sprang to her feet and ran over to the door; she had recognized the voice of her beloved d'Artagnan.

'D'Artagnan, d'Artagnan!' she called. 'Is it you? I'm here!'

'Constance, Constance!' called the young man in reply. 'In Heaven's name, where are you?'

The next moment the door of the cell opened or rather yielded to a powerful impact and half a dozen men burst into the room. Madame Bonacieux had collapsed into an arm-chair and was lying there, as though paralysed.

D'Artagnan was holding a still smouldering pistol in his hand. He threw it into the corner of the room and fell on his knees before his loved one. Athos put his pistol back into his belt, and Porthos and Aramis, who both had drawn swords in their hands, sheathed them.

'Oh d'Artagnan, dearest d'Artagnan!' exclaimed the young woman. 'You've come at last. You haven't deserted me after all; you've really come!'

'Yes, yes, Constance. I've found you at last.'

'*She* kept telling me you wouldn't come. But in my heart of hearts I knew you would. I somehow didn't want to go away with her. Thank God I stayed behind!'

While the lovers had been talking Athos had sat down calmly in a corner of the room. But at the words 'she' and 'her' he sprang to his feet in alarm.

'She? Who d'you mean?' asked d'Artagnan.

'My good friend, my companion here. She wanted to help me escape from the Cardinal's agents. She mistook you for Cardinalists and escaped herself a few minutes ago.'

D'Artagnan went as white as the nun's veil which covered his beloved Constance's head.

'Your companion, your good friend?' he stammered.

'Yes, the woman whose carriage was at the gate just now. She said she was a friend of yours, d'Artagnan, and that you'd told her everything about us.'

'What's her name?' cried d'Artagnan. 'Don't you know her name?'

'Yes, of course I know her name. The Abbess told me. How funny! I can't remember it. I feel quite stupid suddenly and there's something wrong with my eyes.'

D'Artagnan turned to his friends.

'Come here, quick, all of you,' he called. 'Her hands are icy cold. She's ill. Good God, she's fainting!'

Porthos started shouting for help at the top of his voice while Aramis ran over to the table to fetch a glass of water. He stopped dead, however, when he noticed Athos standing by the table with a look of horror on his face, staring dazedly at one of the wine-glasses and muttering to himself:

'No, no, it's impossible. God wouldn't allow that; it's too vile!'

'Water, water!' shouted d'Artagnan.

Athos kept repeating brokenly:

'Poor soul, poor soul!'

D'Artagnan covered his beloved's hands with kisses. At last she opened her eyes.

'She's coming round,' cried the young man. 'Oh thank God, thank God!'

Athos said, pointing to the empty glass on the table:

'Madame Bonacieux, for God's sake tell me whose glass that is.'

Madame Bonacieux replied faintly:

'That's my glass.'

'That glass has had wine in it,' went on Athos. 'Who poured it out for you?'

'She did.'

'Who do you mean? You must know her name.'

'Ah yes, I remember now,' replied Madame Bonacieux. 'Lady de Winter.'

A single cry of horror rang through the room. All four men had cried out together but Athos' voice rose above the rest.

At that moment Madame Bonacieux turned a ghastly leaden colour; a sudden spasm seized her and she slid from the arm-chair on to the floor. Porthos and Aramis rushed to lift her up.

D'Artagnan seized Athos' hands. There was a look of anguish on his face as he said:

'D'you suspect . . .?'

Athos muttered through clenched teeth:

'I suspect the worst.'

'D'Artagnan, where are you?' cried Madame Bonacieux. 'Don't leave me! Don't you see I'm dying?'

D'Artagnan let go of Athos' hands, ran over to his mistress and took her in his arms. Her pretty features were twisted with pain; a film was forming over her eyes; spasms shook her frame and her forehead was damp with sweat.

'In Heaven's name get help, someone! Porthos, Aramis, get help!'

'Nothing can be done,' said Athos. 'There's no antidote to the poison she uses.'

'Yes, yes, get help!' whispered Madame Bonacieux faintly.

Then, summoning all her strength, she took d'Artagnan's head in her hands, looked at him with eyes in which the light of her very soul seemed to shine, and with a sobbing cry pressed her lips to his.

D'Artagnan called out:

'Constance, Constance!'

A sigh escaped from Madame Bonacieux's lips, which d'Artagnan felt like a gentle breath on his cheek. That sigh was Constance's pure, loving soul escaping from its mortal coil and mounting to Heaven.

D'Artagnan, realizing that she was dead, let her fall from his arms, gave a groan of despair and collapsed at her side, as pale and lifeless as she.

The three other men were standing by. Porthos started to weep, Aramis stood with bent head, and Athos crossed himself.

At that moment a figure suddenly appeared in the doorway. It was a man, a stranger. He looked pale and harassed and almost as distressed as the three who had just seen Madame Bonacieux die. He took a quick look round him, staring sharply first at the dead woman and her lover lying unconscious beside her and then at the other three occupants of the room, who were standing motionless with bent heads.

'If I'm not mistaken,' he said, addressing the last-named, 'that's Monsieur d'Artagnan over there, and you gentlemen are his three friends, Monsieur Athos, Monsieur Porthos, and Monsieur Aramis.'

The three musketeers turned and stared at the newcomer in

surprise. They said nothing in reply to his greeting, but all seemed to recollect having seen him before. The stranger continued:

'I suspect that you gentlemen, like myself, are in quest of a certain woman.'

He added with a ghastly smile:

'That corpse there makes me think she must have passed this way not so very long ago.'

Still the three friends said nothing. But the stranger's voice, like his face, seemed familiar, and they all thought they remembered having met him before, though they did not know when or where.

'I see you either don't or won't recognize me, gentlemen,' went on the stranger. 'And yet I think I'm right in saying you saved my life at least twice. So if you'll allow me I'll introduce myself. I'm Lord de Winter, that woman's brother-in-law.'

The three friends gave a start of surprise. Then Athos walked up to de Winter and held out his hand.

'We're delighted to see you, Lord de Winter,' he said. 'Please consider us your friends and join us.'

'I left Portsmouth five hours after she left,' said Lord de Winter. 'I arrived in Boulogne only three hours after and missed her at Saint Omer by a mere twenty minutes. But I lost track of her at Lilliers. I went on searching for her in the neighbourhood, hoping some of the villagers might have seen her. Then I saw you fellows galloping past. I recognized Monsieur d'Artagnan. I called to you but you didn't answer. I tried to follow you but my horse was spent and couldn't keep pace with yours. And yet for all your hurry it looks as though you've arrived too late.'

Athos said nothing but stood aside to let Lord de Winter see Madame Bonacieux's dead body and d'Artagnan lying unconscious beside her. Porthos and Aramis were now trying to revive him.

Lord de Winter frowned anxiously.

'Are they both dead?' he asked.

'No, fortunately,' replied Athos. 'D'Artagnan's only fainted.'

'Thank God for that at least,' said Lord de Winter.

At that moment d'Artagnan regained consciousness. He pushed Porthos and Aramis aside, knelt over the dead woman, took her in his arms again and laid his head on her breast. Athos walked up to him and put his hand affectionately on his shoulder. At this d'Artagnan broke down and began to sob, upon which Athos, to give him courage, said gently:

'D'Artagnan, be a man. Only women mourn the dead. Men avenge them.'

At this d'Artagnan looked up.

'If you're out for revenge I'll go with you to the ends of the earth,' he said.

Seeing that his friend had taken heart again Athos signed to Porthos and Aramis to summon the Abbess.

The two young men found her in the passage. She was still confused and flustered by the sudden sequence of violent events which had disturbed the even tenor of convent life. She summoned several of her nuns and, disregarding the community's strict rule of seclusion, ordered them into the presence of the five men. Athos turned to the Abbess and said:

'Reverend Mother, please take charge of this poor woman's body. She was once an angel on earth; now she's an angel with God in Heaven. Care for her as though she were one of your own sisterhood. One day we'll return and say prayers at her grave.'

At this d'Artagnan laid his head on his friend's shoulder and broke into stifled sobs.

'Weep, young lover,' said Athos. 'Would I could weep with you.'

And with a father's tenderness and the understanding of one who has himself suffered, he took his sorrowing friend's arm and led him gently from the room.

All five men now left the convent, followed by their servants, and walked down the road towards the town, leading their horses by the bridle. The town was only a few hundred yards away and the men stopped at the first inn they saw. D'Artagnan said:

'Aren't we going after that woman?'

'Later,' replied Athos. 'I've got some things to see to first.'

'But she'll get away, Athos,' objected the young man. 'You'll see she'll get away, God help us! And it'll be your fault.'

'I take full responsibility for her,' replied Athos.

D'Artagnan had such trust in his friend that he said no more. The little party now entered the inn.

Porthos and Aramis exchanged glances, for they did not share d'Artagnan's confidence in Athos' word. Lord de Winter thought that the musketeer had spoken as he had merely to ease d'Artagnan's grief.

Athos interviewed the innkeeper, discovered that he had five rooms to let, rejoined his friends and said:

'I suggest, gentlemen, that we all go to bed now. D'Artagnan needs to be alone to weep, and the rest of us to sleep. And don't any of you worry about plans, I'll see to everything.'

De Winter protested:

'I can't help thinking that if we're going to take action against this woman I should be the one responsible. After all, she is my sister-in-law.'

'And she's my wife,' said Athos.

At this d'Artagnan started and felt a chill run down his spine. He knew that Athos would not have betrayed his secret had he not been sure of revenge. Porthos and Aramis went very white. As for Lord de Winter he stared at the musketeer as though he were mad.

Athos continued:

'So you see you can all safely go to bed and leave me, as this woman's husband, to deal with her. Oh, there's just one thing, d'Artagnan. If you haven't lost it would you give me the slip of paper which fell out of that fellow's hat, with the name of the town on it.'

D'Artagnan's eyes lit up.

'Of course!' he said excitedly. 'I remember now; it's written in her handwriting.'

'Yes,' replied Athos. 'You see there is a God in Heaven after all.'

CHAPTER XXVII

The Man in the Red Cloak

HAVING promised his three friends and Lord de Winter that their common account with Lady de Winter would be settled, Athos cast off his habitual apathy and concentrated on the plan of campaign he had already vaguely outlined in his mind. He was the last of the five men to go to his room. He asked the innkeeper for a map of the district and sat poring over it for some time. He discovered that four roads led from Béthune to Armentières and immediately summoned the four servants.

When Planchet, Grimaud, Mousqueton, and Bazin were standing before him he gave them all clear, precise instructions. They were to leave Béthune at dawn the next day and make for Armentières, each by a different road. Planchet, the most intelligent of the four, was to follow the road taken by the carriage which had driven off from the convent door as they had arrived, and which, as we know, was escorted by Rochefort's servant.

Athos decided to send the lackeys to Armentières rather than go himself with his four friends for three reasons. Firstly, they had now been in his and his friends' service for some time and he had begun to appreciate the peculiar merits of each. Secondly, the peasants of the district were less likely to be shy of and more likely to confide in strangers of the servant class than in strangers of the gentleman class. Thirdly, Milady knew the masters but did not know the servants, while the servants knew Milady very well by sight.

All four were to be at Armentières by eleven next morning. If they had discovered where Milady was hiding three of them were to remain and keep watch on her movements, while the fourth was to return to Béthune to report to Athos and act as guide to the four friends and Lord de Winter.

Having received their orders the servants themselves retired to bed.

Athos now got up from his chair, put on his sword and cloak and left the inn. It was already nearly ten o'clock, and at ten o'clock in the evening country lanes were in those days almost entirely deserted. But Athos was obviously searching for someone who could give him some information.

At last he met a belated passer-by. He went up to him and said something in a low voice. The man was evidently alarmed, for he started back and stared at Athos in surprise. After a moment, however, he recovered himself and pointed in a certain direction. Athos offered him half a pistole to come with him and show him the way, but the man refused.

Athos started off in the direction shown by the peasant. But after walking a little way he reached a crossroads and was again in doubt which way to go. The crossroads seemed the most likely spot for an encounter, so he waited here a few minutes. Sure enough a night watchman soon came along. Athos asked him the question he had asked the peasant and the night watchman showed the same alarm and surprise. But he, too, pointed in a certain direction and likewise refused Athos' offer of money to accompany him.

Athos again set off and soon reached the furthermost suburb of the town. Here he again seemed in doubt which road to take and stopped for the third time. Fortunately at that moment a beggar happened to approach him and ask for alms. Athos offered him a crown to accompany him to his destination.

The beggar hesitated a moment; then, seeing the glint of the silver coin in the darkness, he agreed and started to walk ahead of Athos to show him the way. He led him a few hundred yards to where a side road branched off the main street. Here he stopped and pointed to a small, gloomy-looking house standing by itself. Athos started to walk towards it, while the beggar, having been paid his fee, made off in the opposite direction.

When Athos reached the house he had to walk round it to find the door, which was scarcely visible against the dingy red of the walls. No light filtered through the cracks in the shutters. No sound came from inside the house to betray the presence of a living soul. The house itself was as dark and silent as a tomb.

Athos knocked once, twice and then a third time. After the third knock he heard faint footsteps approaching the door. Then the door was half-opened and Athos, peering in, saw a man standing on the threshold, a tall fellow with a pale face and black hair and beard. The musketeer said something to him in a low voice. The man seemed to hesitate; then he pulled the door full open and signed to his caller to enter, closing the door behind him.

Athos was now face to face with the man whom he had come so far and taken such pains to find. His host led him into a laboratory where he had been busy piecing together the bones of a skeleton with wire. He had already assembled the body, but the head still lay separate on a table. Everything in the room revealed that its occupant was a natural scientist. There were bottles containing various species of reptile, all labelled; there were large, black, wooden crates filled with dried lizards which glittered like emeralds. Clumps of scented wild herbs, which doubtless contained therapeutic properties known only to the initiate, hung down from the ceiling in all four corners of the room. And there was not another human soul in the house; the man evidently lived alone, without family or servants.

Athos took a quick look round him. Then, at his host's invitation, he sat down opposite him and started to explain the reason for his visit and what he wished the man to do. But hardly had he stated his request than the man started back in alarm, shaking his head violently to show that he would have nothing to do with it.

At this Athos took a sheet of paper out of his pocket and handed it to his host, who noticed on it two lines of handwriting, a signature, and a seal. When he read the writing his attitude at once changed, and he nodded to Athos to show that he would now do as he was bid and take orders from him. After thanking him Athos bade him good night and walked back along the road by which he had come. When he reached the inn he retired to his room and locked the door.

The next day at dawn d'Artagnan knocked on his door to ask for orders for himself and his three friends.

'Just wait,' replied Athos.

A few moments later a man called at the inn with a message from the Abbess that Madame Bonacieux's funeral would take place that day at noon. As for the murderess nothing more had been heard of her. But footsteps which were clearly hers had been found in the garden, the garden gate had been found locked and the key missing. It was fairly obvious, therefore, that she had escaped that way.

At the hour appointed Lord de Winter and the four friends arrived at the convent. The bells were ringing out a full chime and the chapel door was open; only the wrought-iron gate into the chancel was closed. The murdered woman's body, dressed in novice's robes, lay exposed in the middle of the chancel. The nuns were assembled on either side of the chancel, behind iron gates which opened on to the convent. From here they took part in the service and sang in unison with the priests, hidden from the eyes of the lay congregation.

At the chapel door d'Artagnan felt his courage fail again; he turned round to look for Athos, but his friend had disappeared.

Faithful to his mission of revenge Athos had asked to be taken into the garden. There he had seen the footsteps mentioned by the Abbess, had followed them to the gate which led from the garden into the wood, had asked to have the gate opened and had plunged straight into the forest.

Now all his suspicions were confirmed. The road which the carriage had taken skirted the wood. Athos walked some distance down this road, his eyes fixed on the ground. At intervals along the road he noticed faint bloodstains which he realized must have come from a wound inflicted either on the man who was acting as outrider to the carriage or on one of the horses. After he had gone about two miles and was within a hundred yards of the village of Festubert he noticed a bloodstain considerably larger than the others; here, too, the surface of the road had been trodden down by the horses. Between the forest and this tell-tale spot on the road, a little behind the patch of trampled-on ground, Athos noticed the same small footsteps which he had seen in the garden. Here the carriage had obviously stopped; here Milady had come out of the forest, been picked up by the coachman and outrider and driven on.

Satisfied by this discovery, which confirmed all his previous conjectures, Athos returned to the inn, where he found Planchet waiting impatiently for him. What Planchet told him further confirmed what he suspected. Planchet had also noticed the bloodstains and lit upon the spot where the carriage had stopped. But he had pushed on further than Athos, as far as the village of Festubert. Here he had gone into an inn to have a drink and had learnt by listening to the local gossips that at eighty-thirty the previous night a wounded man had arrived in the village. He had been escorting a lady travelling in a post-chaise but had had to stop in the village as his wound prevented him from going on. According to him the carriage had been attacked by highwaymen in the forest. He had spent the night in the village while the lady in the chaise had hired remounts and continued her journey. Having discovered this Planchet had set off to find the postilion who had driven the lady on the last stage of her journey. He had found him and learned from him that the lady had proceeded to Fromelles and from Fromelles to Armentières. Planchet had taken a short cut across country and arrived in Armentières at seven in the morning.

There was only one inn in Armentières, the Hôtel de la Poste. Planchet had called there, pretending to be a servant on the look-out for a job. Ten minutes' conversation with the host had revealed to him that a lady travelling alone had arrived in the village at eleven o'clock the previous night and had taken a room; she had then summoned the innkeeper and told him that she was staying some time in the neighbourhood.

That was all Planchet wanted to know. He had hurried to the place where he and his three associates were to meet, had found all three waiting for him, taken them back to the inn, posted them where they could watch all the entrances to the building and then returned to report to Athos. Just as Planchet was finishing his tale the three friends came in. They all looked grim, even the gentle Aramis.

'Well, what d'you want us to do?' asked d'Artagnan.

'Wait,' said Athos.

At this all three young men went up to their rooms.

At eight o'clock that evening Athos gave orders for the horses to be saddled and told his friends and Lord de Winter to get ready to start. All four were ready in a moment, with their arms inspected and primed.

When Athos went down he found d'Artagnan already in the saddle.

'You'll have to wait a bit, I'm afraid,' said Athos. 'One of the party hasn't turned up yet.'

His four companions looked at each other in surprise; who could the missing man be?

At that moment Planchet brought up Athos' horse and the musketeer leapt lightly into the saddle.

'Wait for me here,' he said. 'I'll be back in a few minutes.'

And he rode off at the gallop.

He returned a quarter of an hour later, sure enough accompanied by a man in a mask, with a long red cloak wrapped round him.

Lord de Winter and the three musketeers looked at each other with raised eyebrows. All were equally in the dark as to who this mysterious stranger might be. But they accepted him without question, vouched for as he was by Athos, who was in charge of affairs.

At nine o'clock the little cavalcade with Planchet at its head set out along the road taken by the carriage. The six men riding along in silence in the twilight appeared sinister. They were all sunk in their own thoughts and looked stern and solemn, like avenging angels or emissaries of Fate.

CHAPTER XXVIII

The Trial

IT was a dark and stormy night. Heavy clouds scudded across the sky, veiling the light of the stars. The moon was not due to rise till midnight. From time to time flashes of lightning would reveal the road winding white and desolate ahead of the party of riders. Then all would be in shadow again.

More than once Athos had to call d'Artagnan back into line with the rest of the party. The young man kept drawing ahead; he had only one thought in mind, to get on as fast as possible.

The little cavalcade rode in silence through the village of Festubert, where Rochefort's servant had remained to tend his wound. Then it skirted the forest of Richebourg and arrived in Herlier. Here Planchet, who was still acting as guide, branched off to the left.

Lord de Winter, Porthos, and Aramis had all in turn tried to talk to the man in the red cloak. But each time they questioned him he merely bowed and said nothing. They therefore assumed that he had some good reason for not wishing to speak and soon ceased to pester him.

The storm was gradually increasing in violence; the flashes of lightning followed one another rapidly; there were loud claps of thunder and the wind began to whistle across the valley, preluding a hurricane.

The little party now broke into a jog-trot. When it was some way beyond Formelles the storm broke over its head. The men put on their cloaks. They were still about nine miles from their goal and they covered those last nine miles in a deluge of rain.

D'Artagnan had taken off his hat and not put on his cloak. He enjoyed the sensation of the rain streaming down his face and buffeting his body, cooling his fevered nerves.

The six riders had passed through Goskal and were nearing

the next stage when they saw a man step out from behind a tree, advance into the middle of the road and put his finger to his lips. It was Grimaud, who had been sheltering from the rain. D'Artagnan rode up to him.

'What is it?' he said. 'Has she left Armentières?'

Grimaud nodded. D'Artagnan swore under his breath.

'Leave this to me, d'Artagnan,' said Athos. 'You agreed that I should take charge, so it's my business to cross-question Grimaud.'

He turned to his servant.

'Where's she now, Grimaud?' he asked.

Grimaud pointed in the direction of the river Lys.

'Has she gone far?' asked Athos.

Grimaud held up one finger.

'Did she go alone?'

Grimaud nodded.

'Gentlemen,' said Athos. 'She's about a mile from here, over in that direction, somewhere near the river.'

'Good,' said d'Artagnan. 'Take us there, Grimaud!'

Grimaud walked ahead of the party and led them a short cut across country. After about half a mile they came to a stream which they forded. A sudden flash of lightning showed them the village of Erquinheim lying just ahead.

'Is that where she is?' asked d'Artagnan.

Grimaud shook his head.

'Quiet!' insisted Athos.

The little troop rode on.

Soon there was another streak of lightning. Grimaud pointed ahead of him and in the blue-white gleam they made out a little house standing by itself on the banks of the river, about a hundred yards from a ferry boat. In one of the windows of the house a light was shining.

'We're there,' said Athos.

At that moment a man sprang out of the ditch at the side of the field and started running towards them. It was Mousqueton. He pointed to the lighted window.

'She's in there,' he said.

'And where's Bazin?' asked Athos.

'We agreed that I'd watch the window and he'd watch the door.'

'Good,' said Athos. 'You've all done very well.'

The musketeer now dismounted and handed his horse's rein to Grimaud. He then signed to the rest of the party to make for the door of the house, while he himself walked up to the window.

The little house was surrounded by a quickset hedge about three feet in height. Athos leapt over the hedge and stepped right up to the window, which was shutterless but had curtains drawn tightly across it. He climbed on to the stone sill, from where he could see over the curtains into the room.

A lamp was burning in the room and in its rays Athos saw a woman wrapped in a dark cloak seated on a chair near the dying embers of a fire. She had her elbows on the table in front of her and was resting her head in her hands, which were as white as ivory. Athos could not see her face, but as he stood watching her he smiled grimly. There could be no doubt. It was the woman they were looking for.

At that moment one of the horses neighed. Milady looked up, saw Athos' pale face pressed against the window and cried out.

The musketeer saw that she had recognized him. He pressed his elbow and knee against the window until the panes splintered and the frame collapsed. Then, like the Spirit of vengeance, he sprang into the room. Milady ran to the door and opened it. On the threshold stood a figure even sterner and more threatening than Athos – d'Artagnan.

Milady again gave a cry and shrank back into the room. D'Artagnan, fearing that she might have some secret way of escape, drew his pistol from his belt. But Athos called out:

'Put that pistol away, d'Artagnan. This woman has to be tried, not murdered. Patience! You'll soon be even with her. Come in, the rest of you!'

D'Artagnan, awed by Athos' stern manner, obeyed. And now Porthos, Aramis, Lord de Winter, and the man in the red cloak followed him into the room.

The four servants were posted to guard the door and the window.

Milady had fallen back on to her chair and was holding her arms out in front of her as though to banish this terrifying vision. When she caught sight of her brother-in-law she gave another cry and stammered out:

'What do you want, all of you?'

Athos replied:

'We want Anne de Breuil, known first as the Comtesse de la Fère, and then as Clarice, Lady de Winter.'

Milady was dumbfounded.

'Yes, that's me!' she said. 'Why do you want me?'

'We want to try you for your crimes,' said Athos. 'You'll be free to plead your cause and to prove yourself innocent if you can. Monsieur d'Artagnan, I call on you first to bring your charges against this woman.'

D'Artagnan stepped forward.

'Before God and men,' he said, 'I charge this woman with having poisoned Constance Bonacieux, who died last night.'

He turned to Porthos and Aramis, who said in one voice:

'We bear witness to that.'

D'Artagnan continued:

'Before God and men I charge this woman with having tried to poison me with wine which she sent from Villeroy with a forged letter, written to make me believe the wine came from my friends. God protected me, but another died in my place, a man named Brisemont.'

Porthos and Aramis replied again:

'We bear witness to that.'

'Before God and men,' continued d'Artagnan, 'I further charge this woman with having incited me to murder the Comte de Wardes. No one present can bear witness to this charge, but I myself swear to the truth of it. That is the sum of my charges against this woman.'

So saying d'Artagnan went and stood beside Porthos and Aramis in the corner of the room.

'Lord de Winter, will you bring your charges next,' said Athos.

De Winter stepped forward in his turn.

'Before God and men,' he said, 'I charge this woman with having caused the murder of the Duke of Buckingham!'

'The Duke of Buckingham murdered!' cried the four musketeers.

'Yes, murdered,' replied de Winter. 'When I got your warning letter I had this woman arrested and put her in the charge of a man I thought I could trust. But she seduced him; she persuaded him to do this thing; she even put the knife into his hand. And now Felton's to die to atone for this fiend's crime.'

The others standing round felt a thrill of horror at this disclosure of outrages unknown to them.

'I have a further charge to bring,' said Lord de Winter. 'My brother, who made this woman his sole heir in his will, died within three hours of signing it of some mysterious illness, which left purple marks all over his body. Confess, Clarice, how did my brother die?'

'How vile!' cried Porthos and Aramis.

Lord de Winter continued:

'This woman murdered Buckingham, she murdered Felton, she murdered my brother. I demand redress against her and declare that if I don't get it from you here I shall take action on my own.'

Lord de Winter now took his place beside d'Artagnan, Porthos, and Aramis, leaving room for the next accuser to step forward and bring his charge.

Milady was sitting with her head buried in her hands, making frantic efforts to collect her thoughts. But mortal dread had seized her, numbing her wits.

Athos now stepped forward. As he gazed at his former wife he shuddered as a man shudders at the sight of a snake.

'Here's my charge against this woman,' he said. 'I married her when she was a girl, against my family's wishes; I gave her my name and a share in all my worldly goods. One day I discovered she was branded, marked with a fleur-de-lis on her left shoulder.'

At this Milady sprang to her feet and cried:

'I defy anyone to find the court which imposed that wicked sentence on me. And I defy anyone to find the man who executed it.'

At this a voice called out:

'Silence, everybody! I alone can answer that challenge!'

The speaker was the man in the red cloak, who now himself stepped forward.

'Who's that man? Who's that man?' cried Milady in a voice choked with fear.

Her hair was falling loose and now seemed to rise on her head, above her ashen-pale face, like Medusa's serpent-coils.

Everyone was staring at the man in the cloak, for to all but Athos he was a stranger. Athos, too, now looked at him in surprise, for even he did not see how the man could be personally concerned in this terrible drama.

The man walked slowly up to Milady until only the table separated them. Then he took off his mask and stood looking at her. His face was pale and framed in thick black hair, beard and whiskers, and his expression and manner were deadly calm. Milady stared back at him for a moment in silence. Then she suddenly sprang to her feet, shrank back against the wall and cried in a voice hoarse with terror:

'No, no! It can't be! It's a ghost—an evil spirit! Help! Help!'

She now turned her face to the wall and began threshing against it with her arms, as though she were trying to beat a passage through it.

All the others present turned to the stranger and said:

'In Heaven's name, who are you?'

'Ask that woman,' replied the stranger. 'She recognizes me, as you see.'

Milady whipped round.

'The headsman of Lille, the headsman of Lille!' she shrieked.

She was now half-crazed with fear and clung to the wall to prevent herself falling.

Everyone stood aside, leaving the man in the red cloak alone in the middle of the room. Milady, who was standing with her back pressed to the wall, cried out in abject terror:

'Don't kill me, don't kill me! Have pity!'

The stranger waited for a moment. Then he said:

'You see! She does recognize me. Yes, I'm the public executioner of the town of Lille. And here's my charge against this woman.'

All eyes were fixed on him and everyone waited spellbound to hear what he had to say.

'I knew this woman when she was a girl,' he began. 'She was as beautiful then as she is now. She was a nun at the Benedictine convent of Templemar. There was a young priest, a simple, honest fellow, who officiated in the convent chapel. This woman made up her mind to seduce him and succeeded. She'd have seduced a saint.'

He paused and continued:

'Both of them, priest and nun, had taken vows which were sacred and irrevocable. Their relationship couldn't have gone on without bringing disaster to both. She eventually persuaded him to leave the district with her. But they needed money to help them start life in another part of France where they could live in peace. And they were both penniless. So the priest stole the Communion plate from the church and sold it. But both were caught and arrested just as they were leaving the district.

'A week later this woman seduced her gaoler's son and escaped. The young priest was sentenced to ten years in irons and to branding. I was at that time the public executioner of Lille. I had to brand the convict, and the convict, gentlemen, was my own brother!

'I vowed then that this woman, who'd ruined his life, who was more than merely his accomplice, having incited him to commit the crime, should at least share his punishment. I suspected where she was hiding, went after her, found her, bound her hand and foot and branded her with the very iron which I'd used on my brother.

'I then returned to Lille. The day after my return my brother also managed to escape. I was accused of aiding and abetting him, arrested and sentenced to detention in his place until he gave himself up again. My brother never discovered this till later. He'd gone to rejoin this woman, and together they'd fled to Berry, where he managed to procure a small living. He passed this woman off as his sister.

'The lord of the manor and patron of my brother's living met this woman and fell in love with her, so deeply in love that he proposed to her. She didn't hesitate, but left the man whose life she'd ruined and married the man whose life she was destined also to ruin. She became the Comtesse de la Fère.'

At this all eyes were turned on Athos, for of the five men present three knew that this was the musketeer's real name. Athos nodded to show that all the stranger had said was true. The stranger now continued:

'At this my brother became desperate and almost mad with grief. He returned to Lille, and on hearing that I'd been imprisoned in his place gave himself up and that very evening hanged himself in his cell. When his corpse had been identified the authorities released me.

'That, then, is the charge I bring against this woman; that's the crime for which I branded her.'

Now Athos spoke:

'Monsieur d'Artagnan,' he said, 'what punishment do you demand for this woman?'

'Death,' replied d'Artagnan.

'And you, Lord de Winter, what punishment do you demand?'

'Death,' replied Lord de Winter.

'And you, Monsieur Porthos and Monsieur Aramis, you're the judges in this case. What punishment do you call for?'

The two musketeers replied sternly:

'The punishment of death.'

Milady gave an unearthly shriek, sank on her knees, dragged herself across the room and fell prostrate before her judges.

Athos passed sentence on her as she lay there.

'Anne de Breuil,' he said. 'You've wearied God and men with

your crimes. If you've ever prayed in your life, pray now, for you've been found guilty and are to die.'

When Milady heard this and knew that she had no more hope she staggered to her feet and tried to speak. But she could make no sound. And now she felt a strong hand – the executioner's hand – seize her by her hair and start to drag her away. Seeing it was useless to resist she turned and walked quietly out of the house.

Lord de Winter, d'Artagnan, Athos, Porthos, and Aramis walked out behind her, followed by the four servants. The room was left empty with its window broken and its door creaking on its hinges. The smoky lamp still flickered near the hearth, shedding a small circle of light and casting sinister shadows on the walls.

CHAPTER XXIX

The Execution

IT was nearing midnight; the moon, now in its last quarter and reddened by the last traces of the storm, was rising behind the little town of Armentières, whose houses and tall, slender steeple were outlined against its faint glow. The river Lys lay opposite, its waters swirling like molten lead; on the far bank the dense forest rose black against a stormy sky swept with thick copper-edged clouds, which cast a sort of midnight twilight on the scene. To the left stood an old, disused windmill, from whose ruins came at intervals an owl's screech. The meadow land which bordered the road on either side was dotted here and there with low, stunted trees, like misshapen dwarfs squatting on their heels to spy on belated travellers.

From time to time broad, jagged streaks of lightning would illumine the whole landscape, curving scimitar-like over the dark mass of forest, and seeming to cleave the sky. The wind had dropped; the air was sultry; nature lay under a pall of deathly silence; the ground was wet and slippery and the grass and wild flowers smelled sweet after the recent rain.

Two of the servants had hold of Milady, each by one arm, and were urging her forward. The executioner walked behind her, and behind him Lord de Winter, d'Artagnan, Athos, Porthos, and Aramis walked abreast. Planchet and Bazin brought up the rear.

The two servants were leading their prisoner towards the river. She was speechless; only her eyes spoke, and they spoke eloquently enough, as she cast beseeching looks at each of her judges in turn.

At one moment Milady and her two guards found themselves some way ahead of the rest of the party. She whispered quickly to them:

'A thousand pistoles for each of you if you'll help me to escape. If you let your masters have their way with me I've some friends nearby who'll make you pay dearly for my death.' Grimaud was shaken and Mousqueton began to tremble. But Athos had heard Milady speak and walked quickly up to her and her escort, followed by Lord de Winter.

'Send Grimaud and Mousqueton back,' he said. 'She's been talking to them. They're no longer to be trusted.'

Lord de Winter called Planchet and Bazin, who took the places of the other two.

When the procession reached the river bank the executioner went up to Milady and began binding her hands and feet. Suddenly she broke her prolonged silence and cried out:

'Cowards! Murderers! Ten of you butchering one wretched woman! Take care! If I'm not rescued now I'll be avenged later!'

Athos replied coldly:

'You're not a woman! You're not human at all! You're a fiend escaped from Hell and we're sending you back where you belong.'

'Who are you to set yourselves up?' she cried. 'Who are you to appoint yourselves my judges? Remember, anyone who touches a hair of my head's a murderer himself!'

'Executioners can kill without murdering,' said the man in the red cloak, tapping his broad sword. 'They're merely the last judges, the "Nachrichter," as our neighbours the Germans say.'

As he spoke he solemnly continued his work of binding Milady's hands and feet. And now the victim gave two or three unearthly shrieks, which echoed eerily through the night and died away in the dark depths of the forest.

'If I'm guilty of the crimes you accuse me of take me to a court of law, where I can be fairly tried,' she cried. 'None of you here are judges. You can't sentence me!'

'I suggested sending you to Tyburn,' said Lord de Winter. 'Why did you refuse to go?'

'Because I didn't want to die. I'm too young to die.'

'The woman you poisoned at Béthune was even younger than you,' said d'Artagnan. 'And yet she died.'

'I'll retire to a convent. I'll take the veil,' said Milady.

'You were in a convent once,' replied the executioner, 'and you came out of it to ruin my brother's life.'

Milady again gave an unearthly shriek and fell on her knees. The headsman half lifted her in his arms and began to drag her over to the boat.

'O God!' screamed Milady. 'Are you going to drown me?'

Her screams were so dreadful that d'Artagnan, who had at first been the most eager in pursuit of her, now sank down on the stump of a tree, groaned and put his hands to his ears to block out the sound. He was the youngest of the men present and his heart failed him.

'I can't look on at this horrible sight,' he said. 'I can't stand by and watch her die like this.'

Milady heard him and a ray of hope came to her. She cried out:

'D'Artagnan, d'Artagnan, remember I loved you! Remember our hours of perfect happiness together!'

D'Artagnan got up and started to walk towards her. But Athos drew his sword and stood barring his way.

'One step more and it'll be over my dead body,' he said.

D'Artagnan fell on his knees and began to pray. Athos said sternly:

'Headsman, do your duty!'

The headsman replied:

'With all my heart, Sir. For, as I believe in God, so I believe in my right to perform my official duty on this woman.'

'So be it then,' said Athos.

He now approached Milady.

'I forgive you,' he said, 'for the wrong you've done me, for wrecking my life, for bringing shame on me, for defiling my love for you, for destroying my hope of salvation by causing me to despair. Die in peace.'

Lord de Winter now approached the prisoner in his turn.

'I forgive you for murdering my brother,' he said, 'for murdering the Duke of Buckingham, for being the cause of Felton's death, and for your attempts to murder me. Die in peace.'

D'Artagnan now spoke.

'Forgive me, Lady de Winter,' he said, 'for rousing your hatred by my blackguardly conduct. I in return forgive you for murdering Constance Bonacieux and for your savage attacks on me. I forgive you and pity you. Die in peace.'

'I'm lost!' said Milady. 'I'm going to die!'

She had spoken softly, half to herself, but Athos overheard her.

'Yes,' he said. 'You're lost. You're going to die.'

At this Milady rose to her feet and cast a last swift, despairing glance round her. She saw no help anywhere, heard no reassuring voice, saw no friendly face. She was surrounded by enemies.

'Where am I going to die?' she asked.

'On the far bank of the river,' replied the headsman.

Whereupon he motioned her into the boat and was preparing to step in after her when Athos handed him a purse of gold.

'Take this,' he said. 'It's your fee for the execution. Let the prisoner see that we're acting officially as judges.'

'Very well,' said the headsman. 'And now let her see that I'm doing what I'm doing not for money but because I consider it my duty.'

And he threw the purse into the river.

The boat, with the headsman and his prisoner, now started off towards the left bank of the Lys. The rest of the party remained on the right bank; they had fallen on their knees and were praying.

The boat glided slowly along the ferry rope in the shadow of a dark cloud which at that moment hung over the water, intercepting the moon's pale glow. The watchers saw the boat reach the far bank and the two figures silhouetted black against the reddish gleam on the horizon.

On the way across Milady had managed to untie the rope which bound her feet. The moment the boat touched ground she sprang ashore and tried to flee. But the grass was wet and when she reached the top of the bank she slipped and fell on her knees.

Did some superstitious fear now assail her? Did she feel that Heaven and Fate were against her? Or what prompted her to remain motionless on her knees, with her head bowed and her hands folded in front of her, making no further attempt to save herself?

Now the watchers on the far bank saw the executioner slowly raise his arms; they saw the blade of his broadsword glint for a second in the moonlight; they saw his arms fall again; they heard the hiss of the scimitar passing through the air and the victim's shriek; and then the truncated body collapse under the blow, go inert and roll sideways.

And now the executioner took off his red cloak, spread it out on the ground, laid the body in it and then the head, knotted the four ends of the cloak together, hoisted it on to his shoulder and stepped back into the boat.

When he reached the middle of the river he stopped the boat, lifted up his burden, held it over the water and called out in a loud voice:

'I deliver you to God's justice. May His will be done!'

Then he dropped the corpse into the deep, swirling waters, which opened to receive it and closed over it again.

CHAPTER XXX

A Messenger from the Cardinal

THREE days later the four musketeers returned to Paris. Their period of leave was up and they went that same evening to report their return to Monsieur de Tréville. The Captain greeted them heartily.

'Well, gentlemen,' he said, 'did you enjoy your leave?'

Athos had just enough self-control to stammer out:

'Enormously, Sir.'

On 6 September the King left Paris, faithful to his promise to the Cardinal to return to La Rochelle. In the interval he had heard the news of the Duke of Buckingham's murder and was overjoyed.

Although she had been forewarned that her lover was in danger the Queen refused at first to believe the news of his death. Indeed she was rash enough to exclaim in several people's hearing:

'It's a lie! He's just written to me!'

But the next day she received irrefutable proof of the truth of the story. Laporte, who had been temporarily detained in England by Charles I, arrived that day with Buckingham's last and most melancholy gift to the Queen.

The King had been in the seventh heaven of joy, and had made no effort to hide his feelings. On the contrary, he had actually gloated over the event in front of the Queen. Louis XIII, like all weak characters, was ungenerous in victory.

But His Majesty's high spirits never lasted long. He soon became morose again, for he knew that in returning to the camp he was returning to bondage. And yet he felt compelled to obey the Cardinal's summons, for His Eminence had a hypnotic hold on him, like a snake on a helpless bird.

The royal party's return journey to La Rochelle was therefore melancholy in the extreme. And our four friends in no way helped to alleviate the gloom, for they rode along in silence with their heads bowed. Only Athos from time to time looked up, his eyes suddenly bright and a bitter smile on his lips. Then he, too, looked down again and rode along in silence, lost in thought.

One day the King had halted on the route to fly his falcons and the four friends had, as usual, gone to drink a glass of wine in a neighbouring inn. As they were sitting drinking a rider drew rein at the door of the inn and ordered a glass of wine to be brought out to him. He was exhausted and covered in dust, having ridden all the way from La Rochelle at full gallop. While waiting for his wine he happened to glance inside the room where the four friends were seated.

He gave a start of surprise and called out:

'Hullo, there, Monsieur d'Artagnan! It is Monsieur d'Artagnan, isn't it?'

D'Artagnan looked up and also gave a start of surprise. The stranger was none other than his evil genius, his acquaintance of Meung, of the Rue des Fossoyeurs and of Arras. He at once drew his sword and rushed to the door. This time, however, the stranger did not attempt to flee, but dismounted and walked up to him.

'Ha, Sir!' said the young man. 'So we meet at last! You're not going to escape this time!'

'I've no intention of escaping, Sir,' replied the stranger. 'On the contrary, I was looking for you. I arrest you in the King's name.'

'What's that?' cried d'Artagnan. 'What did you say?'

'I said I arrest you in the King's name. You must surrender your sword at once and not try to resist. If you do I warn you it'll be the worse for you.'

D'Artagnan lowered the point of his sword but did not yet surrender it.

'Who are you?' he asked.

The stranger replied:

'Chevalier de Rochefort, Cardinal Richelieu's equerry. I've orders to take you back to His Eminence at La Rochelle.'

Athos had meanwhile come out of the inn and joined them. He said:

'We're all on our way back to La Rochelle now, Sir. You must take Monsieur d'Artagnan's and our word for that.'

'I've orders to have him brought back to camp under escort.'

'We'll act as his escort, Sir,' said Athos. 'You can trust us to bring him back safely.'

Then his face darkened and he added sternly:

'You can also trust us not to hand him over to you.'

De Rochefort glanced behind him and saw that Porthos and Aramis had come out and were standing between him and the inn door. He realized that he was completely at the mercy of these four men.

'Gentlemen,' he said, 'if Monsieur d'Artagnan will surrender his sword to me and give me his word of honour not to escape, I'll consent to your escorting him straight to His Eminence's quarters.'

'I give you my word, Sir,' said d'Artagnan. 'And here's my sword.'

'It really suits me better this way,' said de Rochefort. 'I'm not returning to camp myself. I've got to go on to the north.'

'If you're going to meet Lady de Winter,' said Athos coldly, 'you're going on a fool's errand. You won't find her.'

'Why? What's happened to her?' asked Rochefort sharply.

'Come back to the camp and you'll find out.'

Rochefort thought for a moment. Then he remembered that they were only a day's journey from Surgères, which was the town agreed on as the meeting-place for the King and the Cardinal, and decided to follow Athos' advice and return with the royal party. This plan had the added advantage of enabling him to keep an eye on the prisoner himself.

Shortly afterwards the King took the road again with his escort. At three in the afternoon of the following day the party arrived at Surgères where the Cardinal was awaiting His Majesty. Monarch and minister greeted one another effusively, and exchanged congratulations on the lucky stroke of fate which had rid France of the formidable enemy who had been stirring up Europe against her. Whereupon the Cardinal took leave of the King, inviting him to come next day to inspect the fortifications on the dyke, which were now completed. He had heard from Rochefort that d'Artagnan had been arrested and was keen to cross-question him.

When the Cardinal returned that night to his house on the La Pierre bridge he found d'Artagnan and his three friends standing at his door. D'Artagnan was swordless, but the others were all armed. This time he had the whip hand of them. He looked at them sternly and signed imperiously to d'Artagnan to follow him into the house.

'We'll wait for you, d'Artagnan,' said Athos, just loud enough for the Cardinal to hear.

His Eminence frowned, seemed to hesitate for a moment, and then walked on without a word.

D'Artagnan entered the house behind him, and Rochefort followed d'Artagnan. Sentries were posted on either side of the door.

The Cardinal went into the room which he used as his office and signed to Rochefort to show the young musketeer in. Rochefort obeyed and then retired.

D'Artagnan was now alone with the Cardinal. It was his second interview with the great man and he confessed afterwards that he was certain it would be his last. Richelieu remained standing with his elbow on the mantelpiece; there was a table between him and the young man. He said:

'You've been arrested by my orders, Sir.'

'So I was told, Monseigneur.'

'D'you know why?'

'No, Monseigneur. There's only one charge I could be arrested on, and that Your Eminence doesn't yet know.'

Richelieu stared hard at d'Artagnan.

'Oh?' he asked. 'And what d'you mean by that?'

'If Your Eminence would be good enough to tell me first what crimes I'm charged with I'll tell you what I actually have done.'

'You're charged with crimes that have cost bigger men than you their heads, Sir,' said the Cardinal haughtily.

'What in particular?' asked d'Artagnan calmly.

'You're charged with corresponding with enemies of the State, with intercepting State documents, and with attempting to frustrate your general's plans.'

D'Artagnan suspected that all these charges had been brought by Milady.

'Yes, and who brought these charges against me, Your Eminence?' he asked. 'A woman branded by the law of the land, a woman who married one man in France and another in England, a woman who poisoned her second husband and who once tried to poison me.'

The Cardinal stared at the young man in amazement.

'What are you saying, Sir?' he cried. 'What woman do you mean?'

'Lady de Winter,' replied d'Artagnan. 'Yes, Lady de Winter. I don't suppose Your Eminence knew anything about her crimes when she brought those charges against me.'

'If Lady de Winter's committed the crimes you accuse her of she shall be punished,' said the Cardinal.

'She has been punished, Monseigneur.'

'Who punished her?'

'We did.'

'Is she in prison?'

'She's dead.'

The Cardinal was dumbfounded.

'Dead?' he repeated. 'Did I hear you say she was dead?'

'She made no less than three attempts on my life, and I forgave her. But then she killed the woman I loved, so my friends and I captured her, tried her and sentenced her to death.'

D'Artagnan then related the events of the past few days; how Madame Bonacieux had been poisoned in the Carmelite Convent at Béthune, how they had tried Milady in the little house by the river, and how she had been beheaded on the banks of the Lys.

The Cardinal was not easily impressed. But even he shuddered at this gruesome tale. Then, as though some thought had struck him, the expression on his face, previously stern and anxious, suddenly cleared and he looked quite cheerful again. In gentle tones which contrasted strangely with the threat implied in his words he now said:

'So you all took the law into your own hands? Didn't it occur to you that you had no official right to judge and condemn this woman, and that when you punished her you were committing murder yourselves?'

D'Artagnan replied:

'Monseigneur, I won't try and justify my conduct to you. I'll submit to whatever punishment Your Eminence decides on. I'm not so attached to this life that I'd mind much leaving it.'

The Cardinal smiled and there was a note almost of affection in his voice as he said:

'I know you're brave enough, Monsieur d'Artagnan. So I can tell you here and now you'll have to stand trial and may be found guilty.'

'I might reply that I already have my official pardon in my pocket, Sir. But I won't. I merely say to Your Eminence: "Yours to command, mine to obey".'

'Your pardon?' echoed the Cardinal in astonishment.

'Yes, Monseigneur.'

'Signed by whom? The King?'

There was a hint of scorn in Richelieu's voice as he said this.

'No,' replied d'Artagnan. 'Signed by Your Eminence.'

'By me? What are you talking about? Are you mad?'

'I expect you'll recognize your own handwriting, Sir,' replied the young man.

Whereupon he drew from his pocket the precious scroll of paper which Athos had taken from Milady by force and which he had handed over to d'Artagnan for safe keeping.

His Eminence took the scroll and proceeded to read it aloud slowly, stressing every syllable.

It is by my order and for the benefit of the State that the bearer of this note has done what he has done.

3 December, 1627.   Richelieu.

Having read the two lines the Cardinal sat for a few moments lost in thought. But he did not return the paper to d'Artagnan.

The young man muttered to himself:

'He's thinking out what kind of torture to inflict on me. Well, I'll show him I can die bravely.'

And he indulged in fantasies of himself dying a hero's death on the scaffold.

Richelieu still sat lost in thought, screwing the scroll of paper round in his hand. At last he looked up and fixed his eagle eye on d'Artagnan. When he saw his honest, open, intelligent look and realized from the tears which were coursing down his cheeks how greatly he had suffered during the past month, he was struck for the third or fourth time by the brilliant possibilities in store for this youth of twenty, and saw what treasures of energy, courage, and resource he would provide for a man who knew how to handle him. He compared the qualities of the young man in front of him with Milady's diabolical genius, her sinister intrigues and many crimes, and knew in his heart of hearts that he was on the whole thankful to be rid of such a dangerous accomplice.

He now slowly tore up the scroll of paper which d'Artagnan had so generously handed over to him. The young man thought to himself:

'I'm lost!'

And he made the Cardinal a low bow as though to say:

'Lord, Thy will be done.'

The Cardinal walked over to the table and without sitting down added two lines to a sheet of parchment, two-thirds of which were already written on. Then he set his seal to it.

'That's my death sentence,' thought d'Artagnan. 'He's sparing me the boredom of the Bastille and the slow agony of a trial. It's really very good of him.'

The Cardinal handed him the paper and said:

'I've taken one signed warrant from you and am giving you another in exchange. The name's missing on this commission; write it in yourself.'

D'Artagnan took the paper rather gingerly and shot a quick

glance at it. It was a lieutenant's commission in the Musketeers. He was quite overcome and fell on his knees before the Cardinal.

'Monseigneur,' he said, 'from now on my life's yours. I'll be loyal to you always. But this honour . . . it's too much. I don't deserve it. I've got three friends all of whom deserve it more than I.'

The Cardinal was delighted to have won over this recalcitrant spirit to his side. He patted him familiarly on the shoulder.

'You're a good lad, d'Artagnan,' he said. 'You can do what you like with that commission. The name's left blank, as you see. But don't forget you were the one I meant it for.'

'I won't forget, Monseigneur,' replied the young man. 'I'll never forget. Please believe that.'

The Cardinal now called out:

'Rochefort!'

The equerry, who was probably listening behind the door, was in the room in a flash.

'Rochefort,' said the Cardinal, 'you see Monsieur d'Artagnan here – from now on I'm numbering him among my friends. So make it up, you two. Shake hands and behave yourselves in future, if you value your heads.'

Rochefort and d'Artagnan shook hands rather half-heartedly, but the Cardinal kept his eyes fixed on them to see that they did so. They then left the room together. In the passage outside they said almost in one breath:

'We'll be seeing each other again, won't we?'

'Whenever you like,' said d'Artagnan.

'We'll get a chance soon enough,' said Rochefort.

At that moment the Cardinal opened the door and looked out.

'What were you saying, gentlemen?' he asked.

The two men at once gave each other forced smiles, shook hands again, bowed to His Eminence and walked out of the house.

The musketeer rejoined his friends.

'We were beginning to be worried about you,' said Athos.

'You needn't be,' replied d'Artagnan. 'I'm not only a free man — I'm actually in favour!'

'Tell us about it.'

'Yes, this evening. For the time being we'd better separate.'

That evening d'Artagnan called at Athos' billet. He found him drinking a bottle of Spanish wine, a duty he performed religiously every night. He described in detail his interview with the Cardinal. Then he pulled the commission out of his pocket and handed it to his friend.

'Here's something that falls to you by right, Athos,' he said.

Athos glanced at it and then smiled his sad, gentle smile.

'As Lieutenant Athos I should appear presumptuous,' he said. 'As Lieutenant Comte de la Fère I should appear undignified. No. You keep that commission; it was meant for you. Damn it, you've paid dearly enough for it.'

D'Artagnan now left Athos and went to call on Porthos, whom he found pirouetting in front of the glass in a brand new, magnificent embroidered coat.

'Oh, so it's you, my lad,' said the big man. 'How d'you think this coat suits me?'

'Very well indeed,' answered d'Artagnan. 'But I've come to offer you something which'll suit you better still.'

'What's that?' asked Porthos.

'A commission in the Musketeers.'

D'Artagnan then described his interview with the Cardinal and, taking the commission out of his pocket, said:

'Porthos, just write your name on that. And when you're my officer don't be too harsh with me.'

Porthos glanced at the paper. Then, to d'Artagnan's great surprise, he handed it back to him:

'I'd have liked that very much,' he said, 'but it's too late now. My duchess's husband died while we were on our trip to Béthune and his whole fortune reverts to his widow. If I marry her I shall have the use of it. It's too good a chance to miss. As a matter of fact I was just trying on the coat I'm going to wear at my wedding. You take the commission, old boy. You thoroughly deserve it.'

The young man now called on Aramis. He found him on his

knees at a prie-Dieu, his forehead resting on an open Book of Hours. He described his interview with the Cardinal and, pulling the commission out of his pocket for the third time, said:

'You take this, Aramis. You're our guiding light. You deserve it more than anyone for your good sense and good staff work in our many adventures.'

'Thanks for the offer, d'Artagnan,' replied Aramis. 'But, alas, our last adventure sickened me of soldiering once and for all. I've made up my mind at last. When the siege is over I'm joining the Lazarists. You take the commission, d'Artagnan. A soldier's life suits you. You'll make a first-rate officer.'

D'Artagnan was exceedingly grateful to his friends for their kindness. He walked back to Athos' rooms treading on air. He found his friend still sitting at the table holding up his last glass of Malaga to the lamp.

'Well,' he said, 'the other two also refused the commission.' His friend replied:

'The fact is, d'Artagnan, no one deserves it as much as you.' Whereupon he took up a pen, wrote the name 'd'Artagnan' on the commission and returned it to him.

'Now I'll have no friends any more,' said the young man. 'I shall have nothing but bitter memories.'

'You're young,' replied Athos. 'Your bitter memories will soon change into happy ones.'

EPILOGUE

AFTER Buckingham's death there was no more talk in England of sending a fleet to the help of the Rochellese, and the town surrendered after a year's siege. The capitulation was signed on 28 October 1628. In December of the same year the King made a triumphal entry into Paris, as though he had returned from a victorious campaign, not against Frenchmen, but against an external enemy. He rode down the Faubourg St Jacques under laurel arches.

D'Artagnan took his commission in the Musketeers. Porthos left the army and married Madame Coquenard in the course of the next year. The much-coveted coffer was found to contain eight hundred thousand livres. Mousqueton was given a magnificent livery and got what he had longed for all his life – the right to sit on the box of a gilded coach.

Aramis went on a trip to Lorraine, after which he disappeared entirely and none of his friends heard another word from him. They learned later from one of Madame de Chevreuse's intimate friends that he had embraced what he had always maintained was his true vocation and retired to a monastery, though which monastery no one ever discovered. Bazin became one of the institution's lay brothers.

Athos remained in the King's service until 1633, with d'Artagnan as his officer. In 1633 he went on a trip to Roussillon, after which he, too, left the army on the pretext that he had just inherited a small property in the Blaisois. Grimaud retired with him to the country.

D'Artagnan fought three duels with Rochefort and wounded him three times. The third time he said to the equerry, as he helped him to his feet:

'If we have another fight I shall probably kill you.'

The wounded man replied:

'In that case it would be better for us both to forgive and forget. Damn it all, in some ways I've been a good friend to you. If I'd said a word to the Cardinal after our first fight I could have had your head chopped off.'

Upon which they shook hands, this time in genuine friendship and without any reservations. Rochefort got Planchet posted to the Piedmont regiment as a sergeant.

Monsieur Bonacieux went on living in moderate contentment, quite in the dark as to his wife's fate and not greatly concerned about it. One day, however, he was rash enough to write a letter to the Cardinal to remind him of his existence. The Cardinal sent one of his household begging him to call on him at once and promising to see that thenceforth he lacked for nothing. At seven in the evening of the following day the little draper set out for the Louvre. From that day to this no one in the Rue des Fossoyeurs has seen or heard of him. Rumour has it that his generous patron has been keeping him housed and fed at his own expense in one of the King's castles.